The
Texan Republic
Trilogy

The
Texan Republic
Trilogy

3 Books in One Special Edition

The Texan Star
The Texan Scouts
The Texan Triumph

Joseph A. Altsheler

LEONAUR

The Texan Republic Trilogy
3 Books in One Special Edition
The Texan Star
The Texan Scouts
The Texan Triumph
by Joseph A. Altsheler

First published under the titles
The Texan Star
The Texan Scouts
The Texan Triumph

FIRST EDITION

Leonaur is an imprint
of Oakpast Ltd

Copyright in this form © 2014 Oakpast Ltd

ISBN: 978-1-78282-363-6 (hardcover)
ISBN: 978-1-78282-364-3 (softcover)

http://www.leonaur.com

Publisher's Notes

The views expressed in this book are not necessarily
those of the publisher.

Contents

The Texan Star   9

The Texan Scouts   261

The Texan Triumph   503

The Texan Star

CHAPTER 1

THE PRISONERS

A boy and a man sat in a room of a stone house in the ancient City of Mexico, capital in turn of Aztec, Spaniard and Mexican. They could see through the narrow windows masses of low buildings and tile roofs, and beyond, the swelling shape of great mountains, standing clear against the blue sky. But they had looked upon them so often that the mind took no note of the luminous spectacle. The cry of a water-seller or the occasional jingle of a spur came from the street below, but these, too, were familiar sounds, and they were no longer regarded.

The room contained but little furniture and the door was of heavy oak. Its whole aspect indicated that it was a prison. The man was of middle years, and his face showed a singular blend of kindness and firmness. The pallor of imprisonment had replaced his usual colour. The boy was tall and strong and his cheeks were yet ruddy. His features bore some resemblance to those of his older comrade.

"Ned," said the man at last, "it has been good of you to stay with me here, but a prison is no place for a boy. You must secure a release and go back to our people."

The boy smiled, and his face, in repose rather stern for one so young, was illumined in a wonderful manner.

"I don't want to leave you, Uncle Steve," he said, "and if I did it's not likely that I could. This house is strong, and it's a long way from here to Texas."

"Perhaps I can induce them to let you go," said the man. "Why should they wish to hold one so young?"

Edward Fulton did not reply because he saw that Stephen Austin was speaking to himself rather than his companion. Instead, he looked once more through the window and over the city at the vast white peaks of Popocatepetl and Ixtaccihuatl silent and immutable, forever guarding the sky-line. Yet they seemed to call to him at this moment and tell him of freedom. The words of the man had touched a spring within him and he wanted to go. He could not conceal from himself the fact that he longed for liberty with every pulse and fibre. But he resolved, nevertheless, to stay. He would not desert the one whom he had come to serve.

Stephen Austin, the real founder of Texas, had now been in prison in Mexico more than a year. Coming to Saltillo to secure for the Texans better treatment from the Mexicans, their rulers, he had been seized and held as a criminal. The boy, Edward Fulton, was not really his nephew, but an orphan, the son of a cousin. He owed much to Austin and coming to the capital to help him he was sharing his imprisonment.

"They say that Santa Anna now has the power," said Ned, breaking the sombre silence.

"It is true," said Stephen Austin, "and it is a new and strong reason why I fear for our people. Of all the cunning and ambitious men in Mexico, Antonio Lopez de Santa Anna is the most cunning and ambitious. I know, too, that he is the most able, and I believe that he is the most dangerous to those of us who have settled in Texas. What a country is this Mexico! Revolution after revolution! You make a treaty with one president today and tomorrow another disclaims it! More than one of them has a touch of genius, and yet it is obscured by childishness and cruelty!"

He sighed heavily. Ned, full of sympathy, glanced at him but said nothing. Then his gaze turned back to the mighty peaks which stood so sharp and clear against the blue. Truth and honesty were the most marked qualities of Stephen Austin and he could not understand the vast web of intrigue in which the Mexican capital was continually involved. And to the young mind of the boy, cast in the same mould, it was yet more baffling and repellent.

Ned still stared at the guardian peaks, but his thoughts floated away from them. His head had been full of old romance when he entered the vale of Tenochtitlan. He had almost seen Cortez and the *conquistadores* in their visible forms with their armour clanking about them as they stalked before him. He had gazed eagerly upon the lakes, the mighty mountains, the low houses and the strange people. Here, deeds of which the world still talked had been done centuries ago and his thrill was strong and long. But the feeling was gone now. He had liked many of the Mexicans and many of the Mexican traits, but he had felt with increasing force that he could never reach out his hand and touch anything solid. He thought of volcanic beings on a volcanic soil.

The throb of a drum came from the street below, and presently the shrill sound of fifes was mingled with the steady beat. Ned stood up and pressed his head as far forward as the bars of the window would let him.

"Soldiers, a regiment, I think," he said. "Ah, I can see them now! What brilliant uniforms their officers wear!"

Austin also looked out.

"Yes," he said. "They know how to dress for effect. And their music is good, too. Listen how they play."

It was a martial air, given with a splendid lilt and swing. The tune crept into Ned's blood and his hand beat time on the stone sill. But the music increased his longing for liberty. His thoughts passed away from the narrow street and the marching regiment to the North, to the wild free plains beyond the Rio Grande. It was there that his heart was, and it was there that his body would be.

"It is General Cos who leads them," said Austin. "I can see him now, riding upon a white horse. It's the man in the white and silver uniform, Ned."

"He's the brother-in-law of Santa Anna, is he not?"

"Yes, and I fear him. I know well, Ned, that he hates the Texans—all of us."

"Perhaps the regiment that we see now is going north against our people."

Austin's brows contracted.

"It may be so," he said. "They give soft words all the time, and yet they hold me a prisoner here. It would be like them to strike while pretending to clear away all the troubles between us."

He sighed again. Ned watched the soldiers until the last of them had passed the window, and then he listened to the music, the sound of drum and fife, until it died away, and they heard only the usual murmur of the city. Then the homesickness, the longing for the great free country to the north grew upon him and became almost over-powering.

"Someone comes," said Austin.

They heard the sound of the heavy bar that closed the door being moved from its place.

"Our dinner, doubtless," said Austin, "but it is early."

The door swung wide and a young Mexican officer entered. He was taller and fairer than most of his race, evidently of pure Northern Spanish blood, and his countenance was frank and fine.

11

"Welcome, lieutenant," said Stephen Austin, speaking in Spanish, which he, as well as Ned, understood perfectly. "You know that we are always glad to see you here."

Lieutenant Alfonso de Zavala smiled in a quick, responsive way, but in a moment his face became grave.

"I announce a visitor, a most distinguished visitor, Mr. Austin," he said. "General Antonio Lopez de Santa Anna, President of the Mexican Republic and Commander-in-chief of its armies and navies."

Both Mr. Austin and the boy arose and bowed as a small man of middle years, slender and nervous, strode into the room, standing for a few moments near its centre, and looking about him like a questing hawk. His was, in truth, an extraordinary presence. He seemed to radiate an influence that at once attracted and repelled. His dark features were cut sharply and clearly. His eyes, set closely together, were of the most intense black that Ned had ever seen in a human head. Nor were those eyes ever at rest. They roamed over everything, and they seemed to burn every object for the single instant they fell there. They never met the gaze of either American squarely, although they continually came back to both.

This man was clothed in a white uniform, heavy with gold stripes and gold epaulets. A small sword at his side had a gold hilt set with a diamond. He wore a three-cornered hat shaped like that of Napoleon, but instead of the Corsican's simple gray his was bright in colour and splendid with plumage.

He was at once a powerful and sinister figure. Ned felt that he was in the presence of genius, but it belonged to one of those sinuous creatures, shining and terrible, that are bred under the vivid sun of the tropics. There was a singular sensation at the roots of his hair, but, resolved to show neither fear nor apprehension, he stood and gazed directly at Santa Anna.

"Be seated, Mr. Austin," said the general, "and close the door, de Zavala, but remain with us. Your young relative can remain, also. I have things of importance to say, but it is not forbidden to him, also, to hear them."

Ned sat down and so did Mr. Austin and young de Zavala, but Santa Anna remained standing. It seemed to Ned that he did so because he wished to look down upon them from a height. And all the time the black eyes, like two burning coals, played restlessly about the room.

Ned was unable to take his own eyes away. The figure in its gorgeous uniform was so full of nervous energy that it attracted like a magnet, while at the same time it bade all who opposed to beware. The boy felt as if he were before a splendid leopard with no bars of a cage between.

Santa Anna took three or four rapid steps back and forth. He kept his hat upon his head, a right, it seemed, due to his superiority to other people. He looked like a man who had a great thought which he was shaping into quick words. Presently he stopped before Austin, and shot him one of those piercing glances.

"My friend and guest," he said in the sonorous Spanish.

Austin bowed. Whether the subtle Mexican meant the words in satire or in earnest he did not know, nor did he care greatly.

"When I call you my friend and guest I speak truth," said Santa Anna. "It is true that we had you brought here from Saltillo, and we insist that you accept our continued hospitality, but it is because we know how devoted you are to our common Mexico, and we would have you here at our right hand for advice and help."

Ned saw Mr. Austin smile a little sadly. It all seemed very strange to the boy. How could one talk of friendship and hospitality to those whom he held as prisoners? Why could not these people say what they meant? Again he longed for the free winds of the plains.

"You and I together should be able to quiet these troublesome Texans," continued Santa Anna—and his voice had a hard metallic quality that rasped the boy's nerves. "You know, Stephen Austin, that I and Mexico have endured much from the people whom you have brought within our borders. They shed good Mexican blood at the fort, Velasco, and they have attacked us elsewhere. They do not pay their taxes or obey our decrees, and when I send my officers to make them obey they take down their long rifles."

Austin smiled again, and now the watching boy thought the smile was not sad at all. If Santa Anna took notice he gave no sign.

"But you are reasonable," continued the Mexican, and now his manner was winning to an extraordinary degree. "It was my predecessor, Farias, who brought you here, but I would not see you go, because I love you like a brother, and now I have come to you, that between us we may calm your turbulent Texans."

"But you must bear in mind," said Austin, "that our rights have been taken from us. All the clauses of our charter have been broken, and now your Congress has decreed that we shall have only one soldier to every five hundred inhabitants and that all the rest of us shall be disarmed. How are we, in a wild country, to protect ourselves from the Comanches, Lipans and other Indians who roam everywhere, robbing and murdering?"

Austin's face, usually so benevolent, flushed and his eyes were very bright. Ned looked intently at Santa Anna to see how he would take the daring and truthful indictment. But the Mexican showed no confusion, only astonishment. He threw up his hands in a vivid southern gesture and looked at Austin in surprised reproof.

"My friend," he said in injured but not angry tones, "how can you ask me such a question? Am I not here to protect the Texans? Am I not President of Mexico? Am I not head of the Mexican Army? My gallant soldiers, my horsemen with their lances and sabres, will draw a ring around the Texans through which no Comanche or Lipan, however daring, will be able to break."

He spoke with such fire, such appearance of earnestness, that Ned, despite a mind uncommonly keen and analytical in one so young, was forced to believe for a moment. Texas, however, was far and immense, and there were not enough soldiers in all America to put a ring around the wild Comanches. But the impression remained longer with Austin, who was ever hoping for the best, and ever seeing the best in others.

Ned was a silent boy who had suffered many hardships, and he had acquired the habit of thought which in its turn brought observation and judgment. Yet if Santa Anna was acting he was doing it with consummate skill, and the boy who never said a word watched him all the time.

Santa Anna began to talk now of the great future that awaited the Texans under the banner of Mexico. He poured forth the words with so much Latin fervour that it was almost like listening to a song. Ned felt the influence of the musical roll coming over him again, but, with an effort of the will that was almost physical, he shook it off.

Santa Anna painted the picture of a dream, a gorgeous dream of many colours. Mexico was to become a mighty country and the Texans with their cool courage and martial energy would be no mean factor in it. Austin would be one of his lieutenants, a sharer in his greatness and reward. His eloquence was wonderful, and Ned felt once more the fascination of the serpent. This was a man to whom only the grand and magnificent appealed, and already he had achieved a part of his dream.

Ned moved a little closer to the window. He wished the fresh air to blow upon his face. He saw that Mr. Austin was fully under the spell. Santa Anna was making the most beautiful and convincing promises. He himself was going to Texas. He was the father of his people. He would right every wrong. He loved the Texans, these children of the north who had come to his country for a home. No one could ever say that he appealed in vain to Santa Anna for protection. Texans would be proud that they were a part of Mexico, they would be glad to belong to a nation which already had a glorious history, and to come to a capital which had more splendour and romance than any other in America.

Ned literally withdrew his soul within itself. He sought to shut out the influence that was radiating from this singular and brilliant figure, but he saw that Mr. Austin was falling more deeply under it.

"Look!" said Santa Anna, taking the man by the arm in the familiar manner that one old friend has with another and drawing him to the window. "Is not this a prospect to enchant? Is not this a capital of which you and I can well be proud?"

He lifted a forefinger and swept the half curve that could be seen from the window. It was truly a panorama that would kindle the heart of the dullest. Forty miles away the white crests of Popocatepetl and Ixtaccihuatl still showed against the background of burning blue, like pillars supporting the dome of heaven. Along the whole line of the half curve were mountains in fold on fold. Below the green of the valley showed the waters of the lake both fresh and salt gleaming with gold where the sunlight shot down upon them. Nearer rose the spires of the cathedral, and then the sea of tile roofs burnished by the vivid beams.

Santa Anna stood in a dramatic position, his finger still pointing. There was scarcely a day that Ned did not feel the majesty of this valley of Tenochtitlan, but Santa Anna deepened the spell. Could the world hold another place its equal? Might not the Texans indeed have a glorious future in the land of which this city was the capital? Poetry and romance appealed powerfully to the boy's thoughtful mind, and he felt that here in Mexico he was at their very heart. Nothing else had ever moved him so much.

"You are pleased! It impresses you!" said Santa Anna to Austin. "I can see it on your face. You are with us. You are one of us. Ah, my friend, how noble it is to have a great heart."

"Do I go with your message to the Texans?" asked Austin.

"I must leave now, but I shall come again soon, and I will tell you all. You shall carry words that will satisfy every one of them."

He threw his arms about Austin's shoulders, gave Ned a quick salute, and then left the room, taking young de Zavala with him, Ned heard the heavy bar fall in place on the outside of the door, and he knew that they were shut in as tightly as ever. But Mr. Austin was in a glow.

"What a wonderful, flexible mind!" he said, more to himself than to the boy. "I could have preferred a sort of independence for Texas, but since we're to be ruled from the City of Mexico, Santa Anna will do the best he can for us. As soon as he sweeps away the revolutionary troubles he will repair all our injuries."

Ned was silent. He knew that the generous Austin was still under Santa Anna's magnetic spell, but after his departure the whole room was changed to the boy. He saw clearly again. There were no mists and clouds about his mind. Moreover, the wonderful half curve before the window was changing. Vapours were rolling up from the south and the two great peaks faded from view. Trees and water in the valley changed to gray. The skies which had been so bright now became sombre and menacing.

The boy felt a deep fear at his heart, but Mr. Austin seemed to be yet under the influence of Santa Anna, and talked cheerfully of their speedy return to Texas. Ned listened in silence and unbelief, while the gloom outside deepened, and night presently came over Anahuac. But he had formed his resolution. He owed much to Mr. Austin. He had come a vast distance to be at his side, and to serve him in prison, but he felt now that he could be of more use elsewhere. Moreover, he must carry a message, a warning to those who needed it sorely. One of the windows opened upon the north, and he looked intently through it trying to pierce, with the mind's eye at least, the thousand miles that lay between him and those whom he would reach with the word.

Mr. Austin had lighted a candle. Noticing the boy's gloomy face, he patted him on the head with a benignant hand and said:

"Don't be down of heart, Edward, my lad. We'll soon be on our way to Texas."

"But this is Mexico, and it is Santa Anna who holds us."

"That is true, and it is Santa Anna who is our best friend."

Ned did not dispute the sanguine saying. He saw that Mr. Austin had his opinion, and he had his. The door was opened again in a half hour and a soldier brought them their supper. Young de Zavala, who was their immediate guardian, also entered and stood by while they

16

ate. They had never received poor food, and tonight Mexican hospitality exerted itself—at the insistence of Santa Anna, Ned surmised. In addition to the regular supper there was an ice and a bottle of Spanish wine.

"The president has just given an order that the greatest courtesy be shown to you at all times," said de Zavala, "and I am very glad. I, too, have people in that territory of ours from which you come—Texas."

He spoke with undeniable sympathy, and Ned felt his heart warm toward him, but he decided to say nothing. He feared that he might betray by some chance word the plan that he had in mind. But Mr. Austin, believing in others because he was so truthful and honest himself, talked freely.

"All our troubles will soon be over," he said to de Zavala.

"I hope so, *Senor*," said the young man earnestly.

By and by, when de Zavala and the soldier were gone, Ned went again to the window, stood there a few moments to harden his resolution, and then came back to the man.

"Mr. Austin," he said, "I am going to ask your consent to something."

The Texan looked up in surprise.

"Why, Edward, my lad," he said kindly, "you don't have to ask my consent to anything, after the way in which you have already sacrificed yourself for me."

"But I am not going to stay with you any longer, Mr. Austin—that is, if I can help it. I am going back to Texas."

Mr. Austin laughed. It was a mellow and satisfied laugh.

"So you are, Edward," he said, "and I am going with you. You will help me to bear a message of peace and safety to the Texans."

Ned paused a moment, irresolute. There was no change in his determination. He was merely uncertain about the words to use.

"There may be delays," he said at last, "and—Mr. Austin, I have decided to go alone—and within the next day or two if I can."

The Texan's face clouded.

"I cannot understand you," he said. "Why this hurry? It would in reality be a breach of faith to our great friend, Santa Anna—that is, if you could go. I don't believe you can."

Ned was troubled. He was tempted to tell what was in his mind, but he knew that he would not be believed, so he fell back again upon his infinite capacity for silence. Mr. Austin read resolution in the closed lips and rigid figure.

17

"Do you really mean that you will attempt to steal away?" he asked.

"As soon as I can."

The man shook his head.

"It would be better not to do so," he said, "but you are your own master, and I see I cannot dissuade you from the attempt. But, boy, you will promise me not to take any unnecessary or foolish risks?"

"I promise gladly, and, Mr. Austin, I hate to leave you here."

Their quarters were commodious and Ned slept alone in a small room to the left of the main apartment. It was a bare place with only a bed and a chair, but it was lighted by a fairly large window. Ned examined this window critically. It had a horizontal iron bar across the middle, and it was about thirty feet from the ground. He pulled at the iron bar with both hands but, although rusty with time, it would not move in its socket. Then he measured the two spaces between the bar and the wall.

Hope sprang up in the boy's heart. Then he did a strange thing. He removed nearly all his clothing and tried to press his head and shoulders between the bar and the wall. His head, which was of the long narrow type, so common in the scholar, would have gone through the aperture, had it not been for his hair which was long, and which grew uncommonly thick. His shoulders were very thick and broad and they, too, halted him. He drew back and felt a keen thrill of disappointment.

But he was a boy who usually clung tenaciously to an idea, and, sitting down, he concentrated his mind upon the plan that he had formed. By and by a possible way out came to him. Then he lay down upon the bed, drew a blanket over him because the night was chill in the City of Mexico, and calmly sought sleep.

CHAPTER 2

A HAIRCUT

The optimism of Mr. Austin endured the next morning, but Ned was gloomy. Since it was his habit to be silent, the man did not notice it at first. The breakfast was good, with *tortillas, frijoles*, other Mexican dishes and coffee, but the boy had no appetite. He merely picked at his food, made a faint effort or two to drink his coffee and finally put the cup back almost full in the saucer. Then Mr. Austin began to observe.

"Are you ill, Ned?" he asked. "Is this imprisonment beginning to tell upon you? I had thought that you were standing it well. Can't you eat?"

"I don't believe I'm hungry," replied the boy, "but there is nothing else the matter with me. I'll be all right, Uncle Steve. Don't you bother about me."

He ate a little breakfast, about one half of the usual amount, and then, asking to be excused, went to the window, where he again stared out at the tiled roofs, the green foliage in the valley of Mexico and the ranges and peaks beyond. He was taking his resolution, and he was carrying it out, but it was hard, very hard. He foresaw that he would have to strengthen his will many, many times. Mr. Austin took no further worry on Ned's account, thinking that he would be all right again in a day or two.

But at the dinner which was brought to them in the middle of the day Ned showed a marked failure of appetite, and Mr. Austin felt real concern. The boy, however, was sure that he would be all right before the day was over.

"It must be the lack of fresh air and exercise," said Mr. Austin. "You can really take exercise in here, Ned. Besides, you said that you were going to escape. If you fall ill you will have no chance at all."

He spoke half in jest, but Ned took him seriously.

"I am not ill, Uncle Steve," he said. "I really feel very well, but I have lost my appetite. Maybe I am getting tired of these Mexican dishes."

"Take exercise! take exercise!" said Mr. Austin with emphasis.

"I think I will," said Ned.

Physical exercise, after all, fitted in with his ideas, and that afternoon he worked hard at all the gymnastic feats possible within the three rooms to which they were confined. De Zavala came in and expressed his astonishment at the athletic feats, which Ned continued with unabated zeal despite his presence.

"Why do you do these things?" he asked in wonder.

"To keep myself strong and healthy. I ought to have begun them sooner. The Mexican air is depressing, and I find that I am losing my appetite."

De Zavala's eyes opened wide while Ned deftly turned a handspring. Then the young American sat down panting, his face flushed with as healthy a colour as one could find anywhere.

"You'll have an appetite tonight," said Mr. Austin. But to his great amazement Ned again played with his food, eating only half the usual amount.

"You're surely ill," said Mr. Austin. "I've no doubt de Zavala would allow us to have a physician, and I shall ask him for one."

"Don't do it, Uncle Steve," begged Ned. "There's nothing at all the matter with me, and anyhow I wouldn't want a Mexican doctor fussing over me. I've probably been eating too much."

Mr. Austin was forced to accede. The boy certainly did not look ill, and his appetite was bound to become normal again in a few days. But it did not. As far as Mr. Austin could measure it, Ned was eating less and less. It was obvious that he was thinner. He was also growing much paler, except for a red flush on the cheek bones. Mr. Austin became alarmed, but Ned obstinately refused any help, always asserting with emphasis that he had no ailment of any kind. But the man could see that he had become much lighter, and he wondered at the boy's physical failure. De Zavala, also, expressed his sorrow in sonorous Spanish, but Ned, while thanking them, steadily disclaimed any need of sympathy.

The boy found the days hard, but the nights were harder. For the first time in his life he could not sleep well. He would lie for hours so wide awake that his eyes grew used to the dark, and he could see everything in his room. He was troubled, too, by bad dreams and in many of these dreams he was a living skeleton, wandering about and condemned to live forever without food. More than once he bitterly regretted the resolution he had taken, but having taken it, he would never alter it. His silent, concentrated nature would not let him. Yet he endured undoubted torture day by day. Torture was the only name for it.

"I shall send an application to President Santa Anna to have you allowed a measure of liberty," said Mr. Austin finally. "You are simply pining away here, Edward, my lad. You cannot eat, that is, you eat only a little. I have passed the most tempting and delicate things to you and you always refuse. No boy of your age would do so unless something were very much wrong with his physical system. You have lost many pounds, and if this keeps on I do not know what will happen to you. I shall not ask for more liberty for you, but you must have a doctor at once."

"I do not want any doctor, Uncle Steve," said the boy. "He cannot do me any good, but there is somebody else whom I want."

"Who is he?"

"A barber."

20

"A barber! Now what good can a barber do you?"

"A great deal. What I crave most in the world is a hair-cut, and only a barber can do that for me. My hair has been growing for more than three months, Uncle Steve, and you've seen how extremely thick it is. Now it is so long, too, that it's falling all about my eyes. Its weight is oppressing my brain. I feel a little touch of fever now and then, and I believe it's this awful hair."

He ran his fingers through the heavy locks until his head seemed to be surrounded with a defence like the quills of a porcupine. Beneath the great bush of hair his gray eyes glowed in a pale, thin face.

"There is a lot of it," said Mr. Austin, surveying him critically, "but it is not usual for anybody in our situation to be worrying about the length and abundance of his hair."

"I'm sure I'd be a lot better if I could get it cut close."

"Well, well, if you are taking it so much to heart we'll see what can be done. You are ill and wasted, Edward, and when one is in that condition a little thing can affect his spirits. De Zavala is a friendly sort of young fellow and through him we will send a request to Colonel Sandoval, the commander of the prisons, that you be allowed to have your hair cut."

"If you please, Uncle Steve," said Ned gratefully.

Mr. Austin was not wrong in his forecast about Lieutenant de Zavala. He showed a full measure of sympathy. Hence a petition to Colonel Martin Sandoval y Dominguez, commander of prisons in the City of Mexico, was drawn up in due form. It stated that one Edward Fulton, a Texan of tender years, now in detention at the capital, was suffering from the excessive growth of hair upon his head. The weight and thickness of said hair had heated his brain and destroyed his appetite. In ordinary cases of physical decline a physician was needed most, but so far as young Edward Fulton was concerned, a barber could render the greatest service.

The petition, duly endorsed and stamped, was forwarded to Colonel Martin Sandoval y Dominguez, and, after being gravely considered by him in the manner befitting a Mexican officer of high rank and pure Spanish descent, received approval. Then he chose among the barbers one Joaquin Menendez, a dark fellow who was not of pure Spanish descent, and sent him to the prison with de Zavala to accomplish the needed task.

"I hope you will be happy now, Edward," said Mr. Austin, when the two Mexicans came. "You are a good boy, but it seems to me that you have been making an undue fuss about your hair."

"I'm quite sure I shall recover fast," said Ned.

It was hard for him to hide his happiness from the others. He felt a thrill of joy every time the steel of the scissors clicked together and a lock of hair fell to the floor. But Joaquin Menendez, the barber, had a Southern temperament and the soul of an artist. It pained him to shear away—"shear away" alone described it—such magnificent hair. It was so thick, so long and so glossy.

"Ah," he said, laying some of the clipped locks across his hand and surveying them sorrowfully, "so great is the pity! What *senorita* could resist the young *senor* if these were still growing upon his head!"

"You cut that hair," said Ned with a vicious snap of his teeth, "and cut it close, so close that it will look like the shaven face of a man. I think you will find it so stated in the conditions if you will look at the permit approved in his own handwriting by Colonel Sandoval y Dominguez."

Joaquin Menendez, still the artist, but obedient to the law, heaved a deep sigh, and proceeded with his sad task. Lock by lock the abundant hair fell, until Ned's head stood forth in the shaven likeness of a man's face that he had wished.

"I must tell you," said Mr. Austin, "that it does not become you, but I hope you are satisfied."

"I am satisfied," replied Ned. "I have every cause to be. I know I shall have a stronger appetite tomorrow."

"You are certainly a sensitive boy," said Mr. Austin, looking at him in some wonder. "I did not know that such a thing could influence your feelings and your physical condition so much."

Ned made no reply, but that night he ate supper with a much better appetite than he had shown in many days, bringing words of warm approval and encouragement from Mr. Austin.

An hour or two later, when cheerful goodnights had been exchanged, Ned withdrew to his own little room. He lay down upon his bed, but he was fully clothed and he had no intention of sleep. Instead the boy was transformed. For days he had been walking with a weak and lagging gait. Fever was in his veins. Sometimes he became dizzy, and the walls and floors of the prison swam before him. But now the spirit had taken command of the thin body. Weakness and dizziness were gone. Every vein was infused with strength. Hope was in command, and he no longer doubted that he would succeed.

He rose from the bed and went to the window. The city was silent and the night was dark. Floating clouds hid the moon and stars. The ranges and the city roofs themselves had sunk into the dusk. It seemed to him that all things favoured the bold and persevering. And he had been persevering. No one would ever know how he had suffered, what terrific pangs had assailed him. He could not see now how he had done it, and he was quite sure that he could never go through such an ordeal again. The rack would be almost as welcome.

Ned did not know it, but a deep red flush had come into each pale cheek. He removed most of his clothes, and put his head forward between the iron bar and the window sill. The head went through and the shoulders followed. He drew back, breathing a deep and mighty breath of triumph. Yet he had known that it would be so. When he first tried the space he had been only a shade too large for it. Now his head and shoulders would go between, but with nothing to spare. A sheet of paper could not have been slipped in on either side. Yet it was enough. The triumph of self-denial was complete.

He had thought several times of telling Mr. Austin, but he finally decided not to do so. He might seek to interfere. He would put a thousand difficulties in the way, some real and some imaginary. It would save the feelings of both for him to go quietly, and, when Mr. Austin missed him, he would know why and how he had gone.

Ned stood at the window a little while longer, listening. He heard far away the faint rattle of a sabre, probably some officer of Santa Anna who was going to a place outside a lattice, the sharp cry of a Mexican upbraiding his lazy mule, and the distant note of a woman singing an old Spanish song. It was as dark as ever, with the clouds rolling over the great valley of Tenochtitlan, which had seen so much of human passion and woe. Ned, brave and resolute as he was, shivered. He was oppressed by the night and the place. It seemed to him, for the moment, that the ghosts of stern Cortez, and of the Aztecs themselves were walking out there.

Then he did a characteristic thing. Folding his arms in front of him he grasped his own elbows and shook himself fiercely. The effort of will and body banished the shapes and illusions, and he went to work with firm hands.

He tore the coverings from his bed into strips, and knotted them together stoutly, trying each knot by tying the strip to the bar, and pulling on it with all his strength. He made his rope at least thirty feet long and then gave it a final test, knot by knot. He judged that it was now near midnight and the skies were still very dark. Inside of a half hour he would be gone—to what? He was seized with an intense yearning to wake up Mr. Austin and tell him goodbye. The Texan leader had been so good to him, he would worry so much about him that it was almost heartless to slip away in this manner. But he checked the impulse again, and went swiftly ahead with his work.

He kept on nothing but his underclothing and trousers. The rest he made up into a small package which he tied upon his back. He was sorry that he did not have any weapon. He had been deprived of even his pocket-knife, but he did have a few dollars of Spanish coinage, which he stowed carefully in his trousers pocket. All the while his energy endured despite his wasted form. Hope made a bridge for his weakness.

He let the line out of the window, and his delicate sense told him when it struck against the ground. Six or eight feet were left in his hand, and he tied the end firmly to the bar, knotting it again and again. Then he slipped through the opening and the passage was so close that his ears scraped as they went by. He hung for a few moments on the outside, his feet on the stone sill and his hands clasping the iron bar. He felt sheer and absolute terror. The spires of the cathedral were invisible and only a few far lights showed dimly. It seemed to him that he was suspended over a bottomless pit, and he shivered from head to foot.

But he recalled his courage. Such a black night was best suited to his task. The shivering ceased. Hope ruled once more. He knelt on the stone sill, and, grasping his crude rope with both hands, let himself down from the window. It required almost superhuman exertion to keep himself from dropping sheer away, and the rope burned his palms. But he held on, knowing that he must hold, and the stone wall felt cold to him, as he lay against it, and slid slowly down.

Perhaps his strength, which was more of the mind than of the body, partly gave way under such a severe strain, but he felt pains shooting through his arms, shoulders and chest. His most vivid recollections of the descent were the coldness of the wall against which he lay and the far tinkle of a *mandolin* which came to him with annoying distinctness. The frequent knots where he had tied the strips together were a help, and whenever he came to one he let his hands rest upon it a moment or two lest he slide down too rapidly.

He had been descending, it seemed to him, fully an hour, and he must have come down a mile, when he heard the rattle of a sabre. It was so distinct and so near that it could not be imagination. He looked

24

in the direction of the sound and saw two dark figures in the street. As he stared the two figures shaped themselves into two Mexican officers. Truth, not fancy, told him also that they were not moving. They had seen him escaping and they would come for him! He pressed his body hard against the stone wall, and with his hands resting upon one of the knots clung desperately to the rope. He was hanging in an alley, and the men were on the street at the mouth of it six or seven yards away. They were talking and it must be about him!

He saw them create a light in some manner, and his hands almost slipped from the rope. Then joy flooded back. They were merely lighting cigarettes, and, with a few more words to each other, they walked on. Ned slid slowly down, but when he came to the last knot his strength gave way and he fell. It seemed to him that he was plunging an immeasurable distance through depths of space. Then he struck and with the force of the blow consciousness left him.

When he revived he found himself lying upon a rough stone pavement and it was still dark. He saw above a narrow cleft of sombre sky, and something cold and trailing lay across his face. He shivered with repulsion, snatched at it to throw it off, and found that it was his rope. Then he felt of himself cautiously and fearfully, but found that no bones were broken. Nor was he bruised to any degree and now he knew that he could not have fallen more than two or three feet. Perhaps he had struck first upon the little pack which he had fastened upon his back. It reminded him that he was shoeless and coatless and undoing the pack he reclothed himself fully.

He was quite sure that he had not lain there more than a quarter of an hour. Nothing had happened while he was unconscious. It was a dark little alley in the rear of the prison, and the buildings on the other side that abutted upon it were windowless. He walked cautiously to the mouth of the alley, and looked up and down the street. He saw no one, and, pulling his cap down over his eyes, he started instinctively toward the north, because it was to the far north that he wished to go. He was fully aware that he faced great dangers, almost impossibilities. Practically nothing was in his favour, save that he spoke excellent Spanish and also Mexican versions of it.

He went for several hundred yards along the rough and narrow street, and he began to shiver again. Now it was from cold, which often grows intense at night in the great valley of Mexico. Nor was his wasted frame fitted to withstand it. He was assailed also by a fierce hunger. He had carried self-denial to the utmost limit, and nature was crying out against him in a voice that must be heard.

He resolved to risk all and obtain food. Another hundred yards and he saw crouched in an angle of the street an old woman who offered *tortillas* and *frijoles* for sale. He went a little nearer, but apprehension almost overcame him. It might be difficult for him to pass for a Mexican and she would give the alarm. But he went yet nearer and stood where he could see her face. It was broad, fat and dark, more Aztec than Spaniard, and then he approached boldly, his speed increased by the appetising aroma arising from some flat cakes that lay over burning charcoal.

"I will take these, my mother," he said in Mexican, and leaning over he snatched up half a dozen gloriously hot *tortillas* and *frijoles*. A cry of indignation and anger was checked at the old woman's lips as two small silver coins slipped from the boy's hands, and tinkled pleasantly together in her own.

Holding his spoils in his hands Ned walked swiftly up the street. He glanced back once, and saw that the old Aztec woman had sunk back into her original position. He had nothing to fear from any alarm by her, and he looked ahead for some especially dark nook in which he could devour the precious food. He saw none, but he caught a glimpse beyond of foliage, and he recalled enough of the city of Mexico to know what it was. It was the Zocalo or garden of the cathedral, the Holy Metropolitan Church of Mexico. Above the foliage he could see the dark walls, and above them he saw the dome, as he had seen it from the window of his prison. Over the dome itself rose a beautiful lantern, in which a light was now burning.

Ned entered the garden which contained many trees, and sat down in the thickest group of them. Then he began to eat. He was as ravenous as any wolf, but he had been cultivating the power of will, and he ate like a gentleman, knowing that to do otherwise would not be good for him. But, tempered by discretion, it was a glorious pursuit. It was almost worth the long period of fasting and suffering, for common Mexican food, bought on the street from an old Aztec woman, to taste so well. Strength flowed back into every vein and muscle. He would not now give way to fears and tremblings which were of the body rather than the mind. He stopped when half of the food was gone, put the remainder in his pocket, and stood up. Fine drops of water struck him in the face. It had begun to rain. And a raw wind was moaning in the valley.

Despite the warm food and his returning strength Ned felt the desperate need of shelter. It was growing colder, too. Even as he stood there the fine rain turned to fine snow. It melted as it fell, but when it struck him about the neck and face it had an uncommonly penetrating power and the chill seemed to go into the bone. He must have shelter. He looked at the dark walls of the cathedral and then at the light in the slender lantern far up above the dome. What more truly a shelter than a church! It had been a sanctuary in the dark ages, and he might use it now as such.

He left the trees and stood for a little while by a stone, one of the 124 which formerly enclosed an atrium. Still seeing nothing and hearing nothing but the whistle of the wind which drove the cold drops of snow under his collar he advanced boldly again, sprang over the iron railing, and came to the walls of the old church, where he stood a moment.

Ned knew that in great Catholic cathedrals, like the one of Mexico, there were always side doors or little wickets used by priests or other high officials of the church, and he was hoping to find one that he could open. He passed half way around the building, feeling cautiously along the cold stone. Once he saw a watchman with *sombrero*, heavy cloak and lantern. He pressed into a niche, and the watchman went on his automatic way, little thinking that anyone was near.

The boy continued his circuit and presently he found a wooden door, which he could not force. A little further and he came to a second which opened to his pressure. It was so small an entrance that he stooped as he passed in. He shut it carefully behind him, and stood in what was almost total darkness, until his eyes grew used to the gloom.

Then he saw that he was in a vast interior, Doric in architecture, severe and simple. It was in the form of a Latin cross, with fluted columns dividing the aisles from the nave. Above him rose a noble dome.

He could make out nothing more for the present. It was very still, very imposing, and at another time he would have been awed, but now he had found sanctuary. The cold and the snow were shut out and a grateful warmth took their place. He walked down one of the aisles, careful that his footsteps should make no sound. He saw that there were rows of chapels, seven on either side of the church. It occurred to him that he would be safer in one of these rooms and he chose that which seemed to be used the least.

While on this search he passed the main altar in the centre of the building. He noticed above the stalls a picture of the Virgin. He was a Protestant, but when he saw it he crossed himself devoutly. Was not her church giving him shelter and refuge from his enemies? He also passed the Altar of the Kings, beneath which now lie the heads of great Mexicans who secured the independence of their country from Spain. He looked a little at these before he entered the chapel of his choice.

It was a small room, lighted scarcely at all by a narrow window, and it contained a few straight wooden pews one of which had been turned about facing the wall. He lay down in his pew, and, even in daylight, he would have been hidden from anyone a yard away. The hard wood was soft to him. He put his cap under his head and stretched himself out. Then, without will, he relaxed completely. Nature could stand no more. His eyes closed and he floated off into the far and happy region of sleep.

CHAPTER 3

SANCTUARY

Ned Fulton's sleep was that of exhaustion, and it lasted long. Although fine snow yet fell outside, and the raw wind blew it about, a pleasant warmth pervaded the snug alcove, made by the back of the pew in which he lay. He had been fortunate indeed to find such a place, because the body of the church was gloomy and cold. But he did not hear the winds, and no thought of the snow troubled him, as he slept on hour after hour.

The night passed, the light snow had ceased, no trace of it was left on the earth, and the brilliant sunshine flooded the ancient capital with warmth. People went about their usual pursuits. Old men and old women sold sweets, hot coffee, and *tortillas* and *frijoles*, also hot, in the streets. Little plaster images of the saints and the Virgin were exposed on trays. Donkeys loaded with vegetables, that had been brought across the lakes, bumped one another in the narrow ways. Many officers in fine uniforms and many soldiers in uniforms not so fine could be seen.

Whatever else Mexico might be it was martial. The great Santa Anna whom men called another Napoleon now ruled, and there was talk of war and glory. Much of it was vague, but of one thing they were certain. Santa Anna would soon crush the mutinous Texans in the wild north. Gringos they were, always pushing where they were not wanted, and, however hard their fate, they would deserve it. The vein of cruelty which, despite great virtues, has made Spain a by-word among nations, showed in her descendants.

But the boy, Edward Fulton, sleeping in the chapel of the great cathedral, knew nothing of it all. Nature, too long defrauded, was claiming payment of her debt, and he slept peacefully on, although the hours passed and noon came.

The church had long been open. Priests came and went in the aisles, and entered some of the chapels. Worshipers, most of them women, knelt before the shrines. Service was held at the high altar, and the odour of incense filled the great nave. Yet the boy was still in sanctuary, and a kindly angel was watching over him. No one entered the chapel in which he slept.

It was almost the middle of the afternoon when he awoke. He heard a faint murmur of voices and a pleasant odour came to his nostrils. He quickly remembered everything, and, stirring a little on his wooden couch he found a certain stiffness in the joints. He realised however that all his strength had come back.

But Ned Fulton understood, although he had escaped from prison and had found shelter and sanctuary in the cathedral, that he was yet in an extremely precarious position. The murmur of voices told him that people were in the church, and he had no doubt that the odour came from burning incense.

A little light from the narrow window fell upon him. It came through coloured glass, and made red and blue splotches on his hands, at which he looked curiously. He knew that it was a brilliant day outside, and he longed for air and exercise, but he dared not move except to stretch his arms and legs, until the stiffness and soreness disappeared from his joints. Contact with Spaniard and Mexican had taught him the full need of caution.

He was very hungry again, and now he was thankful for his restraint of the night before. He ate the rest of the food in his pockets and waited patiently.

Ned knew that he had slept a long time, and that it must be late in the day. He was confirmed in his opinion by the angle at which the light entered the window, and he decided that he would lie in the pew until night came again. It was a trying test. School his will as he would he felt at times that he must come from his covert and walk about the chapel. The narrow wooden pew became a casket in which he was held, and now and then he was short of breath. Yet he persisted. He was learning very young the value of will, and he forced himself every day to use it and increase its strength.

In such a position and with so much threatening him his faculties became uncommonly keen. He heard the voices more distinctly, and also the footsteps of the priests in their felt slippers. They passed the door of the chapel in which he lay, and once or twice he thought they were going to enter, but they seemed merely to pause at the door. Then he would hold his breath until they were gone.

At last and with infinite joy he saw the coloured lights fade. The window itself grew dark, and the murmur in the church ceased. But he did not come forth from his secure refuge until it was quite dark. He staggered from stiffness at first, but the circulation was soon restored. Then he looked from the door of the chapel into the great nave. An old priest in a brown robe was extinguishing the candles. Ned watched him until he had put out the last one, and disappeared in the rear of the church.

Then he came forth and standing in the great, gloomy nave tried to decide what to do next. He had found a night's shelter and no more. He had escaped from prison, but not from the City of Mexico, and his Texas was yet a thousand miles away.

Ned found the little door by which he had entered, and passed outside, hiding again among the trees of the Zocalo. The night was very cold and he shivered once more, as he stood there waiting. The night was so dark that the cathedral was almost a formless bulk. But above it, the light in the slender lantern shone like a friendly star. While he looked the great bell of Santa Maria de Guadalupe in the western tower began to chime, and presently the smaller bell of Dona Maria in the eastern tower joined. It was a mellow song they sung and they sang fresh courage into the young fugitive's veins. He knew that he could never again see this cathedral built upon the site of the great Aztec *teocalli*, destroyed by the Spaniards more than three hundred years before, without a throb of gratitude.

Ned's first resolve was to take measures for protection from the cold, and he placed his silver dollars in his most convenient pocket. Then he left the trees and moved toward the east, passing in front of the handsome church Sagrario Metropolitano, and entering a very narrow street that led among a maze of small buildings. The district was lighted faintly by a few hanging lanterns, but as Ned had hoped, some of the shops were yet open. The people who sat here and there in the low doorways were mostly short of stature and dark and broad of face. The Indian in them predominated over the Spaniard, and some were pure Aztec. Ned judged that they would not take any deep interest in the fortunes of their rulers, Spanish or Mexican, royalist or republican.

He pulled his cap over his eyes and a little to one side, and strolled on, humming an old Mexican air. His walk was the swagger of a young Mexican gallant, and in the dimness they would not notice his Northern fairness. Several pairs of eyes observed him, but not with disapproval. They considered him a trim Mexican lad. Some of the men in the doorways took up the air that he was whistling and continued it.

He saw soon the place for which he was looking, a tiny shop in which an old Indian sold *serapes*. He stopped in the doorway, which he filled, took down one of the best and heaviest and held out the number of dollars which he considered an adequate price. The Indian shook his head and asked for nearly twice as much. Ned knew how long they bargained and chaffered in Mexico and what a delight they took in it. After an hour's talk he could secure the *serape*, at the price he offered, but he dared not linger in one place. Already the old Indian was looking at him inquiringly. Doubtless he had seen that this was no Mexican, but Ned judged shrewdly that he would not let the fact interfere with a promising bargain.

The boy acted promptly. He added two more silver dollars to the amount that he had proffered, put the whole in the old Indian's palm, took down the *serape*, folded it over his arm, and with a *"gracias, señor,"* backed swiftly out of the shop. The old Indian was too much astonished to move for at least a half minute. Then tightly clutching the silver in his hand he ran into the street. But the tall young *senor*, with the *serape* already wrapped around his shoulders, was disappearing in the darkness. The Indian opened his palm and looked at the silver. A smile passed over his face. After all, it was two good Spanish dollars more than he had expected, and he returned contentedly to his shop. If such generous young gentlemen came along every night his fortune would soon be made.

Ned soon left the shop far behind. It was a fine *serape*, very large, thick and warm, and he draped himself in it in true Mexican fashion. It kept him warm, and, wrapped in its folds, he looked much more like a genuine Mexican. He had but little money left, but among the more primitive people beyond the capital one might work his way. If suspected he could claim to be English, and Mexico was not at war with England.

He bought a *sombrero* at another shop with almost the last of his money, and then started toward La Viga, the canal that leads from the lower part of the city toward the fresh water lakes, Chalco and Xochimilco. He hoped to find at the canal one of the *bergantins*, or flat-bottomed boats, in which vegetables, fruit and flowers were brought to the city for sale. They were good-natured people, those of the *bergantins*, and they would not scorn the offer of a stout lad to help with sail and oar.

Hidden in his *serape* and *sombrero*, and, secure in his knowledge of Spanish and Mexican, he now advanced boldly through the more populous and better lighted parts of the city. He even lingered a little while in front of a cafe, where men were playing guitar and *mandolin*, and girls were dancing with *castanets*. The sight of light and life pleased the boy who had been so long in prison. These people were diverting themselves and they smiled and laughed. They seemed to have kindly feelings for everybody, but he remembered that cruel Spanish strain, often dormant, but always there, and he hastened on.

Three officers, their swords swinging at their thighs, came down the narrow street abreast. At another time Ned would not have given way, and even now it hurt him to do so, but prudence made him step from the sidewalk. One of them laughed and applied an insulting epithet to the "*peon,*" but Ned bore it and continued, his *sombrero* pulled well down over his eyes.

His course now led him by the great palace of Iturbide, where he saw many windows blazing with light. Several officers were entering and chief among them he recognised General Martin Perfecto de Cos, the brother-in-law of Santa Anna, whom Ned believed to be a treacherous and cruel man. He hastened away from such an unhealthy proximity, and came to La Viga.

He saw a rude wharf along the canal and several boats, all with the sails furled, except two. These two might be returning to the fresh water lakes, and it was possible that he could secure passage. The people of the *bergantins* were always humble peons and they cared little for the intrigues of the capital.

It was now about eleven o'clock and the night had lightened somewhat, a fair moon showing. Ned could see distinctly the boats or *bergantins* as the Mexicans called them. They were large, flat of bottom, shallow of draft, and were propelled with both sail and oar. He was repulsed at the first, where a surly Mexican of middle age told him with a curse that he wanted no help, but at the next which had as a crew a man, a woman, evidently his wife, and two half-grown boys, he was more fortunate. Could he use an oar? He could. Then he might come, because there was little promise of wind, and the sails would be of no use. A strong arm would help, as it was sixteen miles down La Viga to the Lake of Xochimilco, on the shores of which they lived. The boys were tired and sleepy, and he would serve very well in their stead.

Ned took his place in the boat, truly thankful that in this crisis of his life he knew how to row. He saw that his hosts, or rather those for whom he worked, were an ordinary peon family, at least half Indian, sluggish of mind and kind of heart. They had brought vegetables and flowers to the city, and now they were thriftily returning in the night to their home on the lake that Benito Igarritos and his sons might not miss the next day from their work.

Igarritos and Ned took the oars. The two boys stretched themselves on the bottom of the boat and were asleep in an instant. Juana, the wife, spread a *serape* over them, and then sat down in Turkish fashion in the centre of the *bergantin*, a great red and yellow *reboso* about her head and shoulders. Sometimes she looked at her husband, and sometimes at the strange boy. He had spoken to them in good Mexican, he dressed like a Mexican and he walked like a Mexican, but she had not been deceived. She knew that the Mexican part of him ended with the *serape* and *sombrero*. She wondered why he had come, and why he was anxious to go to the Lake of Xochimilco. But she reflected with the patience and resignation of an oppressed race that it was no business of hers. He was a good youth. He had spoken to her with compliments as one speaks to a lady of high degree, and he bent manfully on the oar. He was welcome. But he must have a name and she would know it.

"What do you call yourself?" she asked.

"William," he replied. "I come from a far country, England, and it is my pleasure to travel in new lands and see new peoples."

"Weel-le-am," she said gravely, "you are far from your friends."

Ned bent his head in assent. Her simple words made him feel that he was indeed far from his own land and surrounded by a thousand perils. The woman did not speak again and they moved on with an even stroke down the canal which had an uniform width of about thirty feet. They were still passing houses of stone and others of *adobe*, but before they had gone a mile they were halted by a sharp command from the shore. An officer and three soldiers, one of whom held a lantern, stood on the bank.

Ned had expected that they would be stopped. These were revolutionary times and people could not go in or out of the city unnoticed. Particularly was La Viga guarded. He knew that his fate now rested with Benito Igarritos and his wife Juana, but he trusted them. The officer was peremptory, but the *bergantin* was most innocent in appearance. Merely a humble vegetable boat returning down La Viga after a successful day in the city. "Your family?" Ned heard the officer say to Benito, as he flashed the lantern in turn upon every one.

Taciturn, like most men of the oppressed races, Benito nodded, while his wife sat silent in her great red and yellow *reboso*. Ned leaned carelessly upon the oar, but his face was well hid by the *sombrero*, and his heart was throbbing. When the light of the lantern passed over him he felt as if he were seared by a flame, but the officer had no suspicion, and with a gruff "Pass on" he withdrew from the bank with his men. Benito nodded to Ned and they pulled again into the centre of La Viga. Neither spoke. Nor did the woman.

Ned bent on the oar with renewed strength. He felt that the greatest of his dangers was now passed, and the relief of the spirit brought fresh strength. The night lightened yet more. He saw on the low banks of the canal green shrubs and many plants with spikes and thorns. It seemed to him characteristic of Mexico that nearly everything should have its spikes and thorns. Through the gray night showed the background of the distant mountains.

They overtook and passed two other *bergantins* returning from the city and they met a third on its way thither with vegetables for the morning market. Benito knew the owners and exchanged a brief word with everyone as he passed. Ned pulled silently at his oar.

When it was far past midnight Ned felt a cool breeze rising. Benito began to unfurl the sail.

"You have pulled well, young *senor*," he said to Ned, "but the oar is needed no more. Now the wind will work for us. You will sleep and Carlos will help me."

He awoke the elder of the two boys. Ned was so tired that his arms ached, and he was glad to rest. He wrapped his heavy *serape* about himself, lay down on the bottom of the boat, pillowed his head on his arm, and went to sleep.

When he awoke, it was day and they were floating on a broad sheet of shallow water, which he knew instinctively was Xochimilco. The wind was still blowing, and one of the boys steered the *bergantin*. Be-

34

nito, Juana and the other boy sat up, with their faces turned toward the rosy morning light, as if they were sun-worshipers. Ned also felt the inspiration. The world was purer and clearer here than in the city. In the early morning the grayish, lonely tint which is the prevailing note of Mexico, did not show. The vegetation was green, or it was tinted with the glow of the sun. Near the lower shores he saw the *Chiampas* or floating gardens.

Benito turned the *bergantin* into a cove, and they went ashore. His house, flat roofed and built of adobe, was near, standing in a field, filled with spiky and thorny plants. They gave Ned a breakfast, the ordinary peasant fare of the country, but in abundance, and then the woman, who seemed to be in a sense the spokesman of the family, said very gravely:

"You are a good boy, Weel-le-am, and you rowed well. What more do you wish of us?"

Benito also bent his dark eyes upon him in serious inquiry. Ned was not prepared for any reply. He did not know just what to do and on impulse he answered:

"I would stay with you a while and work. You will not find me lazy."

He waved his hand toward the spiky and thorny field. Benito consulted briefly with his wife and they agreed. For three or four days Ned toiled in the hot field with Benito and the boys and at night he slept on the floor of earth. The work was hard and it made his body sore. The food was of the roughest, but these things were trifles compared with the gift of freedom which he had received. How glorious it was to breathe the fresh air and to have only the sky for a roof and the horizon for walls!

Benito and the older boy again took the *bergantin* loaded with vegetables up La Viga to the city. They did not suggest that Ned go with them. He remained working in the field, and trying to think of some way in which he could obtain money for a journey. The wind was good, the *bergantin* traveled fast, and Benito and his boy returned speedily. Benito greeted Ned with a grave salute, but said nothing until an hour later, when they sat by a fire outside the hut, eating the *tortillas* and *frijoles* which Juana had cooked for them.

"What is the news in the capital?" asked Ned.

Benito pondered his reply.

"The president, the protector of us all, the great General Santa Anna, grows more angry at the Texans, the wild Americans who have

35

come into the wilderness of the far North," he replied. "They talk of an army going soon against them, and they talk, too, of a daring escape."

He paused and contemplatively lit a *cigarrito.*

"What was the escape?" asked Ned, the pulse in his wrist beginning to beat hard.

"One of the Texans, whom the great Santa Anna holds, but a boy they say he was, though fierce, slipped between the bars of his window and is gone. They wish to get him back; they are anxious to take him again for reasons that are too much for Benito."

"Do you think they will find him?"

"How do I know? But they say he is yet in the capital, and there is a reward of one hundred good Spanish dollars for the one who will bring him in, or who will tell where he is to be found."

Benito quietly puffed at his *cigarrito* and Juana, the cooking being over, threw ashes on the coals.

"If he is still hiding within reach of Santa Anna's arm," said Ned, "somebody is sure to betray him for the reward."

"I do not know," said Benito, tossing away the stub of his *cigarrito.* Then he rose and began work in the field.

Ned went out with the elder boy, Carlos, and caught fish. They did not return until twilight, and the others were already waiting placidly while Juana prepared their food. None of them could read; they had little; their life was of the most primitive, but Ned noticed that they never spoke cross words to one another. They seemed to him to be entirely content.

After supper they sat on the ground in front of the *adobe* hut. The evening was clear and already many stars were coming into a blue sky. The surface of the lake was silver, rippling lightly. Benito smoked luxuriously.

"I saw this afternoon a friend of mine, Miguel Lampridi," he said after a while. "He had just come down La Viga from the city."

"What news did he bring?" asked Edward.

"They are still searching everywhere for the young Texan who went through the window—Eduardo Fulton is his name. Truly General Santa Anna must have his reasons. The reward has been doubled."

"Poor lad," spoke Juana, who spoke seldom. "It may be that the young Texan is not as bad as they say. But it is much money that they offer. Someone will find him."

36

"It may be," said Benito. Then they sat a long time in silence. Juana was the first to go into the house and to bed. After a while the two boys followed. Another half hour passed, and Ned rose.

"I go, Benito," he said. "You and your wife have been good to me, and I cannot bring misfortune upon you. Why is it that you did not betray me? The reward is large. You would have been a rich man here."

Benito laughed low.

"Yes, it would have been much money," he replied, "but what use have I for it? I have the wife I wish, and my sons are good sons. We do not go hungry and we sleep well. So it will be all the days of our life. Two hundred silver dollars would bring two hundred evil spirits among us. Thy face, young Texan, is a good face. I think so and my wife, Juana, who knows, says so. Yet it is best that you go. Others will soon learn, and it is hard to live between close stone walls, when the free world is so beautiful. I will call Juana, and she, too, will tell you farewell. We would not drive you away, but since you choose to go, you shall not leave without a kind word, which may go with you as a blessing on your way."

He called at the door of the *adobe* hut. Juana came forth. She was stout, and she had never been beautiful, but her face seemed very pleasant to Ned, as she asked the Holy Virgin to watch over him in his wanderings.

"I have five silver dollars," said Benito. "They are yours. They will make the way shorter."

But Ned refused absolutely to accept them. He would not take the store of people who had been so kind to him. Instead he offered the single dollar that he had left for a heavy knife like a machete. Benito brought it to him and reluctantly took the dollar.

"Do not try the northern way, Texan," he said, "it is too far. Go over the mountains to Vera Cruz, where you will find passage on a ship."

It seemed good advice to Ned, and, although the change of plan was abrupt, he promised to take it. Juana gave him a bag of food which he fastened to his belt under his *serape*, and at midnight, with the blessing of the Holy Virgin invoked for him again, he started. Fifty yards away he turned and saw the man and woman standing before their door and gazing at him. He waved his hand and they returned the salute. He walked on again a little mist before his eyes. They had been very kind to him, these poor people of another race.

He walked along the shore of the lake for a long time, and then bore in toward the east, intending to go parallel with the great road to Vera Cruz. His step was brisk and his heart high. He felt more courage and hope than at any other time since he had dropped from the prison. He had food for several days, and the possession of the heavy knife was a great comfort. He could slash with it, as with a hatchet.

He walked steadily for hours. The road was rough, but he was young and strong. Once he crossed the *pedregal,* a region where an old lava flow had cooled, and which presented to his feet numerous sharp edges like those of a knife. He had good shoes with heavy soles and he knew their value. On the long march before him they were worth as much as bread and weapons, and he picked his way as carefully as a walker on a tight rope. He was glad when he had crossed the dangerous *pedregal* and entered a cypress forest, clustering on a low hill. Grass grew here also, and he rested a while, wrapped in his *serape* against the coldness of the night.

He saw behind and now below him the city, the towers of the churches outlined against the sky. It was from some such place as this that Cortez and his men, embarked upon the world's most marvellous adventure, had looked down for the first time upon the ancient city of Tenochtitlan. But it did not beckon to Ned. It seemed to him that a mighty menace to his beloved Texas emanated from it. And he must warn the Texans.

He sprang to his feet and resumed his journey. At the eastern edge of the hill he came upon a beautiful little spring, leaping from the rock. He drank from it and went on. Lower down he saw some *adobe* huts among the cypresses and cactus. No doubt their occupants were sound asleep, but for safety's sake he curved away from them. Dogs barked, and when they barked again the sound showed they were coming nearer. He ran, rather from caution than fear, because if the dogs attacked he wished to be so far away from the huts that their owners would not be awakened.

Now he gave thanks that he had the machete. He thrust his hands under the *serape* and clasped its strong handle. It was a truly formidable weapon. He came to another little hill, also clothed in cypress, and began to ascend it with decreased speed. The baying of the dogs was growing much louder. They were coming fast. Near the summit he saw a heap of rock, probably an Aztec tumulus, six or seven feet high. Ned smiled with satisfaction. Pressed by danger his mind was quick. He was where he would make his defence, and he did not think it would need to be a long one.

He settled himself well upon the top of the *tumulus* and drew his machete. The dogs, six in number, coursed among the cypresses, and the leader, foam upon his mouth, leaped straight at Ned. The boy involuntarily drew up his feet a little, but he was not shaken from the crouching position that was best suited to a blow. As the hound was in mid-air he swung the machete with all his might and struck straight at the ugly head. The heavy blade crashed through the skull and the dog fell dead without a sound. Another which leaped also, but not so far, received a deep cut across the shoulder. It fell back and retreated with the others among the cypresses, where the unwounded dogs watched with red eyes the formidable figure on the rocks.

But Ned did not remain on the *tumulus* more than a few minutes longer. When he sprang down the dogs growled, but he shook the machete until it glittered in the moonlight. With howls of terror they fled, while he resumed his journey in the other direction.

Near morning he came into country which seemed to him very wild. The soil was hard and dry, but there was a dense growth of giant cactus, with patches here and there of thorny bushes. Guarding well against the spikes and thorns he crept into one of the thickets and lay down. He must rest and sleep and already the touch of rose in the east was heralding the dawn. Sleep by day and flight by night. He was satisfied with himself. He had really succeeded better so far than he had hoped, and, guarded by the spikes and thorns, slumber took him before dawn had spread from east to west.

CHAPTER 4

THE PALM

Ned awoke about noon. The morning had been cold, but having been wrapped very thoroughly in the great serape, he had remained snug and warm all through his long sleep. He rose very cautiously, lest the spikes and thorns should get him, and then went to a comparatively open place among the giant cactus stems whence he could see over the hills and valleys. He saw in the valley nearest him the flat roofs of a small village. Columns of smoke rose from two or three of the adobe houses, and he heard the faint, mellow voices of men singing in a field. Women by the side of a small but swift stream were pounding and washing clothes after the primitive fashion.

Looking eastward he saw hills and a small mountain, but all the

39

As the hound was in mid-air he swung the
machete with all his might.

country in that direction seemed to be extremely arid and repellent. The bare basalt of volcanic origin showed everywhere, and, even at the distance, he could see many deep quarries in the stone, where races older, doubtless, than Aztecs and Toltecs, had obtained material for building. It was always Ned's feeling when in Mexico that he was in an old, old land, not ancient like England or France, but ancient as Egypt and Babylon are ancient.

He had calculated his course very carefully, and he knew that it would lead through this desert, volcanic region, but on the whole he was not sorry. Mexicans would be scarce in such a place. He remained a lad of stout heart, confident that he would succeed.

He ate sparingly and reckoned that with self-denial he had food enough to last three days. He might obtain more on the road by some happy chance or other. Then becoming impatient he started again, keeping well among cypress and cactus, and laying his course toward the small mountain that he saw ahead. He pressed forward the remainder of the afternoon, coming once or twice near to the great road that led to Vera Cruz. On one occasion he saw a small body of soldiers, deep in dust, marching toward the port. All except the officers were peons and they did not seem to Ned to show much martial ardour. But the officers on horseback sternly bade them hasten. Ned, as usual, had much sympathy for the poor peasants, but none for the officers who drove them on.

About sunset he came to a little river, the Teotihuacan he learned afterward, and he still saw before him the low mountain, the name of which was Cerro Gordo. But his attention was drawn from the mountain by two elevations rising almost at the bank of the river. They were pyramidal in shape and truncated, and the larger, which Ned surmised to be anywhere from 500 to 1000 feet square, seemed to rise to a height of two or three hundred feet. The other was about two-thirds the size of the larger, both in area and height.

Although there was much vegetation clinging about them Ned knew that these were pyramids erected by the hand of man. The feeling that this was a land old like Egypt came back to him most powerfully in the presence of these ancient monuments, which were in fact the Pyramid of the Sun and the Pyramid of the Moon. There they stood, desolate and of untold age. The setting sun poured an intense red light upon them, until they stood out vivid and enlarged.

So far as Ned knew, no other human being was anywhere near. The loneliness in the presence of those tremendous ruins was overpowering. He longed for human companionship. A peon, despite the danger otherwise, would have been welcome. The whole land took on fantastic aspects. It was not normal and healthy like the regions from which he came north of the Rio Grande. Every nerve quivered.

Then he did the bravest thing that one could do in such a position, forcing his will to win a victory over weirdness and superstition. He crossed the shallow river and advanced boldly toward the Pyramid of the Sun. His reason told him that there were no such things as ghosts, but it told him also that Mexican peons were likely to believe in them. Hence it was probable that he would be safer about the Pyramid than far from it. The country bade fair to become too rough for night travelling and he would stop there a while, refreshing his strength.

Although the sun was setting, the colour of the skies promised a bright night, and Ned approached boldly. As usual his superstitious fears became weaker as he approached the objects that had called them into existence. But before he reached the pyramids he found that he was among many ruins. They stood all about him, stone fragments of ancient walls, black basalt or lava, and, unless the twilight deceived him, there were also traces of ancient streets. He saw, too, south of the larger pyramids a great earthwork or citadel thirty or forty feet high enclosing a square in which stood a small pyramid. The walls of the earthwork were enormously thick, three hundred feet Ned reckoned, and upon it at regular intervals stood other small pyramids fourteen in number.

Scattered all about, alone or in groups, were *tumuli*, and leading away from the largest group of *tumuli* Ned saw a street or causeway, which, passing by the Pyramid of the Sun, ended in front of the Pyramid of the Moon, where it widened out into a great circle, with a tumulus standing in the centre.

Despite all the courage that he had shown Ned felt a superstitious thrill as he looked at these ancient and solemn ruins. He and they were absolutely alone. Antiquity looked down upon him. The sun was gone now and the moon was coming out, touching pyramids and *tumuli*, earthworks and causeway with ghostly silver, deepening the effect of loneliness and far-off time.

While Ned was looking at these majestic remains he heard the sound of voices, and then the rattle of weapons. He saw through the twilight the glitter of uniforms and of swords and sabres. A company of Mexican soldiers, at least a hundred in number, had come into the ancient city and, no doubt, intended to camp there. Being so absorbed in the strange ruins he had not noticed them sooner.

As the men were already scattering in search of firewood or other needs of the camp Ned saw that he was in great danger. He hid behind a *tumulus*, half covered by the vegetation that had grown from its crevices. He was glad that his *serape* was of a modest brown, instead of the bright colons that most of the Mexicans loved. A soldier passed within ten feet of him, but in the twilight did not notice him. It was enough to make one quiver. Another passed a little later, and he, too, failed to see the fugitive. But a third, if he came, would probably see, and leaving the *tumulus* Ned ran to another where he hid again for a few minutes.

It was the boy's object to make off through the neighbouring forest after passing from *tumulus* to *tumulus*, but he found soon that another body of soldiers was camping upon the far side of the ruined city. He might or might not run the gauntlet in the darkness. The probabilities were that he would not, and hiding behind a *tumulus* almost midway between the two forces he took thought of his next step.

The Pyramid of the Moon rose almost directly before him, its truncated mass spotted with foliage. Ned could see that its top was flat and instantly he took a bold resolution. He made his way to the base of the pyramid and began to climb slowly and with great care, always keeping hidden in the vegetation. He was certain that no Mexican would follow where he was going. They were on other business, and their incurious minds bothered little about a city that was dead and gone for them.

Up he went steadily over uneven terraces, and from below he heard the chatter of the soldiers. A third fire had been lighted much nearer the pyramid, and pausing a moment he looked down. Twenty or thirty soldiers were scattered about this fire. Their muskets were stacked and they were taking their ease. Discipline was relaxed. One man was strumming a *mandolin* already, and two or three began to sing. But Ned saw sentinels walking among the *tumuli* and along the Calle de los Muertos which led from the Citadel to the southern front of the Pyramid of the Moon. He was very glad now that he had sought this lofty refuge, and he renewed his climb.

As he drew himself upon another terrace he saw before him a dark opening into the very mass of the pyramid, which was built either of brick or of stone, he could not tell which. He thought once of creeping in and of hiding there, but after taking a couple of steps into the dark he drew back. He was afraid of plunging into some well and he continued the ascent. He was now about sixty or seventy feet up, but he was not yet half way to the top of the pyramid.

He was so slow and cautious that it took more than a half hour to reach the crest, where he found himself upon a platform about twenty feet square. It was an irregular surface with much vegetation growing from the crevices, and here Ned felt quite safe. Near him and sixty feet above him rose the crest of the Pyramid of the Sun. Beyond were ranges of mountains silvery in the moonlight. He walked to the edge of the pyramid and looked down. Four or five fires were burning now, and the single *mandolin* had grown to four. Several guitars were being plucked vigorously also, and the sound of the instruments joined with that of the singing voices was very musical and pleasant. These Mexicans seemed to be full of good nature, and so they were, with fire, food and music in plenty, but now that he had been their prisoner Ned never forgot how that dormant and Spanish strain of cruelty in their natures could flame high under the influence of passion. The dungeons of Spanish Mexico and of the new Mexico hid many dark stories, and he believed that he had read what lay behind the smiling mask of Santa Anna's face. He would suffer everything to keep out of Mexican hands.

He crept away from the edge of the pyramid, and chose a place near its centre for his lofty camp. There was much vegetation growing out of the ancient masonry, and he had a fear of scorpions and of more dangerous reptiles, perhaps, but he thrashed up the grass and weeds well with his machete. Then he sat down and ate his supper. Fortunately he had drunk copiously at a brook before reaching the ruined city and he did not suffer from thirst.

Then, relying upon the isolation of his perch for safety, he wrapped himself in the invaluable *serape* and lay down. The night was cold as usual, and a sharp wind blew down from northern peaks and ranges, but Ned, protected by vegetation and the heavy *serape*, had an extraordinary feeling of warmth and snugness as he lay on the old pyramid. Held so long within close walls the wild freedom and the fresh air that came across seas and continents were very grateful to him. Even the presence of an enemy, so near, and yet, as it seemed, so little dangerous, added a certain piquancy to his position. The pleasant tinkle of the *mandolins* was wafted upward to him, and it was wonderfully soothing, telling of peace and rest. He inhaled the aromatic odours of strange and flowering southern plants, and his senses were steeped in a sort of luxurious calm.

He fell asleep to the music of the *mandolin*, and when he awoke such a bright sun was shining in his eyes that he was glad to close and open them again several times before they would tolerate the brilliant Mexican sky that bent above him. He lay still about five minutes, listening, and then, to his disappointment, he heard sounds below. He judged by the position of the sun that it must be at least 10 o'clock in the morning, and the Mexicans should be gone. Yet they were undoubtedly still there. He crept to the edge of the pyramid and looked over. There was the Mexican force, scattered about the ruined city, but camped in greatest numbers along the Calle de los Muertos. Their numbers had been increased by two hundred or three hundred, and, as Ned saw no signs of breaking camp, he judged that this was a rendezvous, and that there were more troops yet to come.

He saw at once that his problem was increased greatly. He could not dream of leaving the summit of the pyramid before the next night came. Food he had in plenty but no water, and already as the hot sun's rays approached the vertical he felt a great thirst. Imagination and the knowledge that he could not allay it for the present at least, increased the burning sensation in his throat and the dryness of his lips. He caught a view of the current of the Teotihuacan, the little river by the side of which the pyramids stand, and the sight increased his torments. He had never seen before such fresh and pure water. It sparkled and raced in the sun before him and it looked divine. And yet it was as far out of his reach as if it were all the way across Mexico.

Ned went back to the place where he had slept and sat down. The sight of the river had tortured him, and he felt better when it was shut from view. Now he resolved to see what could be accomplished by will. He undertook to forget the water, and at times he succeeded, but, despite his greatest efforts, the Teotihuacan would come back now and then with the most astonishing vividness. Although he was lying on the *serape* with bushes and shrubs all around, there was the river visible to the eye of imagination, brighter, fresher and more sparkling than ever. He could not control his fancy, but will ruled the body and he did not stir from his place for hours. The sun beat fiercely upon him and the thin bushes and shrubs afforded little protection. Toward the northern edge of the pyramid a small palm was growing out of a large crevice in the masonry, and it might have given some shade, but it was in such an exposed position that Ned did not dare to use it for fear of discovery.

How he hated that sun! It seemed to be drying him up, through and through, causing the very blood in his veins to evaporate. Why should such hot days follow such cold nights? When his tongue touched the roof of his mouth it felt rough and hot like a coal. Perhaps the Mexicans had gone away. It seemed to him that he had not heard any sounds from them for some time. He went to the edge of the pyramid and looked over. No, the Mexicans were yet there, and the sight of them filled him with a fierce anger. They were enjoying themselves. Tents were scattered about and shelters of boughs had been erected. Many soldiers were taking their *siestas*. Nobody was working and there was not the slightest sign that they intended to depart that day. Ned's hot tongue clove to the roof of his hot mouth, but he obstinately refused to look at the river. He did not think that he could stand another sight of it.

He went back to his little lair among the shrubs and prayed for night, blessed night with its cooling touch. He had a horrible apprehension which amounted to conviction that the troops would stay there for several days, awaiting some manoeuvre or perhaps making it a rallying point, and that in his hiding place on the pyramid he was in as bad case as a sailor cast on a desert island without water. Nothing seemed left for him but to steal down and try to escape in darkness. Thus night would be doubly welcome and he prayed for it again and with renewed fervour.

Some hours are ten times as long as others, but the longest of all come to an end at last. The sun began to droop in the west. The vertical glare was gone, yet the masonry where it was bare was yet hot to the touch. It, too, cooled soon. The sun dropped wholly down and darkness came over all the earth. Then the fever in Ned's throat died down somewhat, and the blood began to flow again in his veins. It seemed as if a dew touched his face, delicious, soothing like drops of rain in the burning desert.

He rose and stretched his stiffened limbs. Overhead spread the dark, cool sky, and the bright stars were coming out, one by one. After the first few moments of relief he heard the cry for water again. Despite the night and the coming chill he knew that it would make itself heard often and often, and he began to study the possibilities of a descent. But he saw the fires spread out again on all sides of the Pyramid of the Sun and the Pyramid of the Moon and flame thickly along the Calle de los Muertos. It did not seem that he could pass even on the blackest night.

He moved over toward the northern edge of the pyramid, and

stood under the palm which he had noticed in the day. One of its broad green leaves, swayed by the wind, touched him softly on the face. He looked up. It was a friendly palm. Its very touch was kindly. He stroked the blades and then he examined the stem or body minutely. He was a studious boy who had read much. He had heard of the water palm of the Hawaiian and other South Sea Islands. Might not the water palm be found in Mexico also? In any event, he had never heard of a palm that was poisonous. They were always givers of life.

He raised the machete and slashed the stem of the palm at a point about five feet from the ground. The wound gaped open and a stream of water gushed forth. Ned applied his mouth at once and drank long and deeply. It was not poison, nor was it any bitter juice. This was the genuine water palm, yielding up the living fluid of its arteries for him. He drank as long as the gash gave forth water and then sat down under the blades of the palm, content and thankful, realising that there was always hope in the very heart of despair.

Ned sat a long time, feeling the new life rushing into his veins. He ate from the food of which he had a plentiful supply and once more gave thanks to Benito and Juana. Then he stood up and the broad leaves of the palm waving gently in the wind touched his face again. He reached up his hand and stroked them. The palm was to him almost a thing of life. He went to the edge of the pyramid and strove for a sight of the Teotihuacan. He caught at last a flash of its waters in the moonlight and he shook his fist in defiance. "I can do without you now," was his thought. "The sight of you does not torture me."

He returned to his usual place of sleep. As long as he had a water supply it was foolish of him to attempt an escape through the Mexican lines. He was familiar now with every square inch of the twenty feet square of the crowning platform of the pyramid. It seemed that he had been there for weeks and he began to have the feeling that it was home. Once more, hunger and thirst satisfied, he sought sleep and slept with the deep peace of youth.

Ned awoke from his second night on the pyramid before dawn was complete. There was silvery light in the east over the desolate ranges, but the west was yet a dark blur. He looked down and saw that nearly all the soldiers were still asleep, while those who did not sleep were as motionless as if they were. In the half light the lost city, the tumuli and the ruins of the old buildings took on strange and fantastic shapes. The feeling that he was among the dead, the dead for many centuries, returned to Ned with overpowering effect. He thought of

Aztec and Toltec and people back of all these who had built this city. The Mexicans below were intruders like himself.

He shook himself as if by physical effort he could get rid of the feeling and then went to the water palm in which he cut another gash. Again the fountain gushed forth and he drank. But the palm was a small one. There was too little soil among the crevices of the ancient masonry to support a larger growth, and he saw that it could not satisfy his thirst more than a day or two. But anything might happen in that time, and his courage suffered no decrease.

He retreated toward the centre of the platform as the day was now coming fast after the southern fashion. The whole circle of the heavens seemed to burst into a blaze of light, and, in a few hours, the sun was hotter than it had been before. Many sounds now came from the camp below, but Ned, although he often looked eagerly, saw no signs of coming departure. Shortly after noon there was a great blare of trumpets, and a detachment of lancers rode up. They were large men, mounted finely, and the heads of their long lances glittered as they brandished them in the sun.

Ned's attention was drawn to the leader of this new detachment, an officer in most brilliant uniform, and he started. He knew him at once. It was the brother-in-law of Santa Anna, General Martin Perfecto de Cos, a man in whom that old, cruel strain was very strong, and whom Ned believed to be charged with the crushing of the Texans. Then he was right in his surmise that Mexican forces for the campaign were gathering here on the banks of the Teotihuacan!

More troops came in the afternoon, and the boy no longer had the slightest doubt. The camp spread out further and further, and assumed military form. Not so many men were lounging about and the tinkling of the guitars ceased. Ned could see General de Cos plainly, a heavy man of dark face, autocratic and domineering in manner.

Night came and the boy went once more to the palm. When he struck with his machete the water came forth, but in a much weaker stream. In reality he was yet thirsty after he drank the full flow, but he would not cut into the stem again. He knew that he must practice the severest economy with his water supply.

The third night came and as soon as he was safe from observation Ned slashed the palm once more. The day had been very hot and his thirst was great. The water come forth but with only half the vigour of the morning, which itself had shown a decrease. The poor palm, too, trembled and shook when he cut into it with the machete and the blades drooped. Ned drank what it supplied and then turned away regretfully. It was a kindly palm, a gift to man, and yet he must slay it to save his own life.

He lay down again, but he did not sleep as well as usual. His nerves were upset by the long delay, and the decline of the palm, and he was not refreshed when he awoke in the morning. His head felt hot and his limbs were heavy.

As it was not yet bright daylight he went to the palm and cut into it. The flow of water was only a few mouthfuls. Cautious and doubly economical now he pursed his lips that not a single drop might escape. Then, after eating a little food he lay down, protected as much as possible by the scanty bushes, and also sheltering himself at times from the sun with the serape which he drew over his head. He felt instinctively and with the power of conviction that the Mexicans would not depart. The coming of Cos had taken the hope from him. Cos! He hated the short, brusque name.

It was another day of dazzling brightness and intense heat. Certainly this was a vertical sun. It shot rays like burning arrows straight down. The blood in his veins seemed to dry up again. His head grew hotter. Black specks in myriads danced before his eyes. He looked longingly at his palm. When he first saw it, it stood up, vital and strong. Now it seemed to droop and waver like himself. But it would have enough life to fill its veins and arteries through the day and at night he would have another good drink.

He scarcely stirred throughout the day but spent most of the time looking at the palm. He paid no attention to the sounds below, sure that the Mexicans would not go away. He fell at times into a sort of fevered stupor, and he aroused himself from the last one to find that night had come. He took his machete, went to the tree, and cut quickly, because his thirst was very great.

The gash opened, but not a drop came forth.

Chapter 5

In the Pyramid

Ned stared, half in amazement, half in despair. Yet he had known all the while that this would happen. The palm had emptied every drop from its veins and arteries for him, giving life for life. He had cut so deeply and so often that it would wither now and die. He turned away in sadness, and suddenly a bitter, burning thirst assailed him. It seemed

49

to have leaped into new life with the knowledge that there was nothing now to assuage it.

The boy sat down on a small projection of brickwork, and considered his case. He had been more than twelve hours without water under a fierce sun. His thirst would not increase so fast at night, but it would increase, nevertheless, and the Mexican force might linger below a week. Certainly its camp was of such a character that it would remain at least two or three days, and any risk was preferable to a death of thirst. He could wait no longer.

Now chance which had been so cruel flung a straw his way. The night was darker than usual. The moon and stars did not come out, and troops of clouds stalked up from the southwest. Ned knew that it was a land of little rain, and for a few moments he had a wild hope that in some manner he might catch enough water for his use on the crest of the pyramid. But reason soon drove the hope away. There was no depression which would hold water, and he resolved instead to make the descent under cover of the darkness.

When he had come to this resolution the thirst was not so fierce. Indecision being over, both his physical and mental courage rose. He ate and had left enough food to last for two days, which he fastened securely in a pack to his body. Then, machete in hand, he looked over the edge of the pyramid. There was some noise in the camp, but most of the soldiers seemed to be at rest. Lights flickered here and there, and the ruined city, showing only in fragments through the darkness, looked more ghostly and mournful than ever.

Ned waited a long time. Drops of rain began to fall, and the wind moaned with an almost human note around the pyramids and old walls. The rain increased a little, but it never fell in abundance. It and the wind were very cold, and Ned drew the *serape* very closely about his body. He was anxious now for time to pass fast, because he was beginning to feel afraid, not of the Mexicans, but of the dead city, and the ghosts of those vanished long ago, although he knew there were no such things. But the human note in the wind grew until it was like a shriek, and this shriek was to him a warning that he must go. The pyramid had been his salvation, but his time there was at an end.

He drew the *sombrero* far down over his eyes, and once more calculated the chances. He spoke Spanish well, and he spoke its Mexican variations equally well. If they saw him he might be able to pass for a Mexican. He must succeed.

He lowered himself from the crowning platform of the pyramid and began the descent. The cold rain pattered upon him and his body was weak from privation, but his spirit was strong, and with steady hand and foot he went down. He paused several times to look at the camp. Five or six fires still burned there, but they flickered wildly in the wind and rain. He judged that the sentinels would not watch well. For what must they watch, there in the heart of their own country?

But as he approached the bottom he saw two of these sentinels walking back and forth, their bayonets reflecting a flicker now and then from the flames. He saw also five or six large white tents, and he was quite sure that the largest sheltered at that instant Martin Perfecto de Cos, whom he wished very much to avoid. He intended, when he reached the bottom, to keep as close as he could in the shadow of the pyramid, and then seek the other side of the Teotihuacan.

The rain was still blown about by the wind, and it was very cold. But the influence of both wind and rain were inspiring to the boy. They were a tonic to body and mind, and he grew bolder as he came nearer to the ground. At last he stepped upon the level earth, and stood for a little while black and motionless against the pyramid.

He was aware that the cordon of Cos' army completely enclosed the Pyramid of the Moon, the Pyramid of the Sun, the Calle de los Muertos and the other principal ruins, and he now heard the sentinels much more distinctly as they walked back and forth. Straining his eyes he could see two of them, short, sallow men, musket on shoulder. The beat of one lay directly across the path that he had chosen, reaching from the far edge of the Pyramid of the Moon to a point about twenty yards away. He believed that when this sentinel marched to the other end of his beat he could slip by. At any rate, if he were seen he might make a successful flight, and he slipped his hand to the handle of the machete in his belt in order that he might be ready for resistance.

He saw presently two or three dark heaps near him, and as his eyes grew used to the darkness he made out camp equipage and supplies. The smallest heap which was also nearest to him, consisted of large metal canteens for water, such as soldiers of that day carried. His thirst suddenly made itself manifest again. Doubtless those canteens contained water, and his body which wanted water so badly cried aloud for it.

It was not recklessness but a burning thirst which caused him to creep toward the little heap of canteens at the imminent risk of being discovered. When he reached them he lay flat on the ground and took one from the top. He knew by its lack of weight that it was empty, and he laid it aside. Then he paused for a glance at the sentinel who was still walking steadily on his beat, and whom he now saw very clearly.

He was disappointed to find the first canteen empty, but he was convinced that some in that heap must contain water, and he would persevere. The second and third failed him in like manner, but he would yet persevere. The fourth was heavy, and when he shook it gently he heard the water plash. That thirst at once became burning and uncontrollable. The cry of his body to be assuaged overpowered his will, and while deadly danger menaced he unscrewed the little mouthpiece and drank deep and long. It was not cold and perhaps a little mud lurked at the bottom of the canteen, but like the gift of the water palm it brought fresh life and strength.

He put down the canteen half empty and took another from the heap. It, too, proved to be filled, and he hung it around neck and shoulder by the strap provided for that purpose. He could have found no more precious object for the dry regions through which he intended to make his journey.

Ned went back toward the pyramid, but his joy over finding the water made him a little careless. Great fragments of stone lay about everywhere, and his foot slipped on a piece of black basalt. He fell and the metal of his canteen rang against the stone.

He sprang to his feet instantly, but the sentinel had taken the alarm and as Ned's *sombrero* had slipped back he saw the fair face. He knew that it was the face of no Mexican, and shouting "*Gringo!*" he fired straight at him. Luckily, haste and the darkness prevented good aim, although he was at short range. But Ned felt the swish of the bullet so close to him that every nerve jumped, and he jumped with them. The first jump took him half way to the pyramid and the next landed him at its base. There the second nearest sentinel fired at him and he heard the bullet flatten itself against the stone.

Fortunately for Ned, the silent, thoughtful lad, he had often tried to imagine what he would do in critical junctures, and now, despite the terrible crisis, he was able to take control of his nerves. He remembered to pull the *sombrero* down over his face and to keep close to the pyramid. The shots had caused an uproar in the camp. Men were running about, lights were springing up, and officers were shouting orders. A single fugitive among so many confused pursuers might yet pass for one of them. Chance which had been against him was now for him. The wind suddenly took a wilder sweep and the rain lashed harder. He left the pyramid and darted behind a *tumulus*. He stood there quietly and heard the uproar of the hunt at other points. Presently he slouched away in the manner of a careless *peon*, with his serape drawn about chin as well as body, for which the wind and the rain were a fitting excuse. He also shouted and chattered occasionally with others, and none knew that he was the Gringo at whom the two sentinels had fired.

Ned thought to make a way through the lines, but so many lights now flared up on all the outskirts that he saw it was impossible.

He turned back again to the side of the pyramid, where he was almost hidden by debris and foliage. Two or three false alarms had been sounded on the other side of the great structure, and practically the whole mob of searchers was drawn away in that direction. He formed a quick decision. He would reascend the pyramid. And he would take with him a water supply in the canteen that he still carried over his shoulder. He began to climb, and he noticed as he went up that it was almost the exact point at which he had ascended before.

He heard the tumult below, caught glimpses of lights flashing here and there, and he ascended eagerly. He was almost half way up when he came face to face with a Mexican soldier who carried in his hand a small lantern. The soldier, the only one perhaps who had suspected the pyramid as a place of refuge, had come at another angle, and there on a terrace the two had met.

They were not more than three feet apart. Ned had put his machete back in his belt that he might climb with more ease, but he hit out at once with his clenched right hand. The blow took the Mexican full between the eyes and toppling over backward he dropped the lantern. Then he slid on the narrow terrace and with an instinctive cry of terror fell. Ned was seized with horror and took a hasty glance downward. He was relieved when he saw that the man, grasping at projections and outgrowing vegetation, was sliding rather than falling, and would not be hurt seriously.

He turned to his own case. There lay the lantern on the stone, still glowing. Below rose the tumult, men coming to his side of the pyramid, drawn by his cry. He could no longer reach the top of the pyramid without being seen, but he knew another way. He snatched up the lantern, tucked it under his *serape* and made for the opening which he had noticed in the side of the pyramid at his first ascent. It was scarcely ten feet away, and he boldly stepped in, a thing that he would never have dared to do had it not been for the happy chance of the lantern.

His foot rested on solid stone, and he stood wholly in the dark. Yet the uproar came clearly to his ears. It was a certainty now that more soldiers would ascend the pyramid looking for him, but he believed that ignorance and superstition would keep them from entering it.

The air that came to his nostrils out of the unknown dark was cold and clean, but he did not yet dare to take out his lantern. He felt cautiously in front of him with one foot and touched a stone step below. He also touched narrow walls with his outstretched hand. He descended to the step, and then, feeling sure that the light of his lantern could not be seen from without, he took it from under his *serape* and held it as far in front of him as he could. A narrow flight of stone steps led onward and downward further than he could see, and, driven by imminent necessity, he walked boldly down them.

The way was rough with the decay of time from which stone itself cannot escape, but he always steadied himself with one hand against the wall. The stone was very cold and Ned had the feeling that he was in a tomb. Once more he had that overwhelming sense of old, old things, of things as old as Egypt. At another time, despite every effort of reason, he would have thrilled with superstitious terror, but now it was for his life, and down he went, step by step.

The air remained pure like that of great caves in the States, and Ned did not stop until a black void seemed to open almost before him when he drew back in affright. Calming himself he held up the lantern and looked at the void. It was a deep and square well, its walls faced as far as he could see with squared stones. His lantern revealed no water in the depths and he fancied that it had something to do with ceremonials, perhaps with sacrifice. There was a way around the well, but it was narrow and he chose to go no further. Instead he crouched on the steps where he was safe from a fall, and put the lantern beside him.

It was an oil lamp. Had he possessed any means of relighting it he would have blown it out, and sought sleep in the dark, but once out, out always, and he moved it into a little niche of the wall, where no sudden draught could get at it, and where its hidden light would be no beacon to any daring Mexican who might descend the stairway.

The sense of vast antiquity was still with the boy, but it did not oppress him now as it might have done at another time. His feeling of relief, caused by his escape from the Mexicans, was so great that it created, for the time at least, a certain buoyancy of the mind. The unknown depths of the ancient pyramid were at once a shelter and a protection. He folded the *serape*, in order to make as soft a couch as possible, and soon fell asleep.

When Ned awoke he was lying in exactly the same position on the steps, and the lantern was still burning in the niche. He had no idea how long he had slept, or whether it was day or night, but he did not care. He took the full canteen and drank. It was an unusually large canteen and it contained enough, if he used economy, to last him two days. The cool recesses of the pyramid's interior did not engender thirst like its blazing summit. Then he ate, but whether breakfast, dinner or supper he did not know, nor did he care.

He was tempted to go up to the entrance of the stairway and see what was going forward in the camp, but he resisted the impulse. For the sake of caution he triumphed over curiosity, and remained a long time on the steps, beside the niche in which his lamp sat. Then he began to calculate how much longer the oil would last, and he placed the time at about thirty hours. Surely some decisive event would happen in his favour before the last drop was burned.

After an interminable time the air on the stairway seemed to him to be growing colder, and he inferred that night had come. Taking the lantern he climbed the steps and peered out at the ancient doorway. He saw lights below, and he could discern dimly the shapes of tents. Disappointed, he returned to his place on the steps, and, after another long wait, fell asleep again. When he awoke he calculated by the amount of oil left in the lamp that at least twelve hours had passed since his previous awakening.

Once more he made a great effort of the will in order to achieve a conquest over curiosity and impatience. He would not return to the entrance until the oil had only an hour more to burn. Necessity had proved so stern a master that he was able to keep his resolution. Many long, long hours passed and sometimes he dozed or slept, but he did not go to the entrance. The oil at last marked the final hour, and, taking up the lamp, he went back to the entrance.

Ned looked out and then gave a cry of joy. It was broad daylight, but the army was gone, soldiers, horses, tents, everything. The Calle de los Muertos was once more what its name meant. Silence and desolation had regained the ruined city. He blew out the lantern and set it down at the opening. It had served him well. Then he went out and climbed again to the summit of the pyramid, from which he examined the valley long and well.

He saw no signs of human life anywhere. Traces of the camp remained in abundance, but the army itself had vanished. There were no lurking camp followers to make him trouble. He descended to the ground, and stood a while, drawing in deep draughts of the fresh daylight air. It had not been oppressive in the pyramid, but there is nothing like the open sky above. He went down to the Teotihuacan, and, choosing a safe place, bathed in its waters. Then he resumed the flight across the hills which had been delayed so long. He knew by the sun that it was morning not far advanced, and he wished to travel many miles before night. He saw abundant evidences on the great highway that the army was marching toward Vera Cruz, and as before he travelled on a line parallel with it, but at least a mile away. He passed two sheep herders, but he displayed the machete, and whistling carelessly went on. They did not follow, and he was sure that they took him for a bandit whom it would be wise to let alone.

Ned wandered on for two or three days. In one of his turnings among the mountains he lost the Vera Cruz highway, and came out again upon a wide, sandy plain, dotted with scattered cactus. As he was crossing it a norther came up, and blew with great fierceness. Sand was driven into his face with such force that it stung like shot. The cold became intense, and if it had not been for the *serape* he might have perished.

The storm was still blowing when he reached the far edge of the plain, and came into extremely rough country, with patches of low, thorny forest. Here he found a dilapidated bark hut, evidently used at times by Mexican herdsmen, and, thankful for such shelter, he crept into it and fell asleep. When he awoke he felt very weak. He had eaten the last of his food seven or eight hours before.

Driven by desperate need, Ned ate wild fruits, and, for a while, was refreshed, but that night he fell ill, suffering greatly from internal pains. He was afraid at first that he had poisoned himself, and he knew that he had eaten something not used for food, but by morning the pains were gone, although he was much weaker than before.

Now he felt for the first time the pangs of despair. It was a full two hundred miles yet to Vera Cruz, and he was in the heart of a hostile country. He did not have the strength of a child left, and the chance that he could deliver his message of warning to the Texans seemed to have gone. He rambled about all that day, light-headed at times, and, toward evening, he fell into a stupor. Unable to go any further, he sank down beside a rock, and lapsed wholly into unconsciousness.

CHAPTER 6

THE MARCH WITH COS

When Ned came to himself he was surrounded by men, and at first he thought he was back among his Texans. He was in a vague and dreamy state that was not unpleasant, although he was conscious of a great weakness. He knew that he was lying on the ground upon his own *serape*, and that another *serape* was spread over him. In a little while mind and vision grew more definite and he saw that the soldiers were Mexicans. After his long endurance and ingenuity on the pyramid he had practically walked into their hands. But such was his apathy of mind and body that it roused no great emotion in him. He closed his eyes for a little while, and then fresh strength poured into his veins. When he opened his eyes again his interest in life and his situation was of normal keenness.

They were in a little valley and the soldiers, lancers, seemed to number about two hundred. Their horses were tethered near them, and their lances were stacked in glittering pyramids. It was early morning. Several men were cooking breakfast for the whole troop at large fires. The far edge of the little valley was very rocky and Ned inferred that he had fallen there by a big outcropping of stone, and that the soldiers, looking around for firewood, had found him. But they had not treated him badly, as the *serape* spread over his body indicated.

Feeling so much better he sat up. The odour of the cooking made him realise again that he was fiercely hungry. A Mexican brought him a large tin plate filled with beans and meat chopped small. He ate slowly although only an effort of the will kept him from devouring the food like a famished wild animal. The Mexican who had brought him the plate stood by and watched him, not without a certain sympathy on his face. Several more Mexicans approached and looked at him with keen curiosity, but they did not say or do anything that would offend the young *Gringo*. Knowing that it was now useless, Ned no longer made any attempt to conceal his nationality which was evident to all. He finished the plate and handed it back to the Mexican.

"Many thanks," he said in the native tongue.

"More?" said the soldier, looking at him with understanding.

"I could, without hurting myself," replied Ned with a smile.

A second plate and a cup of water were brought to him. He ate and drank in leisurely fashion, and began to feel a certain relief. He imagined that he would be returned to imprisonment in the City of

Mexico with Mr. Austin. At any rate, he had made a good attempt and another chance might come.

An officer dressed in a very neat and handsome uniform approached and the other Mexicans fell back respectfully. This man was young, not more than thirty-two or three, rather tall, fairer than most of his race, and with a singularly open and attractive face. His dress was that of a colonel, and the boy knew at once that he was commander of the troop. He smiled down at Ned, and Ned, despite himself, smiled back.

"I know you," said he, speaking perfect English. "You are Edward Fulton, the lad who was held in the prison with Stephen Austin, the Texan, the lad who starved himself that he might slip between the bars of his window. There was much talk at the capital about it, and you were not without admirers. You showed so much courage and resource that you deserved to escape, but we could not let you go."

"I got lost and I was without food."

"Rather serious obstacles. They have held many a boy and man. But since I know so much about you and you know nothing about me I will tell you who I am. My name is Juan Nepomuceno Almonte, and I am a colonel in the service of Mexico and of our great Santa Anna. I was educated in that United States of yours, Texan, though you call yourself. That is why I speak the English that you hear. I have friends, too, among your people."

"Well, Colonel Almonte," said Ned, "since I had to be recaptured, I'm glad I fell into your hands."

"I wish I could keep you in them," he said, "but I am under the command of General Cos, and I have to rejoin the main force which he leads."

Ned understood. Cos was a man of another type. But he resolved not to anticipate trouble. Almonte again looked at him curiously, and then leaning forward said confidentially:

"Tell me, was it you who knocked our soldier down on the side of the pyramid and took his lantern? If it is true, it can't do you any harm to acknowledge it now."

"Yes," replied Ned with some pride, "it was I. I came upon him suddenly and I was as much surprised as he. I hit out on the impulse of the moment, and the blow landed in exactly the right place. I hope he was not much hurt."

"He wasn't," replied Almonte, laughing with deep unction. "He was pretty well covered with bruises and scratches, but he forgot them in the awful fright you gave him. He took you to be some demon, some mysterious Aztec god out of a far and dim past, who had smitten him with lightning, because he presumed to climb upon a sacred pyramid. But some of us who were not so credulous, perhaps because we did not have his bruises and scratches, searched all the sides and the top of the pyramid. We failed to find you and we knew that you could not get through our lines. Now, will you tell me where you were?"

His tone was so intent and eager that Ned could not keep from laughing. Besides, the boy had a certain pride in the skill, daring and resource with which he had eluded the men of Cos.

"Did you look inside the pyramid?" he asked.

"Inside it?"

"Yes, inside. There's an opening sixty or seventy feet above the ground. I took your man's lantern when he dropped it and entered. There's a stairway, leading down to a deep, square well, and there's something beyond the well, although I don't know what. I stayed in there until your army went away. Before that I had been for two or three days on top of the pyramid, where a little water palm gave up its life to save me."

Almonte regarded him with wonder.

"I am not superstitious myself—that is, not unnecessarily so," he said, "but yours must be a lucky star. After all that, you should have escaped, and your present capture must be a mere delay. You will slip from us again."

"I shall certainly try," said Ned hopefully.

"It is bound to come true," said Almonte. "All the omens point that way."

Ned smiled. Almonte, young, brilliant and generous, had made him almost feel as if he were a guest and not a prisoner. He did not discern in him that underlying strain of Spanish cruelty, which passion might bring to the surface at any moment. It might be due to his youth, or it might be due to his American education.

"We march in an hour," said Almonte. "We are to rejoin General Cos on the Vera Cruz road, but that will not occur for two or three days. Meanwhile, as the way is rough and you are pretty weak, you can ride on a *burro*. Sorry I can't get you a horse, but our lancers have none to spare. Still, you'll find a *burro* surer of foot and more comfortable over the basalt and lava."

Ned thanked him for his courtesy. He liked this cheerful Mexican better than ever. In another hour they started, turning into the

Vera Cruz road, and following often the path by which great Cortez had come. Ned's *burro*, little but made of steel, picked the way with unerring foot and never stumbled once. He rode in the midst of the lancers, who were full that day of the Latin joy that came with the sun and the great panorama of the Mexican uplands. Now and then they sang songs of the South, sometimes Spanish and sometimes Indian, Aztec, or perhaps even Toltec. Ned felt the influence. Once or twice he joined in the air without knowing the words, and he would have been happy had it not been for his thoughts of the Texans.

The courtesy and kindliness of Almonte must not blind him to the fact that he was the bearer of a message to his own people. That message could not be more important because its outcome was life and death, and he watched all the time for a chance to escape. None occurred. The lancers were always about him, and even if there were an opening his *burro*, sure of foot though he might be, could not escape their strong horses. So he bided his time, for the present, and shared in the gayety of the men who rode through the crisp and brilliant southern air. All the time they ascended, and Ned saw far below him valley after valley, much the same, at the distance, as they were when Cortez and his men first gazed upon them more than three hundred years before.

Yet the look of the land was always different from that to which he was used north of the Rio Grande. Here as in the great valley of Tenochtitlan it seemed ancient, old, old beyond all computation. Here and there, were ruins of which the Mexican peons knew nothing. Sometimes these ruins stood out on a bare slope, and again they were almost hidden by vegetation. In the valleys Ned saw *peons* at work with a crooked stick as a plough, and once or twice they passed swarthy Aztec women cooking *tortillas* and *frijoles* in the open air.

The troop could not advance very rapidly owing to the roughness of the way, and Ned learned from the talk about him that they would not overtake Cos until the evening of the following day. About twilight they encamped in a slight depression in the mountain side. No tents were set, but a large fire was built, partly of dry stems of the giant cactus. The cactus burned rapidly with a light, sparkling blaze, and left a white ash, but the heavier wood, mixed with it, made a bed of coals that glowed long in the darkness.

Ned sat beside the fire on his *serape* with another thrown over his shoulders, as the night was growing very chill with a sharp wind whistling down from the mountains. The kindness of his captors did not

SO HE BIDED HIS TIME, FOR THE PRESENT, AND
SHARED IN THE GAYETY OF THE MEN.

decrease, and he found a genuine pleasure in the human companionship and physical comfort. Almonte found a comfortable place, took a guitar out of a silken case, and hummed and played a love song. No American officer would have done it at such a time and place, but it seemed natural in him.

Ned could not keep from being attracted by the picture that he presented, the handsome young officer bending over his guitar, his heart in the song that he played, but ready at any instant to be the brave and wary soldier. Circumstance and place seemed to the boy so full of wild romance that he forgot, for the time, his own fate and the message that he wished to bear to those far Texans.

It was very cold that night on the heights, and, now and then, a little snow was blown about by the wind, but Ned kept warm by the fire and between the two *serapes*. He fell asleep to the tinkling of Almonte's guitar. They started again at earliest dawn, descended the slopes into a highway to Vera Cruz, and pushed on in the trail of Cos. Ned still rode his *burro*, which trotted along faithfully with the best, and he kept an eager eye for the road and all that lay along it. The silent youth had learned the value of keen observation, and he never neglected it.

Before noon Ned saw a dim, white cone rising on the eastern horizon. It was far away and misty, a thing of beauty which seemed to hang in the air above the clouds.

"Orizaba, the great mountain!" said Almonte.

Ned had seen Popocatepetl and Ixtaccihuatl, but this was a shade loftier and more beautiful than either, shooting up nearly four miles, and visible to sailors far out at sea. It grew in splendour as they approached. Great masses of oak and pine hung on its lofty sides, up the height of three miles, and above the forest rose the sharp cone, gleaming white with snow. The face of Juan Nepomuceno Almonte flushed as he gazed at it.

"It is ours, the great mountain!" he exclaimed. "And the many other magnificent mountains and the valleys and rivers of Mexico. Can you wonder, then, Edward Fulton, that we Mexicans do not wish to lose any part of our country? Texas is ours, it has always been ours, and we will not let the Texans sever it from us!"

"The Texans have not wished to do so," said Ned. "You have been kind to me, Colonel Almonte, and I do not wish to tell you anything but the truth. The Texans will fight oppression and bad faith. You do not know, the Mexicans do not know, how hard they will fight. Our charter has been violated and President Santa Anna would strip our people of arms and leave them at the mercy of savage Indians."

Almonte was about to make a passionate reply, but he checked himself suddenly and said in mild tones:

"It is not fair for me to attack you, a prisoner, even in words. Look how Orizaba grows! It is like a pillar holding up the heavens!"

Ned gazed in admiration. He did not wonder that Almonte loved this country of his, so full of the strange and picturesque. The great mountain grew and grew, until its mighty cone, dark below, and white above, seemed to fill the horizon. But much of the gayety of Almonte departed.

"Before night," he said, "we will be with General Cos, who is my commander. As you know, he is the brother-in-law of General Santa Anna, and—he is much inflamed against the Texans. I fear that he will be hard with you, but I shall do what I can to assuage his severity."

"I thank you, Colonel Almonte," said Ned with a gravity beyond his years. "You are a generous enemy, and chance may help me some day to return your kindness, but whatever treatment General Cos may accord me, I hope I shall be able to stand it."

In another hour they saw a column of dust ahead of them. The column grew and soon Ned saw lances and bayonets shining through it. He knew that this was the army of Cos, and, just as the eastern light began to fade, they joined it. Cos was going into camp by the side of a small stream, and, after a little delay, Almonte took the prisoner to him.

A large tent had been erected for General Cos, but he was sitting before it, eating his supper. A cook was serving him with delicate dishes and another servant filled his glass with red wine. His dark face darkened still further, as he looked at Ned, but he saluted Almonte courteously. It was evident to Ned that through family or merit, probably both, Almonte stood very high in the Mexican service.

"I have the honour to report to you, General Cos," said Almonte, "that we have retaken the young Texan who escaped through the bars of his prison at the capital. We found him in the mountains overcome by exhaustion."

General Cos' lips opened in a slow, cold smile,—an evil smile that struck a chill to Ned's heart. Here was a man far different from the gallant and gay young Almonte. That cruel strain which he believed was in the depths of the Spanish character, dormant though it might usually be, was patent now in General Cos. Moreover, this man was very powerful, and, as brother-in-law of Santa Anna, he was second only to the great dictator. He did not ask Ned to sit down and he was brusque in speech. The air about them grew distinctly colder. Almonte had talked with Ned in English, but Cos spoke Spanish:

"Why did you run away from the capital?" he asked, shortly. "You were treated well there."

"No man can be held in prison and be treated well."

General Martin Perfecto de Cos frowned. The bearing of the young *Gringo* did not please him. Nor did his answer.

"I repeat my question," he said, his voice rising. "Why did you run like a criminal from the capital? You were with the man Austin. You, like he, were the guest of our great and illustrious Santa Anna who does no wrong. Answer me, why did you slip away like a thief?"

"I slipped away, but it was not like a thief nor any other kind of criminal. And if you must know, General Cos, I went because I did not believe the words of the great and illustrious Santa Anna. He promises the Texans redress for their wrongs, and, at the same time, he orders them to give up their weapons. Do you think, and does General Santa Anna think, that the Texans are fools?"

Despite all his study and thought, Ned Fulton was only a boy and he did not have the wisdom of the old. The manner and words of General Cos had angered him, and, on impulse, he gave a direct reply. But he knew at once that it was impolitic. Cos' eyes lowered, and his lips drew back like those of an angry jaguar, showing his strong white teeth. There was no possible doubt now about that Spanish strain of cruelty.

"I presume," he said, and he seemed to Ned to bite each word, "that you meant to go to the Texans with the lying message that the word of the most illustrious General Santa Anna was not to be believed?"

"I meant to go with such a message," said Ned proudly, "but it would not be a lying one."

Knowing that he was already condemned he resolved to seek no subterfuge.

"The president cannot be insulted in my presence," said Cos ominously.

"He is only a boy, general," said Almonte appealingly.

"Boys can do mischief," said Cos, "and this seems to be an unusually cunning and wicked one. You are zealous, Colonel Almonte, I will give you that much credit, but you do not hate the *Gringos* enough."

Almonte flushed, but he bowed and said nothing. Cos turned again to Ned.

"You will bear no message to the Texans," he said. "I think that instead you will stay a long time in this hospitable Mexico of ours."

Ned paled a little. The words were full of menace, and he knew that they came straight from the cruel heart of Cos. But his pride would not permit him to reply.

"You will be kept under close guard," said the general. "I will give that duty to the men of Tlascala. They are infantry and tomorrow you march on foot with them. Colonel Almonte, you did well to take the prisoner, but you need trouble yourself no longer about him."

Two men of the Tlascalan company were summoned and they took Ned with them. The name "Tlascala" had appealed to Ned at first. It was the brave Tlascalan mountaineers who had helped Cortez and who had made possible his conquest of the great Mexican empire. But these were not the Tlascalans of that day. They were a mongrel breed, short, dirty and barefooted. He ate of the food they gave him, said nothing, and lay down on his *serape* to seek sleep. Almonte came to him there.

"I feared this," he said. "I would have saved you from General Cos had I been able."

"I know it," said Ned warmly, "and I want to thank you, Colonel Almonte."

Almonte held out his hand and Ned grasped it. Then the Mexican strode away. Ned lay back again and watched the darkness thin as the moon and stars came out. Far off the silver cone of Orizaba appeared like a spear point against the sky. It towered there in awful solemnity above the strife and passion of the world. Ned looked at it long, and gradually it became a beacon of light to him, his "pillar of flame" by night. It was the last thing he saw as he fell asleep, and there was no thought then in his mind of the swart and menacing Cos.

They resumed the march early in the morning. Ned no longer had his patient *burro*, but walked on foot among the Tlascalans. Often he saw General Cos riding ahead on a magnificent white horse. Sometimes the *peons* stood on the slopes and looked at them but generally they kept far from the marching army. Ned surmised that they had no love of military service.

The way was not easy for one on foot. Clouds of dust arose, and stung nose and throat. The sharp lava or basalt cut through the soles of shoes, and at midday the sun's rays burned fiercely. Weakened already by the hardships of his flight Ned was barely able to keep up. Once when he staggered a horseman prodded him with the butt of his lance. Ned was not revengeful, but he noted the man's face. Had he been armed then he would have struck back at any cost. But he took care not to stagger again, although it required a supreme effort.

They halted about an hour at noon, and Ned ate some rough food and drank water with the Tlascalans. He was deeply grateful for the short rest, and, as he sat trying to keep himself from collapse, Almonte came up and held out a flask.

"It is wine," he said. "It will strengthen you. Drink."

Ned drank. He was not used to wine, but he had been so near exhaustion that he took it as a medicine. When he handed the flask back the colour returned to his face and the blood flowed more vigorously in his veins.

"General Cos does not wish me to see you at all," said Almonte. "He thinks you should be treated with the greatest harshness, but I am not without influence and I may be able to ease your march a little."

"I know that you will do it if you can," said Ned gratefully.

Yet Almonte was able to do little more for him. The march was resumed under equally trying conditions, after the short rest. When night came and the detachment stopped, Ned ached in every bone, and his feet were sore and bleeding. Almonte was sent away in the morning on another service, and there was no one to interfere for him.

He struggled on all of the next day. Most of his strength was gone, but pride still kept him going. Orizaba was growing larger and larger, dominating the landscape, and Ned again drew courage from the lofty white cone that looked down upon them.

Late in the afternoon he heard a trumpet blow, and there was a great stir in the force of Cos. Men held themselves straighter, lines were re-formed, and the whole detachment became more trim and smart. General Cos on his white horse rode to its head, and he was in his finest uniform. Somebody of importance was coming! Ned was keen with curiosity but he was too proud to ask. The Tlascalans had proved a churlish lot, and he would waste no words on them.

The road now led down into a beautiful savanna, thick in grass, and with oaks and pines on all sides. Cos' companies turned into the grass, and Ned saw that another force entering at the far side was doing the same. All the men in the second force were mounted, the officer who was at their head riding a horse even finer than that of Cos. His uniform, too, was more splendid, and his head was surmounted by a great three-cornered hat, heavy with gold lace. He was compact of figure, sat his saddle well, and rode as if the earth belonged to him. Ned recognised him at once. It was the general, the president, the dictator, the father of his country, the illustrious Santa Anna himself.

The mellow trumpet pealed forth again, and Santa Anna advanced to meet his brother, Cos, who likewise advanced to meet him. They met in full view of both forces, and embraced and kissed each other. Then a shout came forth from hundreds of throats at the noble spectacle of fraternal amity. The two forces coalesced with much Latin joy and chatter, and camp was pitched in the *savanna*.

Ned stayed with the Tlascalans, because he had no choice but to do so. They flung him a *tortilla* or two, and he had plenty of water, but what he wanted most was rest. He threw himself on the grass, and, as the Tlascalans did not disturb him, he lay there until long after nightfall. He would have remained there until morning had not two soldiers come with a message that he was wanted by Santa Anna himself.

Ned rose, smoothed out his hair, draped his *serape* as gracefully as he could about his shoulders, and, assuming all the dignity that was possible, went with the men. He had made up his mind that boldness of manner and speech was his best course and it suited his spirit. He was led into a large tent or rather a great marquee, and he stood there for a few moments dazzled.

The floor of the marquee was spread with a thick velvet carpet. A table loaded with silver dishes was between the generals, and a dozen lamps on the walls shed a bright light over velvet carpet, silver dishes and the faces of the two men who held the fortunes of Mexico in the hollows of their hands. General Cos smiled the same cold and evil smile that Ned had noticed at their first meeting, but Santa Anna spoke in a tone half of surprise and half of pity.

"Ah, it is the young Fulton! And he is in evil plight! You would not accept my continued hospitality at the capital, and behold what you have suffered!"

Ned looked steadily at him. He could not fathom the thought that lay behind the words of Santa Anna. The man was always appearing to him in changing colours. So he merely waited.

"It was a pleasure to me," said Santa Anna, "to learn from General Cos that you had been retaken. Great harm might have come to you wandering through the mountains and deserts of the north. You could never have reached the Texans alive, and since you could not do so it was better to have come back to us, was it not?"

"I have not come willingly."

General Cos frowned, but Santa Anna laughed.

"That was frank," he said, "and we will be equally frank with you. You would go north to the Texans, telling them that I mean to come with an army and crush them. Is it not so?"

"It is," replied Ned boldly.

Santa Anna smiled. He did not seem to be offended at all. His manner, swift, subtle and changing, was wholly attractive, and Ned felt its fascination.

"Be your surmise true or not," said the dictator, "it is best for you not to reach Texas. I have discussed the matter with my brother, General Cos, in whom I have great confidence, and we have agreed that since you undertook to reach Vera Cruz you can go there. General Cos will be your escort on the way, and, as I go to the capital in the morning, I wish you a pleasant journey and a happy stay in our chief seaport."

It seemed to Ned that there was the faintest touch of irony in his last word or two, but he was not sure. He was never sure of Santa Anna, that complex man of great abilities and vast ambition. And so after his fashion when he had nothing to say he said nothing.

"You are silent," said Santa Anna, "but you are thinking. You of the north are silent to hide your thoughts, and we of the south talk to hide ours!"

Ned still said nothing, and Santa Anna examined him searchingly. He sent his piercing gaze full into the eyes of the boy. Ned, proud of his race and blood, endured it, and returned it with a firm and steady look. Then the face of Santa Anna changed. He became all at once smiling and friendly, like a man who receives a welcome guest. He put a hand on Ned's shoulder, and apparently he did not notice that the shoulder became rigid under his touch.

"I like you," he said, "I like your courage, your truth, and your bluntness. You Texans, or rather you Americans,—because the Texans are Americans,—have some of the ruder virtues which we who are of the Spanish and Latin blood now and then lack. You are only a boy, but you have in you the qualities that can make a career. The Texans belong to Mexico. Your loyalty is due to Mexico and to me. I have said that you would go to Vera Cruz and take the hospitality that my brother, Cos, will offer you, but there is an alternative."

He stopped as if awaiting a natural question, but still Ned did not speak. A spark appeared in the eye of Santa Anna, but it passed so quickly that it was like a momentary gleam.

"I would make of you," continued the dictator in his mellow, coaxing tone, "a promising young member of my staff, and I would assign to you an immediate and important duty. I would send you to the Texans with a message entirely different from the one you wish to bear. I would have you to tell them that Santa Anna means only their greatest good; that he loves them as his children; that he is glad to have these strong, tall, fair men in the north to fight for him and Mexico; that he is a man who never breaks a promise; that he is the father of his people, and that he loves them all with a heart full of tenderness. To show you how much I trust and value you I would take your word that you would bear such a message, and I would send you with an escort that would make your way safe and easy."

Again he sent his piercing gaze into the eyes of the boy, but Ned was still silent.

"You would tell them," said Santa Anna in the softest and most persuasive tones, "that you have been much with me, that you know me, and that no man has a softer heart or a more just mind."

"I cannot do it," said Ned.

"Why?"

"Because it is not so."

The change on the face of Santa Anna was sudden and startling. His eyes became black with wrath, and his whole aspect was menacing. The hand of Cos flew to the hilt of his sword, and he half rose from his chair. But Santa Anna pushed him back, and then the face of the dictator quickly underwent another transformation. It became that of the ruler, grave but not threatening.

"Softly, Cos, my brother," he said. "Bear in mind that he is only a boy. I offered too much, and he does not understand. He has put away a brilliant career, but, my good brother Cos, he has left to him your hospitality, and you will not be neglectful."

Cos sank back in his chair and laughed. Santa Anna laughed. The two laughs were unlike, one heavy and angry, and the other light and gay, but their effect upon Ned was precisely the same. He felt a cold shiver at the roots of his hair, but he was yet silent, and stood before them waiting.

"You can go," said Santa Anna. "You have missed your opportunity and it will not come again."

Ned turned away without a word. The Tlascalans were waiting at the door of the marquee, and he went with them. Once more he slept under the stars.

CHAPTER 7

THE DUNGEON UNDER THE SEA

Ned, early the next morning, saw Santa Anna with his brilliant escort ride away toward the capital, while General Cos resumed his march to Vera Cruz. Almonte did not reappear at all, and the boy surmised that he was under orders to join the dictator.

Ned continued on foot among the Tlascalans. Cos offered him no kindness whatever, and his pride would not let him ask for it. But when he looked at his sore and bleeding feet he always thought of the patient *burro* that he had lost. They marched several more days, and the road dropped down into the lowlands, into the *tierra caliente*. The air grew thick and hot and Ned, already worn, felt an almost overpowering languor. The vegetation became that of the tropics. Then, passing through marshes and sand dunes, they reached Vera Cruz, the chief port of Mexico, a small, unhealthy city, forming a semicircle about a mile in length about the bay.

Ned saw little of Vera Cruz, as they reached it at nightfall, but the approach through alternations of stagnant marsh and shifting sand affected him most unpleasantly. Offensive odours assailed him and he remembered that this was a stronghold of cholera and yellow fever. He ate rough food with the Tlascalans again, and then Cos sent for him.

"You have reached your home," said the General. "You will occupy the largest and most expensive house in the place, and my men will take you there at once. Do you not thank me?"

"I do not," replied Ned defiantly. Yet he knew that he had much to dread.

"You are an ungrateful young dog of a Texan," said Cos, laughing maliciously, "but I will confer my hospitality upon you, nevertheless. You will go with these men and so I bid you farewell."

Four barefooted soldiers took Ned down through the dirty and evil-smelling streets of the city. He wondered where they were going, but he would not ask. They came presently to the sea and Ned saw before him, about a half mile away, a sombre and massive pile rising upon a rocky islet. He knew that it was the great and ancient Castle of San Juan de Ulua. In the night, with only the moon's rays falling upon its walls, it looked massive and forbidding beyond all description. That cold shiver again appeared at the roots of the boy's hair. He knew now the meaning of all this talk of Santa Anna and Cos about their hospitality. He was to be buried in the gloomiest fortress of the New World. It was a fate that might well make one so young shudder many times. But he said not a word in protest. He got silently into a boat with the soldiers, and they were rowed to the rocky islet on which stood the huge castle.

Not much time was wasted on Ned. He was taken before the governor, his name and age were registered, and then two of the prison guards, one going before and the other behind, led him down a narrow and steep stairway. It reminded him of his descent into the pyramid, but here the air seemed damper. They went down many steps and came into a narrow corridor upon which a number of iron doors opened. The guards unlocked one of the doors, pushed Ned in, relocked the door on him, and went away.

Ned staggered from the rude thrust, but, recovering himself stood erect, and tried to accustom his eyes to the half darkness. He stood in a small, square room with walls of hard cement or plaster. The roof of the same material was high, and in the centre of it was a round hole, through which came all the air that entered the cell. In a corner was a rude pallet of blankets spread upon grass. There was no window. The place was hideous and lonely beyond the telling. He had not felt this way in the pyramid.

Ned now had suffered more than any boy could stand. He threw himself upon the blanket, and only pride kept him from shedding tears. But he was nevertheless relaxed completely, and his body shook as if in a chill. He lay there a long time. Now and then, he looked up at the walls of his prison, but always their sodden gray looked more hideous than ever. He listened but heard nothing. The stillness was absolute and deadly. It oppressed him. He longed to hear anything that would break it; anything that would bring him into touch with human life and that would drive away the awful feeling of being shut up forever.

The air in the dungeon felt damp to Ned. He was glad of it, because damp meant a touch of freshness, but by and by it became chilly, too. The bed was of two blankets, and, lying on one and drawing the other over him, he sought sleep. He fell after a while into a troubled slumber which was half stupor, and from which he awakened at intervals. At the third awakening he heard a noise. Although his other fac-

71

ulties were deadened partially by mental and physical exhaustion, his hearing was uncommonly acute, concentrating in itself the strength lost by the rest. The sound was peculiar, half a swish and half a roll, and although not loud it remained steady. Ned listened a long time, and then, all at once, he recognised its cause.

He was under the sea, and it was the rolling of the waves over his head that he heard. He was in one of the famous submarine dungeons of the Castle of San Juan de Ulua. This was the hospitality of Cos and Santa Anna, and it was a hospitality that would hold him fast. Never would he take any word of warning to the Texans. Buried under the sea! He shivered all over and a cold sweat broke out upon him.

He lay a long time until some of the terror passed. Then he sat up, and looked at the round hole in the cement ceiling. It was about eight inches in diameter and a considerable stream of fresh air entered there. But the pipe or other channel through which it came must turn to one side, as the sea was directly over his head. He could not reach the hole, and even could he have reached it, he was too large to pass through it. He had merely looked at it in a kind of vague curiosity.

Feeling that every attempt to solve anything would be hopeless, he fell asleep again, and when he awoke a man with a lantern was standing beside him. It was a soldier with his food, the ordinary Mexican fare, and water. Another soldier with a musket stood at the door. There was no possible chance of a dash for liberty. Ned ate and drank hungrily, and asked the soldier questions, but the man replied only in monosyllables or not at all. The boy desisted and finished in silence the meal which might be either breakfast, dinner or supper for all he knew. Then the soldier took the tin dishes, withdrew with his comrade, and the door was locked again.

Ned was left to silence and solitude. But he felt that he must now move about, have action of some kind. He threw himself against the door in an effort to shake it, but it did not move a jot. Then he remembered that he had seen cell doors in a row, and that other prisoners might be on either side of him. He kicked the heavy cement walls, but they were not conductors of sound and no answer came.

He grew tired after a while, but the physical exertion had done him good. The languid blood flowed in a better tide in his veins and his mind became more keen. There must be some way out of this. Youth could not give up hope. It was incredible, impossible that he should remain always here, shut off from that wonderful free world outside. The roll of the sea over his head made reply.

After a while he began to walk around his cell, around and around and around, until his head grew dizzy, and he staggered. Then he would reverse and go around and around and around the other way. He kept this up until he could scarcely stand. He lay down and tried to sleep again. But he must have slept a long time before, and sleep would not come. He lay there on the blankets, staring at the walls and not seeing them, until the soldiers came again with his food. Ned ate and drank in silence. He was resolved not to ask a question, and, when the soldiers departed, not a single word had been spoken.

The next day Ned had fever, the day after that he was worse, and on the third day he became unconscious. Then he passed through a time, the length of which he could not guess, but it was a most singular period. It was crowded with all sorts of strange and shifting scenes, some coloured brilliantly, and vivid, others vague and fleeting as moonlight through a cloud. It was wonderful, too, that he should live again through things that he had lived already. He was back with Mr. Austin. He saw the kind and generous face quite plainly and recognised his voice. He saw Benito and Juana, Popocatepetl and Ixtaccihuatl; he was on the pyramid and in it, and he saw the silver cone of Orizaba. Then he shifted suddenly back to Texas and the wild border, the Comanche and the buffalo.

His life now appeared to have no order. Time turned backward. Scenes occurred out of their sequence. Often they would appear for a second or third time. It was the most marvellous jumble that ever ran through any kaleidoscope. His brain by and by grew dizzy with the swift interplay of action and colour. Then everything floated away and blackness and silence came. Nor could he guess how long this period endured, but when he came out of it he felt an extraordinary weakness and a lassitude that was of both mind and body.

His eyes were only half open and he did not care to open them more. He took no interest in anything. But he became slowly conscious that he had emerged from somewhere out of a vast darkness, and that he had returned to his life in the dungeon under the sea.

His eyes opened fully by automatic process rather than by will, and the heavy dark of the dungeon was grateful then, because they, too, like all the rest of him, were very weak. Yet a little light came in as usual with the fresh air from above, and by and by he lifted one hand and looked at it. It was a strange hand, very white, very thin, with the blue veins standing out from the back.

It was almost the hand of a skeleton. He did not know it. Certainly

73

it did not belong to him. He looked at it wondering, and then he did a strange thing. It was his left hand that he was holding before him. He put his right hand upon it, drew that hand slowly over the fingers, then the palm and along the wrist until he reached his shoulder. It was his hand after all. His languid curiosity satisfied he let the hand drop back by his body. It fell like a stone. After a while he touched his head, and found that his hair was cut closely. It seemed thin, too.

He realised that he had been ill, and very ill indeed he must have been to be so weak. He wondered a little how long it had been since he first lapsed into unconsciousness, and then the wonder ceased. Whether the time had been long or short it did not matter. But he shut his eyes and listened for the last thing that he remembered. He heard it presently, that low roll of the sea. He was quite sure of one thing. He was in the same submarine dungeon of the famous Castle of San Juan de Ulua.

His door was opened, and a man, not a soldier, came in with soup in a tin basin. He uttered a low exclamation, when he saw that Ned was conscious, but he made no explanations. Nor did Ned ask him anything. But he ate the soup with a good appetite, and felt very much stronger. His mind, too, began to wake up. He knew that he was going to get well, but it occurred to him that it might be better for him to conceal his returning strength. With a relaxed watch he would have more chance to escape.

The soup had a soothing effect, and his mind shared with his body in the improvement. It was obvious that they had not intended for him to die or they would not have taken care of him in his illness. The shaven head was proof. But he saw nothing that he could do. He must wait upon the action of his jailers. Having come to this conclusion he lay upon his pallet, and let vague thoughts float through his head as they would.

About three hours after they had brought him his soup he heard a scratching at the keyhole of his door. He was not too languid to be surprised. He did not think it likely that any of his jailers would come back so soon, and heretofore the key had always turned in the lock without noise.

Ned sat up. The scratching continued for a few moments, and the door swung open. A tall, thin figure of a man entered, the door closed behind him, and with some further scratching he locked it. Then the man turned and stared at Ned. Ned stared with equal intentness at him.

The figure that he saw was thin and six feet four; the face that he saw was thin and long. The face was also bleached to an indescribable dead white, the effect of which was heightened by the thick and fiery red hair that crowned a head, broad and shaped finely. His hair even in the dark seemed to be vital, the most vital part of him. Ned fancied that his eyes were blue, although in the dimness he could not tell. But he knew that this was no Mexican. A member of his own race stood before him.

"Well," said Ned.

"Well?" replied the man in a singularly soft and pleasant voice.

"Who are you and what do you want?"

"To the first I am Obed White; to the second I want to talk to you, and I would append as a general observation that I am harmless. Evil to him that would evil do."

"The quotation is wrong," said Ned, smiling faintly. "It is 'evil to him who evil thinks.'"

"Perhaps, but I have improved upon it. I add, for your further information, that I am your nearest neighbour. I occupy the magnificent concrete parlour next door to you, where I live a life of undisturbed ease, but I have concluded at last to visit you, and here I am. How I came I will explain later. But I am glad I am with you. One crowded hour of glorious company is worth a hundred years in a solitary cell. I may have got that a little wrong, too, but it sounds well."

He sat down in Turkish fashion on the floor, folding a pair of extremely long legs beneath him, and regarded Ned with a slow, quizzical smile. For the life of him the boy could not keep from smiling back. With the nearer view he could see now that the eyes were blue and honest.

"You may think I'm a Mexican," continued the man in his mellow, pleasant voice, "but I'm not. I'm a Texan—by the way of Maine. As I told you, I live in the next tomb, the one on the right. I'm a watch, clock and tool maker by trade and a bookworm by taste. Because of the former I've come into your cell, and because of the latter I use the ornate language that you hear. But of both those subjects more further on. Meanwhile, I suppose it's you who have been yelling in here at the top of your voice and disturbing a row of dungeons accustomed to peace and quiet."

"It was probably I, but I don't remember anything about it."

"It's not likely that you would, as I see you've had some one of the seven hundred fevers that are customary along this coast. Yours must

75

have been of the shouting kind, as I heard you clean through the wall, and, once when I was listening at the keyhole, you made a noise like the yell of a charging army."

"You don't mean to say that you've been listening at the keyhole of my cell."

"It's exactly what I mean. You wouldn't come to see your neighbour so he decided to come to see you. Good communications correct evil manners. See this?"

He held up a steel pronged instrument about six inches long.

"This was once a fork, a fork for eating, large and crude, I grant you, but a fork. It took me more than a month to steal it, that is I had to wait for a time when I was sure that the soldier who brought my food was so lazy or so stupid that he would not miss it. I waited another week as an additional precaution, and after that my task was easy. If the best watch, clock and instrument maker in the State of Maine couldn't pick any lock with a fork it was time for him to lie on his back and die. I picked the lock of my own door in a minute the first time by dead reckoning, but it took me a full two minutes to open yours, although I'll relock it in half that time when I go out. Where there's a will there will soon be an open door."

He flourished the fork, the two prongs of which now curved at the end, and grinned broadly. He had a look of health despite the dead whiteness of his face, which Ned now knew was caused by prison pallor. Ned liked him. He liked him for many reasons. He liked him because his eyes were kindly. He liked him because he was one of his own race. He liked him because he was a fellow prisoner, and he liked him above all because this was the first human companionship that he had had in a time that seemed ages.

Obed meanwhile was examining him with scrutinizing eyes. He had heard the voice of fever, but he did not expect to find in the "tomb" next to his own a mere boy.

"How does it happen," he asked, "that one as young as you is a prisoner here in a dungeon with the castle of San Juan de Ulua and the sea on top of him?"

Obed White had the mellowest and most soothing voice that Ned had ever heard. Now it was like that of a father speaking to the sick son whom he loved, and the boy trusted him absolutely.

"I was sent here," he replied, "by Santa Anna and his brother-in-law, Cos, because I knew too much, or rather suspected too much. I was held at the capital with Mr. Austin. We were not treated badly.

76

Santa Anna himself would come to see us and talk of the great good that he was going to do for Texas, but I could not believe him. I was sure instead that he was gathering his forces to crush the Texans. So, I escaped, meaning to go to Texas with a message of warning."

"A wise boy and a brave one," said Obed White with admiration. "You suspected but you kept your counsel. Still waters run slowly, but they run."

Ned told all his story, neglecting scarcely a detail. The feeling that came of human companionship was so strong and his trust was so great that he did not wish to conceal anything.

"You've endured about as much as ought to come to one boy," said Obed White, "and you've gone through all this alone. What you need is a partner. Two heads can do what one can't. Well, I'm your partner. As I'm the older, I suppose I ought to be the senior partner. Do you hereby subscribe to the articles of agreement forming the firm of White & Fulton, submarine engineers, tunnel diggers, jail breakers, or whatever form of occupation will enable us to escape from the castle of San Juan de Ulua?"

"Gladly," said Ned, and he held out a thin, white hand. Obed White seized it, but he remembered not to grasp it too firmly. This boy had been ill a long time, and he was white and very weak. The heart of the man overflowed with pity.

"Goodnight, Ned," he said. "I mustn't stay too long, but I'll come again lots of times, and you and I will talk business then. The firm of White & Fulton will soon begin work of the most important kind. Now you watch me unlock that door. They say that *pride goeth before a fall*, but in this case it is going right through an open door."

Obviously he was proud of his skill as he had a full right to be. He inserted the hooked prongs of the fork in the great keyhole, twisted them about a little, and then the lock turned in its groove.

"Goodbye, Ned," said Obed again. "It's time I was back in my own tomb which is just like yours. I hate to lock in a good friend like you, but it must be done."

He disappeared in the hall, the door swung shut and Ned heard the lock slide in the groove again. He was alone once more. The light that had seemed to illuminate his dungeon went with the man, but he left hope behind. Ned would not be alone in the spirit as long as he knew that Obed White was in the cell next to his.

He lay a while, thinking on the chances of fate. They had served him ill, for a long time. Had the turn now come? He did not know it, but it was the human companionship, the friendly voice that had raised such a great hope in his breast. He glided from thought into a peaceful sleep and slept a long time, without dreams or even vague, floating visions. His breath came long and full at regular intervals, and with every beat of his pulse new strength flowed into his body. While he slept nature was hard at work, rebuilding the strong young frame which had yielded only to overpowering circumstances.

Ned ate his breakfast voraciously the next day and wanted more. Dinner also left him hungry, but, carrying out his original plan, he counterfeited weakness, and, before the soldier left, lay down upon the pallet as if he were too languid to care for anything. He disposed of supper in similar fashion, and then waited with a throbbing pulse for the second call from the senior member of the firm of White & Fulton.

After an incredible period of waiting he heard the slight rasping of the fork in the keyhole. Then the door was opened and the older partner entered. Before speaking he carefully relocked the door.

"I believe you're glad to see me," he said to Ned. "You're sitting up. I don't think I ever before saw a boy improve so much in twenty-four hours. I'll just feel your pulse. It will be one of my duties as senior partner to practice medicine for a little while. Yes, it's a strong pulse, a good pulse. You're quite clear of fever. You need nothing now but your strength back again, and we'll wait for that. All things come to him who waits, if he doesn't die of old age first."

His talk was so rapid and cheerful that he seemed fairly to radiate vigour. It was a powerful tonic to Ned who felt so strong that he was prepared to attempt escape at once. But Obed shook his head when he suggested it.

"That strength comes from your feelings," he said. "All that glitters isn't gold or silver or any other precious metal. That false strength would break down under a long and severe test. We'll just wait and plan. For what we're going to undertake you're bound to have every ounce of vigour that you can accumulate."

"You've been able to go out in the hall when you chose, then why haven't you gone away already?" asked Ned.

"I didn't get my key perfected until a few days ago, and then as I heard you yelling in here I decided to find out about you. Two are company; one is none, and so we formed a partnership. Now when the firm acts both partners must act."

Ned did not reply directly. He did not know how to thank him for his generosity.

"Have you explored the hall?" he asked.

"It leads up a narrow stairway, down which I came some time ago when my Mexican brethren decided that I was too much of a Texan patriot. Doubtless you trod the same dark and narrow path. At the head of that is another door which I have not tried, but which I know I can open with this master key of mine. Beyond that I'm ignorant of the territory, but there must be a way out since there was one in. Now, Ned, we must make no mistake. We must not conceal from ourselves that the firm of White & Fulton is confronted by a great task. We must select our time, and have ready for the crisis every particle of strength, courage and quickness that we possess."

Ned knew that he was right, and yet, despite his youth and natural strength, his convalescence was slow. He had passed through too terrible an ordeal to recover entirely in a day or even a week. He would test his strength often and at night Obed White would test it, too, but always he was lacking in some particular. Then Obed would shake his head wisely and say: "Wait."

One night they heard the sea more loudly than ever before. It rolled heavily, just over their heads.

"There must be a great storm on the gulf," said Obed White. "I've lost count of time, but perhaps the period of gales is at hand. If so, I'm not sorry, it'll hide our flight across the water. You'll remember, Ned, that we're a half mile from the mainland."

Fully two weeks passed before they decided that Ned was restored to his old self. Meanwhile they had matured their plan.

"We came in as Texans," said Obed, "but we must go out as Mexicans. There is no other way. It's all simple in the saying, but we've got to be mighty quick in the doing. We must make the change right here in this cell of yours, because, you having been an invalid so long, they're likely to be careless about you."

Ned agreed with him fully, and they began to train their bodies and minds for a supreme effort. They were now able to tell the difference between night and day by the temperature. The air that came through the holes in the ceiling was a little cooler by night, enough for senses trained to preternatural acuteness by long imprisonment to tell it. The guard always came about eight o'clock with Ned's supper and they chose that time for the attempt.

Obed White entered Ned's cell about six o'clock. The boy could scarcely restrain himself and the man's blue eyes were snapping with excitement. But Obed patted Ned on the shoulder.

"We must both keep cool," he said. "The more haste the less likely the deed. The first man comes in with the tray carrying your food. I stand here by the door and he passes by without seeing me. I seize the second, drag him in and slam the door. Then the victory is to the firm of White & Fulton, if it prove to be the stronger. But we'll have surprise in our favour."

They waited patiently. Ned lay upon his pallet. Obed flattened himself against the wall beside the door. Their plan fully arranged, neither now spoke. Overhead they heard the slow roll of the sea, lashed by the waves sweeping in from the gulf. But inside the cell the silence was absolute.

Ned lay in an attitude apparently relaxed. His face was still white. It could not acquire colour in that close cell, but he had never felt stronger. A powerful heart pumped vigorous blood through every artery and vein. His muscles had regained their toughness and flexibility, and above all, the intense desire for freedom had keyed him to supreme effort.

Usually he did not hear the soldier's key turn in the lock, but soon he heard it and his heart pumped. He glanced at White, but the gray figure, flattened against the wall, never moved. The door swung open and the soldier, merely a shambling *peon*, bearing the tray, entered. Behind him according to custom came the second man who stood in the doorway, leaning upon his musket. But he stood there only an instant. A pair of long, powerful arms which must have seemed to him at that moment like the antennae of a devil-fish, reached out, seized him in a fierce grip by either shoulder, and jerked him gun and all into the cell. The door was kicked shut and the grasp of the hands shifted from his shoulders to his throat. He could not cry out although the terrible face that bent over him made his soul start with fear.

The man with the tray heard the noise behind him and turned. Ned sprang like a panther. All the force and energy that he had been concentrating so long were in the leap. The soldier went down as if he had been struck by a cannon ball and his tray and dishes rattled upon him. But he was a wiry fellow and grasping his assailant he struggled fiercely.

"Now stop, my good fellow. Just lie still! That's the way!"

It was Obed White who spoke, and he held the muzzle of a pistol at the man's head. The other soldier lay stunned in the corner. It was from his belt that Obed had snatched the pistol.

"Get up, Ned," said White. "The first step in our escape from the Castle of San Juan de Ulua has been taken. Meanwhile, you lie still, my good fellow; we're not going to hurt you. No, you needn't look at your comrade. I merely compressed his windpipe rather tightly. He'll come to presently. Ned, take that gay red handkerchief out of his pocket and tie his arms. If I were going to be bound I should like for the deed to be done with just such a beautiful piece of cloth. Meanwhile, if you cry out, my friend, I shall have to blow the top of your head off with this pistol. It's not likely that they would hear your cry, but they might hear my pistol shot."

Ned bound the man rapidly and deftly. There was no danger that he would utter a sound, while Obed White held the pistol. Under the circumstances he was satisfied with the *status quo*. The second man was bound in a similar fashion just as he was reviving, and he, too, was content to yield to like threats. Obed drew a loaded pistol from the first man's belt and handed it, too, to Ned. He also looked rather contemptuously at the musket that the guard by the door had dropped.

"A cheap weapon," he said. "A poor substitute for our American rifle, but we'll take it along, Ned. We may need it. You gather their ammunition while I stand handy with this pistol in case they should burst their bonds."

Ned searched the men, taking all their ammunition, their knives and also the key to the door. Then he and Obed divested the two of their outer clothing and put it upon themselves. Fortunately both soldiers had worn their hats and they pulled them down over their own faces.

"If we don't come into too bright a light, Ned," said White, "you'll pass easily for a Mexican. Mexican plumage makes a Mexican bird. Now how do I look?"

"I could take you for Santa Anna himself," said Ned, elated at their success.

"That promises well. There's another advantage. You speak Spanish and so do I."

"It's lucky that we do."

"And now," said Obed White to the two Mexicans, "we will leave you to the hospitality of Cos and Santa Anna, which my young friend and I have enjoyed so long. We feel that it is time for you to share in it. We're going to lock you in this cell, where you can hear the sea rolling over your head, but you will not stay here forever. It's a long lane that does not come somewhere to a happy ending, and your comrades will

81

find you by tomorrow. Farewell."

He went into the hall and they locked the door. They listened beside it a little while but no sound came from within.

"They dare not cry out," said Obed. "They're afraid we'll come back. Now for the second step in our escape. It's pretty dark here. Those fellows must have known the way mighty well to have come down as they did without a lantern."

"There are other prisoners in these cells," said Ned. "Shouldn't we release them? You can probably open any of the doors with your key."

White shook his head.

"I'm sure that we're the only Texans or Americans in San Juan de Ulua, and we couldn't afford to be wasting time on Mexicans whether revolutionaries or criminals. There would merely be a tumult with every one of us sure to be recaptured."

The two now advanced down the passage, which was low and narrow, walled in with massive stone. It was so dark here that they held each other's hands and felt the way before every footstep.

"I think we're going in the right direction," whispered White, "As I remember it this is the way I came in."

"I'm sure of it," Ned whispered back. "Ah, here are more steps."

They had reached the stairway which led down to the hall of the submarine cells, and still feeling their way they ascended it cautiously. As they rose the air seemed to grow fresher, as if they were nearing the openings by which it entered.

"Those fellows who took our places must have left a lamp or a lantern standing somewhere here at the top of these steps," whispered White. "The man who carried the tray could not have gone down them without a light."

"It's probably here," said Ned, "burned out or blown out by a draught of wind."

He smelled a slight smoke and in a niche carved in the stone he found the lamp. The wick was still smoking a little.

"We'll leave it as it is," said Obed White. "Somebody may relight it for those men when they come back again, but that won't be for several hours yet."

Three more steps and they reached the crest of the flight, where they were confronted by a heavy door of oak, ribbed with iron. Obed gently tried the key that they had seized, but it did not fit.

"They must have banged on the door for it to be opened whenever they came back," said Obed. "Now I shall use my fork which is sure to turn the lock if I take long enough. I wasn't the best watch and key maker in Maine for nothing. If first you don't succeed, then keep on trying till you do."

Ned sat down on the steps while White inserted the fork. He could hear it scratching lightly for a minute and then the bolt slid. The boy rose and the man stepped back by his side.

"Draw your pistol and have it ready," he said, "and I'll do as much with the old musket. We don't know what's on the other side of the door but whatever it is we've got to meet it. Thrice armed is he who hath his weapon levelled."

Ned needed no urging. He drew the pistol and held it ready for instant use. What, in truth, was on the other side of the door? His whole fate and that of his comrade might depend upon the revelation. Obed pushed gently and the door opened without noise three or four inches. A shaft of light from the room fell upon them but they could not yet see into the room. They listened, and, hearing nothing, Obed pushed more boldly. Then they saw before them a large apartment, containing little furniture, but with some faded old uniforms hanging about the walls. Evidently it was used as a barracks for soldiers. At the far end was a door and on the side to the right were two windows.

Ned went to the window and looked out. He saw across a small court a high and blank stone wall, but when he looked upward he saw also a patch of sky. It was a black sky, across which clouds were driving before a whistling wind, but it was the most beautiful sight that he had ever seen. The sky, the free, open sky curving over the beautiful earth, was revealed again to him who had been buried for ages in a dungeon under the sea. He would not go back. In the tremendous uplift of feeling he would willingly choose death first. He beckoned to White who joined him and who looked up without being bid.

"It's out there that we're going," he said. "We'll have to cross a stormy sea before we reach freedom, but Ned, you and I are keyed up just high enough to cross. We'll put it to the touch and win it all. Now for the next door."

The second door was not locked and when they pushed it open they entered a small room, furnished handsomely in the Spanish fashion. A lamp burned on a table, at which an officer sat looking over some papers. He heard the two enter and it was too late for them to retreat, as he turned at once and looked at them, inquiry in his face.

"Who are you?" he asked.

"We are the soldiers who have charge of the two Texans in the cells," replied Obed White boldly. "We have just taken them their food and now we are going back to our quarters."

"I have no doubt that you tell the truth," replied the officer, "but your voice has changed greatly since yesterday. You remember that I gave you an order then about the man White."

"Quite true," replied Obed quickly, raising his musket and taking aim, "and now I'm giving the order back to you. It's a poor rule that won't work first one way and then the other. Just you move or cry out and I shoot. I'd hate to do it, because you're not bad looking, but necessity knows the law of self-preservation."

"You need not worry," said the officer, smiling faintly. "I will not move, nor will I cry out. You have too great an advantage, because I see that your aim is good and your hand steady. I surmise that you are the man White himself."

"None other, and this is my young friend, Edward Fulton, who likes San Juan de Ulua as a castle but not as a hotel. Hence he has decided to go away and so have I. Ned, look at those papers on his desk. You might find among them a pass or two which would be mighty useful to us."

"Do you mind if I light a cigarette?" asked the officer. "You can see that my hands and the cigarettes alike are on the table."

"Go ahead," said Obed hospitably, "but don't waste time."

The officer lighted the cigarette and took a satisfied whiff. Ned searched among the papers, turning them over rapidly.

"Yes, here is a pass!" exclaimed he joyfully, "and here is another and here are two more!"

"Two will be enough," said Obed.

"I'll take this one made out to Joaquin de la Barra for you and one to Diego Fernandez for me. Ah, what are these?"

He held up four papers, looking at them in succession.

"What are they?" asked Obed White.

"Death warrants. They are all for men with Mexican names, and they are signed with the name of Antonio Lopez de Santa Anna, General-in-chief and President of the Mexican Republic."

The officer took the cigarette from his mouth and sent out a little smoke through his nostrils.

"Yes, they are death warrants," he said. "I was looking over them when you came in, and I was troubled. The men were to have been executed tomorrow."

"Were to have been?" said Ned. Then a look passed between him and the officer. The boy held the death warrants one by one in the flame of the lamp and burned them to ashes.

"I cannot execute a man without a warrant duly signed," said the officer.

"Which being the case, we'd better go or we might have to help at our own executions," said Obed White. "Now you just sit where you are and have a peaceful and happy mind, while we go out and fight with the storm."

The officer said nothing and the two passed swiftly through the far door, stepping into a paved court, and reaching a few yards further a gate of the castle. It was quite dark when they stepped once more into the open world, and both wind and rain lashed them. But wind and rain themselves were a delight to the two who had come from under the sea. Besides, the darker the better.

Two sentinels were at the gate and Ned thrust the passes before their eyes. They merely glanced at the signatures, opened the gate, and in an instant the two were outside the castle of San Juan de Ulua.

Chapter 8

The Black Jaguar

It was so dark that the two could see but a narrow stretch of masonry on which they stood and a tossing sea beyond. Behind them heaved up the mass of the castle, mighty and sombre. A fierce wind was blowing in from the gulf, and it whistled and screamed about the great walls. The rain, bitter and cold, lashed against them like hail. Shut off so long from the outer air they shivered now, but the shiver was merely of the air. Their spirit was as high as ever and they faced their crisis with undaunted souls.

Yet they were far from escape. The wind was of uncommon strength, seeming to increase steadily in power, and a half mile of wild waters raced between them and the town. Weaker wills would have yielded and turned back to prison, but not they. They ran eagerly along the edge of the masonry, pelted by rain and wind.

"There must be a boat tied up somewhere along here," exclaimed Ned. "The castle, of course, keeps communication with the town!"

"Yes, here it is!" said Obed. "*Fortune favours the persistent.* It's only a small boat, and it's a big sea before us, but, Ned, my lad, we've got to try it. We can't look any further. Listen! That's the alarm in the castle."

They heard shouts and clash of arms above the roaring of the wind. They picked in furious haste at the rope that held the boat, cast it loose, and sprang in, securing the oars. The waves at once lifted them up and tossed them wildly. It was perhaps fortunate that they lost control of their boat for a minute or two. Two musket shots were fired at them, but good aim in the darkness at such a bobbing object was impossible. Ned heard one of the bullets whistle near, and it gave him a queer, creepy feeling to realise that for the first time in his life someone was firing at him to kill.

"Can you row, Ned?" asked White.

"Yes."

"Then pull with all your strength. Bend as low as you can at the same time. They'll be firing at us as long as we are in range."

They strove for the cover of the darkness, but they were compelled to devote most of their efforts to keeping themselves afloat. The little boat was tossed here and there like a bit of plank. Spray from the sea was dashed over them, and, in almost a moment, they were wet through and through. The captured musket lay in the bottom and rolled against their feet. The wind shrieked continually like some wild animal in pain.

Many torches appeared on the wharf that led up to the castle, and there was a noise of men shouting to one another. The torches disclosed the little boat rising and falling with the swell of the sea, and numerous shots were now fired, but all fell short or went wild.

"I don't think we're in much danger from the muskets," said Obed, "so we won't pay any more attention to them. But in another minute they'll have big boats out in pursuit We must make for the land below the town, and get away somehow or other in the brush. If we were to land in the town itself we'd be as badly off as ever. Hark, there goes the alarm!"

A heavy booming report rose above the mutter of the waters and the screaming of the wind. One of the great guns on the castle of San Juan de Ulua had been fired. After a brief interval it was followed by a second shot and then a third. The reports could be heard easily in Vera Cruz, and they said that either a fresh revolution had begun, or that prisoners were escaping. The people would be on the watch. White turned the head of the boat more toward the south.

"Ned," he said, "we must choose the longer way. We cannot run any risk of landing right under the rifles of Santa Anna's troops. Good

God!"

Some gunner on the walls of San Juan de Ulua, of better sight and aim than the others, had sent a cannon ball so close that it struck the sea within ten feet of them. They were deluged by a water spout and again their little vessel rocked fearfully. Obed White called out cheerfully:

"Still right side up! They may shoot more cannon balls at us, Ned, but they won't hit as near as that again!"

"No, it's not likely," said Ned, "but there come the boats!"

Large boats rowed by eight men apiece had now put out, but they, too, were troubled by the wind and the high waves, and the boat they pursued was so small that it was lost to sight most of the time. The wind and darkness while a danger on the one hand were a protection on the other. Fortunately both current and wind were bearing them in the direction they wished, and they struggled with the energy that the love of life can bring. All the large boats save one now disappeared from view, but the exception, having marked them well, came on, gaining. An officer seated in the prow, and wrapped in a long cloak, hailed them in a loud voice, ordering them to surrender.

"Ned," said Obed White, "you keep the boat going straight ahead and I'll answer that man. But I wish this was a rifle in place of a musket."

He picked up the musket and took aim. When he fired the leading rower on the right hand side of the pursuing boat dropped back, and the boat was instantly in confusion. White laid down the musket and seized the oar again.

"Now, Ned," he exclaimed, "if we pull as hard as we can and a little harder, we'll lose them!"

The boat, driven by the oars and the wind, sprang forward. Fortune, as if resolved now to favour fugitives who had made so brave a fight against overwhelming odds, piled the clouds thicker and heavier than ever over the bay. The little boat was completely concealed from its pursuers. Another gun boomed from San Juan de Ulua, and both Ned and Obed saw its flash on the parapet, but, hidden under the kindly veil of the night, they pulled straight ahead with strong arms. The sea seemed to be growing smoother, and soon they saw an outline which they knew to be that of the land.

"We're below the town now," said Obed. "I don't know any particular landing place, but it's low and sandy along here. So I propose that we ride right in on the the highest wave, jump out of the boat when she strikes and leave her."

"Good enough," said Ned. "Yes, that's the land. I can see it plainly now, and here comes our wave."

The crest of the great wave lifted them up, and bore them swiftly inland, the two increasing the speed with their oars. They went far up on a sandy beach, where the boat struck. They sprang out, Obed taking with him the unloaded musket, and ran. The retreating water caught them about the ankles and pulled hard, but could not drag them back. They passed beyond the highest mark of the waves, and then dropped, exhausted, on the ground.

"We've got all Mexico now to escape in," said Obed White, "instead of that pent-up castle."

The alarm gun boomed once more from San Juan de Ulua, and reminded them that they could not linger long there. The rain was still falling, the night was cold, and, after their tremendous strain, they would need shelter as well as refuge.

"They'll be searching the beach soon," said Obed, "and we'd best be off. It's against my inclination just now to stay long in one place. A rolling stone keeps slick and well polished, and that's what I'm after."

"I think our safest course is to travel inland just as fast and as far as we can," said Ned.

"Correct. Good advice needs no bush."

They started in the darkness across the sand dunes, and walked for a long time. They knew that a careful search along the beach would be made for them, but the Mexicans were likely to feel sure when they found nothing that they had been wrecked and drowned.

"I hope they'll think the sea got us," said Ned, "because then they won't be searching about the country for us."

"We weren't destined to be drowned that time," said Obed with great satisfaction. "It just couldn't happen after our running such a gauntlet before reaching the sea. But the further we get away from salt water the safer we are."

"It was my plan at first," said Ned, "to go by way of the sea from Vera Cruz to a Texan port."

"Circumstances alter journeys. It can't be done now. We've got to cut across country. It's something like a thousand miles to Texas, but I think that you and I together, Ned, can make it."

Ned agreed. Certainly they had no chance now to slip through by the way of Vera Cruz, and the sea was not his element anyhow.

The rain ceased, and a few stars came out. They passed from the sand dunes into a region of marshes. Constant walking kept their blood warm, and their clothes were drying upon them. But they were growing very tired and they felt that they must rest and sleep even at the risk of recapture.

"There's a lot of grass growing on the dry ground lying between the marshes," said Ned, "and I suppose that the Mexicans cut it for the Vera Cruz market. Maybe we can find something like a haystack or a windrow. Dry grass makes a good bed."

They hunted over an hour and persistence was rewarded by a small heap of dry grass in a little opening surrounded by thorn bushes. They spread one covering of it on the ground, covered themselves to the mouth with another layer, and then went sound asleep, the old, un-loaded musket lying by Obed White's side.

The two slept the sleep of deep exhaustion, the complete relaxation of both body and mind. Boy and man they had passed through ordeals that few can endure, but, healthy and strong, they suffered merely from weariness and not from shattered nerves. So they slept peacefully and their breathing was long and deep. They were warm as they lay with the grass above and below them like two blankets. It had not rained much here, and the grass had dried before their coming, so they were free from danger of cold.

The night passed and the brilliant Mexican day came, touching with red and gold the town that curved about the bay, and softening the tints of the great fortress that rose on the rocky isle. All was quiet again within San Juan de Ulua and Vera Cruz. It had become known in both castle and town that two Texans, boy and man, had escaped from the dungeons under the sea only to find a grave in the sea above. Their boat had been found far out in the bay where the returning waves carried it, but the fishes would feed on their bodies, and it was well, because the Texans were wicked people, robbers and brigands who dared to defy the great and good Santa Anna, the father of his people.

Meanwhile, the two slept on, never stirring under the grass. It is true that the boy had dreams of a mighty castle from which he had fled and of a roaring ocean over which he had passed, but he landed happily and the dream sank away into oblivion. *Peons* worked in a field not a hundred yards away, but they sought no fugitives, and they had no cruel thoughts about anything. That Spanish strain in them was wholly dormant now. They had heard in the night the signal guns from San Juan de Ulua and the tenderest hearted of them said a prayer under his breath for the boy whom the storm had given to the sea. Then they sang together as they worked, some soft, crooning air of love and sacrifice that had been sung among the hills of Spain before the Moor came. Perhaps if they had known that the boy and man were asleep only a hundred yards away, the tenderest hearted among them at least would have gone on with their work just the same.

Ned was the first to awake and it was past noon. He threw off the grass and stood up refreshed but a little stiff. He awoke Obed, who rose, yawning tremendously and plucking wisps of grass from his hair. The droning note of a song came faintly, and the two listened.

"*Peons* at work in a field," said the boy, looking through the trees. "They don't appear to be very warlike, but we'd better go in the other direction."

"You're right," said Obed. "It's best for us to get away. If we tempt our fate too much it may overtake us, but before we go let's take a last view of our late home, San Juan de Ulua. See it over there, cut out in black against the blue sky. It's a great fortress, but I'm glad to bid it farewell."

"Shall we take the musket?" asked Ned. "It's unloaded, and we have nothing with which to load it."

"I think we'll stick to it," replied Obed, "we may find a use for it, but the first thing we want, Ned, is something to eat, and we've got to get it. Curious, isn't it, how the fear of recapture, the fear of everything, melts away before the demands of hunger."

"Which means that we'll have to go to some Mexican hut and ask for food," said Ned. "Now, I suggest, since we have no money, that we offer the musket for as much provisions as we can carry."

"It's not a bad idea. But our pistols are loaded and we'll keep them in sight. It won't hurt if the humble *peon* takes us for brigands. He'll trade a little faster, and, as this is a time of war so far as we are concerned, we have the right to inspire necessary fear."

They started toward the north and west, anxious to leave the *tierra caliente* as soon as they could and reach the mountains. Ned saw once more the silver cone of Orizaba now on his left. It had not led him on a happy quest before, but he believed that it was a true beacon now. They walked rapidly, staying their hunger as best they could, not willing to approach any hut, until they were a considerable distance from Vera Cruz. It was nearly nightfall when they dared a little *adobe* hut on a hillside.

"We'll claim to be Spaniards out of money and walking to the

City of Mexico," said Obed. "They probably won't believe our statements, but, owing to the sight of these loaded pistols, they will accept them."

It was a poor hut with an *adobe* floor and its owner, a surly Mexican, was at home, but it contained plenty of food of the coarsest Mexican type, and Obed White stated their requests very plainly.

"Food we must have," he said, "sufficient for two or three days. Besides, we want the two *serapes* hanging there on the wall. I think they are clean enough for our use. In return we offer you this most excellent musket, a beautiful weapon made at Seville. Look at it. It is worth twice what we demand for it. Behold the beautifully carved stock and the fine steel barrel."

The Mexican, a dark, heavy-jawed fellow, regarded them maliciously, while his wife and seven half-naked children sat by in silence, but watching the strangers with the wary, shifting eyes of wild animals.

"Yes, it is a good musket," he said, "but may I inquire if it is your own?"

"For the purposes of barter and sale it is my own," replied Obed politely. "In this land as well as some others possession is ten points of the law."

"The words you speak are Spanish but your tone is *Gringo*."

"*Gringo* or Spanish, it does not change the beauty and value of the musket."

"I was in Vera Cruz this morning. Last night there was a storm and the great guns at the mighty Castle of San Juan de Ulua were firing."

"Did they fire the guns to celebrate the storm?"

"No. They gave a signal that two prisoners, vile Texans, were escaping from the dungeons under the sea. But the storm took them, and buried them in the waters of the bay. I heard the description of them. One was a very tall man, thin and with very thick, red hair. The other was a boy, but tall and strong for his age. He had gray eyes and brown hair. Wretched *infidel* Texans they were, but they are gone and may the Holy Virgin intercede for their souls."

He lifted his heavy lashes, and he and Obed White looked gravely into the eyes of each other. They and Ned, too, understood perfectly.

"You were informed wrongly," said Obed. "The man who escaped was short and fat, and he had yellow hair. The boy was very dark with black hair and black eyes. But the statement that they were drowned in the bay is correct."

91

"One might get five hundred good silver *pesos* for bringing in their bodies."

"One might, but one won't, and you, *amigo*, are just concluding an excellent bargain. You get this fine, unloaded musket, and we get the food and the *serapes* for which we have so courteously asked. The entire bargain will be completed inside of two minutes."

The blue eyes and the black eyes met again and the owner of each pair understood.

"It is so," said the Mexican, evenly, and he brought what they wished.

"Good-day, amigo," said Obed politely. "I will repeat that the musket is unloaded, and you cannot find ammunition for it any nearer than Vera Cruz, which will not trouble you as you are here at home in your castle. But our pistols are loaded, and it is a necessary fact for my young friend and myself. We purpose to travel in the hills, where there is great danger of brigands. Fortunately for us we are both able and willing to shoot well. Once more, farewell."

"Farewell," said the Mexican, waving his hand in dignified salute.

"That fellow is no fool," said Obed, as they strode away. "I like a man who can take a hint. A word to the wise is like a stitch in time."

"Will he follow us?"

"Not he. He has that musket which he craved, and at half its value. He does not desire wounds and perhaps death. The chances are ninety-nine out of a hundred that he will never say a word for fear his government will seize his musket."

"And now for the wildest country that we can find," said Ned. "I'm glad it doesn't rain much down here. We can sleep almost anywhere, wrapped in our *serapes*."

They ate as they walked and they kept on a long time after sunset, picking their way by the moonlight. Two or three times they passed *peons* in the path, but their bold bearing and the pistols in their belts always gave them the road. Brigands flourished amid the frequent revolutions, and the humbler Mexicans found it wise to attend strictly to their own business. They slept again in the open, but this time on a hill in a dense thicket. They had previously drunk at a spring at its base, and lacking now for neither food nor water they felt hope rising continually.

Ned had no dreams the second night, and both awoke at dawn. On the far side of the hill, they found a pool in which they bathed, and with breakfast following they felt that they had never been stronger.

Their food was made up in two packs, one for each, and they calculated that with economy it would last two days. They could also reckon upon further supplies from wild fruits, and perhaps more *frijoles* and *tortillas* from the people themselves. When they had summed up all their circumstances, they concluded that they were not in such bad condition. Armed, strong and bold, they might yet traverse the thousand miles to Texas.

Light of heart and foot they started. Off to the left the great silver head of Orizaba looked down at them benignantly, and before them they saw the vast flowering robe of the *tierra caliente* into which they pushed boldly, even as Cortez and his men had entered it.

Ned was almost overpowered by a vegetation so grand and magnificent. Except on the paths which they followed, it was an immense and tangled mass of gigantic trees and huge lianas. Many of the lianas had wound themselves like huge serpents about the trees and had gradually pulled them, no matter how strong, into strange and distorted shapes. Overhead parrots and paroquets chattered amid the vast and gorgeous bloom of red and pink, yellow and white. Ned and Obed were forced to keep to the narrow *peon* paths, because elsewhere one often could not pass save behind an army of axes.

The trees were almost innumerable in variety. They saw mahogany, rosewood, Spanish cedar and many others that they did not know. They also saw the cactus and the palm, turned by the struggle for existence in this tremendous forest, into climbing plants. Obed noted these facts with his sharp eye.

"It's funny that the cactus and the palm have to climb to live," he said, "but they've done it. It isn't any funnier, however, than the fact that the whale lived on land millions of years ago, and had to take to the water to escape being eaten up by bigger and fiercer animals than himself. I'm a Maine man and so I know about whales."

They came now and then to little clearings, in which the *peons* raised many kinds of tropical and semitropical plants, bananas, pineapples, plantains, oranges, cocoa-nuts, mangoes, olives and numerous others. In some places the fruit grew wild, and they helped themselves to it. Twice they asked at huts for the customary food made of Indian corn, and on both occasions it was given to them. The peons were stolid, but they seemed kind and Ned was quite sure they did not care whether the two were *Gringos* or not. Two or three times, heavy tropical rains gushed down in swift showers, and they were soaked through and through, despite their *serapes*, but the hot sun, coming quickly afterward, soon dried them out again. They were very much afraid of chills and fever, but their constitutions, naturally so strong, held them safe.

Deeper and deeper they went into the great tropical wilderness of the *tierra caliente*. Often the heat under the vast canopy of interlacing vines and boughs was heavy and intense. Then they would lie down and rest, first threshing up grass and bushes to drive away snakes, scorpions and lizards. Sometimes they would sleep, and sometimes they would watch the monkeys and parrots darting about and chattering overhead. Twice they saw fierce ocelots stealing among the tree trunks, stalking prey hidden from the man and boy. The first ocelot was a tawny yellow and the second was a reddish gray. Both were marked with black spots in streaks and in lengthened rings. The second was rather the larger of the two. He seemed to be slightly over four feet in length, of which the body was three feet and the tail about a foot.

Ned and Obed were lying flat upon the ground, when the second ocelot appeared, and, as the wind was blowing from him toward them, he did not detect their presence. At the distance the figure of the great cat was enlarged. He looked to them almost like a tiger and certainly he was a ferocious creature, as he stalked his prey. Neither would have cared to meet him even with weapons in hand. Suddenly he darted forward, ran up the trunk of a great tree and disappeared in the dense foliage. As he did not come down again they inferred that he had caught what he was pursuing and was now devouring it.

Ned shivered a little and put his hand on the butt of his loaded pistol.

"Obed," he said, "I don't like the jungle, and I shall be glad when I get out of it. It's too vast, too bewildering, and its very beauty fills me with fear. I always feel that fangs and poison are lurking behind the beauty and the bloom."

"You're not so far wrong, Ned. I believe I'd rather be on the dusty deserts of the North. We'll go through the *tierra caliente* just as quickly as we can."

The next day they became lost among the paths, and did not regain their true direction until late in the afternoon. Sunset found them by the banks of a considerable creek, the waters of which were cold, as if its source were in the high mountains. Being very tired they bathed and arranged couches of grass on the banks. After the heat and perplexity of the jungle they were very glad to see cold, running water. The sight and the pleasant trickle of the flowing stream filled Ned with desires for the north, for the open land beyond the Rio Grande, where cool winds blew, and you could see to the horizon's rim. He was sicker than ever of the jungle, the beauty of which could not hide from him its steam and poison.

"How much longer do you think it will be before we leave the *tierra caliente?*" he asked.

"We ought to reach the intermediate zone between the *tierra caliente* and the higher sierras in three or four days," replied Obed. "It's mighty slow travelling in the jungle, but to get out of it we've only to keep going long enough. Meanwhile, we'll have a good snooze by the side of this nice, clean little river."

As usual after hard travelling, they fell asleep almost at once, but Ned was awakened in the night by some strange sound, the nature of which he could not determine at first. The jungle surrounded them in a vast, high circle, wholly black in the night, but overhead was a blue rim of sky lighted by stars. He raised himself on his elbow. Obed, four or five feet away, was still sleeping soundly on his couch of grass. The little river, silver in the moonlight, flowed with a pleasant trickle, but the trickle was not the sound that had awakened him.

The forest was absolutely silent. Not a breath of wind stirred, but the boy, although awed by the night and the great jungle, still listened intently.

The sound rose again, a low, hoarse rumble. It was distant thunder. A storm was coming. He heard it a third time. It was not thunder. It was the deep growl of some fierce, wild animal. For a moment the boy was afraid. Then he remembered the heavy pistol that never left his belt. It still carried the original load, a large bullet with plenty of gunpowder behind it.

The sounds were repeated and they were nearer. They were like a long drawn *p-u, p-u, p-u.* The tone was of indescribable ferocity. Ned was brave, but he shivered all over and there was a prickly sensation at the roots of his hair. He felt like some primeval youth who with club alone must face the rush of the sabre-toothed tiger. But he drew upon his reserves of pride which were large. He would not awaken Obed, but, drawing the pistol and holding his fingers on trigger and hammer, he walked a little distance down the bank of the stream. That terrible *p-u, p-u, p-u,* suddenly sounded much closer at hand, and Ned shrank back, stiffening with horror.

A great black beast, by far the largest wild animal that he had ever seen, came silently out of the jungle and stood before the boy. He was a good seven feet in length, black as a coal, low but of singularly thick and heavy build. His shoulders and paws were more powerful than those of a tiger. As he stood there before Ned, black and sinister as Satan, he opened his mouth, and emitted again that fearful, rumbling *p-u, p-u, p-u.*

Ned could not move. All his power seemed to have gone into his eyes and he only looked. He saw the red eyes, the black lips wrinkling back from the long, cruel fangs, and the glossy skin rippling over the tremendous muscles. Ned suddenly wrenched himself free from this paralysis of the body, levelled the pistol and fired at a mark midway between the red eyes.

There was a tremendous roar and the animal leaped. Ned sprang to one side. The huge beast with blood pouring from his head turned and would have been upon him at the second leap, but a long barrel and then an arm was projected over Ned's shoulder. A pistol was fired almost in his ear. The monster's spring was checked in mid-flight, and he fell to the earth, dead. Ned too, fell, but in a faint.

Chapter 9

The Ruined Temples

Ned revived and sat up. Cold water which Obed had brought in his hat from the river was dripping from his face. At his feet lay a huge black animal, terrible even in death. There was one wound in his head, where Ned's bullet had gone in, and another through the right eye, where Obed's had entered, reaching the brain. Ned's strength now returned fully and the colour came back to his face. He stood up, but he shuddered nevertheless.

"Obed," he said gratefully, "you came just in time."

"I surely did," said that cheerful artisan. "A bullet in time saved a life like thine. But you had already given him a bad wound."

"What is he, Obed?"

"About the biggest and finest specimen of a black jaguar that ever ravaged a Mexican jungle. I always thought the black kind was found only in Paraguay and the regions down there, but I'm quite sure now that at least one of them has been roaming up here, and he is bound to have kin, too. Ned, isn't he a terror? If he'd got at you he'd have ripped you in pieces in half a minute."

Ned shuddered again. Even in death the great black jaguar was capable of inspiring terror. He had never before seen such a picture of

96

magnificent and sinister strength. He was heavier and more powerful than a tiger, and he knew that the jaguar often became a man-eater.

"I'd like to have that skin to lay upon the parlour of my palatial home, if I ever have one," said Obed, "and I reckon that you and I had better stick pretty close together while we are in this jungle. Our pistols are not loaded now, and we have no more ammunition."

They did not dare to sleep again in the same place, fearing that the jaguar might have a mate which would seek revenge upon them, but, a couple of hundred yards further down, they found in the river a little island, twelve or fifteen feet square. Here they felt that the water would somehow give them security, and they lay down once more.

Ned was awakened a second time by that terrifying *pu-pu-pu*. It approached through the forest but it stopped at the point where the dead body of the black giant lay. He knew that it was the voice of the mate. He listened a long time, but he did not hear it again, and he concluded that the second jaguar, after the brief mourning of animals, had gone away. He fell asleep again, and did not awaken until day.

They were now practically unarmed, but they kept the pistols, for the sake of show in case any peons of the jungle should offer trouble, and pressed forward, with all the speed possible in so dense a tangle of forest. In the deep shade of trees and bushes Ned continually saw the shadows of immense black jaguars. He knew that it was only nerves and imagination, but he did not like to be in a condition that enabled fancy to play him such tricks. He longed more than ever for the open plains, even with dust and thirst.

Already they saw the mountains rising before them, terrace after terrace, and, three days after the encounter with the jaguar, they began to ascend the middle slopes between the *tierra caliente* and the lofty *sierras*. The whole character of the country changed. The tropical jungle ceased. They now entered magnificent forests of oak, pine, plane tree, mimosas, chestnut and many other varieties. They also saw the bamboo, the palm and the cactus. The water was fresher and colder, and they felt as if they had come into a new world.

But the question of food supply returned. They had used the wild fruits in abundance, always economising strictly with their *tortillas* and *frijoles*. Now they had eaten the last of these and a diet of fruit alone would not do.

"We'll have to sell a pistol in the way that we sold the musket," said Ned.

"I hate to do it," said Obed, "but I don't see anything else that we can do. We might seize our food at the first hut we find, but whatever may be the quarrels between the Mexicans and Texans, I'm not willing to rob any of these poor *peons.*"

"Nor I," said Ned with emphasis. "My pistol goes first."

They found the usual *adobe* hut in a pleasant valley, and the noble senor, the proprietor, was at home playing a *mandolin.* He did not suspect them to be *Gringos,* but he was quite sure that they were brigands and he made the exchange swiftly and gladly. Two days later the other pistol went in the same way, and they began to think how they could acquire new weapons and plenty of ammunition for them. They sat in the shade of a great oak while they discussed the question. It was certainly a vital one. Dangerous enough at any time, the long journey through Mexico would become impossible without arms.

"If we could loot them from the soldiers I wouldn't mind at all," said Obed. "The soldiers are to act against Texas, according to the tale you tell, and the tale is true. All's fair in flight and war, and if such a chance comes our way I'm going to take it."

"So am I," said Ned.

But such a chance was in no hurry to present itself. They went on for a number of days and came now to the region, bordering the high sierras, passing through vast forests of oak and pine, and seeing scarcely any habitation. Here, as they walked toward twilight along one of the narrow paths, a voice from the bushes cried: "Halt!"

Ned saw several gun barrels protruding from the foliage, and was obedient to the command. He also threw up his hands and Obed White was no slower than he. Ned judged from the nature of the ambush that they had fallen among brigands, then so prevalent in Mexico, and the thought gave him relief. Soldiers would carry him back to Santa Anna, but surely brigands would not trouble long those who had nothing to lose.

"It is well, friends, that you obey so quickly," said a man in gaudy costume as he stepped from the bushes followed by a half dozen others, evil looking fellows, all carrying guns and pistols. Ned noticed that two of the guns were rifles of long and slender barrel, undoubtedly of American make.

"Good-evening, captain," said Obed White in his smoothest tones. "We were expecting to meet you, as we learned that we are in the territory which you rule so well."

The man frowned and then smiled.

"I see that you are a man of humour, *amigo,*" he said, "and it is well.

Your information is correct. I rule this territory. I am Captain Juan Carossa and these are my men. We collect tribute from all who pass this way."

"A worthy task and, I have no doubt, a profitable one."

"Always worthy but not always profitable. However, I trust that you can make it worth our while."

A look of sadness passed over the expressive features of Obed White.

"You look like a brave and generous man, Senor Juan Carossa," he said sorrowfully, "and it grieves both my young friend and myself to the very centre of our hearts to disappoint you. We have nothing. There is not a cent of either gold or silver upon us. Jewels we admire, but we have them not. You may search."

He held wide his arms and Ned did likewise. Carossa gave an order to one of his men, a tall fellow, swathed in a red serape, to make the search, and he did so in such a rapid and skilful manner that Ned marvelled. He felt hands touching him here and there, as light as the fall of a leaf. Obed was treated in the same fashion, and then the man in the red *serape* turned two empty and expressive palms to his chief.

Carossa swore fluently, and bent a look of deep reproach upon Ned and Obed.

"*Senors,*" he said, "this is an injustice, nay more, it is a crime. You come upon the territory over which we range. You put us to the trouble of stopping you, and you have nothing. All our risk and work are wasted."

Obed shook his head in apology.

"It is not our fault," he said. "We had a little money, but we spent it for food. We had some arms also, but they went for food too, so you see, good kind Captain Carossa, we had nothing left for you."

"But you have two good *serapes,*" said the captain. "Had you money we would not take them from you, but it must not be said of Captain Carossa and his men that they went away with nothing. I trust, *senor,* that you do not think me unreasonable."

Obed White considered. Captain Carossa was a polite man. So was he.

"We can ill afford to part with these cloaks or *serapes,*" he said, "but since it must be we cannot prevent it. Meanwhile, we ask you to offer us your hospitality. We are on the mountains now, and the nights are cold. We would be chilled without our cloaks. Take us with you, and, in the morning, when the warm sunshine comes we will proceed."

Carossa laughed and pulled his long black moustaches. "Santiago, but you have a spirit," he said, "and I like it. You shall have your request and you may come with us but tomorrow you go forth stripped and shorn. My men cannot work for nothing. Spanish or Mexican, English or *Gringo* you must pay. *Gringo* you are, but for that I do not care. It is in truth the reason why I yield to your little request, because you can never bring the soldiers of Santa Anna down upon us."

Obed White smiled. The look upon his face obviously paid tribute to the craft and courage of Juan Carossa, the great, and Carossa therefore was pleased. The brigand captain did not abate one whit from his resolution to have their *serapes* and their coats too, but he would show them first that he was a gentleman. He spoke to his men, and the fellow with the red *serape* led the way along a narrow path through a forest of myrtle oaks. They went in single file, the captain about the middle, and just behind him Obed, with Ned following. Ned as usual was silent, but Obed talked nearly all the time and Carossa seemed to like it. Ned saw that the brigand leader was vain, eager to show his power and resource, but he was sure that, at bottom, he was cruel, and that he would turn them forth stripped and helpless in the forest.

Night came down suddenly, but the man in front lighted a small lantern that he took from under his *serape*, and they continued the march with unabated speed. The forest thinned, and about nine o'clock they came into an open space. The moon was now out and Ned saw a group of four rectangular buildings, elevated on mounds. The buildings, besides being rectangles themselves, were so placed that the group made a rectangle. The structures of stone were partly ruined, and of great age. They followed the uniform plan of those vast and mysterious ruins found so often in Southern and Central Mexico. The same race that erected the pyramids on the Teotihuacan might have raised these buildings.

"My home! The quarters of myself and my men," said Carossa, dramatically, pointing to the largest of the buildings. "We do not know who built it. It goes far beyond the time of Cortez, but it serves us now. The *peon* will not approach it, because Carossa is there and maybe ghosts too."

"I'm not afraid of ghosts," said Obed White. "Lead on, most noble captain. We appreciate your hospitality. We did not know that you were taking us to a palace."

Captain Carossa deigned to be pleased again with himself, and, taking the lantern from the man in the red *serape*, he led the way. He entered the large building by means of a narrow passageway in one of the angles, passed through an unroofed room, and then came to a door at which both Ned and Obed gazed with the most intense curiosity. The doorway was made of only three stones, two huge monolithic door jambs, each seven feet high, nearly as wide and more than two feet thick. Upon them rested a lintel also monolithic, but at least twenty feet in length, with a width of five feet and a thickness of three feet. It was evident to Ned that mighty workmen had once toiled here.

"Is not that an entrance fit for a king?" said the brigand captain, again making a dramatic gesture.

"It is fit for Captain Juan Carossa, which is more," said Obed White with suave courtesy.

Captain Carossa bowed. Once more he deigned to be pleased with himself. Then he led through the doorway and Ned uttered a little cry of admiration. They stood in a great room with a magnificent row of monolithic pillars running down the centre. A stone roof had once covered the room, but it had long since fallen in. The interior of the walls was plain, made of stones and mortar, once covered with cement, deep blood red in colour, of which a few fragments remained. But the walls on the outside were covered with splendid panels of mosaic work varied now and then by sculptured stones. The stone used on the outside was of a light cream colour. But the boy did not see the mosaic panels until later.

Silent and studious, these vast ruins of a mysterious race made a great appeal to Ned. He forgot the rough brigands for a moment, and stood there looking at the walls and great columns, upon which the moon was pouring a flood of beams. What were these outlaws to those mighty builders whom the past had swallowed up so completely?

The brigands were already lighting a fire beside one of the huge monoliths, and Carossa lay down on a *serape*. The fire blazed up, but it did not detract from the weird effect of the Hall of Pillars. One of the men warmed food which he brought from another of the ruined houses, and Carossa told his prisoners to eat.

"What I give you tonight, and what I shall give you tomorrow morning may be the last food that you will have for some time," he said, "so enjoy it as best you may."

He smiled, his lips drawing back from his white teeth, and in some singular way he made Ned think of the black jaguar and his black lips writhing back from his great fangs. Why had Obed spoken of coming with them? Better to have been stripped in the path, and to have gone on alone. But he ate the food, as the long marching had made him hungry, and lay down within the rim of the firelight.

The men also ate, and Ned saw that they were surly. Doubtless they had endured much hardship recently and had secured little spoil. He heard muttered sounds which he knew were curses. He became more uneasy than ever. Certainly little human kindness lurked in the hearts of such as these, and he believed that Carossa was playing with them for his own amusement, just as a trainer with a steel bar makes the animals in a cage do their tricks.

The mutterings among the men increased. Carossa spoke to one of them, who brought forth a stone jar from a recess in the wall. Tin cups were produced and all, including Carossa, drank *pulque* made from the maguey plant. They offered it also to Ned and Obed, but both declined.

The *pulque* did not make the men more quarrelsome, but seemed to plunge them into a lethargy. Two or three of them hummed doleful songs, as if they were thinking of homes to which they could not go. One began to weep, but finally spread out his *serape*, lay down on it and went to sleep. Three or four others soon did the same. Two sat near the great monolithic doorway, with muskets across their knees. Undoubtedly they were intended to be sentinels, but Ned noted that their heads drooped.

"I shall sleep now, my *Gringo* guests," said Carossa, "and I advise you to do the same. You cannot alter anything, and you will need the strength that sleep brings."

"Your advice is good," said Obed, "and we thank you, Captain Carossa, for your advice and courtesy. Manners are the fine finish of a man."

His *serape* had not yet been taken from him, and he rolled himself in it. Ned was already in his, lying with his feet to the smouldering fire. The boy did not wish to sleep, nor could he have slept had he wished. But he saw that Carossa soon slumbered, and the sentinels by the doorway seemed, at least, to doze. He turned slightly on his side, and looked at Obed who lay about eight feet away. He could not see the man's face, but his body did not stir. Perhaps Obed also slept.

A wind was now rising and it made strange sounds among the vast ruins. It was a moan, a shriek and a hoarse sigh. Perhaps the *peons* were not so far wrong! The ghosts did come back to their old abodes. Ned was glad that he was not alone. Even without Obed the company of brigands would have been a help. He lay still a long time.

The coals of the fire went out, one by one, and where they had glowed only black ashes lay. The wind among the ruins played all kinds of strange variations, and Ned was never more awake in his life. He took a last look at the sentinels, and he was sure that they slept, sitting, with their muskets across their laps. Then he rose to his knees and with difficulty checked a cry of astonishment when he saw Obed rising at the same time. They remained on their knees a moment or two looking at each other and then, simultaneously they rose to their feet. Their comprehension was complete.

Ned looked down at Carossa. The brigand chief slept soundly and his face in repose was wholly evil. The gayety and courtesy that they had seen upon it awake were only a mask.

Obed stepped lightly to one of the pillars and Ned followed him. He knew what Obed was seeking. Here was the great chance. The brigands, careless from long immunity, had stacked their guns against the pillar, and Ned and Obed promptly selected the two American rifles that Ned had noticed. Hung by each was a large supply of powder and bullets to fit which they also took. Two of the best machetes were chosen too, and then they were ready to go. With the rifle in his hand, the great weapon with which the pioneer made his way from ocean to ocean, Ned had strength and courage. He believed that Obed and he could defeat the entire force of brigands, but he awaited the signal of his older comrade.

Standing close together behind the massive pillar they could not now see the sentinels at the doorway. Ned was quite sure that they were sleeping and that he and his comrade could steal past them. But Obed turned in another direction and Ned followed without a word. The man had caught a glimpse of a second entrance at the opposite side of this hall of pillars, and the two darted into it.

They found themselves in a passage less than the height of a man, and only about three feet wide, but Obed led on boldly, and Ned, with equal boldness, followed. The wall was about five feet thick, and they came out into a court or patio surrounded by four ruined buildings. The floor of the patio was cement, upon which their footsteps made no noise, and, going through the great apertures in one of the ruined buildings, they stood entirely on the outside of the mass of ancient temples, or whatever it may have been.

"Ned," whispered Obed, "we ought to go right down on our knees and give thanks. We've not only escaped from Carossa and his cutthroats, but we've brought with us two American rifles; good enough for anybody and two or three hundred rounds of ammunition, the things that we needed most of all."

"It must have been more than chance," said Ned with emotion. "It must have been a hand leading us."

"When I proposed to go with them I thought we might have a chance of some kind or other. Well, Captain Carossa, you meant us evil, but you did us good. Come, Ned, the faster we get away from these ghosts the better. Besides, we've got more to carry now."

They had also brought away with them their packs of food, but they did not mind the additional weight of the weapons, which were worth more to them than gold or jewels. They listened a minute or two to see if any alarm had been raised, but no sound came from the Hall of Pillars, and with light steps and strong hearts they began another march on their northward journey.

They travelled by the moon and stars, and, as they were not hindered now by any great tangle of undergrowth, they made many miles before dawn, although they were ascending steadily. They had come upon the edge of the great central plateau of Mexico, which runs far into the north and which includes much of Texas. Before them lay another and great change in the country. They were now to enter a land of little rain, where they would find the ragged yucca tree, the agave and the cactus, the scrubby mesquite bush and clumps of coarse grass. But they had passed through so much that they did not fear it.

They hunted for an hour after sunrise, before they found a small brook, at which they drank, and, in spirit, returned the thanks which Obed had said so emphatically were due. Then, wrapped in the useful *serapes*, they went to sleep once more in a thicket. They had been sure that the Mexicans could not trail them, and their confidence was justified. When they awoke in the afternoon no human being was in sight, and their loaded rifles lay undisturbed beside them.

Then they entered upon the plain, plodding steadily on over a dusty gray landscape, but feeling that their rifles would be ample protection against anything that they might meet. The sun became very hot, and they longed at times for the shade of the forest that they had left behind, but they did not cease their march. Off to their left they saw towering mountains with a green film along their slopes that they knew to be forests of oak and pine; and such was the nature of man that they looked at them regretfully. Obed White, glancing at Ned, caught Ned glancing at him, and both laughed.

"That's it," said Obed. "How precious is the thing that slips away. When we were in the forest we wanted the open country, but now in the open country we want the forest. But we're making progress, Ned. Don't forget that."

"I don't," said Ned. "But when we get further North into the vast stretches of the arid plateau, we must have something more to carry—water bottles."

"That's so. We can't do without them. Maybe, too, Ned, we can pick up a couple of good horses. They'd be a wonderful help."

"We'll hope for everything we need," said Ned cheerfully. "Now I wonder, Obed, if the attack has been made on Texas. Do you think we can yet get there in time?"

"I hope so," replied Obed thoughtfully. "You were a long time in San Juan de Ulua, but armies move slowly, and they have plenty of troubles of their own here in Mexico. I would wager almost anything that no Mexican force in great numbers has yet crossed the Rio Grande."

"Then we may be in time. Obed, we'll push for the north with every ounce of strength we have."

"That's just what we'll do. Courage defeats a multitude of sins."

They travelled now for nearly a week in a direction north slightly by west, suffering at times from heat, and once from a tropical rain storm that deluged them. While the rain poured upon them, they kept their *serapes* wrapped around their powder, and let their bodies take the worst. The rain, for a while, was very cold, but the powder was precious, and after a while the sun came out, drying and warming them again. They were compelled to swim two narrow but deep rivers, a most difficult task, as they had arms, ammunition and food to carry with them.

They noticed stretches of forest again, and passed both scattered houses and villages. Their knowledge of Spanish and their rifles were their protection. But in some places the people seemed to care nothing either about Santa Anna or those who might oppose him. They were content to lead lives in a region which furnished food almost of its own accord. Just before approaching one of these villages Ned shot another jaguar. It was not black like the first, nor so large. It was about five feet in length, and yellowish in colour, with a splendid skin, which, at Obed's suggestion, they removed for purposes of barter. It was a wise idea, as they traded it in the village for two large water bottles. The people there were so indifferent to their identity that they sat in the plaza in the evening, and watched the young people dance the fandango.

It was only a crude little village in the Mexican wilderness. The people were more Indian than Mexican. There was not much melody in their music, and not much rhythm in their dance, but they were human beings, enjoying themselves after labour and without fear. Both Ned and Obed, sitting outside the circle of light with their rifles across their knees, felt it. The sense of human companionship, even of strangers, was very pleasant. The music and the glowing faces appealed very strongly to the boy. Silent, thoughtful, and compelled by circumstances to live a hard life, he was nevertheless young with all the freshness of youth. Obed saw, and he felt a deep sympathy for this lad who had wrapped himself like a younger brother around his heart.

"Just you wait, Ned," he said, "until we reach our own people across the Rio Grande. Then we'll have lots of friends and they'll be friends all the stronger, because you will be the first to bring them news of the treacherous attack that is to be made upon them."

"If we get there in time," said Ned, "and, Obed, I am beginning to believe that we will get there in time."

They passed for hunters, and that night they slept in the village, where they received kindness, and departed again the next morning on the long, long journey that always led to the north.

CHAPTER 10

CACTUS AND MEXICANS

They now came upon bare, windswept plains, which alternated with blazing heat and bitter cold. Once they nearly perished in a norther, which drove down upon them with sheets of hail. Fortunately their serapes were very thick and large, and they found additional shelter among some ragged and mournful yucca trees. But they were much shaken by the experience, and they rested an entire day by the banks of a shallow little brook.

"Oh, for a horse, two horses!" said Obed. "I'd give all our castles in Spain for two noble Barbary steeds to take us swiftly o'er the plain."

"I think we'll keep on walking," said Ned.

"At any rate, we're good walkers. We must be the very best walkers in the world judging from the way we've footed it since we left the castle of San Juan de Ulua."

They refilled their water bottles, despite the muddiness of the stream, and went on for three or four days over the plain, having nothing for scenery save the sandy ridges, the ragged yuccas, dwarfed and ugly mesquite bushes, and the deformed cactus. It was an ugly enough country by day, but, by night, it had a sort of weird charm. The moonlight gave soft tints to the earth. Now and then the wind would pick up the sand and carry it away in whirling gusts. The wind itself had a voice that was almost human and it played many notes. Lean and hungry wolves now appeared and howled mournfully, but were afraid to attack that terrible creature, man.

They saw sheep herders several times, but the herders invariably disappeared over the horizon with great speed. Neither Ned nor Obed meant them any harm, and they would have liked to exchange a few words with human beings.

"They think of course that we're brigands," said Obed. "It's what anybody would take us for. Evil looks corrupt good intentions."

The next day Obed was lucky enough to shoot an antelope, and they had fresh food. It was a fine fat buck, and they jerked and dried the remainder of the body in the sun, taking a long rest at the same time. Obed was continually restraining Ned's eagerness to hurry on.

"The race is to the swift if he doesn't break down," he said, "but you've got to guard mighty well against breaking down. I think we're going to enter a terrible long stretch of dry country, and we want our muscles to be tough and our wind to be good."

Obed was partially right in his prediction as they passed for three days through an absolutely sterile region. It was not sandy, however, but the soil was hard and baked like a stone. Then they saw on their left high but bare and desolate mountains, and soon they came to a little river of clear water, apparently flowing down from the range. The stream was not over twenty feet wide and two feet deep, but its appearance was inexpressibly grateful to both. They sat down on its banks and looked at each other.

"Ned," said Obed, "how much dust of the desert do you think I am carrying upon me? Let your answer be without prejudice. Friendship in this case must not stand in the way of truth."

"Do you mean by weight or by area?"

"Both."

"Answering by guess I should say about three square yards, or about three pounds. Wouldn't you say about the same for me?"

"Just about the same. I should say, too, that we carry at least twelve or fifteen kinds of dirt. It is well soaked in our hair and also in our clothes, and, as we may not get another good chance for a bath in a month, we'd better use our opportunity."

They reviled in the cool waters. They also washed out all their clothing, including their *serapes*, and let the garments dry in the sun. It was the most luxurious stop that they had made and they enjoyed it to the full. Ned, scouting a little distance up the stream, shot a fine fat deer among the bushes, and that night they had a feast of tender steaks. Obed had obtained flint and steel at the Indian village, at which they had seen the *fandango*, and he could light a fire with them, a most difficult thing to do. Their fire was of dried cactus, burning rapidly, but it lasted long enough for their cooking. After the heartiest meal that they had eaten in a long time, they stretched out by the river, listening to its pleasant flow. The remainder of the deer they had hung high in the branches of a myrtle oak about forty yards away.

"We haven't got our horses," said Obed, "but we're making progress. Time and tide will carry man with them if he's ready with his boat."

"Perhaps we've been lucky, too," said Ned, "in passing through what is mostly a wilderness."

"That's so. The desert is a hard road, but in our case it keeps enemies away."

They were lying on their *serapes*, the waters sang softly, the night was dark but very cool and pleasant, and they were happy. But Ned suddenly saw something that made him reach out and touch his companion.

"Look!" he whispered, pointing a finger.

They saw a dark figure creep on noiseless feet toward the tree, from a bough of which hung their deer. It was only a shadow in the night, but they knew that it was a cougar, drawn by the savour of the deer.

"Don't shoot," whispered Obed. "He can't get our meat, but we'll watch him try."

They lay quite still and enjoyed the joke. The cougar sprang again and again, making mighty exertions, but always the rich food swung just out of his reach. Once or twice his nose nearly touched it, but the two or three inches of gulf which he could never surmount were as much as two or three miles. He invariably fell back snarling, and he became so absorbed in the hopeless quest that there was no chance of his noticing the man and boy who lay not far away.

The humour of it appealed strongly to Ned and Obed. The cougar, after so many vain leaps, lay on the ground for a while panting. Then he ran up the tree, and as far out on the bough as he dared. He reached delicately with a forefoot, but he could not touch the strips of bark with which the body was tied. Then he lay flat upon the bough and snarled again and again.

"That's a good punishment for a rascally thief," whispered Obed. "I don't blame him for trying to get something to eat, but it's our deer. Let him go away and do his own hunting."

The cougar came back down the tree, but his descent was made with less spirit than his ascent. Nevertheless he made another try at the jumping. Ned saw, however, that he did not do as well as before. He never came within six inches of the deer now. At last he lay flat again on the ground and panted, staying there a full five minutes. When he got up he made one final and futile jump, and then sneaked away, exhausted and ashamed.

"Now, Ned," said Obed, "since the comedy is over I think we can safely go to sleep."

"Especially as we know our deer is safe," said Ned.

Both slept soundly throughout the remainder of the night. Toward morning the cougar came back and looked longingly at the body of the deer hanging from the bough of the tree. He thought once or twice of leaping for it again, but there was a shift of the wind and he caught the human odour from the two beings who lay forty yards away. He was a large and strong beast of prey, but this odour frightened him, and he slunk off among the trees, not to return.

Ned and Obed stayed two days beside the little river, taking a complete rest, bathing frequently in the fresh waters, and curing as much of the deer as possible for their journey. Then, rather heavily loaded, they started anew, always going northward through a sad and rough land. Now they entered another bare and sterile region of vast extent, walking for five days, without seeing a single trace of surface water. Had it not been for their capacious water bottles they would have perished, and, even with their aid, it was only by the strictest economy that they lived. The evaporation from the heat was so great that after a mouthful or two of water they were invariably as thirsty as ever, inside of five minutes.

They passed from this desert into a wide, dry valley between bare mountains, and entered a great cactus forest, one of the most wonderful things that either of them had ever seen. The ground was almost level, but it was hard and baked. Apparently no more rain fell here than in the genuine desert of shifting sand, and there was not a drop of surface water. Ned, when he first saw the mass of green, took it for a forest of trees, such as one sees in the North, but so great was his interest that he was not disappointed, when he saw that it was the giant cactus.

The strange forest extended many miles. The stems of the cactus rose to a height of sixty feet or more, with a diameter often reaching two feet. Sometimes the stems had no branches, but, in case they did, the branches grew out at right angles from the main stem, and then curving abruptly upward continued their growth parallel to the parent stock.

The stems of these huge plants were divided into eighteen or twenty ribs, within which at intervals of an inch or so were buds, with cushions, yellow and thick, from which grew six or seven large, and many smaller spines.

Most of the cactus trees were gorgeous with flowers, ranging from a deep rich crimson through rose and pink to a creamy white.

The green of the plants and the delicate colours of the flowers were wonderfully soothing to the two who had come from the bare and burning desert. There their eyes had ached with the heat and glare. They had longed for shade as men had longed of old for the shadow of a rock in a weary land. In truth they found little shade in the cactus forest, but the green produced the illusion of it. They expected to find flowing or standing water, but they went on for many miles and the soil remained hard and baked, as it can bake only in the rainless regions of high plateaus.

They found the forest to be fully thirty miles in length and several miles in width. Everywhere the giant cactus predominated, and on its eastern border they found two Indian men and several women and children gathering the fruit, from which they made an excellent preserve. The Indians were short in stature and very dark. All started to run when they saw the white man and boy, both armed with rifles, approaching, but Ned and Obed held up their hands as a sign of amity and, after some hesitation, they stopped. They spoke a dialect which neither Ned nor Obed could understand, but by signs they made a treaty of peace.

They slept that night by the fire of their new friends and the next day they were fortunate enough to shoot a deer, the greater part of which they gave to the Indians. The older of the men then guided them out of the forest at the northern end, and indicated as nearly as he could, by the same sign language, the course they should pursue in order to reach Texas. They had gone too far to the west, and by coming back toward the east they would save distance, as well as pass through a better country. Then he gravely bade them farewell and went back to his people.

Ned and Obed now crossed a low but rugged range of mountains, and came into good country where they were compelled to spend a large part of their time, escaping observation. It was only the troubled state of the people and the extreme division of sentiment among them that saved the two from capture. But they obtained news that filled both with joy. Fighting had occurred in Texas, but no great Mexican army had yet gone into the north.

Becoming bold now from long immunity and trusting to their Mexican address and knowledge of Spanish and its Mexican variants, they turned into the main road and pursued their journey at a good pace. They were untroubled the first day but on the second day they saw a cloud of dust behind them.

"Sheep being driven to market," said Obed.

"I don't know," replied Ned, looking back. "That cloud of dust is at least a mile away, but it seems to me I saw it give out a flash or two."

"What kind of a flash do you mean?"

"Bright, like silver or steel. There, see it!"

"Yes, I see it now, and I think you know what makes it, Ned."

"I should say that it is the sun striking on the steel heads of long lances."

"So should I, and I say also that those lances are carried by Mexican cavalrymen bound for Texas. It may not be a bad guess either that this is the vanguard of the army of Cos. I infer from the volume of dust that it is a considerable force."

"Therefore it is wise for us to leave the road and hide as best we can."

"Correctly spoken. The truth needs no bush. It walks without talking."

They turned aside at once, and entered a field of Indian corn, where they hoped to pass quietly out of sight, but some of the lancers came on very fast and noticed the dusty figures at the far edge of the field. Many of the Mexicans were skilled and suspicious borderers, and the haste with which the two were departing seemed suspicious to them.

Ned and Obed heard loud and repeated shouts to halt, but pretending not to hear passed out of the field and entered a stretch of thin forest beyond.

111

"We must not stop," said Obed. "Being regular soldiers they will surely discover, if they overtake us, that we are not Mexicans, and two or three lance thrusts would probably be the end of us. Now that we are among these trees we'll run for it."

A shout came from the lancers in the cornfield as soon as they saw the two break into a run. Ned heard it, and he felt as the fox must feel when the hounds give tongue. Tremors shook him, but his long and silent mental training came to his aid. His will strengthened his body and he and Obed ran rapidly. Nor did they run without purpose. Both instinctively looked for the roughest part of the land and the thickest stretches of forest. Only there could they hope to escape the lancers who were thundering after them.

Ned more than once wished to use his rifle, but he always restrained the impulse, and Obed glanced at him approvingly. He seemed to know what was passing in the boy's mind.

"Our bullets would be wasted now, even if we brought down a lancer or two," he said, "so we'll just save 'em until we're cornered—if we are. Then they will tell. Look, here are thorn bushes! Come this way."

They ran among the bushes which reached out and took little bits of their clothing as they passed. But they rejoiced in the fact. Horses could never be driven into that dense, thorny growth, and they might evade pursuers on foot. The thorn thicket did not last very long, however. They passed out of it and came into rough ground with a general trend upward. Both were panting now and their faces were wet with perspiration. The breath was dry and hot and the heart constricted painfully. They heard behind them the noise of the pursuit, spread now over a wide area.

"If only these hills continue to rise and to rise fast," gasped Obed White, "we may get away among the rocks and bushes."

There was a rapid tread of hoofs, and two lancers, with their long weapons levelled, galloped straight at them. Obed leaped to one side, but Ned, so startled that he lost command of himself, stopped and stood still. He saw one of the men bearing down upon him, the steel of the lance head glittering in the sunlight, and instinctively he closed his eyes. He heard a sharp crack, something seemed to whistle before his face, and then came a cry which he knew was the death cry of a man. He had shut his eyes only for a moment, and when he opened them he saw the Mexican falling to the ground, where he lay motionless across his lance. Obed White stood near, and his rifle yet smoked.

Ned instantly recovered himself, and fired at the second lancer who, turning about, galloped away with a wound in his shoulder.

"Come Ned," cried Obed White. "There is a time for all things, and it is time for us to get away from here as fast as we can."

He could not be too quick for Ned, who ran swiftly, avoiding another look at the silent and motionless figure on the ground. The riderless horse was crashing about among the trees. From a point three or four hundred yards behind there came the sound of much shouting. Ned thought it to be an outburst of anger caused by the return of the wounded lancer.

"We stung 'em a little," he panted.

"We did," said Obed White. "Remember that when you go out to slay you may be slain. But, Ned, we must reload."

They curved about, and darting into a thick clump of bushes put fresh charges in their rifles. Ned was trembling from excitement and exertion, but his anger was beginning to rise. There must always come a time when the hunted beast will turn and rend if it can. Ned had been the hunted, now he wanted to become the hunter. Obed and he had beaten off the first attack. There were plenty more bullets where the other two had come from, and he was eager to use them. He peered out of the bushes, his face red, his eyes alight, his rifle ready for instant use. But Obed placed one hand on his shoulder:

"Gently, Ned, gently!" he said. "We can't fight an entire Mexican army, but if we slip away to some good position we can beat off any little band that may find us."

It was evident that the Mexicans had lost the trail, for the time being. They were still seeking the quarry but with much noise and confusion. A trumpet was blown as if more help were needed. Officers shouted orders to men, and men shouted to one another. Several shots were fired, apparently at imaginary objects in the bushes.

"While they're running about and bumping into one another we'll regain a little of our lost breath which we'll need badly later," said Obed. "We can watch from here, and when they begin to approach then it's up and away again."

Those were precious minutes. The ground was not good for the lancers who usually advanced in mass, and, after the fall of one man and the wounding of another, the soldiers on foot were not very zealous in searching the thickets. The breathing of the two fugitives became easy and regular once more. The roofs of their mouths were no longer hot and dry, and their limbs did not tremble from excessive exertion. Ned had turned his eyes from the Mexicans and was examining the country in the other direction.

"Obed," he said, "there's a low mountain about a mile back of us, and it's covered with forest. If we ever reach it we can get away."

"Yes—if we reach it," said Obed, "and, Ned, we'll surely try for it. Ah, there they come in this direction now!"

A squad of about twenty men was approaching the thicket rapidly. Ned and Obed sprang up and made at top speed for the mountain. The soldiers uttered a shout and began to fire. But they had only muskets and the bullets did not reach. Ned and Obed, having rested a full ten minutes, ran fast. They were now descending the far side of the hill and meant to cross a slight valley that lay between it and the mountain. When they were near the centre of this valley they heard the hoofs of horsemen, and again saw lancers galloping toward them. These horsemen had gone around the hill, and now the hunt was in full cry again.

Ned and Obed would have been lost had not the valley been intersected a little further on by an arroyo seven or eight feet deep and at least fifteen feet wide. They scrambled down it, then up it and continued their flight among the bushes, while the horsemen, compelled to stop on the bank, uttered angry and baffled cries.

"The good luck is coming with the bad," said Obed. "The foot soldiers will still follow. They know that we're Texans and they want us. Do you see anybody following us now, Ned?"

"I can see the heads of about a dozen men above the bushes."

"Perhaps they are delegated to finish the work. The whole army of Cos can't stop to hunt down two Texans, and when we get on that mountain, Ned, we may be able to settle with these fellows on something like fair terms."

"Let's spurt a little," said Ned.

They put on extra steam, but the Mexicans seemed to have done the same, as presently, appearing a little nearer, they began to shout or fire. Ned heard the bullets pattering on the bushes behind him.

"A hint to the wise is a stitch in time," said Obed White. "Those fellows are getting too noisy. I object to raucous voices making loud outcries, nor does the sound of bullets dropping near please me. I shall give them a hint."

Wheeling about he fired at the nearest Mexican. His rifle was a long range weapon and the man fell with a cry. The others hesitated and the fugitives increased their speed. Now they were at the base of the mountain. Now they were up the slope which was densely clothed with trees and bushes.

Then they came to a great hollow in the stone side of the ridge, an indentation eight or ten feet deep and as many across, while above them the stone arched over their heads at a height of seventy or eighty feet.

"We'll just stay here," said Obed White. "You can run and you can run, but the time comes when you can run no more. They can't get at us from overhead, and they can't get at us from the sides. As for the front, I think that you and I, Ned, can hold it against as many Mexicans as may come."

"At least we'll make a mighty big try," said Ned, whose courage rose high at the sight of their natural fort. They had their backs to the wall, but this wall was of solid stone, and it also curved around on either side of them. Moreover, he had a chance to regain his breath which was once more coming in hot and painful gasps from his chest.

"Let's lie down, Ned," said Obed, "and pull up that log in front of this."

Near them lay the stem of an oak that had fallen years before. All the boughs had decayed and were gone, so it was not a very difficult task to drag the log in front of them, forming a kind of bar across the alcove. As it was fully a foot in diameter it formed an excellent fortification behind which they lay with their rifles ready. It was indeed a miniature fort, the best that a wilderness could furnish at a moment's notice, and the fighting spirit of the two rose fast. If the enemy came on they were ready to give him a welcome.

But the two heard nothing in the dense forest in front of them. The pursuers evidently were aware of the place, in which they had taken refuge, and knew the need of cautious approach. Mexicans do not lack bravery, but both Obed and Ned were sure there would be a long delay.

"I think that all we've got to do for the present," said Obed, "is to watch the woods in front of us, and see that none of them sneaks up near enough for a good shot."

Nearly an hour passed, and they neither saw nor heard anything in the forest. Then there was a rushing sound, a tremendous impact in front of them and something huge bounded and bounded again among the bushes. It was a great rock that had been rolled over the cliff above, in the hope that it would fall upon them, but the arch of stone over their heads was too deep. It struck fully five feet in front of them. Both were startled, although they knew that they were safe, and involuntarily they drew back.

"More will come," said Obed. "Just as one swallow does not make a summer, one stone does not make a flight. Ah, there it is now!"

They heard that same rushing sound through the air, and a bowlder weighing at least half a ton struck in front of their log. It did not bound away like the first, but being so much heavier buried half its weight in the earth and lay there. Obed chuckled and regarded the big stone with an approving look.

"It's an ill stone that doesn't fall to somebody's good," he said. "That big fellow is squarely in the path of anybody who advances to attack us, and adds materially to our breastwork. If they'll only drop a few more they'll make an impregnable fortification for us."

The third came as he spoke, but being a light one rolled away. The fourth was also light, and alighting on the big one bounded back into the alcove, striking just between Ned and Obed. It made both jump and shiver, but they knew that it was a chance not likely to happen again in a hundred times. The bombardment continued for a quarter of an hour without any harm to either of the two, and then the silence came again. Ned and Obed pushed the rock out of the alcove, leaving it in front of them and now their niche had a formidable stone reinforcement.

"They'll be slipping up soon to look at our dead bodies," whispered Obed, "and between you and me, Ned, I think there will be a great surprise in Mexico today."

They lay almost flat and put the muzzles of their rifles across the log. Both, used to life on the border, where the rifle was a necessity, were fine shots and they were also keen of eye and ear. They waited for a while which seemed interminably long to Ned, but which was not more than a quarter of an hour, and then he heard a slight movement among the trees somewhat to their left. He called Obed's attention to it and the man nodded:

"I hear it, too," he whispered. "Those investigators are cautious, but they'll have to come up in front before they can get at us, and then we can get at them, too. We'll just be patient."

Ned was at least quiet and contained, although it was impossible to be patient. They heard the rustling at intervals on their right, then it changed to their front, and he saw a black head, covered with a *sombrero*, peep from behind a tree. The head came a little farther, disclosing a shoulder, and Obed White fired. They heard a yell of pain, and a thrashing among the bushes, but the sound rapidly moved farther and farther away.

"That fellow was stung badly," said Obed White with satisfaction, "and he won't come back. I'm glad to see, Ned, that you held your fire, keeping ready for any other who might come."

Ned glowed at the compliment. He had cocked his rifle, and was ready but he remained cool, wasting no shot.

"I fancy that they now know we are here," said Obed, who loved to talk, "and that we have not been demolished by the several tons of rock that they have sent down from above. A shot to the wise is sufficient. Keep down, Ned! Keep down!"

From a point sixty or seventy yards away Mexicans, lying among the trees or in the undergrowth, suddenly opened a heavy fire upon the rocky fort. The Mexicans were invisible but jets of smoke arose in the brush. Bullets thudded on the log or stones, or upon the stone wall above the two, but both Ned and Obed were sheltered well and they were not touched. Nevertheless it was uncomfortable. The impact of the bullets made an unpleasant sound, and there was always a chance that one of them might angle off from the stone and strike a human target. Obed however was cheerful.

"They're wasting good ammunition," he said. "They'll need that later on when they attack the Texans. After all, Ned, we're serving a good purpose when we induce the Mexicans to shoot good powder and lead here, and not against our people."

Encouraged by the failure of the besieged to reply to their fire the Mexicans came closer and grew somewhat incautious. Ned saw one of them sheltered but partially by a bush and he fired. The man uttered a cry and fell. Ned saw the bush moving and he hoped the man was not slain, but he never knew.

The volleys from the Mexicans ceased, and silence came again in the woods. Wisps of smoke floated here and there among the trees, but a light wind soon caught them and carried them away. Ned and Obed, rolling into easier positions, talked cheerfully.

"I don't think they'll try to rush us," said Obed. "The Mexicans are not afraid to charge breastworks, but they'll hardly think we two are worth the price they would have to pay. Perhaps they'll try to starve us out."

"And that they can't do because we have provisions for several days."

"But they don't know it. Nor do we want to stay here for several

117

days, Ned. Texas is calling to us, and we should be travelling northward instead of lying under a rock besieged by Mexicans."

But they were compelled anew to make heavy drafts upon their patience. The Mexicans kept quiet a long time. Finally a shot fired from some high point grazed Ned's cap, and flattened against the rock behind him. The boy involuntarily ducked against the earth. Obed also lay lower.

"Some Mexican must have climbed a tree," said the Maine man. "He's where he can look over our fortifications and that gives him an advantage. It also gives him a disadvantage because it will be harder for him to come down out of that tree unaided than it was for him to go up in it. We'll stick as close as we can under the log, until he sends in the second shot."

They waited about ten minutes until the Mexican fired again. He was in the boughs of a great oak about fifty yards away, and following the flash of his weapon they saw his chest and shoulders as he leaned forward to take aim and pull the trigger. Obed fired and the soldier dropped to the ground. There was a noise in the underbrush, as if his comrades were dragging him away and then the great silence came again. As Obed reloaded he said grimly:

"I think we're done with the tree-climbers. Evil to him who evil does. They're cured of that habit."

It was now mid-afternoon and the sun was blazing down over the cliffs and forest. It grew very hot in the alcove. No breath of wind reached them there, and they began to pant for air.

"I hope night will come soon," said Ned.

"It will be here before long," said Obed, "but something else will arrive first."

"What is that?"

"Look, there to the right over the trees. See the dark spot in the sky. Ned, my boy, a storm is coming and it is for you and me to say 'let it come.'"

"What will it do for us?"

"Break up the siege, or at least I think so. Unless it drives directly in our faces we will be sheltered out here, but the Mexicans will have no such protection. And, Ned, if you will listen to one who knows, you will understand that storms down here can be terrific."

"Then the more terrific it is the better for us."

"Just so. See, Ned, how that black spot grows! It is a cloud of quite respectable size. Before long it will cover all the skies, and you notice

118

too that there is absolutely no wind."

"It is so. The stillness is so great that I feel it. It oppresses me. It is hard for me to draw my breath."

"Exactly. I feel just the same way. The storm is coming fast and it is going to be a big one. The sun is entirely hidden already, and the air is growing dark. We'll crouch against the wall, Ned, and keep our rifles, powder and ourselves as dry as possible. There goes the thunder, growling away, and here's the lightning! Whew, but that made me jump!"

An intense flash of lightning burned across the sky, and showed the forest and hills for one blazing moment. Then the darkness closed in, thick and black. The two, wrapped closely in their *serapes*, crouched against the stone wall and watched the storm gather in its full majesty and terror.

CHAPTER 11

THE LONG CHASE

Ned, despite his brave heart and strong will, felt a deep awe. Storms on the great uplands of North America often present aspects which are sublime and menacing to the last degree. The thunder which had been growling before now crashed continually like batteries of great guns, and the lightning flashed so fast that there was a rapid alternation of dazzling glare and impervious blackness. Once, the lightning struck in the forest near them with a terrible, rending crash, and trees went down. Far down in the gorges they heard the fierce howl of the wind.

Ned shrank closer and closer against the rocky wall, and, now and then, he veiled his eyes with one hand. If one were to judge by eye and ear alone it would seem that the world was coming to an end. Cast away in the wilderness, he was truly thankful for the human companionship of the man, Obed White, and it is likely that the man, Obed White, was just as thankful for the companionship of the boy, Edward Fulton.

All thought of another attack by the Mexicans passed for the present. They knew that the besiegers themselves would be awed, and would flee for refuge, particularly from the trees falling before the strokes of lightning. It was at least two miles to any such point of safety, and Ned and Obed saw a coming opportunity. Both lightning and thunder ceased so abruptly that it was uncanny. The sudden stillness was heavy and oppressive, and after the continued flare of the lightning, the darkness was so nearly impenetrable that they could not see ten yards in front of them.

Then the rain came in a tremendous cataract, but it came from the south, while they faced the north. Hence it drove over and past their alcove and they remained dry. But it poured so hard and with such a sweep and roar that Obed was forced to shout when he said to Ned:

"I've never been to Niagara and of course I've never been behind the falls there but this must be like it. The luck has certainly turned in our favour, Ned. The Mexicans could never stand it out there without shelter."

"I don't see how it can last long," shouted Ned in reply.

"It can't. It's too violent. But it's the way down here, rushing from one extreme to another. As soon as it begins to ease up, we'll move."

The darkness presently began to thin rapidly, and the heavy drumming of the rain on the rocks and forest turned to a patter.

"I think it's a good time to go, Ned," said Obed. "In fifteen minutes it will stop raining entirely and the Mexicans, if they are not drowned, may come back for us. We can't keep ourselves dry, but we'll protect our rifles and ammunition. We've got a good chance to escape now, especially since night will soon be here."

They left the overhanging cliff which had guarded them so well in more ways than one, and entered the forest, veering off to the left, and picking their way carefully through the underbrush. Ned suddenly sprang aside, shuddering. A Mexican, slain in the battle, lay upon his side. But Obed was practical.

"I know it's unpleasant to touch him," he said, "but he may have what we need. Ah, here is a pistol and bullets for it, and a flask of powder which his own body has helped to keep dry. It's likely that we'll have use for these before we get through, and so I'll take 'em."

He quickly secured the pistol and ammunition, and they went on, travelling rapidly westward. The rain ceased entirely in twenty minutes, and all the clouds passed away, but night came in their place, covering their flight with its friendly mantle. They were wet to the waist and the water dripped from the trees upon them, but these things did not trouble them. They felt all the joy of escape. Ned knew that neither of them, if taken, could expect much mercy from the brutal Cos.

They came after a while to a gorge, through which a torrent rushed, cutting off their way. It was midnight now. They saw that the stream was very muddy and that it bore on its current much debris.

"We'll just sit down here and rest," said Obed. "This is nothing more than a brook raised to a river by the storm, and, in another hour or two, it will be a brook again. Rise fast, fall fast holds true." They sat on a log near the stream and watched it go down. As their muscles relaxed they began to feel cold, and had it not been for the *serapes* they would have been chilled. In two hours the muddy little river was a muddy little brook and they walked across. All the while now, a warm, drying wind was blowing, but they kept on for some time longer in order that the vigorous circulation of the blood might warm their bodies. Then, seeking the best place they could find, they lay down among the bushes, despite the damp, and slept.

Ned was the first to awake the next day, and he saw, by a high sun, that they were on a slope, leading to a pretty valley well grown in grass. He took a few steps and also stretched both arms. He found that his muscles were neither stiff nor sore and his delight was great. Obed still slumbered peacefully, his head upon his arm.

Ned walked a little further down the slope. Then he jumped back and hid behind a bush. He had caught a glimpse of a horse saddled and bridled in the Mexican manner, and it was his first thought that a detachment from the army of Cos was riding straight toward them. But as he stood behind the bush, heart beating, eyes gazing through the leaves, he saw that it was only a single horse. Nor was it coming toward him. It seemed to be moving about slowly in a circle of very limited area. Then, leaving the bush, he saw that the horse was riderless. He watched a long time to see if the owner would appear, and as none came he went back and awakened Obed White.

"What! What!" said Obed, opening his eyes slowly and yawning mightily. "Has the day come? Verily, it is a long night that has no ending. And so you have seen a horse, Ned, a horse saddled and bridled and with no owner! It can't be the one that King Richard offered his kingdom for, and since it isn't we'll just see why this caparisoned animal is there grazing in our valley."

The two went down the slope. The horse was still there, grazing in his grassy circle, and as the two approached he drew away a little but did not seem to be frightened. Then Ned understood, or at least his belief was so strong that it amounted to conviction.

"It's the horse of the soldier whom you shot yesterday," he said. "You remember that he galloped away among the bushes. No doubt, too, he was driven a long distance by the storm. He can't be accounted for in any other manner."

"There are some guesses so good that you know at once they're right," said Obed, "and yours is one of them, Ned. Now that is a valuable horse. One of the most valuable that ever grazed in a valley of Mexico or any other valley. He's so precious because we want him, and we want him so bad that he's worth a million dollars to us."

"That one of us may ride him to Texas."

"Yes, and we may be able to secure another. You stay here, Ned, and let me catch him. Horses like me better than some men do."

Ned sat down and Obed advanced warily, holding out his hand and whistling gently. It was a most persuasive whistle, soft and thrilling and the horse raised his head, looked contemplatively out of large lustrous eyes at the whistler. Obed advanced, still whistling, in the most wonderful, enticing manner. Ned felt that if he were a horse he could not resist it, that he would go to the whistler, expecting to receive oats, corn, and everything else that a healthy horse loves. It seemed to have some such effect upon the quarry that Obed coveted, because the horse, after withdrawing a step, advanced toward the man.

Obed stopped, but continued to whistle, pouring forth the most beautiful and winning trills and quavers. The horse came and Obed, reaching out, seized the bridle which hung loose. He stroked the horse's head and the animal rubbed his nose against his shoulder. The conquest was complete. Bridle in hand, Obed led the way and Ned met him.

"I think our good horse here was lonesome," said Obed, "Horses that are used to human beings miss 'em for a while when they lose 'em, and we're not enslaving our friend by taking him. Here's a lariat coiled at the saddle bow; we'll just tether him by that, and let him go on with his grazing, while we get our breakfast. You will notice, too, Ned, that we've taken more than a horse. See this pair of holster pistols swung across the saddle and ammunition to fit. The enemy is still supplying us with our needs, Ned."

As they ate breakfast they resolved to secure another horse. Obed was of the opinion that the army of Cos was not far away, and he believed that he could steal one. At least, he was willing to try on the following night, and, if he succeeded, their problem would be simplified greatly.

They remained nearly all the morning in the little valley and devoted a large part of the time to developing their acquaintance with the horse, which was a fine animal, amenable to good treatment, and ready to follow his new masters.

"He looks like an American horse," said Obed, with satisfaction, "and maybe he is one, stolen from the Texans. He'll carry one of us over many miles of sand and cactus, and he'll be none the worse for it. But he needs a friend. Horse was not made to live alone. It's my sympathy for him as much as the desire for another mount that drives me to the theft we contemplate."

Ned laughed and lolled on the grass which was now dry.

"You stay here with Bucephalus or Rosinante or whatever you choose to call him," continued Obed, "and I think I'll cross the hills, and see if Cos is near. If we're going to capture a horse, we must first know where the horse is to be found."

"Suppose I go along, too."

"No, it would be easier for the Mexicans to see two than one, and we shouldn't take unnecessary risks. Be sure you stay in the valley, Ned, because I want to know where to find you when I come back. I've an idea that the Mexican army isn't far, as we wound around a good deal during the storm and darkness, and covered no great distance, if it were counted in a straight line. At least I think so."

"You'll find me here."

Obed went toward the east, and Ned continued to make himself comfortable on the grass, which was so long and thick that it almost hid his body. But it was truly luxurious. It seemed that after so much hardship and danger he could not get enough rest. He felt quite safe, too. It would take a careful observer to see him lying there in the deep grass. It was warm and dry where he lay, and the little valley was well hemmed in by forest in which crotons, mimosas, myrtle oaks, *okote* pine and many other trees grew. Some had large rich blossoms and he admired their beauty.

His eyes wandered back from the forest to their new friend, the horse. Besides being an animal of utility the horse added to their comradeship. Ned felt that he still had a friend with him, although Obed was away. Obed had spoken truly. It was a fine horse, a bay, tall, strong and young, grazing with dignified content, at the end of a lariat about forty feet in length.

Ned watched the horse idly, and soon he saw him raise his head, stand perfectly still for a moment or two, and then sniff the wind. The next instant an extraordinary manifestation came from him. He whirled about and galloped so fast to the end of his tether that he was thrown down by the sharp jerk. He regained his feet and stood there, trembling all over. His great eyes were distended. Ned had never before seen such a picture of terror.

The boy raised himself a little in the grass, but not so high that he would be seen by an enemy. It was his first idea that Mexicans had come, but the horse would not show such fright at the presence of human beings. He looked in the direction opposite to the spot on which the horse was standing. At first he saw nothing, but with intent looking he detected a great body crouched in the grass and stealing forward slowly. It was their old enemy, the jaguar, not a black one but tawny in colour.

Ned's rage rose. First a jaguar had attacked him, and now another was stalking their horse. He felt pity for the poor animal which was tied, and which could not escape. Now man who had tied him must save him. Ned knew that if he cut the lariat the horse in its terror might run away and never be retaken. A shot might be heard by the Mexicans, but he believed that the probabilities were against it, and he decided to use the rifle.

He raised himself just a little more, careful to make no noise, and watched the jaguar stealing through the tall grass, so intent on the horse that it failed to notice the most dangerous of all enemies who lay near. But Ned waited until the flank of the animal was well presented, and, taking a sure aim, fired.

The jaguar shot up into the air, as if an electric spring had been released, then came down with a thump and was dead. The horse neighed in terror at sight of his leaping foe and trembled more violently than ever. Ned went to him first, and tried to soothe him which was a long and difficult task. At last, he untethered the horse and led him to the far end of the valley, where he tethered him again at least two hundred yards from the dead body of the jaguar. Returning he looked at the fallen animal, and marked with pleasure the correctness of his aim. He had shot the jaguar squarely through the heart. Then he went back to his place in the grass, but he did not doze or dream. The Mexicans might come, drawn by his shot, and even if they did not, a member of the unpleasant jaguar tribe might take a notion to stalk the only available human being in that grassy little valley.

But no Mexicans appeared, nor did he observe any other jaguar. When the sun set, he began to feel a little uneasy about Obed. His uneasiness increased with the darkness, but he was finally reassured by a whistle from the head of the valley. Then he saw Obed's tall figure striding down the slope in the dusk, and he went forward to meet him.

"I suppose you've spent the afternoon sleeping," said Obed.

"I might have done so, but we had a visitor."

"A visitor? What kind of a visitor?"

"A jaguar. He wanted to eat our horse and as the horse could not get away, being tethered strongly, I had to shoot his jaguarship."

He showed Obed the body, and his comrade approved highly of the shot.

"And now for the history of my own life and adventures during the afternoon," said Obed. "The country to the eastward is not rough, and I made good time through it. Sure enough the army of Cos is there, about five miles away, camped in a plain. It was beaten about a good deal by the storm, and it keeps poor guard, because it is in its own country far from any expected foe, and because the Mexicans are Mexicans. I think, Ned, that we can lift a horse without great trouble or excessive danger. We'll go over there about midnight."

"And we'd better take our present horse with us," said Ned, "or other jaguars may come."

They remained in their own valley until the appointed time, and then set out on a fairly dark night, each taking his turn at riding the horse. They halted at the crest of a low hill, from which they saw the flash of camp fires.

"That's Cos and his army," said Obed. "They're down there, sprawled all about the valley, and I imagine that by this time they're all asleep, including a majority of the sentinels, and that's our opportunity."

They tethered their own horse and crept down the slope. Soon they came to the edge of the woods and saw the camp fires more plainly. All had burned low, but they made out the shapes of tents, and, nearer by, a dark mass which they concluded to be the horses belonging to the lancers and other cavalry. They approached within a hundred yards, and saw no sentinels by the horses, although they were able to discern several moving figures farther on.

"Now, Ned," said Obed, "you stay here and I'll try to cut out a horse, the very best that I can find. Sit down on the ground, and have your rifle ready. If I'm discovered and have to run for it you shoot the first of my pursuers."

Ned obeyed and Obed stole down toward the horses. Ned knew his comrade's skill, and he believed he would employ the soft whistle that had been so effective with the first horse. He watched the dark figure stealing forward, and he admired Obed's skill. It would be almost impossible for anyone to notice so faint a shadow in the darkness. Nevertheless, his heart beat heavily. Despite all that Obed had said it was a dangerous task, requiring both skill and luck.

The faint shadow reached the black blur of the horses and disappeared. Ned waited five minutes, ten, fifteen minutes, while the little pulses beat hard in his temples. Then he saw a shadow detach itself from the black blur. It was the figure of a man and he was on horseback. Obed had succeeded.

Ned remained kneeling, rifle in hand, to guard against any mistake. The man on horseback rode toward him, while the sprawling army of Cos still slept. Then Ned saw clearly that it was Obed, and that he rode a magnificent black horse, sixteen hands high, as fiery as any that could be found in all Mexico.

In another moment Obed was by his side, looking down from the height of his horse. In the moonlight Ned saw that his face was glowing.

"Isn't he a beauty?" he said. "And I think, too, that he likes me. There were three or four sentinels down there by the horses, but all of them were fast asleep, and I had time to pick. I've also brought away a roll of blankets, two for each of us, and I never woke a man. Now, Ned, we're furnished complete, and we're off to Texas with your message."

"The first thing, I suppose, is to introduce our horses to each other."

"Correct. You and I are friends, Ned, and so must our horses be."

They took a last look at the sleeping camp and went away through the woods. Obed dismounted, and led his horse to the place where the second was tied. The two horses whinnied and rubbed noses.

"It's all right," said Obed. "When horse and man agree who can stop us?"

Ned mounted the first, the bay, while Obed retained the black. Then they rode all through the night, coming about dawn to a plain which turned to sand and cactus, as they advanced further into the north. There was no water here, but they had filled their water bottles at the last brook and they had no fear of perishing by thirst. Although they had passed the army of Cos they did not fail to keep a vigilant watch. They knew that patrols of Mexicans would be in the north, and the red men were also to be feared. They were coming into regions across which mounted Indians often passed, doing destruction with rifle and lance, spear and arrow. Both had more apprehension now about Indians than Mexicans.

At noon of that day they saw four horsemen on their left who shaped their course toward theirs in such a manner that if they moved at an equal pace they would meet at the point of a triangle. But the horses that Ned and Obed rode were powerful animals, far superior to the ordinary Mexican mounts, and they rode steadily ahead, apparently taking no notice of the four on their flank.

"They're Mexican scouts," said Obed, "I'm sure of it, but I don't believe that they'll come too close. They see that we have rifles, and they know the deadly nature of the Texan rifle. If we are friends it's all right, if we are Texans it will be wise to keep at a good distance."

Obed was a good prophet. The Mexicans, at a distance of almost a quarter of a mile, raised a great shout. The two took no notice of it, but rode on, their faces toward the north.

"I can talk good Spanish or Mexican," said Obed, "and so can you, but I'm out riding now and I don't feel like stopping for conversation. Ah, there they are shouting again, and as I live, Ned, they're increasing their speed. We'll give 'em a sign."

Obed and Ned wheeled about and raised their rifles. The four Mexicans, who were galloping their ponies, stopped abruptly. Obed and Ned turned and rode on.

"We gave 'em a sign," said Obed, "and they saw it. We're in no danger, Ned. We could beat 'em either in a fight or a run. The battle is sometimes to the strong and the race to the swift."

It was obvious that the Mexicans, who were probably only scouts, did not want a fight with formidable Texans who carried such long rifles. They dropped back until Ned, taking a final look, could not tell their distant figures from the stem of the lonesome cactus.

"Horses and rifles are mighty useful in their place," said Obed. "Add to them wood and water and what little more a man needs he should be able to find."

"It's wood and water that we ought to hunt now."

"We may strike both before night, but if not we'll ride on a while anyhow, and maybe we'll find 'em."

They went deeper into the great upland which was half a desert and half a plain. Occasionally they saw besides the cactus, mesquite and yucca and some clumps of coarse grass.

"Bunch grass," said Obed, "like that which you find further north, and mighty good it is, too, for cattle and horses. We'll have plenty of food for these two noble steeds of ours, and I shouldn't be surprised, too, if we ran across big game. It's always where the bunch grass grows."

They did not reach wood and water by nightfall, but, riding two hours longer in a clear twilight, they found both. The plain rose and fell in deep swells, and in the deepest of the swells to which they had yet to come they found a trickling stream of clear water, free from alkali, fringed on either shore with trees of moderate size.

"Here we are," said Obed, "and here we stay till morning. You never know how fine water looks until you've been a long time without it."

They let their horses drink first, and then, going further up the stream, drank freely of the water themselves. They found it cold and good, and they were refreshed greatly. There was also a belt of excellent grass, extending a hundred yards back on either side of the stream, and, unsaddling and tethering their horses, they let them graze. Both Ned and Obed would have liked a fire, but they deemed it dangerous, and they ate their food cold. After supper, Obed walked up the stream a little distance, examining the ground on either side of the water. When he came back he said to Ned:

"I saw animal tracks two or three hundred yards up the creek, and they were made by big animals. Buffalo range about here somewhere, and we may see 'em before we get through."

"I wouldn't mind having a shot at a fine buffalo," said Ned. But he was not very eager about it. He was thinking more then of sleep. Obed, while thinking of sleep also, was thinking of other things, too, and he was somewhat troubled in his mind. But he bore himself as a man of cheerful countenance.

"Now, Ned," he said, "you and I cannot go forever without sleep. We've been through a good deal and we haven't closed our eyes for thirty-six hours. I feel as if I had pound weights tied to my eyelids."

"Two-pound weights are tied to mine."

"Then we'll prove the value of my foresight in obtaining the two sets of blankets by using them at once."

Each lay down between his blankets, and Ned was soon asleep, but Obed, by a violent effort, kept his eyes open. He could never remember a time when it seemed sweeter to sleep, but he struggled continually against it. When he saw that Ned's slumber was deep he rose and walked up and down the stream again, going a half mile in either direction.

At one point where there was a break in the fringe of trees the imprints of the mighty hoofs were numerous, and, mingled with them, were tracks made by horses' hoofs. It was these that worried Obed so much. They were made by unshod hoofs, but evidently they were two or three days old, and, after all, the riders might have passed on, not to return. Smothering his anxiety as much as possible he went back to their little camp, crept between his two blankets which felt very warm, and began to watch with his eyes and ears, vowing to himself that he would not sleep.

Yet within two hours he slept. Exhausted nature triumphed over will and claimed her own. He was not conscious of any struggle. He was awake and then he was not. The two tethered horses, having eaten all they wanted, also settled themselves comfortably and slept.

But while the two, or rather the four slept, something was moving far out on the plain.

It was an immense black mass with a front of more than a mile, and it was coming toward Ned and Obed. This mass had been disturbed by a great danger and it advanced with mighty heavings and tramplings. Ned and Obed slept calmly for a long time, but as the black front of the moving mass drew closer to the creek and its thin lines of trees, the boy stirred in his blankets. A vague dream came and then a state that was half an awakening. He was conscious in a dim way of a low, thundering sound that approached and he sprang to his feet. The next instant a neigh of terror came from one of the horses and Obed, too, awoke.

"Listen!" exclaimed Ned. "Hear that roar! And it's drawing near, too!"

"Yes, it's a buffalo herd!" said Obed. "We're far enough north now to be within the buffalo ranges, and they're coming down on us fast. But they must be scared or be drawn on by something, because it's not yet dawn."

"All of which means that it's time for us to go."

"Or be trodden to death."

Naturally, they had slept in their clothes and they quickly gathered up their arms and baggage. Then they released their frightened horses, sprang upon their backs and galloped toward the north. They felt secure now, so far as the herd was concerned. Their horses could easily take them out of its reach.

"Maybe they'll stop at the creek," said Ned. "I should think that the water would hold anything in this thirsty land."

Obed shook his head, but offered no further answer. The thunder of the hoofs now filled their ears, and, as the sound advanced steadily, it was evident that the creek had not stopped the buffalo herd.

The dawn suddenly came up sharp and clear after the manner of southern lands. The heavens turned blue, and a rosy light suffused the prairie. Then Ned saw the front of the buffalo herd extending two or three miles to right and to left. And he saw more. He saw the cause of the terror that had smitten the herd.

Brown men, almost naked and on horseback, darted in and out among the buffaloes, shooting and stabbing. They were muscular men, fierce of countenance, and their long black hair streamed out behind them. Some carried rifles and muskets, and others carried lances and bows and arrows.

"Lipans," said Obed, "one of the fiercest of all the south-western tribes. They belong mostly across the Rio Grande, but I suppose they've come for the buffalo. Ned, we're not wanted here."

After the single look they were away toward the north, moving at a smooth and easy gallop. They were truly thankful now that the horses they rode were so large and powerful, evidently of American breed. It was not difficult to increase the distance between them and the herd, and they hoped to slip away before they were seen by any of the Lipans. But a sudden shout behind them, a long, piercing whoop showed that they had reckoned wrong.

The two looked back. A group of warriors had gathered in advance of the band, and it was obvious, as they galloped on, that they had seen the two fugitives. Two or three shook their long lances, and pointed them straight at Ned and Obed. Then uttering that long, menacing whoop again, the group, about twenty in number, rode straight for the two, while the rest continued their work with the herd.

"It's a chase," said Obed. "Those fellows want scalps and they don't care whether we're Texans or Mexicans. Besides, they may have better horses than the Mexican ponies. But it's a long chase that has no turning, and if our horses don't stumble we'll beat them. Look out for potholes and such places."

They rode knee to knee, not yet putting the horses to their full speed, but covering the ground, nevertheless, at a great rate. It seemed play for their fine horses, which arched their necks and sped on, not a drop of perspiration yet staining their glossy skins. Ned felt the thrill, as the ground spun back under his horse's feet, and the air rushed past his face. It did not occur to him that the Lipans could overtake them, and their pursuit merely added a fresh spice to a magnificent ride.

He took another look back. The Lipans, although they had lost ground, were still following. They came in a close group, carrying, besides their arms, shields, made of layers of buffalo hide. Several wore magnificent war bonnets. Otherwise all were naked save for the breech-cloth, and their brown bodies were glistening with war paint. Behind them, yet came the black front of the buffalo herd, but it was a full mile away.

Obed looked also, and his heart smote him. Older and more experienced than Ned, he knew that with the fierce Lipans the most powerful of all lures was the lure of scalps. Just as the wolf can trail down the moose at last, they could follow for days on their tough mustangs. But as he shifted his good rifle a bit he felt better. Both he and Ned were splendid marksmen, and if the chase were a success for the Lipans there would also be a bitter fight at the end of it.

Now he and Ned ceased to talk, the sun blazed down on the plain, and on sped the chase, hour after hour.

Chapter 12

The Trial of Patience

The hours of the afternoon trailed slowly away, one by one. Perspiration appeared at last upon the glossy skins of the horses, but their stride did not abate. The powerful muscles still worked with their full strength and ease. Ned never felt a tremor in the splendid horse beneath him. But when he looked back again there were the Lipans, a little further away, but hanging on as grimly as before, still riding in a close group.

Ned began to understand now the deadly nature of the pursuit. These Lipans would follow not merely for hours, but into the night, and if he and Obed were lost to sight in the darkness they would pick up the trail the next day by the hoof prints on the plain. He felt with absolute certainty that chance had brought upon them one of the deadliest dangers they had yet encountered.

"It's growing a little cooler, Obed," he said.

"So it is. The evening wanes. But, Ned, do you see any sign of forest or high hills ahead?"

"I do not, Obed. There is nothing but the plain which waves like the ripples on a lake, the bunches of buffalo grass here and there, and now and then an ugly yucca."

"You see just what I see, Ned, and as there is no promise of shelter we'd better ease our horses a little. Our lives depend upon them, and even if the Lipans do regain some of their lost ground now it will not matter in the end."

They let the horses drop into a walk, and finally, to put elasticity back into their own stiffened limbs, they dismounted and walked awhile.

"If the Lipans don't rest their horses now they will have to do it later," said Obed, "but as they're mighty crafty they'll probably slow down when we do. Do you see them now, Ned?"

"Yes, there they are on the crest of a swell. They don't seem to gain on us much. I should say they are a full mile away."

"A mile and a half at least. The air of these great uplands is very deceptive, and things look much nearer than they really are."

"Look how gigantic they have grown! They stand squarely in the centre of the sun now."

The sun was low and the Lipans coming out of the southwest were silhouetted so perfectly against it that they seemed black and monstrous, like some product of the primitive world. The fugitives felt a chill of awe, but in a moment or two they threw it off, only to have its place taken a little later by the real chill of the coming night. A wind began to moan over the desolate plain, and their faces were stung now and then by the fine grains of sand blown against them. But as the Lipans were gaining but little, Ned and Obed still walked their horses.

They went on thus nearly an hour. The night came, but it was not dark, and they could yet see the Lipans following as certain as death. Before them the plain still rolled away, bare and brown. There was not a sign of cover. Ned's spirits began to sink. The silent and tenacious pursuit weighed upon him. It was time to rest and sleep. The Lipans had been pursuing for seven or eight hours now, and if they could not catch fugitives in that time they ought to turn back. Nevertheless, there they were, still visible in the moonlight and still coming.

Ned and Obed remounted and rode at a running walk, which was easy but which nevertheless took them on rapidly. But it became evident that the Lipans had increased their pace in the same ratio, as the distance of a mile and a half named by Obed did not decrease. Ned looked up longingly at the sky. There was not a cloud. The moon, round and full, never shone more brightly, and it seemed that countless new stars had arrived that very night. He sighed. They might as well have been riding in broad daylight.

Toward midnight the swells and dips of the plain became accentuated, and they lost sight of the pursuing Lipans. But there was yet no forest to hide them, only the miserable mesquite and the ragged yucca. Save for them the plain stretched away as bare and brown as ever. Two hours more with the Lipans still lost to view, Obed called a halt.

"The Lipans will pick up our trail in the morning," he said. "Though lost to sight we are to their memory dear, and they will hang on. But our horses are faster than theirs, and as they cannot come near us on this bare plain, without being seen we can get away. Whereas, I say, and hence and therefore we might as well rest and let our good steeds rest, too."

"What time would you say it is?"

"About two o' the morning by the watch that I haven't got, and it will be four or five hours until day. Ned, if I were you I'd lie down between blankets. You can relax more comfortably and rest better that way."

Ned did not wish to do it, but Obed insisted so strongly, and was so persuasive that he acceded at last. They had chosen a place on a swell where they could see anything that approached a quarter of a mile away, and Obed stood near the recumbent boy, holding the bridles of the two horses in one hand and his rifle in the other.

The man's eyes continually travelled around the circle of the horizon, but now and then he glanced at the boy. Ned, brave, enduring and complaining so little, had taken a great hold upon his affection. They were comrades, tried by many dangers, and no danger yet to come could induce him to desert the boy.

The moon and stars were still very bright, and Obed, as his eyes travelled the circle of the horizon, saw no sign of the Indian approach. But that the Lipans would come with the dawn, or some time afterward, he did not have the slightest doubt. He glanced once more at Ned and then he smiled. The boy, while never meaning it, was sleeping soundly, and Obed was very glad. This was what he intended, relying upon Ned's utter exhaustion of body and mind.

All through the remaining hours of the night the man, with the bridles of the two horses in one hand and the rifle in the other, kept watch. Now and then he walked in a circle around and around the sleeping boy, and once or twice he smiled to himself. He knew that Ned when he awoke would be indignant because Obed let him sleep, but the man felt quite able to stand such reproaches.

Obed, staunch as he was, felt the weirdness and appalling loneliness of time and place. A wolf howled far out on the plain, and the answer-

133

ing howl of a wolf came back from another point. He shivered a little, but he continued his steady tread around and around the circle.

Dawn shot up, gilding the bare brown plain with silver splendour for a little while. Obed awoke Ned, and laughed at the boy's protests.

"You feel stronger and fresher, Ned," he said, "and nothing has been lost."

"What of you?"

"I? Oh, I'll get my chance later. All things come to him who works while he waits. Meanwhile, I think we'd better take a drink out of our water bottles, eat a quick breakfast and be off before we have visitors."

Once more in the saddle, they rode on over a plain unchanged in character, still the same swells and dips, still the same lonesome yuccas and mesquite, with the occasional clumps of bunch grass.

"Don't you think we have shaken them off?" asked Ned.

"No," replied Obed. "They would scatter toward dawn and the one who picked up the trail would call the others with a whoop or a rifle shot."

"Well, they've been called," said Ned, who was looking back. "See, there, on the highest ridge."

A faint, dark blur had appeared on a crest three or four miles behind them, one that would have been wholly invisible had not the air been so clear and translucent. It was impossible at the distance to distinguish shapes or detach anything from the general mass, but they knew very well that it was the Lipans. Each felt a little chill at this pursuit so tenacious and so menacing.

"I wish that we had some sort of a place like that in which we faced the Mexicans, where we could put our backs to the wall and fight!" exclaimed Ned.

"I know how you feel," said Obed, "because I feel the same way myself, but there isn't any such place, Ned, and this plain doesn't ever give any sign of producing one, so we'll just ride on. We'll trust to time and chance. Something may happen in our favour."

They strengthened their hearts, whistled to their horses and rode ahead. As on the day before the interminable pursuit went on hour after hour. It was another hot day, and their water bottles were almost emptied. The horses had had nothing to drink since the day before and the two fugitives began to feel for them, but about noon they came to a little pool, lying in a dip or hollow between the swells. It was perhaps fifty feet either way, less than a foot deep and the water was yellowish in colour, but it contained no alkali nor any other bitter infusion. Moreover, grass grew around its edges and some wild ducks swam on its surface. It would have been a good place for a camp and they would have stayed there gladly had it not been for that threat which always hung on the southern horizon.

The water was warm, but the horses drank deeply, and Ned and Obed refilled their bottles. The stop enabled the pursuing Lipans to come within a mile of them, but, moving away at an increased pace, they began to lengthen the gap.

"The Lipans will stop and water their ponies and themselves just as we have done," said Obed. "Everything that we have to endure they have to endure, too. It's a poor rule that doesn't work for one side as well as the other."

"It would all look like play," said Ned, "if we didn't know that it was so much in earnest. Just as you said, Obed, they're stopping to drink at the pond."

A shadow seemed to pass between himself and the blazing glare of the sun. He looked up. It was a shadow thrown by a great bird, with black wings, flying low. Others of the same kind circled higher. Ned saw with a shiver that they were vultures. Obed saw them, too, and he also saw Ned's face pale a little.

"You take it as an omen," he said, "and maybe it is, but it's a poor omen that won't work both ways. They're flying back now towards the Indians, so I guess the Lipans had better look out."

Nevertheless, both were depressed by the appearance of the vultures and the heat that afternoon grew more intense than ever. The horses, at last, began to show signs of weariness, but Ned reflected that for every mile they travelled the Lipans must travel one also, and he recalled the words of Obed that chance might come to their aid.

Another night followed, clear and bright, with the great stars dancing in the southern skies, and Ned and Obed rode long after nightfall. Again the Lipans sank from sight, and, as before, the two stopped on one of the swells.

"Now, Obed," said Ned, "it is your time to sleep and mine to watch. I submitted last night and you must submit tonight. You know that you can't go on forever without sleep."

"Your argument is good," said Obed, "and I yield. It isn't worth while for me to tell you to watch well, because I know you'll do it."

He stretched himself out, folded between his blankets, and was soon asleep. The horses tethered to a lonesome yucca found a few blades of grass on the swell, which they cropped luxuriously. Then they lay down. Ned walked about for a long time rifle on shoulder. It turned colder and he wrapped his *serape* around his shoulders and chest. Finally he grew tired of walking, and sat down on the ground, holding his rifle across his lap. He sat on the highest point of the swell, and, despite the night, he could see a considerable distance.

His sight and hearing alike were acute, but neither brought him any alarm. He tried to reconstruct in his mind the Lipan mode of procedure. With the coming of the night and the disappearance of the fugitives from their sight they would spread out in a long line, in order that they might not pass the two without knowing it, and advance until midnight, perhaps. Then they, too, would rest, and pick up the trail again in the morning.

Ned did not know that time could be so long. He had not been watching more than three or four hours, and yet it seemed like as many days. But it was not long until dawn, and then it would be time for them to be up and away again. The horses reposed by the yucca, and, down the far side of the swell, close to the bottom of the dip, was another yucca. Ned's glance wandered toward the second yucca, and suddenly his heart thumped.

There was a shadow within the shadow of the yucca. Then he believed that it must be imagination, but nevertheless he rose to his feet and cocked his rifle. The shadow blended with the shadow of the yucca just behind its stern, but Ned, watching closely, saw in the next instant the two shadows detach and separate. The one that moved was that of a Lipan warrior, naked save for the breech-cloth and horrible with war paint. Ned instantly raised his rifle and fired. The Lipan uttered a cry and fell, then sprang to his feet, and ran away down the dip. In answer to the shot came the fierce note of the war whoop.

"Up, Obed, up!" cried Ned. "The Lipans are coming down upon us. I just shot at one of them in the bush!"

But Obed was up already, running toward the alarmed horses, his blankets under one arm and his rifle under the other. Ned followed, and, in an instant, they were on their horses with their arms and stores. From the next swell behind them came a patter of shots, and, for the second time, the war cry. But the two were now galloping northward at full speed.

"Good work, Ned, my lad," cried Obed. "I didn't have time to see what you shot, but I heard the yell and I knew it must have been a Lipan."

"He was stalking us, a scout, I suppose, and I just got a glimpse of him behind a yucca. I hit him."

"Good eyes and good hand. You saved us. They must have struck our trail in some manner during the night and then they thought they had us. Ah, they still think they have us!"

The last remark was drawn by a shout and another spatter of shots. Two or three bullets struck alarmingly close, and they increased the speed of their horses, while the Lipans urged their ponies to their best.

"They're too eager," said Obed. "It's time to give them a hint that their company is not wanted."

He wheeled and executed with success that most difficult of feats, a running shot. A Lipan fell from his horse, and the others drew back a little for fear of Ned, the second marksman.

"They've taken the hint," said Obed grimly, as he accomplished a second difficult feat, that of reloading his rifle while they were at full gallop. The Lipans did not utter another war cry, but settled down into a steady pursuit.

"I think I'll try a shot, Obed," said Ned.

"All right," said Obed, "but be sure that you hit something. Never waste a good bullet on empty air."

Ned fired. He missed the Lipan at whom he aimed, but he killed the pony the warrior was riding. The Indian leaped on the pony that had been ridden by the warrior slain by Obed and continued in the group of pursuers. Ned looked somewhat chagrined, and Obed noticed it.

"You did very well, Ned," he said. "Of course, no one likes to kill a horse, but it's the horses that bring on the Lipans, and the fewer horses they have the better for us."

Ned also reloaded as they galloped and then said:

"Don't you think they're dropping back a little?"

"Yes, they want to keep out of range. They know that our rifles carry farther than theirs, and they will not take any more risk until they finally corner us, of which they feel sure."

"But of which we are not so sure."

"No, and we are going to be hidden from them, for a while, by something. You haven't noticed, Ned, that the country is rapidly growing much worse, and that we are now in what is practically a sandy desert. You don't see even a yucca, but you do see something whirling there in the southwest. That's a 'dust devil,' and there's a half dozen more whirling in our direction. We're going to have a sand storm."

Ned looked with interest. The "dust devils," rising up like water spouts, danced over the surface of the sand. They were a half dozen, then a dozen, then twenty. A sharp wind struck the faces of the two fugitives, and it had an edge of fine sand that stung. All the "dust devils" were merged and the air darkened rapidly. The cloud of dust about them thickened. They drew their *sombreros* far down over their eyes, and rode very close together. They could not see twenty yards away, and if they became separated in the dust storm it was not likely that they would ever see each other again. But they urged their horses on at a good rate, trusting to the instinct of the animals to take them over a safe course.

Ned had not only pulled the brim of his *sombrero* down over his eyes, but he reinforced it with one hand to keep from being blinded, for the time, by the sand, but it was hard work. As a final resort he let the lids remain open only enough for him to see his comrade who was but three feet away. Meanwhile, he felt the sand going down his collar, and entering every opening of his clothing, scratching and stinging his skin. The wind all the time was roaring in his ears, and now and then the horses neighed in alarm. But they kept onward. Ned knew that they were passing dips and swells, but he knew nothing else.

The storm blew itself out in about three hours. Ned and Obed emerged from an obscurity as great as that of night. The wind ceased shrieking and was succeeded by a stillness that was almost deathly in comparison. The sun came out suddenly, and shone brightly over the dips and swells. But Ned and Obed looked at each other and laughed. Both were so thickly plastered with sand and dust that they had little human semblance.

Ned shook himself, and a cloud of dust flew from him, but so much remained that he could not tell the difference.

"I think we'd better take a drink out of our water bottles," said Obed. "I'd like mighty well to have a bath, too, but I don't see a bath tub convenient. Is there any sign of our friends, the enemy, Ned?"

"None," replied Ned, examining the horizon line. "There is absolutely nothing within view on the plains."

"Don't you fret about 'em. They'll come. They'll spread out and pick up our trail just as they do every morning."

Obed spoke dispassionately, as if he and Ned were not concerned in it. His predictions were justified. Before night they saw the Lipans coming as usual in a close group, now at a distance of about three miles. Ned could not keep from shuddering. They were as implacable as fate. Night, the storm and bullets did not stop them. They could not shake them off in the immense spaces of plain and desert. A kind of horror seized him. Such tenacity must triumph. Was it possible that Obed and he would fall victims after all? At least it seemed sure that in the end they would be overtaken, and Ned began to count the odds in a fight. Anything seemed better than this interminable flight.

They were cheered a little by the aspect of the country, which began to change considerably for the better. The cactus reappeared and then a few trees, lonesome and ragged, but trees, nevertheless. It is wonderful how much humanity a tree has in a sad and sandy land. The soil grew much firmer and soon they saw clumps of buffalo grass. Several small groups of buffalo were also visible.

"There's better country ahead, as you see," said Obed. "Besides, I've been along this way before. We'll strike water by dark."

They reached a tiny brook just as the twilight came, at which both they and their horses drank. They also took the time to wash their hands and faces, but they dared not delay any longer for fear of being overtaken by the Lipans. The night and the following day passed in the same manner as the others, and the horses of Ned and Obed, splendid animals though they were, began to show signs of fatigue. One limped a little. The dreaded was happening. The Indian ponies made only of bone and muscle were riding them down.

On the other hand, the character of the country now encouraged the fugitives. The yucca and the mesquite turned into oak. They passed through large groves and they hoped that they might soon enter a great forest in which they could hide their trail wholly from the Lipans. They crossed two considerable streams, knee deep on the horses, and then they entered the forest for which they had hoped so much. It was of oaks without much undergrowth and the ground was hilly. They rode through it until past midnight. Then they stopped by the edge of a blue pool, and while the other watched with the rifle each took the bath that he had coveted so long.

"I feel that I can fight battles and also run better now that I've got rid of ten pounds of sand and dust," said Obed, "and I guess you feel the same way, Ned. I suppose you've noticed that the other horse has gone lame, too?"

"Yes, I noticed it. I don't believe either could make much speed tomorrow."

"They certainly couldn't unless they had a long rest, and here we stay. There need be no secrets between you and me, Ned, about this pursuit. I think it's likely that we'll have a fight in the morning, and we might as well choose our fort."

The horses were panting and both now limped badly. It was quite evident that they were spent. Beyond the pool was a tiny valley or glade with a good growth of grass, and, after tying the reins to the pommels of the saddles, they released the two faithful beasts there. Obed thought once of tethering them but he reflected that to do so would make them sure targets of the Indian bullets or arrows. They, too, deserved a chance to escape.

Then he and Ned looked around for the fort, of which they had spoken, and they found it beyond the pool in an opening which would have been called a little prairie in the far north. In the centre of this opening grew a rather thick cluster of trees, and there was some fallen wood. A rifle bullet would not reach from any point of the forest to the cluster.

They drew up all the fallen wood they could find, helping to turn the ring of trees into a kind of fortification, refilled their water bottles from the pool, and sat down to wait, with their rifles and pistols ready.

Ned felt a kind of relief, the relief that comes to one who, having faced the worst so long, now knows that it has been realised. The terrible chase had gone on for nights and days. Always the Lipans were behind them. Well, if they were so fond of pursuing, now let them come. By the aid of the dead wood they were fairly well protected from a fire in any direction, and the light was sufficient for them to see an enemy who attempted to cross the open. There was a certain grim pleasure in the situation.

"They've run us down at last," said Obed, "but they haven't got us yet. Before you scalp your man just catch him is a proverb that I would recommend to the Lipans. Now, Ned, suppose we eat a little, and brace ourselves for the arrival of the pursuit."

They ate with a good appetite and then lay propped on their elbows, where they could look just over the logs at the circling forest. It was very quiet. Nothing stirred among the trees. Their eyes, used now to the half dusk, could see almost as well as if it were daylight. Ned finally noticed some dark objects on the boughs of the trees and called Obed's attention to them.

"Wild turkeys," said Obed, after a long look. "The first we've seen and we can't take a shot at them. They must know it or they wouldn't sit there so quiet and easy."

A half hour later, Ned saw something move among the trees at the nearest point of the forest. It looked like a shadow and was gone in an instant. But his heart leaped. He felt sure that it was a Lipan, and told Obed of his suspicion.

"Of course you're right," said the Maine man. "They may have been there in the woods for an hour spying us out. They've dismounted and have left their horses further back among the trees. Suppose you watch to the right while I face to the left. I think the two of us together can cover a whole circle."

Ned felt a singular composure. It seemed to him that he had passed through so many emotions that he had none left now but calm and expectancy. As the night was somewhat cold he even remembered to throw one of the blankets over his body, as he lay behind the log. Obed noticed it and his sharp eyes brightened with approval. It was obvious that the Lipans were now in the woods about them, and that the long chase was at an end, but the boy was as steady as a rock.

Ned looked continually for the second appearance of the shadows. Nothing within the range of his half circle escaped him. He saw the wild turkeys unfold their wings, and fly heavily away, which was absolute proof of the presence of the Lipans. He finally saw the shadow for the second time, and, at almost the same moment, a pink dot appeared in the woods. The crack of a rifle followed, and a bullet knocked up a little dust at least fifty yards short of them. Obed sniffed contemptuously.

"One good bullet wasted," he said, "and one good bullet, I suppose, deserves another, but they won't fire again—yet. It shows that they know we're on guard. They won't rush us. They'll wait for time, thirst and starvation."

Obed was right. Not another shot was fired, nor did any of the Lipans show themselves. Day came, and the forest was as quiet and peaceful as if it were a park. Some little birds of brilliant plumage sang as heralds of dawn, and sunlight flooded the trees and the opening. Ned and Obed moved themselves into more comfortable positions and waited.

They were to have another terrible trial of Indian patience. No attack was made. The two lay behind the logs and watched the circle of the forest, until their eyes grew weary. The silence and peace that had marked the dawn continued through all the hours of the morning. Although the wild turkeys had flown away, the birds that lived in this forest seemed to take no alarm. They hopped peacefully from bough to bough, and sang their little songs as if there were no alien presence. But Ned and Obed had been through too many dangers to be entrapped into a belief that the Lipans had gone. They matched patience with patience. The sun went slowly up toward the zenith, and the earth grew hot, but they were protected from the fiery rays by the foliage of the trees. Yet Ned grew restless. He was continually poking the muzzle of his rifle over the log and seeking a target, although the forest revealed no human being. Finally Obed put his hand upon his arm.

"Easy, now, easy, Ned," he said. "Don't waste your strength and nerves. They can't charge us, at least in the daylight, without our seeing them, and, when they come, we want to be as strong of body and brain as possible. We won't take the fight to them. They must bring it to us."

Ned blushed. Meanwhile the afternoon dragged on, slow and silent, as the morning had been.

Chapter 13

The Texans

Late in the afternoon Ned's nerves began to affect him again. Once more, the old longing for action took such strong hold upon him that he could not cast it off for a long time. But he hid his face from Obed. He did not want his older comrade to see that he was white and trembling. Finally, he took some food from his pack and bit fiercely upon it, as he ate. It was not for the food that he cared, but it was a relief to bring his teeth together so hard. Obed looked at him approvingly.

"You're setting a good example, Ned," he said, "and I'll follow it."

He too ate, and then took a satisfactory drink from his water bottle. Meanwhile the sun was setting in a cloudless sky, and both noticed with satisfaction that it would be a clear night. Eyes, trained like theirs, could see even in the dusk an enemy trying to creep upon them.

"Do you think you could sleep a while, Ned?" said Obed, persuasively. "Of course, I'll awake you at the first alarm, if the alarm itself doesn't do it. Sleep knits us up for the fray, and a man always wants to be at his best when he goes into battle."

"How could a fellow sleep now?"

"Only the brave and resolute can do it," replied Obed, cunningly. "Napoleon slept before Austerlitz, and while no Austerlitz is likely to happen down here in the wilderness of Northern Mexico there is nothing to keep those who are able from copying a great man."

The appeal to Ned's pride was not lost.

"I think I'll try it," he said.

He lay down behind the log with his rifle by his side, and closed his eyes. He had no idea that he could go to sleep, but he wished to show Obed his calmness in face of danger. Yet he did sleep, and he did not awaken until Obed's hand fell upon his shoulder. He would have sprung up, all his faculties not yet regained, but Obed's hand pressed him down.

"Don't forget where you are, Ned," said the Maine man, "and that we are still besieged."

Yet the night was absolutely still and Ned, from his recumbent position, looked up at a clear sky and many glittering stars.

"Has anything happened?" he asked.

"Not a thing. No Lipan has shown himself even among the trees."

"About what time do you think it is?"

"Two or three hours after midnight, and now I'm going to take a nap while you watch. Ned, do you know, I've an idea those fellows are going to sit in the woods indefinitely, safe, beyond range, and wait for us to come out. Doesn't it make you angry?"

"It does, and it makes me angry also to think that they have our horses. Those were good horses."

Obed slept until day, and Ned watched with a vigilance that no creeping enemy could pass. The Lipans made no movement, but the siege, silent and invisible, went on. Ned had another attack of the nerves, but, as his comrade was sleeping soundly, he took no trouble to hide it, and let the spell shake itself out.

The day was bright, burning and hot, and it threatened to pass like its predecessor, in silence and inaction. Ned and Obed had been lying down or sitting down so long that they had grown stiff, and now, knowing that they were out of range they stood up and walked boldly about, tensing and flexing their muscles, and relieving the bodily strain. Ned thought that their appearance might tempt the Lipans to a shot or some other demonstration, but no sound came from the woods, and they could not see any human presence there. "Maybe they have gone away after all," said Ned hopefully.

"If you went over there to the woods you'd soon find out that they hadn't."

"Suppose they really went away. We'd have no way of knowing it and then we'd have to sit here forever all the same."

Obed laughed, despite the grimness of their situation.

"That is a problem," he said, "but if you can't work a problem it will work itself if you only give it enough time."

The morning was without result, but in the afternoon they saw figures stirring in the wood and concluded that some movement was at hand.

"Ned," said Obed, "I think we've either won in the contest of patience, or that something else has occurred to disturb the Lipans. Don't you see horses as well as Indians there among the trees?"

"I can count at least five horses, and I've no doubt there are others."

"All of which to my mind indicates a rush on horseback. Perhaps they think they can gallop over us. We'd better lay our pistols on the logs, where we can get at 'em quick, and be ready."

Ned's sharp eye caught sight of more horses at another point.

"They're coming from all sides," he said.

"You face to the right and I'll face to the left," said Obed, "and be sure your bullet counts. If we bring down a couple of them they will stop. Indians are not fond of charging in the open, and, besides, it will be hard for them to force their horses in among these logs and trees of ours."

Ned did not answer, but he had listened attentively. The muzzle of his rifle rested upon the log beside his pistol, and, with his eye looking down the sights, he was watching for whatever might come.

A sharp whistle sounded from the wood. At the same instant, three bands of Lipans galloped from the trees at different points, and converged upon the little fortress. They were all naked to the waist, and the sun blazed down upon their painted bodies, lighting up their lean faces and fierce eyes. They uttered shout after shout, as they advanced, and as they came closer, bent down behind the shoulders of their ponies or clung to their sides.

The tremor of the nerves seized Ned again, but it was gone in a moment. Then a fierce passion turned the blood in his veins to fire. Why were these savages seeking his life? Why had they hung upon his trail for days and days? And why had they kept up that silent and invincible siege so long? Yet he did not forget his earlier resolution to watch for a good shot, knowing that his life hung upon it. But it was hard to hold one's fire when the thud of those charging hoofs was

144

coming closer.

The horsemen in front of him were four in number, and the leader who wore a brilliant feathered headdress, seemed to be a chief. Ned chose him for his target, but for a few moments the Lipan made his pony bound from side to side in such a manner that he could not secure a good aim. But his chance came. The Lipan raised his head and opened his mouth to utter a great shout of encouragement to his followers. The shout did not pass his lips, because Ned's bullet struck him squarely in the forehead, and he fell backward from his horse, dead before he touched the ground.

Ned heard Obed's rifle crack with his own, but he could not turn his head to see the result. He snatched up his pistol and fired a second shot which severely wounded a Lipan rider, and then all three parties of the Lipans, fearing the formidable hedge, turned and galloped back, leaving two of their number lifeless upon the ground.

Obed had not fired his pistol, but he stood holding it in his hand, his eyes flashing with grim triumph. Ned was rapidly reloading his rifle.

"If we didn't burn their noble Lipan faces then I'm mightily mistaken," said Obed, as he too began to reload his rifle. "A charge that is not pressed home is no charge at all. Hark, what is that?"

There was a sudden crash of rifle shots in the forest, the long whining whoop of the Lipans and then hard upon it a deep hoarse cheer.

"White men!" exclaimed Ned.

"And Texans!" said Obed. "Such a roar as that never came from Mexican throats. It's friends! Do you hear, Ned, it's friends! There go the Indians!"

Across the far edge of the open went the Lipans in wild flight, and, as they pressed their mustangs for more speed, bullets urged them to efforts yet greater. Fifteen or twenty men galloped from the trees, and Ned and Obed, breaking cover, greeted them with joyous shouts, which the men returned in kind.

"You don't come to much," exclaimed Ned, "but we can say to you that never were men more welcome."

"Which I beg to repeat and emphasise," said Obed White.

"Speak a little louder," said the foremost of the men, leaning from his horse and couching one hand behind his ear.

Ned repeated his words in a much stronger tone, and the man nodded and smiled. Ned looked at him with the greatest interest. He was of middle age and medium size. Hair and eyes were intensely

THE LIPAN RAISED HIS HEAD TO UTTER A GREAT SHOUT
OF ENCOURAGEMENT.

black, and his complexion was like dark leather. Dressed in Indian costume he could readily have passed for a warrior. Yet this man had come from the far northern state of New York, and it was only the burning suns of the Texas and North Mexican plains that had turned him to his present darkness.

"Glad to meet you, my boy," he said, leaning from his horse and holding out a powerful hand, burnt as dark as his face. "My name's Smith, Erastus Smith."

Ned grasped his hand eagerly. This was the famous "Deaf" Smith—destined to become yet more famous—although they generally pronounced it D-e-e-f in Texas.

"Guess we didn't come out of season," said Smith with a smile.

"You certainly didn't," broke in Obed. "There's a time for all things, and this was your time!"

"I believe they're real glad to see us. Don't you think so, Jim?" said Smith with a smile.

The man whom he called Jim had been sitting on his horse, silent, and he remained silent yet, but he nodded in reply. Ned's gaze travelled to him and he was certainly a striking figure. He was over six feet in height, with large blue eyes and fair hair. His expression was singularly gentle and mild, but his appearance nevertheless, both face and figure, indicated unusual strength. Obed had not noticed him before, but now he exclaimed joyfully:

"Why, it's Colonel Jim Bowie! Jim, it's me, Obed White! Shake hands!"

"So it is you, Obed," said the redoubtable Bowie, "and here we shake."

The hands of the two met in a powerful clasp. Then they all dismounted and another man, short and thick, shook Obed by the hand and called him by his first name. He was Henry Karnes, the Tennessean, great scout and famous borderer of the Texas plains.

Ned looked with admiration at these men, whose names were great to him. On the wild border where life depended almost continually upon skill and quickness with weapons, "Deaf" Smith, Jim Bowie and Henry Karnes were already heroes to youth. Ned thrilled. He was here with his own people, and with the greatest of them. He had finished his long journey and he was with the Texans. The words shaped themselves again and again in his brain, the Texans! the Texans! the Texans!

"You two seem to have given the Lipans a lot of trouble," said

Bowie, looking at the two fallen warriors.

"We were putting all the obstacles we could in the way of what they wanted," said Obed modestly, "but we don't know what would have happened if you hadn't come. Those fellows had been following us for days, and they must have had some idea that you were near, or they would have waited still longer."

"They must not have known that we were as near as we were," said Bowie, "or they would not have invited our attack. We heard the firing and galloped to it at once. But you two need something better than talk."

He broke off suddenly, because Ned had sat down on one of the logs, looking white and ill. The collapse had come after so many terrible trials and privations, and not even his will could hold him.

"Here, you take a drink of this water, it's good and cold," said "Deaf" Smith kindly as he held out a canteen. "I reckon that no boy has ever passed through more than you have, and if there's any hero you are one."

"Good words," said Bowie.

Ned smiled. These words were healing balm to his pride. To be praised thus by these famous Texans was ample reward. Besides, he had great and vital news to all, and he knew that Obed would wait for him to tell it.

"I think," said Bowie, "that we'd better camp for the night in the clump of trees that served you two so well, and, before it's dark, we'll look around and see what spoil is to be had."

They found three rifles that had been dropped by slain or wounded Lipans, and they were well pleased to get them, as rifles were about to become the most valuable of all articles in Texas. They also recovered Ned and Obed's horses, which the Indians had left in the valley, evidently expecting to take them away, when they secured the scalps of the two fugitives.

Ned, after the cold water and a little rest, fully recovered his strength and poise, but the men would not let him do any work, telling him that he had already done his share. So he sat on his log and watched them as they prepared camp and supper. Besides being the Texans and his own people, to whom he had come after the long journey of perils, they made a wonderful appeal. These were the bold riders, the dauntless, the fearless. He would not find here the pliancy, the cunning, the craft and the dark genius of Santa Anna, but he would find men who talked straight, who shot straight, and who feared nobody.

They were sixteen in number, and all were clad wholly in buckskin, with fur caps upon their heads. They were heavily armed, every man carrying at least a rifle, a pistol, and a formidable knife, invented by Bowie. All were powerful physically, and every face had been darkened by the sun. Ned felt that such a group as this was a match for a hundred Mexicans or Lipans.

They worked dextrously and rapidly, unsaddling their horses and tethering them where they could graze in the open, drawing up the dead wood until it made a heap which was quickly lighted, and then cooking strips of venison over the coals. There was so much life, so much cheerfulness, and so much assurance of strength and invincibility that Ned began to feel as if he did not have a care left. All the men already called him Ned, and he felt that every one of them was his friend.

Karnes put a strip of venison on the sharp end of a stick, and broiled it over the blaze. It gave out a singularly appetizing odour, and when it was done he extended it to the boy.

"Here, Ned," he said, "take this on the end of your knife and eat it. I'll wager that you haven't had any good warm victuals for a week, and it will taste mighty well."

Ned ate it and asked for more. He would have done his own cooking, but they would not let him. They seemed to take a pleasure in helping him, and, used as they were to hardships and danger, they admired all the more the tenacity and courage that had brought a boy so far.

"We can promise you one thing, Ned," said "Deaf" Smith. "We'll see that you and Obed have a full night's good sleep and I guess you'll like that about as much as a big supper."

"We certainly will," said Obed. "Sleep has got a lot of knitting to do in my case."

"The same is true of me," said Ned, who had now eaten about all he wanted, "but before I roll up in the blankets I want to say something to you men."

His voice had suddenly become one of great gravity, and, despite his youth, it impressed them. The darkness had now come, but the fire made a centre of light. They had put themselves in easy attitudes about it, while the horses grazed just beyond them.

"I come from Texas myself," said Ned, "although I was born in Missouri. My parents are dead, and I thought I could make my way in Texas. I met Mr. Austin who is related to me, and he was good to

149

me more than once. When he went to Mexico to talk with the rulers there about our troubles I went with him. I was a prisoner with him in the City of Mexico, and I often saw the dictator, Santa Anna, and his brother-in-law, General Cos."

Ned paused and a deep "Ah!" came from the men. They felt from his face and manner that he was telling no idle tale.

"They said many fine words to Mr. Austin," said Ned, "and always they promised that they were going to do great things for Texas. But much time passed and they did nothing. Also they kept Mr. Austin a prisoner. Then I escaped. I believed that they were preparing to attack Texas. I was right. I was recaptured and both President Santa Anna and General Cos told me so. They told me because they did not believe I could escape again, as they sent me to one of the submarine dungeons under the castle of San Juan de Ulua. But even under the sea I found a friend, Obed here, and we escaped together. We have since seen the army of General Cos, and it is marching straight upon Texas. Santa Anna means to crush us and to execute all our leaders."

Again came that deep murmurous "Ah!" and now it was full of anger and defiance.

"You say you saw the army of Cos?" asked Bowie.

"Yes," replied Ned, "I saw it before I was taken to the castle of San Juan de Ulua and afterward in Northern Mexico, marching straight toward Texas. It is a large force, cannon and lancers, horse and foot."

"And so Santa Anna has been lulling us with promises, while sending an army to destroy us."

Bowie's tone, so gentle and mild before, grew hard and bitter. The firelight flickered across his face and to Ned the blue eyes looked as cold and relentless as death. He had heard strange stories of this man, tales of desperate combats in Mississippi and Louisiana, and he believed now that they were true. He could see the daring and determined soul behind the blue eyes.

While Ned was talking "Deaf" Smith was leaning forward with his hand behind his ear. When the story was finished the dark face grew still darker, but he said nothing. The others, too, were silent but Ned knew their minds. It was a singular little company drawn from different American states, some from the far north, but all alike in their devotion to the vague region then known as Texas.

"I think, Ned," said Bowie, "that you have served Texas well. We have been divided among ourselves. Many have believed in propitiating Santa Anna and Mexico, but how can you propitiate a tiger that is about to devour you? We cannot trust Mexico, and we cannot trust Santa Anna. Your message settles all doubt and gives us time to arm. Thank God we refused to give up our rifles, because we are going to need them more than anything else on earth. It was surely more than luck that brought us this way. We came down here, Ned, on an expedition, half for hunting and half for scouting, and we've found more than we expected. We must start for Texas in the morning. Is it not so, boys?"

"Yes," they answered all together.

"Then, Ned," said Bowie, "you can tell your story to Sam Houston and all our leaders, and I think I know what they will say. We are few, but Santa Anna and all Mexico cannot ride over Texas. And now it's time for you and Obed to go to sleep. I should think that after being chased nearly a week you'd be glad to rest."

"We are," said Obed, answering for them both, "and once more we want to thank you. If you hadn't come the Lipans would certainly have got us."

The night, as usual, was chilly, and Ned spread his blankets in front of the fire. His saddle formed a pillow for his head, and with one blanket beneath him, another above him, and the stalwart Texans all about him, he felt a deep peace, nay more, a great surge of triumph. He had made his way through everything. Santa Anna and Cos could not attack the Texans, unwarned. Neither Mexicans nor Lipans, neither prisons nor storms nor deserts had been able to stop him.

After the triumphant leap of his blood the great peace possessed him entirely. His mind and body relaxed completely. His eyelids drooped and the flames danced before him. The figures of the men became dusky. Sometimes he saw them and sometimes he did not. Then everything vanished, and he fell into a long and sound sleep.

While Ned and Obed slept, the Texans conferred earnestly. They knew that every word Ned had told was true, and they felt that the trouble between Texas and Mexico had now come to a head. It must be war. They were fully aware of the fearful odds, but they did not believe the Texans would flinch. Three or four rode a long distance around the camp and scouted carefully. But, as they had expected, they saw no sign of the Lipans, who undoubtedly were still fleeing southward, carrying in their hearts a healthy fear of the long rifles of the Texans.

After the scouts came back most of the men went to sleep, but Bowie and "Deaf" Smith watched all through the night. Ned moved a little toward the morning and displaced the blanket that lay over him. Bowie gently put it back.

"He's a good boy as well as a brave one," he said to Smith, "and we owe him a lot."

"Never a doubt of that," said Smith, "and he'll be with us in the coming struggle."

When Ned awoke the dawn was barely showing, but all the horses, including his own, were saddled and ready. They ate a brief breakfast, and then they galloped northward over a good country. They did not trouble to look for the army of Cos, as they knew that it was coming and it was their object to spread the alarm as soon as possible through all the Texas settlements. Ned, refreshed and strong, was in the centre of the troop and he rode with a light heart. Obed was on one side of him, and "Deaf" Smith on the other.

"Tonight," said Smith, "we water our horses in the Rio Grande."

"And then on for Texas!" said Obed.

On they sped, their even pace unbroken until noon, when they made a short rest for food and water. Then they sped north once more, Bowie, Smith and Karnes leading the way. They said very little now, but everyone in the group was thinking of the scattered Texans, of the women and children in the little cabins beyond the Rio Grande, harried already by Comanches and Lipans and now threatened by a great Mexican force. They had come from different states and often they were of differing counsels, but a common danger would draw them together. It was significant that Smith, the New Yorker, and Bowie, the Georgian, rode side by side.

All through the hot sun of the afternoon they rode on. Twilight found them still riding. Far in the night they waded and swam the Rio Grande, and the next morning they stood on the soil that now is Texas.

CHAPTER 14

THE RING-TAILED PANTHER

Texas was then a vague and undetermined name in the minds of many. It might extend to the Rio Grande or it might extend only to the Nueces, but to most the Rio Grande was the boundary between them and Mexico. So felt Ned and all his comrades. They were now on the soil which might own the overlordship of Mexico, but for which they, the Texans, were spending their blood. It was strange what an attachment they had for it, although not one of them was born there. Beyond, in the outer world, there was much arguing about the right or wrong of their case, but they knew that they would have to fight for their lives, and for the homes they had built in the wilderness on the faith of promises that had been broken. That to them was the final answer and to people in such a position there could be no other.

The sight of Texas, green and fertile, with much forest along the streams was very pleasant to Ned, and those rough frontiersmen in buckskin who rode with him were the very men whom he had chosen. He had been in a great city, and he had talked with men in brilliant uniforms, but there everything seemed old, so far away in thought and manner from the Texans, and he could never believe the words of the men in brilliant uniforms. There, the land itself looked ancient and worn, but here it was fresh and green, and men spoke the truth.

They rode until nearly noon, when they stopped in a fine grove of oaks and pecans by the side of a clear creek. The grass was also rich and deep here, and they did not take the trouble to tether their horses. Ned was exceedingly glad to dismount as he was stiff and sore from the long ride, and he was also as hungry as a wolf.

"Lay down on the grass, Ned, an' stretch yourself," said Karnes. "When you're tired the best way to rest is to be just as lazy as you can be. The ground will hold you up an' let your lungs do their own breathin'. Don't you go to workin' 'em yourself."

Ned thought it good advice and took it. It was certainly a great luxury to make no physical exertion and just to let the ground hold him up, as Karnes had said. Obed imitated his example, stretching himself out to his great thin length on the soft turf.

"Two are company and twenty are more so," he said, "especially if you're in a wild country. My burden of care isn't a quarter as heavy since we met Jim Bowie, and all the rest of these sure friends and sure shots. This isn't much like San Juan de Ulua is it, Ned? You wouldn't like to be back there."

The boy looked up at the vast blue dome of the heavens, then he listened a moment to the sigh of the free wind which came unchecked a thousand miles and he replied with so much emphasis that his words snapped:

"Not for worlds, Obed!"

Obed White laughed and rolled over in the grass.

"I do believe you mean that, Ned," he said, "and the sentiments

153

that you speak so well are also mine own."

Smith and Karnes went a little distance up the creek, and found some buffalo feeding. They shot a young cow, and in an incredibly short space tender steaks were broiling over a fire. After dinner all but two went to sleep. They understood well the old maxim that the more haste the less speed, and that the sleep and rest through the hours of the afternoon would make them fit for the long riding that was yet before them.

At five o'clock they were in the saddle again, and rode until midnight. The next morning the party separated. The men were to carry the blazing torch throughout the settlements, telling all the Texans that the Mexicans were coming and that they were bringing war with them. But Bowie, "Deaf" Smith and Karnes kept on with Ned and Obed.

"We're taking you to Sam Houston," said Bowie to Ned. "He's to be the general of all the Texan forces, we think, and we want you to tell him what you've told us."

They began now to see signs of settlements in the river bottoms where the forests grew. There were stray little log cabins, almost hidden among the oaks and pecans. Women and children came forth to see the riders go by. The women were tanned like the men, and often they, too, were clothed in buckskin. The children, bare of foot and head, seemed half wild, but all, despite the sun, had the features of the Northern races.

Ned could not keep from waving his hand to them. These were his people, and he was thankful that he should have so large a part in the attempt to save them. But he only had fleeting glimpses because they rode very fast now. He was going to Sam Houston, famous throughout all the Southwest, and Houston was at one of the little new settlements some distance away. He would tell his story again, but he knew that the Texans were already gathering. The messengers detached from the group had now carried the alarm to many a cabin.

Several times at night they saw points of fire on the horizon and they would pause to look at them.

"That's the Texans signalling to one another," said "Deaf" Smith. "They're passing the word westward. They're calling in the buffalo hunters and those who went out to fight the Comanches and Lipans."

Ned had alternations of hope and despondency. He saw anew how few the Texans were. Their numbers could be counted only in thousands, while the Mexicans had millions. Moreover, the tiny settlements were scattered widely. Could such a thin force make a successful defence against the armies of Cos and Santa Anna? But after every moment of despair, the rebound came, and he saw that the spirit of the people was indomitable.

At last, they rode into a straggling little village by the side of a wide and shallow river. All the houses were built of logs or rough boards, and Ned and his companions dismounted before the largest. They had already learned that Sam Houston was inside. Ned felt intense curiosity as they approached. He knew the history of Houston, his singular and picturesque career, and the great esteem in which he was held by the Texans. A man with a rifle on his shoulder stood by the door as guard, but he recognised Smith and Karnes, and held the door open for the four, who went inside without a word.

Several men, talking earnestly were sitting in cane-bottomed chairs, and Ned, although he had never seen him before, knew at once which was Houston. The famous leader sat in the centre of the little group. He was over six feet high, very powerful of build, with thick, longish hair, and he was dressed carefully in a suit of fine dark blue cloth. He rose and saluted the four with great courtesy. Despite his long period of wild life among the Indians his manners were distinguished.

"We welcome you, Smith and Karnes, our faithful scouts," he said, "and we also welcome those with you who, I presume, are the two escaped from the City of Mexico."

It was evident that the story of Ned and Obed had preceded them, but Karnes spoke for them.

"Yes, general," he said. "They are the men, or rather the man and the boy. These are Obed White and Ned Fulton, General Houston."

Houston's glance ran swiftly over them. Evidently he liked both, as he smiled and gave each a hearty hand.

"And now for your story," he said.

Obed nodded toward Ned.

"He's the one who saw it all," he said, "and he's the one who brings the warning."

Ned was a little abashed by the presence of Houston and the other important Texans, but he told the tale once more rapidly and succinctly. Everyone listened closely. They were the chief members of the temporary Texan government, but the room in which they met was all of the frontier. Its floor was of rough boards. Its walls and ceilings were unplastered. There was not a single luxury and not all of the necessities.

When Ned finished, Houston turned to the others and said quietly:

"Gentlemen, we all know that this is war. I think there need be no discussion of the point. It seems necessary to send out more messengers gathering up every Texan who will fight. Do you agree with me?"

All said yes.

"I think, too," said Houston, "that Santa Anna may now send Mr. Austin back to us. He does not know how well informed we are, and doubtless he will believe that such an act will keep us in a state of blindness."

"And you, my brave and resourceful young friend, what do you want to do?"

"Fight under you."

Houston laughed and put his hand affectionately on the boy's shoulder.

"I see that there is something of the courtier in you, too," he said. "It is not a bad quality sometimes, and you shall have the chance that you ask, later on. But meanwhile, you and Mr. White would better rest here, a while. You may have some scouting and skirmishing to do first. We must feel our way."

Ned and Obed now withdrew, and received the hospitality of the little town which was great, at least so far as food was concerned. They longed for action, but the rest was really necessary. Both body and spirit were preparing for greater deeds. Meanwhile, Houston, the scouts and the Texan government went away, but Ned and Obed stayed, awaiting the call. They knew that the signals had now passed through all Texas and they did not think that they would have to remain there long.

They heard soon that Houston's prediction in regard to Austin had come true. Santa Anna had released him, and he had arrived in Texas. But he had not been cajoled. His eyes had been opened at last to the designs of the dictator and immediately upon his return to Texas he had warned his countrymen in a great speech. Meanwhile, the army of Cos was approaching San Antonio, preceded by the heralds of coming Texan ruin.

Ned and Obed sat under the shade of some live oaks, when a horseman came to the little village. He was a strange man, great in size, dressed in buckskin, very brown of countenance and with long hair, tied as the western Indians would wear it. He was something of a genial boaster, was this man, and he was known up and down the Texas border as the Ring Tailed Panther although his right name was Martin Palmer. But he had lived long among the Osage, Kiowa and Pawnee Indians, and he was renowned throughout all the Southwestern country for his bravery, skill and eccentricity. An Indian had killed a white man and eaten his heart. He captured the Indian and compelled him to eat until he died. When his favourite bear dog died he rode sixty miles and brought a minister to preach a sermon over his body. A little boy was captured on the outskirts of a settlement by some Comanche Indians. He followed them alone for three hundred miles, stole the boy away from them in the night, and carried him back safely to his father and mother.

Such was the Ring Tailed Panther, a name that he had originally given to himself and which the people had adopted, one who boasted that he feared no man, the boast being true. He was heavily armed and he rode a black and powerful horse, which he directed straight toward the place where Ned and Obed were sitting.

"You are Ned Fulton an' Obed White, if report tells no lie?" he said in a deep growling voice.

"We are," said Ned, who did not know the identity of their formidable visitor.

"So I knew. I just wanted to see if you'd deny it. Glad to meet you, gentlemen. As for me, I'm the Ring Tailed Panther."

"The Ring Tailed Panther?"

"Exactly. Didn't you hear me say so? I'm the Ring Tailed Panther, an' I can whip anything livin', man or beast, lion or grizzly bear. That's why I'm the Ring Tailed Panther."

"Happy to know you, Mr. Ring Tailed Panther," said Ned, "and having no quarrel with you we don't wish to fight you."

The man laughed, his broad face radiating good humour.

"And I don't want to fight you, either," he said, "'cause all of us have got to fight somebody else. See here, your name's Obed an' yours is Ned, and that's what I'm goin' to call you. No Mistering for me. It don't look well for a Ring Tailed Panther to be givin' handles to people's names."

"Ned and Obed it is," said Ned with warmth.

"Then, Ned an' Obed, it's Mexicans. I've been fightin' Indians a long time. Besides bein' a Ring Tailed Panther, I'm three parts grizzly bear an' one part tiger, an' I want you both to come with guns."

"Is it fighting?" asked Ned, starting up.

"It's ridin' first an' then fightin'. Our people down at Gonzales have a cannon. The Mexicans are comin' to take it away from them, an' I think there's goin' to be trouble over the bargain. The Texans got the gun as a defence against the Indians an' they need it. Some of us are goin' down there to take a hand in the matter of that gun, an' you are goin' with us."

"Of course we are!" said Ned and Obed together. In five minutes they were riding, fully armed, with the Ring Tailed Panther over the prairie. He gave them more details as they rode along.

"Some of our people had been gatherin' at San Felipe to stop the march of Cos if they could," he said, "but they've been drawn off now to help Gonzales. They're comin' from Bastrop, too, an' other places, an' if there ain't a fight then I'm the Ring Tailed Panther for nothing. If we keep a good pace we can join a lot of the boys by nightfall."

"We'll keep it," said Ned. The boy's heart was pounding. Somehow he felt that an event of great importance was at hand, and he was glad to have a share in it. But the three spoke little. The Panther led the way. Ned saw that despite his boasting words he was a man of action. Certainly he was acting swiftly now, and it was quite evident that he knew what he was doing. At last he turned to Ned and said:

"You're only a boy. You know what you're goin' into, of course?"

"A fight, I think."

"And you may get killed?"

"I know it. One can't go into a fight without that risk."

"You're a brave boy. I've heard of what you did, an' you don't talk much. I'm glad of that. I can do all the talkin' that's needed by the three of us. The Lord created me with a love of gab."

The man spoke in a whimsical tone and Ned laughed.

"You can have all my share of the talking, Mr. Palmer," he said.

"The Ring Tailed Panther," corrected the man. "I told you not to be Misterin' me. I like that name, the Ring Tailed Panther. It suits me, because I fit an' I fight till they get me down, then I curl my tail an' I take another round. Once in New Orleans I met a fellow who said he was half horse, half alligator, that he could either claw to death the best man living, stamp him to pieces or eat him alive. I invited him to do any one of these things or all three of them to me."

"What happened?" asked Ned.

A broad smile passed over the man's brown face.

"After they picked up the pieces an' put him back together," he said, "I told him he might try again whenever he felt like it, but he said

158

his challenge was directed to human beings, not to Ring Tailed Panthers. Him an' me got to be great friends an' he's somewhere in Texas now. I may run acrost him before our business with the Mexicans is over, which I take it is goin' to last a good while."

It was now late in the afternoon, and dismounting at a clump of trees the Panther lighted the end of a dead stick and waved the torch around his head many times.

"Watch there in the west for another light like this," he said.

Ned, who sat on his horse, was the first to see the faint circling light far down under the horizon. It was so distant that he could not have seen it had he not been looking for it, but when he pointed it out the Panther ceased to whirl his own torch.

"It's some friends," he said, "an' they're answerin'. They're sayin' that they've seen us an' that they're waitin'. When they get through we'll say that we understan' an' are comin'."

The whirling torch on the horizon stopped presently. The Panther whirled his own for half a minute, then he sprang back upon his horse and the three rode rapidly forward.

The sight of the lights sparkling in the twilight so far across the prairie thrilled Ned. He felt that he was in very truth riding to a fight as the Panther had said. Perhaps it was a part of the force of Cos that was coming to Gonzales. Cos himself had turned from the land route with a part of his force and, coming by sea, had landed at Copano about two weeks before. Ned, having full cause, hated this brutal man, and he hoped that the Texans would come to grips with him.

The night was at hand when they reached four men sitting on horseback and waiting for them. They greeted the Ring Tailed Panther with few words but with warmth. They gave to Ned and Obed, too, the strong handclasp which men in danger give to friends who come. Ned thrilled once more with pride that he should be associated with heroes in great deeds. Such they undoubtedly were to him.

"The Mexicans will be at Gonzales tomorrow," said one of the men. "The place, as you know, has refused to give up its cannon and has defied them, but it's almost bare of men. I don't think they have a dozen there."

"The battle is generally to the strong if they get there in time," said Obed, "and here are seven of us on good horses."

"Not countin' the fact that one of us is a Ring Tailed Panther with claws a foot long an' two sets of teeth in his mouth," said Palmer. "Ride on, boys, an' ride hard."

159

They urged their horses into a gallop and sped over the prairie. At midnight they clattered into the tiny village of Gonzales on the Guadalupe River, where everybody except the little children was awake and watching. Lights flared from the cabins, and the alarm at first, lest they were Mexicans, changed to joy when they were disclosed as Texans.

But the armed force of the place, though stout of heart, was pitifully small. They found only eleven men in Gonzales capable of bearing arms, and no more help could be expected before the Mexicans came the next day. But eleven and seven make eighteen, and now that they were joined, and communicating spirit and hope to one another, the eighteen were more than twice as strong as the eleven had been. The Ring Tailed Panther poured forth a stream of cheer and encouragement. He grew more voluble at the approach of danger. Never had his teeth and claws been longer or sharper.

"I'm afraid of nothin' except that they won't come," he said. "If they don't, my health will give way. I'll be a-droopin' an' a-pinin' an' I'll have to go off an' fight the Comanches an' Lipans to get back my strength."

But he was assured that his health would not suffer. Mexican cavalry, a hundred strong, were coming under a captain, Castenada, sent by Ugartchea, the Mexican commander at San Antonio de Bexar. Scouts had brought that definite news. They were riding from the west and they would have to cross the Guadalupe before they could enter Gonzales. There were fords, but it would be a dangerous task to attempt their passage in face of the Texan rifles.

The ferryboat was tied safely on the Gonzales side, and then the eighteen, every one a fine marksman, distributed themselves at the fords. Ned, Obed and the Ring Tailed Panther stayed together. They did not anticipate the arrival of the Mexican forces before dawn, but Castenada might send spies ahead, and the Mexican scouts were full of wiles and stratagems.

"At any rate," said the Panther, "if we catch any Mexican prowling around here we'll throw him into the river."

"All things, including Mexicans, come to him who waits," said Obed, "and speaking for myself I'd rather they wouldn't come until day. It's more comfortable to sit quiet in the dark."

These three and six others had taken a position under a great oak tree, where they were well shaded but could easily see anyone who approached the ford on the opposite side. Back of them a few lights

160

burned in the little town, where the anxious women watched, but no noise came from it or the second ford, where the other half of the eighteen were on guard. Their horses were tethered some distance in the rear and they, too, rested in quiet. The tree sent up a great gnarled root and Ned sat on the ground, leaning against it. It just fitted into the curve of his back and he was very comfortable. But he did not allow his comfort to lull him into lethargy. Always he watched the river and the farther shore. He had now become no mean scout and sentinel. The faculties develop fast amid the continuous fight for life against all kinds of dangers. Above all, that additional sense which may be defined as prescience, and, which was a development of the other five, was alive within him, ready to warn him of a hostile presence.

But Ned neither saw nor heard anything, nor did his sixth sense warn him that an enemy was near. The Guadalupe, wide, yellow and comparatively shallow like most of the Texas rivers, flowed slowly and without sound. Now and then Obed and the Panther walked down to the other ford, where all, too, was quiet, but Ned kept his place against the root. Toward morning the Panther sat down beside him there.

"Waitin's hard," he said. "I like to jump on the enemy with claws an' nails an' have it out right there an' then. I like to roar an' bite. That's why I'm a Ring Tailed Panther."

Ned laughed.

"If Castenada is coming, and they say he surely is," he said, "we'll soon have use for all our claws and teeth."

"Patience will bring our Mexicans," said Obed White.

At daylight women from the cabins brought them all coffee and warm food, for which they were very grateful. Then the sun rose, and the morning was fresh and crisp, it now being autumn. The men remained by the river, still watching intently and Ned caught a sudden sharp glint which was not that of the sun, far out on the prairie. He knew that it was a brilliant ray reflected from the polished head of a lance, and he said as he pointed a finger:

"The Mexicans are coming."

"So they are," said the Ring Tailed Panther. "I see a horseman, an' another, an' another, an' now a lot of 'em. They must be a hundred at least. It's the troop of Castenada, an' they're after that cannon. Well, I'm glad."

The man seemed to swell and his eyes darkened. He was like some formidable beast about to spring. The boaster was ready to make good his boast.

"Run down to the other ford, Ned," said Palmer, "an' tell the men there that the Mexicans are at hand."

Ned did his errand, but returned very quickly. He was anxious to see the advance of Castenada's troop. The Mexicans, about half of whom were lancers and the rest armed with muskets, came on very steadily. An officer in fine uniform, whom Ned took to be Castenada himself, rode at their head. When they came within rifle shot a white flag was hoisted on a lance.

"A white flag! This is no time for white flags," growled the Ring Tailed Panther. "Never have any faith in a Mexican comin' under a white flag. What we've got to do now is to roar an' rip an' claw."

"Still," said Obed, "it's evil to him who evil does, and we've got to wait till these Mexicans do it. First we've got to hear what they say, and if the saying isn't to our liking, as I'm thinking it won't be, then it's ripping and roaring and clawing and all the other 'ings' to our taste as long as we can stand it."

"Go ahead," growled the Ring Tailed Panther, "I'm not much on talkin'. Fightin's more in my line an' when it's that I come with a hop, a skip an' a jump, teeth an' claws all ready."

"Ned," said Obed, "you speak the best Spanish, so go down there to the bank of the river, and hear what they have to say. Just remember that we're not giving up the cannon, and clothe the answers in what fine words you please. There isn't any rock here, but sooner this rock shall fly from its firm base than the Texans will yield their cannon when they are sure to be attacked by Indians and maybe Mexicans too."

Ned walked down to the edge of the river and the officer, whom he rightly supposed to be Castenada, dismounting, came to the shore at an opposite point.

"What do you want?" cried Ned in pure Spanish across the water.

"Are you empowered to speak for the people of Gonzales?"

"You hear me speaking and you see the other Texans listening."

"Then I have to say that on the order of General Cos I demand your cannon in the name of General Santa Anna and Mexico."

"We've made up our minds to keep it. We're sure to need it later on."

"This is insolent. If you do not give it we shall come and take it."

"Tell him, Ned," growled the Ring Tailed Panther, "that we just hope he'll come an' try to take it, that I'm here roarin' all the time, that I've filed my teeth an' nails 'till they're like the edge of a razor, an' that I'm just hungerin' to rip an' claw."

"The men of Gonzales mean to defend their cannon and themselves," called Ned across the river. "If you come to take the gun it means war. It means more, too. It means that you will lose many of your soldiers. The Texans, as you know, are both able and willing to shoot."

"This is rebellion and treason!" cried Castenada. "The great Santa Anna will come with a mighty force, and when he is through not a Texan will trouble the surface of the earth."

A roar of approval came from the men behind the Mexican captain, but Ned replied:

"Until the earth is rid of us we may make certain spots of it dangerous for you. So, I warn you to draw back. Our bullets carry easily across this river."

Captain Castenada, white with rage, retired with his troop beyond the range of the Texan rifles.

CHAPTER 15

THE FIRST GUN

"Well, Ned, it's sometimes ask and ye shall not receive, isn't it?" said Obed White, looking at the retreating Mexicans.

But the Ring Tailed Panther growled between his shut teeth. Then he opened his mouth and gave utterance to his dissatisfaction.

"It's a cheat, a low Mexican trick," he said, "to come here an' promise a fight an' then go away. I'm willin' to bet my claws that them Mexicans will hang around here two or three days, without tryin' to do a thing."

"An' won't that be all the better for us?" asked Ned. "We're only eighteen and we surely need time for more."

"That's so," admitted the Ring Tailed Panther, "but when you've got all your teeth and claws sharpened for a fight you want it right then an' not next week."

The Mexicans tethered their horses and began to form camp about a half mile from the river. They went about it deliberately, spreading tents for their officers and lighting fires for cooking. The Texans could see them plainly and the Mexicans showed the carelessness and love of pleasure natural to children of the sun. Some lay down on the grass and three or four began to strum mandolins and guitars.

There was a sterner manner on the Texan side of the Guadalupe.

The watch at the fords was not relaxed, but Ned went back into the little town to carry the word to the women and children. Most of the women, like the men, were dressed in deerskin and they, too, volunteered to fight if they were needed. Ned told them what Castenada had asked, and he also told them the reply which was received with grim satisfaction. The women were even more bitter than the men against the Mexicans.

Ned passed a long day by the Guadalupe, keeping his place most of the time at the ford with the Ring Tailed Panther, who was far less patient than he.

"My teeth an' claws will shorely get dull with me a-settin' here an' doin' nothin'," said Palmer. "I can roar an' I can keep on roarin' but what's the good of roarin' when you can't do any bitin' an' tearin'?"

"Patience will have its perfect fight," said Obed, giving one of his misquotations. "I've always heard that every kind of panther would lie very quiet until the chance came for him to spring."

The Ring Tailed Panther growled between his shut teeth.

The sight of the Mexican force in the afternoon became absolutely tantalizing. Although it was early autumn the days were still very hot at times and Castenada's men were certainly taking their ease. Ned could see many of them enjoying the *siesta*, and through a pair of glasses he saw others lolling luxuriously and smoking cigarettes. It was especially irritating to the Ring Tailed Panther, who grew very red in the face but who now only emitted growls between his shut teeth.

It was evident that the Mexicans were going to make no demonstration just yet and the night came, rather dark and cloudy. Now the anxiety in Gonzales increased since the night can be cover for anything, and, besides guarding the fords, several of the defenders were placed at intermediate points.

Ned took a station with Obed in a clump of oaks that grew to the very edge of the Guadalupe. There they sat a long time and watched the surface of the river grow darker and darker. The Mexican camp had been shut from sight long since, and no sounds now came from it. Ned appreciated fully the need of a close watch. The Mexicans might swim the river on their horses in the darkness, and gallop down on the town. So he never ceased to watch, and he also listened with ears which were rapidly acquiring the delicacy and sensitiveness peculiar to those of expert frontiersmen.

Ned was not warlike in temper. He knew, from his reading, all the waste and terrible passions of war, but he was heart and soul with the

Texans. He was one of them, and to him the coming struggle was a fight for home and liberty by an oppressed people. With the ardour of youth flaming in him he was willing for that struggle to begin at once.

Night on the Guadalupe! He felt that the darkness was full of omens and presages for Texas and for him, too, a boy among its defenders. His pulses quivered, and a light moisture broke out on his face. His prescience, the gift of foresight, was at work. It was telling him that the time, in very truth, had come. Yet he could not see or hear a single thing that bore the remotest resemblance to an enemy.

The boy stepped from a clump of trees in order that he might get a better look down the river. There was a crack on the farther shore, a flash of fire, and a bullet sang past his ear. He caught a hasty glimpse of a Mexican with a smoking rifle leaping to cover, and he, too, sprang back into the shelter of the trees.

It was the first shot of the great Texan struggle for independence!

Ned felt all of its significance even then, and so did Obed.

"You saw him?" asked the Maine man.

"I did, and I felt the breath of his bullet on my face, but he gained cover too quick for me to return his fire."

"The first shot was theirs and it was at you. It seems odd, Ned, that you should have been used as a target for the opening of the war."

"I'm proud of the honour."

"So would I be in your place."

Others came, drawn by the shot.

"Was it a Mexican?" asked the Ring Tailed Panther eagerly. "Tell me it was a Mexican and make me happy."

"You can be happy," said Obed. "It was a Mexican and he was shooting with what the law would define as an intent to kill. He sent a rifle bullet across the Guadalupe, aimed at our young friend, Edward Fulton. Ned did not see the bullet, but his sensitiveness to touch showed that it passed within an inch of his face."

Now the Ring Tailed Panther roared, but it was not between his shut teeth.

"By the great horn spoon, I'm glad!" he said, "All the waitin' an' backin' an' fillin' are over. We do our talkin' now with cannon an' rifles."

But not another shot was fired that night. It was merely some scout or skirmisher who had sent the fugitive bullet across the river, but it was enough. The Mexican intentions were now evident.

Ned went off duty toward morning and slept a few hours in one of the cabins. When he awoke he ate a hearty breakfast and went back to the river. About half of the eighteen had taken naps, but they were all gathered once more along the Guadalupe. Ned observed the Mexican camp and saw some movement there. Presently all the soldiers rode out, with Castenada at their head.

"They're comin' to our ford! By the great horn spoon, they are comin'!" roared the Ring Tailed Panther.

It seemed that he was right as the Mexicans were approaching at a gallop, making a gallant show, their lances glittering in the sun.

"Lay down, all!" said the Ring Tailed Panther. "The moment they strike the water turn loose with your rifles an' roar an' scratch an' claw!"

But when they were within one hundred yards of the Guadalupe the Mexicans suddenly sheered off. Evidently they did not like the looks of the Texan rifles which they could plainly see. The defenders of the fords uttered a derisive shout, and some of the Mexicans fired. But their bullets fell short, only a single one of them coming as far as the edge of the Guadalupe. The Texans did not reply. They would not waste ammunition in any such foolish fashion.

The Mexicans stopped, when four or five hundred yards away, and began to wave their lances and utter taunting shouts. The Texans only laughed, all except the Ring Tailed Panther, who growled.

"You see, Ned," said Obed, "that one charge does not make a passage. It appears to me that our friend Castenada does not want his uniform or himself spoiled by our good Texas lead. Now, I take it, we can rest easy awhile longer."

He lay down in the grass under the trees and Ned did likewise, but the Ring Tailed Panther would not be consoled. An opportunity had been lost, and he hurled strange and miscellaneous epithets at the distant Mexicans. Standing upon a little hillock he called them more bad names than Ned had ever before heard. He aspersed the character of their ancestors even to the eighth generation and of their possible descendants also to the eighth generation. He issued every kind of challenge to any kind of combat, and at last, red and panting, descended the hillock.

"Do you feel better?" asked Obed.

"I've whispered a few of my thoughts. Yes, I can re'lly say that the state of my health is improvin'."

"Then sit down and rest. It's never too late to try, try again. Remember that the day is long and the Mexicans may certainly have a chance."

The Ring Tailed Panther growled, but sat down.

In the afternoon the Mexicans again formed in line and trotted down toward the other ford, but as before they did not like the look of the Texan rifles and turned away, after shouting many challenges, brandishing lances and firing random shots. But the Texans contented themselves again with a grim silence, and the Mexicans rode back to their camp. The disgust of the Ring Tailed Panther was so deep that he could not utter a word. But Obed was glad.

"More men will come tonight," he said to Ned. "You know that requests for help were sent in all directions by the people of Gonzales, and if I know our Texans, and I think I do, they'll ride hard to be here. Castenada, in a way, is besieging us now, but—well, the tables may be turned and he'll turn with 'em."

Just at twilight a great shout arose from the women in the village. There was a snorting of horses, a jingling of spurs and embroidered bridle reins, and twenty lean, brown men, very tall and broad of shoulder, rode up. They were the vanguard of the Texan help, and they rejoiced when they found that the Mexican force was still on the west side of the Guadalupe.

Their welcome was not noisy but deep. The eighteen were now the thirty-eight, and tomorrow they would be a hundred or more. The twenty had ridden more than a hundred miles, but they were fresh and zealous for the combat. They went down to the river, and, in the darkness, looked at the Mexican camp fires, while the Ring Tailed Panther roared out his opinion.

"The Mexicans won't bring the fight to us," he said, "so we must carry it to them. They've galloped down here twice an' they've looked at the river an' they've looked at us, an' they've galloped back again. We can't let 'em set over there besiegin' us, we must cross an' besiege them an' get to roarin' an' rippin' an' clawin'.'"

"Tomorrow," said Obed, "more of our friends will be here and when we all get together we will discuss it and make a decision."

"Of course we'll discuss it!" roared the Ring Tailed Panther, "an' then we'll come to a decision, an' there's only one decision that we can come to. We'll cross the river an' mighty quick we'll make them Mexicans wish they'd chose a camp a hundred miles from Gonzales."

The others laughed, but after all, the Ring Tailed Panther had stated their position truly. Every man agreed with him. The watch at the river that night was as vigilant as ever, and the next morning parties of Texans arrived from different points, swelling their numbers to more than one hundred and fifty men, fully equaling the company of Castenada, after allowing for reinforcements received by the Mexican captain.

With one of the Texan troops came a quiet man of confident bearing, dressed like the others in buckskin, but with more authority in his manner. The Ring Tailed Panther greeted him with great warmth, shaking his hand and saying:

"John! John! We're awful glad you've come 'cause there's to be a lot of roarin' an' tearin' an' clawin' to be done."

The man smiled and replied in his quiet tones:

"We know it and that's why we've come. Now, I suggest that while we leave ten men at each ford, we hold a meeting in the village. Everything we have is at stake and as one Texan is as good as another we ought to talk it over."

"Who is he?" asked Ned of Obed.

"That's John Moore. He's been a great Indian fighter and one of the defenders of the frontier. I think it likely that he'll be our leader in whatever we undertake. He's certainly the man for the place."

"Oyez! Oyez!" roared the Ring Tailed Panther with mouth wide open. "Come all ye upon the common, an' hear the case of Texas against Mexico which is now about to be debated. The gentlemen representin' the other side are on the west shore of the river about a mile from here, an' after decidin' upon our argyment an' the manner of it we'll communicate it to 'em later whether they like our decision or not."

They poured upon the common in a tumultuous throng, the women and children forming a continuous fringe about them.

"I move that John Moore be made the Chairman of this here meetin' an' the leader in whatever it decides to do, 'specially as we know already what it's goin' to decide," roared the Ring Tailed Panther, "an' wherever he leads we will follow."

Ned said nothing, but his pulses were leaping. Perhaps the silent boy appreciated more than any other present that this was the beginning of a great epic in the American story. The young student, his head filled with completed dramas of the past, could look further into the future than the veteran men of action around him.

The debate was short. In truth it was no debate at all, because all were of one mind. Since the Mexicans had already fired upon them

168

and would not go away they would cross the river and attack Castenada. As Obed had predicted, Moore was unanimously chosen leader, the title of colonel being bestowed upon him, and they set to work at once for the attack.

Ned and Obed walked together to the cluster of oaks in which the two had spent so much time. Both were grave, appreciating fully the fact that they were about to go into battle.

"Ned," said Obed, "you and I have been through a lot of dangers together and we're not afraid to talk about dangers to come. In case anything should happen to you is there any word you want sent anybody?"

"To nobody except Mr. Austin. He's been very good to me here and in Mexico. I suppose I've got some relatives in Missouri, but they are so distant I've forgotten who they are, and probably they never knew anything about me. If it's the other way about, Obed, what word shall I send?"

"Nothing to nobody. I had a stepfather in Maine, who didn't like me, and my mother died five years after her second marriage. I'm a Texan, Ned, same as if I were born on this soil, and my best friends are around me. I'll live and die with 'em."

The two, the man and the boy, shook hands, but made no further display of feeling. The force was organised in the village, beyond the sight of the Mexicans, who were lounging in the grass, although they had posted sentinels. Every Texan was well armed, carrying a rifle, pistol and knife. Some had in addition the Indian tomahawk.

It was the first day of October and the coolness of late afternoon had come. A fresh breeze was blowing from the southwest. The little command, silent save for the hoof beats of their horses, rode down to the river. The women and children looked after them and they, too, were silent. A strange Indian stoicism possessed them all.

Ned and Obed were side by side. The breeze cooled the forehead and cheeks of the boy, but his pulses beat hard and fast. He looked back at Gonzales and he knew that he would never forget that little village of little log cabins. Then he looked straight before him at the yellow river, and the shore beyond, where the Mexican camp lay.

It was now seven o'clock and the twilight was coming.

"Isn't it late to make an attack?" he said to Obed.

"It depends on what happens. Circumstances alter battles. If we surprise them there'll be time for a fine fight. If they discover our advance it may be better to wait until morning."

They rode into the water twenty abreast, and made for the farther shore. So many horses made much splashing, and Ned expected bullets, but none came. Dripping, they reached the farther shore and went straight toward the Mexican camp. Then came sudden shouts, the flash of rifles and the singing of bullets. The Mexican sentinels had discovered the Texan advance.

Moore ordered his men to halt, and then he held a short conference with the leaders. It was very late, and they would postpone the attack until morning. Hence, they tethered their horses in sight of the Mexican camp, set many sentinels and deliberately began to cook their suppers.

It was all very strange and unreal to Ned. Having started for a battle it was battle he wanted at once and the wait of a night rested heavily upon his nerves.

"Take it easy, Ned," said Obed, who observed him. "Wilful haste makes woeful fight. Eat your supper and then you'd better lie down and sleep if you can. I'd rather go on watch toward morning if I were you, because if anything happens in the night it will happen late."

Ned considered it good advice and he lay down in his blankets, having been notified that he would be called at one o'clock in the morning to take his turn. Once more he exerted will to the utmost in the effort to control nerves and body. He told himself that he was now surrounded by friends, who would watch while he slept, and that he could not be surprised. Slumber came sooner than he had hoped, but at the appointed hour he was awakened and took his place among the sentinels.

Ned found the night cold and dark, but he shook off the chill by vigorous walking to and fro. He discovered, however, that he could not see any better by use, as the darkness was caused by mists rather than clouds. Vapours were rising from the prairie, and objects, seen through them, assumed thin and distorted shapes. He saw west of him and immediately facing him flickering lights which he knew were those of the Mexican camp. The heavy air seemed to act as a conductor of sound, and he heard faintly voices and the tread of horses' hoofs. They were on watch there, also.

He walked back and forth a long time, and the air continued to thicken. A heavy fog was rising from the prairie, and it became so dense that he could no longer see the fires in the Mexican camp. Everything there was shut out from the eye, but he yet heard the faint noises.

It seemed to him toward four o'clock in the morning that the noises were increasing, and curiosity took hold of him. But the sentinel on the left and the sentinel on the right were now hidden by the fog, and, since he could not confer with them at once, he resolved to see what this increase of noise meant.

He cocked his rifle and stole forward over the prairie. He could not see more than ten or fifteen yards ahead, but he went very near to the Mexican camp, and then lay down in the grass. Now he saw the cause of the swelling sounds. The Mexican force, gathering up its arms and horses, was retreating.

Ned stole back to the camp with his news.

"You have done well, Ned, lad," said Moore. "I think it likely, however, that they are merely withdrawing to a stronger position, but they can't escape us. We'll follow 'em, and since they wanted that cannon so badly we'll give 'em a taste of it."

The cannon, a six-pounder, had been brought over on the ferry-boat in the night and was now in the Texan camp.

"Ned," said Moore, "do you, Obed and the Panther ride after those fellows and see what they do. Then come back and report."

It was a dangerous duty, but the three responded gladly. They advanced cautiously through the fog and the Ring Tailed Panther roared softly.

"Runnin' away?" he said. "I'd be ashamed to come for a cannon an' then to slink off with tail droopin' like a cowardly coyote. By the great horn spoon, I hope they are merely seekin' a better position an' will give us a fight. It would be a mean Mexican trick to run clean away."

"The Mexicans are not cowards," said Ned.

"Depends on how the notion strikes 'em," said the Panther. "Sometimes they fight like all creation an' sometimes they hit it for the high grass an' the tall timber. There's never any tellin' what they'll do."

"Hark!" said Obed, "don't you hear their tramp there to our left?"

The three stopped and listened, and they detected sounds which they knew were made by the retreating force. But they could see nothing through the heavy white fog which covered everything like a blanket of snow.

"Suppose we ride parallel with them," whispered Ned. "We can go by the sounds and by the same means we can tell exactly what they do."

"A good idea," said Obed. "We are going over prairie which affords easy riding. We've got nothing to fear unless some lamb strays

171

from the Mexican flock, and blunders upon us. Even then he's more likely to be shorn than to shear."

They advanced for some time, guided by the hoof-beats from the Mexican column. But before the sun could rise and dispel the fog the sound of the hoof-beats ceased.

"They've stopped," whispered the Ring Tailed Panther, joyously. "After all they're not goin' to run away an' they will give us a fight. They are expectin' reinforcements of course, or they wouldn't make a stand."

"But we must see what kind of a position they have taken up," said Obed. "Seeing is telling and you know that when we get back to Colonel Moore we've got to tell everything, or we might as well have stayed behind."

"You're the real article, all wool an' a yard wide, Obed White," said the Ring Tailed Panther. "Now I think we'd better hitch our horses here to these bushes an' creep as close as we can without gettin' our heads knocked off. They might hear the horses when they wouldn't hear us."

"Good idea," said Obed White. "Nothing risk, nothing see."

They tethered the horses to the low bushes, marking well the place, as the heavy, white fog was exceedingly deceptive, distorting and exaggerating when it did not hide. Then the three went forward, side by side. Ned looked back when he had gone a half dozen yards, and already the horses were looming pale and gigantic in the fog. Three or four steps more and they were gone entirely.

But they heard the sounds again in front of them, although they were now of a different character. They were confined in one place, which showed that the Mexicans had not resumed their march, and the tread of horses' hoofs was replaced by a metallic rattle. It occurred to Ned that the Mexicans might be entrenching and he wondered what place of strength they had found.

The boy had the keenest eyes of the three and presently he saw a dark, lofty shape, showing faintly through the fog. It looked to him like an iceberg clothed in mist, and he called the attention of his comrades to it. They went a little nearer, and the Ring Tailed Panther laughed low between his shut teeth.

"We'll have our fight," he said, "an' these Mexicans won't go back to Cos as fine as they were when they started. The tall an' broad thing that you see is a big mound on the prairie an' they're goin' to make a stand on it. It ain't a bad place. A hundred Texans up there could beat off a thousand Mexicans."

They went a little nearer and saw that a fringe of bushes surrounded the base of the mound. Further up the Mexicans were digging in the soft earth with their lances as best they could and throwing up a breastwork. The horses had been tethered in the bushes. Evidently they felt sure that they would be attacked by the Texans. They knew the nature of these riders of the plains.

"I think we've seen enough," said Obed. "We'll go back now to Colonel Moore and the men."

They found their horses undisturbed and were about to gallop back to the main body with the news that the Mexicans were on the mound, when some Mexican sentinels saw them and uttered a shout. The three exchanged shots with them but knowing that a strong force would be upon them in an instant returned to their original intention and went at full speed toward the camp. It was lucky that the fog still held, as the pursuing bullets went wide, but Ned heard more than one sing. The Mexicans showed courage and followed the three until they reached the Texan camp. As Ned and his comrades dismounted they shouted that the Mexicans were on a hill not far away and were fortifying.

Moore promptly had his men run forward that bone of contention, the cannon, and a solid shot was sent humming toward those who had pursued the three. The heavy report came back in sullen echoes from the prairie, and the stream of fire split the fog asunder. But in a moment the mists and vapours closed in again, and the Mexicans were gone. Then the little army stood for a few moments, motionless, but breathing heavily. The cannon shot had made the hearts of everyone leap. They were inured to Indian battle and every kind of danger, but this was a great war.

"Boys," said Moore, "we are here and the enemy is before us."

A deep shout from broad chests and powerful lungs came forth. Then by a single impulse the little army rushed forward, led by Ned, Obed and the Ring Tailed Panther, who took them straight toward the mound. As they ran, the great Texan sun proved triumphant. It seemed to cleave the fog like a sword blade, and then the mists and vapors rolled away on either side, to right and to left of the Texans. The whole plain, dewy and fresh, sprang up in the light of the morning.

They saw the steep mound crowned by the Mexicans, and men still at work on the hasty trench. Again that full-throated cheer came from the Texans and they quickened their pace, but Captain Castenada came down from the mound and a soldier came with him bearing a white flag.

173

"Now, what in thunder can he want?" growled the Ring Tailed Panther to Ned and Obed. "Shorely he ain't goin' to surrender. He's jest goin' to waste our time in talk."

Deep disgust showed on his face.

"By waiting we will see," quoth Obed oracularly. "Now, Panther, don't you be too impatient. Remember that the tortoise beat the hare in the great Greek horse race."

Moore waved his hand and the Texans halted. Castenada on foot came on. Moore also dismounted, and, calling to Ned and Obed to accompany him, went forward to meet him. Ned and Obed, delighted, sprang from their horses, and walked by his side. The Ring Tailed Panther growled between his teeth that he was glad to stay, that he would have no truck with Mexicans.

Castenada, with the soldier beside him, came forward. He was rather a handsome young man of the dark type. As the two little parties met midway between the lines, the forces on the hill and on the plain were alike silent. Every trace of the fog was now gone, and the sun shone with full splendour upon brown faces, upon rifles and lances.

Castenada saluted in Mexican fashion.

"What do you want?" he asked in Spanish, which all understood.

"Your surrender," replied Moore coolly, "either that or the sworn adherence of you and your men to Texas."

Castenada uttered an angry exclamation.

"This is presumption carried to the last degree," he said. "My own honour and the honour of Mexico will not allow me to do either."

"It is that or fight."

"I bid you beware. General Cos is coming with a force that all Texas cannot resist, and after him comes our great Santa Anna with another yet greater. If the Texans make war they will be destroyed. The buffalo will feed where their houses now stand."

"You have already made war. Accept our terms or fight. We deal with you now. We deal with Cos and Santa Anna later on."

"There is nothing more to be said," replied Castenada with haughtiness. "We are here in a strong position and you cannot take us."

He withdrew and Moore turned back with Ned and Obed.

"I don't think he ever meant this parley for anything except to gain time," said Moore. "He's expecting a fresh Mexican force, but we'll see that it comes too late."

Then raising his voice, he shouted to his command:

"Boys, they've chosen to fight, and they are there on the hill. A

174

man cannot rush that hill with his horse, but he can rush it with his two legs."

The face of the Ring Tailed Panther became a perfect full moon of delight. Then he paled a little.

"Do you think there can yet be any new trick to hold us back?" he asked Obed anxiously.

"No," replied Obed cheerfully. "Time and tide wait for no Mexicans, and the tide's at the flood. We charge within a minute."

Even as he spoke, Moore shouted:

"Now, boys, rush 'em!"

For the third time the Texans uttered that deep, rolling cheer. The cannon sent a volley of grape shot into the cluster on the mound and then the Texans rushed forward at full speed, straight at the enemy.

The Mexicans opened a rapid fire with rifles and muskets and the whole mound was soon clothed in smoke. But the rush of the Texans was so great that in an instant they were at the first slope. They stopped to send in a volley and then began the rush up the hill, but there was no enemy.

The Mexicans gave way in a panic at the very first onset, ran down the slope to their horses, leaped upon them and galloped away over the prairie. Many threw away their rifles and lances, and, bending low on the necks of their horses, urged them to greater speed.

Ned had been in the very front of the rush, Obed on one side and the Ring Tailed Panther on the other. His heart was beating hard and there was a fiery mist before his eyes. He heard the bullets whiz past, but once more Providence was good to him. None touched him, and when the first tremors were over he was as eager as any of them to reach the crest of the mound, and come to grips with the enemy. Suddenly he heard a tremendous roar of disgust. The Ring Tailed Panther was the author of it.

"Escaped after all!" he cried. "They wouldn't stay an' fight, when they promised they would!"

"At least, the Mexicans ride well," said Obed.

Ned gazed from the crest of the mound at the flying men, rapidly becoming smaller and smaller as they sped over the prairie.

CHAPTER 16

THE COMING OF URREA

Many of the Texans were hot for pursuit, but Moore recalled them.

His reasons were brief and grim. "You will not overtake them," he said, "and you will need all your energies later on. This is only the beginning."

A number of the Mexicans had been slain, but none of the Texans had fallen, the aim of their opponents being so wild. The triumph had certainly been an easy one, but Ned perhaps rejoiced less than any other one present. The full mind again projected itself into the future, and foresaw great and terrible days. The Texans were but few, scattered thinly over a long frontier, and the rage of Cos and Santa Anna would be unbounded, when they heard of the fight and flight of their troops at Gonzales.

"Obed," he said to his friend, "we are victorious today without loss, but I feel that dark days are coming."

The Maine man looked curiously at the boy. He already considered Ned, despite his youth, superior in some ways to himself.

"You've been a reader and you're a thinker, Ned," he said, "and I like to hear what you say. The dark days may come as you predict, because Santa Anna is a great man in the Mexican way, but night can't come until the day is ended and it's day just now. We won't be gloomy yet."

After the fallen Mexicans had been buried, the little force of voluntary soldiers began to disperse, just as they had gathered, of their own accord. The work there was done, and they were riding for their own little villages or lone cabins, where they would find more work to do. The Mexicans would soon fall on Texas like a cloud, and every one of them knew it.

Ned, Obed and the Ring Tailed Panther rode back to Gonzales, where the women and children welcomed the victors with joyous acclaim.

The three sat down with others to a great feast, spread on tables under the shade of oaks, and consisting chiefly of game, buffalo, deer, squirrels, rabbits and other animals which had helped the early Texans to live. But throughout the dinner Ned and Obed were rather quiet, although the Ring Tailed Panther roared to his heart's content. It was Ned who spoke first the thought that was in the minds of both Obed and himself. Slowly and by an unconscious process he was becoming the leader.

"Obed," he said, "everybody can do as he pleases, and I propose that you and I and the Ring Tailed Panther scout toward San Antonio. Cos and his army are marching toward that town, and while the Texan

176

campaign of defence is being arranged and the leaders are being chosen we might give a lot of help."

"Just what I was thinking," said Obed.

"Jest what I ought to have thought," said the Ring Tailed Panther.

San Antonio was a long journey to the westward, and they started at twilight fully equipped. They carried their usual arms, two blankets apiece, light but warm, food for several days, and double supplies of ammunition, the thing that they would now need most. Gonzales gave them a farewell full of good wishes. Some of the women exclaimed upon Ned's youth, but Obed explained that the boy had lived through hardships and dangers that would have overcome many a veteran pioneer of Texas.

They forded the Guadalupe for the second time on the same day. Then they rode by the mound on which the Mexicans had made their brief stand. The three said little. Even the Ring Tailed Panther had thoughts that were not voiced. The hill, the site of the first battle in their great struggle, stood out, clear and sharp, in the moonlight. But it was very still now.

"We'll date a good many things from that hill," said Ned as they rode on.

They followed in the path of the flying Mexicans who, they were quite sure, would make for Cos and San Antonio. The Ring Tailed Panther knew the most direct course and as the moon was good they could also see the trail left by the Mexicans. It was marked further by grim objects, two wounded horses that had died in the flight, and then by a man succumbing, who had been buried in a grave so shallow that no one could help noticing it.

A little after midnight they saw a light ahead, and they judged by the motions that a man was waving a torch.

"It can't be a trap," said Obed, "because the Mexicans would not stop running until they were long past here."

"An' there ain't no cover where that torch is," added the Ring Tailed Panther.

"Then suppose we ride forward and see what it means," said Ned.

They cocked their rifles, ready for combat if need be, and rode forward slowly. Soon they made out the figure of a man standing on a swell of the prairie, and vigorously waving a torch made of a dead stick lighted at one end. He had a rifle, but it leaned against a bush beside him. His belt held a pistol and knife, but his free hand made no movement toward them, as the three rode up. The man himself was young, slender, and of olive complexion with black hair and eyes. He was a Mexican, but he was dressed in the simple Texan style. Moreover, there were Mexicans born in Texas some of whom, belonging to the Liberal party, inclined to the Texan side. This man was distinctly handsome and the look with which he returned the gaze of the three was frank, free and open.

"I saw you from afar," he said in excellent English. "I climbed the cottonwood there in order to see what might be passing on the prairie, and as my eyes happen to be very good I detected three black dots in the moonlight, coming out of the east. As I saw the men of Santa Anna going west as fast as hoofs would carry them I knew that only Texans could be riding out of the east."

He laughed, threw his torch on the ground and stamped out the light.

"I felt that sooner or later someone would come upon Castenada's track," he said, "and you see that I was not wrong."

He smiled again. Ned's impression was distinctly favourable, and when he glanced at Obed and the Ring Tailed Panther he saw that they, too, were attracted.

"Who are you, stranger?" asked Palmer. "People who meet by night in Texas in these times had best know the names and business of one another."

"Not a doubt of it," replied the young Mexican. "My name is Francisco Urrea, and I was born on the Guadalupe. So, you see, I am a Texan, perhaps more truly a Texan than any of you, because I know by looking at you that all three of you were born in the States. As for my business?"

He grew very serious and looked at the three one after another.

"My business," he said, "is to fight for Texas."

"Well spoke, by the great horn spoon," roared the Ring Tailed Panther.

"Yes, to fight for Texas," resumed young Urrea. "I was on my way to Gonzales to join you. I was too late for the fight, but I saw the men of Castenada, with Castenada himself at their head, flying across the prairie. I assure you there was no delay on their part. First they were here and then they were gone. The prairie rumbled with their hasty tread, their lances glittered for only a single instant, and then they were lost over the horizon."

He laughed again, and his laugh was so infectious that the three laughed with him.

"I know most people in Texas," rumbled the Ring Tailed Panther, "though there are some Mexican families I don't know. But I've heard of the Urreas, an' if you want to go with us an' join in tearin' an' chawin' we'll be glad to have you."

"So we will," said Ned and Obed together, and Obed added: "Three are company, four are better."

"Very well, then," said Urrea, "I shall be happy to become one of your band, and we will ride on together. I've no doubt that I can be of help if you mean to keep a watch on Cos. My horse is tied here in a clump of chaparral. Wait a moment and I will rejoin you."

He came back, riding a fine horse, and he was as well equipped as the Texans. Then the four rode on toward San Antonio de Bexar. They found that Urrea knew much. Cos himself would probably be in San Antonio within a week, and heavy reinforcements would arrive later. The three in return gave him a description of the fight at the mound, and they told how the Texans afterward had scattered for different points on the border.

They were not the only riders that night. Men were carrying along the whole frontier the news that the war had begun, that the death struggle was now on between Mexico and Texas, the giant on one side and the pigmy on the other.

But the ride of the four in the trail of Castenada's flying troop was peaceful enough. About three hours after midnight they stopped under the shelter of some cottonwoods. The Ring Tailed Panther took the watch while the other three slept. Ned lay awake for a little while between his blankets, but he saw that Urrea, who was not ten feet away, had gone sound asleep almost instantly. His olive face lighted dimly by the moon's rays was smooth and peaceful, and Ned was quite sure that he would be a good comrade. Then he, too, entered the land of slumber.

The Ring Tailed Panther stalked up and down, his broad powerful figure becoming gigantic in the moonlight. Belligerent by nature and the born frontiersman, he was very serious now.

He knew that they were riding toward great danger and he glanced at the face of the sleeping boy. The Ring Tailed Panther had a heart within him, and the temptation to make Ned go back, if he could, was very strong. But he quickly dismissed it as useless. The boy would not go. Besides, he was skilful, strong and daring.

The Ring Tailed Panther tramped on. Coyotes howled on the prairie, and the deeper note of a timber wolf came from the right, where there was a thick fringe of trees along a creek. But he paid no attention to them. All the while he watched the circle of the horizon, narrow by night, for horsemen. If they came he believed that his warning must be quick, because they were likely to be either Mexicans or Indians. He saw no riders but toward daylight he saw horses in the west. They were without riders and he walked to the nearest swell to look at them.

He looked down upon a herd of wild horses, many of them clean and fine of build. At their head was a great black stallion and when the Ring Tailed Panther saw him he sighed. At another time, he would have made a try for the stallion's capture, but now there was other business afoot.

The wind shifted. The stallion gave a neigh of alarm and galloped off toward the south, the whole herd with streaming manes and tails following close behind. The Ring Tailed Panther walked back to the cottonwoods and awoke his companions, because it was now full day.

"I saw some wild horses grazing close by," he said, "an' that means that nobody else is near. Mebbe we can ride clean to San Antonio without anybody to stop us."

"And gain great information for the Texans," said Urrea quickly. "Houston is to command the forces of Eastern Texas, and he will be glad enough to know just what Cos is doing."

"And glad will we be to take such news to him," said Ned. "I've seen him and talked with him, Don Francisco. He is a great man. And I've ridden, too, with Jim Bowie and 'Deaf' Smith and Karnes."

Urrea smiled pleasantly at Ned's boyish enthusiasm.

"And they are great men, too," he said, "Bowie, Smith and Karnes. I should not want any one of them to send his bullet at me."

"Jim Bowie is best with the knife," said the Ring Tailed Panther, "but I guess no better shots than 'Deaf' Smith and Hank Karnes were ever born."

"A horseman is coming," said Ned who was in advance. The boy had shaded his eyes from the sun, and his uncommonly keen sight had detected the black moving speck before any of the others could see it.

"It's sure to be a Texan," said Obed. "You won't find any Mexican riding alone on these plains just now."

They rode forward to meet him and the horseman, who evidently had keen eyes, too, came forward with equal confidence. It soon became obvious that he was a Texan as Obed had predicted. His length of limb and body showed despite the fact that he was on horseback, and the long rifle that he carried across the saddle bow was of the frontier type.

"My name is Jim Potter," he said as he came within hailing distance.

"You're welcome, Jim Potter," said the Ring Tailed Panther. "The long, red-headed man here on my right is Obed White, the boy is Ned Fulton; our young Mexican friend, who is a good Texan patriot, is Don Francisco Urrea, an' as for me, I'm Martin Palmer, better an' more properly known as the Ring Tailed Panther."

"I've heard of you, Panther," said Potter, "and you and your friends are just the people I want."

He spoke with great eagerness, and the soul of the Ring Tailed Panther, foreseeing an impending crisis of some kind, responded.

"What is it?" he asked.

"A crowd is gathering to march on Goliad," replied Potter. "The Mexican commander there is treating the people with great cruelty and he is sending out parties to harass lone Texan homes. We mean to smite him."

Potter spoke with a certain solemnity of manner and he had the lean, ascetic face of the Puritan. Ned judged that he was from one of the Northern States of New England, but Obed, a Maine man, was sure of it.

"Friend," said Obed, "from which state do you come, New Hampshire or Vermont? I take it that it is Vermont."

"It is Vermont as you rightly surmise," replied Potter, "and the accent with which you speak, if I mistake not is found only in Maine."

"A good guess, also," said Obed, "but we are both now Texans, heart and soul; is it not so?"

"It is even so," replied Potter gravely. Then he and Obed reached across from their horses and gave each other a powerful clasp.

"You will go with us to Goliad and help smite the heathen?" said Potter.

Obed glanced at his comrades, and all of them nodded.

"We were riding to San Antonio," said the Maine man, "to find out what was going on there, but I see no reason why we should not turn aside to help you, since we seem to be needed."

"Our need of you is great," said Potter in his solemn, unchanging tones, "as we are but few, and the enemy may be wary. Yet we must smite him and smite him hard."

"Then lead the way," said Obed. "It's better to be too soon than too late."

Without another word Potter turned his horse toward the south. He was tall and raw-boned, his face burned well by the sun, but he had an angularity and he bore himself with a certain stiffness that did not belong to the "Texans" of Southern birth. Ned did not doubt that he would be most formidable in combat.

After riding at least two hours without anyone speaking a word, Potter said:

"We will meet the remainder of our friends and comrades about nightfall. We will not exceed fifty, and more probably we shall be scarcely so many as that, but with the strength of a just cause in our arms it is likely that we shall be enough."

"When we charged at Gonzales they stayed for but one look at our faces," said the Ring Tailed Panther. "Then they ran so fast that they were rippin' an' tearin' up the prairie for the next twenty-four hours."

"I have heard of that," said Potter with a grave smile. "The grass so far from growing scarcely bent under their feet. Still, the Mexicans at times will fight with the greatest courage."

Here Urrea spoke.

"My friends," he said, "I must now leave you. I have an uncle and cousins on the San Antonio River, not far above Goliad. Like myself they are devoted adherents of the Texan cause, and it is more than likely that they will suffer terribly at the hands of some raiding party from Goliad, if they are not warned in time. I have tried to steel my heart and go straight with you to Goliad, but I cannot forget those who are so dear to me. However, it is highly probable that I can give them the warning to flee, and yet rejoin you in time for the attack."

"We hate to lose a good man, when there's rippin' an' tearin' ahead of us," said the Ring Tailed Panther.

"But if people of his blood are in such great danger he must even go," said Potter.

Urrea's face was drawn with lines of mental pain. His expressive eyes showed great doubt and anguish. Ned felt very sorry for him.

"It is a most cruel quandary," said Urrea. "I would go with you, and yet I would stay. Texas and her cause have my love, but to us of Mexican blood the family also is very, very dear."

His voice faltered and Latin tears stood in his eyes.

"Go," said Obed. "You must save your kin, and perhaps, as you hope, you can rejoin us in time."

"Farewell," said Urrea, "but you will see me again soon."

He spurred his horse, a powerful animal, and went ahead at a gallop. Soon he disappeared over the swells of the prairie.

"I hate to see him go," growled the Ring Tailed Panther. "Mexicans are uncertain even when they are on your side. But he's a big strong fellow, an' he'd be handy in the fight for which we're lookin'."

But he kept Ned's sympathy.

"He must save his people," said the boy.

Obed and Potter said nothing. At twilight they found the other men waiting for them in a thicket of mesquite, and the total, including the four, was only forty. But with Texan daring and courage they made straight for Goliad, and Ned did not doubt that they would have a fight. Life was now moving fast for him, and it was crowded with incident.

The troop in loose formation rode swiftly, but the hoofs of their horses made little sound on the prairie. The southern moon rode low, and the night was clear. They crossed two or three creeks, and also went through narrow belts of forest, but they never halted or hesitated. Potter and several others knew the way well, and night was the same as day to them.

At midnight Ned saw a wide but shallow stream, much like the Guadalupe. Trees and reeds lined its banks. Potter informed him that this was the San Antonio River, and that they were now below the town of Goliad, where they meant to attack the Mexican force.

"And if Providence favours us," said Potter, "we shall smite them quick and hard."

"Providence favours those who hit first and hard," said Obed, mixing various quotations.

The men forded the river, and, after a brief stop began to move cautiously through thickets of mesquite and chaparral toward the town, the lights of which they could not yet see. At one point the mesquite became so thick that Ned, Obed and the Ring Tailed Panther dismounted, in order to pick their way and led their horses.

Ned, who was in advance, heard a noise, as of something moving in the thicket. At first he thought it was a deer, but the sounds ceased suddenly, as if whatever made them were trying to seek safety in concealment rather than flight. Ned's experience had already made him skillful and daring. The warrior's instinct, born in him, was developing rapidly, and flinging his bridle to Obed he asked him to hold it for a moment.

Before the surprised man could ask why, Ned left him with the reins in his hand, cocked his rifle and crept through the mesquite toward the point whence the sounds had come. He saw a stooping shadow, and then a man sprang up. Quick as a flash Ned covered him with his rifle.

"Surrender!" he cried.

"Gladly," cried the man, throwing up his hands and laughing in a hysterical way. "I yield because you must be a Texan. That cannot be the voice of any Mexican."

Obed and the others came forward and the man strode toward them. He was tall, but gaunt and worn, until he was not much more than a skeleton. His clothing, mere rags, hung loosely on a figure that was now much too narrow for them. Two bloodshot eyes burned in dark caverns.

"Thank God," he cried, "you are Texans, all of you!"

"Why, it's Ben Milam," said Potter. "We thought you were a prisoner at Monterey in Mexico."

"I was," replied Milam, one of the Texan leaders, "but I escaped and obtained a horse. I have ridden nearly seven hundred miles day and night. My horse dropped dead down there in the chaparral and I've been here, trying to take a look at Goliad, uncertain about going in, because I do not know whether it is held by Texans or Mexicans."

"It is held by Mexicans at present," replied Potter, solemnly. "But I think that within an hour or two it will be held by Texans."

"If it ain't there'll be some mighty roarin' an' rippin' an' tearin'," said the Ring Tailed Panther.

"Give me a bite to eat and something to drink," said Milam; "and I'll help you turn Goliad from a Mexican into a Texan town."

Exhausted and nearly starved, he showed, nevertheless, the dauntless spirit of the Texans. Food and drink were given to him and the little party moved toward the town. Presently they saw one or two lights. Far off a dog howled, but it was only at the moon. He had not scented them. By and by the ground grew so rough and the bushes so thick that all dismounted and tethered their horses. Then they crept into the very edge of the town, still unseen and unheard. Potter pointed to a large building.

"That," he said, "is the headquarters of Colonel Sandoval, the commandant, and if you look closely you will see a sentinel walking up and down before the door."

"We will make a rush for that house," said the leader of the Texans, "and call upon the sentinel to yield."

They slipped from the cover and ran toward the house, shouting to the Mexican on guard to surrender. But he fired at them point blank, although his bullet missed, and a shot from one of the Texans slew him. The next moment they were thundering at the door of the house, in which were Sandoval and the larger part of his garrison. The door held fast, and shots were fired at them from the windows.

Some of the Texans ran to the neighbouring houses, obtained axes and smashed in the door. Then they poured in, every man striving to be first, and most of the Mexicans fled through the back doors or the windows, escaping in the darkness into the mesquite and chaparral. Sandoval himself, half dressed, was taken by the Ring Tailed Panther and Obed. He made many threats, but Obed replied:

"You have chosen war and the Texans are giving it to you as best they can. Our bullets fall on all Mexicans, whether just or unjust."

Sandoval said no more, but finished his interrupted toilet. It was clear to Ned, watching his face, that the Mexican colonel considered all the Texans doomed, despite their success of the moment. Sandoval was still in his quarters. His arms had been taken away but he suffered no ill treatment. Despite the rapid flight of the Mexican soldiers twenty-five or thirty had been taken and they were held outside. The Texans not knowing what to do with them decided to release them later on parole.

Ned was about to leave Sandoval's room when he met at the door a young man, perspiring, wild of eye and bearing all the other signs of haste and excitement. It was Francisco Urrea.

"I am too late!" he cried. "Alas! Alas! I would have had a share in this glorious combat! I should like to have taken Sandoval with my own hand! I have cause to hate that man!"

Sandoval was sitting on the edge of his bed, and the eyes of the two Mexicans flashed anger at each other, Urrea went up, and shook his hand in the face of Sandoval. Sandoval shook his in the face of Urrea. Wrath was equal between them. Fierce words were exchanged with such swiftness that Ned could not understand them. He judged that the young Mexican must have some deep cause for hatred of Sandoval. But the Ring Tailed Panther interfered. He did not like this trait of abusing a fallen foe which he considered typically Mexican.

"Come away, Don Francisco," he said. "The rippin' an' tearin' are over an' we can do our roarin' outside!"

He took Urrea by the arm and led him away. Ned preceded them. Outside he met Obed who was in the highest spirits.

"We've done more than capture Mexicans," he said. "It never rains but it turns into a storm. We've gone through the Mexican barracks and we've made a big haul here. Let's take a look."

Ned went with him, and, when he saw, he too exulted. Goliad had been made a place of supply by the Mexicans, and, stored there, the Texans had taken a vast quantity of ammunition, rounds of powder and lead to the scores of thousands, five hundred rifles and three fine cannon. Some of the Texans joined hands in a wild Indian dance, when they saw their spoils, and the eyes of Ned and Obed glistened.

"Unto the righteous shall be given," said Obed. "We've done far better tonight than we hoped. We'll need these in the advance on Cos and San Antonio."

"They will be of the greatest service," said Urrea who joined them at that moment. "How I envy you your glory!"

"What happened to you, Don Francisco?" asked Obed.

"I carried the warning to my uncle and his family," replied Urrea. "I was just in time. Guerrillas of Cos came an hour later, and burned the house to the ground. They destroyed everything, the stables and barns, and they even killed the horses and the cattle. Ah, what a ruin! I rode back by there on my way to Goliad."

The young Mexican pressed his hands over his eyes and Ned thrilled with sympathy.

"What became of your uncle and his family?" asked the boy.

"They rode north for San Felipe de Austin. They will be safe but they lose all."

"Never mind," said Obed, "we'll make the Mexicans pay it back, when we drive 'em out of Texas. I don't believe that any good patriot will suffer."

"Nevertheless," said Urrea, "my uncle is willing to lose and endure for the cause."

Ned slept half through the morning in one of the little *adobe* houses, and at noon he, Obed, the Ring Tailed Panther and others rode toward San Antonio. They slept that night in a pecan grove, and the next day continued their journey, meeting in the morning a Texan who informed them that Cos with a formidable force was in San Antonio. He also confirmed the information that the Texans were gathering from all points for the attack upon this, the greatest Mexican fortress in all Texas. Mr. Austin was commander-in-chief of the forces, but he wished to yield the place to Houston who would not take it.

Late in the afternoon they saw horsemen and rode toward them boldly. The group was sixty or eighty in number and they stopped for the smaller body to approach. Ned's keen eyes recognised them first, and he uttered a cry of joy.

"There's Mr. Bowie," he said, "and there are Smith and Karnes, too! They are all on their way to San Antonio."

He took off his hat and waved it joyously. Smith and Karnes did the same and Bowie smiled gravely as the boy rode up.

"Well, Ned," he said, "we meet again and I judge that we ride on the same errand."

"We do. To San Antonio."

"An' there'll be the biggest fight that was ever seen in Texas," said the Ring Tailed Panther, who knew Bowie well. "If Mexicans an' Texans want to get to roarin' an' rippin' they'll have the chance."

"They will, Panther," said Bowie, still smiling gravely. Then he looked inquiringly at Urrea.

"This is Don Francisco Urrea," said Obed. "He was born in Texas, and he is with us heart and soul. By a hard ride he saved his uncle and family from slaughter by the guerrillas of Cos, and he reached Goliad just a few minutes too late to take part in the capture of the Mexican force."

"Some of the Mexicans born in Texas are with us," said Bowie, "and before we are through at San Antonio, Don Francisco, you will have a good chance to prove your loyalty to Texas."

"I shall prove it," said Urrea vehemently.

"The place for the gathering of our troops is on Salado Creek near San Antonio," said Bowie, "and I think that we shall find both Mr. Austin and General Houston there."

Bowie was extremely anxious to be at a conference with the leaders, and taking Ned, Obed, the Ring Tailed Panther and a few others he rode ahead. Ned suggested that Urrea go too, but Bowie did not seem anxious about him, and he was left behind.

"Maybe he would not be extremely eager to fire upon people of his own blood if we should happen to meet the Mexican lancers," said Bowie. "I don't like to put a man to such a test before I have to do it."

Urrea showed disappointment, but, after some remonstrance, he submitted with a fair grace.

"I'll see you again before San Antonio," he said to Ned.

Ned shook his hand, and galloped away with the little troop, which all told numbered only sixteen. Bowie kept them at a rapid pace until sundown and far after. Ned saw that the man was full of care, and he too appreciated the importance of the situation. Events were coming to a crisis and very soon the Texans and the army of Cos would stand face to face.

They slept on the open prairie, and were in the saddle again before dawn. Bowie now curved a little to the North. They were coming into country over which Mexicans rode, and he did not wish a clash. But the Ring Tailed Panther was not sanguine about a free passage, nor did he seem to care.

"It's likely that the Mexican bands are out ridin'," he said. "Cos ain't no fool, an' he'll be on the lookout for us. There's more timber as you come toward San Antonio, an' there'll be a lot of chances for ambushes."

"I believe you are hoping for one," said Ned.

The Ring Tailed Panther did not answer, but he looked upon this young friend of his of whom he thought so much, and his dark face parted in one of the broadest smiles that Ned had ever seen.

"I ain't runnin' away from the chance of it," he replied.

They saw a little later a belt of timber to their right. Ned's experience told him that it masked the bed of a creek, probably flowing to the San Antonio River, and he noticed, although they were at some distance, that the trees seemed to be of unusually fine growth. This fact first attracted his attention, but he lost sight of it when he saw a glint of unusually bright light among the trunks. He looked more closely. Here again experience was of value. It was the peculiar kind of light that he had seen before, when a ray from the sun struck squarely on the steel head of a lance.

"Look!" he said to Obed and Bowie.

They looked, and Bowie instantly halted his men. The face of the Ring Tailed Panther suddenly lighted up. He too had good eyes, and he said in tones of satisfaction:

"Figures are movin' among the trees, an' they are those of mounted men with lances. Texans don't carry lances an' I think we shall be attacked by a Mexican force within a few minutes, Colonel Bowie."

"It is altogether probable," replied Bowie. "See, they are coming from the wood, and they number at least sixty."

"Nearer seventy, I think," said Obed.

"Whether sixty or seventy, they are not too many for us to handle,"

188

said Bowie.

The Mexicans had seen the little group of Texans and they were coming fast. The wind brought their shouts and they brandished their long lances. Ned observed with admiration how cool Bowie and all the men remained.

"Ride up in a line," said Bowie. "Here, Ned, bring your horse by me and all of you face the Mexicans. Loosen your pistols, and when I give the word to fire let 'em have it with your rifles."

They were on the crest of one of the swells and the sixteen horses stood in a row so straight that a line stretched across their front would have touched the head of every one. They were trained horses, too, and the riders dropped the reins on their necks, while they held their rifles ready.

It was hard for Ned to keep his nerves steady, but Obed was on one side of him and Bowie on the other, while the Ring Tailed Panther was just beyond Obed. Pride as well as necessity kept him motionless and taut like the others.

Doubtless the Mexicans would have turned, had it not been for the smallness of the force opposed to them, but they came on rapidly in a long line, still shouting and brandishing their weapons. Ned saw the flaming eyes of the horses, and he marked the foam upon their jaws. For what was Bowie waiting! Nearer they came, and the beat of the hoofs thundered in his ears. It seemed that the flashing steel of the lances was at his throat. He had already raised his rifle and was taking aim at the man in front of him, all his nerves now taut for the conflict.

"Fire!" cried Bowie, and sixteen rifles were discharged as one.

Not a bullet went astray. The Mexican line was split asunder, and horses and men went down in a mass. A few, horses and men, rose, and ran across the plain. But the wings of the Mexican force closed in, and continued the charge, expecting victory, now that the rifles were empty. But they forgot the pistols. Ned snatched his from the holster, and fired directly into the evil face of a lancer who was about to crash into him. The Mexican fell to the ground and his horse, swerving to one side, galloped on.

The pistols cracked all around Ned, and then, the Mexicans, sheering off, fled as rapidly as they had charged. But they left several behind who would never charge again.

"All right, Ned?" said the cheery voice of Obed.

"Not hurt at all," replied the boy. But as he spoke he gazed down at the face of the man who had tried to crash into him, and he shuddered. He knew that face. At the first glance it had seemed familiar, and at the second he had remembered perfectly. It was the face of the man who had struck him with the butt of a lance on that march in Mexico, when he was the prisoner of Cos. It seemed a vengeance dealt out by the hand of fate. He who had received the blow had given it in return, although not knowing at the time. Ned recognised the justice of fate, but he did not rejoice. Nor did he speak of the coincidence to anyone. It was not a thing of which he wished to talk.

"They're gone," said the Ring Tailed Panther, speaking now in satisfied tones. "They came, they stayed half a minute, an' then they went, but there was some rippin' an tearin' an' chawin'."

"Yes, they've gone, and they've gone to stay," said Bowie. "It was a foolish thing to do to charge Texans armed with rifles on the open prairie."

Ned was looking at the last Mexican as he disappeared over the plain.

CHAPTER 17

THE OLD CONVENT

The Texans gathered up the arms of the fallen Mexicans, except the lances for which they had no use, finding several good rifles and a number of pistols of improved make which were likely to prove of great value, and then they rode on as briskly as if nothing had happened.

The next day they drew near to San Antonio and entered the beautiful valley made by the San Antonio River and the creek to which the Mexicans gave the name San Pedro. Ned found it all very luxuriant and very refreshing to eyes tired of the prairies and the plains. Despite the fact that it was the middle of October the green yet endured in that southern latitude. Splendid forests still in foliage bounded both creek and river. They rode through noble groves of oak and tall pecans. They saw many fine springs spouting from the earth, and emptying into river and creek.

It was a noble land, but, although it had been settled long by Spaniard and Mexican, the wilderness still endured in many of its aspects. Now and then a deer sprang up from the thickets, and the wild turkeys still roosted in the trees. Churches and other buildings, many of massive stone adorned with carved and costly marbles, extended ten or twelve miles down the river, but most of them were abandoned and in decay. The Comanche and his savage brother, the Apache, had raided to the very gates of San Antonio. The deep irrigation ditches, dug by the Spanish priests and their Indian converts, were abandoned, and mud and refuse were fast filling them up. Already an old civilization, sunk in decay, was ready to give place to another, rude and raw, but full of youth and vigour.

It was likely that Ned alone felt these truths, as they reached the lowest outskirts of the missions, and stopped at an abandoned stone convent, built at the very edge of the San Antonio, where the waters of the river, green and clear, flowed between banks clothed in a deep and luxuriant foliage. Half of the troop entered the convent, while the others watched on the horses outside. It impressed Ned with a sense of desolation fully equal to that of the ancient pyramid or the lost city. Everything of value that the nuns had not taken away had been stripped from the place by Comanche, Apache or Lipan.

It was nearly night when they arrived at the convent. The Texan camp still lay some miles away, their horses were very tired, and Bowie decided to remain in the ruined building until morning. The main portion of the structure was of stone, two stories high, but there were some extensions of wood, from one of which the floor had been taken away by plunderers. It was Ned who discovered this floorless room and he suggested that they lead the horses into it, especially as the night was turning quite cold, and there were signs of rain.

"A good thought," said Bowie. "We'll do it."

The horses made some trouble at the door, but when they were finally driven in, and unsaddled and unbridled they seemed content. Two windows, from which the glass was long since gone, admitted an abundance of air, and Ned and several others, taking their big bowie knives, went out to cut grass for them.

On foot, Ned was impressed more than ever by the desolation and loneliness of the place. The grounds had been surrounded by an *adobe* wall, now broken through in many places. On one side had been a little flower garden, and on the other a larger kitchen garden. One or two late roses bloomed in the flower garden, but most of it had been destroyed by weather.

Ned and the others cut armfuls of grass in a little meadow, just beyond the adobe wall, and they hastened the work. They did not like the looks of the night. The skies were darkening very fast, and they saw occasional flashes of lightning in the far southwest. Ned looked back at the convent. It was now an almost formless bulk against the sombre sky, its most prominent feature being the cupola in which a bronze bell still hung.

The wind rose and cold drops of rain struck him. He shivered. It promised to be one of those raw, cold nights frequent in the southwest, and he knew that the rain would be chill and penetrating. He was glad that they had found the convent.

They gave the grass to the horses, and then they went into the main portion of the convent, where Bowie and the rest were already at work. Here the ruin was not so great, as the Spaniards had built in a solid manner, according to their custom. They found a large room, with an open fireplace, in which Ned would have been glad to see wood blazing, but Bowie did not consider it worth while to gather materials for a fire. Adjoining this room was a chapel, in which a pulpit, a desecrated image of the Virgin, and some frames without the pictures, yet remained. Anger filled Ned's heart that anyone should plunder and spoil such a place, and he turned sorrowfully away.

Back of the large rooms were workrooms, kitchen and laundry, all stripped of nearly everything. The narrow stairway that led to the upper floor was in good condition, and, when Ned mounted it, he saw rows of narrow little cell-like rooms in which the nuns had slept. All were bleak and bare, but, from a broken window at the end of the corridor, he looked out upon the San Antonio and the forests of oak and pecan. He could barely see the river, the night had grown so dark. The cold rain increased and was lashed against the building by a moaning wind. Once more Ned shivered, and once more he was glad that they had found the old convent. He was glad to return to the main room, where Bowie and the others were gathered.

The room had been lighted by two windows, facing the San Antonio and two on the side. They had been closed originally by shutters, which were now gone, but as the windows were narrow the driving rain did not enter far. One or two of the men, sharing Ned's earlier feeling, spoke up in favour of a fire. They wanted the cheerfulness that light and warmth give. But Bowie refused again.

"Not necessary," he said. "We are here in the enemy's country, and we do not want to give him warning of our presence. We met the lancers today, and we have no desire to meet them again tonight."

"Right," the Ring Tailed Panther roared gently to Ned. "When you're makin' war you must fight first an' take your pleasure afterward."

192

It was warm enough in the room and the open windows gave them all the air they needed. Every man, except those detailed for the guard, spread his blankets and went to sleep. Ned was on the early watch. He, too, would have liked sleep. He could have felt wonderfully fine rolled in the blankets with the cold rain pattering on the walls outside. But he was chosen for the first watch, and his time would come later.

Ned was posted at a broken door that led to the extension in which the horses were sheltered. The remaining sentinels, three in number, including the Ring Tailed Panther, were stationed in different parts of the building. The boy from his position in the broken doorway could see into the room where his comrades slept, and, when he looked in the other direction, he could also see the horses, some of which were now lying down.

It was all very still in the old convent. So deep was this silence that Ned began to fancy that he heard the breathing of his sleeping comrades. It was only fancy. The horses had ceased to stir. Perhaps they were as glad as the men that they had found shelter. But outside Ned heard distinctly the moaning of the wind, and the lashing of the cold rain against roof and walls.

On the right where the extension had been connected with the main building of stone there was a great opening, and through this Ned looked down toward the *adobe* wall and the San Antonio. He saw dimly across the river a dark waving mass which he knew to be the pecan trees, bending in the wind, but on his own side of the stream he could distinguish nothing. But he watched there unceasingly, save for occasional glances at the horses or his sleeping comrades.

He could now see objects very well within the room. He was able to count his comrades sleeping on the floor. He saw two empty picture frames on the wall, and, near by, a rope, which he surmised led to the bell in the cupola, and which some chance had allowed to remain there. Now and then Ned and one of his comrades of the watch met and exchanged a few words, but they always spoke in whispers, lest they awaken the sleeping men. After these brief meetings Ned would return to his watch at the opening.

The character of the night did not change as time trailed its slow length away. One solid black cloud covered the sky from horizon to horizon. The wind out of the southwest never ceased to moan, and the cold rain blew steadily upon the walls and roof of the ruined convent. It was not a night when either Texans or Mexicans would wish to be abroad, and, as the chill grew sharper and more penetrating, Ned wrapped one of his blankets about his shoulders.

As the night advanced, Ned's sense of oppression deepened. He felt once more as he had felt at the pyramid, that he was among old dead things. Ghosts could walk here as truly as they could walk on the banks of the Teotihuacan. Sometimes as the great cloud lightened the least bit he caught glimpses of the grass and weeds that grew between him and the broken adobe wall which was about fifteen yards away.

Only an hour more, and the second watch would come on. Ned began to think of his place on the floor, and of the deep and dreamless sleep that he knew would be his. Then he was attracted by a glimpse of the *adobe* wall. It seemed to him that he had seen a projection, where there was none before. He looked a second time, and he did not see it. Fancy played strange tricks at midnight in the enemy's country, and in the desolate silence.

Ned shook himself. Although a vivid imagination might be excusable at such a time even in a man, a veteran of many campaigns, he was essentially an uncompromising realist, and he wished to see facts exactly as they were. The work upon which he was engaged allowed no time for the breeding of fancy.

He looked again and there were two projections where he had seen only one before. They resembled knobs on the *adobe* wall, rising perhaps half a foot above it, and the sight troubled Ned. Was fancy to prove too strong, when he had drilled himself so long to see the real? Was he to be played with by the imagination, as if he had no will of his own?

He thought once of speaking to the sentinels at the other doors, but he could not compel himself to do it. They would laugh at him, and it is a bitter thing to be laughed at. So he kept his watch, and while he looked the projections appeared, disappeared and appeared once more.

He could stand it no longer. Putting his rifle under his blanket in order to keep the weapon dry he stepped out of doors, but flattened himself against the wall of the convent. The rain and wind whipped him unmercifully, and the cold ran through him, but he was resolved to see what was happening by the *adobe* wall. The projections were there and they had increased to four. They did not go away.

Ned was now convinced that it was not fancy. His mind had obeyed his will, and he was the true realist, no victim of the imagination. He was about to kneel down in the grass, and crawl toward the wall, when something caused him to change his mind. One of the projections suddenly extended a full yard above the wall, and resolved itself into the shape of a man. But what a man! The body from the waist up was naked, and above it rose a head crested with long hair, black and coarse. Other heads and bodies also savage and naked rose up beside it on the wall. Ned knew in an instant and springing back within the convent he cried:

"Comanches! Comanches! Up men, up!"

At the same moment, acting on impulse, he seized the rope that hung by the wall and pulled it hard, fast and often. Above in the cupola the great bronze bell boomed forth a tremendous solemn note that rose far over the moaning of the wind. From the *adobe* wall came a fierce yell, a sinister cry that swelled until it became a high and piercing volume of sound, and then died away in a menacing note like the howl of wolves. But Ned, impulse still his master, never ceased to pull the bell.

All the Texans were on their feet at once, wide awake, rifles in their hands.

"Lie down, men, by the doors!" cried Bowie, "and shoot anything that tries to come in. Ned, let go the rope, you are in range there, and lie down with us! But you have done well, boy! You have done well! You have saved us all from being scalped, and perhaps the booming of the big bell will bring us help that we may need badly!"

Ned threw himself on the floor just in time to avoid a bullet that sang in at the open doorway. But no other shot was fired then. The Comanches in silence sank back into the darkness and the rain. The defenders lay on the floor, guarding the doorways with open rifles. They could not see much, but they could hear well, and since Ned had given the warning in time every one of the little party felt that they held a fortress.

Ned's pulses were still leaping, but great pride was in his heart. It was he, not one of the veterans, who had saved them, and Bowie had instantly spoken words of high approval. He was now lying flat on the floor, but he looked out once more at the same opening. There were certainly no projections on the wall now, but he could not tell whether the Comanches were inside it or outside. If they crept to the sides of the convent's stone walls the riflemen could not reach them there. He wondered how many they were and how they had happened to raid so near to San Antonio at this time.

Then ensued a long and trying period of silence. Less experienced men than the Texans might have thought that the Comanches had gone away after the failure of their attempt at surprise, but these veterans knew better. Bowie and all of them were trying to divine their point of attack and how to meet it. For the present, they could do nothing but watch the doorways, and guard themselves against a sudden rush of their dangerous foe.

"Panther," said Obed White, "it seems to me that you're getting all the ripping and tearing and chawing that you want on this trip."

"It ain't what you might call monotonous," said the Ring Tailed Panther. "I agree to that much."

It had been fully an hour now since Ned had rung the great bell, and they had heard no noises save the usual ones of that night, the wind and the rain. He surmised at last that the Comanches had taken advantage of the war between the Texans and Mexicans to make a raid on the San Antonio Valley, expecting to gallop in, do their terrible work, and then be away. Doubtless it had not occurred to them that they would meet such a group as that led by Bowie and the Ring Tailed Panther.

"Ned," said Bowie, "creep across the floor there to that rope and ring the bell again. Ring it a long time. Either it will hurry the Comanches into action, or friends of ours will hear it. It's likely that all the Mexicans have now withdrawn into San Antonio, and that only Texans, besides this band of Comanches, are abroad in the valley."

Ned wormed himself across the floor, and then, pressing himself against the wall, reached up for the rope. A strange thought darted into his brain. He had a deep feeling for music, and he could play both the violin and piano. He could also ring chimes. He was keyed to the utmost, every pulse and vein surcharged with the emotion that comes from a desperate situation and a great impulse to save it.

The great bell suddenly began to peal forth the air of The Star Spangled Banner. Some of the notes may have gone wrong, there may have been errors of time and emphasis, but the old tune, then young, was there. Every man lying on the floor, every one of whom was born in the States, knew it, and every heart leaped. Elsewhere it might have been a commonplace thing to do, but there in the night and the storm, surrounded by enemies, on a vast and lonely frontier it was an inspiration. Every Texan in the valley who heard it would know that it was the call of a friend asking for help, and he would come.

Not a Texan moved, but they breathed heavily. Overhead the great bell boomed solemnly on, and Ned, his hand on the rope, put all his heart and strength into the task. A rifle cracked and a bullet entered the doorway, but it passed over the heads of the Texans, and flattened against the stone wall beyond. A rifle inside cracked in response, and a Comanche in the grass and weeds uttered a death yell.

"I was watchin' for just such a chance," said the Ring Tailed Panther in satisfied tones. "I saw him when he rose to fire. Just as you thought, Mr. Bowie, the bell is makin' their nerves raw, an' they feel that they must do somethin' right away."

"What a queer note that was in Ned's tune!" suddenly exclaimed Obed.

Bowie laughed.

"An angry Comanche shot at the bell and hit it. That's what happened," he said. "They can waste as many bullets as they please that way."

But the Comanches wasted no more just then. A noise came from the horses. The shots evidently had alarmed them, and they were beginning to stamp and rear. Four men, at the order of Bowie, slipped into the improvised stable and sought to quiet them. They also remained there to keep a guard at the broken windows. Ned, unconscious how much time had passed, was still ringing the bell.

"You can rest now, Ned," said Bowie. "That was a good idea of yours and you can repeat it later on. I'm thinking that the Comanches will soon act, if they are going to act at all."

But nothing occurred for nearly an hour, when the horses began to rear and stamp again. Two or three of them also uttered shrill neighs. Bowie, with Ned, Obed and the Ring Tailed Panther joined the four already in the improvised stable. The horses would not be quieted. It was quite evident that instinct was warning them of something that human beings could not yet detect.

Ned wondered. He put his hand on the neck of his own horse which knew him well, yet the beast trembled all over, and uttered a sudden shrill neigh. It was quite dark in the place, only a little light coming through the broken windows, yet Ned was quite sure that no Comanches had managed to get inside, and lie in hiding there.

A few moments later the Ring Tailed Panther uttered a fierce cry.

"I smell smoke!" he cried. "That's why the horses are so scared. The demons have managed to set fire to this place which is wood. That's why they've been so quiet!"

Ned, too, now smelt the strong odour of smoke, and a spurt of fire appeared at a crack between two of the planks at the far end of the place. The struggles of the horses increased. They were wild with fright.

Ned instantly recognised the danger. The burning wooden building would fill the stone convent itself with flame and smoke, and make it untenable. The sparks already had become many, and the odour of smoke was increasing. Their situation, suddenly become desperate, was growing more so every instant. But they were Texans, inured to every kind of danger. Bowie shouted for more men to come from the convent, leaving only five or six on guard there.

Then the Texans began to bring method and procedure out of the turmoil. Some held the horses, others, led by Bowie, kicked loose the light planks where the fire had been started, and hurled them outward. They were nearly choked by the smoke but they worked on.

The Comanches, many of whom were hugging the wall, shouted their war cry, and began to fire into the opening that Bowie and his men had made. They could not take much aim, because of the smoke, but their bullets wounded two Texans. Despite the danger Bowie and most of his men were still compelled to work at the fire. The room was full of smoke, and behind them the horses were yet struggling with those who held them.

The Ring Tailed Panther lay down and resting himself on one elbow took aim with his rifle. He was almost clear of the smoke which hung in a bank above him. Ned noticed him and imitated him. He saw a dusky figure outside and when he fired it fell. The Ring Tailed Panther did as well, and Obed joined them. While Bowie and the others were dashing out the fire, three great marksmen were driving back the Comanches who sought to take advantage of the diversion.

"Good! good!" cried Bowie, as they knocked out the last burning plank.

"That ends the fire," said Obed, "and now we've got a hole here which is not so deep as a well, nor so wide as a barn door, but I do not think it will suffice for our friends, the Comanches."

All the men turned their attention to the enemy, and, lying on the ground, they took as good aim as the darkness would permit. The Texan rifles cracked fast and, despite the darkness, the bullets often found the chosen targets. The Comanches had been shouting the war whoop continuously, but now their cries began to die, and their fire died with it. Never a very good marksman, the Indian was no match for the Texans, every one of whom was a sharpshooter, armed with a fine rifle of long range.

The Texans also fired from the shelter of the building, and, as the great cloud was now parting, letting through shafts from the moon, the Comanches were unable to find good hiding in the weeds and grass. The bullets pursued them there. No matter how low they lay the keen eye of some Texan searched them out, and sent in the fatal or wounding bullet. Soon they were driven to the shelter of the adobe wall, where they lay, and for a little while returned a scattering fire which did no harm. After it ceased no Comanche uttered a war whoop and there was silence again, save for the rain which now trickled down softly.

Bowie distributed sentinels at the openings, including the new one made by the fire, and then the Texans took count of themselves. They had not escaped unscathed. One lying on the floor had received a bullet in his head and had died in silence, unnoticed in the battle. Two men had suffered wounds, but they were not severe, and would not keep them from taking part in a renewal of the combat, should it come.

All this reckoning was made in the dusk of the old convent, and with the weariness of both body and soul that comes after a period of great and prolonged exertion. Within the two rooms that they had defended, the odour of burned gunpowder was strong, stinging throat and nostrils. Eddies of smoke hung between floor and ceiling. Many of the men coughed, and it was long before they could reduce the horses to entire quiet.

They wrapped the dead man in his blankets and laid him in the corner. They bound up the hurts of the others, as best they could and then, save for the watching, they relaxed completely. Ned, his back against the wall, sat with his friends Obed and the Ring Tailed Panther. He was utterly exhausted, and even in the dusk the men noticed it.

"Here, Ned," said Obed, "take a chew of this. You may not feel that you need it, but it will be a good thing for you."

He extended a strip of dried venison. Ned thanked him and ate, although he had not felt hungry. By and by he grew stronger, and then Bowie called to him.

"Ned," he said, "crawl across the floor again. Be sure you do not raise your head until you reach the wall. Then ring the bell, until I tell you to stop. I've a notion that somebody will come by morning. Boys, the rest of you be ready with your rifles. It was the bell before that brought on the attack."

Ned slid across the floor, and once more pulled the rope with the old fervour, sending the notes of the tune that he could play best far out over the valley of the San Antonio. But no reply came from the Comanches. They did not dare to rush the place again in the face of those deadly Texan rifles. They made no sound while the bell played on, but the Texans knew that they still lay behind the *adobe* wall, ready for a shot at any incautious head.

Ned rang for a full half hour, before Bowie told him to quit. Then he crept back to his place. He put his head on his folded blanket and, although not intending it, fell asleep, despite the close air of the place. But he awoke before it was dawn, and hastily sat up, ashamed. When he saw in the dark that half the men were asleep he was ashamed no longer. Bowie, who was standing by one of the doors, but sheltered from a shot, smiled at him.

"The sun will rise in a half hour, Ned," he said, "and you've waked up in time to hear the answer to your ringing of the bell. Listen!"

Ned strained his ears, and he heard a faint far sound, musical like his own call. It seemed to him to be the note of a trumpet.

"Horsemen are coming," said Bowie, "and unless I am far wrong they are Texans. Ring again, Ned."

The bell boomed forth once more, and for the last time. Clear and sharp, came the peal of the trumpet in answer. One by one the men awoke. The light was now appearing in the East, the gray trembling into silver. From the valley came the rapid beat of hoofs, a rifle shot and then three or four more. Bowie ran out at the door, and Ned followed him. Across the meadows the Comanches scurried on their ponies, and a group of white men sent a volley after them. Then the white men galloped toward the convent. Bowie walked forward to meet them.

"You were never more welcome, Fannin," he said to the leader of the group.

The man sprang from his horse, and grasped Bowie's hand.

"We rode as fast as we could, but I didn't know it was you, Jim," he said. "Some of our scouts heard a bell somewhere playing The Star Spangled Banner in the night. We thought they were dreaming, but they swore to it. So we concluded it must be a call for help and I came with the troop that you see here. We lost the direction once or twice, but the bell called us back."

"For that," said Bowie, "you have to thank this boy here, a boy in years only, a man in action, and two men in mind and courage. This is Ned Fulton, Colonel Fannin."

Ned blushed and expostulated, but Bowie took nothing back. Fannin looked about him curiously.

"You seem to have had something of a fight here," he said. "Down in the grass and weeds we saw several Comanches who will trouble no more."

"We had all we wanted," said Bowie, "and we shall be glad to ride at once with you to camp. I bring some good men for the cause, and there are more behind."

They buried the fallen man in the old flower garden, and then rode swiftly for the Texan camp on the Salado.

CHAPTER 18

IN SAN ANTONIO

It was a crisp October morning, and as he galloped through the fresh air, all of Ned's spirits came back to him. He would soon be with the full array of the Texans, marching forward boldly to meet Cos himself and all his forces. The great strain of the fight the night before passed away as he inhaled the sparkling air. The red came back to his cheeks, and he felt that he was ready to go wherever the boldest of the Texans led. The Ring Tailed Panther shared his emotions.

"Fine, isn't it?" said he. "Great valley, too, but it oughtn't to belong to the Mexicans. It's been going down under them for a long time. They haven't been able to protect it from Comanches, Apaches and Lipans. The old convent that we held last night had been abandoned for fear of the Indians, an' lots of other work that the Spaniards an' Mexicans did has gone the same way."

The beauty of the country increased, as they rode. Fine springs of cold water gushed from the hills and flowed down into the clear green stream of the San Antonio. The groves of oaks and pecans were superb, but they passed more desolate and abandoned buildings and crossed more irrigation ditches choked up with refuse.

Bowie called Ned up to his side, and had him to relate again all that he had seen and heard in Mexico.

"Mr. Austin is at the camp," said Fannin, "and he has been asking about you."

Ned's heart thrilled. There was a strong bond between him and the gentle, kindly man who strove so hard to serve both Texas and Mexico, and whom Santa Anna had long kept a prisoner for his pains.

"When will we reach the camp?" he asked Bowie.

"In less than a half hour. See, the scouts have already sighted us."

The scouts came up in a few moments, and then they drew near the camp. Ned, eager of eye, observed everything.

The heart of the camp was in the centre of a pecan grove, where a few tents for the leading men stood, but the Texans were spread all about in both groves and meadows, where they slept under the open sky. They wore no uniforms. All were in hunting suits of dressed deerskin or homespun, but they were well armed with the long rifles which they knew how to use with such wonderful skill. They had no military tactics, but they invariably pressed in where the foe was thickest and the danger greatest. They were gathered now in hundreds from all the Texas settlements to defend the homes that they had built in the wilderness, and Cos with his Mexican army did not dare to come out of San Antonio.

The Texans welcomed Bowie and his men with loud acclaim. Ned and his comrades unsaddled, tethered their horses and lay down luxuriously in the grass. Mr. Austin was busy in his tent at a conference of the leaders and Ned would wait until the afternoon to see him. Obed suggested that they take a nap.

"In war eat when you can and sleep when you can," he said. "Sleep lost once is lost forever."

"Obed has got some sense if he don't look like it," chuckled the Ring Tailed Panther. "Here's to followin' his advice."

Ned took it, too, and slept until the afternoon, when a messenger asked him to come to Mr. Austin's tent, a large one, with the sides now open. Obed was invited to come with him, and, as Ned stood in the door of the tent the mild, grave man advanced eagerly, a glow of pleasure and affection on his face.

"My boy! my boy!" he said, putting both hands on Ned's shoulders. "I was sure that I should never see you again, after you made your wonderful escape from our prison in Mexico. But you are here in Texas none the worse, and they tell me you have passed through a very Odyssey of hardship and danger."

Water stood in Ned's eyes. He rejoiced in the affection and esteem of this man, and yet Mr. Austin was very unlike the rest of the Texans. They were rough riders; men of the plains always ready to fight, but he, cultivated and scholarly, was for peace and soft words. He had used his methods, and they had failed, inuring only to the advantage of Santa Anna and Mexico. He had failed most honourably, but he looked very much worn and depressed. He was now heart and soul

202

for the war, knowing that there was no other resort, but for battle he did not feel himself fitted.

Ned introduced Obed as the companion of most of his wanderings, and Obed received a warm greeting. Then other men in the great tent came forward, and Ned, surprised, saw that one of them was Urrea, dressed neatly, handsome and smiling. But the boy was glad to see him.

"Ah, Senor Ned," he said, "you did not expect that I would get here before you. I came by another way, and I have brought information for our leader."

Ned met the other men in the tent, all destined to become famous in the great war, and then he gave in detail once more all that he knew of the Mexicans and their plans. Mr. Austin sat on a little camp stool, as he listened, and Ned noticed how pale and weak he looked. The boy's heart sank, and then flamed up again as he thought of Santa Anna. It was he who had done this. Away from Santa Anna and free from his magnetism he had a heart full of hatred for him. Yet it depressed him to see Mr. Austin who, good man, was obviously unfit for the leadership of an army, about to enter upon a desperate war against great odds.

When Ned was excused, and left the tent he found that Smith, Karnes and the rest of their force had come up. The camp which was more like that of hunters than of an army, was in joyous mood. Several buffaloes had been killed on the plains and the men had brought them in, quartered. Now they were cooking the meat over great fires, scattered about the groves. The younger spirits were in boisterous mood. Several groups were singing, and others were dancing the breakdowns of the border.

Ned and Obed were joined by the Ring Tailed Panther and then by Urrea. Ned felt the high spirits of the young Texans, but he did not join in the singing and dancing. He learned from Urrea that Houston would arrive in a day or two with more volunteers from Eastern Texas, and the young Mexican also told him something about San Antonio.

"Cos has a large force of regular troops," he said, "but he is alarmed. He did not think that the Texans were in such earnest, and that they would dare so much. Now, he is barricading the streets and building breastworks."

The Texans were so resolute and confident that the next day they sent a demand to Cos for his surrender. He would not receive it, and threatened that if another white flag appeared he would fire upon it.

A day or two later, Houston and the Eastern Texans arrived, and Ned, Obed, the Ring Tailed Panther and Urrea planned a daring adventure for the following night. They had heard how Cos was fortifying San Antonio, and as they expected the Texan army to make an assault they intended to see just what he was doing.

They made their way very cautiously toward the town, left on foot when the full dark had come. It was only four miles to San Antonio, and they could reach the line of Mexican sentinels within an hour. The Ring Tailed Panther was growling pleasantly between his teeth. He had tired of inaction. His was a character such as only the rough world of the border could produce. If he did not live by the sword he lived by the rifle, and since childhood he had been in the midst of alarms. Long habit had made anything else tiresome to him beyond endurance, but he was by nature generous and kindly. Like Obed he had formed a strong attachment for Ned who appealed to him as a high-souled and generous youth.

They made their way very cautiously toward the town, passing by abandoned houses and crossing fields, overgrown with weeds. Both the Ring Tailed Panther and Urrea knew San Antonio well, and Obed had been there once. They were of the opinion that the town with its narrow streets, stone and *adobe* houses was adapted particularly to defence, but it was of the greatest importance to know just where the new outworks were placed.

The four came within sight of Mexican lights about nine o'clock. The town was in the midst of gently rolling prairies and as nearly as they could judge these lights—evidently those of camp fires— were about a quarter of a mile from San Antonio. They were three in number and appeared to be two or three hundred yards apart. They watched a little while but they did not see any human outlines passing in front of the fires.

"They are learnin' caution," said the Ring Tailed Panther. "They are afraid of the Texan rifles, an' while those fires light up a lot of ground they keep their own bodies back in the shadow."

"Wise men," said Obed.

The Ring Tailed Panther looked his companions in the eye, one by one.

"We come out here for business," he said. "What we want to ac- quire is learnin', learnin' about the new defences of San Antonio, an' we'd feel cheap if we went back without it. Now, I don't care to feel cheap myself. Good, careful, quiet fellows could slip between them sentinels, an' get into San Antonio. I mean to do it. Are you game to go with me?"

"I am," said Urrea, speaking very quickly and eagerly.

"And I," said Ned.

"To turn back is to confess one's weakness," said Obed.

The Ring Tailed Panther roared gently, and with satisfaction.

"That's the talk I like to hear an' expected to hear," he said. "You boys ain't afraid of rippin' an' tearin', when it's in a good cause. There's pretty good grass here. We'll just kneel down in it, an' crawl."

The Panther marked a point about midway between the nearest two lights and they advanced straight for it on hands and knees, stopping at intervals of a hundred yards or so to rest, as that method of locomotion was neither convenient nor comfortable. As they drew near to the fires they saw the sentinels some distance back of them, and entirely in the shadow, pacing up and down, musket on shoulder. The four were now near enough to have been seen had they been standing erect, but they lay very close to the earth, while they conferred a moment or two.

"There's a patch of bushes between those two sentinels," whispered the Ring Tailed Panther, "an' I think we'd better creep by in its shelter. If either of the sentinels should look suspicious every one of us must lay flat an' hold his breath. We could handle the sentinels, but what we want to do is to get into San Antonio."

They continued their slow and tiresome creeping. Only once did they stop, and then it was because one of the sentinels paused in his walk and took his musket from his shoulder. But it was only to light a cigarette and, relieved, they crept on until they were well beyond the fires, and within the ring of sentinels. Then at the signal of the Ring Tailed Panther they rose to their feet, and stretched their cramped limbs.

"It is certainly good," whispered Obed, "to stand up on two legs again and walk like a man."

They were now very near to the town and they saw the dark shapes of houses, in some of which lights burned. It was the poorer portion of San Antonio, where the Mexican homes were mostly huts or *jacals*, made of *adobe*, and sometimes of mere mud and wattles. As all the four spoke Spanish, they advanced, confident in themselves, and the protecting shadows of the night. A dog barked at them, but Obed cursed him in good, strong Mexican, and he slunk away. Two *peons* wrapped to the eyes in *serapes* passed them but Obed boldly gave them the salutations of the night and they walked on, not dreaming that the dreaded Texans were by.

Fifty yards further they saw a long earthwork, with the spades and shovels lying beside it, as if the Mexicans expected to resume work there in the morning. Toward the north they saw another such defence but they did not go very near, as Mexican soldiers were camped beside it. But Ned retained a very clear idea of the location of the two earthworks.

Then they curved in toward the more important portion of the town, the centre of which was two large squares, commonly called Main Plaza and Military Plaza, separated only by the church of San Fernando. Here were many houses built heavily of stone in the Spanish style. They had thick walls and deep embrasured windows. Often they looked like and were fortresses.

Ned and his comrades were extremely anxious to approach those squares, but the danger was now much greater. They saw barricades on several important streets and many soldiers were passing. They learned from a *peon* that both the squares and many other open places also were filled with the tents of the soldiers.

Ned, Obed and the Ring Tailed Panther having seen so much were eager to see more, but Urrea hung back. He thought they should return with the information they had obtained already, and not risk the loss of everything by capture, but the Ring Tailed Panther was determined.

"I know San Antonio by heart," he said, "an' there's somethin' I want to see. Down this street is the house of the Vice-Governor, Veramendi, and I want to see what is going on there. If the rest of you feel that the risk ain't justified you can turn back, but I'm goin' on."

"If you go I'm going with you," said Ned.

"Me, too," said Obed.

Urrea shrugged his shoulders.

"Very well," he said. "It's against my judgment, but I follow."

They had pulled their slouch hats down over their faces, in the Mexican style, and they handled their rifles awkwardly, after the fashion of Mexican recruits. The Ring Tailed Panther led boldly down the street, until they came to the stone house of Veramendi. Lights shone from the deep embrasured windows of both the first and second floors. The Ring Tailed Panther saw a small door in the stone wall, and he pushed it open.

"Come in! Come quick!" he said to his comrades.

His tone was so sharp and commanding that they obeyed him by impulse, and he quickly closed the door behind the little party. They stood in a small, dark alley that ran beside the house and they heard the sound of music. Crouching against the wall they listened, and heard also the sounds of laughter and feminine voices.

The Ring Tailed Panther grinned in the darkness.

"Some kind of a *fandango* is goin' on," he said. "It's just like the Mexicans to dance and sing at such a time. I wouldn't be s'prised if Cos himself was here, an' I mean to see."

He led the way down the little alley, which was roughly paved with stone, and, as they advanced, the sounds of music and laughter increased. Unquestionably Governor Veramendi was giving a ball, and Ned did not doubt that the Panther's surmise about the presence of Cos would prove correct.

They found a little gate opening from the alley into a large patio or enclosed court. This gate, like the first, was not locked and the Ring Tailed Panther pushed it open also. The patio was filled with palms, flowering plants and a dense shrubbery.

The Ring Tailed Panther again led boldly on, and entered the patio, hiding instantly among the palms and flowers. The others followed and did likewise. Ned quivered with excitement. He knew that the danger was great. He knew also that if they lay close and waited they were likely to hear what was worth hearing.

The boy was in a dense mat of shrubbery. To his right was Obed and to his left were the Ring Tailed Panther and Urrea. He saw that the patio was faced on three sides by *piazzas* or porticos, from which wide doors opened into the house. He heard the music now as clearly as if it were at his side. It was the music of a full band, and it was played with a mellow, gliding rhythm. He saw, also, officers in brilliant uniform and handsome women, as in the dance they passed and repassed the open doors. It was Spanish, Mexican to the core, full of the South, full of warmth and colour. The lean, brown Texans crouching in the shrubbery furnished a striking contrast.

While they waited, several officers and ladies came out on the *piazzas*, ate ices and drank sweet drinks. They were so near that the four easily heard all they said. It was mostly idle chatter, high-pitched compliments, allusions to people in the distant City of Mexico, and now and then a jest at the expense of the Texans. Ned realised that many of the younger Mexicans did not take the siege of San Antonio seriously. They could not understand how a strong city, held by an army of Mexican regulars, could have anything to fear from a few hundred Texan horsemen, mostly hunters in buckskin.

The music began again and the officers and women went in, but presently several older men, also in uniform, came out. Ned instantly recognised in the first the square figure and the dark, lowering face of Cos.

"De La Garcia, Ugartchea, Veramendi," whispered the Ring Tailed Panther, indicating the others. "Now we may hear something."

Cos stood at the edge of the *piazza* and his face was troubled. He held in his hand a small cane, with which he cut angrily at the flowers. The others regarded him uneasily, but for a while he said nothing. Ned hardly breathed, so intense was his interest and curiosity, but when Cos at last spoke his disappointment was great.

The general complimented Veramendi on his house and hospitality, and the vice-governor thanked him in ornate sentences. Some more courtesies were exchanged, but Cos continued to cut off the heads of the flowers with his cane, and Ned knew now that they had come from the ballroom to talk of more important things. Meanwhile, the music flowed on. It was the swaying strains of the dance, and it would have been soothing to anyone, whose mind was not forced elsewhere. The flowers and the palms rippled gently under a light breeze, but Ned did not hear them. He was waiting to hear Cos speak of what was in the mind of himself and the other men on the *piazza*, the same things that were in the minds of the Texans in the shrubbery.

"Have you any further word from the Texan *desperadoes*, general?" asked Veramendi, at last.

Swish went the general's cane, and a flower fell from its stem.

"Nothing direct," he replied, his voice rising in anger.

"They have not sent again demanding my surrender knowing that a messenger would be shot. The impudence of these border horsemen passes all belief. How dare a few hundred such men undertake to besiege us here in San Antonio? What an insult to Mexico!"

"But they can fight," said Ugartchea. "They ride and shoot like demons. They will give us trouble."

"I know it," said Cos, "but the more trouble they make us the more they shall suffer. It was an evil day when the first American was allowed to come into Texas."

"Yet they will attack us here," persisted Ugartchea, "They have driven our men off the prairies. Our lances are not a match for their rifles. Your pardon, general, but it will be wise for us to fortify still further."

Cos frowned and made another wicked sweep with the cane. But he said:

"What you say is truth, Colonel Ugartchea, but with qualifications. Our men are not a match for them on the open prairie, but should they attack us here in the city they will be destroyed."

Then he asked further questions about the fortifications, and Ugartchea, who seemed to be in immediate charge, began to repeat the details. It was for this that the Texans had come into the patio, and Ned leaned forward eagerly. He saw Obed on one side of him and the Ring Tailed Panther on the other do the same. Suddenly there was a noise as of something falling in the shrubbery, and then a sharp whistle. The men on the *piazza* instantly looked in the direction of the hidden Texans. Cos and Ugartchea drew pistols.

The Ring Tailed Panther acted with the greatest promptness and decision.

"We must run for it, boys," he exclaimed in a loud whisper. "Something, I don't know what, has happened to warn them that we are here. Keep your heads low."

Still partly hidden by the palms and flowers they ran for the gate. Cos and Veramendi fired at the flitting forms and shouted for soldiers. Ned felt one of the bullets scorch the back of his hand, but in a few moments he was out of the gate and in the little dark alley. The Ring Tailed Panther was just before him, and Obed was just behind. The Panther, instead of running toward the street continued up the alley which led to a large building of *adobe*, in the rear of the governor's house.

"It's a stable and storehouse," said the Ring Tailed Panther, "an' we'll hide in it while the hunt roars on through the city."

He jerked open a door, and they rushed in. Ned in the dusk saw some horses eating in their stalls, and he also saw a steep ladder leading to lofts above. The Ring Tailed Panther never hesitated, but ran up the ladder and Ned followed sharply after him. He heard Obed panting at his heels.

The lofts contained dried maize and some vegetables, but they were mostly filled with hay. The fugitives plunged into the hay and pulled it around them, until only their heads and the muzzles of their rifles protruded. They lay for a few moments in silence, save for the sound of their own hard breathing, and then Ned suddenly noticed something. They were only three!

"Why, where is Urrea?" he exclaimed.

"Yes, where in thunder is Don Francisco?" said the Ring Tailed

Panther in startled tones.

Urrea was certainly missing, and no one could tell when they had lost him. Their flight had been too hurried to take any count of numbers. There could be only one conclusion. Urrea had been taken in the patio. The Ring Tailed Panther roared between his teeth, low but savagely.

"I don't like many Mexicans," he said, "but I got to like Don Francisco. The Mexicans have shorely got him, an' it will go 'specially hard with him, he bein' of their own race."

Ned sighed. He did not like to think of Don Francisco at the mercy of Cos. But they could do nothing, absolutely nothing. To leave the hay meant certain capture within a few minutes. Already they heard the sounds of the hunt, the shouts of soldiers and the mob, of men calling to one another. Through the chinks in the wall they saw the light of torches in the alley. They lay still for a few minutes and then the noise of the search drifted down toward the plazas. The torches passed out of the alley.

"Did you hear that whistle just before Cos and Ugartchea fired?" asked Ned.

"I did," replied Obed. "I don't understand it, and what I don't understand bothers me."

The Ring Tailed Panther growled, and his growl was the most savage that Ned had ever heard from him. The growl did not turn into words for at least a minute. Then he said:

"I'm like you, Obed; I hate riddles, an' this is the worst one that I was ever mixed up with. Somethin' fell in the shrubbery; then came the whistle, the Mexicans shot, away we went, lickety split, an' now we're here. That's all I know, an' it ain't much."

"I wonder if we'll ever find out," said Ned.

"Doubtful," replied the Ring Tailed Panther. "I'm afeard, boys, they won't waste much time on Urrea, he bein' a spy an' of their own blood, too. It's war an' we've got to make the best of it."

But Ned could not make very well of it. A fugitive hidden there in the hay and the dark, the fate of Urrea seemed very terrible to him. The three sank into silence. Occasionally they heard cries from distant parts of the town, but the hunt did not seem to come back toward them. Ned was thankful that the Ring Tailed Panther had been so ready of wit. The Mexicans would not dream that the Texans were hiding in the vice-governor's own barn, just behind the vice-governor's own house. He made himself cosy in the hay and waited.

After about an hour, the town turned quiet, and Ned inferred that the hunt was over. The Mexicans, no doubt, would assume that the three had escaped from San Antonio, and they would not dare to hunt far out on the prairies. But what of Urrea! Poor Urrea! Ned could not keep from thinking of him, but think as hard as he could he saw no way to find out about his fate. Perhaps the Ring Tailed Panther was right. They would never know.

The three did not stir for a long time. Ned felt very comfortable in the hay. The night was cold without, but here he was snug and warm. He waited for those older and more experienced than himself to decide upon their course and he knew that Obed or the Ring Tailed Panther would speak in time. He was almost in a doze when Obed said that it must be about one o'clock in the morning.

"You ain't far wrong," said the Ring Tailed Panther, "but I'd wait at least another hour. That ball will be over then, if we didn't break it up when we were in the garden."

They waited the full hour, and then they stole from the hay. Veramendi's house was silent and dark, and they passed safely into the street. Ned had a faint hope that Urrea would yet appear from some dark hiding place, but there was no sign of the young Mexican.

They chose the boldest possible course, thinking that it would be safest, claiming to one soldier whom they passed that they were sentinels going to their duty at the farthest outposts. Luck, as it usually does, came to the aid of courage and skill, and they reached the outskirts of San Antonio, without any attempt at interference.

Once more, after long and painful creeping, they stole between the sentinels, took mental note of the earthworks again, and also a last look at the dark bulk that was the town.

"Poor Urrea!" said Ned.

"Poor Urrea," said Obed. "I wonder what in the name of the moon and the stars gave the alarm!"

"Poor Urrea!" said the Ring Tailed Panther. "This is the worst riddle I ever run up ag'inst an' the more I think about it the more riddlin' it gets."

The three sighed together and then sped over the prairie toward the camp on the Salado.

CHAPTER 19

THE BATTLE BY THE RIVER

It was not yet daylight when they approached the Texan camp. Despite the fact that the Texan force was merely a band of volunteer soldiers there was an abundance of sentinels and they were halted when they were within a half mile of the Salado. But they were recognised quickly, and they passed within the lines, where, in the first rosy shoot of the dawn, they saw Bowie going the rounds of the outposts.

"What!" he exclaimed. "Back already! Then you did not get into the town!"

"We went right into it. We split it wide open," said the Ring Tailed Panther.

Bowie's blue eyes glittered.

"But you are only three," he said. "Where is Urrea?"

"We lost him an' we don't know how it happened. We know that he's gone, an' that's all."

Bowie took them to Mr. Austin's tent, where they told to him, Houston, Fannin and the others all that they had seen in San Antonio. In view of the fact, now clearly proved, that Cos was fortifying night and day, Bowie and all the more ardent spirits urged a prompt attack, but Mr. Austin, essentially a man of peace, hung back. He thought their force too small. He was confirmed, too, in the belief of his own unfitness to be a leader in war.

"General," he said, turning to Houston, "you must take the command here. It would be impossible to find one better suited to the place."

But Houston shook his head. He would not agree to it. Able and ambitious, he refused, nevertheless. Perhaps he did not yet understand the full fighting power of the Texans, and he feared to be identified with failure, in case they made the assault upon San Antonio.

When Ned and his comrades withdrew from the tent they went to one of the breakfast fires, where they ate broiled strips of buffalo and deer, and drank coffee. Then Ned rolled in his blankets, and slept under an oak tree. When he awoke about noon he sprang to his feet with a cry of joy and surprise. Urrea was standing beside him, somewhat pale, and with his left hand in a sling, but the young Mexican himself, nevertheless. Ned seized his right hand and gave it a powerful grip.

"We thought you as good as dead, Don Francisco," he said. "We were sure that you had been taken by Cos."

"I thought both things myself for a few wild moments," said Urrea, smiling. "When we rushed from the patio one of the bullets grazed me, but in my excitement as we passed the gate I ran down the alley toward the street, instead of turning in toward the barn, as I have since learned from Mr. White that you did. My wrist was grazed by one of the bullets, fired from the *piazza*, but fortunately I had the presence of mind to wrap it in the *serape* that I wore.

"When I reached the street there was much excitement and many soldiers running about, but being a Mexican it was easy for me to pass unsuspected in the crowd. I reached the home of a relative, at heart a sympathiser with Texas and liberty, where my wound was bound up, and where I lay hidden until morning, when I was smuggled out of the town. Then I made my way among the oaks and pecans, until I came here to our camp on the Salado. I had inquired for you during the night, and, not hearing any news of your capture, I was sure that you were in hiding as I was, and when I came here my best hopes were confirmed by the news of your complete escape. Mr. White has already given me all the details. We have been very lucky indeed, and we should be thankful."

"We are! We truly are!" exclaimed Ned, grasping his hand again.

The news brought by Ned and his comrades was so important that the Texans could not be restrained. A few mornings later Bowie called upon the boy, Obed and the Ring Tailed Panther for a new service.

"Mr. Austin has told me to take a strong party," he said, "and scout up to the very suburbs of San Antonio, because we are going to choose a new and closer position. There are to be ninety of us, including you three, 'Deaf' Smith and Henry Karnes, and we are to retire if the Mexicans undertake an attack upon us, that is, if we have time—you understand, if we have time."

Ned saw Bowie's big eyes glitter, and he understood. The party, the envy of all the others, rode out of the camp in the absence of Urrea. Bowie had not asked him, as he did not seem to fancy the young Mexican, but Ned put it down to racial prejudice. Urrea had not been visible when they started, but Ned thought chagrin at being ignored was the cause of it. Fannin also went along, associated with Bowie in the leadership, but Bowie was the animating spirit. They rode directly toward San Antonio, and, as the distance was very short, they soon saw Mexican sentinels on horseback, some carrying lances and some with rifles or muskets. They would withdraw gradually at the appearance of the Texans, keeping just out of gunshot, but always watching these dangerous horsemen whom they had learned to fear. The Texans were near enough to see from some points the buildings of the town, and the veins of the Ring Tailed Panther swelled with ambition.

"Ned," he said to the boy who rode by his side, "if Bowie would only give the word we would gallop right into town, smashing through the Mexicans."

"We might gallop into it," said Ned, laughing, "but we couldn't gallop out again. No, no, Panther, we mustn't forget that the Mexicans can fight. Besides, Bowie isn't going to give the word."

"No, he ain't," said the Ring Tailed Panther with a sigh, "an' we won't get the chance to make one of the finest dashes ever heard of in war."

"He who doesn't dash but rides away will live to dash another day," said Obed White oracularly.

They rode on in a half circle about the town, keeping a fairly close array, every man sitting his saddle erect and defiant. It seemed to Ned that they were issuing a challenge to the whole army of Cos, and he enjoyed it. It appealed to his youthful spirit of daring. They practically said to the Mexican army in the town: "Come out and fight us if you dare!"

But the Mexicans did not accept the challenge. Save for the little scouting parties that always kept a watch at a safe distance they remained within their entrenchments. But Bowie and Fannin were able to take a look at the fortifications, confirming in every respect all that Ned and his comrades had told them.

They ate in the saddle at noon, having provided themselves with rations when they started, and then rode back on their slow half circle about the town, Mexican scouts riding parallel with them on the inner side of the circle, five hundred yards away. The Texans said little, but they watched all the time.

It made a powerful appeal to Ned, who had been a great reader, and whose mind was surcharged with the old romances. It seemed to him that his comrades and he were like knights, riding around a hostile city and issuing a formal challenge to all who dared to meet them. He was proud to be there in such company. The afternoon waned. Banks of vapour, rose and gold, began to pile up in the southwest, their glow tinting the earth with the same colours. But beauty did not appeal just then to the Ring Tailed Panther, who began to roar.

"A-ridin', an' a-ridin'," he said, "an' nothin' done. Up to San Antonio an' back to camp, an' things are just as they were before."

"A Texas colonel rode out on the prairie with ninety men, and then rode back again," said Obed.

"But we are not going back again!" cried Ned joyfully.

Bowie, who was in the lead, suddenly turned his horse away from the camp and rode toward the river. The others followed him without a word, but nearly every man in the company drew a long breath of satisfaction. Ned knew and all knew that they were not going back to camp that night.

Ned eagerly watched the leader. They rode by the Mission Concepcion, passed through a belt of timber and came abruptly to the river, where Bowie called a halt, and sprang from his horse. Ned leaped down also, and he saw at once the merits of the position into which Bowie had led them. They were in a horseshoe or sharp bend of the river, here a hundred yards in width. The belt of thick timber curved on one side while the river coiled in a half-circle about them and in front of the little tongue of land on which they stood, the bank rose to a height of eighteen feet, almost perpendicular. It was a secluded place, and, as no Mexicans had been following them in the course of the last hour, Ned believed that they might pass a peaceful night there. But the Ring Tailed Panther had other thoughts, although, for the present, he kept them to himself.

They tethered the horses at the edge of the wood, but where they could reach the grass, and then Bowie placed numerous pickets in the wood through which an enemy must come, if he came. Ned was in the first watch and Obed and the Ring Tailed Panther were with him. Ned stood among the trees at a point where he could also see the river, here a beautiful, clear stream with a greenish tint. He ate venison from his knapsack as he walked back and forth, and he watched the last rays of the sun, burning like red fire in the west, until they went out and the heavy twilight came, trailing after it the dark.

Ned's impression of medievalism that he had received in the day when they were riding about San Antonio continued in the night. They had gone back centuries. Hidden here in this horseshoe, water on one side and wood on the other, they seemed to be in an absolutely wild and primitive world. Centuries had rolled back. His vivid imagination made the forest about them what it had been before the white man came.

The surface of the river was now dark. The stream flowed gently, and without noise. It, too, struck upon the boy's imagination. It would be fitting for an Indian canoe to come stealing down in the darkness, and he almost fancied he could see it there. But no canoe came, and Ned walked back and forth in a little space, always watching the wood or the river.

The night was very quiet. The horses, having grazed for an hour or two, now rested content. The men not on guard, used to taking their sleep where they could find it, were already in slumber. There was no wind.

The dark hours as usual were full of chill, but Ned's vigorous walk back and forth kept him warm. He was joined after a while by the famous scout, Henry Karnes, who, like "Deaf" Smith, seemed to watch all the time, although he came and went as he pleased.

"Well, boy," said Karnes, "do you find it hard work, this watching and watching and watching for hours and hours?"

"Not at all," replied Ned, responding to his tone of humorous kindness. "I might have found it so once, but I don't now. I'm always anxious to see what will happen."

"That's a good spirit to have," said Karnes, smiling, "and you need it down here, where a man must always be watching for something. In Texas boys have to be men now."

He walked back and forth with Ned, and the lad felt flattered that so famous a scout should show an interest in him. The two were at the edge of the wood and they could see duskily before them a stretch of bare prairie. Karnes was watching this open space intently, and Ned was watching it also.

The boy saw nothing, but suddenly he heard, or thought he heard, a low sound. It was faint, but, unconsciously bending forward a little, he heard it again. It was a metallic rattle and instantly he called the attention of Karnes to it. The scout stopped his walk and listened. Then Ned saw his form grow rigid and tense.

"Let's put our ears to the ground, Ned," said he.

The two stretched out ear to earth, and then Ned not only heard the noise much more distinctly, but he knew at once what it was. He had heard it more than once in the marching army of Cos. It was the sound made by the approaching wheel of a cannon.

"Artillery," he said in a whisper.

"Beyond a doubt," said Karnes. "It means that the Mexicans have crossed the river—there's a ford two or three hundred yards above—and mean to attack us. It was your good ear, Ned, that gave us the first warning."

Ned flushed with pleasure at the compliment, but, a moment or two later, they saw dark figures rising out of the prairie and advancing toward them.

"Mexicans!" cried Karnes, and instantly fired at a dusky outline. The figures flitted away in the dusk, but the camp of Bowie was aroused at once. Inside of a minute every man was on his feet, rifle in hand, facing the open place in the horseshoe. They knew that they could not be attacked from the river. Bowie came to the side of Ned and Karnes.

"What is it?" he asked.

"Ned heard a sound," Karnes replied, "and when we put our ears to the earth we knew that it was made by artillery. Then I saw their scouts and skirmishers and fired upon them. They must have crossed the river in strong force, colonel."

"Very likely," said Bowie. "Well, we shall be ready for them. Henry, you and Smith and the Ring Tailed Panther scout across the prairie there, and see what has become of them."

"Can't I go, too?" asked Ned.

Bowie patted him on the shoulder.

"You young fire eater!" he replied. "Haven't you done enough for one night? You gave us the first warning that the Mexicans were at hand. I think you'd better rest now, and let these old boys do this job."

The three chosen men disappeared in the darkness, and Ned sat down among the trees with Obed. They, like everybody else, waited as patiently as they could for the reports of the scouts.

"Obed," said Ned, "do you think we're going to have a battle?"

"The signs point that way."

Bowie set everybody to work cutting out undergrowth, in order that they might have a clear field for the work that they expected. By the time this task was completed the scouts returned and their report was alarming.

The Mexicans had crossed the river in heavy force, outnumbering the troop of Texans at least five to one. They had artillery, infantry and cavalry, and they were just out of range, expecting to attack at dawn. The avenue of escape was cut off already.

"Very good," said Bowie. "We'll wait for them."

It was too dark to see, but Ned knew that his blue eyes were glittering. He advanced to the point where the bluff rose nearly ten feet to the edge of the prairie, and took a long look.

"I can see nothing," he said, "but I know you men are right. Now we'll cut steps all along the edge of this bluff, in order that our men can stand in them, and fire at the enemy as he comes. Then we'll have as fine a fort here as anybody could ask."

The men fell to work with hatchets and big knives, cutting steps in the soft earth, at least a hundred of them in order that everybody might have a chance. Meanwhile the hour of dawn was at hand, but a heavy mist had thickened over prairie and river. Beyond the mists and vapours, the sun showed only a yellow blur, and it did not yet cast any glow over the earth.

But Ned could clearly hear the Mexicans; officers shouting to men; men shouting to horses; horses neighing and mules squealing, and he knew from these noises that the report of their great force by the scouts was correct. He also heard the clank of the artillery wheels again, and he feared that the cannon would prove a very dangerous foe to them. All the pulses in his body began to beat fast and hard.

"Will the sun ever get through the fog and let us see?" he exclaimed impatiently. It was hard to wait at such a time.

"It's comin' through now," said the Ring Tailed Panther.

The pale yellow light turned suddenly to full red gold. The banks of mist and vapour dissolved under the shining beams, and floated away in shreds and patches. The river, the forest and the prairie rose up into the light, everything standing out, sharp and clear.

Ned drew a deep breath. There was the Mexican army, massed along the entire open space of the horseshoe, at least five to the Texan one, as the scouts had said, and now not more than two hundred yards from them. Five companies of cavalry were gathered ready to charge; infantry stood just behind them and back of the infantry Ned caught the gleam of the cannon he had heard in the night. Evidently the Mexicans had not yet brought it to the front, because its fire would interfere with the charge of the cavalry which they expected would end the battle in five minutes. There was no chance for the Texans to retreat, but it was not of retreat that they were thinking.

"How's your pulse, Ned?" asked the Ring Tailed Panther.

"It's beating fast and hard, I won't deny that," replied Ned, "but I believe my finger will be steady when it presses the trigger."

"Fine feathers make fine Mexicans," said Obed White. "How they do love colour! That's a gorgeous array out there, and it seems a pity to break it up."

The Mexican force certainly looked well. The cavalry, in brilliant uniforms, presented a long front, their lances gleaming. The Texans, standing in the steps that they had cut in the earth, were in sober attire, but resolute eyes looked out from under their caps or the wide brims of their hats.

"They'll charge in a moment," said Obed, "and they'll try to break

THEY WERE SENDING IN THEIR BULLETS WITH DEADLY
PRECISION.

their way through the wood. They cannot ride down this bluff."

The Ring Tailed Panther raised his rifle, and looked down the sights. His eyes were glittering. He drew the trigger and the sharp lashing report ended the silence. A Mexican officer fell from his horse, and then, with a great shout, the Mexican horsemen charged, presenting a gallant array as they bent forward, their rifles and lances ready. The beat of their horses' hoofs came over the prairie like roiling thunder. They wheeled suddenly toward the wood, and then the infantry, advancing, opened heavy and repeated volleys upon the Texans. The horsemen also fired from their saddles.

It was the heaviest fire under which Ned had ever come, and, for a few moments, he quivered all over. He saw a great blaze in front, above it a cloud of lifting smoke, and he heard over his head the hum of many bullets, like the whistling of hail, driven by a heavy wind. But he was experienced enough now to note that the Mexican fire was wasted. That bank was a wonderful protection.

"It's almost a shame to shoot 'em," roared the Ring Tailed Panther who had reloaded. But up went his rifle, his finger pressed the trigger and another Mexican officer fell from his horse. All along the Texan front ran the rifle fire, a rapid crackling sound like the ripping apart of some great cloth. But the Texans were taking aim. There was no confusion among the hardy veterans of the plains. Lying against the face of the bluff they were sending in their bullets with deadly precision. Horse after horse in the charging host galloped away riderless over the prairie, and the front rank of the infantry was shot down.

Ned, like the others, was loading and firing swiftly, but with care. The imminent danger kept down any feeling that he would have had otherwise. The Mexicans sought their lives, and he must seek theirs. The smoke and the odour of burned gunpowder inflamed him. There was still a blaze in front of him, but he also saw the brown faces of the Mexicans yet pressing forward, and he yet heard the continued thunder of the charging hoofs.

"Another bullet, Ned," roared the Ring Tailed Panther and he and the others around him sent a fresh volley at the horsemen. The Mexican cavalry could stand no more. Five companies strong, they broke and galloped away, seeking only to escape from the deadly fire of the Texan rifles. The infantry also gave back and for a few minutes there was a lull.

"That's the end of Chapter One," said Obed White. "Our Mexican friends came in haste and they will repent at a distance."

The smoke lifted and Ned saw many fallen, both men and horses, on the plain in front of them, and there was confusion in the Mexican force, which was now out of gunshot. Never had the Texan rifles done more deadly service. The Texan loss was small.

Ned dropped down from the steps and sat on the grass. His face was wet with perspiration, and he wiped it on his sleeve. He was compelled to cough once or twice to clear his throat of the smoke. The Ring Tailed Panther also was warm, but satisfied.

"A Texan does best in a fight against odds," he said, "an' we have the odds today. But don't you think, Ned, that it's over already?"

"I don't," said Ned. "I know that they will be up to some new trick soon. They will realise that they underrated us at first."

He sprang back into the steps that he had cut in the bluff, and took a good look at the Mexicans.

"They are nearly ready with Chapter Second, Obed," he said. "They are bringing up that cannon."

"Should have used it in the first place," said the Ring Tailed Panther. "They didn't show much sense."

The Mexicans were running the gun forward to a little mound, whence they could drop shells and shot over the edge of the bluff, directly among the Texans. It was a far more formidable danger than the impulsive charge, and Bowie at once took measures to meet it. He called the best rifle shots. Among them were Ned, Obed and the Ring Tailed Panther.

"There are fifteen of you," said the dauntless leader, "and your rifles will reach that gun. Shoot down every man who tries to handle it. The rest of us will attend to the new charge that is coming."

The second attack was to be more formidable than the first. The Mexican cavalry had massed anew. Ned saw the officers, driving the men into place with the flats of swords, and he heard the note of a trumpet, singing loud and clear over the prairie. Then his eyes turned back to the gun, because there his duty lay.

Ned heard the trumpet peal again, and then the thud of hoofs. He saw the rammers and spongers gather about the gun. The rifle of the Ring Tailed Panther cracked, and the man with the rammer fell. Another picked it up, but he went down before the bullet of Obed. Then a sponger fell, and then the gunner himself was slain by the bullet. The Texans were doing wonderful sharpshooting. The gun could not be fired, because nobody could live near it long enough to fire it. Its entire complement was cleared away by the swift little bullets.

Off to right and left, Ned heard again the rising crackle of the rifle fire, and he also heard the steady monotonous beat of the hoofs. He knew that the charge was still coming on, but Bowie would attend to that. He and his immediate comrades never took their eyes from the gun. New cannoneers, an entire complement, were rushing forward to take the place of their fallen comrades. The Mexicans showed plenty of courage that day but the deadly sharpshooters were slaying them as fast as they came. They were yet unable to fire the gun. Nor could they draw it back from its dangerous position. A second time all about it were slain, but a third body came forward for the trial.

"Greasers or no greasers," cried Obed, "those are men of courage!"

But he continued to shoot straight at them nevertheless, and the third group of cannoneers was fast melting away.

"Some of you aim at the mules hitched to the caisson," cried the Ring Tailed Panther. "I hate to kill a mule, but it will be a help now."

One of the mules was slain and two others, wounded, dashed wildly through the Mexican infantry, adding to the confusion and turmoil. The last of the third group of cannoneers fell and the gun stood alone and untouched, the shell still in place. No one now dared to approach it. The dead now lay in a group all about it. Meanwhile, the second charge broke like the first and the cavalry galloped wildly away.

Ned could turn his eyes now. He saw more riderless horses than before, while the fallen, lying still on the prairie, had doubled in number. Then his eyes turned back to the gun, standing sombre and silent among those who had died for it. The battle-fire gone, for the present, Ned felt pity for the Mexicans who lay so thick about the cannon. Nor did he fail to admire the courage that had been spent so freely, but in vain.

"They won't come again," said the Ring Tailed Panther, dropping to the grass. "They have had enough."

"I don't blame 'em," said Obed, lying down by his side. "They must have lost a third of their number, and they'd have lost another third if they had charged once more."

"They're not going away," said Ned, who had remained on his perch. "They're coming again."

A third time the Mexicans charged and a third time they were driven back by the rifles. Then they formed on the prairie beyond gunshot, and marched away to San Antonio, leaving behind the mournful and silent cannon as proof alike of their courage and defeat.

CHAPTER 20
THE WHEEL OF FIRE

Ned watched the Mexicans marching away until the last lance had disappeared behind a swell of the prairie. Then he joined in the cheer that the Texans gave, after which he and his comrades went out upon the field, and gazed upon their work. The killed among the Mexicans nearly equalled in numbers the whole Texan force, sixteen lying dead around the cannon alone, and many of them also had been wounded, while the Texans had escaped with only a single man slain, and but few hurt. But Ned quickly left the field. The sight of it was not pleasant to him, although he was still heart and soul with the Texans, in what he regarded as a defensive war.

Bowie drew his forces out of the horseshoe and they rode for the Texan camp, carrying with them the trophies of arms that they had taken. On their way they met Mr. Austin and a strong force who had heard of their plight and who were now coming to their relief. They, too, rejoiced greatly at the victory, and all went back in triumph to the Salado.

"Now that they have seen how we can fight I reckon that Mr. Austin and Houston will order an attack right away on San Antonio," said the Ring Tailed Panther.

"I don't believe they will," said Obed White. "Seeing is sometimes doubting. I believe that they still fear our failure."

Ned inclined to Obed's belief but he said nothing. At twilight Urrea came back, rejoicing and also full of regrets. He rejoiced over the victory and he regretted that he had not been there.

"Seems to me, Don Francisco," said the Ring Tailed Panther, "that you're missin' a lot of things."

"There's many a slip 'twixt Francisco and the fight-o," said Obed.

Ned was hurt by the irony of his friends, but Urrea only laughed as he spread his blanket in a good place, and lay down on it.

"I will admit, gentlemen," he said in his precise English, "that I seem always to be absent when anything important happens, but it is owing to the nature of the service that I can best render the Texans. Being of the Mexican race and knowing the country so thoroughly, I am of most value as a seeker after information. I had gone off on a long scout about San Antonio, and I have news which I have given to Mr. Austin."

"Spyin' is a dangerous business, but it's got to be done," said the

Ring Tailed Panther. Ned saw that he again looked with disfavour upon Urrea, but he ascribed it as before to racial aversion.

Obed was right. Despite the brilliant victory of Bowie, Houston and Austin still held back, and the Ring Tailed Panther roared long and loud. But his roaring was cut short by an order for him, Obed, Ned and Urrea to ride eastward to some of the little Texan towns in search of help. The leaders were anxious that their utmost strength be gathered when they should at last make the attack upon San Antonio. Since he could not have just what he wished, the Panther was glad to get the new task, and the others were content.

They rode away the next morning, armed and provisioned well. Their horses, having rested long and fed abundantly, were strong and fresh, and they went at a good pace, until they came to the last swell from which they could see San Antonio. The town was distant, but it was magnified in the clear Texas sunlight. It looked to Ned, sitting there on his horse, like a large city. It had come to occupy a great place in his mind and just now it was to him the most important town in the world. He wondered if they would ever take it. Urrea, who was watching him, smiled.

"I know what you are thinking," he said, "and I will wager that it was just the same that I was thinking."

"I was trying to read the future and tell whether we would take San Antonio," said Ned.

"Exactly. Those were my thoughts, too."

"I reckon you two wasn't far away from my trail either," said the Ring Tailed Panther, "'cause I was figgerin' that we'd take it inside of a month."

"Count me in, too," said Obed. "Great minds go in bunches. I was calculating that we would capture it some day, but I left out the limit of time."

They turned their horses, and when they reached the crest of the next swell San Antonio was out of sight. Before them stretched the prairies, now almost as desolate as they had been when the Indians alone roamed over them. They passed two or three small cabins, each built in a cluster of trees near a spring, but the occupants had gone, fled to a town for shelter. One seemed to have been abandoned only an hour or two ago, as the ashes were scarcely cold on the hearth, and a bucket of water, with its gourd in it, still stood on the shelf. The sight moved the Ring Tailed Panther to sentiment.

"Think of the women an' children havin' to sleep out on the prairie," he said. "It ain't right an' fittin'."

"We'll bring them all back before we are through," said Obed.

They left the little cabin, exactly as they had found it, and then rode at an increased pace toward the north and the east, making for the settlements on the Brazos. A little while before nightfall, they met a buffalo hunter who told them there were reports of a Mexican cavalry force far north of San Antonio, although he could not confirm the truth of the rumors. Urrea shook his head vigorously.

"Impossible! impossible!" he said. "The Mexicans would not dare to come away so far from their base at San Antonio."

The hunter, an old man, looked at him with curiosity and disapproval.

"That's more than you an' me can say," he said, "although you be a Mexican yourself and know more about your people than I do. I jest tell what I've heard."

"Mr. Urrea is one of the most ardent of the Texan patriots," said Ned.

"I jest tell what I've heard," said the old man, whistling to his pony and riding away.

"Obstinate!" said Urrea, laughing in his usual light, easy manner. "These old hunters are very narrow. You cannot make them believe that a Mexican, although born on Texas soil, which can be said of very few Texans, is a lover of liberty and willing to fight against aggression from the capital."

At night they rode into a splendid belt of forest, and made their camp by a cool spring that gushed from a rock and flowed away among the trees. Ned and Obed scouted a little, and found the country so wild that the deer sprang up from the bushes. It was difficult to resist the temptation of a shot, but they were compelled to let them go, and returning to camp they reported to Urrea and the Ring Tailed Panther that they seemed to have the forest to themselves, so far as human beings were concerned.

"Do you think it is safe to light a fire?" asked Urrea.

"I see no danger in it," replied Obed, "that is, none in a little one. There are so many bushes about us that it couldn't be seen fifty yards away."

It was now November and as the night had become quite cold Urrea's suggestion of a fire seemed good to Ned. He showed much zeal in gathering the dry wood, and then they deftly built a fire, one that would throw out little flame, but which would yet furnish much heat. The Ring Tailed Panther, who had the most skill in wilderness life, kindled it with flint and steel, and while the flames, held down by brush, made hot coals beneath, the smoke was lost among the trees and the darkness.

The horses were tethered near, and they warmed their food by the coals before eating it. The place was snug, a little cup set all around by bushes and high trees, and the heat of the fire was very grateful. While Ned sat before it, eating his food, he noticed great numbers of last year's fallen leaves lying about, and he picked the very place where he would make his bed. He would draw great quantities of the leaves there under the big beech, and spread his blankets upon them.

They were tired after the long day's journey, and they did not talk much. The foliage about them was so thick, making it so dark within the little shade that the need of a watch seemed small, but they decided to keep it, nevertheless. The Ring Tailed Panther would take the first half of the night and Urrea the second half. The next night would be divided between Obed and Ned.

Ned raked up the leaves at the place that he had selected, folded himself between his blankets, and was asleep in five minutes. The last thing that he remembered seeing was the broad figure of the Ring Tailed Panther, sitting with his back against a tree, and his rifle across his knees.

But Ned awoke hours later—after midnight in fact—although it was not a real awakening, instead a sort of halfway station from slumber-land. He did not move, but opened his eyes partly, and saw that Urrea was now on guard. The young Mexican was not sitting as the Ring Tailed Panther had been, but was standing some yards away, with his rifle across his shoulder. Ned thought in a vague way that he looked trim and strong, and then his heavy lids dropped down again. But he did not fall back into the deep sleep from which he had come. The extra sense, his remarkable power of intuition or divination was at work. Without any effort of his will the mechanism of his brain was moving and gave him a signal. He heard a slight noise and he lifted the heavy lids.

Urrea had walked to the other side of the little glade, his feet brushing some of the dry leaves as he went. There was nothing unusual in such action on the part of a sentinel, but something in Urrea's attitude seemed to Ned to denote expectancy. His whole figure was drawn close together like that of one about to spring, and he leaned forward a little. Yet this meant nothing. Any good man on guard would be attentive to every sound of the forest, whether the light noise made by a squirrel, as he scampered along the bark of a tree, or a stray puff of wind rustling the leaves.

Ned made another effort of the will, and closed his eyes for the second time, but the warning sense, the intuitive note out of the infinite, would not be denied. He was compelled to open his eyes once more and now his faculties were clear. Urrea had moved again and now he was facing the sleepers. He regarded them attentively, one by one, and in the dusk he could not see that Ned's eyelids were not closed. The boy did not stir, but a cold shiver ran down his spine. He felt with all the power of second sight that something extraordinary was going to happen.

Urrea walked to the smouldering fire, and now Ned dropped his eyelids, until he looked only through a space as narrow as the edge of a knife blade. Urrea stooped and took from the dying heap a long stick, still burning at the end. Then he took another look at the three and suddenly disappeared among the bushes, carrying with him the burning stick. He was so light upon his feet that he made no sound as he went.

Ned was startled beyond measure, but he was like a spring released by a key. He felt that the need of instant action was great, and, as light of foot as Urrea himself, he sprang up, rifle in hand, and followed the young Mexican. He was thankful for the wilderness training that he had been compelled to acquire. He caught sight of Urrea about twenty yards ahead, still moving swiftly on soundless feet. He moved thus a hundred yards or more, with Ned, as his shadow, as dark and silent as he, and then he stopped by the side of a great tree.

Ned felt instinctively, when Urrea halted that he would look back to see if by chance he were followed, and he sank down in the bushes before the Mexican turned. Urrea gave only a glance or two in that direction and, satisfied, began to examine the tree which was certainly worthy of attention, as it rose to an uncommon height, much above its fellows.

Ned's amazement grew. Why should Urrea be so particular about the size or height of a tree? It grew still further, when he saw Urrea lay his rifle down at the foot of the tree, spring up, grasp the lowest branch with one hand, and then deftly draw himself up, taking with him the burning stick. He paused a moment on the bough, looked again toward the little camp and then climbed upward with a speed and dexterity worthy of a great monkey.

Ned saw the Mexican's figure going up and up, a dark blur against the stem of the tree, and it was hard to persuade himself that it was reality. He saw also the bright spark on the end of the stick that he carried with him. The tree rose to a height of nearly 150 feet, and when Urrea passed above the others that surrounded it, the moon's rays, unobstructed, fell upon him. Then, although he became smaller and smaller, Ned saw him more clearly. The boy was so much absorbed now in the story that was unfolding before him that he did not have time to wonder.

Urrea went up as high as the stem would sustain him. Then he rested his feet on a bough, wrapped his left arm around the tree, and, with his right arm, began to whirl the burning stick rapidly. The spark leaped up, grew into a blaze, and Ned saw a wheel of fire. He had seen many strange things, but this, influenced by circumstances of time and place, was the most uncanny of them all.

Far above his head, and above the body of the forest revolved the wheel of fire. Urrea's own body had melted away in the darkness, until it was fused with the tree. Ned now saw only the fiery signal, for such it must be, and his heart rose in fierce anger against Urrea. Once he lifted his rifle a little, and studied the possibilities of a shot at such range, but he put the rifle down again. He would watch and wait.

The wheel ceased presently to revolve, and Ned saw Urrea again, torch in hand, but motionless. He, too, was waiting. He did not stir for a full quarter of an hour, but all the while the torch burned steadily. Then he suddenly began to whirl it again, but in a direction opposite to that made by the first wheel of fire. Around and around went the burning brand for some minutes. When he stopped, he waited at least ten minutes longer. Then, as if he had received the answer that he wished, making the claim of communication complete, he dropped the torch. Ned saw it falling, a trail of light, until it struck among the bushes, where it went out. Then Urrea began to descend the tree, but he came down more slowly than he had gone up.

Ned slipped forward, seized Urrea's rifle, and then slipped back among the bushes. He put the Mexican's weapon at his feet, cocked his own and waited.

Urrea, coming slowly down the tree, stopped and stood there for a few moments as if in contemplation. A shaft of moonlight piercing through the foliage fell upon his face illumining the olive complexion and the well-cut features. It was hard for Ned to believe what he had seen. What could it be but a signal? and that signal to the enemies of the Texans! And yet Urrea did not look like a villain and traitor. There was certainly no malevolence in his face, which on the other hand had rather a melancholy cast, as he stood there on the bough before swinging to the ground.

Ned strengthened his will. He had seen what he had seen. Such things could not be passed over in times when lives were the forfeit of weakness. Urrea let himself lightly to the earth, and stooped down for his rifle. It was not there, and when he straightened up again Ned saw that his face was ghastly pale in the moonlight. Urrea, with his quick perceptions, was bound to know from the absence of the rifle that he had been followed and was caught. His hand went down toward his belt where a pistol hung, but Ned instantly called from the bush:

"Hands up, Don Francisco, or I shoot!"

His tone was stern and menacing, and Urrea's hands went up by the side of his head. But the paleness left his face, and his manner became careless and easy.

"Is that you, Ned?" he called in the most friendly tones. "Is it a joke that you play upon me? Ah, you Anglo-Saxons, you seem rough in your play to us Latins."

"It is no joke, Don Francisco. I was never more earnest in my life," said Ned, stepping from the bush, but still keeping Urrea covered with his rifle. "Your merits as a climber of trees are great, but you interested me more with your wheel of fire. I think I can account now for your absences, when any fighting with the Mexicans was to be done. You are a spy and you were signalling with that torch to our enemies."

Urrea laughed lightly, musically, and he regarded Ned with a look of amusement. It seemed to say to him that he was only a boy, that one so young was bound to make mistakes, but that the Mexican was not offended because he was making one now at his cost. The laugh was irritating to the last degree, and yet it implanted in the boy's mind a doubt, a fear that he might have been mistaken.

"Signalling to friends, not enemies, you mean," said Urrea. "This forest ends but a few hundred yards beyond, and I learned when I was scouting about San Antonio that some allies of ours in this region were waiting night and day for the news from us to come. I took this method to communicate with them, a successful method, too, I am happy to say, as they answered. In a wild region one must do strange things."

His tone was so light, so easy, and it rang so true that Ned hesitated. But it was only for a moment. Manner could not change substance.

He cleared away the mists and vapours made by Urrea's light tone and easy assurance, and came back to the core of the matter.

"Don Francisco," he said, "I have liked you, and I believed that you were a true Texan patriot, but I cannot believe the story that you tell me. It seems too improbable. If you wished to make these signals to friends, why did you not tell us that you were going to do so?"

"I did not know of the possibility of such a signal until I saw this tree and its great height. Then, as all of you were asleep, I concluded to make my signal, achieve the result and give you a pleasant surprise. Come now, Senor Edward, hand me my rifle, and let us end this unpleasant joke."

Ned shook his head. It was hard to resist Urrea's assurance, but manner was not all. His logical mind rejected the story.

"I'm sorry, Don Francisco," he said, "but I must refer this to my comrades, Mr. Palmer and Mr. White. Meanwhile, I am compelled to hold you a prisoner. You will walk before me to the camp, keeping your hands up."

Urrea shrugged his shoulders and gave Ned a glance, which seemed to be a mixture of disgust and contempt.

"Very well, if you will have it so," he said. "There is nothing like the stubbornness of a boy."

"March!" said Ned, who felt his temper rising.

Urrea, hands up, walked toward the camp, and Ned came behind him, carrying the two rifles, one of them cocked and ready for instant use. The Mexican never looked back, but walked with unhesitating step straight to the camp. The Ring Tailed Panther and Obed were still sound asleep, but, when Ned called sharply to them, they sprang to their feet, gazing in astonishment at the spectacle of Urrea with his hands up, and the boy standing behind him with the two rifles.

"Things seem to have happened while I slept," said Obed.

"Looks as if there might have been some rippin' an' tearin'," said the Ring Tailed Panther. "What have you been up to, Urrea?"

Urrea gave the Ring Tailed Panther a malignant glance.

"I have not been up to anything, to use your own common language," he replied. "If you want any explanation, you can ask it of your suspicious young friend there. As for me, I am tired of holding my hands as high as my head, and I intend to light a cigarette. Three of you, I suppose, are sufficient to watch me."

There were still a few embers and touching his cigarette to one of them he sat down, leaned against the trunk of a tree and began to puff, as if the future of the case had no interest for him.

"Just hand me that pistol at your belt, will you?" said Obed. "There seems to be some kind of a difference of opinion between you and Ned, and, without knowing anything about it, I'm for Ned."

Urrea took the pistol and tossed it toward Obed. The Maine man caught it deftly and thrust it in his own belt. He did not seem to be at all offended by the young Mexican's contemptuous manner.

"Besides being one of the best watch makers the State of Maine ever produced," he said, "I'm pretty good at sleight-of-hand. I could catch loaded pistols all day, Urrea, if you were to pitch them at me."

Urrea did not deign a reply and Obed and the Ring Tailed Panther looked at Ned, who told them all he had seen. Urrea did not deny a thing or say a word throughout the narrative. When Ned finished the Ring Tailed Panther roared in his accustomed fashion.

"Signalin' to the enemy from a tree top while we was asleep an' he was supposed to be on guard!" he exclaimed. "What have you got to say to this, Urrea?"

"Our young paragon of knowledge and wilderness lore has given you my statement," replied Urrea. "You can believe it or not as you choose. I shall not waste another word on thickheads."

The teeth of the Ring Tailed Panther came together with a click, and he looked ominously at Urrea.

"You may not say anything," he growled, "but I will. I didn't trust you at first, Don Francisco, an' there have been times all along since then when I didn't trust you. You're a smooth talker, but your habit of disappearin' has been too much for me. I believe just as Ned does that you were signallin' to the enemy an' that you meant Texas harm, lots of harm. It was a lucky thing that the boy awoke. Now, what do you think, Obed?"

"Appearances are deceitful sometimes but not always. Don Francisco seems to have spun a likely yarn to Ned, but I've heard better and they were not so mighty much."

"You see the jury is clean ag'inst you, Don Francisco," said the Ring Tailed Panther, "an' it's goin' to hold you to a higher court. Did you hear what I said?"

Urrea nodded.

"Yes, I heard you," he replied, "but I heard only foolishness."

The Ring Tailed Panther growled, but he had the spirit of a gentleman. He would not upbraid a prisoner.

"The verdict of the jury bein' given," he said soberly, "we've got

231

to hold the prisoner till we reach the higher court. We ain't takin' no chances, Urrea, an' for that reason we've got to tie you. Ned, cut off a piece of that lariat."

Urrea leaped to his feet. He was stung at last.

"I will not be bound," he cried.

"Yes, you will," said the Ring Tailed Panther. "I ain't goin' to hurt you, 'cause I'm pretty handy at that sort of thing, but I'll tie you so you won't get loose in a hurry. Better set down an' take it easy."

Urrea, after the single flash of anger, sat down, and resuming his careless air, held out his hands.

"Since you intend to act like barbarians as well as fools," he said, "I will not seek to impede you."

None of the three replied. The Ring Tailed Panther handily tied his wrists together, and then his ankles, but in such fashion that he could still sit in comfort, leaning against the tree, although the pleasure of the cigarette was no longer for him.

"If you don't mind," he said, "I think I shall go to sleep."

"No objections a-tall, a-tall," said the Ring Tailed Panther. "Have nice dreams."

Urrea closed his eyes, and his chest soon rose and fell in the regular manner of one who sleeps. Ned could not tell whether he really slept. A feeling of compassion for Urrea rose again in his heart. What if he should be telling the truth after all? Wild and improbable tales sometimes came true. He was about to speak of his thoughts to the men, but he checked himself. Disbelief was returning. It was best to take every precaution.

"You go to sleep, Ned," said Obed. "You've done a good job and you are entitled to a rest. The Panther and I will watch till day."

Ned lay down between his blankets and everything was so still that contrary to his expectations, he fell asleep, and did not awaken again until after dawn, when Obed told him that they would resume the march, eating their breakfast as they went. Urrea was unbound, although he was first searched carefully for concealed weapons.

"I wouldn't have a man to ride with his arms tied," said the Ring Tailed Panther, "but we'll keep on both sides of you an' you needn't try to make a bolt of it, Urrea."

"I shall not try to make any bolt of it," said Urrea scornfully, "but you will pay dearly to Austin and Houston for the indignity that you have put upon me."

The Ring Tailed Panther, true to his principle of never taunting a prisoner, did not reply, and they mounted. The Panther rode ahead and Obed and Ned, with Urrea between them, followed. Urrea was silent, his face melancholy and reproachful.

The belt of timber extended only a few hundred yards farther, when they came upon the open prairie extending to the horizon. Far to the left some antelope were feeding, but there was no other sign of life of any kind.

"I don't see anything of them friends of ours to whom you were signallin'," said the Ring Tailed Panther.

Urrea would not reply. The Panther said nothing further, and they rode on over the prairie. But both the Ring Tailed Panther and Obed were watching the ground, and, when they had gone about two miles, they reined in their horses.

"See!" they exclaimed simultaneously.

They had come to a broad trail cutting directly across their path. It was made by at least a hundred horses, and the veriest novice could not have missed it. The trail was that of shod hoofs, indicating the presence of white men.

"What is this, Don Francisco?" asked the Ring Tailed Panther.

"I do not have to reply to you unless I wish," said Urrea, "but I am willing to tell you that it is undoubtedly the trail of the Texan reinforcements to which I was signalling last night."

Ned looked quickly at him. Again the young Mexican's voice had the ring of truth. Was the wild and improbable tale now coming true? If so, he could never forgive himself for the manner in which he had treated Urrea. Still, it was for the older men to act now, and he continued his silence.

"Maybe Texans made this trail, and maybe they didn't," said Obed, "but I think we'd better follow it for a while and see. About how old would you say this trail is, Panther?"

"Not more'n two hours."

They turned their course, and followed the broad path left by the horsemen across the prairie. Thus they rode at a good pace, until nearly noon, and the trail was now so fresh that they could not be far away. The change of direction had brought them toward forest, heavy with undergrowth. It was evident that the horsemen had gone into this forest as the trail continued to lead straight to it, and the Ring Tailed Panther approached with the greatest caution.

"Can you see anything, Ned, in there among them trees an' bushes?" he asked. "You've got the sharpest eyes of all."

"Not a thing," replied Ned, "nor do I see a bough or bush moving."

"It would be hard for such a big party to hide themselves," said Obed, "so I think we'd better ride straight in."

They entered the forest, still following the trail among the trampled bushes, riding slowly over rough ground, and watching wanly to right and left. Urrea had not said a word, but when they were about a mile within the wood, he suddenly leaned from his horse, snatched the knife from the belt of the Ring Tailed Panther and slashed at him. Fortunately, the range was somewhat long for such work, and, as the Panther threw up his arm, the blade merely cut his buckskin sleeve from wrist to elbow, only grazing his skin. Urrea, quick as lightning, turned his horse, threw him against that of Obed which was staggered, and then started at a gallop among the trees.

The Ring Tailed Panther raised his rifle, but Urrea threw himself behind his horse, riding with all the dexterity of a Comanche in the fashion of an Indian who wishes to protect himself; that is, hanging on the far side of the horse by only hands and toes. The Panther shifted his aim and shot the horse through the head. But Urrea leaped clear of the falling body, avoided Obed's bullet, and darted into the thickest of the bushes. As he disappeared a sharp, piercing whistle rose. Ned did not have time to think, but when he heard the whistle, instinct warned him that it was a signal. He had heard that whistle once before in exciting moments, and by a nervous action as it were, he pulled hard upon the reins of his horse. In this emergency it was the boy whose action was the wisest.

"Come back, Obed, you and Panther!" he shouted. "He may have led us into an ambush!"

Obed and the Ring Tailed Panther were still galloping after Urrea, and, even as Ned shouted to them, a flash of flame burst from the undergrowth. He saw Obed's horse fall, but Obed himself sprang clear. The Panther did not seem to be hurt, but, in an instant, both were surrounded by Mexicans. Obed was seized on the ground and the Panther was quickly dragged from his horse. But the Maine man, even in such a critical moment, did not forget the boy for whom he had such a strong affection. He shouted at the top of his voice:

"Ride, Ned! Ride for your life!"

Ned, still guided by impulse, wheeled his horse and galloped away. It was evident that his comrades had been taken, and he alone was left to carry out their mission. Shots were fired at him and bullets whistled past, but none touched him, and he only urged his horse to greater speed.

The boy felt a second impulse. It was to turn back and fall, or be taken with the two comrades whom he liked so well. But then reason came. He could do more for them free than a captive, and now he began to take full thought for himself. He bent far over on his horse's neck, in order to make as small a target as possible, holding the reins with one hand and his rifle with the other. A minute had taken him clear of the undergrowth, and once more he was on the prairie.

Ned did not look back for some time. He heard several shots, but he judged by the reports that he was practically out of range. Now he began to feel sanguine. His horse was good and true, and he rode well. As long as the bullets could not reach and weaken, he felt that the chances were greatly in his favour. He was riding almost due north and the prairie stretched away without limit, although the forest extended for a long distance on his right.

He now straightened up somewhat in the saddle, but he did not yet look back, fearing that he might check his speed by doing so, and knowing that every moment was of the utmost value. But he listened attentively to the pursuing hoofs and he was sure that the beat was steadily growing fainter. The gap must be widening.

He glanced back for the first time and saw about twenty Mexicans spread out in the segment of a circle. They rode ponies and two or three were recoiling lariats which they had evidently got ready in the hope of a throw. Ned smiled to himself when he saw the lariats. Unless something happened to his horse they could never come near enough for a cast. He measured the gap and he believed that his rifle of long range would carry it.

One of the Mexicans rode a little in front of the others and Ned judged him to be the leader. Twisting in his saddle he took aim at him. It is difficult to shoot backward from a flying horse, but Ned had undergone the wilderness training and he felt that he could make the hit. He pulled the trigger. The jet of smoke leaped forth and the man, swaying, fell from his saddle, but sprang to his feet and clapped his hands to his shoulder, where the boy's bullet had struck.

There was confusion among the Mexicans, as it was really their leader whom Ned had wounded, and, before the pursuit was resumed with energy, the fugitive had gained another hundred yards. After that, the gap widened steadily, and, when he looked back a second time, the Mexicans were a full quarter of a mile in the rear. He maintained his speed and in another hour they were lost behind the swells.

Sure that he had now made good his escape, Ned pulled his horse down to a walk. The good animal was dripping with foam and perspiration and he did not allow him to cool too fast. Without his horse he would be lost. But when they had gone on another hour at a walk, he stopped and let him have a complete rest.

Ned was not able to see anything of the Mexicans. The prairie, as far as he could tell, was bare of human life save himself. To his right was the dark line of the forest, but everywhere else the open extended to the horizon. He had escaped!

They had started as four and now but one was left. Urrea had proved to be a traitor and his good friends, Obed and the Ring Tailed Panther were captured or—he refused to consider the alternative. They were alive. Two men, so strong and vital as they, could not have fallen.

Now that his horse had rested, Ned mounted again, and rode at a trot for the forest. He knew the direction in which the settlements lay, and he could go on with his mission. Men would say that he had shown great skill and presence of mind in escaping from the ambush, when those older and more experienced had been trapped. But when the alternatives were presented to Ned's mind he had not hesitated. They were lingering before San Antonio and the call for volunteers was not so urgent. He was going back to rescue his comrades or be taken or fall in the attempt.

One of the great qualities in Ned's mind was gratitude. Had it not been for Obed he might yet be under the sea in a dungeon of the Castle of San Juan de Ulua. The Ring Tailed Panther had done him a hundred services, and would certainly risk his life, if need be, to save Ned's. He would never desert them.

The forest was not so near as it looked on the prairie, but two hours' riding brought him to it. He knew that it was the same forest in which Obed and the Panther had been taken, here extending for many miles.

He believed that the Mexicans, being far north of their usual range, would remain in the forest, and he was glad of it. He could work much better under cover than on the prairie. This was undoubtedly the Mexican band of which the old hunter had spoken, and Urrea had given his signal to it from the tree. Ned did not believe that it would remain long in this region, but would go swiftly south, probably to reinforce Cos in San Antonio. He must act with speed.

It was several hours until night, and he rode southward through the forest which consisted chiefly of oak, ash, maple and sweet gum. There was not much undergrowth here, and he did not have any great fear of ambush. Turning in, yet farther to the right, he saw a fine creek, and he followed its course until the undergrowth began to grow thick again. Then he dismounted and fastened his horse at the end of his lariat.

The boy had already come to his conclusion. The presence of the creek had decided him. He believed that the Mexicans, for the sake of water, had encamped somewhere along its course, and all he had to do was to follow its stream. He marked well the spot at which he was leaving his horse, and began what he believed to be the last stage of his journey.

Ned was glad now that the undergrowth was dense. It concealed him well, and he had acquired skill enough to go through it swiftly and without noise. He advanced two or three miles, when he saw a faint light ahead, and he was quite sure that it came from the Mexican camp. As he went nearer, he heard the sound of many voices, and, when he came to the edge of a thicket, belief became certainty.

The entire Mexican force was encamped in a semi-circular glade next to the creek. The horses were tethered at the far side, and the men, eighty or a hundred in number, were lying or standing about several fires that burned brightly. It was a cold night, and the Mexicans were making themselves comfortable. They were justified in doing so, as they knew that there was no Texan force anywhere within a day's ride. They had put out no sentinels, quite sure that wandering Texans who might see them would quickly go the other way.

Ned crept up as close as he dared, and, lying on his side in a dense thicket, watched them. Their fires were large, and a bright moon was shining. The whole glade was filled with light. The Mexicans talked much, after their fashion, and there was much moving about from fire to fire. Presently the eyes of the boy watching in the bush lighted up with a gleam which was not exactly that of benevolence.

Urrea was passing before one of the fires. Ned saw him clearly now, the trim, well-knit figure, and the handsome, melancholy face. But he was no prisoner. Many of the Mexicans made way for him and all showed him deference. Ned had liked Urrea, but he could not understand how a man could play the spy and traitor in such a manner, and his heart flamed with bitterness against him.

The Mexicans continued to shift about, and when two more men came into view Ned's heart leaped. They were alive! Prisoners they were, but yet alive. He had believed that two so vivid and vital as they could not perish, and he was right.

Obed and the Ring Tailed Panther sat with their backs against the same tree. They were unbound but the armed Mexicans were all about them, and they did not have a chance. They were thirty yards away, and Ned could see them very plainly, yet there was a wall between him and these trusty comrades of his.

Obed and the Panther remained motionless against the tree. Apparently they took no interest in the doings of the Mexicans. Ned, yet seeing no way in which he could help them, watched them a long time. He saw Urrea, after a while, come up and stand before them. The light was good enough for him to see that Urrea's expression was sneering and triumphant. Again Ned's heart swelled with rage. The traitor was exulting over the captives.

Urrea began to speak. Ned could not hear his words, but he knew by the movement of the man's lips that he was talking fast. Undoubtedly he was taunting the prisoners with words as well as looks. But neither Obed nor the Ring Tailed Panther made any sign that he heard. They continued to lean carelessly against the tree, and Urrea, his desire to give pain foiled for the time, went away.

Now Ned bestirred his mind. Here were the Mexicans, and here were his friends. How should he separate them? He could think of nothing at present and he drew back deeper into the forest. There, lying very close among the bushes, he pondered a long time. He might try to stampede the horses, but the attempt would be more than doubtful, and he gave up the idea.

It was now growing late and the fires in the Mexican camp were sinking. The wind began to blow, and the leaves rustled dryly over Ned's head. Best thoughts sometimes spring from little things, and it was the dry rustle of the leaves that gave Ned his idea. It was a desperate chance, but he must take it. The increasing strength of the wind increased his hope. It was blowing from him directly toward the camp.

He retreated about a quarter of a mile. Then he hunted until he found where the fallen leaves lay thickest, and he raked them into a great heap. Drawing both the flint and steel which he, like other borderers, always carried, he worked hard until the spark leaped forth and set the leaves on fire. Then he stood back.

The forest was dry like tinder. Ned had nothing to do but to set the torch. In an instant the leaves leaped into a roaring flame. The blaze ran higher, took hold of the trees and ran from bough to bough.

It sprang to other trees, and, in an incredibly brief space, a forest fire, driven by the wind, sending forth sparks in myriads, and roaring and crackling, was racing down upon the Mexican camp.

Ned kept behind the fire and to one side. Sparks fell upon him, and the smoke was in his eyes and ears, but he thought little just then of such things. The fire, like many others of its kind, took but a narrow path. It was as if a flaming sword blade were slashed down across the woods.

Ned saw it through the veil of smoke rush upon the Mexican camp. He saw the startled Mexicans running about, and he heard the shrill neigh of frightened horses. Never was a camp abandoned more quickly. The men sprang upon their horses and scattered in every direction through the woods. Two on horseback crowded by Ned. They did not see him, nor did he pay any attention to them, but when a third man on foot came, running at the utmost speed, the boy seized him by the shoulder, and was dragged from his feet.

"It is I, Obed!" he cried. "It is I, Ned Fulton!"

Obed White stopped abruptly and the Ring Tailed Panther, unable to check himself, crashed into him. The three, men and boy, went to the ground, where they lay for a few moments among the bushes, half stunned. It was a fortunate chance, as Urrea, who had retained his presence of mind, was on horseback looking for the prisoners, and he passed so near that he would have seen them had they been standing.

The three rose slowly to their feet and the two men gazed in admiration at Ned.

"You did it!" they exclaimed together.

"I did," replied Ned with pride, "and it has worked beautifully."

"I was never so much in love with a forest fire before," said the Ring Tailed Panther. "How it roars an' tears an' bites! An' just let it roar an' tear an' bite!"

"We'd better go on the back track," said Obed. "The Mexicans are all running in other directions."

"My horse is back that way, too," said Ned. "Come on."

They started back, running along the edge of the burned area. Before they had gone far the Ring Tailed Panther caught a saddled and bridled horse which was galloping through the woods, and, they were so much emboldened, that they checked their flight, and hunted about until they found a second.

"There must be at least thirty or forty of 'em dashin' about through the woods, mad with fright," said Obed.

"Three are all we can use, includin' Ned's," said the Ring Tailed Panther, "but I wish we had more weapons."

They had found across the saddle of one of the horses a couple of pistols in holsters, but they had no other weapons except those that Ned carried. But they were free and they had horses. The Ring Tailed Panther's customary growl between his teeth became a chant of triumph.

"Did the Mexicans capture Obed an' me?" he said. "They did. Did they keep us? They didn't. Why didn't they? There was a boy named Ned who escaped. He was a smart boy, a terribly smart boy. Did he run away an' leave us? He didn't. There was only one trick in the world that he could work to save us, an' he worked it. Oh, it was funny to see the Mexicans run with the fire scorchin' the backs of their ears. But that boy, Ned, ain't he smart? He whipped a hundred Mexicans all by himself."

Ned blushed.

"Stop that, you Panther," he said, "or I'll call for Urrea to come and take you back."

"Having horses," said Obed, "there is no reason why we shouldn't ride. Here, jump up behind me, Ned."

They were very soon back at the point where Ned had left his own horse, and found him lying contentedly on his side. Then, well mounted each on his own horses they resumed their broken journey.

CHAPTER 21

THE TEXAN STAR

Just after the three started, they looked back and saw a faint light over the trees, which they knew was caused by the forest fire still travelling northward.

"It seemed almost a sin to set the torch to the woods," said the boy, "but I couldn't think of any other way to get you two loose from the Mexicans."

"It's a narrow fire," said the Ring Tailed Panther, "an' I guess it will burn itself out ag'inst some curve of the creek a few miles further on."

This, in truth, was what happened, as they learned later, but for the present they could bestow the thought of only a few moments upon the subject. Despite the Mexican interruption they intended to go on with their mission. With good horses beneath them they expected to reach the Brazos settlements the next day unless some new danger intervened.

They turned from the forest into the prairie and rode northward at a good gait.

"That was a fine scheme of yours, Ned," repeated the Ring Tailed Panther, "an' nobody could have done it better. You set the fire an' here we are, together ag'in."

"I was greatly helped by luck," said Ned modestly.

"Luck helps them that think hard an' try hard. Didn't that fellow, Urrea, give you the creeps? I had my doubts about him before, but I never believed he was quite as bad as he is."

But Ned felt melancholy. It seemed to him that somebody whom he liked had died.

"I saw him talking to you and Obed," he said. "What was he saying?"

The Ring Tailed Panther frowned and Ned heard his teeth grit upon one another.

"He was sayin' a lot of things," he replied. "He was talkin' low down, hittin' at men who couldn't hit back, abusin' prisoners, which the same was Obed an' me. He was doin' what I guess you would call tauntin', tellin' of all the things we would have to suffer. He said that they'd get you, too, before mornin' an' that we'd all be hanged as rebels an' traitors to Mexico. He laughed at the way he fooled us. He said that spat he had with Sandoval was only make-believe. He said that we'd never get San Antonio; that he'd kept Cos informed about all our movements an' that Santa Anna was comin' with a great army. He said that most of us would be chawed right up, an' that them that wasn't chawed up would wish they had been before Santa Anna got through with 'em."

"Many a threatened man who runs away lives to fight another day," said Obed cheerfully.

"That's so," said the Ring Tailed Panther, "an' I say it among us three that if we don't take San Antonio we'll have a mighty good try at it, an' if it comes to hangin' an' all that sort of business there's Texan as well as Mexican ropes."

They reached another belt of forest about 3 o'clock in the morning, and they concluded to rest there and get some sleep. They felt no fear of the Mexicans who, they were sure, were now riding southward. They slept here four or five hours, and late the next afternoon reached the first settlement on the Brazos.

Ned and his companions spent a week on the river and when they rode south again they took with them nearly a hundred volunteers for the attack on San Antonio, the last draft that the little settlements could furnish. Very few, save the women and children, were left behind.

On their return journey they passed through the very forest in which Ned had made his singular rescue of Obed and the Ring Tailed Panther. They saw the camp and they saw the swath made by the fire, a narrow belt, five or six miles in length, ending as the Ring Tailed Panther had predicted at a curve of the creek. The Mexicans, as they now knew definitely, were gone days ago from that region.

"Perhaps we'll meet Urrea when we attack San Antonio," said Ned.

"Maybe," said Obed.

They rode to the camp on the Salado without interruption, and found that indecision still reigned there. The blockade of San Antonio was going on, and the men were eager for the assault, but the leaders were convinced that the force was too small and weak. They would not consent to what they considered sure disaster. The recruits that the three brought were welcomed, but Ned noticed a state of depression in the camp. He found yet there his old friends, Bowie, Smith, Karnes, and the others. His news that Urrea was a spy and traitor created a sensation.

Ned was asked by "Deaf" Smith the morning after his arrival to go with him on a scout, and he promptly accepted. A rest of a single day was enough for him and he was pining for new action.

The two rode toward the town, and then curved away to one side, keeping to the open prairie where they might see the approach of a superior enemy, in time. They observed the Mexican sentinels at a distance, but the two forces had grown so used to each other that no hostile demonstration was made, unless one or the other came too close.

Smith and Ned rode some distance, and then turned on another course, which brought them presently to a hill covered with ash and oak. They rode among the trees and from that point of vantage searched the whole horizon. Ned caught the glint of something in the south, and called Smith's attention to it.

"What do you think it is?" he asked after Smith had looked a long time.

"It's the sun shining on metal, either a lance head or a rifle barrel.

Ah, now I see horsemen riding this way."

"And they are Mexicans, too," said Ned. "What does it mean?"

A considerable force of mounted Mexicans was coming into view, and Smith's opinion was formed at once.

"It's reinforcements for Cos," he cried. "We heard that Ugartchea was going to bring fresh troops from Laredo, and that he would also have with him mule loads of silver to pay off Cos' men. We'll just cut off this force and take their silver. We'll ride to Bowie!"

They galloped at full speed to the camp and found the redoubtable Georgian, who instantly gathered together a hundred men including the Ring Tailed Panther and Obed and raced back. The Mexican horsemen were still in the valley, seeming to move slowly, and Bowie at once formed up the Texans for a charge. But before he could give the word a trumpet pealed, and the Mexicans rode at full speed toward a great gully at the end of the valley into which they disappeared. The last that the Texans saw were some heavily-loaded mules following their master into the ravine.

The Ring Tailed Panther burst into a laugh.

"Them's not reinforcements," he cried, "an' them's not mules loaded with silver. They're carryin' nothin' but grass. These men have been out there cuttin' feed in the meadow for Cos' horses."

"You're right, Panther," said "Deaf" Smith, somewhat crestfallen.

"But we'll attack, just the same," said Bowie. "Our men need action. We'll follow 'em into that gully. On, men, on!"

A joyous shout was his reply and the men galloped into the plain. They were about to charge for the gully when Bowie cried to them to halt. A new enemy had appeared. A heavy force of cavalry with two guns was coming from San Antonio to rescue the grass cutters. They rode forward with triumphant cheers, but the Texans did not flinch. They would face odds of at least three to one with calmness and confidence.

"Rifles ready, men!" cried Bowie. "They're about to charge."

The trumpets pealed out the signal again, and the Mexicans charged at a gallop. Up went the Texans' rifles. A hundred fingers pressed a hundred triggers, and a hundred bullets crashed into the front of the Mexican line. Down went horses and men, and the Mexican column stopped. But it opened in a few moments, and, through the breach, the two cannon began to fire, the heavy reports echoing over the plain. The Texans instinctively lengthened their line, making it as thin as possible, and continued their deadly rifle fire.

Ned, Obed and the Ring Tailed Panther as usual kept close together, and "Deaf" Smith also was now with them. All of them were aiming as well as they could through the smoke which was gathering fast, but the Mexicans, in greatly superior force, supported by the cannon, held their ground. The grass cutters in the gully also opened fire on the Texan flank, and for many minutes the battle swayed back and forth on the plain, while the clouds of smoke grew thicker, at times almost hiding the combatants from one another.

The Texans now began to press harder, and the Mexicans, despite their numbers and their cannon, yielded a little, but the fire from the men in the gully was stinging their flank. If they pushed forward much farther they would be caught between the two forces and might be destroyed. It was an alarming puzzle, but at that moment a great shout rose behind them. The sound of the firing had been heard in the main Texan camp and more Texans were coming by scores.

"It's all over now," said Obed.

The Texans divided into two forces. One drove the main column of the Mexicans in confusion back upon the town, and the other, containing Ned and his friends, charged into the gully and put to flight or captured all who were hidden there. They also took the mules with their loads of grass which they carried back to their own camp.

Ned, the Ring Tailed Panther, Obed and "Deaf" Smith rode back together to the Salado. It had been a fine victory, won as usual against odds, but they were not exultant. In the breast of every one of them had been a hope that the whole Texan army would seize the opportunity and charge at once upon Cos and San Antonio. Instead, they had been ordered back.

They made their discontent vocal that and the following evenings. There was no particular order among the Texans. They usually acted in groups, according to the localities from which they came, and some, believing that nothing would be done, had gone home disgusted. Mr. Austin himself had left, and Houston had persisted in his refusal to command. Burleson, a veteran Indian fighter, had finally been chosen for the leadership. Houston soon left, and Bowie, believing that nothing would be done, followed him.

It was only a few days after the grass fight, and despite that victory, Ned felt the current of depression. It seemed that their fortune was melting away without their ever putting it to the touch. Although new men had come their force was diminishing in numbers and San Antonio was farther from their hands than ever.

"If we don't do something before long," said Henry Karnes, "we'll just dissolve like a snow before a warm wind."

"An' all our rippin' an' tearin' will go for nothin'," growled the Ring Tailed Panther. "We've won every fight we've been in, an' yet they won't let us go into that town an' have it out with Cos."

"We'll get it yet," said Obed cheerfully. "In war it's a long lane that has no battle at the end. Just you be patient, Panther. Patience will have her good fight. I've tested it more than once myself."

Ned did not say anything. He had made himself a comfortable place, and, as the cold night wind was whistling among the oaks and pecans, the fire certainly looked very good to him. He watched the flames leap and sink, and the great beds of coals form, and once more he was very glad that he was not alone again on the Mexican mountains. He resolutely put off the feeling of depression. They might linger and hesitate now, but he did not doubt that the cause of Texas would triumph in the end.

Ned was restless that night, so restless that he could not sleep, and, after a futile effort, he rose, folded up his blankets and wandered about the camp. It was a body of volunteers drawn together by patriotism and necessity for a common purpose, and one could do almost as one pleased. There was a ring of sentinels, but everybody knew everybody else and scouts, skirmishers and foragers passed at will.

Ned was fully armed, of course, and, leaving the camp, he entered an oak grove that lay between it and the city. As there was no underbrush here and little chance for ambush he felt quite safe. Behind him he saw the camp and the lights of the scattered fires now dying, but before him he saw only the trunks of the trees and the dusky horizon beyond.

Ned had no definite object in view, but he thought vaguely of scouting along the river. One could never know too much about the opposing force, and experience added to natural gifts had given him great capabilities.

He advanced deeper into the pecan grove, and reached the point where the trees grew thickest. There, where the moonlight fell he saw a shadow lying along the ground, the shadow of a man. Ned sprang behind a tree and lay almost flat. The shadow had moved, but he could still see a head. He felt sure that its owner was behind another tree not yet ten feet distant. Perhaps some Mexican scout like himself. On the other hand, it might be Smith or Karnes, and he called softly.

No answer came to his call. Some freak of the moonlight still kept the shadowy head in view, while its owner remained completely hidden, unconscious, perhaps, that any part of his reflection was showing. Ned did not know what to do. After waiting a long time, and, seeing that the shadow did not move, he edged his way partly around the trunk, and stopped where he was still protected by the ground and the tree. He saw the shadowy head shift to the same extent that he had moved, but he heard no sound.

He called again and more loudly. He said: "I am a Texan; if you are a friend, say so!" No one would mistake his voice for that of a Mexican. No reply came from behind the tree.

Ned was annoyed. This was most puzzling and he did not like puzzles. Moreover, his situation was dangerous. If he left his tree, the man behind the other one—and he did not doubt now that he was an enemy—could probably take a shot at him.

He tried every manoeuvre that he knew to draw the shot, while he yet lay in ambush, but none succeeded. His wary enemy knew every ruse. Had it not been for the shadowy head, yet visible in the moonlight, Ned might have concluded that he had gone. He had now been behind the tree a full half hour, and during all that time he had not heard a single sound from his foe. The singular situation, so unusual in its aspect, and so real in its danger, began to get upon his nerves.

He thought at last of something which he believed would draw the fire of the ambushed Mexican. He carried a pistol as well as a rifle, and, carefully laying the cocked rifle by his side, he drew the smaller weapon. Then he crept about the tree, purposely making a little noise. He saw the shadowy head move, and he knew that his enemy was seeking a shot. He heard for the first time a slight sound, and he could tell from it exactly where the man lay.

Raising his pistol he fired, and the bark flew from the right side of the tree. A man instantly sprang out, rifle in hand, and rushed toward him expecting to take him, unarmed. Like a flash Ned seized his own cocked rifle and covered the man. When he looked down the sights he saw that it was Urrea.

Urrea halted, taken by surprise. His own rifle was not levelled, and Ned held his life at his gun muzzle.

"Stop, Don Francisco, or I fire," said the boy. "I did not dream that it was you, and I am sorry that I was wrong."

Urrea recovered very quickly from his surprise. He did not seek to raise his rifle, knowing that it was too late.

"Well," he said, "why don't you fire?"

"I don't know," replied Ned.

"I would do it in your place."

"I know it, but there is a difference between us and I am glad of that difference, egotistical as it may sound."

"There is another difference which perhaps you do not have in mind. You are a Texan, an American, and I am a Mexican. That is why I came among you and claimed to be one of you. You were fools to think that I, Francisco Urrea, could ever fight for Texas against Mexico."

"It seems that we were," said Ned.

Urrea laughed somewhat scornfully.

"There are some Mexicans born here in Texas who are so foolish," he said, "but they do not know Mexico. They do not know the greatness of our nation, or the greatness of Santa Anna. What are your paltry numbers against us? You will fail here against San Antonio, and, even if you should take the town, Santa Anna will come with a great army and destroy you. And then, remember that there is a price to be paid. Much rope will be used to good purpose in Texas."

"You have eaten our bread, you have received kindness from us, and yet you talk of executions."

"I ate your bread, because it was my business to do so. I am not ashamed of anything that I have done. I do not exaggerate, when I say that I have rendered my nation great service against the Texan rebels. It was I who brought them against you more than once."

"I should not boast of it. I should never pretend to belong to one side in war and work for another."

"Again there is a difference between us. Now, what do you purpose to do? I am, as it were, your prisoner, and it is for you to make a beginning."

Ned was embarrassed. He was young and he could not enforce all the rigors of war. He knew that if he took Urrea to the camp the man would be executed as a spy and traitor. The Mexicans had already committed many outrages, and the Texans were in no forgiving mood. Ned could not forget that this man had broken bread with his comrades and himself, and once he had liked him. Even now his manner, which contained no fear nor cringing, appealed to him.

"Go," he said at last, "I cannot take your life, nor can I carry you to those who would take it. Doubtless I am doing wrong, but I do not know what else to do."

"Do you mean that you let me go free?"

"I do. You cannot be a spy among us again, and as an open enemy you are only as one among thousands. Of course you came here to-night to spy upon us, and it was an odd chance that brought us together. Take the direction of San Antonio, but don't look back. I warn you that I shall keep you covered with my rifle."

Urrea turned without another word and walked away. Ned watched him for a full hundred yards. He noticed that the man's figure was as trim and erect as ever. Apparently, he was as wanting in remorse as he was in fear.

When Urrea had gone a hundred yards Ned turned and went swiftly back to the camp. He said nothing about the incident either to Obed or the Ring Tailed Panther. The next day Urrea was crowded from his mind by exciting news. A sentinel had hailed at dawn three worn and unkempt Texans who had escaped from San Antonio, where they had long been held prisoners by Cos. They brought word that the Mexican army was disheartened. The heavy reinforcements, promised by Santa Anna, had not come.

A great clamour for an immediate attack arose. The citizen army gathered in hundreds around the tent of Burleson, the leader, and de-manded that they be led against San Antonio. Fannin and Milam were there, and they seconded the demands of the men. Ned stood on the outskirts of the crowd. The Ring Tailed Panther on one side of him uttering a succession of growls, but Obed on the other was silent.

"It looks like a go this time," said Ned.

"I think it is," said Obed, "and if it isn't a go now it won't be one at all. Waiting wears out the best of men."

The Ring Tailed Panther continued to growl.

A great shout suddenly arose. The Panther ceased to growl and his face beamed. Burleson had consented to the demand of the men. It was quickly arranged that they should attack San Antonio in the morning, and risk everything on the cast.

The short day—it was winter now—was spent in preparations. Ned and his comrades cleaned their rifles and pistols and provided themselves with double stores of ammunition. Ned did not seek to conceal from himself, nor did the men seek to hide from him the greatness and danger of their attempt.

"They outnumber us and they hold a fortified town," said Obed. "Whatever we do we three must stick together. In union there is often safety."

"We stick as long as we stand," said the Ring Tailed Panther. "If

248

one falls the other two must go on, an', if two fall, the last must go on as long as he can."

"Agreed," said Ned and Obed.

They were ready long before night, but after dark an alarming story spread through the little army. Part of it at least proved to be true. One of the scouts, sent out after the decision to attack had been taken, had failed to come in. It was believed that he had deserted to the Mexicans with news of the intended Texan advance. The leaders had counted upon surprise, as a necessary factor in their success, and without it they would not advance. Gloom settled over the army, but it was not a silent gloom. These men spoke their disappointment in words many and loud. Never had the Ring Tailed Panther roared longer, without taking breath.

The Texans were still talking angrily about the fires, when another shout arose. The missing scout came in and he brought with him a Mexican deserter, who confirmed all the reports about the discouragement of the garrison. Once more, the Texans crowded about Burleson's tent, and demanded that the attack be made upon San Antonio. At last Burleson exclaimed:

"Well, if you can get volunteers to attack, go and attack!"

Milam turned, faced the crowd and raised his hand.

There was a sudden hush save for the deep breathing of many men. Then in a loud, clear voice Milam spoke only ten words. They were:

"Who will go with old Ben Milam into San Antonio?"

And a hundred voices roared a single word in reply. It was: "I!"

"That settles it," said the Ring Tailed Panther with deep satisfaction. "Old Satan himself couldn't stop the attack now."

The word was given that the volunteers for the direct attack, three hundred in number, would gather at an old mill half way between the camp and the town. Thence they would march on foot for the assault. Ned and his comrades were among the first to gather at the mill and he waited as calmly as he could, while the whole force was assembled, three hundred lean, brown men, large of bone and long of limb.

No light was allowed, and the night was cold. The figures of the men looked like phantoms in the dusk. Ned stood with his friends, while Milam gave the directions. They were to be divided into two forces. One under Milam was to enter the town by the street called Acequia, and the other under Colonel Johnson was to penetrate by Soledad Street. They relied upon the neglect of the Mexicans to get so far, before the battle began. Burleson, with the remainder of his men would attack the ancient mission, then turned into a fort, called the Alamo.

"Deaf" Smith, who knew the town thoroughly, led Johnson's column, and Ned, Obed and the Ring Tailed Panther were just behind him.

Ned was quivering in every nerve with excitement and suspense, but he let no one see it. He moved forward with steady step and he heard behind him the soft tread of the men who intended to get into San Antonio without being seen. He looked back at them. They came in the dusk like so many shadows and no one spoke. It was like a procession of ghosts, moving into a sleeping town. The chill wind cut across their faces, but no one at that moment took notice of cold.

High over Ned's head a great star danced and twinkled, and it seemed to him that it was the Texan Star springing out.

The houses of the town rose out of the darkness. Ned saw off to right and left fresh earthworks and rifle pits, but either no men were stationed there or they slept. The figure of Smith led steadily on and behind came the long and silent file. How much farther would they go without being seen or heard? It seemed amazing to Ned that they had come so far already.

They were actually at the edge of the town. Now they were in it, going up the narrow Soledad Street between the low houses directly toward the main plaza, which was fortified by barricades and artillery. A faint glimmer of dawn was just beginning to appear in the east.

A dusky figure suddenly appeared in the street in front of them and gave a shout of alarm. "Deaf" Smith fired and the man fell. A bugle pealed from the plaza and a cannon was fired down the street, the ball whistling over the heads of the Texans. In an instant the garrison of Cos was awake, and the alarm sounded from every point of San Antonio. Lights flashed, arms rattled and men called to one another.

"Into this house" cried "Deaf" Smith. "We cannot charge up the narrow street in face of the cannon!"

They were now within a hundred yards of the plaza, but they saw that the guide was right. They dashed into the large, solid house that he had indicated, and Ned did not notice until he was inside that it was the very house of the Vice-Governor, Veramendi, into which he had come once before. Just as the last of the Texans sprang through the doors another cannon ball whistled down the street, this time low enough. Milam's division, meanwhile, had rushed into the house of

De La Garcia, near by.

As Ned and the others sprang to cover he trampled upon the flowers in a patio, and he saw a little fountain playing. Then he knew. It was the house of Veramendi, and he thought it a singular chance that had brought him to the same place. But he had little time for reflection. The column of Texans, a hundred and fifty in number, were taking possession of every part of the building, the occupants of which had fled through the rear doors.

"To the roof!" cried "Deaf" Smith. "We can best meet the attack from there."

The doors and windows were already manned, but Smith and many of the best men rushed to the flat roof, and looked over the low stone coping. It was not yet day and they could not see well. Despite the lack of light, the Mexicans opened a great fire of cannon and small arms. The whole town resounded with the roar and the crash and also with the shouting. But most of the cannon balls and bullets flew wide, and the rest spent themselves in vain on the two houses.

The Texans, meanwhile, held their fire, and waited for day. Ned, Smith and the others on the roof lay down behind the low coping. They had achieved their long wish. They were in San Antonio, but what would happen to them there?

Ned peeped over the coping. He saw many flashes down the street toward the *plaza* and he heard the singing of bullets. His finger was on the trigger and the temptation to reply was great, but like the others he waited.

The faint light in the east deepened and the sun flashed out. The full dawn was at hand and the two forces, Texans and Mexicans, faced each other.

CHAPTER 22

THE TAKING OF THE TOWN

The December sun, clear and cold, bathed the whole town in light. Houses, whether of stone, *adobe* or wood, were tinted a while with gold, but everywhere in the streets and over the roofs floated white puffs of smoke from the firing, which had never ceased on the part of the Mexicans. The crash of rifles and muskets was incessant, and every minute or two came the heavy boom of the cannon with which Cos swept the streets. The Texans themselves now pulled the trigger but little, calmly waiting their opportunity.

Ned and his comrades still lay on the roof of the Veramendi house. The boy's heart beat fast but the scene was wild and thrilling to the last degree. He felt a great surge of pride that he should have a share in so great an event. From the other side of the river came the rattle of rifle fire, and he knew that it was the detachment from Burleson attacking the Alamo. But presently the sounds there died.

"They are drawing off," said Obed, "and it is right. It is their duty to help us here, but I don't see how they can ever get into San Antonio. I wish the Mexicans didn't have those cannon which are so much heavier than ours."

The Texans had brought with them a twelve pounder and a six pounder, but the twelve pounder had already been dismounted by the overpowering Mexican fire, and, without protection they were unable to use the six pounder which they had drawn into the patio, where it stood silent.

Ned from his corner could see the mouths of the guns in the heavy Mexican battery at the far end of the *plaza*, and he watched the flashes of flame as they were fired one by one. In the intervals he saw a lithe, strong figure appear on the breastwork, and he was quite sure that it was Urrea.

An hour of daylight passed. From the house of De La Garcia the other division of Texans began to fire, the sharp lashing of their rifles sounding clearly amid the duller crash of musketry and cannon from the Mexicans. The Texans in the lower part of the Veramendi house were also at work with their rifles. Every man was a sharpshooter, and, whenever a Mexican came from behind a barricade, he was picked off. But the Mexicans had also taken possession of houses and they were firing with muskets from windows and loopholes.

"We must shoot down the cannoneers," shouted the Ring Tailed Panther to "Deaf" Smith.

Smith nodded. The men on the roof were fifteen in number and now they devoted their whole attention to the battery. Despite the drifting smoke they hit gunner after gunner. The fever in Ned's blood grew. Everything was red before him. His temples throbbed like fire. The spirit of battle had taken full hold of him, and he fired whenever he caught a glimpse of a Mexican.

"Deaf" Smith was on Ned's right, and he picked off a gunner. But to do so he had lifted his head and shoulders above the coping. A figure rose up behind the Mexican barricade and fired in return. "Deaf" Smith uttered a little cry, and clapped his hand to his shoulder.

252

"Never mind," he said in reply to anxious looks. "It's in the fleshy part only, and I'm not badly hurt."

The bullet had gone nearly through the shoulder and was just under the skin on the other side. The Ring Tailed Panther cut it out with his bowie knife and bound up the wound tightly with strips from his hunting shirt. But Ned, although it was only a fleeting glimpse, had recognised the marksman. It was Urrea who had sent the bullet through "Deaf" Smith's shoulder. He was proving himself a formidable foe.

But the men on the roof continued their deadly sharpshooting, and now, the battery, probably at Urrea's suggestion, began to turn its attention to them. Ned was seized suddenly by Obed and pulled flat. There was a roaring and hissing sound over his head as a twelve pound cannon ball passed, and Ned said to Obed: "I thank you." The cannon shot was followed by a storm of bullets and then by more cannon shots. The Mexican guns were served well that day. The coping was shot away and the Texans were in imminent danger from the flying pieces. They were glad when the last of it was gone.

But they did not yet dare to raise themselves high enough for a shot. Balls, shell, and bullets swept the roof without ceasing. Ned lay on his side, almost flat. He listened to the ugly hissing and screaming over his head until it became unbearable. He turned over on his other side and looked at Smith, their leader. Smith was pale and weak from his wound, but he smiled wanly.

"You don't speak, but your face asks your question, Ned," he said. "I hate to say it, but we can't hold this roof. I never knew the Mexicans to shoot so well before, and their numbers and cannon give them a great advantage. Below, lads, as soon as you can!"

They crept down the stairway, and found that the house itself was suffering from the Mexican cannon. Holes had been smashed in the walls, but here the Texans were always replying with their rifles. They also heard the steady fire in the house of De La Garcia and they knew that their comrades were standing fast. Ned, exhausted by the great tension, sat down on a willow sofa. His hands were trembling and his face was wet with perspiration. The Ring Tailed Panther sat down beside him.

"Good plan to rest a little, Ned," he said. "We've come right into a hornets' nest an' the hornets are stingin' us hard. Listen to that, will you!"

A cannon ball smashed through the wall, passed through the room in which they were sitting, and dropped spent in another room beyond. Obed joined them on the sofa.

"A cannon ball never strikes in the same place twice," misquoted Obed. "So it's safer here than it is anywhere else in this Veramendi house. I'd help with the rifles but there's no room for me at the windows and loopholes just now."

"Our men are giving it back to them," said Ned. "Listen how the rifles crackle!"

The battle was increasing in heat. The Mexicans, despite their artillery, and their heavy barricades, were losing heavily at the hands of the sharpshooters. The Texans, sheltered in the buildings, were suffering little, but their position was growing more dangerous every minute. They were inside the town, but the force of Burleson outside was unable to come to their aid. Meanwhile, they must fight five to one, but they addressed themselves with unflinching hearts to the task. Even in the moment of imminent peril they did not think of retreat, but clung to their original purpose of taking San Antonio.

Ned, tense and restless, was unable to remain more than a few minutes on the sofa. He wandered into another room and saw a large table spread with food. Bread and meat were in the dishes, and there were pots of coffee. All was now cold. Evidently they had been making ready for early breakfast in the Veramendi house when the Texans came. Ned called to his friends.

"Why shouldn't we use it!" he said, "even if it is cold?"

"Why shouldn't we?" said Obed. "Even though we fight we must live."

They took the food and coffee, cold as it was, to the men, and they ate and drank eagerly. Then they searched everywhere and found large supplies of provisions in the house, so much, in fact, that the Ring Tailed Panther growled very pleasantly between his teeth.

"There's enough here," he said, "to last two or three days, an' it's well when you're in a fort, ready to stand a siege, to have something to eat."

Some of the men now left the windows and loopholes to get a rest and Ned found a place at one of them. Peeping out he saw the bare street, torn by shot and shell. He saw the flash of the Texan rifles from the De La Garcia house and he saw the blaze of the Mexican cannon in the *plaza*. Mexican men, women and children on the flat roofs, out of range, were eagerly watching the battle. Clouds of smoke drifted over the city.

While Ned was at the window, a second cannon ball smashed through the wall of the Veramendi house, and caused the debris to fall in masses. The colonel grew uneasy. The cannon gave the Mexicans an immense advantage, and they were now using it to the utmost. The house would be battered down over the heads of the Texans, and they could not live in the streets, which the Mexicans, from their dominating position, could sweep with cannon and a thousand rifles and muskets. A third ball crashed through the wall and demolished the willow sofa on which the three had been sitting. Plaster rained down upon the Texans. They looked at one another. They could not stay in the house nor could they go out. A boy suddenly solved the difficulty.

"Let's dig a trench across the street to the De La Garcia house!" cried Ned, "and join our comrades there!"

"That's the thing!" they shouted. They had not neglected to bring entrenching tools with them, and they found spades and shovels about the house. But in order to secure the greatest protection for their work they decided to wait until night, confident that they could hold their present position throughout the day.

It was many hours until the darkness, and the fire rose and fell at intervals. More shattered plaster fell upon them, but they were still holding the wreck of a house, when the welcome twilight deepened and darkened into the night. Then they began work just inside the doorway, cutting fast through plaster and *adobe*, and soon reaching the street. They made the trench fairly wide, intending to get their six pounder across also. Just behind those who worked with spade and shovel came the riflemen.

A third of the way across, and the Mexicans discovered what was going on. Once more a storm of cannon, rifle and musket balls swept the street, but the Texans, bent down in their trench, toiled on, throwing the dirt above their heads and out on either side. The riflemen behind them, sheltered by the earth, replied to the Mexican fire, and, despite the darkness, picked off many men.

Ned was just behind Obed, and the Ring Tailed Panther was following him. All three were acting as riflemen. Obed was seeking a glimpse of Urrea, but he did not get it. Ned was watching for a shot at the gunners.

Once the Mexicans under the cover of their artillery undertook to charge down the street, but the sharpshooters in the trench quickly drove them back.

Thus they burrowed like a great mole all the way across Soledad

Street, and joined their comrades in the strong house of De La Garcia. They also succeeded in getting both of their cannon into the house, and, now united, the Texans were encouraged greatly. Ned found all the rooms filled with men. A party broke through the joint wall and entered the next house, thus taking them nearer to the *plaza* and the Mexican fortifications.

All through the night intermittent firing went on. The Mexicans increased their fortifications, preparing for a desperate combat on the morrow. They threw up new earthworks, and they loop-holed many of the houses that they held. Cos, his dark face darker with rage and fury, went among them, urging them to renewed efforts, telling them that they were bound to take prisoners all the Texans whom they did not slay in battle, and that they should hang every prisoner. Great numbers of the women and children had hidden in the Alamo on the other side of the river. San Antonio itself was stripped for battle, and the hatred between Texan and Mexican, so unlike in temperament, flamed into new heat.

Ned was worn to the bone. His lips were burnt with his feverish breath. The smoke stung his eyes and nostrils, and his limbs ached. He felt that he must rest or die, and, seeing two men sound asleep on the floor of one of the rooms, he flung himself down beside them. He slept in a few minutes and Obed and the Ring Tailed Panther seeing him there did not disturb him.

"If any boy has been through more than he has," said Obed, "I haven't heard of him."

"An' I guess that he an' all of us have got a lot more comin'," said the Ring Tailed Panther grimly. "Cos ain't goin' to give up here without the terriblest struggle of his life. He can't afford to do it."

"Reckon you're right," said Obed.

Ned awoke the next morning with the taste of gunpowder in his mouth, but the Texans, besides finding food in the houses, had brought some with them, and he ate an ample breakfast. Then ensued a day that he found long and monotonous. Neither side made any decided movement. There was occasional firing, but they rested chiefly on their arms. In the course of the second night the Mexicans opened another trench, from which they began to fire at dawn, but the Texan rifles quickly put them to flight.

The Texans now began to grow restless. Cooped up in two houses they were in the way of one another and they demanded freedom and action. Henry Karnes suggested that they break into another house closer to the plaza. Milam consented and Karnes, followed closely by Ned, Obed, the Ring Tailed Panther and thirty others, dashed out, smashed in the door of the house, and were inside before the astonished Mexicans could open an accurate fire upon them. Here they at once secured themselves and their bullets began to rake the *plaza*. The Mexicans were forced to throw up more and higher entrenchments.

Again the combat became intermittent. There were bursts of rifle fire, and occasional shots from the cannon, and, now and then, short periods of almost complete silence. Night came on and Ned, watching from the window, saw Colonel Milam, their leader, pass down the trench and enter the courtyard of the Veramendi house. He stood there a moment, looking at the Mexican position. A musket cracked and the Texan, throwing up his arms, fell. He was dead by the time he touched the ground. The ball had struck him in the centre of the forehead.

Ned uttered a cry of grief, and it was taken up by all the Texans who had seen their leader fall. A half dozen men rushed forward and dragged away his body, but that night they buried it in the patio. His death only incited them to new efforts. As soon as his burial was finished they rushed another house in their slow advance, one belonging to Antonio Navarro, a solid structure only one block from the great *plaza*. They also stormed and carried a redoubt which the Mexicans had erected in the street beside the house. It now being midnight they concluded to rest until the morrow. Meanwhile, they had elected Johnson their leader.

Ned was in the new attack and with Obed and the Ring Tailed Panther he was in the Navarro house. It was the fourth that he had occupied since the attack on San Antonio. He felt less excitement than on the night before. It seemed to him that he was becoming hardened to everything. He looked at his comrades and laughed. They were no longer in the semblance of white men. Their faces were so blackened with smoke, dirt and burned gunpowder that they might have passed for negroes.

"You needn't laugh, Ned," said Obed. "You're just as black as we are. This thing of changing your boarding house every night by violence and the use of firearms doesn't lead to neatness. If fine feathers make fine birds then we three are about the poorest flock that ever flew."

"But when we go for a house we always get it," said the Ring Tailed Panther. "You notice that. This place belongs to Antonio Navarro. I've met him in San Antonio, an' I don't like him, but I'm willin' to take his roof an' bed."

Ned took the roof but not the bed. He could not sleep that night, and it was found a little later that none would have a chance to sleep. The Mexicans, advancing over the other houses, the walls of all of which joined, cut loopholes in the roof of the Navarro house and opened fire upon the Texans below. The Texans, with surer aim, cleared the Mexicans away from the loopholes, then climbed to the roof and drove them off entirely.

But no one dared to sleep after this attack, and Ned watched all through the dark hours. Certainly they were having action enough now, and he was wondering what the fourth day would bring forth. From an upper window he watched the chilly sun creep over the horizon once more, and the dawn brought with it the usual stray rifle and musket shots. Both Texan and Mexican sharpshooters were watching at every loophole, and whenever they saw a head they fired at it. But this was only the beginning, the crackling prelude to the event that was to come.

"Come down, Ned," said Obed, "and get your breakfast. We've got coffee and warm corn cakes and we'll need 'em, as we're already tired of this boarding house and we intend to find another."

"Can't stay more than one night in a place while we're in San Antonio," said the Ring Tailed Panther, growling pleasantly. "A restless lot we are an' it's time to move on again."

Ned ate and drank in silence. His nerves were quite steady, and he had become so used to battle that he awaited whatever they were going to attempt, almost without curiosity.

"Ain't you wantin' to know what we're goin' to do, Ned?" asked the Ring Tailed Panther.

"I'm thinking that I'll find out pretty quick," replied Ned.

"Now this boy is shorely makin' a fine soldier," said the Panther to Obed. "He don't ask nothin' about what he's goin' to do, but just eats an' waits orders."

Ned smiled and ate another corn cake.

"Maybe," said Obed, "we'll meet our friend Urrea in the attack we're going to make. If so, I'll take a shot at him, and I won't have any remorse about it, either, if I hit him."

They did not wait long. A strong body of the Texans gathered on the lower floor, many carrying, in addition to their weapons, heavy iron crowbars. The doors were suddenly thrown open and they rushed out into the cool morning air, making for a series of stone houses called the Zambrano Row, the farthest of which opened upon the main *plaza*, where the Mexicans were fortified so strongly. Scattering shots from muskets and rifles greeted them, but as usual, when any sudden movement occurred, the Mexicans fired wildly, and the Texans broke into the first of the houses, before they could take good aim.

Ned was one of the last inside. He had lingered with the others to repel any rush that the Mexicans might make. He was watching the Mexican barricade, and he saw heads rise above it. One rose higher than the rest and he recognised Urrea. The Mexican saw Ned also, and the eyes of the two met. Urrea's were full of anger and malice, and raising his rifle he fired straight at the boy. Ned felt the bullet graze his cheek, and instantly he fired in reply. But Urrea had quickly dropped down behind the barricade and the bullet missed. Then Ned rushed into the house.

The boy was blazing with indignation. He had spared Urrea's life, and yet the Mexican had sought at the first opportunity to kill him. He could not understand a soul of such calibre. But the incident passed from his mind, for the time being, in the strenuous work that they began now to do.

They broke through partition wall after wall with their powerful picks and crowbars. Stones fell about them. Plaster and dust rained down, but the men relieving one another, the work with the heavy tools was never stopped until they penetrated the interior of the last house in the row. Then the Texans uttered a grim cry of exultation. They looked from the narrow windows directly over the main *plaza* and their rifles covered the Mexican barricades. The Mexicans tried to drive them out of the houses with the guns, but the solid stone walls resisted balls and shells, and the Texan rifles shot down the gunners.

Then ensued another silence, broken by distant firing, caused by another attack upon the Texan camp outside the town. It was driven off quickly and the Texans in the houses lay quiet until evening. Then they heard a great shouting, the occasion of which they did not know until later. Ugartchea with six hundred men had arrived from the Rio Grande to help Cos. But it would not have made any difference with the Texans had they known. They were determined to take San Antonio, and all the time they were pressing harder on Cos.

That night, the Texans, Ned with them, seized another large building called the Priests' House, which looked directly over the *plaza*, and now their command of the Mexican situation was complete. Nothing could live in the square under their fire, and in the night Ned saw the

Mexicans withdrawing, leaving their cannon behind.

Exhaustion compelled the boy to sleep from midnight until day, when he was roused by Obed.

"The Mexicans have all gone across the river to the Alamo," said the Maine man. "San Antonio is ours."

Ned went forth with his comrades. Obed had told the truth. The great seat of the Mexican power in the north was theirs. Three hundred daring men, not strongly supported by those whom they had left behind, had penetrated to the very heart of the city through house after house, and had driven out the defenders who were five to their one.

The *plaza* and Soledad Street presented a sombre aspect. The Mexican dead, abandoned by their comrades, lay everywhere. The Texan rifles had done deadly work. The city itself was silent and deserted.

"Most of the population has gone with the Mexican army to the Alamo," said Obed. "I suppose we'll have to attack that, too."

But Cos, the haughty and vindictive general, did not have the heart for a new battle with the Texans. He sent a white flag to Burleson and surrendered. Ned was present when the flag came, and the leader of the little party that brought it was Urrea. The young Mexican had lost none of his assurance.

"You have won now," he said to Ned, "but bear in mind that we will come again. You have yet to hear from Mexico and Santa Anna."

"When Santa Anna comes he will find us here ready to meet him," replied Ned.

The Texans in the hour of their great and marvellous victory behaved with humanity and moderation. Cos and his army, which still doubled in numbers both the Texans who had been inside and outside San Antonio, were permitted to retire on parole beyond the Rio Grande. They left in the hands of the Texans twenty-one cannon and great quantities of ammunition. Rarely has such a victory been won by so small a force and in reality with the rifle alone. All the Texans felt that it was a splendid culmination to a perilous campaign.

Ned, Obed and the Ring Tailed Panther, seated on their horses, watched the captured army of Cos march away.

"Well, Texas is free," said the Ring Tailed Panther.

"And San Antonio is ours," said Obed.

"But Santa Anna will come," said Ned, remembering the words of Urrea.

The Texan Scouts

CHAPTER 1
IN THE STORM

The horseman rode slowly toward the west, stopping once or twice to examine the wide circle of the horizon with eyes that were trained to note every aspect of the wilderness. On his right the plains melted away in gentle swell after swell, until they met the horizon. Their brown surface was broken only by the spiked and thorny cactus and stray bits of chaparral.

On his left was the wide bed of a river which flowed through the sand, breaking here and there into several streams, and then reuniting, only to scatter its volume a hundred yards further into three or four channels. A bird of prey flew on strong wing over the water, dipped and then rose again, but there was no other sign of life. Beyond, the country southward rolled away, gray and bare, sterile and desolate.

The horseman looked most often into the south. His glances into the north were few and brief, but his eyes dwelled long on the lonely land that lay beyond the yellow current. His was an attractive face. He was young, only a boy, but the brow was broad and high, and the eyes, grave and steady, were those of one who thought much. He was clad completely in buckskin, and his hat was wide of brim. A rifle held in one hand lay across the pommel of his saddle and there were weapons in his belt. Two light, but warm, blankets, folded closely, were tied behind him. The tanned face and the lithe, strong figure showed a wonderful degree of health and strength.

Several hours passed and the horseman rode on steadily though slowly. His main direction was toward the west, and always he kept the river two or three hundred yards on his left. He never failed to search the plains on either side, but chiefly in the south, with the eager, intent gaze that missed nothing. But the lonesome gray land, cut by the coiling yellow river, still rolled before him, and its desolation and chill struck to his heart. It was the depth of the Texan winter, and, at times, icy gusts, born in far mountains, swept across the plains.

The rider presently turned his horse toward the river and stopped on a low bluff overlooking it. His face showed a tinge of disappointment, as if his eyes failed to find objects for which they sought. Again he gazed long and patiently into the south, but without reward.

He resumed his ride parallel with the river, but soon stopped a second time, and held up an open hand, like one who tests the wind. The air was growing perceptibly colder. The strong gusts were now fusing into a steady wind. The day, which had not been bright at any time, was turning darker. The sun was gone and in the far north banks of mists and vapour were gathering. A dreary moaning came over the plain.

Ned Fulton, tried and brave though he was, beheld the omens with alarm. He knew what they portended, and in all that vast wilderness he was alone. Not a human being to share the danger with him! Not a hand to help!

He looked for chaparral, something that might serve as a sort of shelter, but he had left the last clump of it behind, and now he turned and rode directly north, hoping that he might find some deep depression between the swells where he and his horse, in a fashion, could hide.

Meanwhile the norther came down with astonishing speed. The temperature fell like a plummet. The moan of the wind rose to a shriek, and cold clouds of dust were swept against Ned and his horse. Then snow mingled with the dust and both beat upon them. Ned felt his horse shivering under him, and he shivered, too, despite his will. It had turned so dark that he could no longer tell where he was going, and he used the wide brim of his hat to protect himself from the sand.

Soon it was black as night, and the snow was driving in a hurricane. The wind, unchecked by forest or hill, screamed with a sound almost human. Ned dismounted and walked in the lee of his horse. The animal turned his head and nuzzled his master, as if he could give him warmth.

Ned hoped that the storm would blow itself out in an hour or two, but his hope was vain. The darkness did not abate. The wind rose instead of falling, and the snow thickened. It lay on the plain several inches deep, and the walking grew harder. At last the two, the boy and the horse, stopped. Ned knew that they had come into some kind of a depression, and the full force of the hurricane passed partly over their heads.

It was yet very dark, and the driving snow scarcely permitted him to open his eyes, but by feeling about a little he found that one side of the dip was covered with a growth of dwarf bushes. He led the horse into the lower edge of these, where some protection was secured, and, crouching once more in the lee of the animal, he unfolded the two blankets, which he wrapped closely about himself to the eyes.

Ned, for the first time since the norther rushed down upon him, felt secure. He would not freeze to death, he would escape the fate that sometimes overtook lone hunters or travelers upon those vast plains. Warmth from the blankets began gradually to replace the chill in his bones, and the horse and the bushes together protected his face from the driven snow which had been cutting like hail. He even had, in some degree, the sense of comfort which one feels when safe inside four walls with a storm raging past the windows. The horse whinnied once and rubbed his nose against Ned's hand. He, too, had ceased to shiver.

All that afternoon the norther blew with undiminished violence. After a while the fall of snow thinned somewhat, but the wind did not decrease. Ned was devoutly thankful for the dip and the bushes that grew within it. Nor was he less thankful for the companionship of his horse. It was a good horse, a brave horse, a great bay mustang, built powerfully and with sinews and muscles of steel. He had secured him just after taking part in the capture of San Antonio with his comrades, Obed White and the Ring Tailed Panther, and already the tie between horse and rider had become strong and enduring. Ned stroked him again, and the horse, twisting his neck around, thrust his nose under his arm.

"Good old boy! Good fellow!" said Ned, pinching his ear. "We were lucky, you and I, to find this place."

The horse neighed ever so gently, and rubbed his nose up and down. After a while the darkness began to increase. Ned knew that it was not a new development of the storm, but the coming of night, and he grew anxious again. He and his horse, however secure at the present moment, could not stay always in that dip among the bushes. Yet he did not dare to leave it. Above on the plain they would receive the full sweep of the wind, which was still bitterly cold.

He was worn by the continued buffetings of blast and snow, but he did not dare to lie down, even in the blankets, lest he never wake again, and while he considered he saw darker shadows in the darkness above him. He gazed, all attention, and counted ten shadows, following one another, a dusky file. He knew by the set of their figures, short and stocky, that they were Mexicans, and his heart beat heavily. These were the first Mexicans that anyone had seen on Texan soil since the departure of Cos and his army on parole from captured San Antonio. So the Mexicans had come back, and no doubt they would return in great force!

Ned crouched lower, and he was very glad that the nose of the horse was still under his arm. He would not have a chance to whinny to his kind that bore the Mexicans. But the horse made no attempt to move, and Ned watched them pass on and out of sight. He had not heard the sound of footsteps or voices above the wind, and after they were gone it seemed to him that he had seen a line of phantoms.

But he was sure that his own mortal eyes had beheld that for which he was looking. He and his comrades had been watching the Rio Grande to see whether the Mexicans had crossed, and now he at least knew it.

He waited patiently three or four hours longer, until the wind died and the fall of snow ceased, when he mounted his horse and rode out of the dip. The wind suddenly sprang up again in about fifteen minutes, but now it blew from the south and was warm. The darkness thinned away as the moon and stars came out in a perfect sky of southern blue. The temperature rose many degrees in an hour and Ned knew that the snow would melt fast. All danger of freezing was past, but he was as hungry as a bear and tired to death.

He unwrapped the blankets from his body, folded them again in a small package which he made fast to his saddle, and once more stroked the nose of his horse.

"Good Old Jack," he murmured—he had called him Old Jack after Andrew Jackson, then a mighty hero of the south and west, "you passed through the ordeal and never moved, like the silent gentleman that you are."

Old Jack whinnied ever so softly, and rubbed his nose against the boy's coat sleeve. Ned mounted him and rode out of the dip, pausing at the top of the swell for a long look in every direction. The night was now peaceful and there was no noise, save for the warm wind that blew out of the south with a gentle sighing sound almost like the note of music. Trickles of water from the snow, already melting, ran down the crests. Lighter and lighter grew the sky. The moon seemed to Ned to be poised directly overhead, and close by. New stars were springing out as the last clouds floated away.

Ned sought shelter, warmth and a place in which to sleep, and to secure these three he felt that he must seek timber. The scouts whom he had seen were probably the only Mexicans north of the Rio Grande, and, as he believed, there was not one chance in a thousand of meeting such enemies again. If he should be so lucky as to find shelter he would sleep there without fear.

He rode almost due north for more than two hours, seeing patches of chaparral on both right and left. But, grown fastidious now and not thinking them sufficient for his purpose, he continued his northern course. Old Jack's feet made a deep sighing sound as they sank in the snow, and now there was water everywhere as that soft but conquering south wind blew steadily over the plain.

When he saw a growth of timber rising high and dark upon a swell he believed that he had found his place, and he urged his horse to renewed speed. The trees proved to be pecans, aspens and oaks growing so densely that he was compelled to dismount and lead Old Jack before they could force an entrance. Inside he found a clear space, somewhat like the openings of the north, in shape an irregular circle, but not more than fifteen feet across. Great spreading boughs of oaks had protected it so well that but little snow had fallen there, and that little had melted. Already the ground in the circle was drying.

Ned uttered an exclamation of relief and gratitude. This would be his camp, and to one used to living in the wilderness it furnished good shelter. At one edge of the opening was an outcropping of flat rock now quite dry, and there he would spread his bed. He unsaddled and unbridled his horse, merely tethering him with a lariat, and spread the horse blanket upon the flat rock. He would lie upon this and cover himself with his own blankets, using the saddle as a pillow.

But the security of the covert tempted the boy, who was now as hungry as a bear just come from winter quarters. He felt weak and relaxed after his long hours in the snow and storm, and he resolved to have warm food and drink.

There was much fallen wood among the trees, and with his strong hunting knife he whittled off the bark and thin dry shavings until he had a fine heap. Working long with flint and steel, he managed to set fire to the shavings, and then he fed the flames with larger pieces of wood until he had a great bed of glowing coals. A cautious wilderness rover, learning always from his tried friends, Ned never rode the plains without his travelling equipment, and now he drew from his pack a small tin coffee pot and tiny cup of the same material. Then with quick and skilful hands he made coffee over the coals and warmed strips of deer and buffalo meat.

He ate and drank hungrily, while the horse nibbled the grass that grew within the covert. Glorious warmth came again and the worn feeling departed. Life, youthful, fresh and abounding, swelled in every vein.

He now put out all the coals carefully, throwing wet leaves upon them, in order that not a single spark might shine through the trees to be seen by an enemy upon the plain. He relied upon the horse to give warning of a possible approach by man, and to keep away wolves.

Then he made his bed upon the rock, doing everything as he had arranged it in his mind an hour before, and, wrapped in his blankets, fell into the soundest of sleeps. The south wind still blew steadily, playing a low musical song among the trees. The beads of water on the twigs and the few leaves that remained dried fast. The grass dried, too, and beyond the covert the snow, so quick to come, was equally quick to go.

The horse ceased to nibble the grass, looked at the sleeping boy, touched his blankets lightly with his nose, and walked to the other side of the opening, where he lay down and went to his own horse heaven of sleep.

It was not many hours until day and Old Jack was a light sleeper. When he opened his eyes again he saw a clear and beautiful winter day of the far south. The only clouds in the sky were little drifting bits of fine white wool, and the warm wind still blew. Old Jack, who was in reality Young Jack, as his years were not yet four, did not think so much of the covert now, as he had already eaten away all the grass within the little opening but his sense of duty was strong. He saw that his human master and comrade still slept, apparently with no intention of awakening at any very early date, and he set himself to gleaning stray blades of grass that might have escaped his notice the night before.

Ned awoke a little after the noon hour, and sprang to his feet in dismay. The sun was almost directly over his head, showing him how late it was. He looked at his horse as if to reproach his good comrade for not waking him sooner, but Old Jack's large mild eyes gave him such a gaze of benignant unconcern that the boy was ashamed of himself.

"It certainly was not your fault," he said to his horse, "and, after all, it probably doesn't matter. We've had a long sound sleep and rest, and I've no doubt that both of us will profit by it. Nothing seems to be left in here for you to eat, but I'll take a little breakfast myself."

He did not relight the fire, but contented himself with cold food. Then resaddling, he left the grove and rode northward again until he came to a hill, or, rather, a swell, that was higher than the rest. Here he stopped his horse and took a glance at the sun, which was shining with uncommon brilliancy. Then he produced a small mirror from the pocket of his hunting shirt and held it in such a position that it made a focus of the sun's rays, throwing them in a perfect blazing lance of light.

He turned the flaming lance around the horizon, until it completed the circle and then he started around with it again. Meantime he was keeping a close watch upon every high point. A hill rose in the north, and he looked at it longest, but nothing came from it. There was another, but lower, hill in the west, and before he had completed the second round with his glass a light flashed from it. It was a brilliant light, almost like a sheaf of white incandescent rays. He lowered his own mirror and the light played directly upon his hill. When it ceased he sent back answering rays, to which, when he stopped, a rejoinder came in like fashion. Then he put the little mirror back in the safe pocket of his hunting shirt and rode with perfect confidence toward that western hill.

The crest that Ned sought was several miles away, although it looked much nearer in the thin clear air of the plains, but he rode now at increased speed, because there was much to draw him on. Old Jack seemed to share in his lightness of spirit, raising his head once and neighing, as if he were sending forth a welcome.

The boy soon saw two figures upon the hill, the shapes of horse and man, outlined in black against the sun, which was now declining in the west. They were motionless and they were exaggerated into gigantic stature against the red background. Ned knew them, although the distance was far too great to disclose any feature. But signal had spoken truly to signal, and that was enough. Old Jack made a fresh burst of speed and presently neighed once more. An answering neigh came back from the hill.

Ned rode up the slope and greeted Obed White and the Ring Tailed Panther with outstretched hands.

"And it's you, my boy," said Obed, his eyes glistening. "Until we saw your signal we were afraid that you might have frozen to death in the norther, but it's a long lane that has no happy ending, and here we are, all three of us, alive, and as well as ever."

269

"That's so," said the Panther, "but even when the storm was at its worst I didn't give up, Ned. Somehow, when things are at the blackest I'm always hopin'. I don't take any credit fur it. I was just born with that kind of a streak in me."

Ned regarded him with admiration. The Ring Tailed Panther was certainly a gorgeous object. He rode a great black horse with a flowing mane. He was clad completely in a suit of buckskin which was probably without a match on the border. It and his moccasins were adorned with thick rows of beads of many colours, that glittered and flashed as the sunlight played upon them. Heavy silver spurs were fastened to his heels, and his hat of broad brim and high cone in the Mexican fashion was heavy with silver braid. His saddle also was of the high, peaked style, studded with silver. The Panther noticed Ned's smile of appraisement and smiled back.

"Ain't it fine?" he said. "I guess this is about the beautifullest outfit to be found in either Texas or Mexico. I bought it all in honour of our victory just after we took San Antonio, and it soothes my eyes and makes my heart strong every time I look at it."

"And it helps out the prairies," said Obed White, his eyes twinkling. "Now that winter has made 'em brown, they need a dash of colour and the Panther gives it to 'em. Fine feathers don't keep a man from being a man for a' that. What did you do in the storm, Ned?"

"I found shelter in a thick grove, managed to light a fire, and slept there in my blankets."

"We did about the same."

"But I saw something before I reached my shelter."

"What was that?" exclaimed the two, noting the significance in Ned's tone.

"While I was waiting in a dip I saw ten Mexican horsemen ride by. They were heavily armed, and I've no doubt they were scouts belonging to some strong force."

"And so they are back on this side of the Rio Grande," said Obed White thoughtfully. "I'm not surprised. Our Texans have rejoiced too early. The full storm has not burst yet."

The Panther began to bristle. A giant in size, he seemed to grow larger, and his gorgeous hunting suit strained at the seams.

"Let 'em come on," he said menacingly. "Let Santa Anna himself lead 'em. We Texans can take care of 'em all."

But Obed White shook his head sadly.

"We could if we were united," he said, "but our leaders have taken to squabbling. You're a cheerful talker, Panther, and you deserve both your names, but to tell you the honest truth I'm afraid of the Mexican advance."

"I think the Mexicans probably belonged to Urrea's band," said Ned.

"Very likely," said Obed. "He's about the most energetic of their partisan leaders, and it may be that we'll run against him pretty soon."

They had heard in their scouting along the Rio Grande that young Francisco Urrea, after the discovery that he was a spy and his withdrawal from San Antonio with the captured army of Cos, had organized a strong force of horsemen and was foremost among those who were urging a new Mexican advance into Texas.

"It's pretty far west for the Mexicans," said the Panther. "We're on the edge of the Indian country here."

But Obed considered it all the more likely that Urrea, if he meditated a raid, would come from the west, since his approach at that point would be suspected the least. The three held a brief discussion and soon came to an agreement. They would continue their own ride west and look for Urrea. Having decided so, they went into the task heart and soul, despite its dangers.

The three rode side by side and three pairs of skilled eyes examined the plain. The snow was left only in sheltered places or among the trees. But the further they went the scarcer became the trees, and before night they disappeared entirely.

"We are comin' upon the buffalo range," said the Panther. "A hundred miles further west we'd be likely to strike big herds. When we're through fightin' the Mexicans I'm goin' out there again. It's the life fur me."

The night came, dark and cold, but fortunately without wind. They camped in a dip and did not light any fire, lying as Ned had done the night before on their horse blankets and wrapping themselves in their own. The three horses seemed to be contented with one another and made no noise.

They deemed it wise now to keep a watch, as they might be near Urrea's band or Lipans might pass, and the Panther, who said he was not sleepy at all, became sentinel. Ned, although he had not risen until noon, was sleepy again from the long ride, and his eyes closed soon. The last object that he saw was the Panther standing on the crest of the swell just beyond them, rifle on shoulder, watching the moonlit plains. Obed White was asleep already.

The Panther walked back and forth a few times and then looked down at his comrades in the dip. His trained eyes saw their chests rising and falling, and he knew that they were far away in the land of Nowhere. Then he extended his walk back and forth a little further, scanning carefully the dusky plain.

A light wind sprang up after a while, and it brought a low but heavy and measured tread to his ears. The Panther's first impulse was to awaken his friends, because this might be the band of Urrea, but he hesitated a moment, and then lay down with his ear to the earth. When he rose his uneasiness had departed and he resumed his walk back and forth. He had heard that tread before many times and, now that it was coming nearer, he could not mistake it, but, as the measured beat indicated that it would pass to one side, it bore no threat for his comrades or himself.

The Panther did not stop his walk as from a distance of a few hundred yards he watched the great buffalo herd go by. The sound was so steady and regular that Ned and Obed were not awakened nor were the horses disturbed. The buffaloes showed a great black mass across the plain, extending for fully a mile, and they were moving north at an even gait. The Panther watched until the last had passed, and he judged that there were fully a hundred thousand animals in the herd. He saw also the big timber wolves hanging on the rear and flanks, ready to cut out stray calves or those weak from old age. So busy were the wolves seeking a chance that they did not notice the gigantic figure of the man, rifle on shoulder, who stood on the crest of the swell looking at them as they passed.

The Panther's eyes followed the black line of the herd until it disappeared under the northern rim of darkness. He was wondering why the buffaloes were travelling so steadily after daylight and he came to the conclusion that the impelling motive was not a search for new pastures. He listened a long time until the last rumble of the hundred thousand died away in a faint echo, and then he awakened his comrades.

"I'm thinkin'," he said, "that the presence of Urrea's band made the buffaloes move. Now I'm not a Ring Tailed Panther an' a cheerful talker for nothin', an' we want to hunt that band. Like as not they've been doin' some mischief, which we may be able partly to undo. I'm in favour of ridin' south, back on the herd track an' lookin' for 'em."

"So am I," said Obed White. "My watch says it's one o'clock in the morning, and my watch is always right, because I made it myself. We've had a pretty good rest, enough to go on, and what we find may be worth finding. A needle in a haystack may be well hid, but you'll find it if you look long enough."

They rode almost due south in the great path made by the buffalo herd, not stopping for a full two hours when a halt was made at a signal from the Panther. They were in a wide plain, where buffalo grass yet grew despite the winter, and the Panther said with authority that the herd had been grazing here before it was started on its night journey into the north.

"An' if we ride about this place long enough," he said, "we'll find the reason why the buffaloes left it."

He turned his horse in a circuit of the plain and Ned and Obed followed the matchless tracker, who was able, even in the moonlight, to note any disturbance of the soil. Presently he uttered a little cry and pointed ahead. Both saw the skeleton of a buffalo which evidently had been killed not long and stripped of its meat. A little further on they saw another and then two more.

"That tells it," said the Panther succinctly. "These buffaloes were killed for food an' most likely by Mexicans. It was the shots that set the herd to runnin'. The men who killed 'em are not far away, an' I'm not a Ring Tailed Panther an' a cheerful talker if they don't belong to Urrea's band."

"Isn't that a light?" said Ned, pointing to the west, "or is it a firefly or something of the kind?"

A glowing spark was just visible over the plain, but as it neither moved nor went out the three concluded that it was made by a distant fire.

"I think it's in chaparral or among trees," said Obed, "or we would see it more plainly. It's a poor camp fire that hides its light under a bushel."

"I think you're right an' it must be chaparral," said the Panther. "But we'll ride toward it an' soon answer our own questions."

The light was more than a mile away and, as they advanced slowly, they saw it grow in size and intensity. It was surely a campfire, but no sound that they could yet hear came from it. They did not expect to hear any. If it was indeed Urrea and his men they would probably be sleeping soundly, not expecting any foe to be near. The Panther now dismounted, and the other two did likewise.

"No need to show too high above the plain," he said, "an' if we have to run it won't take a second to jump back on our horses."

Ned did not take the bridle of his horse as the others did. He knew that Old Jack would follow as faithful as any dog to his master, and he was right. As they advanced slowly the velvet nose more than once pressed trustfully against his elbow.

They saw now that an extensive growth of chaparral rose before them, from the centre of which the light seemed to be shining. The Panther lay down on the prairie, put his ear to the ground, and listened a long time.

"I think I hear the feet of horses movin' now an' then," he said, "an' if so, one of us had better stay behin' with ours. A horse of theirs might neigh an' a horse of ours might answer. Yon can't tell. Obed, I guess it'll be for you to stay. You've got a most soothin' disposition with animals."

"All right," said Obed philosophically, "I'd rather go on, but, if it's better for me to stay, I'll stay. They also serve who stand and hold the reins. If you find you've got to leave in a hurry I'll be here waiting."

He gathered up the reins of the three horses and remained quietly on the plain, while Ned and the Panther went forward, making straight for the light.

When they came to the edge of the chaparral they knelt among the bushes and listened. Now both distinctly heard the occasional movement of horses, and they saw the dusky outlines of several figures before the fire, which was about three hundred yards away.

"They are bound to be Mexicans," whispered the Panther, "'cause there are no Texans in this part of the country, an' you an' me, Ned, must find out just who they are."

"You lead the way, Panther," said Ned. "I'll follow wherever you go."

"Then be mighty careful. Look out for the thorns an' don't knock your rifle against any bush."

The Panther lay almost flat. His huge figure seemed to blend with the earth, and he crept forward among the thorny bushes with amazing skill. He was like some large animal, trained for countless generations to slip through thickets. Ned, just behind him, could hear only the faintest noise, and the bushes moved so little that one, not knowing, might have credited it to the wind.

The boy had the advantage of following in the path made by the man's larger figure, and he, too, was successful in making no sound. But he could hear the stamp of horses' feet clearly now, and both to left and right he caught glimpses of them tethered in the thickets. His comrade stopped at last. They were not more than a hundred yards from the fire now, and the space in front of them was mostly open. The Panther, crouching among the bushes, raised his finger slowly and pointed toward the fire.

Ned, who had moved to one side, followed the pointing finger and saw Urrea. He was the dominant figure in a group of six or seven gathered about the flames. He was no longer in any disguise, but wore an officer's gorgeous uniform of white and silver. A splendid cocked hat was on his head, and a small gold hilted rapier swung by his side.

It may have been partly the effect of the night and the red flame, but the face of Urrea had upon Ned an effect much like that of Santa Anna. It was dark and handsome, but full of evil. And evil Ned knew Urrea to be. No man with righteous blood in his veins would play the spy and traitor as he had done.

"I could shoot him from here," whispered the Panther, who evidently was influenced in a similar way, "then reach our horses an' get away. It might be a good deed, an' it might save our lives, Ned, but I'm not able to force myself to do it."

"Nor I," said Ned. "I can't shoot an enemy from ambush."

Urrea and the other men at the fire, all of whom were in the dress of officers, were in a deep talk. Ned inferred that the subject must be of much importance, since they sat awake, discussing it between midnight and morning.

"Look beyond the fire at the figures leanin' against the trees," whispered the Panther.

Ned looked and hot anger rose in his veins.

CHAPTER 2

THE CAPTIVES

Ned had not noticed at first, but, since his eyes were growing used to the dim light, and since the Panther had pointed the way, he saw a dozen men, arms bound tightly behind them, leaning against the trees. They were prisoners and he knew instinctively that they were Texans. His blood, hot at first, now chilled in his veins. They had been captured by Urrea in a raid, and as Santa Anna had decreed that all Texans were rebels who should be executed when taken, they would surely die, unless rescue came.

"What shall we do?" he whispered.

275

"Nothing now," replied the Panther, in the same soft tone, "but if you an' Obed are with me we'll follow this crowd, an' maybe we can get the Texans away from 'em. It's likely that Urrea will cross the Rio Grande an' go down into Mexico to meet Cos or Santa Anna. Are you game enough to go, Ned? I'm a Ring Tailed Panther an' a roarin' grizzly bear, but I don't like to follow all by myself."

"I'm with you," said Ned, "if I have to go all the way back to the City of Mexico, an' I know that I can speak for Obed, too."

"I jest asked as a matter of form," said the Panther. "I knowed before askin' that you an' Obed would stick to me."

There was a sudden gust of wind at that moment and the light of the fire sprang higher. The flames threw a glow across the faces of the prisoners. Most of them were asleep, but Ned saw them very distinctly now. One was a boy but little older than himself, his face pale and worn. Near him was an old man, with a face very uncommon on the border. His features were those of a scholar and ascetic. His cheeks were thin, and thick white hair crowned a broad white brow. Ned felt instinctively that he was a man of importance.

Both the boy and the man slept the sleep of utter exhaustion.

Urrea rose presently and looked at his prisoners. The moonlight was shining on his face, and it seemed to Ned to be that of some master demon. The boy was far from denying many good qualities to the Mexicans, but the countenance of Urrea certainly did not express any of them that night. It showed only savage exultation as he looked at the bound men, and Ned knew that this was a formidable enemy of the Texans, one who would bring infinite resources of cunning and enterprise to crush them.

Urrea said a few words to his officers and then withdrew into a small tent which Ned had not noticed hitherto. The officers lay down in their blankets, but a dozen sentinels watched about the open space. Ned and the Panther crept slowly back toward the plain.

"What is our best plan, Panther?" whispered the boy.

"We can't do anything yet but haul off, watch an' then follow. The chaparral runs along for a mile or two an' we can hide in the north end of it until they march south an' are out of sight. Then we'll hang on."

They found Obed standing exactly where they had left him, the reins of the three horses in his hands.

"Back at last," he said. "All things come to him who waits long enough, if he doesn't die first. Did you see anything besides a lot of

Mexican *vaqueros*, fuddled with liquor and sound asleep?"

"We did not see any *vaqueros*," replied the Panther, "but we saw Urrea an' his band, an' they had among them a dozen good Texans bound fast, men who will be shot if we three don't stand in the way. You have to follow with us, Obed, because Ned has already promised for you."

The Maine man looked at them and smiled.

"A terribly good mind reader, that boy, Ned," he said. "He knew exactly what I wanted. There's a lot of things in the world that I'd like to do, but the one that I want to do most just now is to follow Urrea and that crowd of his and take away those Texans. You two couldn't keep me from going."

The Panther smiled back.

"You are shorely the right stuff, Obed White," he said. "We're only three in this bunch, but two of 'em besides me are ring-tailed panthers. Now we'll just draw off, before it's day, an' hide in the chaparral up there."

They rode a mile to the north and remained among dense bushes until daylight. At dawn they saw a column of smoke rise from Urrea's camp.

"They are cookin' breakfast now," said the Panther. "It's my guess that in an hour they'll be ridin' south with their prisoners."

The column of smoke sank after a while, and a couple of hours later the three left the chaparral. From one of the summits they dimly saw a mass of horsemen riding toward Mexico.

"There's our men," said the Panther, "an' now we'll follow all day at this good, safe distance. At night we can draw up closer if we want to do it."

The Mexicans maintained a steady pace, and the three pursuers followed at a distance of perhaps two miles. Now and then the swells completely shut Urrea's band from sight, but Ned, Obed and the Panther followed the broad trail without the slightest difficulty.

"They'll reach the river before noon," said the Panther. "There ain't any doubt now that they're bound for Mexico. It's jest as well for what we want to do, 'cause they're likely to be less watchful there than they are in Texas."

The band of Urrea, as nearly as they could judge, numbered about fifty, all mounted and armed well. The Mexicans were fine horsemen, and with good training and leadership they were dangerous foes. The three knew them well, and they kept so far behind that they were not likely to be observed.

It was only a half hour past noon when Urrea's men reached the Rio Grande, and without stopping made the crossing. They avoided the quicksands with experienced eyes, and swam their horses through the deep water, the prisoners always kept in the centre of the troop. Ned, Obed and the Panther watched them until they passed out of sight. Then they, too, rode forward, although slowly, toward the stream.

"We can't lose 'em," said the Panther, "so I think we'd better stay out of sight now that they're on real Mexican soil. Maybe our chance will come tonight, an' ag'in maybe it won't."

"Patience will have its perfect rescue, if we only do the right things," said Obed.

"An' if we think hard enough an' long enough we're bound to do 'em, or I'm a Ring Tailed Panther an' a Cheerful Talker fur nothin'," said the Panther.

Waiting until they were certain that the Mexicans were five or six miles ahead, the three forded the Rio Grande, and stood once more on Mexican soil. It gave Ned a curious thrill. He had passed through so much in Mexico that he had not believed he would ever again enter that country. The land on the Mexican side was about the same as that on the Texan, but it seemed different to him. He beheld again that aspect of infinite age, of the long weariness of time, and of physical decay.

They rode more briskly through the afternoon and at darkness saw the camp fires of Urrea glimmering ahead of them. But the night was not favourable to their plans. The sky was the usual cloudless blue of the Mexican plateau, the moon was at the full and all the stars were out. What they wanted was bad weather, hoping meanwhile the execution of the prisoners would not be begun until the Mexicans reached higher authority than Urrea, perhaps Santa Anna himself.

They made their own camp a full two miles from Urrea's, and Obed and the Panther divided the watch.

Urrea started early the next morning, and so did the pursuing three. The dawn was gray, and the breeze was chill. As they rode on, the wind rose and its edge became so sharp that there was a prospect of another norther. The Panther unrolled from his pack the most gorgeous serape that Ned had ever seen. It was of the finest material, coloured a deep scarlet and it had a gold fringe.

"Fine feathers are seen afar," said Obed.

"That's so," said the Panther, "but we're not coming near enough to the Mexicans for them to catch a glimpse of this, an' such bein' the case I'm goin' to put it between me an' the cold. I'm proud of it, an' when I wrap it aroun' me I feel bigger an' stronger. Its red colour helps me. I think I draw strength from red, just as I do from a fine, tender buffalo steak."

He spoke with much earnestness, and the other two did not contradict him. Meanwhile he gracefully folded the great *serape* about his shoulders, letting it fall to the saddle. No Mexican could have worn it more rakishly.

"That's my shield and protector," he said. "Now blow wind, blow snow, I'll keep warm."

It blew wind, but it did not blow snow. The day remained cold, but the air undoubtedly had a touch of damp.

"It may rain, and I'm sure the night will be dark," said Obed. "We may have our chance. *Fortune favours those who help themselves.*"

The country became more broken, and the patches of scrub forest increased in number. Often the three rode quite near to Urrea's men and observed them closely. The Mexicans were moving slowly, and, as the Americans had foreseen, discipline was relaxed greatly.

Near night drops of rain began to fall in their faces, and the sun set among clouds. The three rejoiced. A night, dark and wet, had come sooner than they had hoped. Obed and Ned also took out *serapes*, and wrapped them around their shoulders. They served now not only to protect their bodies, but to keep their firearms dry as well. Then they tethered their horses among thorn bushes about a mile from Urrea's camp, and advanced on foot.

They saw the camp fire glimmering feebly through the night, and they advanced boldly. It was so dark now that a human figure fifty feet away blended with the dusk, and the ground, softened by the rain, gave back no sound of footsteps. Nevertheless they saw on their right a field which showed a few signs of cultivation, and they surmised that Urrea had made his camp at the lone hut of some *peon*.

They reckoned right. They came to clumps of trees, and in an opening enclosed by them was a low *adobe* hut, from the open door of which a light shone. They knew that Urrea and his officers had taken refuge there from the rain and cold and, under the boughs of the trees or beside the fire, they saw the rest of the band sheltering themselves as best they could. The prisoners, their hands bound, were in a group in the open, where the slow, cold rain fell steadily upon them. Ned's heart swelled with rage at the sight.

Order and discipline seemed to be lacking. Men came and went as they pleased. Fully twenty of them were making a shelter of canvas and thatch beside the hut. Others began to build the fire higher in order to fend off the wet and cold. Ned did not see that the chance of a rescue was improved, but the Panther felt a sudden glow when his eyes alighted upon something dark at the edge of the woods. A tiny shed stood there and his keen eyes marked what was beneath it.

"What do you think we'd better do, Panther?" asked Obed.

"No roarin' jest now. We mustn't raise our voices above whispers, but we'll go back in the brush and wait. In an hour or two all these Mexicans will be asleep. Like as not the sentinels, if they post any, will be asleep first."

They withdrew deeper into the thickets, where they remained close together. They saw the fire die in the Mexican camp. After a while all sounds there ceased, and again they crept near. The Panther was a genuine prophet, known and recognised by his comrades. Urrea's men, having finished their shelters, were now asleep, including all the sentinels except two. There was some excuse for them. They were in their own country, far from any Texan force of importance, and the night could scarcely have been worse. It was very dark, and the cold rain fell with a steadiness and insistence that sought and finally found every opening in one's clothing. Even the stalking three drew their *serapes* closer, and shivered a little.

The two sentinels who did not sleep were together on the south side of the glade. Evidently they wished the company of each other. They were now some distance from the dark little shed toward which the Panther was leading his comrades, and their whole energies were absorbed in an attempt to light two *cigarritos*, which would soothe and strengthen them as they kept their rainy and useless watch.

The three completed the segment of the circle and reached the little shed which had become such an object of importance to the Panther.

"Don't you see?" said the Panther, his grim joy showing in his tone.

They saw, and they shared his satisfaction. The Mexicans had stacked their rifles and muskets under the shed, where they would be protected from the rain.

"It's queer what foolish things men do in war," said Obed. "Whom the gods would destroy they first deprive of the sense of danger. They do not dream that Richard, meaning the Panther, is in the chaparral."

"If we approach this shed from the rear the sentinels, even if they look, will not be able to see us," said the Panther. "By the great horn spoon, what an opportunity! I can hardly keep from roarin' an' ravin' about it. Now, boys, we'll take away their guns, swift an' quiet."

A few trips apiece and all the rifles and muskets with their ammunition were carried deep into the chaparral, where Obed, gladly sacrificing his own comfort, covered them against the rain with his serape. Not a sign had come meanwhile from the two sentinels on the far side of the camp. Ned once or twice saw the lighted ends of their *cigarritos* glowing like sparks in the darkness, but the outlines of the men's figures were very dusky.

"An' now for the riskiest part of our job, the one that counts the most," said the Panther, "the one that will make everything else a failure if it falls through. We've got to secure the prisoners."

The captives were lying under the boughs of some trees about twenty yards from the spot where the fire had been built. The pitiless rain had beaten upon them, but as far as Ned could judge they had gone to sleep, doubtless through sheer exhaustion. The Panther's plan of action was swift and comprehensive.

"Boys," he said, "I'm the best shot of us three. I don't say it in any spirit of boastin', 'cause I've pulled trigger about every day for thirty years, an' more'n once a hundred times in one day. Now you two give me your rifles and I'll set here in the edge of the bushes, then you go ahead as silent as you can an' cut the prisoners loose. If there's an alarm I'll open fire with the three rifles and cover the escape."

Handing the rifles to the Panther, the two slipped forward. It was a grateful task to Ned. Again his heart swelled with wrath as he saw the dark figures of the bound men lying on the ground in the rain. He remembered the one who was youthful of face like himself and he sought him. As he approached he made out a figure lying in a strained position, and he was sure that it was the captive lad. A yard or two more and he knew absolutely. He touched the boy on the shoulder, whispered in his ear that it was a friend, and, with one sweep of his knife, released his arms.

"Crawl to the chaparral there," said Ned, in swift sharp tones, pointing the way. "Another friend is waiting at that point."

The boy, without a word, began to creep forward in a stiff and awkward fashion. Ned turned to the next prisoner. It was the elderly man whom he had seen from the chaparral, and he was wide awake, staring intently at Ned.

"Is it rescue?" he whispered. "Is it possible?"

"It is rescue. It is possible," replied Ned, in a similar whisper. "Turn a little to one side and I will cut the cords that bind you."

The man turned, but when Ned freed him he whispered:

"You will have to help me. I cannot yet walk alone. Urrea has already given me a taste of what I was to expect."

Ned shuddered. There was a terrible significance in the prisoner's tone. He assisted him to rise partly, but the man staggered. It was evident that he could not walk. He must help this man, but the others were waiting to be released also. Then the good thought came.

"Wait a moment," he said, and he cut the bonds of another man.

"Now you help your friend there," he said.

He saw the two going away together, and he turned to the others. He and Obed worked fast, and within five minutes the last man was released. But as they crept back toward the chaparral the slack sentinels caught sight of the dusky figures retreating. Two musket shots were fired and there were rapid shouts in Mexican jargon. Ned and Obed rose to their feet and, keeping the escaped prisoners before them, ran for the thickets.

A terrific reply to the Mexican alarm came from the forest. A volley of rifle and pistol shots was fired among the soldiers as they sprang to their feet and a tremendous voice roared:

"At 'em, boys! At 'em! Charge 'em! Now is your time! Rip an' t'ar an' roar an' chaw! Don't let a single one escape! Sweep the scum off the face of the earth!"

The Ring Tailed Panther had a mighty voice, issuing from a mighty throat. Never had he used it in greater volume or to better purpose than on that night. The forest fairly thundered with the echoes of the battle cry, and as the dazed Mexicans rushed for their guns only to find them gone, they thought that the whole Texan army was upon them. In another instant a new terror struck at their hearts. Their horses and mules, driven in a frightful stampede, suddenly rushed into the glade and they were now busy keeping themselves from being trampled to death.

Truly the Panther had spent well the few minutes allotted to him. He fired new shots, some into the frightened herd. His tremendous voice never ceased for an instant to encourage his charging troops, and to roar out threats against the enemy. Urrea, to his credit, made an attempt to organize his men, to stop the panic, and to see the nature of the enemy, but he was borne away in the frantic mob of men and horses which was now rushing for the open plain.

Ned and Obed led the fugitives to the place where the rifles and muskets were stacked. Here they rapidly distributed the weapons and then broke across the tree trunks all they could not use or carry. Another minute and they reached their horses, where the Panther, panting from his huge exertions, joined them. Ned helped the lame man upon one of the horses, the weakest two who remained, including the boy, were put upon the others, and led by the Panther they started northward, leaving the chaparral.

It was a singular march, but for a long time nothing was said. The sound of the Mexican stampede could yet be heard, moving to the south, but they, rescuers and rescued, walked in silence save for the sound of their feet in the mud of the wind-swept plain. Ned looked curiously at the faces of those whom they had saved, but the night had not lightened, and he could discern nothing. They went thus a full quarter of an hour. The noise of the stampede sank away in the south, and then the Panther laughed.

It was a deep, hearty, unctuous laugh that came from the very depths of the man's chest. It was a laugh with no trace of merely superficial joy. He who uttered it laughed because his heart and soul were in it. It was a laugh of mirth, relief and triumph, all carried to the highest degree. It was a long laugh, rising and falling, but when it ceased and the Panther had drawn a deep breath he opened his mouth again and spoke the words that were in his mind.

"I shorely did some rippin' an' roarin' then," he said. "It was the best chance I ever had, an' I guess I used it. How things did work for us! Them sleepy sentinels, an' then the stampede of the animals, carryin' Urrea an' the rest right away with it."

"Fortune certainly worked for us," said Ned.

"And we can find no words in which to describe to you our gratitude," said the crippled man on the horse. "We were informed very clearly by Urrea that we were rebels and, under the decree of Santa Anna, would be executed. Even our young friend here, this boy, William Allen, would not have been spared."

"We ain't all the way out of the woods yet," said the Panther, not wishing to have their hopes rise too high and then fall. "Of course Urrea an' his men have some arms left. They wouldn't stack 'em all under the shed, an' they can get more from other Mexicans in these parts. When they learn from their trailers how few we are they'll follow."

The rescued were silent, save one, evidently a veteran frontiersman, who said:

"Let 'em come. I was took by surprise, not thinkin' any Mexicans was north of the Rio Grande. But now that I've got a rifle on one shoulder an' a musket on the other I think I could thrash an acre-lot full of 'em."

"That's the talk," said Obed White. "We'll say to 'em: 'Come one, come all, this rock from its firm base may fly, but we're the boys who'll never say die.'"

They relapsed once more into silence. The rain had lightened a little, but the night was as dark as ever. The boy whom the man had called William Allen drew up by the side of Ned. They were of about the same height, and each was as tall and strong as a man.

"Have you any friends here with you?" asked Ned.

"All of them are my friends, but I made them in captivity. I came to Texas to find my fortune, and I found this."

The boy laughed, half in pity of himself, and half with genuine humour.

"But I ought not to complain," he added, "when we've been saved in the most wonderful way. How did you ever happen to do it?"

"We've been following you all the way from the other side of the Rio Grande, waiting a good chance. It came tonight with the darkness, the rain, and the carelessness of the Mexicans. I heard the man call you William Allen. My name is Fulton, Edward Fulton, Ned to my friends."

"And mine's Will to my friends."

"And you and I are going to be friends, that's sure."

"Nothing can be surer."

The hands of the two boys met in a strong grasp, signifying a friendship that was destined to endure.

The Panther and Obed now began to seek a place for a camp. They knew that too much haste would mean a breakdown, and they meant that the people whom they had rescued should have a rest. But it took a long time to find the trees which would furnish wood and partial shelter. It was Obed who made the happy discovery some time after midnight. Turning to their left, they entered a grove of dwarf oaks, covering a half acre or so, and with much labor and striving built a fire. They made it a big fire, too, and fed it until the flames roared and danced. Ned noticed that all the rescued prisoners crouched close to it, as if it were a giver of strength and courage as well as warmth, and now the light revealed their faces. He looked first at the crippled man, and the surprise that he had felt at his first glimpse of him increased.

The stranger was of a type uncommon on the border. His large features showed cultivation and the signs of habitual and deep thought. His thick white hair surmounted a broad brow. His clothing, although torn by thorns and briars, was of fine quality. Ned knew instinctively that it was a powerful face, one that seldom showed the emotions behind it. The rest, except the boy, were of the border, lean, sun-browned men, dressed in tanned deerskin.

The Panther and Obed also gazed at the crippled man with great curiosity. They knew the difference, and they were surprised to find such a man in such a situation. He did not seem to notice them at first, but from his seat on a log leaned over the fire warming his hands, which Ned saw were large, white and smooth. His legs lay loosely against the log, as if he were suffering from a species of paralysis. The others, soaked by the rain, which, however, now ceased, were also hovering over the fire which was giving new life to the blood in their veins. The man with the white hands turned presently and, speaking to Ned, Obed and the Panther, said:

"My name is Roylston, John Roylston."

Ned started.

"I see that you have heard of it," continued the stranger, but without vanity. "Yes, I am the merchant of New Orleans. I have lands and other property in this region for which I have paid fairly. I hold the deeds and they are also guaranteed to me by Santa Anna and the Mexican Congress. I was seized by this guerilla leader, Urrea. He knew who I was, and he sought to extract from me an order for a large sum of money lying in a European bank in the City of Mexico. There are various ways of procuring such orders, and he tried one of the most primitive methods. That is why I cannot walk without help. No, I will not tell what was done. It is not pleasant to hear. Let it pass. I shall walk again as well as ever in a month."

"Did he get the order?" asked Obed curiously.

Roylston laughed deep in his throat.

"He did not," he said. "It was not because I valued it so much, but my pride would not permit me to give way to such crude methods. I must say, however, that you three came just in time, and you have done a most marvellous piece of work."

Ned shuddered and walked a little space out on the plain to steady his nerves. He had never deceived himself about the dangers that the Texans were facing, but it seemed that they would have to fight every kind of ferocity. When he returned, Obed and the Panther were building the fire higher.

"We must get everybody good and dry," said the Panther. "Pursuit will come, but not tonight, an' we needn't worry about the blaze. We've food enough for all of you for a day, but we haven't the horses, an' for that I'm sorry. If we had them we could git away without a doubt to the Texan army."

"But not having them," said Obed, "we'll even do the best we can, if the Mexicans, having run away, come back to fight another day."

"So we will," said a stalwart Texan named Fields. "That Urrea don't get me again, and if I ain't mistook your friend here is Mr. Palmer, better known in our parts as the Ring Tailed Panther, ain't he?"

Ned saw the Panther's huge form swell. He still wore the great serape, which shone in the firelight with a deep blood-red tinge.

"I am the Ring Tailed Panther," he said proudly.

"Then lemme shake your hand. You an' your pards have done a job tonight that ain't had its like often, and me bein' one of them that's profited by it makes it look all the bigger to me."

The Panther graciously extended an enormous palm, and the great palm of Fields met it in a giant clasp. A smile lighted up the sombre face of Mr. Roylston as he looked at them.

"Often we find powerful friends when we least expect them," he said.

"As you are the worst hurt of the lot," said the Panther, "we're going to make you a bed right here by the fire. No, it ain't any use sayin' you won't lay down on it. If you won't we'll jest have to put you down."

They spread a blanket, upon which the exhausted merchant lay, and they covered him with a *serape*. Soon he fell asleep, and then Fields said to Ned and his comrades:

"You fellows have done all the work, an' you've piled up such a mountain of debt against us that we can never wipe it out. Now you go to sleep and four of us will watch. And, knowin' what would happen to us if we were caught, we'll watch well. But nothing is to be expected tonight."

"Suits us," said Obed. "Some must watch while others sleep, so runs the world away. Bet you a dollar, Ned, that I'm off to Slumberland before you are."

"I don't take the bet," said Ned, "but I'll run you an even race."

In exactly five minutes the two, rolled in their own blankets, slept soundly. All the others soon followed, except four, who, unlike the Mexicans, kept a watch that missed nothing.

CHAPTER 3

THE FIGHT WITH URREA

Morning came. Up rose the sun, pouring a brilliant light over the desolate plains. Beads of water from the rain the night before sparkled a little while and then dried up. But the day was cold, nevertheless, and a sharp wind now began to search for the weakest point of every one. Ned, Obed and the Panther were up betimes, but some of the rescued still slept.

Ned, at the suggestion of the Panther, mounted one of the horses and rode out on the plain a half mile to the south. Those keen eyes of his were becoming all the keener from life upon the vast rolling plains. But no matter how he searched the horizon he saw only a lonesome cactus or two shivering in the wind. When he returned with his report the redoubtable Panther said:

"Then we'll just take our time. The pursuit's goin' to come, but since it ain't in sight we'll brace up these new friends of ours with hot coffee an' vittles. I guess we've got coffee enough left for all."

They lighted the fire anew and soon pleasant odours arose. The rescued prisoners ate and drank hungrily, and Mr. Roylston was able to limp a little. Now that Ned saw him in the full daylight he understood more clearly than ever that this was indeed a most uncommon man. The brow and eyes belonged to one who thought, planned and organized. He spoke little and made no complaint, but when he looked at Ned he said:

"You are young, my boy, to live among such dangers. Why do you not go north into the states where life is safe?"

"There are others as young as I, or younger, who have fought or will fight for Texas," said Ned. "I belong here and I've got powerful friends. Two of them have saved my life more than once and are likely to do so again."

He nodded toward Obed and the Panther, who were too far away to hear. Roylston smiled. The two men were in singular contrast, but each was striking in his way. Obed, of great height and very thin, but exceedingly strong, was like a steel lath. The Panther, huge in every aspect, reminded one, in his size and strength, of a buffalo bull.

"They are uncommon men, no doubt," said Roylston. "And you expect to remain with them?"

"I'd never leave them while this war lasts! Not under any circumstances!"

Ned spoke with great energy, and again Roylston smiled, but he said no more.

"It's time to start," said the Panther.

Roylston again mounted one of the horses. Ned saw that it hurt his pride to have to ride, but he saw also that he would not complain when complaints availed nothing. He felt an increasing interest in a man who seemed to have perfect command over himself.

The boy, Will Allen, was fresh and strong again. His youthful frame had recovered completely from all hardships, and now that he was free, armed, and in the company of true friends his face glowed with pleasure and enthusiasm. He was tall and strong, and now he carried a good rifle with a pistol also in his belt. He and Ned walked side by side, and each rejoiced in the companionship of one of his own age.

"How long have you been with them?" asked Will, looking at Obed and the Panther.

"I was first with Obed away down in Mexico. We were prisoners together in the submarine dungeon of San Juan de Ulua. I'd never have escaped without him. And I'd never have escaped a lot more things without him, either. Then we met the Panther. He's the greatest frontiersman in all the southwest, and we three somehow have become hooked together."

Will looked at Ned a little enviously.

"What comrades you three must be!" he said. "I have nobody."

"Are you going to fight for Texas?"

"I count on doing so."

"Then why don't you join us, and we three will turn into four?"

Will looked at Ned, and his eyes glistened.

"Do you mean that?" he asked.

"Do I mean it? I think I do. Ho, there, Panther! You and Obed, just a minute or two!"

The two turned back. Ned and Will were walking at the rear of the little company.

"I've asked Will to be one of us," said Ned, "to join our band and to share our fortunes, good or bad."

"Can he make all the signs, an' has he rid the goat?" asked the

Panther solemnly.

"Does he hereby swear never to tell any secret of ours to Mexican or Indian?" asked Obed. "Does he swear to obey all our laws and by-laws wherever he may be, and whenever he is put to the test?"

"He swears to everything," replied Ned, "and I know that he is the kind to make a trusty comrade to the death."

"Then you are declared this minute a member of our company in good standin'," said the Panther to Will, "an' with this grip I give you welcome."

He crushed the boy's hand in a mighty grasp that made him wince, and Obed followed with one that was almost equally severe. But the boy did not mind the physical pain. Instead, his soul was uplifted. He was now the chosen comrade of these three paladins, and he was no longer alone in the world. But he merely said:

"I'll try to show myself worthy."

They were compelled to stop at noon for rather a long rest, as walking was tiresome. Fields, who was a good scout, went back and looked for pursuers, but announced that he saw none, and, after an hour, they started again.

"I'm thinkin'," said the Panther, "that Urrea has already organized the pursuit. Mebbe he has pow'ful glasses an' kin see us when we can't see him. He may mean to attack tonight. It's a lucky thing for us that we can find timber now an' then."

"It's likely that you're right about tonight," said Obed, "but there's no night so dark that it doesn't have its silver lining. I guess everybody in this little crowd is a good shot, unless maybe it's Mr. Roylston, and as we have about three guns apiece we can make it mighty hot for any force that Urrea may bring against us."

They began now to search for timber, looking especially for some clump of trees that also enclosed water. They did not anticipate any great difficulty in regard to the water, as the winter season and the heavy rains had filled the dry creek beds, and had sent torrents down the arroyos. Before dark they found a stream about a foot deep running over sand between banks seven or eight feet high toward the Rio Grande. A mile further on a small grove of myrtle oaks and pecans grew on its left bank, and there they made their camp.

Feeling that they must rely upon their valour and watchfulness, and not upon secrecy, they built a fire, and ate a good supper. Then they put out the fire and half of them remained on guard, the other half going to sleep, except Roylston, who sat with his back to a tree, his injured legs resting upon a bed of leaves which the boys had raked up for him. He had been riding Old Jack and the horse had seemed to take to him, but after the stop Ned himself had looked after his mount.

The boy allowed Old Jack to graze a while, and then he tethered him in the thickest of the woods just behind the sleeping man. He wished the horse to be as safe as possible in case bullets should be flying, and he could find no better place for him. But before going he stroked his nose and whispered in his ear.

"Good Old Jack! Brave fellow!" he said. "We are going to have troublous times, you and I, along with the others, but I think we are going to ride through them safely."

The horse whinnied ever so softly, and nuzzled Ned's arm. The understanding between them was complete. Then Ned left him, intending to take a position by the bank of the creek as he was on the early watch. On the way he passed Roylston, who regarded him attentively.

"I judge that your leader, Mr. Palmer, whom you generally call the Panther, is expecting an attack," said the merchant.

"He's the kind of man who tries to provide for everything," replied Ned.

"Of course, then," said Roylston, "he provides for the creek bed. The Mexican skirmishers can come up it and yet be protected by its banks."

"That is so," said the Panther, who had approached as he was speaking. "It's the one place that we've got to watch most, an' Ned an' me are goin' to sit there on the banks, always lookin'. I see that you've got the eye of a general, Mr. Roylston."

The merchant smiled.

"I'm afraid I don't count for much in battle," he said, "and least of all hampered as I am now. But if the worst comes to the worst I can sit here with my back to this tree and shoot. If you will kindly give me a rifle and ammunition I shall be ready for the emergency."

"But it is your time to sleep, Mr. Roylston," said the Panther.

"I don't think I can sleep, and as I cannot I might as well be of use."

The Panther brought him the rifle, powder and bullets, and Roylston, leaning against the tree, rifle across his knees, watched with bright eyes. Sentinels were placed at the edge of the grove, but the Panther and Ned, as arranged, were on the high bank overlooking the bed of the creek. Now and then they walked back and forth, meeting at intervals, but most of the time each kept to his own particular part of the ground.

Ned found an oak, blown down on the bank by some hurricane, and as there was a comfortable seat on a bough with the trunk as a rest for his back he remained there a long time. But his ease did not cause him to relax his vigilance. He was looking toward the north, and he could see two hundred yards or more up the creek bed to a point where it curved. The bed itself was about thirty feet wide, although the water did not have a width of more than ten feet.

Everything was now quite dry, as the wind had been blowing all day. But the breeze had died with the night, and the camp was so still that Ned could hear the faint trickle of the water over the sand. It was a fair night, with a cold moon and cold stars looking down. The air was full of chill, and Ned began to walk up and down again in order to keep warm. He noticed Roylston still sitting with eyes wide open and the rifle across his lap.

As Ned came near in his walk the merchant turned his bright eyes upon him.

"I hear," he said, "that you have seen Santa Anna."

"More than once. Several times when I was a prisoner in Mexico, and again when I was recaptured."

"What do you think of him?"

The gaze of the bright eyes fixed upon Ned became intense and concentrated.

"A great man! A wickedly great man!"

Roylston turned his look away, and interlaced his fingers thoughtfully.

"A good description, I think," he said. "You have chosen your words well. A singular compound is this Mexican, a mixture of greatness, vanity and evil. I may talk to you more of him some day. But I tell you now that I am particularly desirous of not being carried a prisoner to him."

He lifted the rifle, put its stock to his shoulder, and drew a bead.

"I think I could hit at forty or fifty yards in this good moonlight," he said.

He replaced the rifle across his knees and sighed. Ned was curious, but he would not ask questions, and he walked back to his old position by the bank. Here he made himself easy, and kept his eyes on the deep trench that had been cut by the stream. The shadows were dark against the bank, but it seemed to him that they were darker than they had been before.

Ned's blood turned a little colder, and his scalp tingled. He was startled but not afraid. He looked intently, and saw moving figures in the river bed, keeping close against the bank. He could not see faces, he could not even discern a clear outline of the figures, but he had no doubt that these were Urrea's Mexicans. He waited only a moment longer to assure himself that the dark moving line was fact and not fancy. Then, aiming his rifle at the foremost shape, he fired. While the echo of the sharp crack was yet speeding across the plain he cried:

"Up, men! up! Urrea is here!"

A volley came from the creek bed, but in an instant the Panther, Obed, Will and Fields were by Ned's side.

"Down on your faces," cried the Panther, "an' pot 'em as they run! So they thought to go aroun' the grove, come down from the north an' surprise us this way! Give it to 'em, boys!"

The rifles flashed and the dark line in the bed of the creek now broke into a huddle of flying forms. Three fell, but the rest ran, splashing through the sand and water, until they turned the curve and were protected from the deadly bullets. Then the Panther, calling to the others, rushed to the other side of the grove, where a second attack, led by Urrea in person, had been begun. Here men on horseback charged directly at the wood, but they were met by a fire which emptied more than one saddle.

Much of the charge was a blur to Ned, a medley of fire and smoke, of beating hoofs and of cries. But one thing he saw clearly and never forgot. It was the lame man with the thick white hair sitting with his back against a tree calmly firing a rifle at the Mexicans. Roylston had time for only two shots, but when he reloaded the second time he placed the rifle across his knees as before and smiled.

Most Mexican troops would have been content with a single charge, but these returned, encouraged by shouts and driven on by fierce commands. Ned saw a figure waving a sword. He believed it to be Urrea, and he fired, but he missed, and the next moment the horseman was lost in the shadows.

The second charge was beaten back like the first, and several skirmishers who tried to come anew down the bed of the creek were also put to flight. Two Mexicans got into the thickets and tried to stampede the horses, but the quickness of Obed and Fields defeated their aim. One of the Mexicans fell there, but the other escaped in the darkness.

When the second charge was driven back and the horses were quieted the Panther and Obed threshed up the woods, lest some Mexican musketeer should lie hidden there.

Nobody slept any more that night. Ned, Will and the Panther kept a sharp watch upon the bed of the creek, the moon and stars fortunately aiding them. But the Mexicans did not venture again by that perilous road, although toward morning they opened a scattering fire from the plain, many of their bullets whistling at random among the trees and thickets. Some of the Texans, crawling to the edge of the wood, replied, but they seemed to have little chance for a good shot, as the Mexicans lay behind a swell. The besiegers grew tired after a while and silence came again.

Three of the Texans had suffered slight wounds, but the Panther and Fields bound them up skillfully. It was still light enough for these tasks. Fields was particularly jubilant over their success, as he had a right to be. The day before he could look forward only to his own execution. Now he was free and victorious. Exultantly he hummed:

You've heard, I s'pose, of New Orleans,
It's famed for youth and beauty;
There are girls of every hue, it seems,
From snowy white to sooty.
Now Packenham has made his brags,
If he that day was lucky,
He'd have the girls and cotton bags
In spite of Old Kentucky.

But Jackson, he was wide awake,
And was not scared at trifles,
For well he knew Kentucky's boys,
With their death-dealing rifles.
He led them down to cypress swamp,
The ground was low and mucky;
There stood John Bull in martial pomp,
And here stood old Kentucky.

"Pretty good song, that of yours," said the Panther approvingly. "Where did you get it?"

"From my father," replied Fields. "He's a Kentuckian, an' he fit at New Orleans. He was always hummin' that song, an' it come back to me after we drove off the Mexicans. Struck me that it was right timely."

Ned and Will, on their own initiative, had been drawing all the fallen logs that they could find and move to the edge of the wood, and having finished the task they came back to the bed of the creek. Roylston, the rifle across his knees, was sitting with his eyes closed, but he opened them as they approached. They were uncommonly large and bright eyes, and they expressed pleasure.

"It gratifies me to see that neither of you is hurt," he said. "This has been a strange night for two who are as young as you are. And it is a strange night for me, too. I never before thought that I should be firing at any one with intent to kill. But events are often too powerful for us."

He closed his eyes again.

"I am going to sleep a little, if I can," he said.

But Ned and Will could not sleep. They went to Ned's old position at the edge of the creek bed, and together watched the opening dawn. They saw the bright sun rise over the great plains, and the dew sparkle for a little while on the brown grass. The day was cold, but apparently it had come with peace. They saw nothing on the plain, although they had no doubt that the Mexicans were waiting just beyond the first swell. But Ned and Will discerned three dark objects lying on the sand up the bed of the creek, and they knew that they were the men who had fallen in the first rush. Ned was glad that he could not see their faces.

At the suggestion of the Panther they lighted fires and had warm food and coffee again, thus putting heart into all the defenders. Then the Panther chose Ned for a little scouting work on horseback. Ned found Old Jack seeking blades of grass within the limits allowed by his lariat. But when the horse saw his master he stretched out his head and neighed.

"I think I understand you," said Ned. "Not enough food and no water. Well, I'll see that you get both later, but just now we're going on a little excursion."

The Panther and Ned rode boldly out of the trees, and advanced a short distance upon the plain. Two or three shots were fired from a point behind the first swell, but the bullets fell far short.

"I counted on that," said the Panther. "If a Mexican has a gun it's mighty hard for him to keep from firing it. All we wanted to do was to uncover their position an' we've done it. We'll go back now, an' wait fur them to make the first move."

But they did not go just yet. A man on horseback waving a large white handkerchief appeared on the crest of the swell and rode toward them. It was Urrea.

"He knows that he can trust us, while we don't know that we can trust him," said the Panther, "so we'll just wait here an' see what he has to say."

Urrea, looking fresh and spirited, came on with confidence and saluted in a light easy fashion. The two Americans did not return the salute, but waited gravely.

"We can be polite, even if we are enemies," said Urrea, "so I say good morning to you both, former friends of mine."

"I have no friendship with spies and traitors," growled the Panther.

"I serve my country in the way I think best," said Urrea, "and you must remember that in our view you two are rebels and traitors."

"We don't stab in the back," said the Panther.

Urrea flushed through his swarthy skin.

"We will not argue the point any further," he said, "but come at once to the business before us. First, I will admit several things. Your rescue of the prisoners was very clever. Also you beat us off last night, but I now have a hundred men with me and we have plenty of arms. We are bound to take you sooner or later."

"Then why talk to us about it?" said the Panther.

"Because I wish to save bloodshed."

"Wa'al, then, what do you have to say?"

"Give us the man, Roylston, and the rest of you can go free."

"Why are you so anxious to have Roylston?"

Ned eagerly awaited the answer. It was obvious that Roylston had rather minimized his own importance. Urrea flicked the mane of his mustang with a small whip and replied:

"Our president and general, the illustrious Santa Anna, is extremely anxious to see him. Secrets of state are not for me. I merely seek to do my work."

"Then you take this from me," said the Panther, a blunt frontiersman, "my comrades an' me ain't buyin' our lives at the price of nobody else's."

"You feel that way about it, do you?"

"That's just the way we feel, and I want to say, too, that I wouldn't take the word of either you or your Santa Anna. If we was to give up Mr. Roylston—which we don't dream of doin'—you'd be after us as hot an' strong as ever."

Urrea's swarthy cheeks flushed again.

"I shall not notice your insults," he said. "They are beneath me. I am a Mexican officer and gentleman, and you are mere riders of the plains."

"All the same," said the Panther grimly, "if you are goin' to talk you have to talk with us."

"That is true," said Urrea lightly, having regained complete control of his temper. "In war one cannot choose his enemies. I make you the proposition once more. Give us Roylston and go. If you do not accept we shall nevertheless take him and all of you who do not fall first. Remember that you are rebels and traitors and that you will surely be shot or hanged."

"I don't remember any of them things," said the Panther grimly. "What I do remember is that we are Texans fightin' fur our rights. To hang a man you've first got to catch him, an' to shoot him you've first got to hit him. An' since things are to be remembered, remember that what you are tryin' to do to us we may first do to you. An' with that I reckon we'll bid you good day, Mr. Urrea."

Urrea bowed, but said nothing. He rode back toward his men, and Ned and the Panther returned to the grove. Roylston was much better that morning and he was able to stand, leaning against a tree.

"May I ask the result of your conference," he said.

"There ain't no secret about it," replied the Panther, "but them Mexicans seem to be almighty fond of you, Mr. Roylston."

"In what way did they show it?"

"Urrea said that all of us could go if we would give up you."

"And your answer?"

The Panther leaned forward a little on his horse.

"You know something about the Texans, don't you, Mr. Roylston?"

"I have had much opportunity to observe and study them."

"Well, they've got plenty of faults, but you haven't heard of them buyin' their lives at the price of a comrade's, have you?"

"I have not, but I wish to say, Mr. Palmer, that I'm sorry you returned this answer. I should gladly take my chances if the rest of you could go."

"We'd never think of it," said the Panther. "Besides, them Mexicans wouldn't keep their word. They're goin' to besiege us here, hopin' maybe that starvation or thirst will make us give you up. Now the first thing for us to do is to get water for the horses."

This presented a problem, as the horses could not go down to the creek, owing to the steep high banks, but the Texans soon solved it. The cliff was soft and they quickly cut a smooth sloping path with their knives and hatchets. Old Jack was the first to walk down it and Ned led him. The horse hung back a little, but Ned patted his head and talked to him as a friend and equal. Under such persuasion Old Jack finally made the venture, and when he landed safely at the bottom he drank eagerly. Then the other two horses followed. Meanwhile two riflemen kept a keen watch up and down the creek bed for lurking Mexican sharpshooters.

But the watering of the horses was finished without incident, and they were tethered once more in the thicket. Fields and another man kept a watch upon the plain, and the rest conferred under the trees. The Panther announced that by a great reduction of rations the food could be made to last two days longer. It was not a cheerful statement, as the Mexicans must know the scanty nature of their supplies, and would wait with all the patience of Indians.

"All things, including starvation, come to him who waits long enough," said Obed White soberly.

"We'll jest set the day through," said the Panther, "an' see what turns up."

But the day was quite peaceful. It was warmer than usual and bright with sunshine. The Mexicans appeared on some of the knolls, seemingly near in the thin clear air, but far enough away to be out of rifle shot, and began to play cards or loll on their serapes. Several went to sleep.

"They mean to show us that they have all the time in the world," said Ned to Will, "and that they are willing to wait until we fall like ripe apples into their hands."

"Do you think they will get us again?" asked Will anxiously.

"I don't. We've got food for two days and I believe that something will happen in our favour within that time. Do you notice, Will, that it's beginning to cloud up again? In winter you can't depend upon bright sunshine to last always. I think we're going to have a dark night and it's given me an idea."

"What is it?"

"I won't tell you, because it may amount to nothing. It all depends upon what kind of night we have."

The sun did not return. The clouds banked up more heavily, and in the afternoon Ned went to the Panther. They talked together earnestly, looking frequently at the skies, and the faces of both expressed satisfaction. Then they entered the bed of the creek and examined it critically. Will was watching them. When the two separated and Ned came toward him, he said:

"I can guess your idea now. We mean to escape tonight up the bed of the creek."

Ned nodded.

"Your first guess is good," he said. "If the promise of a dark night keeps up we're going to try."

The promise was fulfilled. The Mexicans made no hostile movement throughout the afternoon, but they maintained a rigid watch.

When the sun had set and the thick night had come down the Panther told of the daring enterprise they were about to undertake, and all approved. By nine o'clock the darkness was complete, and the little band gathered at the point where the path was cut down into the bed of the creek. It was likely that Mexicans were on all sides of the grove, but the Panther did not believe that any of them, owing to bitter experience, would enter the cut made by the stream. But, as leader, he insisted upon the least possible noise. The greatest difficulty would be with the horses. Ned, at the head of Old Jack, led the way.

Old Jack made the descent without slipping and in a few minutes the entire force stood upon the sand. They had made no sound that anyone could have heard thirty yards away.

"Now Mr. Roylston," whispered the Panther to the merchant, "you get on Ned's horse an' we'll be off."

Roylston sighed. It hurt his pride that he should be a burden, but he was a man of few words, and he mounted in silence. Then they moved slowly over the soft sand. They had loaded the extra rifles and muskets on the other two horses, but every man remained thoroughly armed and ready on the instant for any emergency.

The Panther and Obed led. Just behind them came Ned and Will. They went very slowly in order to keep the horses' feet from making any sound that listening Mexican sentinels might hear. They were fortunate in the sand, which was fine and soundless like a carpet. Ned thought that the Mexicans would not make any attempt upon the grove until late at night, and then only with skirmishers and snipers. Or they might not make any attempt at all, content with their cordon.

But it was thrilling work as they crept along on the soft sand in the darkness and between the high banks. Ned felt a prickling of the blood. An incautious footstep or a stumble by one of the horses might bring the whole Mexican force down upon them at any moment. But there was no incautious footstep. Nor did any horse stumble. The silent procession moved on, passed the curve in the bed of the creek and continued its course.

Urrea had surrounded the grove completely. His men were on both sides of the creek, but no sound came to them, and they had a healthy respect for the deadly Texan rifles. Their leader had certainly been wise in deciding to starve them out. Meanwhile the little procession in the bed of the creek increased its speed slightly.

The Texans were now a full four hundred yards from the grove, and their confidence was rising.

"If they don't discover our absence until morning," whispered Ned to Will, "we'll surely get away."

"Then I hope they won't discover it until then," said Will fervently. "I don't want to die in battle just now, nor do I want to be executed in Mexico for a rebel or for anything else."

They were now a full mile from the grove and the banks of the creek were decreasing in height. They did not rise anywhere more than three or four feet. But the water increased in depth and the margin of sand was narrower. The Panther called a halt and they listened. They heard no sound but the faint moaning of the wind among the dips and swells, and the long lone howl of a lonesome coyote.

"We've slipped through 'em! By the great horn spoon, we've slipped through 'em!" said the Panther exultantly. "Now, boys, we'll take to the water here to throw 'em off our track, when they try to follow it in the mornin'."

The creek was now about three feet in depth and flowing slowly like most streams in that region, but over a bed of hard sand, where the trace of a footstep would quickly vanish.

"The water is likely to be cold," said the Panther, "an' if any fellow is afraid of it he can stay behind and consort with the Mexicans who don't care much for water."

"Lead on, Macduff," said Obed, "and there's nobody who will cry 'hold, enough.'"

The Panther waded directly into the middle of the stream, and all the others followed. The horses, splashing the water, made some noise, but they were not so careful in that particular now since they had put a mile between themselves and the grove. In fact, the Panther urged them to greater speed, careless of the sounds, and they kept in the water for a full two miles further. Then they quit the stream at a point where the soil seemed least likely to leave traces of their footsteps, and stood for a little while upon the prairie, resting and shivering. Then they started at a rapid pace across the country, pushing for the Rio Grande until noon. Then Fields stalked and shot an antelope, with which they renewed their supply of food. In the afternoon it rained heavily, but by dark they reached the Rio Grande, across which they made a dangerous passage, as the waters had risen, and stood once more on the soil of Texas.

"Thank God!" said Will.

"Thank God!" repeated Ned.

Then they looked for shelter, which all felt they must have.

CHAPTER 4

THE CABIN IN THE WOODS

It proved a difficult matter to find shelter. All the members of the little group were wet and cold, and a bitter wind with snow began to whistle once more across the plain. But every one strove to be cheerful and the relief that their escape had brought was still a tonic to their spirits. Yet they were not without comment upon their condition.

"I've seen hard winters in Maine," said Obed White, "but there you were ready for them. Here it tricks you with warm sunshine and then with snow. You suffer from surprise."

"We've got to find a cabin," said the Panther.

"Why not make it a whole city with a fine big hotel right in the centre of it?" said Obed. "Seems to me there's about as much chance of one as the other."

"No, there ain't," said the Panther. "There ain't no town, but there are huts. I've rid over this country for twenty year an' I know somethin' about it. There are four or five settlers' cabins in the valleys of the creeks runnin' down to the Rio Grande. I had a mighty good dinner at one of 'em once. They're more'n likely to be abandoned now owin' to the war an' their exposed situation, but if the roofs haven't fell in any of 'em is good enough for us."

"Then you lead on," said Obed. "The quicker we get there the happier all of us will be."

"I may not lead straight, but I'll get you there," replied the Panther confidently.

Roylston, at his own urgent insistence, dismounted and walked a little while. When he betook himself again to the back of Old Jack he spoke with quiet confidence.

"I'm regaining my strength rapidly," he said. "In a week or two I shall be as good as I ever was. Meanwhile my debt to you, already great, is accumulating."

The Panther laughed.

"You don't owe us nothin'," he said. "Why, on this frontier it's one man's business to help another out of a scrape. If we didn't do that we couldn't live."

"Nevertheless, I shall try to pay it," said Roylston, in significant tones.

"For the moment we'll think of that hut we're lookin' for," said the Panther.

"It will be more than a hut," said Will, who was of a singularly cheerful nature. "I can see it now. It will be a gorgeous palace. Its name will be the Inn of the Panther. Menials in gorgeous livery will show us to our chambers, one for every man, where we will sleep between white sheets of the finest linen."

"I wonder if they will let us take our rifles to bed with us," said Ned, "because in this country I don't feel that I can part with mine, even for a moment."

"That is a mere detail which we will discuss with our host," said Obed. "Perhaps, after you have eaten of the chicken and drunk of the wine at this glorious Inn of the Panther, you will not be so particular about the company of your rifle, Mr. Fulton."

The Panther uttered a cry of joy.

"I've got my b'arin's exactly now," he said. "It ain't more'n four miles to a cabin that I know of, an' if raiders haven't smashed it it'll give us all the shelter we want."

"Then lead us swiftly," said Obed. "There's no sunset or anything to give me mystical lore, but the coming of that cabin casts its shadow before, or at least I want it to do it."

The Panther's announcement brought new courage to every one and they quickened their lagging footsteps. He led toward a dark line of timber which now began to show through the driving snow, and when they passed among the trees he announced once more and with exultation:

"Only a mile farther, boys, an' we'll be where the cabin stands, or stood. Don't git your feelin's too high, 'cause it may have been wiped off the face of the earth."

A little later he uttered another cry, and this was the most exultant of all.

"There she is," he said, pointing ahead. "She ain't been wiped away by nobody or nothin'. Don't you see her, that big, stout cabin ahead?"

"I do," said young Allen joyously, "and it's the Inn of the Panther as sure as you live."

"But I don't see any smoke coming out of the chimney," said Ned, "and there are no gorgeous menials standing on the doorstep waiting for us."

"It's been abandoned a long time," said the Panther. "I can tell that by its looks, but I'm thinkin' that it's good enough fur us an' mighty welcome. An' there's a shed behind the house that'll do for the horses. Boys, we're travellin' in tall luck."

The cabin, a large one, built of logs and *adobe*, was certainly a consoling sight. They had almost reached the limit of physical endurance, but they broke into a run to reach it. The Panther and Ned were the first to push open a heavy swinging door, and they entered side by side. It was dry within. The solid board roof did not seem to be damaged at all, and the floor of hard, packed earth was as dry as a bone also. At one end were a wide stone fireplace, cold long since, and a good chimney of mud and sticks. There were two windows, closed with heavy clapboard shutters.

There was no furniture in the cabin except two rough wooden benches. Evidently the original owners had prepared well for their flight, but it was likely that no one had come since. The lonely place among the trees had passed unobserved by raiders. The shed behind the cabin was also in good condition, and they tethered there the horses, which were glad enough to escape from the bitter wind and driving snow.

The whole party gathered in the cabin, and as they no longer feared pursuit it was agreed unanimously that they must have luxury. In this case a fire meant the greatest of all luxuries.

They gathered an abundance of fallen wood, knocked the snow from it and heaped it on either side of the fireplace. They cut with infinite difficulty dry shavings from the inside of the logs in the wall of the house, and after a full hour of hard work lighted a blaze with flint and steel. The rest was easy, and soon they had a roaring fire. They fastened the door with the wooden bar which stood in its place and let the windows remain shut. Although there was a lack of air, they did not yet feel it, and gave themselves up to the luxury of the glowing heat.

They took off their clothes and held them before the fire. When they were dry and warm they put them on again and felt like new beings. Strips of the antelope were fried on the ends of ramrods, and they ate plentifully. All the chill was driven from their bodies, and in its place came a deep pervading sense of comfort. The bitter wind yet howled without and they heard the snow driven against the door and windows. The sound heightened their feeling of luxury. They were like a troop of boys now, all of them—except Roylston. He sat on one of the piles of wood and his eyes gleamed as the others talked.

"I vote that we enlarge the name of our inn," said Allen. "Since our leader has black hair and black eyes, let's call it the Inn of the Black Panther. All in favour of that motion say 'Aye.'"

"Aye!" they roared.

"All against it say 'no.'"

Silence.

"The Inn of the Black Panther it is," said Will, "an' it is the most welcome inn that ever housed me."

The Panther smiled benevolently.

"I don't blame you boys for havin' a little fun," he said. "It does feel good to be here after all that we've been through."

The joy of the Texans was irrepressible. Fields began to pat and three or four of them danced up and down the earthen floor of the cabin. Will watched with dancing eyes. Ned, more sober, sat by his side.

However, the highest spirits must grow calm at last, and gradually the singing and dancing ceased. It had grown quite close in the cabin now, and one of the window shutters was thrown open, permitting a rush of cool, fresh air that was very welcome. Ned looked out. The wind was still whistling and moaning, and the snow, like a white veil, hid the trees.

The men one by one went to sleep on the floor. Obed and Fields kept watch at the window during the first half of the night, and the Panther and Ned relieved them for the second half. They heard nothing but the wind, and saw nothing but the snow. Day came with a hidden sun, and the fine snow still driven by the wind, but the Panther, a good judge of weather, predicted a cessation of the snow within an hour.

The men awoke and rose slowly from the floor. They were somewhat stiff, but no one had been overcome, and after a little stretching of the muscles all the soreness disappeared. The horses were within the shed, unharmed and warm, but hungry. They relighted the fire and broiled more strips of the antelope, but they saw that little would be left. The Panther turned to Roylston, who inspired respect in them all.

"Now, Mr. Roylston," he said, "we've got to agree upon some course of action an' we've got to put it to ourselves squar'ly. I take it that all of us want to serve Texas in one way or another, but we've got only three horses, we're about out of food, an' we're a long distance from the main Texas settlements. It ain't any use fur us to start to rippin' an' t'arin' unless we've got somethin' to rip an' t'ar with."

"Good words," said Obed White. "A speech in time saves errors nine."

"I am glad you have put the question, Mr. Palmer," said Roylston. "Our affairs have come to a crisis, and we must consider. I, too, wish to help Texas, but I can help it more by other ways than battle."

It did not occur to any of them to doubt him. He had already established over them the mental ascendency that comes from a great mind used to dealing with great affairs.

"But we are practically dismounted," he continued. "It is winter and we do not know what would happen to us if we undertook to roam over the prairies as we are. On the other hand, we have an abundance of arms and ammunition and a large and well-built cabin. I suggest that we supply ourselves with food, and stay here until we can acquire suitable mounts. We may also contrive to keep a watch upon any Mexican armies that may be marching north. I perhaps have more reason than any of you for hastening away, but I can spend the time profitably in regaining the use of my limbs."

"Your little talk sounds mighty good to me," said the Panther. "In fact, I don't see anything else to do. This cabin must have been built an' left here 'speshully fur us. We know, too, that the Texans have all gone home, thinkin' that the war is over, while we know different an' mebbe we can do more good here than anywhere else. What do you say, boys? Do we stay?"

"We stay," replied all together.

They went to work at once fitting up their house. More firewood was brought in. Fortunately the men had been provided with hatchets, in the frontier style, which their rescuers had not neglected to bring away, and they fixed wooden hooks in the walls for their extra arms and clothing. A half dozen scraped away a large area of the thin snow and enabled the horses to find grass. A fine spring two hundred yards away furnished a supply of water.

After the horses had eaten Obed, the Panther and Ned rode away in search of game, leaving Mr. Roylston in command at the cabin.

The snow was no longer falling, and that which lay on the ground was melting rapidly.

"I know this country," said the Panther, "an' we've got four chances for game. It may be buffalo, it may be deer, it may be antelope, and it may be wild turkeys. I think it most likely that we'll find buffalo. We're so fur west of the main settlements that they're apt to hang 'roun' here in the winter in the creek bottoms, an' if it snows they'll take to the timber fur shelter."

"And it has snowed," said Ned.

"Jest so, an' that bein' the case we'll search the timber. Of course big herds couldn't crowd in thar, but in this part of the country we gen'rally find the buffalo scattered in little bands."

They found patches of forest, generally dwarfed in character, and looked diligently for the great game. Once a deer sprang out of a thicket, but sped away so fast they did not get a chance for a shot. At length Obed saw large footprints in the thinning snow, and called the Panther's attention to them. The big man examined the traces critically.

"Not many hours old," he said. "I'm thinkin' that we'll have buffalo steak fur supper. We'll scout all along this timber. What we want is a young cow. Their meat is not tough."

They rode through the timber for about two hours, when Ned caught sight of moving figures on the far side of a thicket. He could just see the backs of large animals, and he knew that there were their buffalo. He pointed them out to the Panther, who nodded.

"We'll ride 'roun' the thicket as gently as possible," he said, "an' then open fire. Remember, we want a tender young cow, two of 'em if we can get 'em, an' don't fool with the bulls."

Ned's heart throbbed as Old Jack bore him around the thicket. He had fought with men, but he was not yet a buffalo hunter. Just as they turned the flank of the bushes a huge buffalo bull, catching their odor, raised his head and uttered a snort. The Panther promptly fired at a young cow just beyond him. The big bull, either frightened or angry, leaped head down at Old Jack. The horse was without experience with buffaloes, but he knew that those sharp horns meant no good to him, and he sprang aside with so much agility that Ned was almost unseated.

The big bull rushed on, and Ned, who had retained his hold upon his rifle, was tempted to take a shot at him for revenge, but, remembering the Panther's injunction, he controlled the impulse and fired at a young cow.

When the noise and confusion were over and the surviving buffaloes had lumbered away, they found that they had slain two of the young cows and that they had an ample supply of meat.

"Ned," said the Panther, "you know how to go back to the cabin, don't you?"

"I can go straight as an arrow."

"Then ride your own horse, lead the other two an' bring two men. We'll need 'em with the work here."

The Panther and Obed were already at work skinning the cows. Ned sprang upon Old Jack, and rode away at a trot, leading the other two horses by their lariats. The snow was gone now and the breeze was almost balmy. Ned felt that great rebound of the spirits of which the young are so capable. They had outwitted Urrea, they had taken his prisoners from him, and then had escaped across the Rio Grande. They had found shelter and now they had obtained a food supply. They were all good comrades together, and what more was to be asked?

He whistled as he rode along, but when he was half way back to the cabin he noticed something in a large tree that caused him to stop. He saw the outlines of great bronze birds, and he knew that they were wild turkeys. Wild turkeys would make a fine addition to their larder, and, halting Old Jack, he shot from his back, taking careful aim at the largest of the turkeys. The huge bird fell, and as the others flew away Ned was lucky enough to bring down a second with a pistol shot.

His trophies were indeed worth taking, and tying their legs together with a withe he hung them across his saddle bow. He calculated that the two together weighed nearly sixty pounds, and he rode triumphantly when he came in sight of the cabin.

Will saw him first and gave a shout that drew the other men.

"What luck?" hailed young Allen.

"Not much," replied Ned, "but I did get these sparrows."

He lifted the two great turkeys from his saddle and tossed them to Will. The boy caught them, but he was borne to his knees by their weight. The men looked at them and uttered approving words.

"What did you do with the Panther and Obed?" asked Fields.

"The last I saw of them they had been dismounted and were being chased over the plain by two big bull buffaloes. The horns of the buffaloes were then not more than a foot from the seats of their trousers. So I caught their horses, and I have brought them back to camp."

"I take it," said Fields, "that you've had good luck."

"We have had the finest of luck," replied Ned. "We ran into a group of fifteen or twenty buffaloes, and we brought down two fine, young cows. I came back for two more men to help with them, and on my way I shot these turkeys."

Fields and another man named Carter returned with Ned. Young Allen was extremely anxious to go, but the others were chosen on account of their experience with the work. They found that Obed and the Panther had already done the most of it, and when it was all finished Fields and Carter started back with the three horses, heavily laden. As the night promised to be mild, and the snow was gone, Ned, Obed and the Panther remained in the grove with the rest of their food supply.

They also wished to preserve the two buffalo robes, and they staked them out upon the ground, scraping them clean of flesh with their knives. Then they lighted a fire and cooked as much of the tender meat as they wished. By this time it was dark and they were quite ready to rest. They put out the fire and raked up the beds of leaves on which they would spread their blankets. But first they enjoyed the relaxation of the nerves and the easy talk that come after a day's work well done.

"It certainly has been a fine day for us," said Obed. "Sometimes I like to go through the bad days, because it makes the good days that follow all the better. Yesterday we were wandering around in the snow, and we had nothing, today we have a magnificent city home, that is to say, the cabin, and a beautiful country place, that is to say, this grove. I can add, too, that our nights in our country place are spent to the accompaniment of music. Listen to that beautiful song, won't you?"

A long, whining howl rose, sank and died. After an interval they heard its exact duplicate and the Panther remarked tersely:

"Wolves. Mighty hungry, too. They've smelled our buffalo meat and they want it. Guess from their big voices that they're timber wolves and not coyotes."

Ned knew that the timber wolf was a much larger and fiercer animal than his prairie brother, and he did not altogether like this whining sound which now rose and died for the third time.

"Must be a dozen or so," said the Panther, noticing the increasing volume of sound. "We'll light the fire again. Nothing is smarter than a wolf, an' I don't want one of those hulkin' brutes to slip up, seize a fine piece of buffalo and dash away with it. But fire will hold 'em. How a wolf does dread it! The little red flame is like a knife in his heart."

They lighted four small fires, making a rude ring which enclosed their leafy beds and the buffalo skins and meat. Before they finished the task they saw slim dusky figures among the trees and red eyes glaring at them. The Panther picked up a stick blazing like a torch, and made a sudden rush for one of the figures. There was a howl of terror and a sound of something rushing madly through the bushes.

The Panther flung his torch as far as he could in the direction of the sounds and returned, laughing deep in his throat.

"I think I came pretty near hittin' the master wolf with that," he said, "an' I guess he's good an' scared. But they'll come back after a while, an' don't you forget it. For that reason, I think we'd better keep a watch. We'll divide it into three hours apiece, an' we'll give you the first, Ned."

Ned was glad to have the opening watch, as it would soon be over and done with, and then he could sleep free from care about any watch to come. The Panther and Obed rolled in their blankets, found sleep almost instantly, and the boy, resolved not to be a careless sentinel, walked in a circle just outside the fires.

Sure enough, and just as the Panther had predicted, he saw the red eyes and dusky forms again. Now and then he heard a faint pad among the bushes, and he knew that a wolf had made it. He merely changed from the outside to the inside of the fire ring, and continued his walk. With the fire about him and his friends so near he was not afraid of wolves, no matter how big and numerous they might be.

Yet their presence in the bushes, the light shuffle of their feet and their fiery eyes had an uncanny effect. It was unpleasant to know that such fierce beasts were so near, and he gave himself a reassuring glance at the sleeping forms of his partners. By and by the red eyes melted away, and he heard another soft tread, but heavier than that of the wolves. With his rifle lying in the hollow of his arm and his finger on the trigger he looked cautiously about the circle of the forest.

Ned's gaze at last met that of a pair of red eyes, a little further apart than those of the wolves. He knew then that they belonged to a larger animal, and presently he caught a glimpse of the figure. He was sure that it was a puma or cougar, and so far as he could judge it was a big brute. It, too, must be very hungry, or it would not dare the fire and the human odour.

Ned felt tentatively of his rifle, but changed his mind. He remembered the Panther's exploit with the firebrand, and he decided to imitate it, but on a much larger scale. He laid down his rifle, but kept his left hand on the butt of the pistol in his belt. Then selecting the largest torch from the fire he made a rush straight for the blazing eyes, thrusting the flaming stick before him. There was a frightened roar, and then the sound of a heavy body crashing away through the undergrowth. Ned returned, satisfied that he had done as well as the Panther and better.

Both the Panther and Obed were awake and sitting up. They looked curiously at Ned, who still carried the flaming brand in his hand.

"A noise like the sound of thunder away off wakened me up," said the Panther. "Now, what have you been up to, young 'un?"

"Me?" said Ned lightly. "Oh, nothing important. I wanted to make some investigations in natural history out there in the bushes, and as I needed a light for the purpose I took it."

"An' if I'm not pressin' too much," said the Panther, in mock humility, "may I make so bold as to ask our young Solomon what is natural history?"

"Natural history is the study of animals. I saw a panther in the bushes and I went out there to examine him. I saw that he was a big fellow, but he ran away so fast I could tell no more about him."

"You scared him away with the torch instead of shooting," said Obed. "It was well done, but it took a stout heart. If he comes again tell him I won't wake up until it's time for my watch."

He was asleep again inside of a minute, and the Panther followed him quickly. Both men trusted Ned fully, treating him now as an experienced and skilled frontiersman. He knew it, and he felt proud and encouraged.

The panther did not come back, but the wolves did, although Ned now paid no attention to them. He was growing used to their company and the uncanny feeling departed. He merely replenished the fires and sat patiently until it was time for Obed to succeed him. Then he, too, wrapped himself in his blankets and slept a dreamless sleep until day.

The remainder of the buffalo meat was taken away the next day, but anticipating a long stay at the cabin they continued to hunt, both on horseback and on foot. Two more buffalo cows fell to their rifles. They also secured a deer, three antelope and a dozen wild turkeys.

Their hunting spread over two days, but when they were all assembled on the third night at the cabin general satisfaction prevailed. They had ranged over considerable country, and as game was plentiful and not afraid the Panther drew the logical conclusion that man had been scarce in that region.

"I take it," he said, "that the Mexicans are a good distance east, and that the Lipans and Comanches are another good distance west. Just the same, boys, we've got to keep a close watch, an' I think we've got more to fear from raidin' parties of the Indians than from the Mexicans. All the Mexicans are likely to be ridin' to some point on the Rio Grande to meet the forces of Santa Anna."

"I wish we had more horses," said Obed. "We'd go that way ourselves and see what's up."

"Well, maybe we'll get 'em," said the Panther. "Thar's a lot of horses on these plains, some of which ought to belong to us an' we may find a way of claimin' our rights."

They passed a number of pleasant days at the cabin and in hunting and foraging in the vicinity. They killed more big game and the dressed skins of buffalo, bear and deer were spread on the floor or were hung on the walls. Wild turkeys were numerous, and they had them for food every day. But they discovered no signs of man, white or red, and they would have been content to wait there had they not been so anxious to investigate the reported advance of Santa Anna on the Rio Grande.

Roylston was the most patient of them all, or at least he said the least.

"I think," he said about the fourth or fifth day, "that it does not hurt to linger here. The Mexican power has not yet gathered in full. As for me, personally, it suits me admirably. I can walk a full two hundred yards now, and next week I shall be able to walk a mile."

"When we are all ready to depart, which way do you intend to go Mr. Roylston?" asked Ned.

"I wish to go around the settlements and then to New Orleans," replied Roylston. "That city is my headquarters, but I also have establishments elsewhere, even as far north as New York. Are you sure, Ned, that you cannot go with me and bring your friend Allen, too? I could make men of you both in a vast commercial world. There have been great opportunities, and greater are coming. The development of this mighty southwest will call for large and bold schemes of organization. It is not money alone that I offer, but the risk, the hopes and rewards of a great game, in fact, the opening of a new world to civilization, for such this southwest is. It appeals to some deeper feeling than that which can be aroused by the mere making of money."

Ned, deeply interested, watched him intently as he spoke. He saw Roylston show emotion for the first time, and the mind of the boy responded to that of the man. He could understand this dream. The image of a great Texan republic was already in the minds of men. It possessed that of Ned. He did not believe that the Texans and Mexicans could ever get along together, and he was quite sure that Texas could never return to its original position as part of a Mexican state.

"You can do much for Texas there with me in New Orleans," said Roylston, as if he were making a final appeal to one whom he looked upon almost as a son. "Perhaps you could do more than you can here in Texas."

Ned shook his head a little sadly. He did not like to disappoint this man, but he could not leave the field. Young Allen also said that he would remain.

"Be it so," said Roylston. "It is young blood. Never was there a truer saying than 'Young men for war, old men for counsel.' But the time may come when you will need me. When it does come send the word."

Ned judged from Roylston's manner that dark days were ahead, but the merchant did not mention the subject again. At the end of a week, when they were amply supplied with everything except horses, the Panther decided to take Ned and Obed and go on a scout toward the Rio Grande. They started early in the morning and the horses, which had obtained plenty of grass, were full of life and vigour.

They soon left the narrow belt of forest far behind them, maintaining an almost direct course toward the southeast. The point on the river that they intended to reach was seventy or eighty miles away, and they did not expect to cover the distance in less than two days.

They rode all that day and did not see a trace of a human being, but they did see both buffalo and antelope in the distance.

"It shows what the war has done," said the Panther. "I rode over these same prairies about a year ago an' game was scarce, but there were some men. Now the men are all gone an' the game has come back. Cur'us how quick buffalo an' deer an' antelope learn about these things."

They slept the night through on the open prairie, keeping watch by turns. The weather was cold, but they had their good blankets with them and they took no discomfort. They rode forward again early in the morning, and about noon struck an old but broad trail. It was evident that many men and many wagons had passed here. There were deep ruts in the earth, cut by wheels, and the traces of footsteps showed over a belt a quarter of a mile wide.

"Well, Ned, I s'pose you can make a purty good guess what this means?" said the Panther.

"This was made weeks and weeks ago," replied Ned confidently, "and the men who made it were Mexicans. They were soldiers, the army of Cos, that we took at San Antonio, and which we allowed to retire on parole into Mexico."

"There's no doubt you're right," said the Panther. "There's no other force in this part of the world big enough to make such a wide an' lastin' trail. An' I think it's our business to follow these tracks. What do you say, Obed?"

"It's just the one thing in the world that we're here to do," said the Maine man. "Broad is the path and straight is the way that leads before us, and we follow on."

"Do we follow them down into Mexico?" said Ned.

"I don't think it likely that we'll have to do it," replied the Panther, glancing at Obed.

Ned caught the look and he understood.

"Do you mean," he asked, "that Cos, after taking his parole and pledging his word that he and his troops would not fight against us, would stop at the Rio Grande?"

"I mean that an' nothin' else," replied the Panther. "I ain't talkin' ag'in Mexicans in general. I've knowed some good men among them, but I wouldn't take the word of any of that crowd of generals, Santa Anna, Cos, Sesma, Urrea, Gaona, Castrillon, the Italian Filisola, or any of them."

"There's one I'd trust," said Ned, with grateful memory, "and that's Almonte."

"I've heard that he's of different stuff," said the Panther, "but it's best to keep out of their hands."

They were now riding swiftly almost due southward, having changed their course to follow the trail, and they kept a sharp watch ahead for Mexican scouts or skirmishers. But the bare country in its

312

winter brown was lone and desolate. The trail led straight ahead, and it would have been obvious now to the most inexperienced eye that an army had passed that way. They saw remains of camp fires, now and then the skeleton of a horse or mule picked clean by buzzards, fragments of wornout clothing that had been thrown aside, and once a brokendown wagon. Two or three times they saw little mounds of earth with rude wooden crosses stuck upon them, to mark where some of the wounded had died and had been buried.

They came at last to a bit of woodland growing about a spring that seemed to gush straight up from the earth. It was really an open grove with no underbrush, a splendid place for a camp. It was evident that Cos's force had put it to full use, as the earth nearly everywhere had been trodden by hundreds of feet, and the charred pieces of wood were innumerable. The Panther made a long and critical examination of everything.

"I'm thinkin'," he said, "that Cos stayed here three or four days. All the signs p'int that way. He was bound by the terms we gave him at San Antonio to go an' not fight ag'in, but he's shorely takin' his time about it. Look at these bones, will you? Now, Ned, you promisin' scout an' skirmisher, tell me what they are."

"Buffalo bones," replied Ned promptly.

"Right you are," replied the Panther, "an' when Cos left San Antonio he wasn't taking any buffaloes along with him to kill fur meat. They staid here so long that the hunters had time to go out an' shoot game."

"A long lane's the thief of time," said Obed, "and having a big march before him, Cos has concluded to walk instead of run."

"'Cause he was expectin' somethin' that would stop him," said the Panther angrily. "I hate liars an' traitors. Well, we'll soon see."

Their curiosity became so great that they rode at a swift trot on the great south trail, and not ten miles further they came upon the unmistakable evidences of another big camp that had lasted long.

"Slower an' slower," muttered the Panther. "They must have met a messenger. Wa'al, it's fur us to go slow now, too."

But he said aloud:

"Boys, it ain't more'n twenty miles now to the Rio Grande, an' we can hit it by dark. But I'm thinkin' that we'd better be mighty keerful now as we go on."

"I suppose it's because Mexican scouts and skirmishers may be watching," said Ned.

"Yes, an' 'specially that fellow Urrea. His uncle bein' one of Santa Anna's leadin' gen'rals, he's likely to have freer rein, an', as we know, he's clever an' active. I'd hate to fall into his hands again."

They rode more slowly, and three pairs of eyes continually searched the plain for an enemy. Ned's sight was uncommonly acute, and Obed and the Panther frequently appealed to him as a last resort. It flattered his pride and he strove to justify it.

Their pace became slower and slower, and presently the early twilight of winter was coming. A cold wind moaned, but the desolate plain was broken here and there by clumps of trees. At the suggestion of the Panther they rode to one of these and halted under cover of the timber.

"The river can't be much more than a mile ahead," said the Panther, "an' we might run into the Mexicans any minute. We're sheltered here, an' we'd better wait a while. Then I think we can do more stalkin'."

Obed and Ned were not at all averse, and dismounting they stretched themselves, easing their muscles. Old Jack hunted grass and, finding none, rubbed Ned's elbow with his nose suggestively.

"Never mind, old boy," said Ned, patting the glossy muzzle of his faithful comrade. "This is no time for feasting and banqueting. We are hunting Mexicans, you and I, and after that business is over we may consider our pleasures."

They remained several hours among the trees. They saw the last red glow that the sun leaves in the west die away. They saw the full darkness descend over the earth, and then the stars come trooping out. After that they saw a scarlet flush under the horizon which was not a part of the night and its progress. The Panther noted it, and his great face darkened. He turned to Ned.

"You see it, don't you? Now tell me what it is."

"That light, I should say, comes from the fires of an army. And it can be no other army than that of Cos."

"Right again, ain't he, Obed?"

"He surely is. Cos and his men are there. He who breaks his faith when he steals away will have to fight another day. How far off would you say that light is, Panther?"

"'Bout two miles, an' in an hour or so we'll ride fur it. The night will darken up more then, an' it will give us a better chance for lookin' an listenin'. I'll be mightily fooled if we don't find out a lot that's worth knowin'."

True to Obed's prediction, the night deepened somewhat within the hour. Many of the stars were hidden by floating wisps of cloud, and objects could not be seen far on the dusky surface of the plain. But the increased darkness only made the scarlet glow in the south deepen. It seemed, too, to spread far to right and left.

"That's a big force," said the Panther. "It'll take a lot of fires to make a blaze like that."

"I'm agreeing with you," said Obed. "I'm thinking that those are the camp fires of more men than Cos took from San Antonio with him."

"Which would mean," said Ned, "that another Mexican army had come north to join him."

"Anyhow, we'll soon see," said the Panther.

They mounted their horses and rode cautiously toward the light.

CHAPTER 5

SANTA ANNA'S ADVANCE

The three rode abreast, Ned in the centre. The boy was on terms of perfect equality with Obed and the Panther. They treated him as a man among men, and respected his character, rather grave for one so young, and always keen to learn.

The land rolled away in swells as usual throughout a great part of Texas, but they were not of much elevation and the red glow in the south was always in sight, deepening fast as they advanced. They stopped at last on a little elevation within the shadow of some myrtle oaks, and saw the fires spread before them only four or five hundred yards away, and along a line of at least two miles. They heard the confused murmur of many men. The dark outlines of cannon were seen against the firelight, and now and then the musical note of a mandolin or guitar came to them.

"We was right in our guess," said the Panther. "It's a lot bigger force than the one that Cos led away from San Antonio, an' it will take a heap of rippin' an' t'arin' an' roarin' to turn it back. Our people don't know how much is comin' ag'in 'em."

The Panther spoke in a solemn tone. Ned saw that he was deeply impressed and that he feared for the future. Good cause had he. Squabbles among the Texan leaders had reduced their army to five or six hundred men.

"Don't you think," said Ned, "that we ought to find out just exactly what is here, and what this army intends?"

"Not a doubt of it," said Obed. "Those who have eyes to see should not go away without seeing."

The Panther nodded violently in assent.

"We must scout about the camp," he said. "Mebbe we'd better divide an' then we can all gather before daybreak at the clump of trees back there."

He pointed to a little cluster of trees several hundred yards back of them, and Ned and Obed agreed. The Panther turned away to the right, Obed to the left and Ned took the centre. Their plan of dividing their force had a great advantage. One man was much less likely than three to attract undue attention.

Ned went straight ahead a hundred yards or more, when he was stopped by an *arroyo* five or six feet wide and with very deep banks. He looked about, uncertain at first what to do. Obed and the Panther had already disappeared in the dusk. Before him glowed the red light, and he heard the distant sound of many voices.

Ned quickly decided. He remembered how they had escaped up the bed of the creek when they were besieged by Urrea, and if one could leave by an *arroyo*, one could also approach by it. He rode to the group of trees that had been designated as the place of meeting, and left his horse there. He noticed considerable grass within the ring of trunks, and he was quite confident that Old Jack would remain there until his return. But he addressed to him words of admonition:

"Be sure that you stay among these trees, old friend," he said, "because it's likely that when I want you I'll want you bad. Remain and attend to this grass."

Old Jack whinnied softly and, after his fashion, rubbed his nose gently against his master's arm. It was sufficient for Ned. He was sure that the horse understood, and leaving him he went back to the arroyo, which he entered without hesitation.

Ned was well armed, as every one then had full need to be. He wore a *sombrero* in the Mexican fashion, and flung over his shoulders was a great *serape* which he had found most useful in the winter. With his perfect knowledge of Spanish and its Mexican variants he believed that if surprised he could pass as a Mexican, particularly in the night and among so many.

The *arroyo* led straight down toward the plain upon which the Mexicans were encamped, and when he emerged from it he saw that the fires which at a distance looked like one continuous blaze were scores in number. Many of them were built of buffalo chips and others of light wood that burned fast. Sentinels were posted here and there, but they kept little watch. Why should they? Here was a great Mexican army, and there was certainly no foe amounting to more than a few men within a hundred miles.

Ned's heart sank as he beheld the evident extent of the Mexican array. The little Texan force left in the field could be no match for such an army as this.

Nevertheless, his resolution to go through the Mexican camp hardened. If he came back with a true and detailed tale of their numbers the Texans must believe and prepare. He drew the brim of his *sombrero* down a little further, and pulled his *serape* up to meet it. The habit the Mexicans had of wrapping their *serapes* so high that they were covered to the nose was fortunate at this time. He was now completely disguised, without the appearance of having taken any unusual precaution.

He walked forward boldly and sat down with a group beside a fire. He judged by the fact that they were awake so late that they had but little to do, and he saw at once also that they were Mexicans from the far south. They were small, dark men, rather amiable in appearance. Two began to play guitars and they sang a plaintive song to the music. The others, smoking *cigarritos*, listened attentively and luxuriously. Ned imitated them perfectly. He, too, lying upon his elbow before the pleasant fire, felt the influence of the music, so sweet, so murmurous, speaking so little of war. One of the men handed him a *cigarrito*, and, lighting it, he made pretence of smoking—he would not have seemed a Mexican had he not smoked the *cigarrito*.

Lying there, Ned saw many tents, evidence of a camp that was not for the day only, and he beheld officers in bright uniforms passing among them. His heart gave a great jump when he noticed among them a heavy-set, dark man. It was Cos, Cos the breaker of oaths. With him was another officer whose uniform indicated the general. Ned learned later that this was Sesma, who had been dispatched with a brigade by Santa Anna to meet Cos on the Rio Grande, where they were to remain until the dictator himself came with more troops.

The music ceased presently and one of the men said to Ned:

"What company?"

Ned had prepared himself for such questions, and he moved his hand vaguely toward the left.

"Over there," he said.

They were fully satisfied, and continued to puff their *cigarritos*, resting their heads with great content upon pillows made of their saddles and blankets. For a while they said nothing more, happily watching the rings of smoke from their *cigarritos* rise and melt into the air. Although small and short, they looked hardy and strong. Ned noticed the signs of bustle and expectancy about the camp. Usually Mexicans were asleep at this hour, and he wondered why they lingered. But he did not approach the subject directly.

"A hard march," he said, knowing that these men about him had come a vast distance.

"Aye, it was," said the man next on his right. "Santiago, but was it not, Jose?"

Jose, the second man on the right, replied in the affirmative and with emphasis:

"You speak the great truth, Carlos. Such another march I never wish to make. Think of the hundreds and hundreds of miles we have tramped from our warm lands far in the south across mountains, across bare and windy deserts, with the ice and the snow beating in our faces. How I shivered, Carlos, and how long I shivered! I thought I should continue shivering all my life even if I lived to be a hundred, no matter how warmly the sun might shine."

The others laughed, and seemed to Ned to snuggle a little closer to the fire, driven by the memory of the icy plains.

"But it was the will of the great Santa Anna, surely the mightiest man of our age," said Carlos. "They say that his wrath was terrible when he heard how the Texan bandits had taken San Antonio de Bexar. Truly, I am glad that I was not one of his officers, and that I was not in his presence at the time. After all, it is sometimes better to be a common soldier than to have command."

"Aye, truly," said Ned, and the others nodded in affirmation.

"But the great Santa Anna will finish it," continued Carlos, who seemed to have the sin of garrulity. "He has defeated all his enemies in Mexico, he has consolidated his power and now he advances with a mighty force to crush these insolent and miserable Texans. As I have said, he will finish it. The rope and the bullet will be busy. In six months there will be no Texans."

Ned shivered, and when he looked at the camp fires of the great army he saw that this *peon* was not talking foolishness. Nevertheless his mind returned to its original point of interest. Why did the Mexican army remain awake so late?

"Have you seen the president?" he asked of Carlos.

"Often," replied Carlos, with pride. "I fought under him in the great battle on the plain of Guadalupe less than two years ago, when we defeated Don Francisco Garcia, the governor of Zacatecas. Ah, it was a terrible battle, my friends! Thousands and thousands were killed and all Mexicans. Mexicans killing Mexicans. But who can prevail against the great Santa Anna? He routed the forces of Garcia, and the City of Zacatecas was given up to us to pillage. Many fine things I took that day from the houses of those who presumed to help the enemy of our leader. But now we care not to kill Mexicans, our own people. It is only the miserable Texans who are really *Gringos*."

Carlos, who had been the most amiable of men, basking in the firelight, now rose up a little and his eyes flashed. He had excited himself by his own tale of the battle and loot of Zacatecas and the coming slaughter of the Texans. That strain of cruelty, which in Ned's opinion always lay embedded in the Spanish character, was coming to the surface.

Ned made no comment. His *serape*, drawn up to his nose, almost met the brim of his *sombrero* and nobody suspected that the comrade who sat and chatted with them was a *Gringo*, but he shivered again, nevertheless.

"We shall have a great force when it is all gathered," he said at length.

"Seven thousand men or more," said José proudly, "and nearly all of them are veterans of the wars. We shall have ten times the numbers of the Texans, who are only hunters and *rancheros*."

"Have you heard when we march?" asked Ned, in a careless tone.

"As soon as the great Santa Anna arrives it will be decided, I doubt not," said Jose. "The general and his escort should be here by midnight."

Ned's heart gave a leap. So it was that for which they were waiting. Santa Anna himself would come in an hour or two. He was very glad that he had entered the Mexican camp. Bidding a courteous good night to the men about the fire, he rose and sauntered on. It was easy enough for him to do so without attracting attention, as many others were doing the same thing. Discipline seldom amounted to much in a Mexican army, and so confident were both officers and soldiers of an overwhelming victory that they preserved scarcely any at all. Yet the expectant feeling pervaded the whole camp, and now that he knew that Santa Anna was coming he understood.

Santa Anna was the greatest man in the world to these soldiers. He had triumphed over everything in their own country. He had exhibited qualities of daring and energy that seemed to them supreme, and his impression upon them was overwhelming. Ned felt once more that little shiver. They might be right in their view of the Texan war.

He strolled on from fire to fire, until his attention was arrested suddenly by one at which only officers sat. It was not so much the group as it was one among them who drew his notice so strongly. Urrea was sitting on the far side of the fire, every feature thrown into clear relief by the bright flames. The other officers were young men of about his own age and they were playing dice. They were evidently in high good humour, as they laughed frequently.

Ned lay down just within the shadow of a tent wall, drew his *serape* higher about his face, and rested his head upon his arm. He would have seemed sound asleep to an ordinary observer, but he was never more wide awake in his life. He was near enough to hear what Urrea and his friends were saying, and he intended to hear it. It was for such that he had come.

"You lose, Francisco," said one of the men as he made a throw of the dice and looked eagerly at the result. "What was it that you were saying about the general?"

"That I expect an early advance, Ramon," replied Urrea, "a brief campaign, and a complete victory. I hate these Texans. I shall be glad to see them annihilated."

The young officer whom he called Ramon laughed.

"If what I hear be true, Francisco," he said, "you have cause to hate them. There was a boy, Fulton, that wild buffalo of a man, whom they call the Panther, and another who defeated some of your finest plans."

Urrea flushed, but controlled his temper.

"It is true, Ramon," he replied. "The third man I can tell you is called Obed White, and they are a clever three. I hate them, but it hurts my pride less to be defeated by them than by any others whom I know."

"Well spoken, Urrea," said a third man, "but since these three are fighters and will stay to meet us, it is a certainty that our general will scoop them into his net. Then you can have all the revenge you wish."

"I count upon it, Ambrosio," said Urrea, smiling. "I also hope that we shall recapture the man Roylston. He has great sums of money in

320

the foreign banks in our country, and we need them, but our illustrious president cannot get them without an order from Roylston. The general would rather have Roylston than a thousand Texan prisoners."

All of them laughed, and the laugh made Ned, lying in the shadow, shiver once more. Urrea glanced his way presently, but the recumbent figure did not claim his notice. The attention of his comrades and himself became absorbed in the dice again. They were throwing the little ivory cubes upon a blanket, and Ned could hear them click as they struck together. The sharp little sound began to flick his nerves. Not one to cherish resentment, he nevertheless began to hate Urrea, and he included in that hatred the young men with him. The Texans were so few and poor. The Mexicans were so many, and they had the resources of a nation more than two centuries old.

Ned rose by and by and walked on. He could imitate the Mexican gait perfectly, and no one paid any attention to him. They were absorbed, moreover, in something else, because now the light of torches could be seen dimly in the south. Officers threw down cards and dice. Men straightened their uniforms and Cos and Sesma began to form companies in line. More fuel was thrown on the fires, which sprang up, suffusing all the night with colour and brightness. Ned with his rifle at salute fell into place at the end of one of the companies, and no one knew that he did not belong there. In the excitement of the moment he forgot all about the Panther and Obed.

A thrill seemed to run through the whole Mexican force. It was the most impressive scene that Ned had ever beheld. A leader, omnipotent in their eyes, was coming to these men, and he came at midnight out of the dark into the light.

The torches grew brighter. A trumpet pealed and a trumpet in the camp replied. The Mexican lines became silent save for a deep murmur. In the south they heard the rapid beat of hoofs, and then Santa Anna came, galloping at the head of fifty horsemen. Many of the younger officers ran forward, holding up torches, and the dictator rode in a blaze of light.

Ned looked once more upon that dark and singular face, a face daring and cruel, that might have belonged to one of the old conquistadores. In the saddle his lack of height was concealed, but on the great white horse that he rode Ned felt that he was an imposing, even a terrible, figure. His eyes were blazing with triumph as his army united with torches to do him honour. It was like Napoleon on the night before Austerlitz, and what was he but the Napoleon of the New World? His figure swelled and the gold braid on his cocked hat and gorgeous uniform reflected the beams of the firelight.

A mighty cheer from thousands of throats ran along the Mexican line, and the torches were waved until they looked like vast circles of fire. Santa Anna lifted his hat and bowed three times in salute. Again the Mexican cheer rolled to right and to left. Santa Anna, still sitting on his horse, spread out his hands. There was instant silence save for the deep breathing of the men.

"My children," he said, "I have come to sweep away these miserable Texans who have dared to raise the rebel flag against us. We will punish them all. Houston, Austin, Bowie and the rest of their leaders shall feel our justice. When we finish our march over their prairies it shall be as if a great fire had passed. I have said it. I am Santa Anna."

The thunderous cheer broke forth again. Ned had never before heard words so full of conceit and vainglory, yet the strength and menace were there. He felt it instinctively. Santa Anna believed himself to be the greatest man in the world, and he was certainly the greatest in Mexico. His belief in himself was based upon a deep well of energy and daring. Once more Ned felt a great and terrible fear for Texas, and the thin line of skin-clad hunters and ranchmen who were its sole defence. But the feeling passed as he watched Santa Anna. A young officer rushed forward and held his stirrup as the dictator dismounted. Then the generals, including those who had come with him, crowded around him. It was a brilliant company, including Sesma, Cos, Duque, Castrillon, Tolsa, Gaona and others, among whom Ned noted a man of decidedly Italian appearance. This was General Vincente Filisola, an Italian officer who had received a huge grant of land in Texas, and who was now second in command to Santa Anna.

Ned watched them as they talked together and occasionally the crowd parted enough for him to see Santa Anna, who spoke and gesticulated with great energy. The soldiers had been drawn away by the minor officers, and were now dispersing to their places by the fires where they would seek sleep.

Ned noticed a trim, slender figure on the outer edge of the group around Santa Anna. It seemed familiar, and when the man turned he recognised the face of Almonte, the gallant young Mexican colonel who had been kind to him. He was sorry to see him there. He was sorry that he should have to fight against him.

Santa Anna went presently to a great marquee that had been prepared for him, and the other generals retired also to the tents that had been set about it. The dictator was tired from his long ride and must not be disturbed. Strict orders were given that there should be no noise in the camp, and it quickly sank into silence.

Ned lay down before one of the fires at the western end of the camp wrapped as before in his serape. He counterfeited sleep, but nothing was further from his mind. It seemed to him that he had done all he could do in the Mexican camp. He had seen the arrival of Santa Anna, but there was no way to learn when the general would order an advance. But he could infer from Santa Anna's well-known energy and ability that it would come quickly.

Between the slit left by the brim of his *sombrero* and his *serape* he watched the great fires die slowly. Most of the Mexicans were asleep now, and their figures were growing indistinct in the shadows. But Ned, rising, slouched forward, imitating the gait of the laziest of the Mexicans. Yet his eyes were always watching shrewdly through the slit. Very little escaped his notice. He went along the entire Mexican line and then back again. He had a good mathematical mind, and he saw that the estimate of 7,000 for the Mexican Army was not too few. He also saw many cannon and the horses for a great cavalry force. He knew, too, that Santa Anna had with him the best regiments in the Mexican service.

On his last trip along the line Ned began to look for the Panther and Obed, but he saw no figures resembling theirs, although he was quite sure that he would know the Panther in any disguise owing to his great size. This circumstance would make it more dangerous for the Panther than for either Obed or himself, as Urrea, if he should see so large a man, would suspect that it was none other than the redoubtable frontiersman.

Ned was thinking of this danger to the Panther when he came face to face with Urrea himself. The young Mexican captain was not lacking in vigilance and energy, and even at that late hour he was seeing that all was well in the camp of Santa Anna. Ned was truly thankful now that Mexican custom and the coldness of the night permitted him to cover his face with his serape and the brim of his *sombrero*.

"Why are you walking here?" demanded Urrea.

"I've just taken a message to General Castrillon," replied Ned.

He had learned already that Castrillon commanded the artillery, and as he was at least a mile away he thought this the safest reply.

"From whom?" asked Urrea shortly.

"Pardon, sir," replied Ned, in his best Spanish, disguising his voice as much as possible, "but I am not allowed to tell."

Ned's tone was courteous and apologetic, and in ninety-nine cases out of a hundred Urrea would have contented himself with an impatient word or two. But he was in a most vicious temper. Perhaps he had been rebuked by Santa Anna for allowing the rescue of Roylston.

"Why don't you speak up?" he exclaimed. "Why do you mumble your words, and why do you stand in such a slouching manner. Remember that a soldier should stand up straight."

"Yes, my captain," said Ned, but he did not change his attitude. The tone and manner of Urrea angered him. He forgot where he was and his danger.

Urrea's swarthy face flushed. He carried in his hand a small riding whip, which he switched occasionally across the tops of his tall, military boots.

"Lout!" he cried. "You hear me! Why do you not obey!"

Ned stood impassive. Certainly Urrea had had a bad half hour somewhere. His temper leaped beyond control.

"Idiot!" he exclaimed.

Then he suddenly lashed Ned across the face with the little riding whip. The blow fell on *serape* and *sombrero* and the flesh was not touched, but for a few moments Ned went mad. He dropped his rifle, leaped upon the astonished officer, wrenched the whip from his hands, slashed him across the cheeks with it until the blood ran in streams, then broke it in two and threw the pieces in his face. Ned's *serape* fell away. Urrea had clasped his hands to his cheeks that stung like fire, but now he recognised the boy.

"Fulton!" he cried.

The sharp exclamation brought Ned to a realisation of his danger. He seized his rifle, pulled up the *serape* and sprang back. Already Mexican soldiers were gathering. It was truly fortunate for Ned that he was quick of thought, and that his thoughts came quickest when the danger was greatest. He knew that the cry of "Fulton!" was unintelligible to them, and he exclaimed:

"Save me, comrades! He tried to beat me without cause, and now he would kill me, as you see!"

Urrea had drawn a pistol and was shouting fiery Mexican oaths. The soldiers, some of them just awakened from sleep, and all of them dazed, had gathered in a huddle, but they opened to let Ned pass. Excessive and cruel punishment was common among them. A man might be flogged half to death at the whim of an officer, and instinctively they protected their comrade.

As the Mexican group closed up behind him, and between him and Urrea, Ned ran at top speed toward the west where the *arroyo* cut across the plain. More Mexicans were gathering, and there was great confusion. Everybody was asking what was the matter. The boy's quick wit did not desert him. There was safety in ignorance and the multitude.

He quickly dropped to a walk and he, too, began to ask of others what had caused the trouble. All the while he worked steadily toward the *arroyo*, and soon he left behind him the lights and the shouting. He now came into the dark, passed beyond the Mexican lines, and entered the cut in the earth down which he had come.

He was compelled to sit down on the sand and relax. He was exhausted by the great effort of both mind and body which had carried him through so much danger. His heart was beating heavily and he felt dizzy. But his eyes cleared presently and his strength came back. He considered himself safe. In the darkness it was not likely that any of the Mexicans would stumble upon him.

He thought of the Panther and Obed, but he could do nothing for them. He must trust to meeting them again at the place appointed. He looked at the Mexican camp. The fires had burned up again there for a minute or two, but as he looked they sank once more. The noise also decreased. Evidently they were giving up the pursuit.

Ned rose and walked slowly up the *arroyo*. He became aware that the night was very cold and it told on his relaxed frame. He pulled up the *serape* again, and now it was for warmth and not for disguise. He stopped at intervals to search the darkness with his eyes and to listen for noises. He might meet with an enemy or he might meet with one of his friends. He was prepared for either. He had regained control of himself both body and mind, and his ready rifle rested in the hollow of his arm.

He met neither. He heard nothing but the usual sighing of the prairie wind that ceased rarely, and he saw nothing but the faint glow on the southern horizon that marked the Mexican camp where he had met his enemy.

He left the *arroyo*, and saw a dark shadow on the plain, the figure of a man, rifle in hand, Ned instantly sprang back into the *arroyo* and the stranger did the same. A curve in the line of this cut in the earth now hid them from each other, and Ned, his body pressed against the bank, waited with beating heart. He had no doubt that it was a Mexican sentinel or scout more vigilant than the others, and he felt his danger.

Ned in this crisis used the utmost caution. He did not believe that any other would come, and it must be a test of patience between him and his enemy. Whoever showed his head first would be likely to lose in the duel for life. He pressed himself closer and closer against the bank, and sought to detect some movement of the stranger. He saw nothing and he did not hear a sound. It seemed that the man had absolutely vanished into space. It occurred to Ned that it might have been a mere figment of the dusk and his excited brain, but he quickly dismissed the idea. He had seen the man and he had seen him leap into the *arroyo*. There could be no doubt of it.

There was another long wait, and the suspense became acute. The man was surely on the other side of that curve waiting for him. He was held fast. He was almost as much a prisoner as if he lay bound in the Mexican camp. It seemed to him, too, that the darkness was thinning a little. It would soon be day and then he could not escape the notice of horsemen from Santa Anna's army. He decided that he must risk an advance and he began creeping forward cautiously. He remembered now what he had forgotten in the first moments of the meeting. He might yet, even before this sentinel or scout, pass as a Mexican.

He stopped suddenly when he heard a low whistle in front of him. While it could be heard but a short distance, it was singularly sweet. It formed the first bars of an old tune, "The World Turned Upside Down," and Ned promptly recognised it. The whistle stopped in a moment or two, but Ned took up the air and continued it for a few bars more. Then, all apprehension gone, he sprang out of the *arroyo* and stood upon the bank. Another figure was projected from the arroyo and stood upon the bank facing him, not more than twenty feet away.

Simultaneously Obed White and Edward Fulton advanced, shook hands and laughed.

"You kept me here waiting in this gully at least half an hour," said Obed. "Time and I waited long on you."

"But no longer than I waited on you," said Ned. "Why didn't you think of whistling the tune sooner?"

"Why didn't you?"

They laughed and shook hands again.

"At any rate, we're here together again, safe and unharmed," said

Ned. "And now to see what has become of the Panther."

"You'd better be lookin' out for yourselves instead of the Panther," growled a voice, as a gigantic figure upheaved itself from the *arroyo* eight or ten yards behind them. "I could have picked you both off while you were standin' there shakin' hands, an' neither of you would never have knowed what struck him."

"The Panther!" they exclaimed joyously, and they shook hands with him also.

"An' now," said the Panther, "it will soon be day. We'd better make fur our horses an' then clear out. We kin tell 'bout what we've seen an' done when we're two or three miles away."

They found the horses safe in the brushwood, Old Jack welcoming Ned with a soft whinny. They were in the saddle at once, rode swiftly northward, and none of them spoke for a half hour. When a faint tinge of gray appeared on the eastern rim of the world the Panther said:

"My tale's short. I couldn't get into the camp, 'cause I'm too big. The very first fellow I saw looked at me with s'picion painted all over him. So I had to keep back in the darkness. But I saw it was a mighty big army. It can do a lot of rippin', an' t'arin', an' chawin'."

"I got into the camp," said Obed, after a minute of silence, "but as I'm not built much like a Mexican, being eight or ten inches too tall, men were looking at me as if I were a strange specimen. One touch of difference and all the world's staring at you. So I concluded that I'd better stay on the outside of the lines. I hung around, and I saw just what Panther saw, no more and no less. Then I started back and I struck the *arroyo*, which seemed to me a good way for leaving. But before I had gone far I concluded I was followed. So I watched the fellow who was following, and the fellow who was following watched me for about a year. The watch was just over when you came up, Panther. It was long, but it's a long watch that has no ending."

"And I," said Ned, after another wait of a minute, "being neither so tall as Obed nor so big around as the Panther, was able to go about in the Mexican camp without any notice being taken of me. I saw Santa Anna arrive to take the chief command."

"Santa Anna himself?" exclaimed the Panther.

"Yes, Santa Anna himself. They gave him a great reception. After a while I started to come away. I met Urrea. He took me for a *peon*, gave me an order, and when I didn't obey it tried to strike me across the face with a whip."

"And what did you do?" exclaimed the two men together.

"I took the whip away from him and lashed his cheeks with it. I was recognised, but in the turmoil and confusion I escaped. Then I had the encounter with Obed White, of which he has told already."

"Since Santa Anna has come," said the Panther, "they're likely to move at any moment. We'll ride straight for the cabin an' the boys."

CHAPTER 6

FOR FREEDOM'S SAKE

Evidently the horses had found considerable grass through the night, as they were fresh and strong, and the miles fell fast behind them. At the gait at which they were going they would reach the cabin that night. Meanwhile they made plans. The little force would divide and messengers would go to San Antonio, Harrisburg and other points, with the news that Santa Anna was advancing with an immense force.

And every one of the three knew that the need was great. They knew how divided counsels had scattered the little Texan army. At San Antonio, the most important point of all, the town that they had triumphantly taken from a much greater force of Mexicans, there were practically no men, and that undoubtedly was Santa Anna's destination. Unconsciously they began to urge their horses to great and yet greater speed, until the Panther recalled them to prudence.

"Slower, boys! slower!" he said. "We mustn't run our horses out at the start."

"And there's a second reason for pulling down," said Ned, "since there's somebody else on the plain."

His uncommon eyesight had already detected before the others the strange presence. He pointed toward the East.

"Do you see that black speck there, where the sky touches the ground?" he said. "If you'll watch it you'll see that it's moving. And look! There's another! and another! and another!"

The Panther and Obed now saw the black specks also. The three stopped on the crest of a swell and watched them attentively.

"One! two! three! four! five! six! seven! eight! nine! ten! eleven! twelve! thirteen!" counted the far-sighted boy.

"An' them thirteen specks are thirteen men on horseback," continued the Panther, "an' now I wonder who in the name of the great horn spoon they are!"

"Suppose we see," said Obed. "All things are revealed to him who looks—at least most of the time. It is true that they are more than four to our one, but our horses are swift, and we can get away."

"That's right," said the Panther. "Still, we oughtn't to take the risk unless everybody is willin'. What do you say, Ned?"

"I reply 'yes,' of course," said the boy, "especially as I've an idea that those are not Mexicans. They look too big and tall, and they sit too straight up in their saddles for Mexicans."

"Them ideas of yours are ketchin'," said the Panther. "Them fellers may be Mexicans, but they don't look like Mexicans, they don't act like Mexicans, an' they ain't Mexicans."

"Take out what isn't, and you have left what is," said Obed.

"We'll soon see," said Ned.

A few minutes more and there could be no further doubt that the thirteen were Texans or Americans. One rode a little ahead of the others, who came on in an even line. They were mounted on large horses, but the man in front held Ned's attention.

The leader was tall and thin, but evidently muscular and powerful. His hair was straight and black like an Indian's. His features were angular and tanned by the winds of many years. His body was clothed completely in buckskin, and a raccoon skin cap was on his head. Across his shoulder lay a rifle with a barrel of unusual length.

"Never saw any of them before," said the Panther. "By the great horn spoon, who can that feller in front be? He looks like somebody."

The little band rode closer, and its leader held up his hand as a sign of amity.

"Good friends," he said, in a deep clear voice, "we don't have very close neighbours out here, and that makes a meeting all the pleasanter. You are Texans, I guess."

"You guess right," said the Panther, in the same friendly tone. "An' are you Texans, too?"

"That point might be debated," replied the man, in a whimsical tone, "and after a long dispute neither I nor my partners here could say which was right and which was wrong. But while we may not be Texans, yet we will be right away."

His eyes twinkled as he spoke, and Ned suddenly felt a strong liking for him. He was not young and, despite his buckskin dress and careless grammar, there was something of the man of the world about him. But he seemed to have a certain boyishness of spirit that appealed strongly to Ned.

"I s'pose," he continued, "that a baptism will make us genuine Texans, an' it 'pears likely to me that we'll get that most lastin' of all baptisms, a baptism of fire. But me an' Betsy here stand ready for it."

He patted lovingly the stock of his long rifle as he spoke the word "Betsy." It was the same word "Betsy" that gave Ned his sudden knowledge.

"I'm thinking that you are Davy Crockett," he said.

The man's face was illumined with an inimitable smile.

"Correct," he said. "No more and no less. Andy Jackson kept me from going back to Washington, an' so me an' these twelve good friends of mine, Tennesseans like myself, have come here to help free Texas."

He reached out his hand and Ned grasped it. The boy felt a thrill. The name of Davy Crockett was a great one in the southwest, and here he was, face to face, hands gripped with the great borderer.

"This is Mr. Palmer, known all over Texas as the Panther, and Mr. Obed White, once of Maine, but now a Texan," said Ned, introducing his friends.

Crockett and the Panther shook hands, and looked each other squarely in the eye.

"Seems to me," said Crockett, "that you're a man."

"I was jest thinkin' the same of you," said the Panther.

"An' you," said Crockett to Obed White, "are a man, too. But they certainly do grow tall where you come from."

"I'm not as wide as a barn door, but I may be long enough to reach the bottom of a well," said Obed modestly. "Anyway, I thank you for the compliment. Praise from Sir Davy is sweet music in my ear, indeed. And since we Texans have to stand together, and since to stand together we must know about one another, may I ask you, Mr. Crockett, which way you are going?"

"We had an idea that we would go to San Antonio," said Crockett, "but I'm never above changin' my opinion. If you think it better to go somewhere else, an' can prove it, why me an' Betsy an' the whole crowd are ready to go there instead."

"What would you say?" asked the Panther, "if we told you that Santa Anna an' 7,000 men were on the Rio Grande ready to march on San Antonio?"

"If you said it, I'd say it was true. I'd also say that it was a thing the Texans had better consider. If I was usin' adjectives I'd call it alarm-in'."

"An' what would you say if I told you there wasn't a hundred Texan soldiers in San Antonio to meet them seven thousand Mexicans comin' under Santa Anna?"

"If you told me that I'd say it was true. I'd say also, if I was usin' adjectives, that it was powerful alarmin'. For Heaven's sake, Mr. Panther, the state of affairs ain't so bad as that, is it?"

"It certainly is," replied the Panther. "Ned Fulton here was all through their camp last night. He can talk Mexican an' Spanish like lightnin' an' he makes up wonderful—an' he saw their whole army. He saw old Santa Anna, too, an' fifty or a hundred generals, all covered with gold lace. If we don't get a lot of fightin' men together an' get 'em quick, Texas will be swept clean by that Mexican army same as if a field had been crossed by millions of locusts."

It was obvious that Crockett was impressed deeply by these blunt statements.

"What do you wish us to do?" he asked the Panther.

"You an' your friends come with us. We've got some good men at a cabin in the woods that we can reach tonight. We'll join with them, raise as many more as we can, spread the alarm everywhere, an' do everything possible for the defence of San Antonio."

"A good plan, Mr. Panther," said Crocket. "You lead the way to this cabin of yours, an' remember that we're servin' under you for the time bein'."

The Panther rode on without another word and the party, now raised from three to sixteen, followed. Crockett fell in by the side of Ned, and soon showed that he was not averse to talking.

"A good country," he said, nodding at the landscape, "but it ain't like Tennessee. It would take me a long time to git used to the lack of hills an' runnin' water an' trees which just cover the state of Tennessee."

"We have them here, too," replied Ned, "though I'll admit they're scattered. But it's a grand country to fight for."

"An' as I see it we'll have a grand lot of fightin' to do," said Davy Crockett.

They continued at good speed until twilight, when they rested their horses and ate of the food that they carried. The night promised to be cold but clear, and the crisp air quickened their blood.

"How much further is it?" asked Crockett of Ned.

"Fifteen or eighteen miles, but at the rate we're going we should be there in three hours. We've got a roof. It isn't a big one, and we don't know who built it, but it will shelter us all."

"I ain't complainin' of that," rejoined Davy Crockett. "I'm a lover of fresh air an' outdoors, but I don't object to a roof in cold weather. Always take your comfort, boy, when it's offered to you. It saves wear an' tear."

A friendship like that between him and Bowie was established already between Ned and Crockett. Ned's grave and serious manner, the result of the sufferings through which he had gone, invariably attracted the attention and liking of those far older than himself.

"I'll remember your advice, Mr. Crockett," he said.

A rest of a half hour for the horses and they started riding rapidly. After a while they struck the belt of forest and soon the cabin was not more than a mile away. But the Panther, who was still in the lead, pulled up his horse suddenly.

"Boys," he exclaimed, "did you hear that?"

Every man stopped his horse also and with involuntary motion bent forward a little to listen. Then the sound that the Panther had heard came again. It was the faint ping of a rifle shot, muffled by the distance. In a moment they heard another and then two more. The sounds came from the direction of their cabin.

"The boys are attacked," said the Panther calmly, "an' it's just as well that we've come fast. But I can't think who is after 'em. There was certainly no Mexicans in these parts yesterday, an' Urrea could not possibly have got ahead of us with a raidin' band. But at any rate we'll ride on an' soon see."

They proceeded with the utmost caution, and they heard the faint ping of the rifles a half dozen times as they advanced. The nostrils of the Panther began to distend, and streaks of red appeared on his eyeballs. He was smelling the battle afar, and his soul rejoiced. He had spent his whole life amid scenes of danger, and this was nature to him. Crockett rode up by his side, and he, too, listened eagerly. He no longer carried Betsy over his shoulder but held the long rifle across the pommel of his saddle, his hand upon hammer and trigger.

"What do you think it is, Panther?" he asked. Already he had fallen into the easy familiarity of the frontier.

"I can't make it out yet," replied the Panther, "but them shots shorely came from the cabin an' places about it. Our fellows are besieged, but I've got to guess at the besiegers, an' then I'm likely to guess wrong."

They were riding very slowly, and presently they heard a dozen shots, coming very clearly now.

"I think we'd better stop here," said the Panther, "an' do a little scoutin'. If you like it, Mr. Crockett, you an' me an' Ned, here, will dismount, slip forward an' see what's the trouble. Obed will take command of the others, an' wait in the bushes till we come back with the news, whatever it is."

"I'll go with you gladly," said Davy Crockett. "I'm not lookin' for trouble with a microscope, but if trouble gets right in my path I'm not dodgin' it. So I say once more, lead on, noble Mr. Panther, an' if Betsy here must talk she'll talk."

The Panther grinned in the dusk. He and Davy Crockett had instantly recognised congenial souls, each in the other.

"I can't promise you that thar'll be rippin' an' t'arin' an' roarin' an' chawin' all the time," he said, "but between you an' me, Davy Crockett, I've an' idee that we're not goin' to any sort of prayer meetin' this time of night."

"No, I'm thinkin' not," said Crockett, "but if there is a scene of turbulence before us lead on. I'm prepared for my share in it. The debate may be lively, but I've no doubt that I'll get my chance to speak. There are many ways to attract the attention of the Speaker. Pardon me, Mr. Panther, but I fall naturally into the phrases of legislative halls."

"I remember that you served two terms in Congress at Washington," said the Panther.

"An' I'd be there yet if it wasn't for Andy Jackson. I wanted my way in Tennessee politics an' he wanted his. He was so stubborn an' headstrong that here I am ready to become a statesman in this new Texas which is fightin' for its independence. An' what a change! From marble halls in Washington to a night in the brush on the frontier, an' with an unknown enemy before you."

They stopped talking now and, kneeling down in a thicket, began to creep forward. The cabin was not more than four or five hundred yards away, but a long silence had succeeded the latest shots, and after an advance of thirty or forty yards they lay still for a while. Then they heard two shots ahead of them, and saw little pink dots of flame from the exploding gunpowder.

"It cannot be Mexicans who are besieging the cabin," said Ned. "They would shout or make some kind of a noise. We have not heard a thing but the rifle shots."

"Your argyment is good," whispered the Panther. "Look! Did you see that figure passin' between us an' the cabin?"

"I saw it," said Davy Crockett, "an' although it was but a glimpse an' this is night it did not seem to me to be clad in full Christian raiment. I am quite sure it is not the kind of costume that would be admitted to the galleries of Congress."

"You're right, doubly right," said the Panther. "That was an Injun you saw, but whether a Comanche or a Lipan I couldn't tell. The boys are besieged not by Mexicans, but by Injuns. Hark to that!"

There was a flash from the cabin, a dusky figure in the woods leaped into the air, uttered a death cry, fell and lay still.

"An', as you see," continued the Panther, in his whisper, "the boys in the house are not asleep, dreamin' beautiful dreams. Looks to me as if they was watchin' mighty sharp for them fellers who have broke up their rest."

Crack! went a second shot from the house, but there was no answering cry, and they could not tell whether it hit anything. But they soon saw more dark figures flitting through the bushes, and their own position grew very precarious. If a band of the Indians stumbled upon them they might be annihilated before they gave their besieged comrades any help.

"I make the motion, Mr. Panther," said Crockett, "that you form a speedy plan of action for us, an' I trust that our young friend Ned here will second it."

"I second the motion," said Ned.

"It is carried unanimously. Now, Mr. Panther, we await your will."

"It's my will that we git back to the rest of the men as soon as we can. I reckon, Mr. Crockett, that them Tennesseans of yours wouldn't head in the other direction if a fight grew hot."

"I reckon that wild horses couldn't drag 'em away," said Crockett dryly.

"Then we'll go back an' j'in 'em."

"To hold a caucus, so to speak."

"I don't know what a cow-cuss is."

"It's Congressional for a conference. Don't mind these parliamentary expressions of mine, Mr. Panther. They give me pleasure an' they hurt nobody."

They reached the Tennesseans without interruption, and the Panther quickly laid his plan before them. They would advance within a quarter of a mile of the cabin, tie their horses in the thickest of the brush, leave four men to guard them, then the rest would go forward to help the besieged.

334

Crockett's eyes twinkled when the Panther announced the campaign in a few words.

"Very good; very good," he said. "A steering committee could not have done better. That also is parliamentary, but I think you understand it."

They heard detached shots again and then a long yell.

"They're Comanches," said the Panther. "I know their cry, an' I guess there's a lot of them."

Ned hoped that the shout did not mean the achieving of some triumph. They reached presently a dense growth of brush, and there the horses were tied. Four reluctant Tennesseans remained with them and the rest crept forward. They did not hear any shot after they left the horses until they were within three hundred yards of the house. Then an apparition caused all to stop simultaneously.

A streak of flame shot above the trees, curved and fell. It was followed by another and another. Ned was puzzled, but the Panther laughed low.

"This can't be fireworks on election night," said Davy Crockett. "It seems hardly the place for such a display."

"They're fireworks, all right," said the Panther, "but it's not election night. You're correct about that part of it. Look, there goes the fourth an' the fifth."

Two more streaks of flame curved and fell, and Ned and Crockett were still puzzled.

"Them's burnin' arrers," said the Panther. "It's an old trick of the Injuns. If they had time enough they'd be sure to set the cabin on fire, and then from ambush they'd shoot the people as they ran out. But what we're here for is to stop that little game of theirs. The flight of the arrers enables us to locate the spot from which they come an' there we'll find the Comanches."

They crept toward the point from which the lighted arrows were flying, and peering; from the thicket saw a score or more of Comanches gathered in the bushes and under the trees. One of the Tennesseans, seeking a better position, caused a loud rustling, and the alert Comanches, instantly taking alarm, turned their attention to the point from which the sound had come.

"Fire, boys! Fire at once!" cried the Panther.

A deadly volley was poured into the Comanche band. The Indians replied, but were soon compelled to give way. The Panther, raising his voice, shouted in tremendous tones:

"Rescue! Rescue! We're here, boys!"

The defenders of the cabin, hearing the volleys and the shouts of their friends, opened the door and rushed out of the cabin, rifle in hand. Caught between two forces, the Comanches gave up and rushed to the plain, where they had left their ponies. Jumping upon the backs of these, they fled like the wind.

The two victorious parties met and shook hands.

"We're mighty glad to see you, Panther," said Fields, grinning. "You don't look like an angel, but you act like one, an' I see you've brought a lot of new angels with you."

"Yes," replied the Panther, with some pride in his voice, "an' the first of the angels is Davy Crockett. Mr. Crockett, Mr. Fields."

The men crowded around to shake hands with the renowned Davy. Meanwhile a small party brought the four Tennesseans and the horses. Fortunately the Comanches had fled in the other direction. But it was not all joy in the Texan camp. Two silent figures covered with *serapes* were stretched on the floor in the cabin, and several others had wounds, although they had borne their part in the fighting.

"Tell us how it happened," said the Panther, after they had set sentinels in the forest.

"They attacked us about an hour after dark," replied Fields. "We knew that no Mexicans were near, but we never thought of Indians raiding this far to the eastward. Some of the men were outside looking after jerked meat when they suddenly opened fire from the brush. Two of the boys, Campbell and Hudson, were hurt so badly that they died after they were helped into the house by the others. The Comanches tried to rush in with our own men, but we drove them off and we could have held the cabin against 'em forever, if they hadn't begun to shoot the burning arrows. Then you came."

Campbell and Hudson were buried. Ned had been welcomed warmly by Allen, and the two boys compared notes. Will's face glowed when he heard of Ned's adventures within the Mexican lines.

"I could never have done it," he said. "I couldn't have kept steady enough when one crisis after another came along. I suppose this means, of course, that we must try to meet Santa Anna in some way. What do you think we can do, Ned?"

"I don't know, but just at present I'm going to sleep. The Panther, Davy Crockett and Obed will debate the plans."

Ned, who was becoming inured to war and danger, was soon asleep, but Will could not close his eyes. He had borne a gallant part in the defence, and the sounds of rifle shots and Indian yells still resounded in his excited ear. He remained awake long after he heard the heavy breathing of the men about him, but exhausted nerves gave way at last and he, too, slept.

The next morning their news was debated gravely by all. There was not one among them who did not understand its significance, but it was hard to agree upon a policy. Davy Crockett, who had just come, and who was practically a stranger to Texas, gave his opinions with hesitation.

"It's better for you, Mr. Panther, an' you, Mr. White, to make the motions," he said, "an' I an' my Tennesseans will endorse them. But it seems, boys, that if we came for a fight it is offered to us the moment we get here."

"Yes," said the twelve Tennesseans all together.

"I shall be compelled to leave you," said Roylston. "Pray, don't think it's because I'm afraid to fight the Mexicans. But, as I told you before, I can do far greater good for the Texan cause elsewhere. As I am now as well as ever, and I am able to take care of myself, I think I shall leave at once."

"I've known you only a few hours, Mr. Roylston," said Crockett, "but I've knocked around a hard world long enough to know a man when I see him. If you say you ought, you ought to go."

"That's so," said the Panther. "We've seen Mr. Roylston tried more than once, and nobody doubts his courage."

A good horse, saddled and bridled, and arms and ammunition, were given to Roylston. Then he bade them farewell. When he was about twenty yards away he beckoned to Ned. When the boy stood at his saddle bow he said very earnestly:

"If you fall again into the hands of Santa Anna, and are in danger of your life, use my name with him. It is perhaps a more potent weapon than you think. Do not forget."

"I will not," said Ned, "and I thank you very much, Mr. Roylston. But I hope that no such occasion will arise."

"So do I," said Roylston with emphasis. Then he rode away, a square, strong figure, and never looked back.

"What was he saying, Ned?" asked Will, when the boy returned.

"Merely promising help if we should need it, hereafter."

"He looks like a man who would give it."

After some further talk it was decided that Ned, Will, Obed and the Panther should ride south to watch the advance of Santa Anna, while Crockett, Fields and the remainder should go to San Antonio and raise such troops as they could.

"An' if you don't mind my sayin' it to you, Mr. Crockett," said the Panther, "keep tellin' 'em over an' over again that they have need to beware. Tell 'em that Santa Anna, with all the power of Mexico at his back, is comin'."

"Fear not, my good friend," said Davy Crockett. "I shall tell them every hour of the day. I shall never cease to bring the information before the full *quorum* of the House. Again I am parliamentary, but I think you understand, Mr. Panther."

"We all understan'," said the Panther, and then Crockett rode away at the head of the little troop which tacitly made him commander. Ned's eyes followed his figure as long as he was in sight. Little did he dream of what was to pass when they should meet again, scenes that one could never forget, though he lived a thousand years.

"A staunch man and true," said Obed. "He will be a great help to Texas."

Then they turned back to the cabin, the four of them, because they did not intend to go forth until night. They missed their comrades, but the cabin was a pleasant place, well stored now with meat of buffalo, deer and wild turkey. Floor and walls alike were covered with dressed skins.

"Why not fasten it up just as tightly as we can before we go away," said Allen. "The Comanches are not likely to come back, the war is swinging another way, and maybe we'll find it here handy for us again some day."

"You're talkin' sense, Will Allen," said the Panther. "It's been a shelter to us once, and it might be a shelter to us twice. The smell of the meat will, of course, draw wolves an' panthers, but we can fix it so they can't get in."

Taking sufficient provisions for themselves, they put the rest high up on the rafters. Then they secured the windows, and heaped logs before the door in such a manner that the smartest wolves and panthers in the world could not force an entrance. As they sat on their horses in the twilight preparatory to riding away, they regarded their work with great content.

"There it is, waiting for us when we come again," said Obed White. "It's a pleasant thing to have a castle for refuge when your enemies are making it too hot for you out in the open."

"So it is," said the Panther, "and a man finds that out more than once in his life."

Then they turned their horses and rode southward in the dusk. But before long they made an angle and turned almost due west. It was their intention to intersect the settlements that lay between the Rio Grande and San Antonio and give warning of the approach of Santa Anna.

They went on steadily over a rolling country, mostly bare, but with occasional clumps of trees.

CHAPTER 7

THE HERALD OF ATTACK

About midnight they rode into the thickest part of the woods that they could find, and slept there until day. Then they continued their course toward the west, and before night they saw afar small bands of horsemen.

"What do you say they are?" asked the Panther of Ned when they beheld the first group. "Seems to me they are Mexican."

Ned looked long before returning an answer. Then he replied with confidence:

"Yes, they are Mexicans. The two men in the rear have lances, and no Texan ever carried such a weapon."

"Then," said Obed White, "it behooves us to have a care. We're scouts now and we're not looking for a battle. He who dodges the fight and runs away may live to scout another day."

The Mexican horsemen were on their right, and the four continued their steady course to the west. They were reassured by the fact that the Mexicans were likely to take them in the distance for other Mexicans. It became evident now that Santa Anna was taking every precaution. He was sending forward scouts and skirmishers in force, and the task of the four was likely to become one of great danger.

Toward night an uncommonly raw and cold wind began to blow. That winter was one of great severity in Northern Mexico and Southern Texas, noted also for its frequent northers. Although the time for the Texan spring was near at hand, there was little sign of it. Not knowing what else to do they sought the shelter of timber again and remained there a while. By and by they saw for the second time a red glow in the south, and they knew that it came from the camp fires of Santa Anna. But it was now many miles north of the Rio Grande.

Santa Anna was advancing.

"He's pressin' forward fast," said the Panther, "an' his skirmishers are scourin' the plain ahead of him. We've got to keep a sharp lookout, because we may run into 'em at any time. I think we'd better agree that if by any luck we get separated an' can't reunite, every fellow should ride hard for San Antonio with the news."

The plan seemed good to all, and, after a long wait, they rode to another clump of trees four or five hundred yards further south. Here they saw the red glow more plainly. It could not be more than two miles away, and they believed that to approach any nearer was to imperil their task. Before the first light appeared the next day they would turn back on San Antonio as the heralds of Santa Anna's advance.

The four sat on their horses among the trees, darker shadows in the shadow. Beyond the little grove they saw the plain rolling away on every side bare to the horizon, except in the south, where the red glow always threatened. Ned rode to the western edge of the grove in order to get a better view. He searched the plain carefully with his keen vision, but he could find no sign of life there in the west.

He turned Old Jack in order to rejoin his comrades, when he suddenly heard a low sound from the east. He listened a moment, and then, hearing it distinctly, he knew it. It was the thud of hoofs, and the horsemen were coming straight toward the grove, which was two or three hundred yards in width.

Owing to the darkness and the foliage Ned could not see his comrades, but he started toward them at once. Then came a sudden cry, the rapid beat of hoofs, the crack of shots, and a Mexican body of cavalry dashed into the wood directly between the boy and his comrades. He heard once the tremendous shout of the Panther and the wild Mexican yells. Two horsemen fired at him and a third rode at him with extended lance.

It was Old Jack that saved Ned's life. The boy was so startled that his brain was in a paralysis for a moment. But the horse shied suddenly away from the head of the lance, which was flashing in the moonlight. Ned retained both his seat and his rifle. He fired at the nearest of the Mexicans, who fell from his saddle, and then, seeing that but one alternative was left him he gave Old Jack the rein and galloped from the grove into the west.

Amid all the rush and terrific excitement of the moment, Ned thought of his comrades. It was not possible for him to join them now, but they were three together and they might escape. The Panther was

340

a wonderful borderer, and Obed White was not far behind him. He turned his attention to his own escape. Two more shots were fired at him, but in both cases the bullets went wide. Then he heard only the thud of hoofs, but the pursuing horsemen were very near.

Something whizzed through the air and instinctively he bent forward almost flat on the neck of Old Jack. A coiling shape struck him on the head, slipped along his back, then along the quarters of his horse and fell to the ground. He felt as if a deadly snake had struck at him, and then had drawn its cold body across him. But he knew that it was a lasso. The Mexicans would wish to take him alive, as they might secure valuable information from him. Now he heard them shouting to one another, every one boasting that his would be the successful throw. As Ned's rifle was empty, and he could not reload it at such speed, they seemed to fear nothing for themselves.

He looked back. They numbered seven or eight, and they were certainly very near. They had spread out a little and whenever Old Jack veered a yard or two from the pursuers some one gained. He saw a coil of rope fly through the air and he bent forward again. It struck Old Jack on the saddle and fell to the ground. Ned wondered why they did not fire now, but he remembered that their rifles or muskets, too, might be empty, and suddenly he felt a strange exultation. He was still lying forward on his horse's neck, and now he began to talk to him.

"On! On! Old Jack," he said, "show 'em the cleanest heels that were ever seen in Texas! On! On! my beauty of a horse, my jewel of a horse! Would you let miserable Mexican ponies overtake you? You who were never beaten! Ah, now we gain! But faster! faster!"

It seemed that Old Jack understood. He stretched out his long neck and became a streak in the darkness. A third Mexican threw his lasso, but the noose only touched his flying tail. A fourth threw, and the noose did not reach him at all.

They were far out on the plain now, where the moonlight revealed everything, and the horse's sure instinct would guide. Ned felt Old Jack beneath him, running strong and true without a jar like the most perfect piece of machinery. He stole a glance over his shoulder. All the Mexicans were there, too far away now for a throw of the lasso, but several of them were trying to reload their weapons. Ned knew that if they succeeded he would be in great danger. No matter how badly they shot a chance bullet might hit him or his horse. And he could afford for neither himself nor Old Jack to be wounded.

Once more the boy leaned far over on his horse's neck and cried in his ear:

"On, Old Jack, on! Look, we gain now, but we must gain more. Show to them what a horse you are!"

And again the great horse responded. Fast as he was going it seemed to Ned that he now lengthened his stride. His long head was thrust out almost straight, and his great body fairly skimmed the earth. But the Mexicans hung on with grim tenacity. Their ponies were tough and enduring, and, spread out like the arc of a bow, they continually profited by some divergence that Old Jack made from the straight line. Aware of this danger Ned himself, nevertheless, was unable to tell whether the horse was going in a direct course, and he let him have his head.

"Crack!" went a musket, and a bullet sang past Ned's face. It grazed Old Jack's ear, drawing blood. The horse uttered an angry snort and fairly leaped forward. Ned looked back again. Another man had succeeded in loading his musket and was about to fire. Then the boy remembered the pistol at his belt. Snatching it out he fired at the fellow with the loaded musket.

The Mexican reeled forward on his horse's neck and his weapon dropped to the ground. Whether the man himself fell also Ned never knew, because he quickly thrust the pistol back in his belt and once more was looking straight ahead. Now confidence swelled again in his heart. He had escaped all their bullets so far, and he was still gaining. He would escape all the others and he would continue to gain.

He saw just ahead of him one of the clumps of trees that dotted the plain, but, although it might give momentary protection from the bullets he was afraid to gallop into it, lest he be swept from his horse's back by the boughs or bushes. But his direct course would run close to the left side of it, and once more he sought to urge Old Jack to greater speed.

The horse was still running without a jar. Ned could not feel a single rough movement in the perfect machinery beneath him. Unless wounded Old Jack would not fail him. He stole another of those fleeting glances backward.

Several of the Mexicans, their ponies spent, were dropping out of the race, but enough were left to make the odds far too great. Ned now skimmed along the edge of the grove, and when he passed it he turned his horse a little, so the trees were between him and his nearest pursuers. Then he urged Old Jack to his last ounce of speed. The

342

plain raced behind him, and fortunate clouds, too, now came, veiling the moon and turning the dusk into deeper darkness. Ned heard one disappointed cry behind him, and then no sound but the flying beat of his own horse's hoofs.

When he pulled rein and brought Old Jack to a walk he could see or hear nothing of the Mexicans. The great horse was a lather of foam, his sides heaving and panting, and Ned sprang to the ground. He reloaded his rifle and pistol and then walked toward the west, leading Old Jack by the bridle. He reckoned that the Mexicans would go toward the north, thinking that he would naturally ride for San Antonio, and hence he chose the opposite direction.

He walked a long time and presently he felt the horse rubbing his nose gently against his arm. Ned stroked the soft muzzle.

"You've saved my life. Old Jack," he said, "and not for the first time. You responded to every call."

The horse whinnied ever so softly, and Ned felt that he was not alone. Now he threw the bridle reins back over the horse's head, and then the two walked on, side by side, man and beast.

They stopped at times, and it may be that the horse as well as the boy then looked and listened for a foe. But the Mexicans had melted away completely in the night. It was likely now that they were going in the opposite direction, and assured that he was safe from them for the time Ned collapsed, both physically and mentally. Such tremendous exertions and such terrible excitement were bound to bring reaction. He began to tremble violently, and he became so weak that he could scarcely stand. The horse seemed to be affected in much the same way and walked slowly and painfully.

Ned saw another little grove, and he and the horse walked straight toward it. It was fairly dense, and when he was in the centre of it he wrapped his rifle and himself in his serape and lay down. The horse sank on his side near him. He did not care for anything now except to secure rest. Mexicans or Comanches or Lipans might be on the plain only a few hundred yards away. It did not matter to him. He responded to no emotion save the desire for rest, and in five minutes he was in a deep sleep.

Ned slept until long after daylight. He was so much exhausted that he scarcely moved during all that time. Nor did the horse. Old Jack had run his good race and won the victory, and he, too, cared for nothing but to rest.

Before morning some Lipan buffalo hunters passed, but they took no notice of the grove and soon disappeared in the west. After the dawn a detachment of Mexican lancers riding to the east to join the force of Santa Anna also passed the clump of trees, but the horse and man lay in the densest part of it, and no pair of Mexican eyes was keen enough to see them there. They were answering the call of Santa Anna, and they rode on at a trot, the grove soon sinking out of sight behind them.

Ned was awakened at last by the sun shining in his face. He stirred, recalled in a vague sort of way where he was and why he was there, and then rose slowly to his feet. His joints were stiff like those of an old man, and he rubbed them to acquire ease. A great bay horse, saddle on his back, was searching here and there for the young stems of grass. Ned rubbed his eyes. It seemed to him that he knew that horse. And a fine big horse he was, too, worth knowing and owning. Yes, it was Old Jack, the horse that had carried him to safety.

His little store of provisions was still tied to the saddle and he ate hungrily. At the end of the grove was a small pool formed by the winter's rains, and though the water was far from clear he drank his fill. He flexed and tensed his muscles again until all the stiffness and soreness were gone. Then he made ready for his departure.

He could direct his course by the sun, and he intended to go straight to San Antonio. He only hoped that he might get there before the arrival of Santa Anna and his army. He could not spare the time to seek his comrades, and he felt much apprehension for them, but he yet had the utmost confidence in the skill of the Panther and Obed White.

It was about two hours before noon when Ned set out across the plain. Usually in this region antelope were to be seen on the horizon, but they were all gone now. The boy considered it a sure sign that Mexican detachments had passed that way. It was altogether likely, too, so he calculated, that the Mexican Army was now nearer than he to San Antonio. His flight had taken him to the west while Santa Anna was moving straight toward the Texan outworks. But he believed that by steady riding he could reach San Antonio within twenty-four hours.

The afternoon passed without event. Ned saw neither human beings nor game on the vast prairie. He had hoped that by some chance he might meet with his comrades, but there was no sign of them, and he fell back on his belief that their skill and great courage had saved them. Seeking to dismiss them from his thoughts for the time in order that he might concentrate all his energies on San Antonio, he rode on. The horse had recovered completely from his great efforts of the preceding night, and once more that magnificent piece of machinery worked without a jar. Old Jack moved over the prairie with long, easy strides. It seemed to Ned that he could never grow weary. He patted the sinewy and powerful neck.

"Gallant comrade," he said, "you have done your duty and more. You, at least, will never fail."

Twilight came down, but Ned kept on. By and by he saw in the east, and for the third time, that fatal red glow extending far along the dusky horizon. All that he had feared of Santa Anna was true. The dictator was marching fast, whipping his army forward with the fierce energy that was a part of his nature. It was likely, too, that squadrons of his cavalry were much further on. A daring leader like Urrea would certainly be miles ahead of the main army, and it was more than probable that bands of Mexican horsemen were now directly between him and San Antonio.

Ned knew that he would need all his strength and courage to finish his task. So he gave Old Jack a little rest, although he did not seem to need it, and drew once more upon his rations.

When he remounted he was conscious that the air had grown much colder. A chill wind began to cut him across the cheek. Snow, rain and wind have played a great part in the fate of armies, and they had much to do with the struggle between Texas and Mexico in that fateful February. Ned's experience told him that another norther was about to begin, and he was glad of it. One horseman could make much greater progress through it than an army.

The wind rose fast and then came hail and snow on its edge. The red glow in the east disappeared. But Ned knew that it was still there. The norther had merely drawn an icy veil between. He shivered, and the horse under him shivered, too. Once more he wrapped around his body the grateful folds of the *serape* and he drew on a pair of buckskin gloves, a part of his winter equipment.

Then he rode on straight toward San Antonio as nearly as he could calculate. The norther increased in ferocity. It brought rain, hail and snow, and the night darkened greatly. Ned began to fear that he would get lost. It was almost impossible to keep the true direction in such a driving storm. He had no moon and stars to guide him, and he was compelled to rely wholly upon instinct. Sometimes he was in woods, sometimes upon the plain, and once or twice he crossed creeks, the waters of which were swollen and muddy.

The norther was not such a blessing after all. He might be going directly away from San Antonio, while Santa Anna, with innumerable guides, would easily reach there the next day. He longed for those faithful comrades of his. The four of them together could surely find a way out of this.

He prayed now that the norther would cease, but his prayer was of no avail. It whistled and moaned about him, and snow and hail were continually driven in his face. Fortunately the brim of the *sombrero* protected his eyes. He floundered on until midnight. The norther was blowing as fiercely as ever, and he and Old Jack were brought up by a thicket too dense for them to penetrate.

Ned understood now that he was lost. Instinct had failed absolutely. Brave and resourceful as he was he uttered a groan of despair. It was torture to be so near the end of his task and then to fail. But the despair lasted only a moment. The courage of a nature containing genuine greatness brought back hope.

He dismounted and led his horse around the thicket. Then they came to a part of the woods which seemed thinner, and not knowing anything else to do he went straight ahead. But he stopped abruptly when his feet sank in soft mud. He saw directly before him a stream yellow, swollen and flowing faster than usual.

Ned knew that it was the San Antonio River, and now he had a clue. By following its banks he would reach the town. The way might be long, but it must inevitably lead him to San Antonio, and he would take it.

He remounted and rode forward as fast as he could. The river curved and twisted, but he was far more cheerful now. The San Antonio was like a great coiling rope, but if he followed it long enough he would certainly come to the end that he wished. The norther continued to blow. He and his horse were a huge moving shape of white. Now and then the snow, coating too thickly upon his *serape*, fell in lumps to the ground, but it was soon coated anew and as thick as ever. But whatever happened he never let the San Antonio get out of his sight.

He was compelled to stop at last under a thick cluster of oaks, where he was somewhat sheltered from the wind and snow. Here he dismounted again, stamped his feet vigorously for warmth and also brushed the snow from his faithful horse. Old Jack, as usual, rubbed his nose against the boy's arm.

HE FLOUNDERED ON UNTIL MIDNIGHT.

The horse was a source of great comfort and strength to Ned. He always believed that he would have collapsed without him. As nearly as he could guess the time it was about halfway between midnight and morning, and in order to preserve his strength he forced himself to eat a little more.

A half hour's rest, and remounting he resumed his slow progress by the river. The rest had been good for both his horse and himself, and the blood felt warmer in his veins. He moved for some time among trees and thickets that lined the banks, and after a while he recognised familiar ground. He had been in some of these places in the course of the siege of San Antonio, and the town could not be far away.

It was probably two hours before daylight when he heard a sound which was not that of the norther, a sound which he knew instantly. It was the dull clank of bronze against bronze. It could be made only by one cannon striking against another. Then Santa Anna, or one of his generals, despite the storm and the night, was advancing with his army, or a part of it. Ned shivered, and now not from the cold.

The Texans did not understand the fiery energy of this man. They would learn of it too late, unless he told them, and it might be too late even then. He pressed on with as much increase of speed as the nature of the ground would allow. In another hour the snow and hail ceased, but the wind still blew fiercely, and it remained very cold.

The dawn began to show dimly through drifting clouds. Ned did not recall until long afterward that it was the birthday of the great Washington. By a singular coincidence Santa Anna appeared before Taylor with a vastly superior force on the same birthday eleven years later.

It was a hidden sun, and the day was bleak with clouds and driving winds. Nevertheless the snow that had fallen began to disappear. Ned and Old Jack still made their way forward, somewhat slowly now, as they were stiff and sore from the long night's fight with darkness and cold. On his right, only a few feet away, was the swollen current of the San Antonio. The stream looked deep to Ned, and it bore fragments of timber upon its muddy bosom. It seemed to him that the waters rippled angrily against the bank. His excited imagination—and full cause there was—gave a sinister meaning to everything.

A heavy fog began to rise from the river and wet earth. He could not see far in front of him, but he believed that the town was now only a mile or two away. Soon a low, heavy sound, a measured stroke, came out of the fog. It was the tolling of the church bell in San Antonio, and for some reason its impact upon Ned's ear was like the stroke of death. A strange chilly sensation ran down his spine.

He rode to the very edge of the stream and began to examine it for a possible ford. San Antonio was on the other side, and he must cross. But everywhere the dark, swollen waters threatened, and he continued his course along the bank.

A thick growth of bushes and a high portion of the bank caused him presently to turn away from the river until he could make a curve about the obstacles. The tolling of the bell had now ceased, and the fog was lifting a little. Out of it came only the low, angry murmur of the river's current.

As Ned turned the curve the wind grew much stronger. The bank of fog was split asunder and then floated swiftly away in patches and streamers. On his left beyond the river Ned saw the roofs of the town, now glistening in the clear morning air, and on his right, only four or five hundred yards away, he saw a numerous troop of Mexican cavalry. In the figure at the head of the horsemen he was sure that he recognised Urrea.

Ned's first emotion was a terrible sinking of the heart. After all that he had done, after all his great journeys, hardships and dangers, he was to fail with the towers and roofs of San Antonio in sight. It was the triumphant cry of the Mexicans that startled him into life again. They had seen the lone horseman by the river and they galloped at once toward him. Ned had made no mistake. It was Urrea, pressing forward ahead of the army, who led the troop, and it may be that he recognised the boy also.

With the cry of the Mexicans ringing in his ears, the boy shouted to Old Jack. The good horse, as always, made instant response, and began to race along the side of the river. But even his mighty frame had been weakened by so much strain. Ned noticed at once that the machinery jarred. The great horse was labouring hard and the Mexican cavalry, comparatively fresh, was coming on fast. It was evident that he would soon be overtaken, and so sure were the Mexicans of it that they did not fire.

There were deep reserves of courage and fortitude in this boy, deeper than even he himself suspected. When he saw that he could not escape by speed, the way out flashed upon him. To think was to do. He turned his horse without hesitation and urged him forward with a mighty cry.

Never had Old Jack made a more magnificent response. Ned felt the mighty mass of bone and muscle gather in a bunch beneath him. Then, ready to expand again with violent energy, it was released as if by the touch of a spring. The horse sprang from the high bank far out into the deep river.

Ned felt his *serape* fly from him and his rifle dropped from his hand. Then the yellow waters closed over both him and Old Jack. They came up again, Ned still on the horse's back, but with an icy chill through all his veins. He could not see for a moment or two, as the water was in his eyes, but he heard dimly the shouts of the Mexicans and several shots. Two or three bullets splashed the water around him and another struck his *sombrero*, which was floating away on the surface of the stream.

The horse, turning somewhat, swam powerfully in a diagonal course across the stream. Ned, dazed for the moment by the shock of the plunge from a height into the water, clung tightly to his back. He sat erect at first, and then remembering that he must evade the bullets leaned forward with the horse's neck between him and the Mexicans.

More shots were fired, but again he was untouched, and then the horse was feeling with his forefeet in the muddy bank for a hold. The next instant, with a powerful effort, he pulled himself upon the shore. The violent shock nearly threw Ned from his back, but the boy seized his mane and hung on.

The Mexicans shouted and fired anew, but Ned, now sitting erect, raced for San Antonio, only a mile away.

CHAPTER 8

IN THE ALAMO

Most of the people in San Antonio were asleep when the dripping figure of a half unconscious boy on a great horse galloped toward them in that momentous dawn. He was without hat or *serape*. He was bareheaded and his rifle was gone. He was shouting "Up! Up! Santa Anna and the Mexican Army are at hand!" But his voice was so choked and hoarse that he could not be heard a hundred feet away.

Davy Crockett, James Bowie and a third man were standing in the main *plaza*. The third man, like the other two, was of commanding proportions. He was a full six feet in height, very erect and muscular, and with full face and red hair. He was younger than the others, not more than twenty-eight, but he was Colonel William Barrett Travis, a North Carolina lawyer, who was now in command of the few Texans in San Antonio.

The three men were talking very anxiously. Crockett had brought word that the army of Santa Anna was on the Texan side of the Rio Grande, but it had seemed impossible to rouse the Texans to a full sense of the impending danger. Many remained at their homes following their usual vocations. Mr. Austin was away in the states trying to raise money. Dissensions were numerous in the councils of the new government, and the leaders could agree upon nothing.

Travis, Bowie and Crockett were aware of the great danger, but even they did not believe it was so near. Nevertheless they were full of anxiety. Crockett, just come to Texas, took no command and sought to keep in the background, but he was too famous and experienced a man not to be taken at once by Travis and Bowie into their councils. They were discussing now the possibility of getting help.

"We might send messengers to the towns further east," said Travis, "and at least get a few men here in time."

"We need a good many," said Bowie. "According to Mr. Crockett the Mexican army is large, and the population here is unfriendly."

"That is so," said Travis, "and we have women and children of our own to protect."

It was when he spoke the last words that they heard the clatter of hoofs and saw Ned dashing down the narrow street toward the main *plaza.* They heard him trying to shout, but his voice was now so hoarse that he could not be understood.

But Ned, though growing weaker fast, knew two of the men. He could never forget the fair-haired Bowie nor the swarthy Crockett, and he galloped straight toward them. Then he pulled up his horse and half fell, half leaped to the ground. Holding by Old Jack's mane he pulled himself into an erect position. He was a singular sight The water still fell from his wet hair and dripped from his clothing. His face was plastered with mud.

"Santa Anna's army, five thousand strong, is not two miles away!" he said. "I tell you because I have seen it!"

"Good God!" cried Bowie. "It's the boy, Ned Fulton. I know him well. What he says must be truth."

"It is every word truth!" croaked Ned. "I was pursued by their vanguard! My horse swam the river with me! Up! Up! for Texas!"

Then he fainted dead away. Bowie seized him in his powerful arms and carried him into one of the houses occupied by the Texans, where men stripped him of his wet clothing and gave him restoratives. But

Bowie himself hurried out into the main *plaza*. He had the most unlimited confidence in Ned's word and so had Crockett. They and Travis at once began to arrange the little garrison for defence.

Many of the Texans even yet would not believe. So great had been their confidence that they had sent out no scouting parties. Only a day or two before they had been enjoying themselves at a great dance. The boy who had come with the news that Santa Anna was at hand must be distraught. Certainly he had looked like a maniac.

A loud cry suddenly came from the roof of the church of San Fernando. Two sentinels posted there had seen the edge of a great army appear upon the plain and then spread rapidly over it. Santa Anna's army had come. The mad boy was right. Two horsemen sent out to reconnoitre had to race back for their lives. The flooded stream was now subsiding and only the depth of the water in the night had kept the Mexicans from taking cannon across and attacking.

Ned's faint was short. He remembered putting on clothing, securing a rifle and ammunition, and then he ran out into the square. From many windows he saw the triumphant faces of Mexicans looking out, but he paid no attention to them. He thought alone of the Texans, who were now displaying the greatest energy. In the face of the imminent and deadly peril Travis, Crockett, Bowie and the others were cool and were acting with rapidity. The order was swiftly given to cross to the Alamo, the old mission built like a fortress, and the Texans were gathering in a body. Ned saw a young lieutenant named Dickinson catch up his wife and child on a horse, and join the group of men. All the Texans had their long rifles, and there were also cannon.

As Ned took his place with the others a kindly hand fell upon his shoulder and a voice spoke in his ear.

"I was going to send for you, Ned," said Bowie, "but you've come. Perhaps it would have been better for you, though, if you had been left in San Antonio."

"Oh, no, Mr. Bowie!" cried Ned. "Don't say that. We can beat off any number of Mexicans!"

Bowie said nothing more. Much of Ned's courage and spirit returned, but he saw how pitifully small their numbers were. The little band that defiled across the plain toward the Alamo numbered less than one hundred and fifty men, and many of them were without experience.

They were not far upon the plain when Ned saw a great figure coming toward him. It was Old Jack, who had been forgotten in the haste and excitement. The saddle was still on his back and his bridle trailed on the ground. Ned met him and patted his faithful head. Already he had taken his resolution. There would be no place for Old Jack in the Alamo, but this good friend of his should not fall into the hands of the Mexicans.

He slipped off saddle and bridle, struck him smartly on the shoulder and exclaimed:

"Goodbye, Old Jack, goodbye! Keep away from our enemies and wait for me."

The horse looked a moment at his master, and, to Ned's excited eyes, it seemed for a moment that he wished to speak. Old Jack had never before been dismissed in this manner. Ned struck him again and yet more sharply.

"Go, old friend!" he cried.

The good horse trotted away across the plain. Once he looked back as if in reproach, but as Ned did not call him he kept on and disappeared over a swell. It was to Ned like the passing of a friend, but he knew that Old Jack would not allow the Mexicans to take him. He would fight with both teeth and hoofs against any such ignominious capture.

Then Ned turned his attention to the retreat. It was a little band that went toward the Alamo, and there were three women and three children in it, but since they knew definitely that Santa Anna and his great army had come there was not a Texan who shrank from his duty. They had been lax in their watch and careless of the future, faults frequent in irregular troops, but in the presence of overwhelming danger they showed not the least fear of death.

They reached the Alamo side of the river. Before them they saw the hewn stone walls of the mission rising up in the form of a cross and facing the river and the town. It certainly seemed welcome to a little band of desperate men who were going to fight against overwhelming odds. Ned also saw not far away the Mexican cavalry advancing in masses. The foremost groups were lancers, and the sun glittered on the blades of their long weapons.

Ned believed that Urrea was somewhere in one of these leading groups. Urrea he knew was full of skill and enterprise, but his heart filled with bitterness against him. He had tasted the Texan salt, he had broken bread with those faithful friends of his, the Panther and Obed White, and now he was at Santa Anna's right hand, seeking to destroy the Texans utterly.

"Looks as if I'd have a lot of use for Old Betsy," said a whimsical voice beside him. "Somebody said when I started away from Tennessee that I'd have nothing to do with it, might as well leave my rifle at home. But I 'low that Old Betsy is the most useful friend I could have just now."

It was, of course, Davy Crockett who spoke. He was as cool as a cake of ice. Old Betsy rested in the hollow of his arm, the long barrel projecting several feet. His raccoon skin cap was on the back of his head. His whole manner was that of one who was in the first stage of a most interesting event. But as Ned was looking at him a light suddenly leaped in the calm eye.

"Look there! look there!" said Davy Crockett, pointing a long finger. "We'll need food in that Alamo place, an' behold it on the hoof!"

About forty cattle had been grazing on the plain. They had suddenly gathered in a bunch, startled by the appearance of so many people, and of galloping horsemen.

"We'll take 'em with us! We'll need 'em! Say we can do it, colonel!" shouted Crockett to Travis.

Travis nodded.

"Come on, Ned," cried Crockett, "an' come on the rest of you fleet-footed fellows! Every mother's son of you has driv' the cows home before in his time, an' now you kin do it again!"

A dozen swift Texans ran forward with shouts, Ned and Davy Crockett at their head. Crockett was right. This was work that every one of them knew how to do. In a flash they were driving the whole frightened herd in a run toward the gate that led into the great *plaza* of the Alamo. The swift motion, the sense of success in a sudden manoeuvre, thrilled Ned. He shouted at the cattle as he would have done when he was a small boy.

They were near the gate when he heard an ominous sound by his side. It was the cocking of Davy Crockett's rifle, and when he looked around he saw that Old Betsy was levelled, and that the sure eye of the Tennessean was looking down the sights.

Some of the Mexican skirmishers seeing the capture of the herd by the daring Texans were galloping forward to check it. Crockett's finger pressed the trigger. Old Betsy flashed and the foremost rider fell to the ground.

"I told that Mexican to come down off his horse, and he came down," chuckled Crockett.

The Mexicans drew back, because other Texan rifles, weapons that they had learned to dread, were raised. A second body of horsemen charged from a different angle, and Ned distinctly saw Urrea at their head. He fired, but the bullet missed the partisan leader and brought down another man behind him.

"There are good pickings here," said Davy Crockett, "but they'll soon be too many for us. Come on, Ned, boy! Our place is behind them walls!"

"Yes," repeated Bowie, who was near. "It's the Alamo or nothing. No matter how fast we fired our rifles we'd soon be trod under foot by the Mexicans."

They passed in, Bowie, Crockett and Ned forming the rear guard. The great gates of the Alamo were closed behind them and barred. For the moment they were safe, because these doors were made of very heavy oak, and it would require immense force to batter them in. It was evident that the Mexican horsemen on the plain did not intend to make any such attempt, as they drew off hastily, knowing that the deadly Texan rifles would man the walls at once.

"Well, here we are, Ned," said the cheerful voice of Davy Crockett, "an' if we want to win glory in fightin' it seems that we've got the biggest chance that was ever offered to anybody. I guess when old Santa Anna comes up he'll say: 'By nations right wheel; forward march the world.' Still these walls will help a little to make up the difference between fifty to one."

As he spoke he tapped the outer wall.

"No Mexican on earth," he said, "has got a tough enough head to butt through that. At least I think so. Now what do you think, Ned?"

His tone was so whimsical that Ned was compelled to laugh despite their terrible situation.

"It's a pity, though," continued Crockett, "that we've got such a big place here to defend. Sometimes you're the stronger the less ground you spread over."

Ned glanced around. He had paid the Alamo one hasty visit just after the capture of San Antonio by the Texans, but he took only a vague look then. Now it was to make upon his brain a photograph which nothing could remove as long as he lived.

He saw in a few minutes all the details of the Alamo. He knew already its history. This mission of deathless fame was even then more than a century old. Its name, the Alamo, signified "the Cottonwood tree," but that has long since been lost in another of imperishable grandeur.

The buildings of the mission were numerous, the whole arranged, according to custom, in the form of a cross. The church, which was now without a roof, faced town and river, but it contained arched rooms, and the sacristy had a solid roof of masonry. The windows, cut for the needs of an earlier time, were high and narrow, in order that attacking Indians might not pour in flights of arrows upon those who should be worshipping there. Over the heavy oaken doors were images and carvings in stone worn by time.

To the left of the church, beside the wing of the cross, was the *plaza* of the convent, about thirty yards square, with its separate walls more than fifteen feet high and nearly four feet thick.

Ned noted all these things rapidly and ineffaceably, as he and Crockett took a swift but complete survey of their fortress. He saw that the convent and hospital, each two stories in height, were made of *adobe* bricks, and he also noticed a sally-port, protected by a little redoubt, at the south-eastern corner of the yard.

They saw beyond the convent yard the great *plaza* into which they had driven the cattle, a parallelogram covering nearly three acres, enclosed by a wall eight feet in height and three feet thick. Prisons, barracks and other buildings were scattered about. Beyond the walls was a small group of wretched jacals or huts in which some Mexicans lived. Water from the San Antonio flowed in ditches through the mission.

It was almost a town that they were called upon to defend, and Ned and Crockett, after their hasty look, came back to the church, the strongest of all the buildings, with walls of hewn stone five feet thick and nearly twenty-five feet high. They opened the heavy oaken doors, entered the building and looked up through the open roof at the sky. Then Crockett's eyes came back to the arched rooms and the covered sacristy.

"This is the real fort," he said, "an' we'll put our gunpowder in that sacristy. It looks like sacrilege to use a church for such a purpose, but, Ned, times are goin' to be very hot here, the hottest we ever saw, an' we must protect our powder."

He carried his suggestion to Travis, who adopted it at once, and the powder was quickly taken into the rooms. They also had fourteen pieces of cannon which they mounted on the walls of the church, at the stockade at the entrance to the *plaza* and at the redoubt. But the Texans, frontiersmen and not regular soldiers, did not place much reliance upon the cannon. Their favourite weapon was the rifle, with which they rarely missed even at long range.

It took the Texans but little time to arrange the defence, and then came a pause. Ned did not have any particular duty assigned to him, and went back to the church, which now bore so little resemblance to a house of worship. He gazed curiously at the battered carvings and images over the door. They looked almost grotesque to him now, and some of them threatened.

He went inside the church and looked around once more. It was old, very old. The grayness of age showed everywhere, and the silence of the defenders on the walls deepened its ancient aspect. But the norther had ceased to blow, and the sun came down, bright and un-clouded, through the open roof.

Ned climbed upon the wall. Bowie, who was behind one of the cannon, beckoned to him. Ned joined him and leaned upon the gun as Bowie pointed toward San Antonio.

"See the Mexican masses," he said. "Ned, you were a most timely herald. If it had not been for you our surprise would have been total. Look how they defile upon the plain."

The army of Santa Anna was entering San Antonio and it was spread out far and wide. The sun glittered on lances and rifles, and brightened the bronze barrels of cannon. The triumphant notes of a bugle came across the intervening space, and when the bugle ceased a Mexican band began to play.

It was fine music. The Mexicans had the Latin ear, the gift for melody, and the air they played was martial and inspiring. One could march readily to its beat. Bowie frowned.

"They think it nothing more than a parade," he said. "But when Santa Anna has taken us he will need a new census of his army."

He looked around at the strong stone walls, and then at the reso-lute faces of the men near him. But the garrison was small, pitifully small.

Ned left the walls and ate a little food that was cooked over a fire lighted in the convent *plaza*. Then he wandered about the place look-ing at the buildings and enclosures. The Alamo was so extensive that he knew Travis would be compelled to concentrate his defence about the church, but he wanted to examine all these places anyhow.

He wandered into one building that looked like a storehouse. The interior was dry and dusty. Cobwebs hung from the walls, and it was empty save for many old barrels that stood in the corner. Ned looked casually into the barrels and then he uttered a shout of joy. A score of so of them were full of shelled Indian corn in perfect condition, a hundred bushels at least. This was truly treasure trove, more valuable than if the barrels had been filled with coined gold.

He ran out of the house and the first man he met was Davy Crockett.

"Now what has disturbed you?" asked Crockett, in his drawling tone. "Haven't you seen Mexicans enough for one day? This ain't the time to see double."

"I wish I could see double in this case, Mr. Crockett," replied Ned, "because then the twenty barrels of corn that I've found would be forty."

He took Crockett triumphantly into the building and showed him the treasure, which was soon transferred to one of the arched rooms beside the entrance of the church. It was in truth one of the luckiest finds ever made. The cattle in the *plaza* would furnish meat for a long time, but they would need bread also. Again Ned felt that pleasant glow of triumph. It seemed that fortune was aiding them.

He went outside and stood by the ditch which led a shallow stream of water along the eastern side of the church. It was greenish in tint, but it was water, water which would keep the life in their bodies while they fought off the hosts of Santa Anna.

The sun was now past the zenith, and since the norther had ceased to blow there was a spring warmth in the air. Ned, conscious now that he was stained with the dirt and dust of flight and haste, bathed his face and hands in the water of the ditch and combed his thick brown hair as well as he could with his fingers.

"Good work, my lad," said a hearty voice beside him. "It shows that you have a cool brain and an orderly mind."

Davy Crockett, who was always neat, also bathed his own face and hands in the ditch.

"Now I feel a lot better," he said, "and I want to tell you, Ned, that it's lucky the Spanish built so massively. Look at this church. It's got walls of hewn stone, five feet through, an' back in Tennessee we build 'em of planks a quarter of an inch thick. Why, these walls would turn the biggest cannon balls."

"It surely is mighty lucky," said Ned. "What are you going to do next, Mr. Crockett?"

"I don't know. I guess we'll wait on the Mexicans to open the battle. Thar, do you hear that trumpet blowin' ag'in? I reckon it means that they're up to somethin'."

"I think so, too," said Ned. "Let's go back upon the church walls,

Mr. Crockett, and see for ourselves just what it means."

The two climbed upon the great stone wall, which was in reality a parapet. Travis and Bowie, who was second in command, were there already. Ned looked toward San Antonio, and he saw Mexicans everywhere. Mexican flags hoisted by the people were floating from the flat roofs of the houses, signs of their exultation at the coming of Santa Anna and the expulsion of the Texans.

The trumpet sounded again and they saw three officers detach themselves from the Mexican lines and ride forward under a white flag. Ned knew that one of them was the young Urrea.

"Now what in thunder can they want?" growled Davy Crockett. "There can be no talk or truce between us an' Santa Anna. If all that I've heard of him is true I'd never believe a word he says."

Travis called two of his officers, Major Morris and Captain Martin, and directed them to go out and see what the Mexicans wanted. Then, meeting Ned's eye, he recalled something.

"Ah, you speak Spanish and Mexican Spanish perfectly," he said. "Will you go along, too?"

"Gladly," said Ned.

"An', Ned," said Davy Crockett, in his whimsical tone, "if you don't tell me every word they said when you come back I'll keep you on bread an' water for a week. There are to be no secrets here from me."

"I promise, Mr. Crockett," said Ned.

The heavy oaken doors were thrown open and the three went out on foot to meet the Mexican officers who were riding slowly forward. The afternoon air was now soft and pleasant, and a light, soothing wind was blowing from the south. The sky was a vast dome of brilliant blue and gold. It was a picture that remained indelibly on Ned's mind like many others that were to come. They were etched in so deeply that neither the colours nor the order of their occurrence ever changed. An odour, a touch, or anything suggestive would make them return to his mind, unfaded and in proper sequence like the passing of moving pictures.

The Mexicans halted in the middle of the plain and the three Texans met them. The Mexicans did not dismount. Urrea was slightly in advance of the other two, who were older men in brilliant uniforms, generals at least. Ned saw at once that they meant to be haughty and arrogant to the last degree. They showed it in the first instance by not dismounting. It was evident that Urrea would be the chief spokesman, and his manner indicated that it was a part he liked. He, too, was in a fine uniform, irreproachably neat, and his handsome olive face was flushed.

"And so," he said, in an undertone and in Spanish to Ned, "we are here face to face again. You have chosen your own trap, the Alamo, and it is not in human power for you to escape it now."

His taunt stung, but Ned merely replied:

"We shall see."

Then Urrea said aloud, speaking in English, and addressing himself to the two officers:

"We have come by order of General Santa Anna, President of Mexico and Commander-in-Chief of her officers, to make a demand of you."

"A conference must proceed on the assumption that the two parties to it are on equal terms," said Major Morris, in civil tones.

"Under ordinary circumstances, yes," said Urrea, without abating his haughty manner one whit, "but this is a demand by a paramount authority upon rebels and traitors."

He paused that his words might sink home. All three of the Texans felt anger leap in their hearts, but they put restraint upon their words.

"What is it that you wish to say to us?" continued Major Morris. "If it is anything we should hear we are listening."

Urrea could not subdue his love of the grandiose and theatrical.

"As you may see for yourselves," he said, "General Santa Anna has returned to Texas with an overpowering force of brave Mexican troops. San Antonio has fallen into his hands without a struggle. He can take the Alamo in a day. In a month not a man will be left in Texas able to dispute his authority."

"These are statements most of which can be disputed," said Major Morris. "What does General Santa Anna demand of us?"

His quiet manner had its effect upon Urrea.

"He demands your unconditional surrender," he said.

"And does he say nothing about our lives and good treatment?" continued the major, in the same quiet tones.

"He does not," replied Urrea emphatically. "If you receive mercy it will be due solely to the clemency of General Santa Anna toward rebels."

Hot anger again made Ned's heart leap. The tone of Urrea was almost insufferable, but Major Morris, not he, was spokesman.

"I am not empowered to accept or reject anything," continued

Major Morris. "Colonel Travis is the commander of our force, but I am quite positive in my belief that he will not surrender."

"We must carry back our answer in either the affirmative or the negative," said Urrea.

"You can do neither," said Major Morris, "but I promise you that if the answer is a refusal to surrender—and I know it will be such—a single cannon shot will be fired from the wall of the church."

"Very well," said Urrea, "and since that is your arrangement I see nothing more to be said."

"Nor do I," said Major Morris.

The Mexicans saluted in a perfunctory manner and rode toward San Antonio. The three Texans went slowly back to the Alamo. Ned walked behind the two men. He hoped that the confidence of Major Morris was justified. He knew Santa Anna too well. He believed that the Texans had more to fear from surrender than from defence.

They entered the Alamo and once more the great door was shut and barred heavily. They climbed upon the wall, and Major Morris and Captain Martin went toward Travis, Bowie and Crockett, who stood together waiting. Ned paused a little distance away. He saw them talking together earnestly, but he could not hear what they said. Far away he saw the three Mexicans riding slowly toward San Antonio.

Ned's eyes came back to the wall. He saw Bowie detach himself from the other two and advance toward the cannon. A moment later a flash came from its muzzle, a heavy report rolled over the plain, and then came back in faint echoes.

The Alamo had sent its answer. A deep cheer came from the Texans. Ned's heart thrilled. He had his wish.

The boy looked back toward San Antonio and his eyes were caught by something red on the tower of the Church of San Fernando. It rose, expanded swiftly, and then burst out in great folds. It was a blood-red flag, flying now in the wind, the flag of no quarter. No Texan would be spared, and Ned knew it. Nevertheless his heart thrilled again.

CHAPTER 9

THE FLAG OF NO QUARTER

Ned gazed long at the great red flag as its folds waved in the wind. A chill ran down his spine, a strange, throbbing sensation, but not of fear. They were a tiny islet there amid a Mexican sea which threatened to roll over them. But the signal of the flag, he realised, merely told him that which he had expected all the time. He knew Santa Anna. He would show no quarter to those who had humbled Cos and his forces at San Antonio.

The boy was not assigned to the watch that night, but he could not sleep for a long time. Among these borderers there was discipline, but it was discipline of their own kind, not that of the military martinet. Ned was free to go about as he chose, and he went to the great *plaza* into which they had driven the cattle. Some supplies of hay had been gathered for them, and having eaten they were now all at rest in a herd, packed close against the western side of the wall.

Ned passed near them, but they paid no attention to him, and going on he climbed upon the portion of the wall which ran close to the river. Some distance to his right and an equal distance to his left were sentinels. But there was nothing to keep him from leaping down from the wall or the outside and disappearing. The Mexican investment was not yet complete. Yet no such thought ever entered Ned's head. His best friends, Will Allen, the Panther and Obed White, were out there somewhere, if they were still alive, but his heart was now here in the Alamo with the Texans.

He listened intently, but he heard no sound of any Mexican advance. It occurred to him that a formidable attack might be made here, particularly under the cover of darkness. A dashing leader like the younger Urrea might attempt a surprise.

He dropped back inside and went to one of the sentinels who was standing on an abutment with his head just showing above the wall. He was a young man, not more than two or three years older than Ned, and he was glad to have company.

"Have you heard or seen anything?" asked Ned.

"No," replied the sentinel, "but I've been looking for 'em down this way."

They waited a little longer and then Ned was quite sure that he saw a dim form in the darkness. He pointed toward it, but the sentinel could not see it at all, as Ned's eyes were much the keener: But the shape grew clearer and Ned's heart throbbed.

The figure was that of a great horse, and Ned recognised Old Jack. Nothing could have persuaded him that the faithful beast was not seeking his master, and he emitted a low soft whistle. The horse raised his head, listened and then trotted forward.

"He is mine," said Ned, "and he knows me."

"He won't be yours much longer," said the sentinel. "Look, there's a Mexican creeping along the ground after him."

Ned followed the pointing finger, and he now noticed the Mexican, a *vaquero*, who had been crouching so low that his figure blurred with the earth. Ned saw the coiled lariat hanging over his arm, and he knew that the man intended to capture Old Jack, a prize worth any effort.

"Do you think I ought to shoot him?" asked the sentinel.

"Not yet, at least," replied Ned. "I brought my horse into this danger, but I think that he'll take himself out of it."

Old Jack had paused, as if uncertain which way to go. But Ned felt sure that he was watching the Mexican out of the tail of his eye. The *vaquero* emboldened by the prospect of such a splendid prize, crept closer and closer, and then suddenly threw the lasso. The horse's head ducked down swiftly, the coil of rope slipped back over his head, and he dashed at the Mexican.

The *vaquero* was barely in time to escape those terrible hoofs. But howling with terror he sprang clear and raced away in the darkness. The horse whinnied once or twice gently, waited, and, when no answer came to his calls, trotted off in the dusk.

"No Mexican will take your horse," said the sentinel.

"You're right when you say that," said Ned. "I don't think another will ever get so near him, but if he should you see that my horse knows how to take care of himself."

Ned wandered back toward the convent yard. It was now late, but a clear moon was shining. He saw the figures of the sentinels clearly on the walls, but he was confident that no attack would be made by the Mexicans that night. His great tension and excitement began to relax and he felt that he could sleep.

He decided that the old hospital would be a good place, and, taking his blankets, he entered the long room of that building. Only the moonlight shone there, but a friendly voice hailed him at once.

"It's time you were hunting rest, Ned," said Davy Crockett. "I saw you wanderin' 'roun' as if you was carryin' the world on your shoulders, but I didn't say anything. I knew that you would come to if left to yourself. There's a place over there by the wall where the floor seems to be a little softer than it is most everywhere else. Take it an' enjoy it."

Ned laughed and took the place to which Crockett was pointing. The hardness of a floor was nothing to him, and with one blanket under him and another over him he went to sleep quickly, sleeping the night through without a dream. He awoke early, took a breakfast of fresh beef with the men in the convent yard, and then, rifle in hand, he mounted the church wall.

All his intensity of feeling returned with the morning. He was eager to see what was passing beyond the Alamo, and the first object that caught his eye was the blood-red flag of no quarter hanging from the tower of the Church of San Fernando. No wind was blowing and it drooped in heavy scarlet folds like a pall.

Looking from the flag to the earth, he saw great activity in the Mexican lines. Three or four batteries were being placed in position, and Mexican officers, evidently messengers, were galloping about. The flat roofs of the houses in San Antonio were covered with people. Ned knew that they were there to see Santa Anna win a quick victory and take immediate vengeance upon the Texans. He recognised Santa Anna himself riding in his crouched attitude upon a great white horse, passing from battery to battery and hurrying the work. There was proof that his presence was effective, as the men always worked faster when he came.

Ned saw all the Texan leaders, Travis, Bowie, Crockett and Bonham, watching the batteries. The whole Texan force was now manning the walls and the heavy cedar palisade at many points, but Ned saw that for the present all their dealings would be with the cannon.

Earthworks had been thrown up to protect the Mexican batteries, and the Texan cannon were posted for reply, but Ned noticed that his comrades seemed to think little of the artillery. In this desperate crisis they fondled their rifles lovingly.

He was still watching the batteries, when a gush of smoke and flame came from one of the cannon. There was a great shout in the Mexican lines, but the round shot spent itself against the massive stone walls of the mission.

"They'll have to send out a stronger call than that," said Davy Crockett contemptuously, "before this 'coon comes down."

Travis went along the walls, saw that the Texans were sheltering themselves, and waited. There was another heavy report and a second round shot struck harmlessly upon the stone. Then the full bombardment began. A half dozen batteries rained shot and shell upon the Alamo. The roar was continuous like the steady roll of thunder, and it beat upon the drums of Ned's ears until he thought he would become deaf.

He was crouched behind the stone parapet, but he looked up often enough to see what was going on. He saw a vast cloud of smoke gathering over river and town, rent continually by flashes of fire from the muzzles of the cannon. The air was full of hissing metal, shot and shell poured in a storm upon the Alamo. Now and then the Texan cannon replied, but not often.

The cannon fire was so great that for a time it shook Ned's nerves. It seemed as if nothing could live under such a rain of missiles, but when he looked along the parapet and saw all the Texans unharmed his courage came back.

Many of the balls were falling inside the church, in the convent yard and in the *plazas*, but the Texans there were protected also, and as far as Ned could see not a single man had been wounded.

The cannonade continued for a full hour and then ceased abruptly. The great cloud of smoke began to lift, and the Alamo, river and town came again into the brilliant sunlight. The word passed swiftly among the defenders that their fortress was uninjured and not a man hurt.

As the smoke rose higher Ned saw Mexican officers with glasses examining the Alamo to see what damage their cannon had done. He hoped they would feel mortification when they found it was so little. Davy Crockett knelt near him on the parapet, and ran his hand lovingly along the barrel of Betsy, as one strokes the head of a child.

"Do you want some more rifles, Davy?" asked Bowie.

"Jest about a half dozen," replied Crockett. "I think I can use that many before they clear out."

Six of the long-barrelled Texan rifles were laid at Crockett's feet. Ned watched with absorbed interest. Crockett's eye was on the nearest battery and he was slowly raising Betsy.

"Which is to be first, Davy?" asked Bowie.

"The one with the rammer in his hand."

Crockett took a single brief look down the sights and pulled the trigger. The man with the rammer dropped to the earth and the rammer fell beside him. He lay quite still. Crockett seized a second rifle and fired. A loader fell and he also lay still. A third rifle shot, almost as quick as a flash, and a gunner went down, a fourth and a man at a wheel fell, a fifth and the unerring bullet claimed a sponger, a sixth and a Mexican just springing to cover was wounded in the shoulder. Then Crockett remained with the seventh rifle still loaded in his hands, as there was nothing to shoot at, all the Mexicans now being hidden.

But Crockett, kneeling on the parapet, the rifle cocked and his finger on the trigger, watched in case any of the Mexicans should expose himself again. He presented to Ned the simile of some powerful animal about to spring. The lean, muscular figure was poised for instant action, and all the whimsicality and humour were gone from the eyes of the sharpshooter.

A mighty shout of triumph burst from the Texans. Many a good marksman was there, but never before had they seen such shooting. The great reputation of Davy Crockett, universal in the southwest, was justified fully. The crew of the gun had been annihilated in less than a minute.

For a while there was silence. Then the Mexicans, protected by the earthwork that they had thrown up, drew the battery back a hundred yards. Even in the farther batteries the men were very careful about exposing themselves. The Texans, seeing no sure target, held their fire. The Mexicans opened a new cannonade and for another half hour the roar of the great guns drowned all other sounds. But when it ceased and the smoke drifted away the Texans were still unharmed.

Ned was now by the side of Bowie, who showed great satisfaction.

"What will they do next?" asked Ned.

"I don't know, but you see now that it's not the biggest noise that hurts the most. They'll never get us with cannon fire. The only way they can do it is to attack the lowest part of our wall and make a bridge of their own bodies."

"They are doing something now," said Ned, whose far-sighted vision always served him well. "They are pulling down houses in the town next to the river."

"That's so," said Bowie, "but we won't have to wait long to see what they're about."

Hundreds of Mexicans with wrecking hooks had assailed three or four of the houses, which they quickly pulled to pieces. Others ran forward with the materials and began to build a bridge across the narrow San Antonio.

"They want to cross over on that bridge and get into a position at once closer and more sheltered," said Bowie, "but unless I make a big mistake those men at work there are already within range of our rifles. Shall we open fire, colonel?"

He asked the question of Travis, who nodded. A picked band of Mexicans under General Castrillon were gathered in a mass and were rapidly fitting together the timbers of the houses to make the narrow

366

bridge. But the reach of the Texan rifles was great, and Davy Crockett was merely the king among so many sharpshooters.

The rifles began to flash and crack. No man fired until he was sure of his aim, and no two picked the same target. The Mexicans fell fast. In five minutes thirty or forty were killed, some of them falling into the river, and the rest, dropping the timbers, fled with shouts of horror from the fatal spot. General Castrillon, a brave man, sought to drive them back, but neither blows nor oaths availed. Santa Anna himself came and made many threats, but the men would not stir. They preferred punishment to the sure death that awaited them from the muzzles of the Texan rifles.

The light puffs of rifle smoke were quickly gone, and once more the town with the people watching on the flat roofs came into full view. A wind burst out the folds of the red flag of no quarter on the tower of the church of San Fernando, but Ned paid no attention to it now. He was watching for Santa Anna's next move.

"That's a bridge that will never be built," said Davy Crockett. "'Live an' learn' is a good sayin', I suppose, but a lot of them Mexicans neither lived nor learned. It's been a great day for 'Betsy' here."

Travis, the commander, showed elation.

"I think Santa Anna will realise now," he said, "that he has neither a promenade nor a picnic before him. Oh, if we only had six or seven hundred men, instead of less than a hundred and fifty!"

"We must send for help," said Bowie. "The numbers of Santa Anna continually increase, but we are not yet entirely surrounded. If the Texans know that we are beleaguered here they will come to our help."

"I will send messengers tomorrow night," said Travis. "The Texans are much scattered, but it is likely that some will come."

It was strange, but it was characteristic of them, nevertheless, that no one made any mention of escape. Many could have stolen away in the night over the lower walls. Perhaps all could have done so, but not a single Texan ever spoke of such a thing, and not one ever attempted it.

Santa Anna moved some of his batteries and also erected two new ones. When the work on the latter was finished all opened in another tremendous cannonade, lasting for fully an hour. The bank of smoke was heavier than ever, and the roaring in Ned's ears was incessant, but he felt no awe now. He was growing used to the cannon fire, and as it did so little harm he felt no apprehension.

While the fire was at its height he went down in the church and cleaned his rifle, although he took the precaution to remain in one of the covered rooms by the doorway. Davy Crockett was also there busy with the same task. Before they finished a cannon ball dropped on the floor, bounded against the wall and rebounded several times until it finally lay at rest.

"Somethin' laid a big egg then," said Crockett. "It's jest as well to keep a stone roof over your head when you're under fire of a few dozen cannon. Never take foolish risks, Ned, for the sake of showin' off. That's the advice of an old man."

Crockett spoke very earnestly, and Ned remembered his words. Bonham called to them a few minutes later that the Mexicans seemed to be meditating some movement on the lower wall around the grand plaza.

"Like as not you're right," said Crockett. "It would be the time to try it while our attention was attracted by the big cannonade."

Crockett himself was detailed to meet the new movement, and he led fifty sharpshooters. Ned was with him, his brain throbbing with the certainty that he was going into action once more. Great quantities of smoke hung over the Alamo and had penetrated every part of it. It crept into Ned's throat, and it also stung his eyes. It inflamed his brain and increased his desire for combat. They reached the low wall on a run, and found that Bonham was right. A large force of Mexicans was approaching from that side, evidently expecting to make an opening under cover of the smoke.

The assailants were already within range, and the deadly Texan rifles began to crack at once from the wall. The whole front line of the Mexican column was quickly burned away. The return fire of the Mexicans was hasty and irregular and they soon broke and ran.

"An' that's over," said Crockett, as he sent a parting shot. "It was easy, an' bein' sheltered not a man of ours was hurt. But, Ned, don't let the idea that we have a picnic here run away with you. We've got to watch an' watch an' fight an' fight all the time, an' every day more Mexicans will come."

"I understand, Mr. Crockett," said Ned. "You know that we may never get out of here alive, and I know it, too."

"You speak truth, lad," said Crockett, very soberly. "But remember that it's a chance we take every day here in the southwest. An' it's pleasant to know that they're all brave men here together. You haven't seen any flinchin' on the part of anybody an' I don't think you ever will."

"What are you going to do now?" asked Ned.

"I'm goin' to eat dinner, an' after that I'll take a nap. My advice to you is to do the same, 'cause you'll be on watch tonight."

"I know I can eat," said Ned, "and I'll try to sleep."

He found that his appetite was all right, and after dinner he lay down in the long room of the hospital. Here he heard the cannon of Santa Anna still thundering, but the walls softened the sound somewhat and made it seem much more distant. In a way it was soothing and Ned, although sure that he could not sleep, slept. All that afternoon he was rocked into deeper slumber by the continuous roar of the Mexican guns. Smoke floated over the convent yard and through all the buildings, but it did not disturb him. Now and then a flash of rifle fire came from the Texans on the walls, but that did not disturb him, either.

Nature was paying its debt. The boy lying on his blankets breathed deeply and regularly as he slept. The hours of the afternoon passed one by one, and it was dark when he awoke. The fire of the cannon had now ceased and two or three lights were burning in the hospital. Crockett was already up, and with some of the other men was eating beefsteak at a table.

"You said you'd try to sleep, Ned," he exclaimed, "an' you must have made a big try, 'cause you snored so loud we couldn't hear Santa Anna's cannon."

"Why, I'm sure I don't snore, Mr. Crockett," said Ned, red in the face.

"No, you don't snore, I'll take that back," said Davy Crockett, when the laugh subsided, "but I never saw a young man sleep more beautifully an' skilfully. Why, the risin' an' fallin' of your chest was as reg'lar as the tickin' of a clock."

Ned joined them at the table. He did not mind the jests of those men, as they did not mind the jests of one another. They were now like close blood-kin. They were a band of brethren, bound together by the unbreakable tie of mortal danger.

Ned spent two-thirds of the night on the church wall. The Mexicans let the cannon rest in the darkness, and only a few rifle shots were fired. But there were many lights in San Antonio, and on the outskirts two great bonfires burned. Santa Anna and his generals, feeling that their prey could not escape from the trap, and caring little for the peons who had been slain, were making a festival. It is even said that Santa Anna on this campaign, although he left a wife in the city of Mexico, exercised the privileges of an Oriental ruler and married another amid great rejoicings.

Ned slept soundly when his watch was finished, and he awoke again the next day to the thunder of the cannonade, which continued almost without cessation throughout the day, but in the afternoon Travis wrote a letter, a noble appeal to the people of Texas for help. He stated that they had been under a continual bombardment for more than twenty-four hours, but not a man had yet been hurt. "I shall never surrender or retreat," he said. "Then I call on you in the name of liberty, of patriotism, and of everything dear to the American character, to come to our aid with all dispatch." He closed with the three words, "Victory or death," not written in any vainglory or with any melodramatic appeal, but with the full consciousness of the desperate crisis, and a quiet resolution to do as he said.

The heroic letter is now in the possession of the State of Texas. Most of the men in the Alamo knew its contents, and they approved of it. When it was fully dark Travis gave it to Albert Martin. Then he looked around for another messenger.

"Two should go together in case of mishap," he said.

His eye fell upon Ned.

"If you wish to go I will send you," he said, "but I leave it to your choice. If you prefer to stay, you stay."

Ned's first impulse was to go. He might find Obed White, Will Allen and the Panther out there and bring them back with him, but his second impulse told him that it was only a chance, and he would abide with Crockett and Bowie.

"I thank you for the offer, but I think, sir, that I'll stay," he said.

He saw Crockett give him a swift approving glance. Another was quickly chosen in his stead, and Ned was in the grand *plaza* when they dropped over the low wall and disappeared in the darkness. His comrades and he listened attentively a long time, but as they heard no sound of shots they were sure that they were now safe beyond the Mexican lines.

"I don't want to discourage anybody," said Bowie, "but I'm not hoping much from the messengers. The Texans are scattered too widely."

"No, they can't bring many," said Crockett, "but every man counts. Sometimes it takes mighty little to turn the tale, and they may turn it."

"I hope so," said Bowie.

The Mexican cannon were silent that night and Ned slept deeply, awaking only when the dawn of a clear day came. He was astonished at the quickness with which he grew used to a state of siege and imminent danger. All the habits of life now went on as usual. He ate breakfast with as good an appetite as if he had been out on the prairie with his friends, and he talked with his new comrades as if Santa Anna and his army were a thousand miles away.

But when he did go upon the church wall he saw that Santa Anna had begun work again and at a new place. The Mexican general, having seen that his artillery was doing no damage, was making a great effort to get within much closer range where the balls would count. Men protected by heavy planking or advancing along trenches were seeking to erect a battery within less than three hundred yards of the entrance to the main *plaza*. They had already thrown up a part of a breastwork. Meanwhile the Texan sharpshooters were waiting for a chance.

Ned took no part in it except that of a spectator. But Crockett, Bowie and a dozen others were crouched on the wall with their rifles. Presently an incautious Mexican showed above the earthwork. It was Crockett who slew him, but Bowie took the next. Then the other rifles flashed fast, eight or ten Mexicans were slain, and the rest fled. Once more the deadly Texan rifles had triumphed.

Ned wondered why Santa Anna had endeavoured to place the battery there in the daytime. It could be done at night, when it was impossible for the Texans to aim their rifles so well. He did not know that the pride of Santa Anna, unable to brook delay in the face of so small a force, had pushed him forward.

Knowing now what might be done at night, Ned passed the day in anxiety, and with the coming of the twilight his anxiety increased.

CHAPTER 10

CROCKETT AND BOWIE

Unluckily for the Texans, the night was the darkest of the month. No bonfires burned in San Antonio, and there were no sounds of music. It seemed to Ned that the silence and darkness were sure indications of action on the part of the foe.

He felt more lonely and depressed than at any other time hitherto in the siege, and he was glad when Crockett and a young Tennessean whom he called the Bee-Hunter joined him. Crockett had not lost any of his whimsical good humour, and when Ned suggested that Santa Anna was likely to profit by the dark he replied:

371

"If he is the general I take him to be he will, or at least try, but meanwhile we'll just wait, an' look, an' listen. That's the way to find out if things are goin' to happen. Don't turn little troubles into big ones. You don't need a cowskin for a calf. We'll jest rest easy. I'm mighty nigh old enough to be your grandfather, Ned, an' I've learned to take things as they come. I guess men of my age were talkin' this same way five thousand years ago."

"You've seen a lot in your life, Mr. Crockett," said Ned, to whom the Tennessee an was a great hero.

Crockett laughed low, but deep in his throat, and with much pleasure.

"So I have! So I have!" he replied, "an', by the blue blazes, I can say it without braggin'. I've seen a lot of water go by since I was runnin' 'roun' a bare-footed boy in Tennessee. I've ranged pretty far from east to west, an' all the way from Boston in the north to this old mission, an' that must be some thousands of miles. An' I've had some big times in New York, too."

"You've been in New York," said Ned, with quick interest. "It must be a great town."

"It is. It's certainly a bulger of a place. There are thousands an' thousands of houses, an' you can't count the sails in the bay. I saw the City Hall an' it's a mighty fine buildin', too. It's all marble on the side looking south, an' plain stone on the side lookin' north. I asked why, an' they said all the poor people lived to the north of it. That's the way things often happen, Ned. An' I saw the great, big hotel John Jacob Astor was beginnin' to build on Broadway just below the City Hall. They said it would cost seven hundred thousand dollars, which is an all-fired lot of money, that it would cover mighty nigh a whole block, an' that there would be nothin' else in America comin' up to it."

"I'd like to see that town," said Ned.

"Maybe you will some day," said Crockett, "'cause you're young. You don't know how young you look to me. I heard a lot there, Ned, about that rich man, Mr. Astor. He got his start as a fur trader. I guess he was about the biggest fur trader that ever was. He was so active that all them animals that wore furs on their backs concluded they might as well give up. I heard one story there about an otter an' a beaver talkin'. Says the otter to the beaver, when he was tellin' the beaver goodbye after a visit: 'Farewell, I never expect to see you again, my dear old friend.' 'Don't be too much distressed,' replies the beaver, 'you an' I, old comrade, will soon meet at the hat store.'"

Ned and the Bee-Hunter laughed, and Crockett delved again into his past life and his experiences in the great city, relatively as great then to the whole country as it is now.

"I saw a heap of New York," he continued, "an' one of the things I liked best in it was the theaters. Lad, I saw the great Fanny Kemble play there, an' she shorely was one of the finest women that ever walked this troubled earth. I saw her first as Portia in that play of Shakespeare's called, called, called—"

"*The Merchant of Venice*," suggested Ned.

"Yes, that's it, *The Merchant of Venice*, where she was the woman lawyer. She was fine to see, an' the way she could change her voice an' looks was clean mirac'lous. If ever I need a lawyer I want her to act for me. She had me mad, an' then she had me laughin', an' then she had the water startin' in my eyes. Whatever she wanted me to see I saw, an' whatever she wanted me to think I thought. An' then, too, she was many kinds of a woman, different in turn. In fact, Ned, she was just like a handsome piece of changeable silk—first one colour an' then another, but always clean."

He paused and the others did not interrupt him.

"I don't like cities," he resumed presently. "They crowd me up too much, but I do like the theater. It makes you see so many things an' so many kinds of people that you wouldn't have time to see if you had to travel for 'em. We don't have much chance to travel right now, do we, Bee-Hunter?"

"A few hundred yards only for our bodies," replied the young Tennessean, "but our spirits soar far;

Up with your banner, Freedom,
Thy champions cling to thee,
They'll follow where'er you lead them
To death or victory.
Up with your banner, Freedom.

He merely hummed the words, but Ned caught his spirit and he repeated to himself: "*Up with your banner, Freedom.*"

"I guess you've heard enough tales from an old fellow like me," said Crockett. "At least you won't have time to hear any more 'cause the Mexicans must be moving out there. Do you hear anything, Ned?"

"Nothing but a little wind."

"Then my ears must be deceivin' me. I've used 'em such a long time that I guess they feel they've got a right to trick me once in a while."

But Ned was thinking just then of the great city which he wanted to see some day as Crockett had seen it. But it seemed to him at that moment as far away as the moon. Would his comrades and he ever escape from those walls?

His mind came back with a jerk. He did hear something on the plain. Crockett was right. He heard the tread of horses and the sound of wheels moving. He called the attention of Crockett to the noises.

"I think I know what causes them," said Crockett. "Santa Anna is planting his battery under the cover of the night an' I don't see, boys, how we're goin' to keep him from doin' it."

The best of the Texan sharpshooters lined the walls, and they fired occasionally at indistinct and flitting figures, but they were quite certain that they did no execution. The darkness was too great. Travis, Bowie and Crockett considered the possibility of a sortie, but they decided that it had no chance of success. The few score Texans would be overwhelmed in the open plain by the thousands of Mexicans.

But all the leaders were uneasy. If the Mexican batteries were brought much closer, and were protected by earthworks and other fortifications, the Alamo would be much less defensible. It was decided to send another messenger for help, and Ned saw Bonham drop over the rear wall and slip away in the darkness. He was to go to Goliad, where Fannin had 300 men and four guns, and bring them in haste.

When Bonham was gone Ned returned to his place on the wall. For hours he heard the noises without, the distant sound of voices, the heavy clank of metal against metal, and he knew full well that Santa Anna was planting his batteries. At last he went to his place in the long room of the hospital and slept.

When dawn came he sprang up and rushed to the wall. There was the battery of Santa Anna only three hundred yards from the entrance to the main *plaza* and to the southeast, but little further away, was another. The Mexicans had worked well during the night.

"They're creepin' closer, Ned. They're creepin' closer," said Crockett, who had come to the wall before him, "but even at that range I don't think their cannon will do us much harm. Duck, boy, duck! They're goin' to fire!"

The two batteries opened at the same time, and the Mexican masses in the rear, out of range, began a tremendous cheering. Many of the balls and shells now fell inside the mission, but the Texans stayed well under cover and they still escaped without harm. The Mexican

374

gunners, in their turn, kept so well protected that the Texan riflemen had little chance.

The great bombardment lasted an hour, but when it ceased, and the smoke lifted, Ned saw a heavy mass of Mexican cavalry on the eastern road.

Both Ned and Crockett took a long look at the cavalry, a fine body of men, some carrying lances and others muskets. Ned believed that he recognised Urrea in the figure of their leader, but the distance was too great for certainty. But when he spoke of it to Crockett the Tenessean borrowed Travis' fieldglasses.

"Take these," he said, "an' if it's that beloved enemy of yours you can soon tell."

The boy, with the aid of the glasses, recognised Urrea at once. The young leader in the uniform of a Mexican captain and with a cocked and plumed hat upon his head sat his horse haughtily. Ned knew that he was swelling with pride and that he, like Santa Anna, expected the trap to shut down on the little band of Texans in a day or two. He felt some bitterness that fate should have done so much for Urrea.

"I judge by your face," said Crockett whimsically, "that it is Urrea. But remember, Ned, that you can still be hated and live long."

"It is indeed Urrea," said Ned. "Now what are they gathering cavalry out there for? They can't expect to gallop over our walls."

"Guess they've an idea that we're goin' to try to slip out an' they're shuttin' up that road of escape. Seems to me, Ned, they're comin' so close that it's an insult to us."

"They're almost within rifle shot."

"Then these bad little Mexican boys must have their faces scorched as a lesson. Just you wait here, Ned, till I have a talk with Travis an' Bowie."

It was obvious to Ned that Crockett's talk with the commander and his second was satisfactory, because when he returned his face was in a broad grin. Bowie, moreover, came with him, and his blue eyes were lighted up with the fire of battle.

"We're goin' to teach 'em the lesson, Ned, beginnin' with a b c," said Crockett, "an' Jim here, who has had a lot of experience in Texas, will lead us. Come along, I'll watch over you."

A force of seventy or eighty was formed quickly, and hidden from the view of the Mexicans, they rushed down the *plaza*, climbed the low walls and dropped down upon the plain. The Mexican cavalry outnumbered them four or five to one, but the Texans cared little for such odds.

"Now, boys, up with your rifles!" cried Bowie. "Pump it into 'em!"

Bowie was a product of the border, hard and desperate, a man of many fierce encounters, but throughout the siege he had been singularly gentle and considerate in his dealings with his brother Texans. Now he was all warrior again, his eyes blazing with blue fire while he shouted vehement words of command to his men.

The sudden appearance of the Texan riflemen outside the Alamo look Urrea by surprise, but he was quick of perception and action, and his cavalrymen were the best in the Mexican army. He wheeled them into line with a few words of command and shouted to them to charge. Bowie's men instantly stopped, forming a rough line, and up went their rifles. Urrea's soldiers who carried rifles or muskets opened a hasty and excited fire at some distance.

Ned heard the bullets singing over his head or saw them kicking up dust in front of the Texans, but only one of the Texans fell and but few were wounded. The Mexican rifles or muskets were now empty, but the Mexican lancers came on in good order and in an almost solid group, the yellow sunlight flashing across the long blades of their lances.

It takes a great will to face sharp steel in the hands of horsemen thundering down upon you, and Ned was quite willing to own afterward that every nerve in him was jumping, but he stood. All stood, and at the command of Bowie their rifles flashed together in one tremendous explosion.

The rifles discharged, the Texans instantly snatched out their pistols, ready for anything that might come galloping through the smoke. But nothing came. When the smoke lifted they saw that the entire front of the Mexican column was gone. Fallen men and horses were thick on the plain and long lances lay across them. Other horses, riderless, were galloping away to right and left, and unhorsed men were running to the rear. But Urrea had escaped unharmed. Ned saw him trying to reform his shattered force.

"Reload your rifles, men!" shouted Bowie. "You can be ready for them before they come again!"

These were skilled sharpshooters, and they rammed the loads home with startling rapidity. Every rifle was loaded and a finger was on every trigger when the second charge of Urrea swept down upon them. No need of a command from Bowie now. The Texans picked their targets and fired straight into the dense group. Once more the front of the Mexican column was shot away, and the lances fell clattering on the plain.

"At 'em, boys, with your pistols!" shouted Bowie. "Don't give 'em a second chance!"

The Texans rushed forward, firing their pistols. Ned in the smoke became separated from his comrades, and when he could see more clearly he beheld but a single horseman. The man was Urrea.

The two recognised each other instantly. The Mexican had the advantage. He was on horseback and the smoke was in Ned's eyes, not his own. With a shout of triumph, he rode straight at the boy and made a fierce sweep with his cavalry sabre. It was fortunate for Ned that he was agile of both body and mind. He ducked and leaped to one side. He felt the swish of the heavy steel over his head, but as he came up again he fired.

Urrea was protected largely by his horse's neck, and Ned fired at the horse instead, although he would have greatly preferred Urrea as a target. The bullet struck true and the horse fell, but the rider leaped clear and, still holding the sabre, sprang at his adversary. Ned snatched up his rifle, which lay on the ground at his feet, and received the slash of the sword upon its barrel. The blade broke in two, and then, clubbing his rifle, Ned struck.

It was fortunate for Urrea, too, that he was agile of mind and body. He sprang back quickly, but the butt of the rifle grazed his head and drew blood. The next moment other combatants came between, and Urrea dashed away in search of a fresh horse. Ned, his blood on fire, was rushing after him, when Bowie seized his arm and pulled him back.

"No further, Ned!" he cried. "We've scattered their cavalry and we must get back into the Alamo or the whole Mexican army will be upon us!"

Ned heard far away the beat of flying hoofs. It was made by the horses of the Mexican cavalry fleeing for their lives. Bowie quickly gathered together his men, and carrying with them two who had been slain in the fight they retreated rapidly to the Alamo, the Texan cannon firing over their heads at the advancing Mexican infantry. In three or four minutes they were inside the walls again and with their comrades.

The Mexican cavalry did not reappear upon the eastern road, and the Texans were exultant, yet they had lost two good men and their joy soon gave way to more solemn feelings. It was decided to bury the slain at once in the *plaza*, and a common grave was made for them. They were the first of the Texans to fall in the defence, and their fate made a deep impression upon everybody.

It took only a few minutes to dig the grave, and the men, laid side by side, were covered with their cloaks. While the spades were yet at work the Mexican cannon opened anew upon the Alamo. A ball and a bomb fell in the *plaza*. The shell burst, but fortunately too far away to hurt anybody. Neither the bursting of the shell nor any other part of the cannonade interrupted the burial.

Crockett, a public man and an orator, said a few words. They were sympathetic and well chosen. He spoke of the two men as dying for Texas. Others, too, would fall in the defence of the Alamo, but their blood would water the tree of freedom. Then they threw in the dirt. While Crockett was speaking the cannon still thundered without, but every word could be heard distinctly.

When Ned walked away he felt to the full the deep solemnity of the moment. Hitherto they had fought without loss to themselves. The death of the two men now cast an ominous light over the situation. The Mexican lines were being drawn closer and closer about the Alamo, and he was compelled to realise the slenderness of their chances.

The boy resumed his place on the wall, remaining throughout the afternoon, and watched the coming of the night. Crockett joined him, and together they saw troops of Mexicans marching away from the main body, some to right and some to left.

"Stretchin' their lines," said Crockett. "Santa Anna means to close us in entirely after a while. Now, by the blue blazes, that was a close shave!"

A bullet sang by his head and flattened against the wall. He and Ned dropped down just in time. Other bullets thudded against the stone. Nevertheless, Ned lifted his head above the edge of the parapet and took a look. His eyes swept a circle and he saw little puffs of smoke coming from the roofs and windows of the *jacals* or Mexican huts on their side of the river. He knew at once that the best of the Mexican sharpshooters had hidden themselves there, and had opened fire not with muskets, but with improved rifles. He called Crockett's attention to this point of danger and the frontiersman grew very serious.

"We've got to get 'em out some way or other," he said. "As I said before, the cannon balls make a big fuss, but they don't come so often an' they come at random. It's the little bullets that have the sting of the wasp, an' when a man looks down the sights, draws a bead on you, an' sends one of them lead pellets at you, he gen'rally gets you. Ned, we've got to drive them fellers out of there some way or other."

The bullets from the *jacals* now swept the walls and the truth of Crockett's words became painfully evident. The Texan cannon fired upon the huts, but the balls went through the soft adobe and seemed to do no harm. It was like firing into a great sponge. Triumphant shouts came from the Mexicans. Their own batteries resumed the cannonade, while their sheltered riflemen sent in the bullets faster and faster.

Crockett tapped the barrel of Betsy significantly.

"The work has got to be done with this old lady an' others like her," he said. "We must get rid of them *jacals*."

"How?" asked Ned.

"You come along with me an' I'll show you," said Crockett. "I'm goin' to have a talk with Travis, an' if he agrees with me we'll soon wipe out that wasps' nest."

Crockett briefly announced his plan, which was bold in the extreme. Sixty picked riflemen, twenty of whom bore torches also, would rush out at one of the side gates, storm the *jacals*, set fire to them, and then rush back to the Alamo.

Travis hesitated. The plan seemed impossible of execution in face of the great Mexican force. But Bowie warmly seconded Crockett, and at last the commander gave his consent. Ned at once asked to go with the daring troop, and secured permission. The band gathered in a close body by one of the gates. The torches were long sticks lighted at the end and burning strongly. The men had already cocked their rifles, but knowing the immense risk they were about to take they were very quiet. Ned was pale, and his heart beat painfully, but his hand did not shake.

The Texan cannon, to cover the movement, opened fire from the walls, and the riflemen, posted at various points, helped also. The Mexican cannonade increased. When the thunder and crash were at their height the gate was suddenly thrown open and the sixty dashed out. Fortunately the drifting smoke hid them partially, and they were almost upon the *jacals* before they were discovered.

A great shout came from the Mexicans when they saw the daring Texans outside, and bullets from the *jacals* began to knock up grass and dust about them. But Crockett himself, waving a torch, led them on, shouting:

"It's only a step, boys! It's only a step! Now, let 'em have it!"

The Texans fired as they rushed, but they took care to secure good aim. The Mexicans were driven from the roofs and the windows and then the Texans carrying the torches dashed inside. Every house contained something inflammable, which was quickly set on fire, and two or three huts made of wood were lighted in a dozen places.

The dry materials blazed up fast. A light wind fanned the flames, which joined together and leaped up, a roaring pyramid. The Mexicans, who had lately occupied them, were scuttling like rabbits toward their main force, and the Texan bullets made them jump higher and faster.

Crockett, with a shout of triumph, flung down his torch.

"Now, boys," he cried. "Here's the end of them *jacals*. Nothin' on earth can put out that fire, but if we don't make a foot race back to the Alamo the end of us will be here, too, in a minute."

The little band wheeled for its homeward rush. Ned heard a great shout of rage from the Mexicans, and then the hissing and singing of shells and cannon balls over his head. He saw Mexicans running across the plain to cut them off, but his comrades and he had reloaded their rifles, and as they ran they sent a shower of bullets that drove back their foe.

Ned's heart was pumping frightfully, and myriads of black specks danced before his eyes, but he remembered afterward that he calculated how far they were from the Alamo, and how far the Mexicans were from them. A number of his comrades had been wounded, but nobody had fallen and they still raced in a close group for the gate, which seemed to recede as they rushed on.

"A few more steps, Ned," cried Crockett, "an' we're in! Ah, there go our friends!"

The Texan cannon over their heads now fired into the pursuing Mexican masses, and the sharpshooters on the walls also poured in a deadly hail. The Mexicans recoiled once more and then Crockett's party made good the gate.

"All here!" cried Crockett, as those inside held up torches. He ran over the list rapidly himself and counted them all, but his face fell when he saw his young friend the Bee-Hunter stagger. Crockett caught him in his arms and bore him into the hospital. He and Ned watched by his side until he died, which was very soon. Before he became unconscious he murmured some lines from an old Scotch poem:

But hame came the saddle, all bluidy to see.
And hame came the steed, but never hame came he.

They buried him that night beside the other two, and Ned was more solemn than ever when he sought his usual place in the hospital by the wall. It had been a day of victory for the Texans, but the omens, nevertheless, seemed to him to be bad.

The next day he saw the Mexicans spreading further and further about the Alamo, and they were in such strong force that the Texans could not now afford to go out and attack any of these bands. A light cold rain fell, and as he was not on duty he went back to the hospital, where he sat in silence.

He was deeply depressed and the thunder of the Mexican cannon beat upon his ears like the voice of doom. He felt a strange annoyance at the reports of the guns. His nerves jumped, and he became angry with himself at what he considered a childish weakness.

Now, and for the first time, he felt despair. He borrowed a pencil and a sheet of paper torn from an old memorandum book and made his will. His possessions were singularly few, and the most valuable at hand was his fine long-barrelled rifle, which he left to his faithful friend, Obed White. He bequeathed his pistol and knife to the Panther, and his clothes to Will Allen. He was compelled to smile at himself when he had finished his page of writing. Was it likely that his friends would ever find this paper, or, if finding it, was it likely that any one of them could ever obtain his inheritance? But it was a relief to his feelings and, folding the paper, he put it in the inside pocket of his hunting shirt.

The bombardment was renewed in the afternoon, but Ned stayed in his place in the hospital. After a while Davy Crockett and several others joined him there. Crockett as usual was jocular, and told more stories of his trips to the large eastern cities. He had just finished an anecdote of Philadelphia, when he turned suddenly to Ned.

"Boy," he said, "you and I have fought together more than once now, an' I like you. You are brave an' you've a head full of sense. When you grow older you'll be worth a lot to Texas. They'll need you in the council. No, don't protest. This is the time when we can say what is in us. The Mexican circle around the Alamo is almost complete. Isn't that so, boys?"

"It is."

"Then I'll say what we all know. Three or four days from now the

381

chances will be a hundred to one against any of us ever gettin' out of here. An' you're the youngest of the defence, Ned, so I want you to slip out tonight while there's yet time. Mebbe you can get up a big lot of men to come to our help."

Ned looked straight at Crockett, and the veteran's eyes wavered.

"It's a little scheme you have," said Ned, "to get me out of the way. You think because I'm the youngest I ought to go off alone at night and save my own life. Well, I'm not going. I intend to stay here and fight it out with the rest of you."

"I meant for the best, boy, I meant for the best," said Crockett. "I'm an old fellow an' I've had a terrible lot of fun in my time. About as much, I guess, as one man is entitled to, but you've got all your life before you."

"Couldn't think of it," said Ned lightly; "besides, I've got a password in case I'm taken by Santa Anna."

"What's that?" asked Crockett curiously.

"It's the single word 'Roylston.' Mr. Roylston told me if I were taken by Santa Anna to mention his name to him."

"That's queer, an' then maybe it ain't," said Crockett musingly. "I've heard a lot of John Roylston. He's about the biggest trader in the southwest. I guess he must have some sort of a financial hold on Santa Anna, who is always wantin' money. Ned, if the time should ever come, don't you forget to use that password."

The next night was dark and chilly with gusts of rain. In the afternoon the Mexican cannonade waned, and at night it ceased entirely. The Alamo itself, except for a few small lights within the buildings, was kept entirely dark in order that skulking sharpshooters without might not find a target.

Ned was on watch near one of the lower walls about the *plaza*. He wrapped his useful *serape* closely about his body and the lower part of his face in order to protect himself from the cold and wet, and the broad brim of his sombrero was drawn down to meet it. The other Texans on guard were protected in similar fashion, and in the flitting glimpses that Ned caught of them they looked to him like men in disguise.

The time went on very slowly. In the look backward every hour in the Alamo seemed to him as ten. He walked back and forth a long time, occasionally meeting other sentinels, and exchanging a few words with them. Once he glanced at their cattle, which were packed closely under a rough shed, where they lay, groaning with content. Then he went back to the wall and noticed the dim figure of one of

382

the sentinels going toward the convent yard and the church.

Ned took only a single glance at the man, but he rather envied him. The man was going off duty early, and he would soon be asleep in a warm place under a roof. He did not think of him again until a full hour later, when he, too, going off duty, saw a figure hidden in *serape* and *sombrero* passing along the inner edge of the *plaza*. The walk and figure reminded him of the man whom he had seen an hour before, and he wondered why any one who could have been asleep under shelter should have returned to the cold and rain.

He decided to follow, but the figure flitted away before him down the *plaza* and toward the lowest part of the wall. This was doubly curious. Moreover, it was ground for great suspicion. Ned followed swiftly. He saw the figure mounting the wall, as if to take position there as a sentinel, and then the truth came to him in a flash. It was Urrea playing the congenial role of spy.

Ned rushed forward, shouting. Urrea turned, snatched a pistol and fired. The bullet whistled past Ned's head. The next moment Urrea dropped over the wall and fled away in the darkness. The other sentinels were not able to obtain a shot at him.

CHAPTER 11

THE DESPERATE DEFENCE

Ned's report created some alarm among the defenders of the Alamo, but it passed quickly.

"I don't see just how it can help 'em," said Crockett. "He's found out that we're few in number. They already knew that. He's learned that the Alamo is made up of a church an' other buildings with walls 'roun' them. They already knew that, too, an' so here we all are, Texans an' Mexicans, just where we stood before."

Nevertheless, the bombardment rose to a fiercer pitch of intensity the next day. The Mexicans seemed to have an unlimited supply of ammunition, and they rained balls and shells on the Alamo. Many of the shells did not burst, and the damage done was small. The Texans did not reply from the shelter of their walls for a long time. At last the Mexicans came closer, emboldened perhaps by the thought that resistance was crushed, and then the Texan sharpshooters opened fire with their long-barrelled rifles.

The Texans had two or three rifles apiece, and they poured in a fast and deadly fire. So many of the Mexicans fell that the remainder retreated with speed, leaving the fallen behind them. But when the smoke lifted others came forward under a white flag, and the Texans allowed them to take away their dead.

The cannonade now became spasmodic. All the Mexican cannon would fire continuously for a half hour or so, and then would ensue a silence of perhaps an hour.

In the afternoon Bowie was taken very ill, owing to his great exertions, and a bed was made for him in the hospital. Ned sat there with him a while. The gentle mood that had distinguished the Georgian throughout the siege was even more marked now.

"Ned," he said, "you ought to have gone out the other night when we wanted you to go. Fannin may come to our help or he may not, but even if he should come I don't think his force is sufficient. It would merely increase the number of Texans in the trap."

"I've quite made up my mind that I won't go," said Ned.

"I'm sorry," said Bowie. "As for me, it's different. I'm a man of violence, Ned. I don't deny it. There's human blood on my hands, and some of it is that of my own countrymen. I've done things that I'd like to call back, and so I'm glad to be here, one of a forlorn hope, fighting for Texas. It's a sort of atonement, and if I fall I think it will be remembered in my favour."

Ned was singularly impressed. Crockett had talked in much the same way. Could these men, heroes of a thousand dangers, have really given up? Not to give up in the sense of surrender, but to expect death fighting? But for himself he could not believe such a thing possible. Youth was too strong in him.

He was on the watch again for part of the next night, and he and Crockett were together. They heard sounds made by the besiegers on every side of them. Mexicans were calling to Mexicans. Bridle bits rattled, and metal clanked against metal.

"I suppose the circle is complete," said Ned.

"Looks like it," said Crockett, "but we've got our cattle to eat an' water to drink an' only a direct attack in force can take us. They can bang away with their cannon till next Christmas an' they won't shake our grip on the Alamo."

The night was fairly dark, and an hour later Ned heard a whistle. Crockett heard it, too, and stiffened instantly into attention.

"Did that sound to you like a Mexican whistling?" he asked.

"No, I'd say it came from American lips, and I'd take it also for a signal."

"An' so it is. It's just such a whistle as hunters use when they want to talk to one another without words. I've whistled to my pardners that way in the woods hundreds of times. I think, Ned, that some Texans are at hand waitin' a chance to slip in."

Crockett emitted a whistle, low but clear and penetrating, almost like the song of a night bird, and in a half minute came the rejoinder. He replied to it briefly, and then they waited. Others had gathered at the low *plaza* wall with them. Hidden to the eyes, they peered over the parapet.

They heard soft footsteps in the darkness, and then dim forms emerged. Despite the darkness they knew them to be Texans, and Crockett spoke low:

"Here we are, boys, waitin' for you! This way an' in a half minute you're in the Alamo!"

The men ran forward, scaled the wall and were quickly inside. They were only thirty-two. Ned had thought that the Panther, Obed, and Will Allen might be among them, but they were not there. The new men were shaking hands with the others and were explaining that they had come from Gonzales with Captain Smith at their head. They were all well armed, carried much ammunition, and were sure that other parties would arrive from different points.

The thirty-two were full of rejoicings over their successful entry, but they were worn, nevertheless, and they were taken into one of the buildings, where food and water were set before them. Ned stood by, an eager auditor, as they told of their adventures.

"We had a hard time to get in here to you," said Captain Smith, "and from the looks of things I reckon we'll have as hard a time to get out. There must be a million Mexicans around the Alamo. We tried to get up a bigger force, but we couldn't gather any more without waiting, and we thought if you needed us at all you needed us in a hurry."

"Reckon you're right about the need of bein' in a hurry," said Crockett. "When you want help you want it right then an' there."

"So you do," said Smith, as he took a fresh piece of steak, "and we had it in mind all the time. The wind was blowing our way, and in the afternoon we heard the roaring of cannon a long distance off. Then as we came closer we heard Mexicans buzzing all around the main swarm, scouts and skirmishers everywhere.

"We hid in an *arroyo* and waited until dark. Then we rode closer and found that there would never be any chance to get into the Alamo on horseback. We took the saddles and bridles off our horses, and turned them loose on the prairie. Then we undertook to get in here, but it was touch and go. I tell you it was touch and go. We wheeled and twisted and curved and doubled, until our heads got dizzy. Wherever we went we found Mexicans, thousands of 'em."

"We've noticed a few ourselves," said Crockett.

"It was pretty late when we struck an opening, and then not being sure we whistled. When we heard you whistle back we made straight for the wall, and here we are."

"We're mighty glad to see you," said Crockett, "but we ain't welcomin' you to no picnic, I reckon you understand that, don't you, Jim Smith?"

"We understand it, every one of us," replied Smith gravely. "We heard before we started, and now we've seen. We know that Santa Anna himself is out there, and that the Mexicans have got a big army. That's the reason we came, Davy Crockett, because the odds are so heavy against you."

"You're a true man," said Crockett, "and so is every one of these with you."

The new force was small—merely a few more for the trap—but they brought with them encouragement. Ned shared in the general mental uplift. These new faces were very welcome, indeed. They gave fresh vigour to the little garrison, and they brought news of that outside world from which he seemed to have been shut off so long. They told of numerous parties sure to come to their relief, but he soon noticed that they did not particularize. He felt with certainty that the Alamo now had all the defenders that it would ever have.

Repeated examinations from the walls of the church confirmed Ned in his belief. The Mexican circle was complete, and their sheltered batteries were so near that they dropped balls and shells whenever they pleased inside the Alamo. Duels between the cannon and the Texan sharpshooters were frequent. The gunners as they worked their guns were forced to show themselves at times, and every exposure was instantly the signal for a Texan bullet which rarely missed. But the Mexicans kept on. It seemed that they intended to wear out the defenders by the sheer persistency of their cannon fire.

Ned became so hardened to the bombardment that he paid little attention to it. Even when a ball fell inside the Alamo the chances were several hundred to one that it would not hit him. He had amused himself with a mathematical calculation of the amount of space he occupied compared with the amount of space in the Alamo. Thus he arrived at the result, which indicated comparatively little risk for himself.

The shrewdest calculations are often wrong. As he passed through the convent yard he met Crockett, and the two walked on together. But before they had gone half a dozen steps a bomb hissed through the air, fell and rolled to their feet. It was still hissing and smoking, but Ned, driven by some unknown impulse, seized it and with a mighty effort hurled it over the wall, where it burst. Then he stood licking his burned fingers and looking rather confusedly at Crockett. He felt a certain shyness over what he had done.

The veteran frontiersman had already formed a great affection for the boy. He knew that Ned's impulse had come from a brave heart and a quick mind, and that he had probably saved both their lives. He took a great resolution that this boy, the youngest of all the defenders, should be saved.

"That was done well, Ned," he said quietly. "I'm glad, boy, that I've known you. I'd be proud if you were a son of mine. We can talk plainly here with death all around us. You've got a lot in that head of yours. You ought to make a great man, a great man for Texas. Won't you do what I say and slip out of the Alamo while there's still a chance?"

Ned was much moved, but he kept his resolution as he had kept it before. He shook his head.

"You are all very good to me here," he said. "Mr. Bowie, too, has asked me to go, but if I should do so and the rest of you were to fall I'd be ashamed of myself all the rest of my life. I'm a Texan now, and I'm going to see it through with the rest of you."

"All right," said Crockett lightly. "I've heard that you can lead a horse to the water, but you can't make him drink, an' if a boy don't want to go you can't make him go. So we'll just go into this little improvised armoury of ours, an' you an' I will put in our time mouldin' bullets."

They entered one of the *adobe* buildings. A fire had been built on the hearth, and a half dozen Texans were already busy there. But they quickly made room for Crockett and Ned. Crockett did not tell Ned that their supplies of powder and lead were running low, and that they must reduce their fire from the walls in order that they might have sufficient to meet an attack in force.

But it was a cheerful little party that occupied itself with moulding bullets. Ned put a bar of lead into a ladle, and held it over the fire until the bar became molten. Then he poured it into the mould until it was full, closed it, and when he opened it again a shining bullet dropped out. He worked hour after hour. His face became flushed with the heat, but with pride he watched his heap of bullets grow.

Crockett at last said they had done enough for one day, and Ned was glad when they went outside and breathed the fresh air again. There was no firing at that time, and they climbed once more upon the church wall. Ned looked out upon the scene, every detail of which was so familiar to him now. But conspicuous, and seeming to dominate all, was the blood-red flag of no quarter floating from the tower of the church of San Fernando. Wind and rain had not dimmed its bright colour. The menace in its most vivid hue was always there.

Travis, who was further along the wall with a pair of strong field glasses, came back and joined Ned and Crockett.

"If you would like to see Santa Anna you can," he said to Ned. "He is on the church of San Fernando now with his generals looking at us. Take these glasses and your gaze may meet his."

Ned took the glasses, and there was Santa Anna standing directly under the folds of the banner with his own glasses to his eyes, studying the Alamo and its defenders. About him stood a half dozen generals. Ned's heart swelled with anger. The charm and genius of Santa Anna made him all the more repellent now. Ned knew that he would break any promise if it suited him, and that cunning and treachery were his most potent tools.

Santa Anna, at that very moment, was discussing with Sesma, Cos, Gaona and others the question of an immediate assault with his whole army upon the Alamo. They had heard rumors of an advance by Fannin with help for the Texans, but, while some of the younger spirits wished prompt attack, Santa Anna decided on delay.

The dictator doubted whether Fannin would come up, and if he did he would merely put so many more rats in the trap. Santa Anna felt secure in his vast preponderance of numbers. He would take the Texans in his own good time, that is, whenever he felt like it. He did not care to hurry, because he was enjoying himself greatly in San Antonio. Capable of tremendous energy at times, he gave himself up at other times to Babylonian revels.

Ned handed the glasses to Crockett, who also took a long look. "I've heard a lot of Santa Anna," he said, "an' maybe I'll yet meet him eye to eye."

"It's possible," said Travis, "but, Davy, we've got to wait on the

Mexicans. It's always for them to make the move, and then we'll meet it if we can. I wish we could hear from Bonham. I'm afraid he's been taken."

"Not likely," said Crockett. "One man, all alone, an' as quick of eye an' foot as Bonham, would be pretty sure to make his way safely."

"I certainly hope so," said Travis. "At any rate, I intend to send out another letter soon. If the Texans are made to realise our situation they will surely come, no matter how far away they may be."

"I hope they will," said Crockett. But Ned noticed that he did not seem to speak with any great amount of confidence. Balancing everything as well as he could, he did not see how much help could be expected. The Texan towns were tiny. The whole fringe of Texan settlements was small. The Texans were but fifty or sixty thousands against the seven or eight millions of Mexico, and now that they knew a great Mexican army was in Texas the scattered borderers would be hard put to it to defend themselves. He did not believe that in any event they could gather a force great enough to cut its way through the coil of Santa Anna's multitude.

But Travis' faith in Bonham, at least, was justified. The next night, about halfway between midnight and morning, in the darkest hour, a man scaled the wall and dropped inside the *plaza*. It proved to be Bonham himself, pale, worn, covered with mud and dust, but bringing glad tidings. Ned was present when he came into the church and was met by Travis. Bowie, Crockett and Smith. Only a single torch lighted up the grim little group.

"Fannin has left Goliad with 300 men and four cannon to join us," Bonham said. "He started five days ago, and he should be here soon. With his rifles and big guns he'll be able to cut his way through the Mexicans and enter the Alamo."

"I think so, too," said Travis, with enthusiasm.

But Ned steadily watched Bowie and Crockett. They were the men of experience, and in matters such as these they had minds of uncommon penetration. He noticed that neither of them said anything, and that they showed no elation.

Everybody in the Alamo knew the next day that Bonham had come from Fannin, and the whole place was filled with new hope. As Ned reckoned, it was about one hundred and fifty miles from San Antonio de Bexar to Goliad; but, according to Bonham, Fannin had already been five days on the way, and they should hear soon the welcome thunder of his guns. He eagerly scanned the southeast, in which direction lay Goliad, but the only human beings he saw were Mexicans. No sound came to his ears but the note of a Mexican trumpet or the crack of a *vaquero's* whip.

He was not the only one who looked and listened. They watched that day and the next through all the bombardment and the more dangerous rifle fire. But they never saw on the horizon the welcome flash from any of Fannin's guns. No sound that was made by a friend reached their ears. The only flashes of fire they saw outside were those that came from the mouths of Mexican cannon, and the only sounds they heard beyond the Alamo were made by the foe. The sun, huge, red and vivid, sank in the prairie and, as the shadows thickened over the Alamo, Ned was sure in his heart that Fannin would never come.

★★★★★★

A few days before the defenders of the Alamo had begun to scan the southeast for help a body of 300 men were marching toward San Antonio de Bexar. They were clad in buckskin and they were on horseback. Their faces were tanned and bore all the signs of hardship. Near the middle of the column four cannon drawn by oxen rumbled along, and behind them came a heavy wagon loaded with ammunition.

It was raining, and the rain was the raw cold rain of early spring in the southwest. The men, protecting themselves as well as they could with cloaks and *serapes*, rarely spoke. The wheels of the cannon cut great ruts in the prairie, and the feet of the horses sank deep in the mud.

Two men and a boy rode near the head of the column. One of these would have attracted attention anywhere by his gigantic size. He was dressed completely in buckskin, save for the raccoon skin cap that crowned his thick black hair. The rider on his right hand was long and thin with the calm countenance of a philosopher, and the one on his left was an eager and impatient boy.

"I wish this rain would stop," said the Panther, his ensanguined eye expressing impatience and anger. "I don't mind gettin' cold an' I don't mind gettin' wet, but there is nothin' stickier or harder to plough through than the Texas mud. An' every minute counts. Them boys in that Alamo can't fight off thousands of Mexicans forever. Look at them steers! Did you ever see anything go as slow as they do?"

"I'd like to see Ned again," said Will Allen. "I'd be willing to take my chance with him there."

"That boy of ours is surely with Crockett and Bowie and Travis

390

and the others, helping to fight off Santa Anna and his horde," said Obed White. "Bonham couldn't have made any mistake about him. If we had seen Bonham himself we could have gone with him to the Alamo."

"But he gave Ned's name to Colonel Fannin," said Will, "and so it's sure to be he."

"Our comrade is certainly there," said Obed White, "and we've got to help rescue him as well as help rescue the others. It's hard not to hurry on by ourselves, but we can be of most help by trying to push on this force, although it seems as if everything had conspired against us."

"It shorely looks as if things was tryin' to keep us back," exclaimed the Panther angrily. "We've had such a hard time gettin' these men together, an' look at this rain an' this mud! We ought to be at Bexar right now, a-roarin', an' a-t'arin', an' a-rippin', an' a-chawin' among them Mexicans!"

"Patience! Patience!" said Obed White soothingly. "Sometimes the more haste the oftener you trip."

"Patience on our part ain't much good to men sixty or eighty miles away, who need us yellin' an' shootin' for them this very minute."

"I'm bound to own that what you say is so," said Obed White.

They relapsed into silence. The pace of the column grew slower. The men were compelled to adapt themselves to the cannon and ammunition wagon, which were now almost mired. The face of the Panther grew black as thunder with impatience and anger, but he forced himself into silence.

They stopped a little while at noon and scanty rations were doled out. They had started in such haste that they had only a little rice and dried beef, and there was no time to hunt game.

They started again in a half hour, creeping along through the mud, and the Panther was not the only man who uttered hot words of impatience under his breath. They were nearing the San Antonio River now, and Fannin began to show anxiety about the fort. But the Panther was watching the ammunition wagon, which was sinking deeper and deeper into the mire. It seemed to him that it was groaning and creaking too much even for the deep mud through which it was passing.

The driver of the ammunition wagon cracked his long whip over the oxen and they tugged at the yoke. The wheels were now down to the hub, and the wagon ceased to move. The driver cracked his whip again and again, and the oxen threw their full weight into the effort. The wheels slowly rose from their sticky bed, but then something cracked with a report like a pistol shot. The Panther groaned aloud, because he knew what had happened.

The axle of the wagon had broken, and it was useless. They distributed the ammunition, including the cannon balls, which they put in sacks, as well as they could, among the horsemen, and went on. They did not complain, but every one knew that it was a heavy blow. In two more hours they came to the banks of the muddy San Antonio, and stared in dismay at the swollen current. It was evident at once to everybody that the passage would be most difficult for the cannon, which, like the ammunition wagon, were drawn by oxen.

The river was running deep, with muddy banks, and a muddy bottom, and, taking the lightest of the guns, they tried first to get it across. Many of the men waded neck deep into the water and strove at the wheels. But the stream went completely over the cannon, which also sank deeper and deeper in the oozy bottom. It then became an effort to save the gun. The Panther put all his strength at the wheel, and, a dozen others helping, they at last got it back to the bank from which they had started.

Fannin, not a man of great decision, looked deeply discouraged, but the Panther and others urged him on to new attempts. The Panther, himself, as he talked, bore the aspect of a huge river god. Yellow water streamed from his hair, beard, and clothing, and formed a little pool about him. But he noticed it not at all, urging the men on with all the fiery energy which a dauntless mind had stored in a frame so great and capable.

"If it can be done the Panther will get the guns across," said Will to Obed.

"That's so," said Obed, "but who'd have thought of this? When we started out we expected to have our big fight with an army and not with a river."

They took the cannon into the water a second time, but the result was the same. They could not get it across, and with infinite exertion they dragged it back to the bank. Then they looked at one another in despair. They could ford the river, but it seemed madness to go on without the cannon. While they debated there, a messenger came with news that the investment of the Alamo by Santa Anna was now complete. He gave what rumor said, and rumor told that the Mexican army numbered ten or twelve thousand men with fifty or sixty guns.

Santa Anna's force was so great that already he was sending off large bodies to the eastward to attack Texan detachments wherever they could be found.

Fannin held an anxious council with his officers. It was an open talk on the open prairie, and anybody who chose could listen. Will Allen and Obed White said nothing, but the Panther was vehement.

"We've got to get there!" he exclaimed. "We can't leave our people to die in the Alamo! We've got to cut our way through, an', if the worst comes to the worst, die with them!"

"That would benefit nobody," said Fannin. "We've made every human effort to get our cannon across the river, and we have failed. It would not profit Texas for us to ride on with our rifles merely to be slaughtered. There will be other battles and other sieges, and we shall be needed."

"Does that mean we're not goin' on?" asked the Panther.

"We can't go on."

Fannin waved his hand at the yellow and swollen river.

"We must return to Goliad," he said, "I have decided. Besides, there is nothing else for us to do. About face, men, and take up the march."

The men turned slowly and reluctantly, and the cannon began to plough the mud on the road to Goliad, from which they had come.

The Panther had remounted, and he drew to one side with Will and Obed, who were also on their horses. His face was glowing with anger. Never had he looked more tremendous as he sat on his horse, with the water still flowing from him.

"Colonel Fannin," he called out, "you can go back to Goliad, but as for me an' my pardners, Obed White an' Will Allen, we're goin' to Bexar, an' the Alamo."

"I have no control over you," said Fannin, "but it would be much better for you three to keep with us."

"No," said the Panther firmly. "We hear the Alamo callin'. Into the river, boys, but keep your weapons an' ammunition dry."

Their horses, urged into the water, swam to the other bank, and, without looking back the three rode for San Antonio de Bexar.

★★★★★★

While the Panther, Obed White and Will Allen were riding over the prairie, Ned Fulton sat once more with his friend. Davy Crockett, in one of the *adobe* buildings. Night had come, and they heard outside the fitful crackle of rifle fire, but they paid no attention to it. Travis, at a table with a small tallow candle at his elbow, was writing his last

393

message.

Ned was watching the commander as he wrote. But he saw no expression of despair or even discouragement on Travis' fine face. The letter, which a messenger succeeded in carrying through the lines that night, breathed a noble and lofty courage. He was telling again how few were his men, and how the balls and bombs had rained almost continuously for days upon the Alamo. Even as his pen was poised they heard the heavy thud of a cannon, but the pen descended steadily and he wrote:

I shall continue to hold it until I get relief from my countrymen, or perish in its defence.

He wrote on a little longer and once more came the heavy thud of a great gun. Then the pen wrote:

Again I feel confident that the determined spirit and desperate courage heretofore exhibited by my men will not fail them in the last struggle, and, although they may be sacrificed to the vengeance of a Gothic enemy, the victory will cost that enemy so dear that it will be worse than a defeat.

"*Worse than a defeat!*" Travis never knew how significant were the words that he penned then. A minute or two later the sharp crack of a half dozen rifles came to them, and Travis wrote:

A blood-red flag waves from the church of Bexar and in the camp above us, in token that the war is one of vengeance against rebels.

They heard the third heavy thud of a cannon, and a shell, falling in the court outside, burst with a great crash. Ned went out and returned with a report of no damage. Travis had continued his letter, and now he wrote:

These threats have no influence upon my men, but to make all fight with desperation, and with that high-souled courage which characterizes the patriot who is willing to die in defence of his country, liberty and his own honour, God and Texas.
Victory or death.

He closed the letter and addressed it. An hour later the messenger was beyond the Mexican lines with it, but Travis sat for a long time at the table, unmoving and silent. Perhaps he was blaming himself for not having been more watchful, for not having discovered the advance of Santa Anna. But he was neither a soldier nor a frontiersman, and since the retreat into the Alamo he had done all that man could do.

He rose at last and went out. Then Crockett said to Ned, knowing that it was now time to speak the full truth:

"He has given up all hope of help."

"So have I," said Ned.

"But we can still fight," said Crockett.

The day that followed was always like a dream to Ned, vivid in some ways, and vague in others. He felt that the coil around the Alamo had tightened. Neither he nor any one else expected aid now, and they spoke of it freely one to another. Several who could obtain paper wrote, as Ned had done, brief wills, which they put in the inside pockets of their coats. Always they spoke very gently to one another, these wild spirits of the border. The strange and softening shadow which Ned had noticed before was deepening over them all.

Bowie was again in the hospital, having been bruised severely in a fall from one of the walls, but his spirit was as dauntless as ever.

"The assault by the Mexicans in full force cannot be delayed much longer," he said to Ned. "Santa Anna is impatient and energetic, and he surely has brought up all his forces by this time."

"Do you think we can beat them off?" asked Ned.

Bowie hesitated a little, and then he replied frankly:

"I do not. We have only one hundred and seventy or eighty men to guard the great space that we have here. But in falling we will light such a flame that it will never go out until Texas is free."

Ned talked with him a little longer, and always Bowie spoke as if the time were at hand when he should die for Texas. The man of wild and desperate life seemed at this moment to be clothed about with the mantle of the seer.

The Mexican batteries fired very little that day, and Santa Anna's soldiers kept well out of range. They had learned a deep and lasting respect for the Texan rifles. Hundreds had fallen already before them, and now they kept under cover.

The silence seemed ominous and brooding to Ned. The day was bright, and the flag of no quarter burned a spot of blood-red against the blue sky. Ned saw Mexican officers occasionally on the roofs of the higher buildings, but he took little notice of them. He felt instinctively that the supreme crisis had not yet come. They were all waiting, waiting.

The afternoon drew its slow length away in almost dead silence, and the night came on rather blacker than usual. Then the word was passed for all to assemble in the courtyard. They gathered there, Bowie dragging his sick body with the rest. Every defender of the Alamo was present. The cannon and the walls were for a moment deserted, but the Mexicans without did not know it.

There are ineffaceable scenes in the life of every one, scenes which, after the lapse of many years, are as vivid as of yesterday. Such, the last meeting of the Texans, always remained in the mind of Ned. They stood in a group, strong, wiry men, but worn now by the eternal vigilance and danger of the siege. One man held a small torch, which cast but a dim light over the brown faces.

Travis stood before them and spoke to them.

"Men," he said, "all of you know what I know, that we stand alone. No help is coming for us. The Texans cannot send it or it would have come. For ten days we have beaten off every attack of a large army. But another assault in much greater force is at hand. It is not likely that we can repel it. You have seen the red flag of no quarter flying day after day over the church, and you know what it means. Santa Anna never gives mercy. It is likely that we shall all fall, but, if any man wishes to go, I, your leader, do not order him to stay. You have all done your duty ten times over. There is just a chance to escape over the walls and in the darkness. Now go and save your lives if you can."

"We stay," came the deep rumble of many voices together. One man slipped quietly away a little later, but he was the only one. Save for him, there was no thought of flight in the minds of that heroic band.

Ned's heart thrilled and the blood pounded in his ears. Life was precious, doubly so, because he was so young, but he felt a strange exaltation in the face of death, an exaltation that left no room for fear.

The eyes of Travis glistened when he heard the reply.

"It is what I expected," he said. "I knew that every one of you was willing to die for Texas. Now, lads, we will go back to the walls and wait for Santa Anna."

CHAPTER 12

BEFORE THE DICTATOR

Ned's feeling of exaltation lasted. The long siege, the incessant danger and excitement, and the wonderful way in which the little band of Texans had kept a whole army at bay had keyed him up to a pitch in which he was not himself, in which he was something a little more than human. Such extraordinary moments come to few people, and his vivid, imaginative mind was thrilled to the utmost.

He was on the early watch, and he mounted the wall of the church. The deep silence which marked the beginning of the night still prevailed. They had not heard any shots, and for that reason they all felt that the messenger had got through with Travis' last letter.

It was very dark that night and Ned could not see the red flag on the tower of the church of San Fernando. But he knew it was there, waving a little in the soft wind which blew out of the southwest, herald of spring. Nothing broke the silence. After so much noise, it was ominous, oppressive, surcharged with threats. Fewer lights than usual burned in the town and in the Mexican camp. All this stillness portended to Ned the coming storm, and he was right.

His was a short watch, and at 11 o'clock he went off duty. It was silent and dark in the convent yard, and he sought his usual place for sleep in the hospital, where many of the Texans had been compelled to go, not merely to sleep, but because they were really ill, worn out by so many alarms, so much fighting and so much watching. But they were all now asleep, overpowered by exhaustion. Ned crept into his own dark little corner, and he, too, was soon asleep.

But he was awakened about four hours later by some one pulling hard at his shoulder. He opened his eyes, and stared sleepily. It was Crockett bending over him, and, Bowie lying on his sick bed ten feet away, had raised himself on his elbow. The light was so faint that Ned could scarcely see Crockett's face, but it looked very tense and eager.

"Get up, Ned! Get up!" said Crockett, shaking him again. "There's great work for you to do!"

"Why, what is it?" exclaimed the boy, springing to his feet.

"It's your friends, Roylston, an' that man, the Panther, you've been tellin' me about," replied Crockett in quick tones. "While you were asleep a Mexican, friendly to us, sneaked a message over the wall, sayin' that Roylston, the Panther, an' others were layin' to the east with a big force not more'n twenty miles away—not Fannin's crowd, but another one that's come down from the north. They don't know whether we're holdin' out yet or not, an' o' course they don't want to risk destruction by tryin' to cut through the Mexican army to reach us when we ain't here. The Mexican dassent go out of San Antonio. He won't try it, 'cause, as he says, it's sure death for him, an' so somebody must go to Roylston with the news that we're still alive, fightin' an' kickin'. Colonel Travis has chose you, an' you've got to go. No, there's no letter. You're just to tell Roylston by word of mouth to come on with his men."

The words came forth popping like pistol shots. Ned was swept off his feet. He did not have time to argue or ask questions. Bowie also added a fresh impetus. "Go, Ned, go at once!" he said. "You are chosen for a great service. It's an honor to anybody!"

"A service of great danger, requirin' great skill," said Crockett, "but you can do it, Ned, you can do it."

Ned flushed. This was, in truth, a great trust. He might, indeed, bring the help they needed so sorely.

"Here's your rifle an' other weapons an' ammunition," said Crockett. "The night's at its darkest an' you ain't got any time to waste. Come on!"

So swift was Crockett that Ned was ready almost before he knew it. The Tennessean never ceased hurrying him. But as he started, Bowie called to him:

"Goodbye, Ned!"

The boy turned back and offered his hand. The Georgian shook it with unusual warmth, and then lay back calmly on his blankets.

"Goodbye, Ned," he repeated, "and if we don't meet again I hope you'll forget the dark things in my life, and remember me as one who was doing his best for Texas."

"But we will meet again," said Ned. "The relieving force will be here in two or three days and I'll come with it."

"Out with you!" said Crockett. "That's talk enough. What you want to do now is to put on your invisible cap an' your seven league boots an' go like lightnin' through the Mexican camp. Remember that you can talk their lingo like a native, an' don't forget, neither, to keep always about you a great big piece of presence of mind that you can use on a moment's notice."

Ned wore his *serape* and he carried a pair of small, light but very warm blankets, strapped in a pack on his back. His haversack contained bread and dried beef, and, with his smaller weapons in his belt, and his rifle over his shoulder, he was equipped fully for a long and dangerous journey.

Crockett and the boy passed into the convent yard.

The soft wind from the southwest blew upon their faces, and from the high wall of the church a sentinel called: "All's well!" Ned felt an extraordinary shiver, a premonition, but it passed, unexplained. He and Crockett went into the main *plaza* and reached the lowest part of the wall.

"Ought I to see Colonel Travis?" asked Ned, as they were on the way.

"No, he asked me to see to it, 'cause there ain't no time to waste. It's about three o'clock in the mornin' now, an' you've got to slip through in two or three hours, 'cause the light will be showin' then. Now, Ned, up with you an' over."

Ned climbed to the summit of the wall. Beyond lay heavy darkness, and he neither saw nor heard any human being. He looked back, and extended his hand to Crockett as he had to Bowie.

"Goodbye, Mr. Crockett," he said, "you've been very good to me."

The great brown hand of the frontiersman clasped his almost convulsively.

"Aye, Ned," he said, "we've cottoned to each other from the first. I haven't knowed you long, but you've been like a son to me. Now go, an' God speed you!"

Ned recalled afterward that he did not say anything about Roylston's relieving force. What he thought of then was the deep feeling in Crockett's words.

"I'm coming back," he said, "and I hope to hunt buffalo with you over the plains of a free Texas."

"Go! go! Hurry, Ned!" said Crockett.

"Goodbye," said Ned, and he dropped lightly to the ground.

He was outside the Alamo after eleven days inside, that seemed in the retrospect almost as many months. He flattened himself against the wall, and stood there for a minute or two, looking and listening. He thought he might hear Crockett again inside, but evidently the Tennessean had gone back at once. In front of him was only the darkness, pierced by a single light off toward the west.

Ned hesitated. It was hard for him to leave the Alamo and the friends who had been knitted to him by so many common dangers, yet his errand was one of high importance—it might save them all— and he must do it. Strengthening his resolution he started across an open space, walking lightly. As Crockett had truly said, with his perfect knowledge of the language he might pass for a Mexican. He had done so before, and he did not doubt his ability to do so again.

He resolved to assume the character of a Mexican scout, looking into the secrets of the Alamo, and going back to report to Santa Anna.

As he advanced he heard voices and saw earthworks from which the muzzles of four cannon protruded. Behind the earthwork was a small fire, and he knew that men would be sitting about it. He turned aside, not wishing to come too much into the light, but a soldier near the earthwork hailed him, and Ned, according to his plan, replied briefly that he was on his way to General Santa Anna in San Antonio.

But the man was talkative.

"What is your name?" he asked.

"Pedro Miguel Alvarado," replied Ned on the spur of the moment.

"Well, friend, it is a noble name, that of Alvarado."

"But it is not a noble who bears it. Though a descendant of the great Alvarado, who fought by the side of the glorious and mighty *conquistador*, Hernando Cortez, I am but a poor peasant offering my life daily for bread in the army of General Santa Anna."

The man laughed.

"You are as well off as I am," he said. "But what of the wicked Texans? Are they yet ready to surrender their throats to our knives? The dogs hold us over long. It is said that they number scarce two hundred within the mission. Truly they fight hard, and well they may, knowing that death only is at the end."

Ned shuddered. The man seemed to take it all so lightly. But he replied in a firm voice:

"I learned little of them save that they still fight. I took care not to put myself before the muzzle of any of their rifles."

The Mexican laughed again.

"A lad of wisdom, you," he said. "They are demons with their rifles. When the great assault is made, many a good man will speed to his long home before the Alamo is taken."

So, they had already decided upon the assault. The premonition within the Alamo was not wrong. It occurred to Ned that he might learn more, and he paused.

"Has it been finally settled?" he asked. "We attack about three days from now, do we not?"

"Earlier than that," replied the Mexican. "I know that the time has been chosen, and I think it is tomorrow morning."

Ned's heart beat heavily. Tomorrow morning! Even if he got through, how could he ever bring Roylston and the relief force in time?

"I thank you," he said, "but I must hurry with my report."

"*Adios, Senor,*" said the man politely, and Ned repeated his "*Adios*" in the same tone. Then he hurried forward, continually turning in toward the east, hoping to find a passage where the Mexican line was thinnest. But the circle of the invaders was complete, and he saw that he must rely upon his impersonation of a Mexican to take him through.

He was in a fever of haste, knowing now that the great assault was to come so soon, and he made for a point between two smouldering camp fires fifty or sixty yards apart. Boldness only would now avail, and with the brim of his *sombrero* pulled well down over his face he walked confidently forward, coming fully within the light of the fire on his left.

A number of Mexican soldiers were asleep around the fire, but at least a half dozen men were awake. They called to Ned as he passed and he responded readily, but Fortune, which had been so kind to him for a long time, all at once turned her back upon him. When he spoke, a man in officer's uniform who had been sitting by the fire rose quickly.

"Your name?" he cried.

"Pedro Miguel Alvarado," replied Ned instantly. At the same moment he recognised Urrea.

"It is not so!" cried Urrea. "You are one of the Texans, young Fulton. I know your voice. Upon him, men! Seize him!"

His action and the leap of the Mexicans were so sudden that Ned did not have time to aim his rifle. But he struck one a short-arm blow with the butt of it that sent him down with a broken head, and he snatched at his pistol as three or four others threw themselves upon him. Ned was uncommonly strong and agile, and he threw off two of the men, but the others pressed him to the ground, until, at Urrea's command, his arms were bound and he was allowed to rise.

Ned was in despair, not so much for himself but because there was no longer a chance that he could get through to Roylston. It was a deep mortification, moreover, to be taken by Urrea. But he faced the Mexican with an appearance of calmness.

"Well," he said, "I am your prisoner."

"You are," said Urrea, "and you might have passed, if I had not known your voice. But I remind you that you come from the Alamo. You see our flag, and you know its meaning."

The black eyes of the Mexican regarded Ned malignantly. The boy knew that the soul of Urrea was full of wicked triumph. The officer could shoot him down at that moment, and be entirely within orders. But Ned recalled the words of Roylston. The merchant had told him to use his name if he should ever fall again into the hands of Santa Anna.

"I am your prisoner," he repeated, "and I demand to be taken before General Santa Anna. Whatever your red flag may mean, there are reasons why he will spare me. Go with me and you will see."

He spoke with such boldness and directness that Urrea was impressed.

"I shall take you to the general," he said, "not because you demand it, but because I think it well to do so. It is likely that he will want to examine you, and I believe that in his presence you will tell all you know. But it is not yet 4 o'clock in the morning, and I cannot awaken him now. You will stay here until after daylight."

"Very well," said Ned, trying to be calm as possible. "As you have bound me I cannot walk, but if you'll put me on a blanket there by the fire I'll sleep until you want me."

"We won't deny you that comfort," replied Urrea grimly.

When Ned was stretched on his blanket he was fairly easy so far as the body was concerned. They had bound him securely, but not painfully. His agony of mind, though, was great. Nevertheless he fell asleep, and slept in a restless way for three or four hours, until Urrea awoke him, and told him they were going to Santa Anna.

It was a clear, crisp dawn and Ned saw the town, the river, and the Alamo. There, only a short distance away, stood the dark fortress, from which he had slipped but a few hours before with such high hopes. He even saw the figures of the sentinels, moving slowly on the church walls, and his heart grew heavy within him. He wished now that he was back with the defenders. Even if he should escape it would be too late. At Urrea's orders he was unbound.

"There is no danger of your escaping now," said the young Mexican. "Several of my men are excellent marksmen, and they will fire at the first step you take in flight. And even should they miss, what chance do you think you have here?"

He swept his right hand in a circle, and, in the clear morning air, Ned saw batteries and troops everywhere. He knew that the circle of steel about the Alamo was complete. Perhaps he would have failed in his errand even had he got by. It would require an unusually strong force to cut through an army as large as that of Santa Anna, and he did not know where Roylston could have found it. He started, as a sudden suspicion smote him. He remembered Crockett's hurried manner, and his lack of explanation. But he put it aside. It could not be true.

"I see that you look at the Alamo," said Urrea ironically. "Well, the rebel flag is still there, but it will not remain much longer. The trap is about ready to shut down."

Ned's colour rose.

"It may be so," he said, "but for every Texan who falls the price will be five Mexicans."

"But they will fall, nevertheless," said Urrea. "Here is food for you. Eat, and I will take you to the general."

They offered him Mexican food, but he had no appetite, and he ate little. He stretched and tensed his limbs in order to restore the full flood of circulation, and announced that he was ready. Urrea led the way, and Ned followed with a guard of four men about him.

The boy had eyes and ears for everything around him, but he looked most toward the Alamo. He could not, at the distance, recognise the figures on the wall, but all those men were his friends, and his eyes filled with tears at their desperate case. Out here with the Mexicans, where he could see all their overwhelming force and their extensive preparations, the chances of the Texans looked worse than they did inside the Alamo.

They entered the town and passed through the same streets, along which Ned had advanced with the conquering army of the Texans a few months before. Many evidences of the siege remained. There were tunnels, wrecked houses and masses of stone and *adobe*. The appearance of the young prisoner aroused the greatest curiosity among both soldiers and people. He heard often the word "*Texano*." Women frequently looked down at him from the flat roofs, and some spoke in pity.

Ned was silent. He was resolved not to ask Urrea any questions or to give him a chance to show triumph. He noticed that they were advancing toward the *plaza*, and then they turned into the Veramendi house, which he had cause to remember so well.

"This was the home of the vice-governor," said Urrea, "and General Santa Anna is here."

"I know the place," said Ned. "I am proud to have been one of the Texans who took it on a former occasion."

"We lost it then, but we have it now and we'll keep it," said Urrea. "My men will wait with you here in the courtyard, and I'll see if our illustrious general is ready to receive you."

Ned waited patiently. Urrea was gone a full half hour, and, when he returned, he said:

"The general was at breakfast with his staff. He had not quite finished, but he is ready to receive you now."

Then Urrea led the way into the Veramendi house. Luxurious fittings had been put in, but many of the rents and scars from the old combat were yet visible. They entered the great dining room, and, once more, Ned stood face to face with the most glorious general, the most illustrious dictator, Don Antonio Lopez de Santa Anna. But Ned alone stood. The dictator sat at the head of the table, about which were Castrillon, Sesma, Cos, Gaona, the Italian, Filisola and others. It seemed to Ned that he had come not only upon a breakfast but upon a conference as well.

The soldiers who had guarded Ned stepped back, Urrea stood by the wall, and the boy was left to meet the fixed gaze of Santa Anna. The dictator wore a splendid uniform, as usual. His face seemed to Ned fuller and more flushed than when they had last met in Mexico. The marks of dissipation were there. Ned saw him slip a little silver box from the pocket of his waistcoat and take from it a pinch of a dark drug, which he ate. It was opium, but the Mexican generals seemed to take no note of it.

Santa Anna's gaze was fixed and piercing, as if he would shoot terror into the soul of his enemy—a favourite device of his—but Ned withstood it. Then Santa Anna, removing his stare from his face, looked him slowly up and down. The generals said nothing, waiting upon their leader, who could give life or death as he chose. Ned was sure that Santa Anna remembered him, and, in a moment, he knew that he was right.

"It is young Fulton, who made the daring and ingenious escape from our hospitality in the capital," he said, "and who also departed in an unexpected manner from one of the submarine dungeons of our castle of San Juan de Ulua. Fate does not seem to reward your courage and enterprise as they deserve, since you are in our hands again."

The dictator laughed and his generals laughed obediently also. Ned said nothing.

"I am informed by that most meritorious young officer, Captain Urrea," continued Santa Anna, "that you were captured about three o'clock this morning trying to escape from the Alamo."

"That is correct," said Ned.

"Why were you running away in the dark?"

404

Ned flushed, but, knowing that it was an unworthy and untruthful taunt, he remained silent.

"You do not choose to answer," said Santa Anna, "but I tell you that you are the rat fleeing from the sinking ship. Our cannon have wrecked the interior of the Alamo. Half of your men are dead, and the rest would gladly surrender if I should give them the promise of life."

"It is not true!" exclaimed Ned with heat. "Despite all your fire the defenders of the Alamo have lost but a few men. You offer no quarter and they ask none. They are ready to fight to the last."

There was a murmur among the generals, but Santa Anna raised his hand and they were silent again.

"I cannot believe all that you say," he continued. "It is a boast. The Texans are braggarts. Tomorrow they die, every one of them. But tell us the exact condition of everything inside the Alamo, and perhaps I may spare your life."

Ned shut his teeth so hard that they hurt. A deep flush surged into the dark face of Santa Anna.

"You are stubborn. All the Texans are stubborn. But I do not need any information from you. I shall crush the Alamo, as my fingers would smash an eggshell."

"But your fingers will be pierced deep," Ned could not keep from replying. "They will run blood."

"Be that as it may," said Santa Anna, who, great in some things, was little enough to taunt an enemy in his power, "you will not live to see it. I am about to give orders to have you shot within an hour."

His lips wrinkled away from his white teeth like those of a great cat about to spring, and his cruel eyes contracted. Holding all the power of Mexico in his hands he was indeed something to be dreaded. The generals about the table never spoke. But Ned remembered the words of Roylston.

"A great merchant named John Roylston has been a good friend to me," he said. "He told me that if I should ever fall into your hands I was to mention his name to you, and to say that he considered my life of value."

The expression of the dictator changed. He frowned, and then regarded Ned intently, as if he would read some secret that the boy was trying to hide.

"And so you know John Roylston," he said at length, "and he wishes you to say to me that your life is of value."

Ned saw the truth at once. He had a talisman and that talisman was the name of Roylston. He did not know why it was so, but it was a wonderful talisman nevertheless, because it was going to save his life for the time being, at least. He glanced at the generals, and he saw a look of curiosity on the face of every one of them.

"I know Roylston," said Santa Anna slowly, "and there are some matters between us. It may be to my advantage to spare you for a while."

Ned's heart sprang up. Life was sweet. Since he was to be spared for a while it must mean ultimately exchange or escape. Santa Anna, a reader of the human face, saw what was in his mind.

"Be not too sanguine," he said, "because I have changed my mind once it does not mean that you are to be free now or ever. I shall keep you here, and you shall see your comrades fall."

A sudden smile, offspring of a quick thought and satanic in its nature, passed over his face.

"I will make you a spectator of the defeat of the Texans," he said. "A great event needs a witness, and since you cannot be a combatant you can serve in that capacity. We attack at dawn tomorrow, and you shall miss nothing of it."

The wicked smile passed over his face again. It had occurred to Ned, a student of history, that the gladiatorial cruelty of the ancient Romans had descended to the Spaniards instead of the Italians. Now he was convinced that it was so.

"You shall be kept a prisoner in one of our strongest houses," said Santa Anna, "and Captain Urrea, whose vigilance prevented your escape, will keep guard over you. I fancy it is a task that he does not hate."

Santa Anna had also read the mind of the young Mexican. Urrea smiled. He liked this duty. He hated Ned and he, too, was not above taunting a prisoner. He advanced, and put a hand upon Ned's shoulder, but the boy shook it off.

"Don't touch me," said Ned. "I'll follow without resistance."

Santa Anna laughed.

"Let him have his way for the present, Captain Urrea," he said. "But remember that it is due to your gentleness and mercy. *Adios*, Senor Fulton, we meet again tomorrow morning, and if you survive I shall report to Mr. Roylston the manner in which you may bear yourself."

"Good-day," said Ned, resolved not to be outdone, even in ironical courtesy. "And now, Captain Urrea, if you will lead the way, I'll follow."

Urrea and his soldiers took Ned from the Veramendi house and across the street to a large and strong stone building.

"You are fortunate," said Urrea, "to have escaped immediate death. I do not know why the name of Roylston was so powerful with our general, but I saw that it was."

"It seemed to have its effect," said Ned.

Urrea led the way to the flat roof of the house, a space reached by a single narrow stairway.

"I shall leave you here with two guards," he said. "I shall give them instructions to fire upon you at the slightest attempt on your part to escape, but I fancy that you will have sense enough not to make any such attempt."

Urrea departed, but the two sentinels sat by the entrance to the stairway, musket in hand. He had not the faintest chance to get by them, and knowing it he sat down on the low stone coping of the roof. He wondered why Urrea had brought him there instead of locking him up in a room. Perhaps it was to mock him with the sight of freedom so near and yet unattainable.

His gaze turned instinctively to the Alamo like the magnet to the pole. There was the fortress, gray and grim in the sunshine, with the dim figures of the watchers on the walls. What were they doing inside now? How were Crockett and Bowie? His heart filled with grief that he had failed them. But had he failed them? Neither Urrea nor any other Mexican had spoken of the approach of a relieving force under Roylston. There was no sign that the Mexicans were sending any part of their army to meet it.

The heavy thud of a great gun drew his attention, and he saw the black smoke from the discharge rising over the plain. A second, a third and a fourth cannon shot were fired, but no answer came from the walls of the Alamo. At length he saw one of the men in the nearest battery to the Alamo expose himself above the earthwork. There was a flash from the wall of the church, a little puff of smoke, and Ned saw the man fall as only dead men fall. Perhaps it was Davy Crockett, the great marksman, who had fired that shot. He liked to think that it was so, and he rejoiced also at this certain evidence that the little garrison was as dauntless as ever. He watched the Alamo for nearly an hour, and he saw that the firing was desultory. Not more than a dozen cannon shots were fired during that time, and only three or four rifles replied from the Alamo. Toward noon the firing ceased entirely, and Ned knew that this was in very fact and truth the lull before the storm.

His attention wandered to his guards. They were mere *peons*, but, although watchful, they were taking their ease. Evidently they liked their task. They were resting with the complete relaxation of the body that only the Southern races know. Both had lighted *cigarritos*, and were puffing at them contentedly. It had been a long time since Ned had seen such a picture of lazy ease.

"You like it here?" he said to the nearest.

The man took the *cigarrito* from his mouth, emitted smoke from his nose and replied politely:

"It is better to be here lying in the sun than out there on the grass with a Texan bullet through one's body. Is it not so, Fernando?"

"Aye, it is so," replied his comrade. "I like not the Texan bullets. I am glad to be here where they cannot reach me. It is said that Satan sights their rifles for them, because they do not miss. They will die hard tomorrow. They will die like the bear in its den, fighting the hunters, when our army is poured upon them. That will be an end to all the Texans, and we will go back to the warm south."

"But are you sure," asked Ned, "that it will be an end of the Texans? Not all the Texans are shut up in the Alamo."

"What matters it?" replied Fernando, lightly. "It may be delayed, but the end will be the same. Nothing can resist the great, the powerful, the most illustrious Santa Anna. He is always able to dig graves for his enemies."

The men talked further. Ned gathered from them that the whole force of Santa Anna was now present. Some of his officers wanted him to wait for siege artillery of the heaviest calibre that would batter down the walls of the Alamo, but the dictator himself was impatient for the assault. It would certainly take place the next morning.

"And why is the young *senor* here?" asked Fernando. "The order has been issued that no Texan shall be spared, and do you not see the red flag waving there close by us?"

Ned looked up. The red flag now flaunted its folds very near to him. He could not repress a shiver.

"I am here," he replied, "because someone who has power has told General Santa Anna that I am not to be put to death."

"It is well for you, then," said Fernando, "that you have a friend of such weight. It is a pity to die when one is so young and so straight and strong as you. Ah, my young *senor*, the world is beautiful. Look how green is the grass there by the river, and how the sun lies like gold across it!"

Ned had noticed before the love of beauty that the humblest *peon* sometimes had, and there was a certain touch of brotherly feeling between him and this man, his jailer.

"The world is beautiful," said the boy, "and I am willing to tell you that I have no wish to leave it."

"Nor I," said Fernando. "Why are the Texans so foolish as to oppose the great Santa Anna, the most illustrious and powerful of all generals and rulers? Did they not know that he would come and crush them, every one?"

Ned did not reply. The *peon*, in repose at least, had a gentle heart, and the boy knew that Santa Anna was to him omnipotent and omniscient. He turned his attention anew to the Alamo, that magnet of his thoughts. It was standing quiet in the sun now. The defiant flag of the defenders, upon which they had embroidered the word "Texas," hung lazily from the staff.

The guards in the afternoon gave him some food and a jug of water, and they also ate and drank upon the roof. They were yet amply content with their task and their position there. No bullets could reach them. The sunshine was golden and pleasant. They had established friendly relations with the prisoner. He had not given them the slightest trouble, and, before and about them, was spread the theatre upon which a mighty drama was passing, all for them to see. What more could be asked by two simple peasants of small wants?

Ned was glad that they let him remain upon the roof. The Alamo drew his gaze with a power that he could not break if he would. Since he was no longer among the defenders he was eager to see every detail in the vast drama that was now unfolding.

But the afternoon passed in inaction. The sun was brilliant and toward evening turned to a deep, glowing red. It lighted up for the last time the dim figures that stood on the walls of the Alamo. Ned choked as he saw them there. He felt the premonition.

Urrea came upon the roof shortly before twilight. He was not sneering or ironical, and Ned, who had no wish to quarrel at such a time, was glad of it.

"As General Santa Anna told you," said Urrea, "the assault is to be made in overwhelming force early in the morning. It will succeed, of course. Nothing can prevent it. Through the man Roylston, you have some claim upon the general, but it may not be strong enough to save you long. A service now might make his pardon permanent."

"What do you mean by a service now?"

"A few words as to the weaker points of the Alamo, the best places for our troops to attack. You cannot do anything for the defenders. You cannot alter their fate in any particular, but you might do something for yourself."

Ned did not wish to appear dramatic. He merely turned his back upon the young Mexican.

"Very well," said Urrea, "I made you the offer. It was for you to accept it or not as you wish."

He left him upon the roof, and Ned saw the last rim of the red sun sink in the plain. He saw the twilight come, and the Alamo fade into a dim black bulk in the darkness. He thought once that he heard a cry of a sentinel from its walls, "All's well," but he knew that it was only fancy. The distance was far too great. Besides, all was not well.

When the darkness had fully come, he descended with his two benevolent jailers to a lower part of the house, where he was assigned to a small room, with a single barred window and without the possibility of escape. His guards, after bringing him food and water, gave him a polite good night and went outside. He knew that they would remain on watch in the hall.

Ned could eat and drink but little. Nor could he yet sleep. The night was far too heavy upon him for slumber. Besides, it had brought many noises, significant noises that he knew. He heard the rumble of cannon wheels over the rough pavements, and the shouts of men to the horses or mules. He heard troops passing, now infantry, and then cavalry, the hoofs of their horses grinding upon the stones.

He pressed his face against the barred window. He was eager to hear and yet more eager to see. He caught glimpses only of horse and foot as they passed, but he knew what all those sights and sounds portended. In the night the steel coil of the Mexicans was being drawn closer and closer about the Alamo.

Brave and resolute, he was only a boy after all. He felt deserted of all men. He wanted to be back there with Crockett and Bowie and Travis and the others. The water came into his eyes, and unconsciously he pulled hard at the iron bars.

He remained there a long time, listening to the sounds. Once he heard a trumpet, and its note in the night was singularly piercing. He knew that it was a signal, probably for the moving of a regiment still closer to the Alamo. But there were no shots from either the Mexicans or the mission. The night was clear with many stars.

410

After two or three hours at the window Ned tried to sleep. There was a narrow bed against the wall, and he lay upon it, full length, but he did not even close his eyes. He became so restless that at last he rose and went to the window again. It must have been then past midnight. The noises had ceased. Evidently the Mexicans had everything ready. The wind blew cold upon his face, but it brought him no news of what was passing without.

He went back to the bed, and by and by he sank into a heavy slumber.

CHAPTER 13

TO THE LAST MAN

Ned awoke after a feverish night, when there was yet but a strip of gray in the east. It was Sunday morning, but he had lost count of time, and did not know it. He had not undressed at all when he lay down, and now he stood by the window, seeking to see and hear. But the light was yet dim and the sounds were few. Nevertheless the great pulse in his throat began to leap. The attack was at hand.

The door of the room was unlocked and the two *peons* who had guarded him upon the roof came for him. Ned saw in the half gloom that they were very grave of countenance.

"We are to take you to the noble Captain Urrea, who is waiting for you," said Fernando.

"Very well," said Ned. "I am ready. You have been kind to me, and I hope that we shall meet again after today."

Both men shook their heads.

"We fear that is not to be," said Fernando.

They found Urrea and another young officer waiting at the door of the house. Urrea was in his best uniform and his eyes were very bright. He was no coward, and Ned knew that the gleam was in anticipation of the coming attack.

"The time is at hand," he said, "and it will be your wonderful fortune to see how Mexico strikes down her foe."

His voice, pitched high, showed excitement, and a sense of the dramatic. Ned said nothing, and his own pulses began to leap again. The strip of gray in the east was broadening, and he now saw that the whole town was awake, although it was not yet full daylight. Santa Anna had been at work in the night, while he lay in that feverish sleep. He heard everywhere now the sound of voices, the clank of arms and

411

the beat of horses' hoofs. The flat roofs were crowded with the Mexican people. Ned saw Mexican women there in their dresses of bright colours, like Roman women in the *Coliseum*, awaiting the battle of the gladiators. The atmosphere was surcharged with excitement, and the sense of coming triumph.

Ned's breath seemed to choke in his throat and his heart beat painfully. Once more he wished with all his soul that he was with his friends, that he was in the Alamo. He belonged with them there, and he would rather face death with those familiar faces around him than be here, safe perhaps, but only a looker-on. It was with him now a matter of the emotions, and not of reasoned intellect. Once more he looked toward the old mission, and saw the dim outline of the buildings, with the dominating walls of the church. He could not see whether anyone watched on the walls, but he knew that the sentinels were there. Perhaps Crockett, himself, stood among them now, looking at the great Mexican coil of steel that was wrapping itself tighter and tighter around the Alamo. Despite himself, Ned uttered a sigh.

"What is the matter with you?" asked Urrea, sharply. "Are you already weeping for the conquered?"

"You know that I am not," replied Ned. "You need not believe me, but I regret that I am not in the Alamo with my friends."

"It's an idle wish," said Urrea, "but I am taking you now to General Santa Anna. Then I leave, and I go there! Look, the horsemen!"

He extended his hand, and Ned saw his eyes kindling. The Mexican cavalry were filing out in the dim dawn, troop after troop, the early light falling across the blades of the lances, spurs and bridles jingling. All rode well, and they made a thrilling picture, as they rode steadily on, curving about the old fortress.

"I shall soon be with them," said Urrea in a tone of pride. "We shall see that not a single one of your Texans escapes from the Alamo."

Ned felt that choking in his throat again, but he deemed it wiser to keep silent. They were going toward the main *plaza* now, and he saw masses of troops gathered in the streets. These men were generally silent, and he noticed that their faces expressed no elation. He divined at once that they were intended for the assault, and they had no cause for joy. They knew that they must face the deadly Texan rifles.

Urrea led the way to a fortified battery standing in front of the main *plaza*. A brilliant group stood behind an earthen wall, and Ned saw Santa Anna among them.

"I have brought the prisoner," said Urrea, saluting.

"Very good," replied the dictator, "and now, Captain Urrea, you can join your command. You have served me well, and you shall have your share in the glory of this day."

Urrea flushed with pride at the compliment, and bowed low. Then he hurried away to join the horse. Santa Anna turned his attention.

"I have brought you here at this moment," he said, "to give you a last chance. It is not due to any mercy for you, a rebel, but it is because you have been so long in the Alamo that you must know it well. Point out to us its weakest places, and you shall be free. You shall go north in safety. I promise it here, in the presence of my generals."

"I have nothing to tell," replied Ned.

"Are you sure?"

"Absolutely sure."

"Then it merely means a little more effusion of blood. You may stay with us and see the result."

All the ancient, inherited cruelty now shone in Santa Anna's eyes. It was the strange satanic streak in him that made him keep his captive there in order that he might see the fall of his own comrades. A half dozen guards stood near the person of the dictator, and he said to them:

"If the prisoner seeks to leave us, shoot him at once."

The manner of Santa Anna was arrogant to the last degree, but Ned was glad to stay. He was eager to see the great panorama which was about to be unrolled before him. He was completely absorbed in the Alamo, and he utterly forgot himself. Black specks were dancing before his eyes, and the blood was pounding in his ears, but he took no notice of such things.

The gray bar in the east broadened. A thin streak of shining silver cut through it, and touched for a moment the town, the river, the army and the Alamo. Ned leaned against an edge of the earthwork, and breathed heavily and painfully. He had not known that his heart could beat so hard.

The same portentous silence prevailed everywhere. The men and women on the roofs of the houses were absolutely still. The cavalry, their line now drawn completely about the mission, were motionless. Ned, straining his eyes toward the Alamo, could see nothing there. Suddenly he put up his hand and wiped his forehead. His fingers came away wet. His blood prickled in his veins like salt. He became impatient, angry. If the mine was ready, why did they not set the match? Such waiting was the pitch of cruelty.

413

"Cos, my brother," said Santa Anna to the swart general, "take your command. It was here that the Texan rebels humiliated you, and it is here that you shall have full vengeance."

Cos saluted, and strode away. He was to lead one of the attacking columns.

"Colonel Duque," said Santa Anna to another officer, "you are one of the bravest of the brave. You are to direct the attack on the northern wall, and may quick success go with you."

Duque glowed at the compliment, and he, too, strode away to the head of his column.

"Colonel Romero," said Santa Anna, "the third column is yours, and the fourth is yours, Colonel Morales. Take your places and, at the signal agreed, the four columns will charge with all their strength. Let us see which will be the first in the Alamo."

The two colonels saluted as the others had done, and joined their columns.

The bar of gray in the east was still broadening, but the sun itself did not yet show. The walls of the Alamo were still dim, and Ned could not see whether any figures were there. Santa Anna had put a pair of powerful glasses to his eyes, but when he took them down he said nothing of what he had seen.

"Are all the columns provided?" he said to General Sesma, who stood beside him.

"They have everything," replied Sesma, "crowbars, axes, scaling ladders. Sir, they cannot fail!"

"No, they cannot," said Santa Anna exultantly. "These Texan rebels fight like demons, but we have now a net through which they cannot break. General Gaona, see that the bands are ready and direct them to play the *Deguelo* when the signal for the charge is given."

Ned shivered again. The "*Deguelo*" meant the "cutting-of-throats," and it, too, was to be the signal of no quarter. He remembered the red flag, and he looked up. It hung, as ever, on the tower of the church of San Fernando, and its scarlet folds moved slowly in the light morning breeze. General Gaona returned.

"The bands are ready, general," he said, "and when the signal is given they will play the air that you have chosen."

A Mexican, trumpet in hand, was standing near. Santa Anna turned and said to him the single word:

"Blow!"

The man lifted the trumpet to his lips, and blew a long note that

414

swelled to its fullest pitch, then died away in a soft echo.

It was the signal. A tremendous cry burst from the vast ring of the thousands, and it was taken up by the shrill voices of the women on the flat roofs of the houses. The great circle of cavalrymen shook their lances and sabres until they glittered.

When the last echo of the trumpet's dying note was gone the bands began to play with their utmost vigour the murderous tune that Santa Anna had chosen. Then four columns of picked Mexican troops, three thousand strong, rushed toward the Alamo. Santa Anna and the generals around him were tremendously excited. Their manner made no impression upon Ned then, but he recalled the fact afterward.

The boy became quickly unconscious of everything except the charge of the Mexicans and the Alamo. He no longer remembered that he was a prisoner. He no longer remembered anything about himself. The cruel throb of that murderous tune, the *Deguelo*, beat upon the drums of his ears, and mingled with it came the sound of the charging Mexicans, the beat of their feet, the clank of their arms, and the shouts of their officers.

Whatever may be said of the herded masses of the Mexican troops, the Mexican officers were full of courage. They were always in advance, waving their swords and shouting to their men to come on. Another silver gleam flashed through the gray light of the early morning, ran along the edges of swords and lances, and lingered for a moment over the dark walls of the Alamo.

No sound came from the mission, not a shot, not a cry. Were they asleep? Was it possible that every man, overpowered by fatigue, had fallen into slumber at such a moment? Could such as Crockett and Bowie and Travis be blind to their danger? Such painful questions raced through Ned's mind. He felt a chill run down his spine. Yet his breath was like fire to his lips.

"Nothing will stop them!" cried Santa Anna. "The Texans cower before such a splendid force! They will lay down their arms!"

Ned felt his body growing colder and colder, and there was a strange tingling at the roots of the hair. Now the people upon the roofs were shouting their utmost, and the voices of many women united in one shrill, piercing cry. But he never turned to look at them. His eyes were always on the charging host which converged so fast upon the Alamo.

The trumpet blew another signal, and there was a crash so loud that it made Ned jump. All the Mexican batteries had fired at once over the heads of their own troops at the Alamo. While the gunners reloaded the smoke of the discharge drifted away and the Alamo still stood silent. But over it yet hung a banner on which was written in great letters the word, "Texas."

The Mexican troops were coming close now. The bands playing the *Deguelo* swelled to greater volume and the ground shook again as the Mexican artillery fired its second volley. When the smoke drifted away again the Alamo itself suddenly burst into flame. The Texan cannon at close range poured their shot and shell into the dense ranks of the Mexicans. But piercing through the heavy thud of the cannon came the shriller and more deadly crackle of the rifles. The Texans were there, every one of them, on the walls. He might have known it. Nothing on earth could catch them asleep, nor could anything on earth or under it frighten them into laying down their arms.

Ned began to shout, but only hoarse cries came from a dry throat through dry lips. The great pulses in his throat were leaping again, and he was saying: "The Texans! The Texans! Oh, the brave Texans!"

But nobody heard him. Santa Anna, Filisola, Castrillon, Tolsa, Gaona and the other generals were leaning against the earthwork, absorbed in the tremendous spectacle that was passing before them. The soldiers who were to guard the prisoner forgot him and they, too, were engrossed in the terrible and thrilling panorama of war. Ned might have walked away, no one noticing, but he, too, had but one thought, and that was the Alamo.

He saw the Mexican columns shiver when the first volley was poured upon them from the walls. In a single glance aside he beheld the exultant look on the faces of Santa Anna and his generals die away, and he suddenly became conscious that the shrill shouting on the flat roofs of the houses had ceased. But the Mexican cannon still poured a cloud of shot and shell over the heads of their men at the Alamo, and the troops went on.

Ned, keen of ear and so intent that he missed nothing, could now separate the two fires. The crackle of the rifles which came from the Alamo dominated. Rapid, steady, incessant, it beat heavily upon the hearing and nerves. Pyramids and spires of smoke arose, drifted and arose again. In the intervals he saw the walls of the church a sheet of flame, and he saw the Mexicans falling by dozens and scores upon the plain. He knew that at the short range the Texan rifles never missed, and that the hail of their bullets was cutting through the Mexican ranks like a fire through dry grass.

416

"God, how they fight!" he heard one of the generals—he never knew which—exclaim.

Then he saw the officers rushing about, shouting to the men, striking them with the flats of their swords and urging them on. The Mexican army responded to the appeal, lifted itself up and continued its rush. The fire from the Alamo seemed to Ned to increase. The fortress was a living flame. He had not thought that men could fire so fast, but they had three or four rifles apiece.

The silence which had replaced the shrill shouting in the town continued. All the crash was now in front of them, and where they stood the sound of the human voice would carry. In a dim far-away manner Ned heard the guards talking to one another. Their words showed uneasiness. It was not the swift triumphal rush into the Alamo that they had expected. Great swaths had been cut through the Mexican Army. Santa Anna paled more than once when he saw his men falling so fast.

"They cannot recoil! They cannot!" he cried.

But they did. The column led by Colonel Duque, a brave man, was now at the northern wall, and the men were rushing forward with the crowbars, axes and scaling ladders. The Texan rifles, never more deadly, sent down a storm of bullets upon them. A score of men fell all at once. Among them was Duque, wounded terribly. The whole column broke and reeled away, carrying Duque with them.

Ned saw the face of Santa Anna turn purple with rage. He struck the earthwork furiously with the flat of his sword.

"Go! Go!" he cried to Gaona and Tolsa. "Rally them! See that they do not run!"

The two generals sprang from the battery and rushed to their task. The Mexican cannon had ceased firing, for fear of shooting down their own men, and the smoke was drifting away from the field. The morning was also growing much lighter. The gray dawn had turned to silver, and the sun's red rim was just showing above the eastern horizon.

The Texan cannon were silent, too. The rifles were now doing all the work. The volume of their fire never diminished. Ned saw the field covered with slain, and many wounded were drifting back to the shelter of the earthworks and the town.

Duque's column was rallied, but the column on the east and the column on the west were also driven back, and Santa Anna rushed messenger after messenger, hurrying up fresh men, still driving the

417

whole Mexican army against the Alamo. He shouted orders incessantly, although he remained safe within the shelter of the battery.

Ned felt an immense joy. He had seen the attack beaten off at three points. A force of twenty to one had been compelled to recoil. His heart swelled with pride in those friends of his. But they were so few in number! Even now the Mexican masses were reforming. The officers were among them, driving them forward with threats and blows. The great ring of Mexican cavalry, intended to keep any of the Texans from escaping, also closed in, driving their own infantry forward to the assault.

Ned's heart sank as the whole Mexican army, gathering now at the northern or lower wall, rushed straight at the barrier. But the deadly fire of the rifles flashed from it, and their front line went down. Again they recoiled, and again the cavalry closed in, holding them to the task.

There was a pause of a few moments. The town had been silent for a long time, and the Mexican soldiers themselves ceased to shout. Clouds of smoke eddied and drifted about the buildings. The light of the morning, first gray, then silver, turned to gold. The sun, now high above the earth's rim, poured down a flood of rays.

Everything stood out sharp and clear. Ned saw the buildings of the Alamo dark against the sun, and he saw men on the walls. He saw the Mexican columns pressed together in one great force, and he even saw the still faces of many who lay silent on the plain.

He knew that the Mexicans were about to charge again, and his feeling of exultation passed. He no longer had hope that the defenders of the Alamo could beat back so many. He thought again how few, how very few, were the Texans.

The silence endured but a moment or two. Then the Mexicans rushed forward in a mighty mass at the low northern wall, the front lines firing as they went. Flame burst from the wall, and Ned heard once more the deadly crackle of the Texan rifles. The ground was littered by the trail of the Mexican fallen, but, driven by their officers, they went on.

Ned saw them reach the wall and plant the scaling ladders, many of them. Scores of men swarmed up the ladders and over the wall. A heavy division forced its way into the redoubt through the sally-port, and as Ned saw he uttered a deep gasp. He knew that the Alamo was doomed. And the Mexicans knew it, too. The shrill screaming of the women began again from the flat roofs of the houses, and shouts burst from the army also.

"We have them! We have them!" cried Santa Anna, exultant and excited.

Sheets of flame still burst from the Alamo, and the rifles still poured bullets on the swarming Mexican forces, but the breach had been made. The Mexicans went over the low wall in an unbroken stream, and they crowded through the sally-port by hundreds. They were inside now, rushing with the overwhelming weight of twenty to one upon the little garrison. They seized the Texan guns, cutting down the gunners with lances and sabres, and they turned the captured cannon upon the defenders.

Some of the buildings inside the walls were of adobe, and they were soon shattered by the cannon balls. The Texans, covered with smoke and dust and the sweat of battle, were forced back by the press of numbers into the convent yard, and then into the church and hospital. Here the cannon and rifles in hundreds were turned upon them, but they still fought. Often, with no time to reload their rifles, they clubbed them, and drove back the Mexican rush.

The Alamo was a huge volcano of fire and smoke, of shouting and death. Those who looked on became silent again, appalled at the sights and sounds. The smoke rose far above the mission, and caught by a light wind drifted away to the east. The Mexican generals brought up fresh forces and drove them at the fortress. A heavy column, attacking on the south side, where no defenders were now left, poured over a stockade and crowded into the mission. The circle of cavalry about the Alamo again drew closer, lest any Texan should escape. But it was a useless precaution. None sought flight.

In very truth, the last hope of the Alamo was gone, and perhaps there was none among the defenders who did not know it. There were a few wild and desperate characters of the border, whom nothing in life became so much as their manner of leaving it. In the culminating moment of the great tragedy they bore themselves as well as the best.

Travis, the commander, and Bonham stood in the long room of the hospital with a little group around them, most of them wounded, the faces of all black with powder smoke. But they fought on. Whenever a Mexican appeared at the door an unerring rifle bullet struck him down. Fifty fell at that single spot before the rifles, yet they succeeded in dragging up a cannon, thrust its muzzle in at the door and fired it twice loaded with grape shot into the room.

The Texans were cut down by the shower of missiles, and the

whole place was filled with smoke. Then the Mexicans rushed in and the few Texans who had survived the grape shot fell fighting to the last with their clubbed rifles. Here lay Travis of the white soul and beside him fell the brave Bonham, who had gone out for help, and who had returned to die with his comrades. The Texans who had defended the room against so many were only fifteen in number, and they were all silent now. Now the whole attack converged on the church, the strongest part of the Alamo, where the Texans were making their last stand. The place was seething with fire and smoke, but above it still floated the banner upon which was written in great letters the word, "Texas."

The Mexicans, pressing forward in dense masses, poured in cannon balls and musket balls at every opening. Half the Texans were gone, but the others never ceased to fire with their rifles. Within that raging inferno they could hardly see one another for the smoke, but they were all animated by the same purpose, to fight to the death and to carry as many of their foes with them as they could.

Evans, who had commanded the cannon, rushed for the magazine to blow up the building. They had agreed that if all hope were lost he should do so, but he was killed on his way by a bullet, and the others went on with the combat.

Near the entrance to the church stood a great figure swinging a clubbed rifle. His raccoon skin cap was lost, and his eyes burned like coals of fire in his swarthy face. It was Crockett, gone mad with battle, and the Mexicans who pressed in recoiled before the deadly sweep of the clubbed rifle. Some were awed by the terrific figure, dripping blood, and wholly unconscious of danger.

"Forward!" cried a Mexican officer, and one of his men went down with a shattered skull. The others shrank back again, but a new figure pressed into the ring. It was that of the younger Urrea. At the last moment he had left the cavalry and joined in the assault.

"Don't come within reach of his blows!" he cried. "Shoot him! Shoot him!"

He snatched a double-barrelled pistol from his own belt and fired twice straight at Crockett's breast. The great Tennessean staggered, dropped his rifle and the flame died from his eyes. With a howl of triumph his foes rushed upon him, plunged their swords and bayonets into his body, and he fell dead with a heap of the Mexican slain about him.

A bullet whistled past Urrea's face and killed a man beyond him.

He sprang back. Bowie, still suffering severe injuries from a fall from a platform, was lying on a cot in the arched room to the left of the entrance. Unable to walk, he had received at his request two pistols, and now he was firing them as fast as he could pull the triggers and reload.

"Shoot him! Shoot him at once!" cried Urrea.

His own pistol was empty now, but a dozen musket balls were fired into the room. Bowie, hit twice, nevertheless raised himself upon his elbow, aimed a pistol with a clear eye and a steady hand, and pulled the trigger. A Mexican fell, shot through the heart, but another volley of musket balls was discharged at the Georgian. Struck in both head and heart he suddenly straightened out and lay still upon the cot. Thus died the famous Bowie.

Mrs. Dickinson and her baby had been hidden in the arched room on the other side for protection. The Mexicans killed a Texan named Walters at the entrance, and, wild with ferocity, raised his body upon a half dozen bayonets while the blood ran down in a dreadful stream upon those who held it aloft.

Urrea rushed into the room and found the cowering woman and her baby. The Mexicans followed, and were about to slay them, too, when a gallant figure rushed between. It was the brave and humane Almonte. Sword in hand, he faced the savage horde. He uttered words that made Urrea turn dark with shame and leave the room. The soldiers were glad to follow.

At the far end of the church a few Texans were left, still fighting with clubbed rifles. The Mexicans drew back a little, raised their muskets and fired an immense shattering volley. When the smoke cleared away not a single Texan was standing, and then the troops rushed in with sword and bayonet.

It was nine o'clock in the morning, and the Alamo had fallen. The defenders were less than nine score, and they had died to the last man. A messenger rushed away at once to Santa Anna with the news of the triumph, and he came from the shelter, glorying, exulting and crying that he had destroyed the Texans.

Ned followed the dictator. He never knew exactly why, because many of those moments were dim, like the scenes of a dream, and there was so much noise, excitement and confusion that no one paid any attention to him. But an overwhelming power drew him on to the Alamo, and he rushed in with the Mexican spectators.

Ned passed through the sally-port and he reeled back aghast for a moment. The Mexican dead, not yet picked up, were strewn everywhere. They had fallen in scores. The lighter buildings were smashed by cannon balls and shells. The earth was gullied and torn. The smoke from so much firing drifted about in banks and clouds, and it gave forth the pungent odor of burned gunpowder.

The boy knew not only that the Alamo had fallen, but that all of its defenders had fallen with it. The knowledge was instinctive. He had been with those men almost to the last day of the siege, and he had understood their spirit.

He was not noticed in the crush. Santa Anna and the generals were running into the church, and he followed them. Here he saw the Texan dead, and he saw also a curious crowd standing around a fallen form. He pressed into the ring and his heart gave a great throb of grief.

It was Crockett, lying upon his back, his body pierced by many wounds. Ned had known that he would find him thus, but the shock, nevertheless, was terrible. Yet Crockett's countenance was calm. He bore no wounds in the face, and he lay almost as if he had died in his bed. It seemed to Ned even in his grief that no more fitting death could have come to the old hero.

Then, following another crowd, he saw Bowie, also lying peacefully in death upon his cot. He felt the same grief for him that he had felt for Crockett, but it soon passed in both cases. A strange mood of exaltation took its place. They had died as one might wish to die, since death must come to all. It was glorious that these defenders of the Alamo, comrades of his, should have fallen to the last man. The full splendour of their achievement suddenly burst in a dazzling vision before him. Texans who furnished such valour could not be conquered. Santa Anna might have twenty to one or fifty to one or a hundred to one, in the end it would not matter.

The mood endured. He looked upon the dead faces of Travis and Bonham also, and he was not shaken. He saw others, dozens and dozens whom he knew, and the faces of all of them seemed peaceful to him. The shouting and cheering and vast chatter of the Mexicans did not disturb him. His mood was so high that all these things passed as nothing.

Ned made no attempt to escape. He knew that while he might go about almost as he chose in this crowd of soldiers, now disorganized, the ring of cavalry beyond would hold him. The thought of escape, however, was but little in his mind just then. He was absorbed in the great tomb of the Alamo. Here, despite the recent work of the cannon, all things looked familiar. He could mark the very spots where he had stood and talked with Crockett or Bowie. He knew how the story of the immortal defence would spread like fire throughout Texas and beyond. When he should tell how he had seen the faces of the heroes, every heart must leap.

He wandered back to the church, where the curious still crowded. Many people from the town, influential Mexicans, wished to see the terrible Texans, who yet lay as they had fallen. Some spoke scornful words, but most regarded them with awe. Ned looked at Crockett for the second time, and a hand touched him on the shoulder. It was Urrea.

"Where are your Texans now?" he asked.

"They are gone," replied Ned, "but they will never be forgotten." And then he added in a flash of anger. "Five or six times as many Mexicans have gone with them."

"It is true," said the young Mexican thoughtfully. "They fought like cornered mountain wolves. We admit it. And this one, Crockett you call him, was perhaps the most terrible of them all. He swung his clubbed rifle so fiercely that none dared come within its reach. I slew him."

"You?" exclaimed Ned.

"Yes, I! Why should I not? I fired two pistol bullets into him and he fell."

He spoke with a certain pride. Ned said nothing, but he pressed his teeth together savagely and his heart swelled with hate of the sleek and triumphant Urrea.

"General Santa Anna, engrossed in much more important matters, has doubtless forgotten you," continued the Mexican, "but I will see that you do not escape. Why he spares you I know not, but it is his wish."

He called to two soldiers, whom he detailed to follow Ned and see that he made no attempt to escape. The boy was yet so deeply absorbed in the Alamo that no room was left in his mind for anything else. Nor did he care to talk further with Urrea, who he knew was not above aiming a shaft or two at an enemy in his power. He remained in the crowd until Santa Anna ordered that all but the troops be cleared from the Alamo.

Then, at the order of the dictator, the bodies of the Texans were taken without. A number of them were spread upon the ground, and

423

were covered with a thick layer of dry wood and brush. Then more bodies of men and heaps of dry wood were spread in alternate layers until the funeral pile was complete.

Young Urrea set the torch, while the Mexican army and population looked on. The dry wood flamed up rapidly and the whole was soon a pyramid of fire and smoke. Ned was not shocked at this end, even of the bodies of brave men. He recalled the stories of ancient heroes, the bodies of whom had been consumed on just such pyres as this, and he was willing that his comrades should go to join Hercules, Hector, Achilles and the rest.

The flames roared and devoured the great pyramid, which sank lower, and at last Ned turned away. His mood of exaltation was passing. No one could remain keyed to that pitch many hours. Overwhelming grief and despair came in its place. His mind raged against everything, against the cruelty of Santa Anna, who had hoisted the red flag of no quarter, against fate, that had allowed so many brave men to perish, and against the overwhelming numbers that the Mexicans could always bring against the Texans.

He walked gloomily toward the town, the two soldiers who had been detailed as guards following close behind him. He looked back, saw the sinking blaze of the funeral pyre, shuddered and walked on.

San Antonio de Bexar was rejoicing. Most of its people, Mexican to the core, shared in the triumph of Santa Anna. The terrible Texans were gone, annihilated, and Santa Anna was irresistible. The conquest of Texas was easy now. No, it was achieved already. They had the dictator's own word for it that the rest was a mere matter of gathering up the fragments.

Some of the graver and more kindly Mexican officers thought of their own losses. The brave and humane Almonte walked through the courts and buildings of the Alamo, and his face blanched when he reckoned their losses. A thousand men killed or wounded was a great price to pay for the nine score Texans who were sped. But no such thoughts troubled Santa Anna. All the vainglory of his nature was aflame. They were decorating the town with all the flags and banners and streamers they could find, and he knew that it was for him. At night they would illuminate in his honour. He stretched out his arm toward the north and west, and murmured that it was all his. He would be the ruler of an empire half the size of Europe. The scattered and miserable Texans could set no bounds to his ambition. He had proved it.

He would waste no more time in that empty land of prairies and plains. He sent glowing dispatches about his victory to the City of Mexico and announced that he would soon come. His subordinates would destroy the wandering bands of Texans. Then he did another thing that appealed to his vanity. He wrote a proclamation to the Texans announcing the fall of the Alamo, and directing them to submit at once, on pain of death, to his authority. He called for Mrs. Dickinson, the young wife, now widow, whom the gallantry of Almonte had saved from massacre in the Alamo. He directed her to take his threat to the Texans at Gonzales, and she willingly accepted. Mounting a horse and alone save for the baby in her arms, she rode away from San Antonio, shuddering at the sight of the Mexicans, and passed out upon the desolate and dangerous prairies.

The dictator was so absorbed in his triumph and his plans for his greater glory that for the time he forgot all about Ned Fulton, his youthful prisoner, who had crossed the stream and who was now in the town, attended by the two *peons* whom Urrea had detailed as his guards. But Ned had come out of his daze, and his mind was as keen and alert as ever. The effects of the great shock of horror remained. His was not a bitter nature, but he could not help feeling an intense hatred of the Mexicans. He was on the battle line, and he saw what they were doing. He resolved that now was his time to escape, and in the great turmoil caused by the excitement and rejoicing in San Antonio he did not believe that it would be difficult.

He carefully cultivated the good graces of the two soldiers who were guarding him. He bought for them *mescal* and other fiery drinks which were now being sold in view of the coming festival. Their good nature increased and also their desire to get rid of a task that had been imposed upon them. Why should they guard a boy when everybody else was getting ready to be merry?

They went toward the main *plaza*, and came to the Zambrano Row, where the Texans had fought their way when they took San Antonio months before. Ned looked up at the buildings. They were still dismantled. Great holes were in the walls and the empty windows were like blind eyes. He saw at once that their former inhabitants had not yet returned to them, and here he believed was his chance.

When they stood beside the first house he called the attention of his guards to some Mexican women who were decorating a doorway across the street. When they looked he darted into the first of the houses in the Zambrano Row. He entered a large room and at the corner saw a stairway. He knew this place. He had been here in the siege of San Antonio by the Texans, and now he had the advantage over his guards, who were probably strangers.

He rushed for the staircase and, just as he reached the top, one of the guards, who had followed as soon as they noticed the flight of the prisoner, fired his musket. The discharge roared in the room, but the bullet struck the wall fully a foot away from the target. Ned was on the second floor, and out of range the next moment. He knew that the soldiers would follow him, and he passed through the great hole, broken by the Texans, into the next house.

Here he paused to listen, and he heard the two soldiers muttering and breathing heavily. The distaste which they already felt for their task had become a deep disgust. Why should they be deprived of their part in the festival to follow up a prisoner? What did a single captive amount to, anyhow? Even if he escaped now the great, the illustrious Santa Anna, whose eyes saw all things, would capture him later on when he swept all the scattered Texans into his basket.

Ned went from house to house through the holes broken in the party walls, and occasionally he heard his pursuers slouching along and grumbling. At the fourth house he slipped out upon the roof, and lay flat near the stone coping.

He knew that if the soldiers came upon the roof they would find him, but he relied upon the *mescal* and their lack of zeal. He heard them once tramping about in the room below him, and then he heard them no more.

Ned remained all the rest of the afternoon upon the roof, not daring to leave his cramped position against the coping. He felt absolutely safe there from observation, Mexicans would not be prowling through dismantled and abandoned houses at such a time. Now and then gay shouts came from the streets below. The Mexicans of Bexar were disturbed little by the great numbers of their people who had fallen at the Alamo. The dead were from the far valleys of Mexico, and were strangers.

Ned afterward thought that he must have slept a little toward twilight, but he was never sure of it. He saw the sun set, and the gray and silent Alamo sink away into the darkness. Then he slipped from the roof, anxious to be away before the town was illuminated. He had no difficulty at all in passing unnoticed through the streets, and he made his way straight for the Alamo.

He was reckoning very shrewdly now. He knew that the superstitious Mexicans would avoid the mission at night as a place thronged with ghosts, and that Santa Anna would not need to post any guard within those walls. He would pass through the enclosures, then over the lower barriers by which the Mexicans had entered, and thence into the darkness beyond.

It seemed to him the best road to escape, and he had another object also in entering the Alamo. The defenders had had three or four rifles apiece, and he was convinced that somewhere in the rooms he would find a good one, with sufficient ammunition.

It was with shudders that he entered the Alamo, and the shudders came again when he looked about the bloodstained courts and rooms, lately the scene of such terrible strife, but now so silent. In a recess of the church which had been used as a little storage place by himself and Crockett he found an excellent rifle of the long-barrelled Western pattern, a large horn of powder and a pouch full of bullets. There was also a supply of dried beef, which he took, too.

Now he felt himself a man again. He would find the Texans and then they would seek vengeance for the Alamo. He crossed the main *plaza*, dropped over the low wall and quickly disappeared in the dusk.

CHAPTER 14

THE NEWS OF THE FALL

Five days before the fall of the Alamo a little group of men began to gather at the village of Washington, on the Brazos river in Texas. The name of the little town indicated well whence its people had come. All the houses were new, mostly of unpainted wood, and they contained some of the furniture of necessity, none of luxury. The first and most important article was the rifle which the Texans never needed more than they did now.

But this new and little Washington was seething with excitement and suspense, and its population was now more than triple the normal. News had come that the Alamo was beleaguered by a force many times as numerous as its defenders, and that Crockett, Bowie, Travis and other famous men were inside. They had heard also that Santa Anna had hoisted the red flag of no quarter, and that Texans everywhere, if taken, would be slaughtered as traitors. The people of Washington had full cause for their excitement and suspense.

The little town also had the unique distinction of being a capi-

427

tal for a day or two. The Texans felt, with the news that Santa Anna had enveloped the Alamo, that they must take decisive action. They believed that the Mexicans had broken every promise to the Texans. They knew that not only their liberty and property, but their lives, also, were in peril. Despite the great disparity of numbers it must be a fight to the death between Texas and Mexico. The Texans were now gathering at Washington.

One man who inspired courage wherever he went had come already. Sam Houston had ridden into town, calm, confident and talking only of victory. He was dressed with a neatness and care unusual on the border, wearing a fine black suit, while his face was shaded by the wide brim of a white *sombrero*. The famous scouts, "Deaf" Smith and Henry Karnes, and young Zavala, whom Ned had known in Mexico, were there also.

Fifty-eight delegates representing Texas gathered in the largest room of a frame building. "Deaf" Smith and Henry Karnes came in and sat with their rifles across their knees. While some of the delegates were talking Houston signalled to the two, and they went outside.

"What do you hear from the Alamo, Smith?" asked Houston.

"Travis has fought off all the attacks of the Mexicans," replied the great borderer, "but when Santa Anna brings up his whole force an' makes a resolute assault it's bound to go under. The mission is too big an' scattered to be held by Travis an' his men against forty or fifty times their number."

"I fear so. I fear so," said Houston sadly, "and we can't get together enough men for its relief. All this quarrelling and temporizing are our ruin. Heavens, what a time for disagreements!"

"There couldn't be a worse time, general," said Henry Karnes. "Me an' 'Deaf' would like mighty well to march to the Alamo. A lot of our friends are in there an' I reckon we've seen them for the last time."

The fine face of Houston grew dark with melancholy.

"Have you been anywhere near San Antonio?" he asked Smith.

"Not nearer than thirty miles," replied Smith, "but over at Goliad I saw a force under Colonel Fannin that was gettin' ready to start to the relief of Travis. With it were some friends of mine. There was Palmer, him they call the Panther, the biggest and strongest man in Texas; Obed White, a New Englander, an' a boy, Will Allen. I've knowed 'em well for some time, and there was another that belonged to their little band. But he's in the Alamo now, an' they was wild to rescue him."

"Do you think Fannin will get through?" asked Houston.

"I don't," replied Smith decidedly, "an' if he did it would just mean the loss of more good men for us. What do you think about it, Hank?"

"The same that you do," replied Karnes.

Houston pondered over their words a long time. He knew that they were thoroughly acquainted with Texas and the temper of its people, and he relied greatly on their judgment. When he went back in the room which was used as a convention hall Smith and Karnes remained outside.

Smith sat down on the grass, lighted a pipe and began to smoke deliberately. Karnes also sat down on the grass, lighted his own pipe and smoked with equal deliberation. Each man rested his rifle across his knees.

"Looks bad," said Smith.

"Powerful bad."

"Almighty bad."

"Talkin's no good when the enemy's shootin'."

"Reckon there's nothin' left for us but this," tapping the barrel of his rifle significantly.

"Only tool that's left for us to use."

"Reckon we'll soon have as many chances as we want to use it, an' more."

"Reckon you're Almighty right."

"An' we'll be there every time."

The two men reached over and shook hands deliberately. Houston by and by came out again, and saw them sitting there smoking, two images of patience and quiet.

"Boys," he said, "you're not taking much part in the proceedings."

"Not much, just yet, Colonel Sam," replied Smith, "but we're waitin'. I reckon that tomorrow you'll declare Texas free an' independent, a great an' good republic. An' as there ain't sixty of you to declare it, mebbe you'll need the help of some fellows like Hank an' me to make them resolutions come true."

"We will," said Houston, "and we know that we can rely upon you."

He was about to pass on, but he changed his mind and sat down with the men. Houston was a singular character. He had been governor of an important state, and he had lived as a savage among savages. He could adapt himself to any company.

"Boys," he said, "you know a merchant, John Roylston, who has headquarters in New Orleans, and also offices in St. Louis and Cincinnati?"

"We do," said Smith, "an' we've seen him, too, more than once. He's been in these parts not so long ago."

"He's in New Orleans now," said Houston. "He's the biggest trader along the coast. Has dealings with Santa Anna himself, but he's a friend of Texas, a powerful one. Boys, I've in my pocket now an order from him good for a hundred thousand dollars. It's to be spent buying arms and ammunition for us. And when the time comes there's more coming from the same place. We've got friends, but keep this to yourselves."

He walked on and the two took a long and meditative pull at their pipes.

"I reckon Roylston may not shoot as straight as we can," said Smith, "but mebbe at as long range as New Orleans he can do more harm to the Mexicans than we can."

"Looks like it. I ain't much of a hand at money, but I like the looks of that man Roylston, an' I reckon the more rifles and the more ammunition we have the fewer Mexicans will be left."

The two scouts, having smoked as long as they wished, went to their quarters and slept soundly through the night. But Houston and the leading Texans with him hardly slept at all. There was but one course to choose, and they were fully aware of its gravity, Houston perhaps more so than the rest, as he had seen more of the world. They worked nearly all night in the bare room, and when Houston sought his room he was exhausted.

Houston's room was a bare little place, lighted by a tallow candle, and although it was not long until day he sat there a while before lying down. A man of wide experience, he alone, with the exception of Roylston, knew how desperate was the situation of the Texans. In truth, it was the money of Roylston sent from New Orleans that had caused him to hazard the chance. He knew, too, that, in time, more help would arrive from the same source, and he believed there would be a chance against the Mexicans, a fighting chance, it is true, but men who were willing to die for a cause seldom failed to win. He blew out the candle, got in bed and slept soundly.

"Deaf" Smith and Henry Karnes were up early—they seldom slept late—and saw the sun rise out of the prairie. They were in a house which had a small porch, looking toward the Brazos. After breakfast they lighted their cob pipes again, smoked and meditated.

"Reckon somethin' was done by our leadin' statesmen last night," said Smith.

"Reckon there was," said Karnes.

"Reckon I can guess what it was."

"Reckon I can, too."

"Reckon I'll wait to hear it offish-ul-ly before I speak."

"Reckon I will, too. Lots of time wasted talkin'."

"Reckon you're right."

They sat in silence for a full two hours. They smoked the first hour, and they passed the second in their chairs without moving. They had mastered the borderer's art of doing nothing thoroughly, when nothing was to be done. Then a man came upon the porch and spoke to them. His name was Burnet, David G. Burnet.

"Good mornin'. How is the new republic?" said "Deaf" Smith.

"So you know," said Burnet.

"We don't know, but we've guessed, Hank an' me. We saw things as they was comin'."

"I reckon, too," said Karnes, "that we ain't a part of Mexico any more."

"No, we're a free an' independent republic. It was so decided last night, and we've got nothing more to do now but to whip a nation of eight millions, the fifty thousand of us."

"Well," said Smith philosophically, "it's a tough job, but it might be did. I've heard tell that them old Greeks whipped the Persians when the odds were powerful high against them."

"That is true," said Burnet, "and we can at least try. We give the reason for declaring our independence. We assert to the world that the Mexican republic has become a military despotism, that our agents carrying petitions have been thrown in dungeons in the City of Mexico, that we have been ordered to give up the arms necessary for our defence against the savages, and that we have been deprived of every right guaranteed to us when we settled here."

"We're glad it's done, although we knew it would be done," said Smith. "We ain't much on talkin', Mr. President, Hank an' me, but we can shoot pretty straight, an' we're at your call."

"I know that, God bless you both," said Burnet. "The talking is over. It's rifles that we need and plenty of them. Now I've to see Houston. We're to talk over ways and means."

He hurried away, and the two, settling back into their chairs on the porch, relighted their pipes and smoked calmly.

"Reckon there'll be nothin' doin' for a day or two, Hank," said Smith.

"Reckon not, but we'll have to be doin' a powerful lot later, or be hoofin' it for the tall timber a thousand miles north."

"You always was full of sense, Hank. Now there goes Sam Houston. Queer stories about his leavin' Tennessee and his life in the Indian Territory."

"That's so, but he's an honest man, looks far ahead, an' 'tween you an' me, 'Deaf,' it's a thousand to one that he's to lead us in the war."

"Reckon you're guessin' good."

Houston, who had just awakened and dressed, was walking across the grass and weeds to meet Burnet. Not even he, when he looked at the tiny village and the wilderness spreading about it, foresaw how mighty a state was to rise from beginnings so humble and so small. He and Burnet went back into the convention hall, and he wrote a fiery appeal to the people. He said that the Alamo was beleaguered and "the citizens of Texas must rally to the aid of our army or it will perish."

Smith and Karnes remained while the convention continued its work. They did little ostensibly but smoke their cob pipes, but they observed everything and thought deeply. On Sunday morning, five days after the men had gathered at Washington, as they stood at the edge of the little town they saw a man galloping over the prairie. Neither spoke, but watched him for a while, as the unknown came on, lashing a tired horse.

"'Pears to be in a hurry," said Smith.

"An' to be in a hurry generally means somethin' in these parts," said Karnes.

"I'm makin' a guess."

"So am I, an' yours is the same as mine. He comes from the Alamo."

Others now saw the man, and there was a rush toward him. His horse fell at the edge of the town, but the rider sprang to his feet and came toward the group, which included both Houston and Burnet. He was a wild figure, face and clothing covered with dust. But he recognised Houston and turned to him at once.

"You're General Houston, and I'm from the Alamo," he said. "I bring a message from Colonel Travis."

There was a sudden and heavy intake of breath in the whole group.

"Then the Alamo has not fallen?" said Houston.

432

"Not when I left, but that was three days ago. Here is the letter."

It was the last letter of Travis, concluding with the words: "God and Texas; victory or death." But when the messenger put the letter into the hands of Houston the Alamo had fallen two hours before.

The letter was laid before the convention, and the excitement was great and irrepressible. The feelings of these stern men were moved deeply. Many wished to adjourn at once and march to the relief of the Alamo, but the eloquence of Houston, who had been re-elected Commander-in-chief, prevailed against the suggestion. Then, with two or three men, he departed for Gonzales to raise a force, while the others elected Burnet President of the new Texas, and departed for Harrisburg on Buffalo Bayou.

"Deaf" Smith and Henry Karnes did not go just then with Houston. They were scouts, hunters and rough riders, and they could do as they pleased. They notified General Sam Houston, commander-in-chief of the Texan armies, that they would come on later, and he was content.

When the Texan government and the Texan army, numbering combined about a hundred men, followed by most of the population, numbering fifty or sixty more, filed off for Gonzales, the two sat once more on the same porch, smoking their cob pipes. They were not ordinary men. They were not ordinary scouts and borderers. One from the north and one from the south, they were much alike in their mental processes, their faculties of keen observation and deep reasoning. Both were now stirred to the core, but neither showed a trace of it on his face. They watched the little file pass away over the prairie until it was lost to sight behind the swells, and then Smith spoke:

"I reckon you an' me, Hank, will ride toward the Alamo."

"I reckon we will, Deaf, and that right away."

Inside of five minutes they were on the road, armed and provisioned, the best two borderers, with the single exception of the Panther, in all the southwest. They were mounted on powerful mustangs, which, with proper handling and judicious rests, could go on forever. But they pushed them a little that afternoon, stopped for two hours after sundown, and then went on again. They crossed the Colorado River in the night, swimming their horses, and about a mile further on stopped in dense chaparral. They tethered the mustangs near them, and spread out their blankets.

"If anything comes the horses will wake us," said Smith.

"I reckon they will," said Karnes.

Both were fast asleep in a few minutes, but they awoke shortly after sunrise. They made a frugal breakfast, while the mustangs had cropped short grass in the night. Both horses and men, as tough and wiry as they ever become, were again as fresh as the dawn, and, with not more than a dozen words spoken, the two mounted and rode anew on their quest. Always chary of speech, they became almost silence itself as they drew nearer to San Antonio de Bexar. In the heart of each was a knowledge of the great tragedy, not surmise, but the certainty that acute intelligence deduces from facts.

They rode on until, by a simultaneous impulse, the two reined their horses back into a cypress thicket and waited. They had seen three horsemen on the sky line, coming, in the main, in their direction. Their trained eyes noticed at once that the strangers were of varying figure. The foremost, even at the distance, seemed to be gigantic, the second was very long and thin, and the third was normal. Smith and Karnes watched them a little while, and then Karnes spoke in words of true conviction.

"It would be hard, Deaf, for even a bad eye to mistake the foremost."

"Right you are, Hank. You might comb Texas with a fine-tooth comb an' you'd never rake out such another."

"If that ain't Mart Palmer, the Ring Tailed Panther, I'll go straight to Santa Anna an' ask him to shoot me as a fool."

"You won't have to go to Santa Anna."

Smith rode from the covert, put his curved hand to his mouth, and uttered a long piercing cry. The three horsemen stopped at once, and the giant in the lead gave back the signal in the same fashion. Then the two little parties rode rapidly toward each other. While they were yet fifty yards apart they uttered words of hail and good fellowship, and when they met they shook hands with the friendship that has been sealed by common hardships and dangers.

"You're goin' toward the Alamo?" said Smith.

"Yes," replied the Panther. "We started that way several days ago, but we've been delayed. We had a brush with one little party of Mexicans, and we had to dodge another that was too big for us. I take it that you ride for the same place."

"We do. Were you with Fannin?"

The dark face of the Panther grew darker.

"We were," he replied. "He started to the relief of the Alamo, but the ammunition wagon broke down, an' they couldn't get the cannon

434

across the San Antonio River. So me an' Obed White an' Will Allen here have come on alone."

"News for news," said Smith dryly. "Texas has just been made a free an' independent republic, an' Sam Houston has been made commander-in-chief of all its mighty armies, horse, foot an' cannon. We saw all them things done back there at Washington settlement, an' we, bein' a part of the army, are ridin' to the relief of the Alamo."

"We j'in you, then," said the Panther, "an' Texas raises two armies of the strength of three an' two to one of five. Oh, if only all the Texans had come what a roarin' an' rippin' an' t'arin' and chawin' there would have been when we struck Santa Anna's army, no matter how big it might be."

"But they didn't come," said Smith grimly, "an' as far as I know we five are all the Texans that are ridin' toward San Antonio de Bexar an' the Alamo."

"But bein' only five won't keep us from ridin' on," said the Panther.

"And things are not always as bad as they look," said Obed White, after he had heard of the messenger who had come to Houston and Unmet. "It's never too late to hope."

The five rode fast the remainder of the day. They passed through a silent and desolate land. They saw a few cabins, but every one was abandoned. The deep sense of tragedy was over them all, even over young Will Allen. They rarely spoke, and they rode along in silence, save for the beat of their horses' hoofs. Shortly before night they met a lone buffalo hunter whom the Panther knew.

"Have you been close to San Antonio, Simpson?" asked the Panther, after the greeting.

"I've been three or four days hangin' 'roun' the neighbourhood," replied the hunter. "I came down from the northwest when I heard that Santa Anna was advancing an' once I thought I'd make a break an' try to get into the Alamo, but the Mexican lines was drawed too thick an' close."

"Have you heard anything about the men inside?" asked the Panther eagerly.

"Not a thing. But I've noticed this. A mornin' an' evenin' gun was fired from the fortress every day until yesterday, Sunday, an' since then—nothin'."

The silence in the little band was as ominous as the silence of the morning and evening gun. Simpson shook his head sadly.

435

"Boys," he said, "I'm goin' to ride for Gonzales an' join Houston. I don't think it's any use for me to be hangin' aroun' San Antonio de Bexar any longer. I wish you luck in whatever you're tryin' to do."

He rode away, but the five friends continued their course toward the Alamo, without hope now, but resolved to see for themselves. Deep in the night, which fortunately for their purpose was dark, heavy clouds shutting out the moon and stars, they approached San Antonio from the east. They saw lights, which they knew were those of the town, but there was darkness only where they knew the Alamo stood.

They tethered their horses in some bushes and crept closer, until they could see the dim bulk of the Alamo. No light shone there. They listened long and intently, but not a single sound came from the great hecatomb. Again they crept nearer. There were no Mexican guards anywhere. A little further and they stood by the low northern wall.

"Boys," said the Panther, "I can't stand it any longer. Queer feelin's are runnin' all over me. No, I'm goin' to take the risk, if there is any, all alone. You wait for me here, an' if I don't come back in an hour then you can hunt for me."

The Panther climbed over the wall and disappeared. The others remained in the deepest shadow waiting and silent. They were oppressed by the heavy gloom that hung over the Alamo. It was terrifying to young Will Allen, not the terror that is caused by the fear of men, but the terror that comes from some tragic mystery that is more than half guessed.

Nearly an hour passed, when a great figure leaped lightly from the wall and joined them. The swarthy face of the Panther was as white as chalk, and he was shivering.

"Boys," he whispered, "I've seen what I never want to see ag'in. I've seen red, red everywhere. I've been through the rooms of the Alamo, an' they're red, splashed with the red blood of men. The water in the ditch was stained with red, an' the earth all about was soaked with it. Somethin' awful must have happened in the Alamo. There must have been a terrible fight, an' I'm thinkin' that most of our fellows must have died before it was took. But it's give me the creeps, boys, an' I think we'd better get away."

"We can't leave any too quick to please me," said Will Alien. "I'm seeing ghosts all the time."

"Now that we know for sure the Alamo has fallen," said Smith, "nothin' is to be gained by stayin' here. It's for Sam Houston to lead us to revenge, and the more men he has the better. I vote we ride for

Gonzales."

"Seein' what we can see as we go," said Karnes. "The more information we can pick up on the way about the march of the Mexicans the better it will be for Houston."

"No doubt of that," said the Panther. "When we go to roarin' an' rippin' an' t'arin' we must know what we're about. But come on, boys, all that red in the Alamo gives me conniption fits."

They rode toward the east for a long time until they thought they were beyond the reach of Mexican skirmishing parties, and then they slept in a cypress thicket, Smith and Karnes standing guard by turns. As everybody needed rest they did not resume their journey the next day until nearly noon, and they spent most of the afternoon watching for Mexican scouts, although they saw none. They had a full rest that night and the next day they rode slowly toward Gonzales.

About the middle of the afternoon, as they reached the crest of a swell, Will Allen uttered an exclamation, and pointed toward the eastern horizon. There they saw a single figure on horseback, and another walking beside it. The afternoon sun was very bright, casting a glow over the distant figures, and, shading their eyes with their hands, they gazed at them a long time.

"It's a woman that's ridin'," said Smith at last, "an' she's carryin' some sort of a bundle before her."

"You're shorely right, Deaf," said Karnes, "an' I think the one walkin' is a black fellow. Looks like it from here."

"I'm your way of thinkin'," said the Panther, "an' the woman on the horse is American, or I'm mightily fooled in my guess. S'pose we ride ahead faster an' see for shore."

They increased the speed of their mustangs to a gallop and rapidly overhauled the little party. They saw the woman trying to urge her horse to greater speed. But the poor beast, evidently exhausted, made no response. The woman, turning in the saddle, looked back at her pursuers.

"By all that's wonderful!" exclaimed Obed White, "the bundle that she's carrying is a baby!"

"It's so," said Smith, "an' you can see well enough now that she's one of our own people. We must show her that she's got nothin' to fear from us."

He shouted through his arched hands in tremendous tones that they were Texans and friends. The woman stopped, and as they galloped up she would have fallen from her horse had not Obed White promptly seized her and, dismounting, lifted her and the baby tenderly to the ground. The coloured boy who had been walking stood by and did not say anything aloud, but muttered rapidly: "Thank the Lord! Thank the Lord!"

Three of the five were veteran hunters, but they had never before found such a singular party on the prairie. The woman sat down on the ground, still holding the baby tightly in her arms, and shivered all over. The Texans regarded her in pitying silence for a few minutes, and then Obed White said in gentle tones:

"We are friends, ready to take you to safety. Tell us who you are."

"I am Mrs. Dickinson," she replied.

"Deaf" Smith looked startled.

"There was a Lieutenant Dickinson in the Alamo," he said.

"I am his wife," she replied, "and this is our child."

"And where is—" Smith stopped suddenly, knowing what the answer must be.

"He is dead," she replied. "He fell in the defence of the Alamo."

"Might he not be among the prisoners?" suggested Obed White gently.

"Prisoners!" she replied. "There were no prisoners. They fought to the last. Every man who was in the Alamo died in its defence."

The five stared at her in amazement, and for a little while none spoke.

"Do you mean to say," asked Obed White, "that none of the Texans survived the fall of the Alamo?"

"None," she replied.

"How do you know?"

Her pale face filled with colour. It seemed that she, too, at that moment felt some of the glow that the fall of the Alamo was to suffuse through Texas.

"Because I saw," she replied. "I was in one of the arched rooms of the church, where they made the last stand. I saw Crockett fall and I saw the death of Bowie, too. I saw Santa Anna exult, but many, many Mexicans fell also. It was a terrible struggle. I shall see it again every day of my life, even if I live to be a hundred."

She covered her face with her hands, as if she would cut out the sight of that last inferno in the church. The others were silent, stunned for the time.

"All gone," said Obed White, at last. "When the news is spread that every man stood firm to the last I think it will light such a fire in Texas that Santa Anna and all his armies cannot put it out."

"Did you see a boy called Ned Fulton in the Alamo, a tall, hand-some fellow with brown hair and gray eyes?" asked Obed White.

"Often," replied Mrs. Dickinson. "He was with Crockett and Bowie a great deal."

"And none escaped?" said Will Allen.

"Not one," she repeated, "I did not see him in the church in the final assault. He doubtless fell in the hospital or in the convent yard. Ah, he was a friend of yours! I am sorry."

"Yes, he was a friend of ours," said the Panther. "He was more than that to me. I loved that boy like a son, an' me an' my comrades here mean to see that the Mexicans pay a high price for his death. An' may I ask, ma'am, how you come to be here?"

She told him how Santa Anna had provided her with the horse, and had sent her alone with the proclamation to the Texans. At the Salado Creek she had come upon the negro servant of Travis, who had escaped from San Antonio, and he was helping her on the way.

"An' now, ma'am," said "Deaf" Smith, "we'll guard you the rest of the way to Gonzales."

The two little groups, now fused into one, resumed their journey over the prairie.

CHAPTER 15

IN ANOTHER TRAP

When Ned Fulton scaled the lowest wall of the Alamo and dropped into the darkness he ran for a long time. He scarcely knew in what direction he was going, but he was anxious to get away from that terrible town of San Antonio de Bexar. He was filled with grief for his friends and anger against Santa Anna and his people. He had passed through an event so tremendous in its nature, so intense and fiery in its results, that his whole character underwent a sudden change. But a boy in years, the man nevertheless replaced the boy in his mind. He had looked upon the face of awful things, so awful that few men could bear to behold them.

There was a certain hardening of his nature now. As he ran, and while the feeling of horror was still upon him, the thought of vengeance swelled into a passion. The Texans must strike back for what had been done in the Alamo. Surely all would come when they heard the news that he was bringing.

He believed that the Texans, and they must be assembled in force somewhere, would be toward the east or the southeast, at Harrisburg or Goliad or some other place. He would join them as soon as he could, and he slackened his pace to a walk. He was too good a borderer now to exhaust himself in the beginning.

He was overpowered after a while by an immense lethargy. A great collapse, both physical and mental, came after so much exhaustion. He felt that he must rest or die. The night was mild, as the spring was now well advanced in Texas, and he sought a dense thicket in which he might lie for a while. But there was no scrub or chaparral within easy reach, and his feeling of lassitude became so great that he stopped when he came to a huge oak and lay down under the branches, which spread far and low.

He judged that he was about six miles from San Antonio, a reasonably safe distance for the night, and, relaxing completely, he fell asleep. Then nature began her great work. The pulses which were beating so fast and hard in the boy's body grew slower and more regular, and at last became normal. The blood flowed in a fresh and strong current through his veins. The great physician, minute by minute, was building up his system again.

Ned's collapse had been so complete that he did not stir for hours. The day came and the sun rose brilliant in red and gold. The boy did not stir, but not far away a large animal moved. Ned's tree was at the edge of a little grassy plain, and upon this the animal stood, with a head held high and upturned nose sniffing the breeze that came from the direction of the sleeper.

It was in truth a great animal, one with tremendous teeth, and after hesitating a while it walked toward the tree under which the boy lay. Here it paused and again sniffed the air, which was now strong with the human odour. It remained there a while, staring with great eyes at the sleeping form, and then went back to the grassy little meadow. It revisited the boy at intervals, but never disturbed him, and Ned slept peacefully on.

It was nearly noon when Ned awoke, and he might not have awakened then had not the sun from its new position sent a shaft of light directly into his eyes. He saw that his precious rifle was still lying by his side, and then he sprang to his feet, startled to find by the sun that it was so late. He heard a loud joyous neigh, and a great bay horse trotted toward him.

It was Old Jack, the faithful dumb brute, of which he had thought so rarely during all those tense days in the Alamo. The Mexicans had not taken him. He was here, and happy chance had brought him and his master together again. It was so keen a joy to see a friend again, even an animal, that Ned put his arm around Old Jack's neck, and for the first time tears came to his eyes.

"Good Old Jack!" he said, patting his horse's nose. "You must have been waiting here all the time for me. And you must have fared well, too. I never before saw you looking so fat and saucy."

The finding of the horse simplified Ned's problem somewhat. He had neither saddle nor bridle, but Old Jack always obeyed him beautifully. He believed that if it came to the pinch, and it became necessary for him to ride for his life, he could guide him in the Indian fashion with the pressure of the knees.

He made a sort of halter of withes which he fastened on Old Jack's head, and then he sprang upon his bare back, feeling equal to almost anything. He rode west by south now, his course taking him toward Goliad, and he went on at a good gait until twilight. A little later he made out the shapes of wild turkeys, then very numerous in Texas among the boughs of the trees, and he brought a fine fat one down at the first shot. After some difficulty he lighted a fire with the flint and steel, which the Mexicans fortunately had not taken from him, toasted great strips over the coals, and ate hungrily of juicy and tender wild turkey.

He was all the time aware that his fire might bring danger down upon him, but he was willing to chance it. After he had eaten enough he took the remainder of his turkey and rode on. It was a clear, starry night and, as he had been awake only since noon, he continued until about ten o'clock, when he again took the turf under a tree for a couch. He slipped the rude halter from Old Jack, patted him on the head and said:

"Old Jack, after the lofty way in which you have behaved I wouldn't disgrace you by tying you up for the night. Moreover, I know that you're the best guard I could possibly have, and so, trusting you implicitly, I shall go to sleep."

His confidence was justified, and the next morning they were away again over the prairie. Ned was sure that he would meet roving Texans or Mexicans before noon, but he saw neither. He surmised that the news of Santa Anna's great force had sent all the Texans eastward, but the loneliness and desolation nevertheless weighed upon him.

He crossed several streams, all of them swollen and deep from spring rains, and every time he came to one he returned thanks again because he had found Old Jack. The great horse always took the flood without hesitation, and would come promptly to the other bank.

He saw many deer, and started up several flights of wild turkeys, but he did not disturb them. He was a soldier now, not a hunter, and he sought men, not animals. Another night came and found him still alone on the prairie. As before, he slept undisturbed under the boughs of a tree, and he awoke the next morning thoroughly sound in body and much refreshed in mind. But the feeling of hardness, the desire for revenge, remained. He was continually seeing the merciless face of Santa Anna and the sanguinary interior of the Alamo. The imaginative quality of his mind and his sensitiveness to cruelty had heightened the effect produced upon him.

He continued to ride through desolate country for several days, living on the game that his rifle brought. He slept one night in an abandoned cabin, with Old Jack resting in the grass that was now growing rankly at the door. He came the next day to a great trail, so great in truth that he believed it to have been made by Mexicans. He did not believe that there was anywhere a Texan force sufficient to tread out so broad a road.

He noticed, too, that the hoofs of the horses were turned in the general direction of Goliad or Victoria, nearer the sea, and he concluded that this was another strong Mexican army intended to complete the ruin of infant Texas. He decided to follow, and near nightfall he saw the camp fires of a numerous force. He rode as near as he dared and reckoned that there were twelve or fifteen hundred men in the camp. He was sure that it was no part of the army with which Santa Anna had taken the Alamo.

Ned rode a wide circuit around the camp and continued his ride in the night. He was forced to rest and sleep a while toward morning, but shortly after daylight he went forward again to warn he knew not whom. Two or three hours later he saw two horsemen on the horizon, and he rode toward them. He knew that if they should prove to be Mexicans Old Jack was swift enough to carry him out of reach. But he soon saw that they were Texans, and he hailed them.

The two men stopped and watched him as he approached. The fact that he rode a horse without saddle or bridle was sufficient to attract their attention, and they saw, too, that he was wild in appearance, with long, uncombed hair and torn clothing. They were hunters who had come out from the little town of Refugio.

Ned hailed them again when he came closer.

"You are Texans and friends?" he said.

"Yes, we are Texans and friends," replied the older of the two men. "Who are you?"

"My name is Fulton, Edward Fulton, and I come from the Alamo."

"The Alamo? How could that be? How could you get out?"

"I was sent out on an errand by Colonel Crockett, a fictitious errand for the purpose of saving me, I now believe. But I fell at once into the hands of Santa Anna. The next morning the Alamo was taken by storm, but every Texan in it died in its defence. I saw it done."

Then he told to them the same tale that Mrs. Dickinson had told to the Panther and his little party, adding also that a large Mexican force was undoubtedly very near.

"Then you've come just in time," said the older man. "We've heard that a big force under General Urrea was heading for the settlements near the coast, and Captain King and twenty-five or thirty men are now at Refugio to take the people away. We'll hurry there with your news and we'll try to get you a saddle and bridle, too."

"For which I'll be thankful," said Ned.

But he was really more thankful for human companionship than anything else. He tingled with joy to be with the Texans again, and during the hours that they were riding to Refugio he willingly answered the ceaseless questions of the two men, Oldham and Jackson, who wanted to know everything that had happened at the Alamo. When they reached Refugio they found there Captain King with less than thirty men who had been sent by Fannin, as Jackson had said, to bring away the people.

Ned was taken at once to King, who had gathered his men in the little *plaza*. He saw that the soldiers were not Texans, that is, men who had long lived in Texas, but fresh recruits from the United States, wholly unfamiliar with border ways and border methods of fighting. The town itself was an old Mexican settlement with an ancient stone church or mission, after the fashion of the Alamo, only smaller.

"You say that you were in the Alamo, and that all the defenders have fallen except you?" said the captain, looking curiously at Ned.

"Yes," replied the boy.

"And that the Mexican force dispatched against the Eastern settlements is much nearer than was supposed?"

"Yes," replied Ned, "and as proof of my words there it is now."

He had suddenly caught the gleam of lances in a wood a little distance to the west of the town, and he knew that the Mexican cavalry, riding ahead of the main army, was at hand. It was a large force, too, one with which the little band of recruits could not possibly cope in the open. Captain King seemed dazed, but Ned, glancing at the church, remembered the Alamo. Every Spanish church or mission was more or less of a fortress, and he exclaimed:

"The church, captain, the church! We can hold it against the cavalry!"

"Good!" cried the captain. "An excellent idea!"

They rushed for the church and Ned followed. Old Jack did not get the saddle and bridle that had been promised to him. When the boy leaped from his back he snatched off the halter of withes and shouted loudly to him: "Go!"

It pained him to abandon his horse a second time under compulsion, but there was no choice. Old Jack galloped away as if he knew what he ought to do, and then Ned, running into the church with the others, helped them to bar the doors.

The church was a solid building of stone with a flat roof, and with many loopholes made long ago as a defence against the Indians. Ned heard the cavalry thundering into the village as they barred the doors, and then he and half a dozen men ran to the roof. Lying down there, they took aim at the charging horsemen.

These were raw recruits, but they knew how to shoot. Their rifles flashed and four or five saddles were emptied. The men below were also firing from the loopholes, and the front rank of the Mexican cavalry was cut down by the bullets. The whole force turned at a shout from an officer, and galloped to the shelter of some buildings. Ned estimated that they were two hundred in number, and he surmised that young Urrea led them.

He descended from the roof and talked with King. The men understood their situation, but they were exultant. They had beaten off the enemy's cavalry, and they felt that the final victory must be theirs. But Ned had been in the Alamo, and he knew that the horsemen had merely hoped to surprise and overtake them with a dash. Stone fortresses are not taken by cavalry. He was sure that the present force would remain under cover until the main army came up with cannon. He suggested to Captain King that he send a messenger to Fannin for help.

King thought wisely of the suggestion and chose Jackson, who slipped out of the church, escaped through an oak forest and disappeared. Ned then made a careful examination of the church, which was quite a strong building with a supply of water inside and some dried corn. The men had brought rations also with them, and they were amply supplied for a siege of several days. But Ned, already become an expert in this kind of war, judged that it would not last so long. He believed that the Mexicans, flushed by the taking of the Alamo, would push matters.

King, lacking experience, leaned greatly on young Fulton. The men, who believed implicitly every word that he had said, regarded him almost with superstition. He alone of the defenders had come alive out of that terrible charnel house, the Alamo.

"I suspect," said King, "that the division you saw is under General Urrea."

"Very probably," said Ned. "Of course, Santa Anna, no longer having any use for his army in San Antonio, can send large numbers of troops eastward."

"Which means that we'll have a hard time defending this place," said King gloomily.

"Unless Fannin sends a big force to our help."

"I'm not so sure that he'll send enough," said King. "His men are nearly all fresh from the States, and they know nothing of the country. It's hard for him to tell what to do. We started once to the relief of the Alamo, but our ammunition wagon broke down and we could not get our cannon across the San Antonio River. Things don't seem to be going right with us."

Ned was silent. His thoughts turned back to the Alamo. And so Fannin and his men had started but had never come! Truly "things were going wrong!" But perhaps it was just as well. The victims would have only been more numerous, and Fannin's men were saved to fight elsewhere for Texas.

He heard a rattle of musketry, and through one of the loopholes he saw that the Mexican cavalry in the wood had opened a distant fire. Only a few of the bullets reached the church, and they fell spent against the stones. Ned saw that very little harm was likely to come from such a fire, but he believed it would be wise to show the Mexicans that the defenders were fully awake.

"Have you any specially good riflemen?" he asked King.

"Several."

"Suppose you put them at the loopholes and see if they can't pick off some of those Mexican horsemen. It would have a most healthy effect."

Six young men came forward, took aim with their long-barrelled rifles, and at King's command fired. Three of the saddles were emptied, and there was a rapid movement of the Mexicans, who withdrew further into the wood. The defenders reloaded and waited.

Ned knew better than Captain King or any of his men the extremely dangerous nature of their position. Since the vanguard was already here the Mexican army must be coming on rapidly, and this was no Alamo. Nor were these raw recruits defenders of an Alamo.

He saw presently a man, holding a white handkerchief on the end of a lance, ride out from the wood. Ned recognised him at once. It was young Urrea. As Ned had suspected, he was the leader of the cavalry for his uncle, the general.

"What do you think he wants?" asked King.

"He will demand our surrender, but even if we were to yield it is likely that we should be put to death afterward."

"I have no idea of surrendering under any circumstances. Do you speak Spanish?"

"Oh, yes," said Ned, seizing the opportunity.

"Then, as I can't, you do the talking for us, and tell it to him straight and hard that we're going to fight."

Ned climbed upon the roof, and sat with only his head showing above the parapet, while Urrea rode slowly forward, carrying the lance and the white flag jauntily. Ned could not keep from admiring his courage, as the white flag, even, in such a war as this might prove no protection. He stopped at a distance of about thirty yards and called loudly in Spanish:

"Within the church there! I wish to speak to you!"

Ned stood up, his entire figure now being revealed, and replied:

"I have been appointed spokesman for our company. What do you want?"

Urrea started slightly in his saddle, and then regarded Ned with a look of mingled irony and hatred.

"And so," he said, "our paths cross again. You escaped us at the Alamo. Why General Santa Anna spared you then I do not know, but he is not here to give new orders concerning you!"

"What do you want?" repeated Ned.

"We want the church, yourself and all the other bandits who are within it."

446

Ned's face flushed at Urrea's contemptuous words and manner, and his heart hardened into a yet deeper hatred of the Mexicans. But he controlled his voice and replied evenly.

"And if we should surrender, what then?"

"The mercy of the illustrious General Santa Anna, whatever it may be."

"I saw his mercy at the Alamo," replied Ned, "and we want none of it. Nor would we surrender, even if we could trust your most illustrious General Santa Anna."

"Then take your fate," said Urrea. "Since you were at the Alamo you know what befell the defenders there, and this place, mostly in ruins, is not nearly so strong. *Adios!*"

"*Adios!*" said Ned, speaking in a firm tone. But he felt that there was truth in Urrea's words. Little was left of the mission but its strong walls. Nevertheless, they might hold them.

"What did he say?" asked King.

"He demanded our surrender."

"On what terms?"

"Whatever Santa Anna might decree, and if you had seen the red flag of no quarter waving in sight of the Alamo you would know his decree."

"And your reply?"

"I told him that we meant to hold the place."

"Good enough," said King. "Now we will go back to business. I wish that we had more ammunition."

"Fannin's men may bring plenty," said Ned. "And now, if you don't mind, Captain King, I'm going to sleep down there at the foot of the wall, and tonight I'll join the guard."

"Do as you wish," said King, "you know more about Texas and these Mexicans than any of us."

"I'd suggest a very thorough watch when night comes. Wake me up about midnight, won't you?"

Ned lay down in the place that he had chosen. It was only the middle of the afternoon, but he had become so inured to hardship that he slept quickly. Several shots were fired before twilight came, but they did not awaken him. At midnight King, according to his request, took him by the shoulder and he stood up.

"Nothing of importance has happened," said King.

"You can see the camp fires of the Mexicans in the wood, but as far as we can tell they are not making any movement."

"Probably they are content to wait for the main force," said Ned.

"Looks like it," said King.

"If you have no objection, captain," said Ned, "I think I'll go outside and scout about a little."

"Good idea, I think," said King.

They opened the door a moment and Ned slipped forth. The night was quite dark and, with the experience of border work that he was rapidly acquiring, he had little fear of being caught by the Mexicans. He kept his eye on the light burning in the wood and curved in a half circle to the right. The few houses that made up the village were all dark, but his business was with none of them. He intended to see, if he could, whether the main Mexican force was approaching. If it should prove to be at hand with the heavy cannon there would be no possible chance of holding the mission, and they must get away.

He continued in his wide curve, knowing that in this case the longest way around was the best and safest, and he gradually passed into a stretch of chaparral beyond the town. Crossing it, he came into a meadow, and then he suddenly heard the soft pad of feet. He sought to spring back into the chaparral, but a huge dim figure bore down upon him, and then his heart recovered its normal beat when he saw that it was only Old Jack.

Ned stroked the great muzzle affectionately, but he was compelled to put away his friend.

"No, faithful comrade," he said. "I can't take you with me. I'd like to do it, but there's no room in a church for a horse as big as you are. Go now! Go at once, or the Mexicans will get you!"

He struck the horse smartly on the jaw. Old Jack looked at him reproachfully, but turned and trotted away from the town. Ned continued his scout. This proof of affection from a dumb brute cheered him.

An hour's cautious work brought him to the far side of the wood. As well as he could judge, nearly all the Mexican troopers were asleep around two fires, but they had posted sentinels who walked back and forth, calling at intervals "*Sentinela alerte*" to one another. Obviously there had been no increase in their force. They were sufficient to maintain a blockade of the church, but too few to surround it completely.

He went two or three miles to the west and, seeing no evidence that the main force was approaching, he decided to return to the church. His original curve had taken him by the south side of the

448

wood, and he would return by the north side in order that his examination might be complete.

He walked rapidly, as the night was far advanced, and the sky was very clear, with bright stars twinkling in myriads. He did not wish day to catch him outside the mission. It was a prairie country, with patches of forest here and there, and as he crossed from one wood to another he was wholly without cover.

He was within a mile of the mission when he heard the faint tread of horses' hoofs, and he concluded that Old Jack, contrary to orders, was coming forward to meet him again. He paused, but the faint tread suddenly became rapid and heavy. A half dozen horsemen who had ridden into the prairie had caught sight of him and now they were galloping toward him. The brightness of the night showed Ned at once that they were Mexican cavalrymen, and as he was on foot he was at a great disadvantage.

He ran at full speed for the nearest grove. The Mexicans fired several musket shots at him, but the bullets all went wild. He did not undertake a reply, as he was straining every effort to reach the trees. Several pistols also were emptied at him, but he yet remained unhurt.

Nevertheless, the horsemen were coming alarmingly near.

He heard the thunder of hoofs in his ears, and he heard also a quick hiss like that of a snake.

Ned knew that the hissing sound was made by a lasso, and as he dodged he felt the coil, thrown in vain, slipping from his shoulders. He whirled about and fired at the man who had thrown the lasso. The rider uttered a cry, fell backward on his horse, and then to the ground.

As Ned turned for the shot he saw that Urrea was the leader of the horsemen. Whether Urrea had recognised him or not he did not know, but the fact that he was there increased his apprehension. He made a mighty effort and leaped the next instant into the protection of the trees and thickets. Fortune favoured him now. A wood alone would not have protected him, but here were vines and bushes also.

He turned off at a sharp angle and ran as swiftly and with as little noise as he could. He heard the horses floundering in the forest, and the curses of their riders. He ran a hundred yards further and, coming to a little gully, lay down in it and reloaded his rifle. Then he stayed there until he could regain his breath and strength. While he lay he heard the Mexicans beating up the thickets, and Urrea giving sharp orders.

Ned knew that his hiding place must soon be discovered, and he began to consider what would be the best movement to make next. His heart had now returned to its normal beat, and he felt that he was good for another fine burst of speed.

He heard the trampling of the horses approaching, and then the voice of Urrea telling the others that he was going straight ahead and to follow him. Evidently they had beaten up the rest of the forest, and now they were bound to come upon him. Ned sprang from the gully, ran from the wood and darted across the prairie toward the next little grove.

He was halfway toward the coveted shelter when Urrea caught sight of him, gave a shout, and fired his pistol. Ned, filled with hatred of Urrea, fired in return. But the bullet, instead of striking the horseman, struck the horse squarely in the head. The horse fell instantly, and Urrea, hurled violently over his head, lay still.

Ned caught it all in a fleeting glance, and in a few more steps he gained the second wood. He did not know how much Urrea was hurt, nor did he care. He had paid back a little, too. He was sure, also, that the pursuit would be less vigorous, now that its leader was disabled.

The second grove did not contain so many vines and bushes, but, hiding behind a tree there, Ned saw the horsemen hold off. Without Urrea to urge them on they were afraid of the rifle that the fugitive used so well. Two, also, had stopped to tend Urrea, and Ned decided that the others would not now enter the grove.

He was right in his surmise. The horsemen rode about at a safe distance from the trees. Ned, taking his time, reloaded his rifle again and departed for the mission. There was now fairly good cover all the way, but he heard other troops of Mexicans riding about, and blowing trumpets as signals. No doubt the shots had been heard at the main camp, and many men were seeking their cause.

But Ned, fortunately for himself, was now like the needle in the haystack. While the trumpets signalled and the groups of Mexican horsemen rode into one another he stole back to the old mission and knocked upon the door with the butt of his rifle. Answering King's questions through the loophole, he was admitted quickly.

"The main army hasn't come up yet," he said, in reply to the eager inquiries of the defenders. "Fannin's men may get here in time, and if they are in sufficient force to beat off the cavalry detachment I suggest that we abandon the mission before we are caught in a trap, and retreat toward Fannin. If we linger the whole Mexican army will be around us."

"Sounds right," said King, "but we've got to hear from Fannin first. Now you look pretty tired, Fulton. Suppose you roll up in some blankets there by the wall and take a nap."

"I don't want to sleep now," said Ned. "You remember that I slept until nearly midnight. But I would like to stretch out a while. It's not very restful to be hunted through woods by Mexicans, even if you do get away."

Ned lay by the wall upon the blankets and watched the sun go slowly up the arch of the heavens. It seemed a hard fate to him that he should again be trapped thus in an old mission. Nor did he have here the strength and support of the great borderers like Bowie and Crockett. He missed them most of all now.

The day passed slowly and with an occasional exchange of shots that did little harm. Toward the twilight one of the sentinels on the wall uttered a great and joyous shout.

"The reinforcements!" he cried. "See, our friends are coming!"

Ned climbed upon the wall and saw a force of more than a hundred men, obviously Texans, approaching. They answered the hail of the sentinel and came on more swiftly. His eyes turned to the wood, in which the Mexican camp yet lay. Their cavalry would still outnumber the Texan force two or three to one, but the Mexicans invariably demanded greater odds than that before they would attack the Texans. Ned saw no stir in the wood. Not a shot was fired as the new men came forward and were joyously admitted to the church.

The men were one hundred and twenty in number, led by Colonel Ward, who by virtue of his rank now commanded all the defenders. As soon as they had eaten and rested a council, at which Ned was present, was held. King had already told the story of young Fulton to Ward, and that officer looked very curiously at Ned as he came forward. He asked him briefly about the Alamo, and Ned gave him the usual replies. Then he told of what he had seen before he joined King.

"How large do you think this force was?" asked Ward.

"About fifteen hundred men."

"And we've a hundred and fifty here. You were not much more than a hundred and fifty in the Alamo, and you held it two weeks against thousands. Why should we retreat?"

"But the Alamo fell at last," said Ned, "and this Refugio mission is not so defensible as the Alamo was."

"You think, then, we should retreat?"

451

"I do. I'm sure the place cannot be held against a large army."

There was much discussion. Ned saw that all the men of the new force were raw recruits from the States like King's. Many of them were mere boys, drawn to Texas by the love of adventure. They showed more curiosity than alarm, and it was evident to Ned that they felt able to defeat any number of Mexicans.

Ned, called upon again for his opinion, urged that they withdraw from the church and the town at once, but neither Ward nor King was willing to make a retreat in the night. They did not seem especially anxious to withdraw at all, but finally agreed to do so in the morning.

Ned left the council, depressed and uneasy. He felt that his countrymen held the Mexicans too lightly. Were other tragedies to be added to that of the Alamo? He was no egotist, but he was conscious of his superiority to all those present in the grave affairs with which they were now dealing.

He took his rifle and went upon the wall, where he resolved to watch all through the night. He saw the lights in the wood where the Mexicans were camped, but darkness and silence prevailed everywhere else. He had no doubt that young Urrea had sent messengers back to hurry up the main force. He smiled to himself at the thought of Urrea. He was sure that the young Mexican had sustained no fatal injury, but he must have painful wounds. And Ned, with the Alamo as vivid as ever in his mind, was glad that he had inflicted them.

Midnight came, and Ward told Ned that he need not watch any longer when the second relay of sentinels appeared. But the boy desired to remain and Ward had no objection.

"But you'll be sleepy," he said, in a good-humoured tone, "when we start at the break of day, and you won't have much chance to rest on a long march."

"I'll have to take the risk," said Ned. "I feel that I ought to be watching."

Toward morning the men in the mission were awakened and began to prepare for the march. They made considerable noise as they talked and adjusted their packs, but Ned paid no attention to them. He was listening instead to a faint sound approaching the town from the south. No one in the church or on the walls heard it but himself, but he knew that it was steadily growing louder.

Ned, moreover, could tell the nature of that sound, and as it swelled his heart sank within him. The first spear of light, herald of dawn, appeared in the east and Ward called out cheerfully:

"Well, we are all ready to go now."

"It is too late," said Ned. "The whole Mexican Army is here."

CHAPTER 16

FANNIN'S CAMP

When Ned made his startling announcement he leaped down lightly from the wall.

"If you will look through the loophole there," he said to Colonel Ward, "you will see a great force only a few hundred yards away. The man on the large horse in front is General Urrea, who commands them. He is one of Santa Anna's most trusted generals. His nephew, Captain Urrea, led the cavalry who besieged us yesterday and last night."

Captain Ward looked, but the Mexicans turned into the wood and were hidden from sight. Then the belief became strong among the recruits that Ned was mistaken. This was only a little force that had come, and Ward and King shared their faith. Ward, against Ned's protest, sent King and thirteen men out to scout.

Ned sadly watched them go. He was one of the youngest present, but he was first in experience, and he knew that he had seen aright. General Urrea and the main army were certainly at hand. But he deemed it wiser to say nothing more. Instead, he resumed his place on the wall, and kept sharp watch on the point where he thought the Mexican force lay. King and his scouts were already out of sight.

Ned suddenly heard the sound of shots, and he saw puffs of smoke from the wood. Then a great shout arose and Mexican cavalry dashed from the edge of the forest. Some of the other watchers thought the mission was about to be attacked, but the horsemen bore down upon another point to the northward. Ned divined instantly that they had discovered King and his men and were surrounding them.

He leaped once more from the wall and shouted the alarm to Ward.

"The men out there are surrounded," he cried. "They will have no chance without help!"

Ward was brave enough, and his men, though lacking skill, were brave enough, too. At his command they threw open the gate of the mission and rushed out to the relief of their comrades. Ned was by the side of Ward, near the front. As they appeared in the opening they heard a great shouting, and a powerful detachment of cavalry galloped toward their right, while an equally strong force of infantry moved on their left. The recruits were outnumbered at least five to one, but in such a desperate situation they did not blench.

"Take good aim with your rifles," shouted Ward. And they did. A shower of bullets cut gaps in the Mexican line, both horse and foot. Many riderless horses galloped through the ranks of the foe, adding to the confusion. But the Mexican numbers were so great that they continued to press the Texans. Young Urrea, his head in thick bandages, was again with the cavalry, and animated by more than one furious impulse he drove them on.

It became evident now even to the rawest that the whole Mexican army was present. It spread out to a great distance, and enfolded the Texans on three sides, firing hundreds of muskets and keeping up a great shouting, Ned's keen ear also detected other firing off to the right, and he knew that it was King and his men making a hopeless defence against overpowering numbers.

"We cannot reach King," groaned Ward.

"We have no earthly chance of doing so," said Ned, "and I think, colonel, that your own force will have a hard fight to get back inside the mission."

The truth of Ned's words was soon evident to everyone. It was only the deadly Texan rifles that kept the Mexican cavalry from galloping over them and crushing them at once. The Mexican fire itself, coming from muskets of shorter range, did little damage. Yet the Texans were compelled to load and pull trigger very fast, as they retreated slowly upon the mission.

At last they reached the great door and began to pass rapidly inside. Now the Mexicans pressed closer, firing heavy volleys.

A score of the best Texan marksmen whirled and sent their bullets at the pursuing Mexicans with such good aim that a dozen saddles were emptied, and the whole force reeled back. Then all the Texans darted inside, and the great door was closed and barricaded. Many of the men sank down, breathless from their exertions, regardless of the Mexican bullets that were pattering upon the church. Ward leaned against the wall, and wiped the perspiration from his face.

"My God!" he exclaimed. "What has become of King?"

There was no answer. The Mexicans ceased to fire and shout, and retreated toward the wood. Ward was destined never to know what had become of King and his men, but Ned soon learned the terrible facts, and they only hardened him still further. The thirteen had been compelled to surrender to overwhelming numbers. Then they were immediately tied to trees and killed, where their skeletons remained upright until the Texans found them.

"You were right, Fulton," said Ward, after a long silence. "The Mexican army was there, as we have plenty of evidence to show."

He smiled sadly, as he wiped the smoke and perspiration from his face. Ned did not reply, but watched through a loophole. He had seen a glint of bronze in the wood, and presently he saw the Mexicans pushing a cannon from cover.

"They have artillery," he said to Ward. "See the gun. But I don't think it can damage our walls greatly. They never did much with the cannon at the Alamo. When they came too close there, we shot down all their cannoneers, and we can do the same here."

Ward chose the best sharpshooters, posting them at the loopholes and on the walls. They quickly slew the Mexicans who tried to man the gun, and General Urrea was forced to withdraw it to such a distance that its balls and shells had no effect whatever upon the strong walls of the church.

There was another period of silence, but the watchers in the old mission saw that much movement was going on in the wood and presently they beheld the result. The Mexican army charged directly upon the church, carrying in its centre men with heavy bars of wood to be used in smashing in the door. But they yielded once more to the rapid fire of the Texan rifles, and did not succeed in reaching the building. Those who bore the logs and bars dropped them, and fled out of range.

A great cheer burst from the young recruits. They thought victory complete already, but Ned knew that the Mexicans would not abandon the enterprise. General Urrea, after another futile charge, repulsed in the same deadly manner, withdrew some distance, but posted a strong line of sentinels about the church.

Having much food and water the recruits rejoiced again and thought themselves secure, but Ned noticed a look of consternation on the face of Ward, and he divined the cause.

"It must be the ammunition, colonel," he said in a whisper.

"It is," replied Ward. "We have only three or four rounds left. We could not possibly repel another attack."

"Then," said young Fulton, "there is nothing to do but for us to slip out at night, and try to cut our way through."

"That is so," said Ward. "The Mexican general doubtless will not expect any such move on our part, and we may get away."

He said nothing of his plan to the recruits until the darkness came, and then the state of the powder horns and the bullet pouches was announced. Most of the men had supposed that they alone were suffering from the shortage, and something like despair came over them when they found that they were practically without weapons. They were more than willing to leave the church, as soon as the night deepened, and seek refuge over the prairie.

"You think that we can break through?" said Ward to Ned.

"I have no doubt of it," replied Ned, "but in any event it seems to me, colonel, that we ought to try it. All the valour and devotion of the men in the Alamo did not suffice to save them. We cannot hold the place against a determined assault."

"That is undoubtedly true," said Ward, "and flushed by the success that they have had elsewhere it seems likely to me that the Mexicans will make such an attack very soon."

"In any event," said Ned, "we are isolated here, cut off from Fannin, and exposed to imminent destruction."

"We start at midnight," said Ward.

Ned climbed upon the walls, and examined all the surrounding country. He saw lights in the wood, and now and then he discerned the figures of Mexican horsemen, riding in a circle about the church, members of the patrol that had been left by General Urrea. He did not think it a difficult thing to cut through this patrol, but the Texans, in their flight, must become disorganized to a certain extent. Nevertheless it was the only alternative.

The men were drawn up at the appointed time, and Ward told them briefly what they were to do. They must keep as well together as possible, and the plan was to make their way to Victoria, where they expected to rejoin Fannin. They gave calabashes of water and provisions to several men too badly wounded to move, and left them to the mercy of the Mexicans, a mercy that did not exist, as Urrea's troops massacred them the moment they entered the church.

Luckily it was a dark night, and Ned believed that they had more than half a chance of getting away. The great door was thrown silently open, and, with a moving farewell to their wounded and disabled comrades, they filed silently out, leaving the door open behind them.

Then the column of nearly one hundred and fifty men slipped away, every man treading softly. They had chosen a course that lay directly away from the Mexican army, but they did not expect to escape without an alarm, and it came in five minutes. A Mexican horseman, one of the patrol, saw the dark file, fired a shot and gave an alarm. In an instant all the sentinels were firing and shouting, and Urrea's army in the wood was awakening.

But the Texans now pressed forward rapidly. Their rifles cracked, quickly cutting a path through the patrol, and before Urrea could get up his main force they were gone through the forest and over the prairie.

Knowing that the whole country was swarming with the Mexican forces, they chose a circuitous course through forests and swamps and pressed on until daylight. Some of the Mexicans on horseback followed them for a while, but a dozen of the best Texan shots were told off to halt them. When three or four saddles were emptied the remainder of the Mexicans disappeared and they pursued their flight in peace.

Morning found them in woods and thickets by the banks of a little creek of clear water. They drank from the stream, ate of their cold food, and rested. Ned and some others left the wood and scouted upon the prairie. They saw no human being and returned to their own people, feeling sure that they were safe from pursuit for the present.

Yet the Texans felt no exultation. They had been compelled to retreat before the Mexicans, and they could not forget King and his men, and those whom they had left behind in the church. Ned, in his heart, knowing the Mexicans so well, did not believe that a single one of them had been saved.

They walked the whole day, making for the town of Victoria, where they expected to meet Fannin, and shortly before night they stopped in a wood, footsore and exhausted. Again their camp was pitched on the banks of a little creek and some of the hunters shot two fine fat deer further up the stream.

Seeking as much cheer as they could they built fires, and roasted the deer. The spirits of the young recruits rose. They would meet Fannin tomorrow or the next day and they would avenge the insult that the Mexicans had put upon them. They were eager for a new action in which the odds should not be so great against them, and they felt sure of victory. Then, posting their sentinels, they slept soundly.

But Ned did not feel so confident. Toward morning he rose from his blankets. Yet he saw nothing. The prairie was bare. There was not a single sign of pursuit. He was surprised. He believed that at least the younger Urrea with the cavalry would follow.

Ned now surmised the plan that the enemy had carried out. Instead of following the Texans through the forests and swamps they had gone straight to Victoria, knowing that the fugitives would make for that point. Where Fannin was he could not even guess, but it was certain that Ward and his men were left practically without ammunition to defend themselves as best they could against a horde of foes.

The hunted Texans sought the swamps of the Guadalupe, where Mexican cavalry could not follow them, but where they were soon overtaken by skirmishers. Hope was now oozing from the raw recruits. There seemed to be no place in the world for them. Hunted here and there they never found rest. But the most terrible fact of all was the lack of ammunition. Only a single round for every man was left, and they replied sparingly to the Mexican skirmishers.

They lay now in miry woods, and on the other side of them flowed the wide and yellow river. The men sought, often in vain, for firm spots on which they might rest. The food, like the ammunition, was all gone, and they were famished and weak. The scouts reported that the Mexicans were increasing every hour.

It was obvious to Ned that Ward must surrender. What could men without ammunition do against many times their number, well armed? He resolved that he would not be taken with them, and shortly before day he pulled through the mud to the edge of the Guadalupe. He undressed and made his clothes and rifle into a bundle. He had been very careful of his own ammunition, and he had a half dozen rounds left, which he also tied into the bundle.

Then shoving a fallen log into the water he bestrode it, holding his precious pack high and dry. Paddling with one hand he was able to direct the log in a diagonal course across the stream. He toiled through another swamp on that shore, and, coming out upon a little prairie, dressed again.

He looked back toward the swamp in which the Texans lay, but he saw no lights and he heard no sounds there. He knew that within a short time they would be prisoners of the Mexicans. Everything seemed to be working for the benefit of Santa Anna. The indecision of the Texans and the scattering of their forces enabled the Mexicans to present overwhelming forces at all points. It seemed to Ned that fortune, which had worked in their favour until the capture of San Antonio, was now working against them steadily and with overwhelming power.

He gathered himself together as best he could, and began his journey southward. He believed that Fannin would be at Goliad or near it. Once more that feeling of vengeance hardened within him. The tremendous impression of the Alamo had not faded a particle, and now the incident of Ward, Refugio and the swamps of the Guadalupe was cumulative. Remembering what he had seen he did not believe that a single one of Ward's men would be spared when they were taken as they surely would be. There were humane men among the Mexicans, like Almonte, but the ruthless policy of Santa Anna was to spare no one, and Santa Anna held all the power.

He held on toward Goliad, passing through alternate regions of forest and prairie, and he maintained a fair pace until night. He had not eaten since morning, and all his venison was gone, but strangely enough he was not hungry. When the darkness was coming he sat down in one of the little groves so frequent in that region, and he was conscious of a great weariness. His bones ached. But it was not the ache that comes from exertion. It seemed to go to the very marrow. It became a pain rather than exhaustion.

He noticed that everything about him appeared unreal. The trees and the earth itself wavered. His head began to ache and his stomach was weak. Had the finest of food been presented to him he could not have eaten it. He had an extraordinary feeling of depression and despair.

Ned knew what was the matter with him. He was suffering either from overwhelming nervous and physical exhaustion, or he had contracted malaria in the swamps of the Guadalupe. Despite every effort of the will, he began to shake with cold, and he knew that a chill was coming. He had retained his blankets, his frontiersman's foresight not deserting him, and now, knowing that he could not continue his flight for the present, he sought the deepest part of the thicket. He crept into a place so dense that it would have been suited for an animal's den, and lying down there he wrapped the blankets tightly about himself, his rifle and his ammunition.

In spite of his clothing and the warm blankets he grew colder and colder. His teeth chattered and he shivered all over. He would not have minded that so much, but his head ached with great violence, and the least light hurt his eyes. It seemed to him the culmination. Never had he been more miserable, more lost of both body and soul. The pain in his head was so violent that life was scarcely worth the price.

He sank by and by into a stupor. He was remotely conscious that he was lying in a thicket, somewhere in boundless Texas, but it did not really matter. Cougars or bears might come there to find him, but he was too sick to raise a hand against them. Besides, he did not care. A million Mexicans might be beating up those thickets for him, and they would be sure to find him. Well, what of it? They would shoot him, and he would merely go at once to some other planet, where he would be better off than he was now.

It seems that fate reserves her severest ordeals for the strong and the daring, as if she would respond to the challenges they give. It seems also that often she brings them through the test, as if she likes the courage and enterprise that dare her, the all-powerful, to combat. Ned's intense chill abated. He ceased to shake so violently, and after a while he did not shake at all. Then fever came. Intolerable heat flowed through every vein, and his head was ready to burst. After a while violent perspiration broke out all over him, and then he became unconscious.

Ned lay all night in the thicket, wrapped in the blankets, and breathing heavily. Once or twice he half awoke, and remembered things dimly, but these periods were very brief and he sank back into stupor. When he awoke to stay awake the day was far advanced, and he felt an overwhelming lassitude. He slowly unwound himself from his blankets and looked at his hand. It was uncommonly white, and it seemed to him to be as weak as that of a child.

He crept out of the thicket and rose to his feet. He was attacked by dizziness and clutched a bush for support. His head still ached, though not with the violence of the night before, but he was conscious that he had become a very weak and poor specimen of the human being. Everything seemed very far away, impossible to be reached.

He gathered strength enough to roll up his blankets and shoulder his rifle. Then he looked about a little. There was the same alternation of woods and prairie, devoid of any human being. He did not expect to see any Texans, unless, by chance, Fannin came marching that way, but a detachment of Mexican lancers might stumble upon him at any moment. The thought, however, caused him no alarm. He felt so much weakness and depression that the possibility of capture or death could not add to it.

Young Fulton was not hungry,—the chill and following fever had taken his appetite away so thoroughly,—but he felt that he must eat. He found some early berries in the thickets and they restored his strength a little, but the fare was so thin and unsubstantial that he decided to look for game. He could never reach Fannin or anybody else in his present reduced condition.

He saw a line of oaks, which he knew indicated the presence of a water-course, probably one of the shallow creeks, so numerous in Eastern Texas, and he walked toward it, still dizzy and his footsteps dragging. His head was yet aching, and the sun, which was now out in full brightness, made it worse, but he persisted, and, after an interminable time, he reached the shade of the oaks, which, as he surmised, lined both sides of a creek.

He drank of the water, rested a while, and then began a search of the oaks. He was looking for squirrels, which he knew abounded in these trees, and, after much slow and painful walking, he shot a fine fat one among the boughs. Then followed the yet more mighty task of kindling a fire with sticks and tinder, but just when he was completely exhausted, and felt that he must fail, the spark leaped up, set fire to the white ash that he had scraped with his knife, and in a minute later a good fire was blazing.

He cooked the tenderest parts of the squirrel and ate, still forcing his appetite. Then he carefully put out the fire and went a mile further up the creek. He felt stronger, but he knew that he was not yet in any condition for a long journey. He was most intent now upon guarding against a return of the chill. It was not the right time for one to be ill. Again he sought a place in a thicket, like an animal going to its den, and, wrapping himself tightly in the blankets, lay down.

He watched with anxiety for the first shiver of the dreaded chill. Once or twice imagination made him feel sure that it had come, but it always passed quickly. His body remained warm, and, while he was still watching for the chill, he fell asleep, and slept soundly all through the night.

The break of day aroused him. He felt strong and well, and he was in a pleasant glow, because he knew now that the chill would not come. It had been due to overtaxed nerves, and there was no malaria in his system.

He hunted again among the big trees until he found a squirrel on one of the high boughs. He fired at it and missed. He found another soon and killed it at the first shot. But the miss had been a grave matter. He had only four bullets left. He took them out and looked at them, little shining pellets of lead. His life depended upon these four, and he must not miss again.

It took him an hour to start his fire, and he ate only half of the squirrel, putting the remainder into his bullet pouch for future needs. Then, much invigorated, he resumed his vague journey. But he was compelled very soon to go slowly and with the utmost caution. There were even times when he had to stop and hide. Mexican cavalry appeared upon the prairies, first in small groups and then in a detachment of about three hundred. Their course and Ned's was the same, and he knew then that he was going in the right direction. Fannin was surely somewhere ahead.

But it was most troublesome travelling for Ned. If they saw him they could easily ride him down, and what chance would he have with only four bullets in his pouch? Or rather, what chance would he have if the pouch contained a hundred?

The only thing that favoured him was the creek which ran in the way that he wanted to go. He kept in the timber that lined its banks, and, so long as he had this refuge, he felt comparatively safe, since the Mexicans, obviously, were not looking for him. Yet they often came perilously near. Once, a large band rode down to the creek to water their horses, when Ned was not fifty feet distant. He instantly lay flat among some bushes, and did not move. He could hear the horses blowing the water back with their noses, as they drank.

When the horses were satisfied, the cavalrymen turned and rode away, passing so near that it seemed to him they had only to look down and see him lying among the bushes. But they went on, and, when they were out of sight, he rose and continued his flight through the timber.

But this alternate fleeing and dodging was most exhausting work, and before the day was very old he decided that he would lie down in a thicket, and postpone further flight until night. Just when he had found such a place he heard the faint sound of distant firing. He put his ear to the earth, and then the crackle of rifles came more distinctly. His ear, experienced now, told him that many men must be engaged, and he was sure that Fannin and the Mexican army had come into contact.

Young Fulton's heart began to throb. The dark vision of the Alamo came before him again. All the hate that he felt for the Mexicans flamed up. He must be there with Fannin, fighting against the hordes of Santa Anna. He rose and ran toward the firing. He saw from the crest of a hillock a wide plain with timber on one side and a creek on the other. The center of the plain was a shallow valley, and there the firing was heavy.

Ned saw many flashes and puffs of smoke, and presently he heard the thud of cannon. Then he saw near him Mexican cavalry galloping through the timber. He could not doubt any longer that a battle was in progress. His excitement increased, and he ran at full speed through the bushes and grass into the plain, which he now saw took the shape of a shallow saucer. The firing indicated that the defensive force stood in the centre of the saucer, that is, in the lowest and worst place.

A terrible fear assailed young Fulton, as he ran. Could it be possible that Fannin also was caught in a trap, here on the open prairie, with the Mexicans in vastly superior numbers on the high ground around him? He remembered, too, that Fannin's men were raw recruits like those with Ward, and his fear, which was not for himself, increased as he ran.

He noticed that there was no firing from one segment of the ring in the saucer, and he directed his course toward it. As soon as he saw horses and men moving he threw up his hands and cried loudly over and over again: "I'm a friend! Do not shoot!" He saw a rifle raised and aimed at him, but a hand struck it down. A few minutes later he sprang breathless into the camp, and friendly hands held him up as he was about to pitch forward with exhaustion.

His breath and poise came back in a few moments, and he looked about him. He had made no mistake. He was with Fannin's force, and it was already pressed hard by Urrea's army. Even as he drew fresh, deep breaths he saw a heavy mass of Mexican cavalry gallop from the wood, wheel and form a line between Fannin and the creek, the only place where the besieged force could obtain water.

"Who are you?" asked an officer, advancing toward Ned.

Young Fulton instantly recognized Fannin.

"My name is Edward Fulton, you will recall me, colonel," he replied. "I was in the Alamo, but went out the day before it fell. I was taken by the Mexicans, but escaped, fled across the prairie, and was in the mission at Refugio when some of your men under Colonel Ward came to the help of King."

"I have heard that the church was abandoned, but where is Ward, and where are his men?"

Ned hesitated and Fannin read the answer in his eyes.

"You cannot tell me so!" he exclaimed.

"I'm afraid that they will all be taken," said Ned. "They had no ammunition when I slipped away, and the Mexicans were following them. There was no possibility of escape."

463

Fannin paled. But he pressed his lips firmly together for a moment and then said to Ned:

"Keep this to yourself, will you? Our troops are young and without experience. It would discourage them too much."

"Of course," said Ned. "But meanwhile I wish to fight with you."

"There will be plenty of chance," said Fannin. "Hark to it!"

The sound of firing swelled on all sides of them, and above it rose the triumphant shouts of the Mexicans.

CHAPTER 17

THE SAD SURRENDER

Ned took another look at the beleaguered force, and what he saw did not encourage him. The men, crowded together, were standing in a depression seven or eight feet below the surface of the surrounding prairie. Near by was an ammunition wagon with a broken axle. The men themselves, three ranks deep, were in a hollow square, with the cannon at the angles and the supply wagons in the centre. Every face looked worn and anxious, but they did not seem to have lost heart.

Yet, as Ned had foreseen, this was quite a different force from that which had held the Alamo so long, and against so many. Most of the young faces were not yet browned by the burning sun of Texas. Drawn by the reports of great adventure they had come from far places, and each little company had its own name. There were the "Grays" from New Orleans, the "Mustangs" from Kentucky, the "Red Rovers" from Alabama and others with fancy names, but altogether they numbered, with the small reinforcements that had been received, only three hundred and fifty men.

Ned could have shed tears, when he looked upon the force. He felt himself a veteran beside them. Yet there was no lack of courage among them. They did not flinch, as the fire grew heavier, and the cannon balls whistled over their heads. Ned was sure now that General Urrea was around them with his whole army. The presence of the cannon indicated it, and he saw enough to know that the Mexican force outnumbered the Texan four or five to one.

He heard the Mexican trumpets pealing presently, and then he saw their infantry advancing in dark masses with heavy squadrons of cavalry on either flank. But as soon as they came within range, they were swept by the deadly fire of the Texan rifles and were driven back in confusion. Ned noticed that this always happened. The Mexicans could never carry a Texan position by a frontal attack. The Texans, or those who were called the Texans, shot straight and together so fast that no Mexican column could withstand their hail of bullets.

A second time the Mexicans charged, and a second time they were driven back in the same manner. Exultation spread among the recruits standing in the hollow, but they were still surrounded. The Mexicans merely drew out of range and waited. Then they attacked a third time, and, from all sides, charging very close, infantry and cavalry. The men in the hollow were well supplied with rifles, and their square fairly blazed. Yet the Mexicans pressed home the charge with a courage and tenacity that Ned had never seen among them before. These were Mexico's best troops, and, even when the men faltered, the officers drove them on again with the point of the sword. General Urrea himself led the cavalry, and the Mexicans pressed so close that the recruits saw both lance and bayonet points shining in their faces.

The hollow in which the Texans stood was a huge cloud of flame and smoke. Ned was loading and firing so fast that the barrel of his rifle grew hot to the touch. He stood with two youths but little older than himself, and the comradeship of battle had already made them friends. But they scarcely saw the faces of one another. The little valley was filled with the smoke of their firing. They breathed it and tasted it, and it inflamed their brains.

Ned's experience had made him a veteran, and when he heard the thunder of the horse's hoofs and saw the lance points so near he knew that the crisis had come.

"One more volley. One for your lives!" he cried to those around him.

The volley was forthcoming. The rifles were discharged at the range of only a few yards into the mass of Mexican cavalry. Horses and men fell headlong, some pitching to the very feet of the Texans and then one of the cannon poured a shower of grape shot into the midst of the wavering square. It broke and ran, bearing its general away with it, and leaving the ground cumbered with fallen men and horses.

The Mexican infantry was also driven back at every point, and retreated rapidly until they were out of range. Under the cloud of smoke wounded men crept away. But when the cloud was wholly gone, it disclosed those who would move no more, lying on every side. The defenders had suffered also. Fannin lay upon the ground, while two of his men bound up a severe wound in the thigh that he had sustained from a Mexican bullet. Many others had been wounded and some had been killed. Most alarming of all was the announcement that the cannon could be fired only a few times more, as there was no water for the sponges when they became heated and clogged. But this discouraged only the leaders, not the recruits themselves, who had ultimate faith in their rifles.

Ned felt an extreme dizziness. All his old strength had not yet returned, and after such furious action and so much excitement there was a temporary collapse. He lay back on the grass, closed his eyes, and waited for the weakness to pass. He heard around him the talk and murmur of the men, and the sounds of new preparations. He heard the recruits telling one another that they had repulsed four Mexican attacks, and that they could repulse four more. Yet the amount of talking was not great. The fighting had been too severe and continuous to encourage volubility. Most of them reloaded in silence and waited.

Ned felt that his weakness had passed, opened his eyes, and sat up again. He saw that the Mexicans had drawn a circle of horsemen about them, but well beyond range. Behind the horsemen their army waited. Fannin's men were rimmed in by steel, and Ned believed that Urrea, after his great losses in the charges, would now wait.

Ned stretched himself and felt his muscles. He was strong once more and his head was clear. He did not believe that the weakness and dizziness would come again. But his tongue and throat were dry, and one of the youths who had stood with him gave him a drink from his canteen. Ned would gladly have made the drink a deep one, but he denied himself, and, when he returned the canteen, its supply was diminished but little. He knew better than the giver how precious the water would become.

Ned was standing at the edge of the hollow, and his head was just about on a level with the surrounding prairie. After his look at the Mexican circle, something whistled by his ear. It was an unpleasant sound that he knew well, one marking the passage of a bullet, and he dropped down instantly. Then he cautiously raised himself up again, and, a half dozen others who had heard the shot did the same. One rose a little higher than the rest and he fell back with a cry, a bullet in his shoulder.

Ned was surprised and puzzled. Whence had come these shots? There was the line of Mexican cavalry, well out of range, and, beyond the horsemen, were the infantry. He could see nothing, but the wounded shoulder was positive proof that some enemy was near.

There was a third crack, and a man fell to the bottom of the hollow, where he lay still. The bullet had gone through his head. Ned saw a wreath of smoke rising from a tiny hillock, a hundred yards away, and then he saw lifted for only a moment a coppery face with high cheek bones and coarse black hair. An Indian! No one could ever mistake that face for a white man's. Many more shots were fired and he caught glimpses of other faces, Indian in type like the first.

Every hillock or other inequality of the earth seemed to spout bullets, which were now striking among the Texans, cooped up in the hollow, killing and wounding. But the circle of Mexican horsemen did not stir.

"What are they?" called Fannin, who was lying upon a pallet, suffering greatly from his wound.

"Indians," replied Ned.

"Indians!" exclaimed Fannin in surprise. "I did not know that there were any in this part of the country."

"Nor did I," replied Ned, "but they are surely here, colonel, and if I may make a suggestion, suppose we pick sharpshooters to meet them."

"It is the only thing to do," said Fannin, and immediately the best men with the rifle were placed along the edge of the hollow. It was full time, as the fire of the red sharpshooters was creeping closer, and was doing much harm. They were Campeachy Indians, whom the Mexicans had brought with them from their far country and, splendid stalkers and skirmishers, they were now proving their worth. Better marksmen than the Mexicans, naked to the waist, their dark faces inflamed with the rage to kill, they wormed themselves forward like snakes, flattened against the ground, taking advantage of every hillock or ridge, and finding many a victim in the hollow. Far back, the Mexican officers sitting on their horses watched their work with delighted approval.

Ned was not a sharpshooter like the Panther or Davy Crockett, but he was a sharpshooter nevertheless, and, driven by the sternest of all needs, he was growing better all the time. He saw another black head raised for a moment above a hillock, and a muzzle thrust forward, but he fired first. The head dropped back, but the rifle fell from the arms and lay across the hillock. Ned knew that his bullet had sped true, and he felt a savage joy.

The other sharpshooters around him were also finding targets. The Indian bullets still crashed into the crowded ranks in the hollow, but the white marksmen picked off one after another in the grass. The moment a red face showed itself a bullet that rarely missed was sent toward it. Here was no indiscriminate shooting. No man pulled the trigger until he saw his target. Ned had now fired four times, and he knew that he had not missed once. The consuming rage still possessed him, but it was for the Mexicans rather than the Indians against whom he was sending his bullets. Surely they were numerous enough to fight the Texans. They ought to be satisfied with ten to one in their favour, without bringing Indians also against the tiny settlements! The fire mounted to his brain, and he looked eagerly for a fifth head.

It was a singular duel between invisible antagonists. Never was an entire body seen, but the crackling fire and the spurts of flame and smoke were incessant. After a while the line of fire and smoke on the prairie began to retreat slowly. The fire of the white sharpshooters had grown too hot and the Indians were creeping away, leaving their dead in the grass. Presently their fire ceased entirely and then that of the white marksmen ceased also.

No sounds came from the Mexicans, who were all out of range. In the hollow the wounded, who now numbered one-fifth of the whole, suppressed their groans, and their comrades, who bound up their hurts or gave them water, said but little. Ned's own throat had become parched again, but he would not ask for another drop of water.

The Texans had used oxen to drag their cannon and wagons, and most of them now lay dead about the rim of the shallow crater, slain by the Mexican and Indian bullets. The others had been tied to the wagons to keep them, when maddened by the firing, from trampling down the Texans themselves. Now they still shivered with fear, and pulled at their ropes. Ned felt sorry for the poor brutes. Full cause had they for fright.

The afternoon was waning, and he ate a little supper, followed by a single drink of water. Every man received a similar drink and no more from the canteens. The coming twilight brought a coolness that was refreshing, but the Indians, taking advantage of the dusk, crept forward, and began to fire again at the Texans cooped up in the crater. These red sharpshooters had the advantage of always knowing the position of their enemy, while they could shift their own as they saw fit.

The Texan marksmen, worn and weary though they were, returned to their task. They could not see the Indians, but they used an old device, often successful in border warfare. Whenever an Indian fired a spurt of smoke shot up from his rifle's muzzle. A Texan instantly pulled trigger at the base of the smoke, and oftener than not the bullet hit his dusky foe.

This new duel in the dark went on for two hours. The Indians could fire at the mass in the hollow, while the Texans steadily picked out their more difficult targets. The frightened oxen uttered terrified lowings and the Indians, now and then aiming at the sounds, killed or wounded more of the animals. The Texans themselves slew those that were wounded, unwilling to see them suffer so much.

The skill of the Texans with the rifle was so great that gradually they prevailed over the Indians a second time in the trial of sharp-shooting. The warriors were driven back on the Mexican cavalry, and abandoned the combat. The night was much darker than usual, and a heavy fog, rising from the plain, added to its density and dampness. The skies were invisible, hidden by heavy masses of floating clouds and fog.

Ned saw a circle of lights spring up around them. They were the camp fires of the Mexican army, and he knew that the troops were comfortable there before the blaze. His heart filled with bitterness. He had expected so much of Fannin's men, and Crockett and Bowie before him had expected so much! Yet here they were, beleaguered as the Texans had been beleaguered in the Alamo, and there were no walls behind which they could fight. It seemed to Ned that the hand of fate itself had resolved to strike down the Texans. He knew that Urrea, one of Santa Anna's ablest and most tenacious generals, would never relax the watch for an instant. In the darkness he could hear the Mexican sentinels calling to one another: "*Sentinela Alerte!*"

The cold damp allayed the thirst of the young recruits, but the crater was the scene of gloom. They did not dare to light a fire, know-ing it would draw the Indian bullets at once, or perhaps cannon shots. The wounded in their blankets lay on the ground. A few of the un-hurt slept, but most of them sat in silence looking sombrely at one another.

Fannin lay against the breech of one of the cannon, blankets hav-ing been folded between to make his position easy. His wound was severe and he was suffering greatly, but he uttered no complaint. He had not shown great skill or judgment as a leader, but he was cool and undaunted in action. Now he was calling a council to see what they could do to release themselves from their desperate case. Officers and men alike attended it freely.

"Boys," said Fannin, speaking in a firm voice despite his weakness and pain, "we are trapped here in this hole in the prairie, but if you are trapped it does not follow that you have to stay trapped. I don't seek to conceal anything from you. Our position could not well be worse. We have cannon, but we cannot use them any longer because they are choked and clogged from former firing, and we have no water to wash them out. Shortly we will not have a drop to drink. But you are brave, and you can still shoot. I know that we can break through the Mexican lines tonight and reach the Coleto, the water and the timber. Shall we do it?"

Many replied yes, but then a voice spoke out of the darkness:

"What of the wounded, colonel? We have sixty men who can't move."

There was an instant's silence, and then a hundred voices said in the darkness:

"We'll never leave them. We'll stay here and fight again!"

Ned was standing with those nearest Fannin, and although the darkness was great his eyes had become so used to it that he could see the pale face of the leader. Fannin's eyes lighted up at the words of his men, and a little colour came into his cheeks.

"You speak like brave men rather than wise men," he said, "but I cannot blame you. It is a hard thing to leave wounded comrades to a foe such as the one who faces us. If you wish to stay here, then I say stay. Do you wish it?"

"We do!" thundered scores of voices, and Fannin, moving a little to make himself easier, said simply:

"Then fortify as best you can."

They brought spades and shovels from the wagons, and began to throw up an earthwork, toiling in the almost pitchy darkness. They reinforced it with the bodies of the slain oxen, and, while they toiled, they saw the fires where the Mexican officers rested, sure that their prey could not break from the trap. The Texans worked on. At midnight they were still working, and when they rested a while there was neither food nor drink for them. Every drop of water was gone long since, and they had eaten their last food at supper. They could have neither food nor drink nor sleep.

Ned had escaped from many dangers, but it is truth that this time he felt despair. His feeling about the hand of fate striking them down became an obsession. What chance had men without an ounce of food or a drop of water to withstand a siege?

But he communicated his fears to no one. Two or three hours before day, he became so sore and weary from work with the spade that he crawled into one of the half-wrecked wagons, and tried to go to sleep. But his nerves were drawn to too high a pitch. After a quarter of an hour's vain effort he got out of the wagon and stood by the wheel. The sky was still black, and the heavy clouds of fog and vapour rolled steadily past him. It seemed to him that everything was closing on them, even the skies, and the air was so heavy that he found it hard to breathe.

He would have returned to work, but he knew that he would over-task his worn frame, and he wanted to be in condition for the battle that he believed was coming with the morrow. They had not tried to cut out at night, then they must do it by day, or die where they stood of thirst.

He sat down at last on the ground, and leaned against a wagon wheel, drawing a blanket over his shoulders for warmth. He found that he could rest better here than inside the wagon, and, in an hour or two, he dozed a little, but when he awoke the night was still very dark.

The men finished their toil at the breastwork just before day and then, laying aside their shovels and picks and taking up their rifles, they watched for the first shoot of dawn in the east. It came presently, disclosing the long lines of Mexican sentinels and behind them the army. The enemy was on watch and soon a terrible rumour, that was true, spread among the Texans. They were caught like the men of Refugio. Only three or four rounds of ammunition were left. It was bad enough to be without food and water, but without powder and bullets either they were no army. Now Ned knew that his presages were true. They were doomed.

The sun rose higher, pouring a golden light upon the plain. The distance to the Mexican lines was in appearance reduced half by the vivid light. Then Ned of the keen eye saw a dark line far off to their right on the prairie. He watched them a little, and saw that they were Mexican cavalry, coming to swell still further Urrea's swollen force. He also saw two cannon drawn by mules.

Ned pointed out the column to Wallace, a major among the Texans, and then Wallace used a pair of glasses.

"You are right," he said. "They are Mexicans and they have two pieces of artillery. Oh, if we could only use our own guns!"

But the Texan cannon stood as worthless as if they had been spiked, and the Texans were compelled to remain silent and helpless, while the Mexicans put their new guns in position, and took aim with deliberation, as if all the time in the world was theirs. Ned tried to console himself with the reflection that Mexican gunners were not often accurate, but the first thud and puff of smoke showed that these were better than usual.

A shower of grape shot coming from a superior height swept their camp, killing two or three of the remaining oxen, smashing the wagons to pieces, and wounding more men. Another shower from the second gun struck among them with like result, and the case of the Texans grew more desperate.

They tried to reach the gunners with their rifles, but the range was too great, and, after having thrown away nearly all the ammunition that was left, they were forced to stand idly and receive the Mexican fire. The Mexicans must have divined the Texan situation, as a great cheer rose from their lines. It became evident to Ned that the shallow crater would soon be raked through and through by the Mexican artillery.

Fannin, lying upon his pallet, was already calling a council of his officers, to which anyone who chose might listen. The wounded leader was still resolute for battle, saying that they might yet cut their way through the Mexicans. But the others had no hope. They pointed to the increased numbers of the foe, and the exhausted condition of their own men, who had not now tasted food or water for many hours. If Urrea offered them good terms they must surrender.

Ned stood on one side, saying nothing, although his experience was perhaps greater than that of anybody else present. But he had seen the inevitable. Either they must yield to the Mexicans or rush boldly on the foe and die to the last man, as the defenders of the Alamo had done. Yet Fannin still opposed.

"We whipped them off yesterday, and we can do it again today," he said.

But he was willing to leave it to the others, and, as they agreed that there was no chance to hold out any longer, they decided to parley with the Mexicans. A white cloth was hoisted on the muzzle of a rifle. The Mexican fire ceased, and they saw officers coming forward. The sight was almost more than Ned could stand. Here was a new defeat, a new tragedy.

"I shall meet them myself," said Fannin, as he rose painfully. "You come with me. Major Wallace, but we do not speak Spanish, either of us."

His eye roved over the recruits, and caught Ned's glance.

"I have been much in Mexico," said Ned. "I speak Spanish and also

472

several Mexican variations of it."

"Good," said Fannin, "then you come with us, and you, too, Durangue. We may need you both."

The two officers and the two interpreters walked out of the hollow, passing the barricade of earth and dead oxen that had been of no avail, and saw four Mexican officers coming toward them. A silk handkerchief about the head of one was hidden partly by a cocked hat, and Ned at once saw that it was Urrea, the younger. His heart swelled with rage and mortification. It was another grievous pang that Urrea should be there to exult.

They met about midway between the camps, and Urrea stepped forward. He gave Ned only a single glance, but it made the boy writhe inwardly. The young Mexican was now all smoothness and courtesy, although Ned was sure that the cruel Spanish strain was there, hidden under his smiling air, but ready to flame up at provocation.

"I salute you as gallant foes," said Urrea in good English, taking off his hat. "My comrades and associates here are Colonel Salas, Lieutenant Colonel Holzinger and Lieutenant Gonzales, who are sent with myself by my uncle, General Urrea, to inquire into the meaning of the white flag that you have hoisted."

Each of the Mexican officers, as his name was called, took off his hat and bowed.

"I am Colonel Fannin," began the Texan leader.

All four Mexicans instantly bowed again.

"And you are wounded," said Urrea. "It shows the valour of the Texans, when their commander himself shares their utmost dangers."

Fannin smiled rather grimly.

"There was no way to escape the dangers," he said. "Your fire was heavy."

Urrea smiled in a gratified way, and then waited politely for Fannin to continue. The leader at once began to treat with the Mexican officers. Ned, Durangue and Urrea translated, and the boy did not miss a word that was said. It was agreed that the Texans should surrender, and that they should be treated as prisoners of war in the manner of civilized nations. Prompt and special attention would be given to the wounded.

Then the Mexican officers saluted courteously and went back toward their own ranks. It had all seemed very easy, very simple, but Ned did not like this velvet smoothness, this willingness of the Mexicans to agree to the most generous terms. Fannin, however, was elated. He had won no victories, but he had saved the lives of his men.

Their own return was slow, as Fannin's wound oppressed him, but when they reached their camp, and told what had been done, the recruits began silently to stack their arms, half in gladness and half in sorrow. More Mexican officers came presently and still treated them with that same smooth and silky courtesy. Colonel Holzinger received the surrendered arms, and, as he did so, he said to Ned, who stood by:

"Well, it's liberty and home in ten days for all you gentlemen."

"I hope so," said Ned gravely, although he had no home.

The Mexican courtesy went so far that the arms of the officers were nailed up in a box, with the statement that they would be given back to them as soon as they were released.

"I am sorry that we cannot consider you an officer, Senor Fulton," said young Urrea to Ned, "then you would get back your rifle and pistols."

"You need not bother about it," said Ned. "I am willing to let them go. I dare say that when I need them I can get others."

"Then you still mean to fight against us?" said Urrea.

"If I can get an exchange, and I suppose I can."

"You are not content even yet! You saw what happened at the Alamo. You survived that by a miracle, but where are all your companions in that siege? Dead. You escaped and joined the Texans at Refugio. Where are the defenders of Refugio? In the swamps of the Guadalupe, and we have only to put forth our hands and take them. You escaped from Refugio to find Fannin and his men. Where are Fannin and his men now? Prisoners in our hands. How many of the Texans are left? There is no place in all Texas so far that the arm of the great Santa Anna cannot reach it."

Ned was stung by his taunts and replied:

"You forget Houston."

Urrea laughed.

"Houston! Houston!" he said. "He does nothing. And your so-called government does nothing, but talk. They, too, will soon feel the might and wrath of Santa Anna. Nothing can save them but a swift flight to the States."

"We shall see," said Ned, although at that moment he was far from confident. "Remember how our men died at the Alamo. The Texans cannot be conquered."

Urrea said nothing further, as if he would not exult over a fallen enemy, although Ned knew that he was swelling with triumph, and went back to his uncle's camp. The Texan arms were taken ahead on some wagons, and then the dreary procession of the Texans themselves marched out of the hollow. They were all on foot and without arms. Those hurt worst were sustained by their comrades, and, thus, they marched into the Mexican camp, where they expected food and water, but General Urrea directed them to walk on to Goliad.

Fainting from hunger and thirst, they took up their march again. The Mexican cavalry rode on either side of them, and many of the horsemen were not above uttering taunts which, fortunately, few of the prisoners could understand. Young Urrea was in command of this guard and he rode near the head of the column where Ned could see him. Now and then a Mexican *vaquero* cracked his long whip, and every report made Ned start and redden with anger.

Some of the recruits were cheerful, talked of being exchanged and of fighting again in the war, but the great majority marched in silence and gloom. They felt that they had wasted themselves. They had marched into a trap, which the Mexicans were able to close upon them before they could strike a single blow for Texas. Now they were herded like cattle being driven to a stable.

They reached the town of Goliad, and the Mexican women and children, rejoicing in the triumph of their men, came out to meet them, uttering many shrill cries as they chattered to one another. Ned understood them, but he was glad that the others did not. Young Urrea rode up by the side of him and said:

"Well, you and your comrades have now arrived at our good town of Goliad. You should be glad that your lives have been spared, because you are rebels and you deserve death. But great is the magnanimity of our most illustrious president and general, Antonio Lopez de Santa Anna."

Ned looked up quickly. He thought he had caught a note of cruelty in that soft, measured voice. He never trusted Urrea, nor did he ever trust Santa Anna.

"I believe it is customary in civilized warfare to spare the lives of prisoners," he said.

"But rebels are rebels, and freebooters are freebooters," said Urrea.

It seemed to Ned that the young Mexican wanted to draw him into some sort of controversy, and he refused to continue. He felt that there was something sinister about Urrea, or that he represented something sinister, and he resolved to watch rather than talk. So, gazing straight ahead, he walked on in silence. Urrea, waiting for an answer, and seeing that he would get none, smiled ironically, and, turning his horse, galloped away.

The prisoners were marched through the town, and to the church. All the old Spanish or Mexican towns of Texas contained great stone churches, which were also fortresses, and Goliad was no exception. This was of limestone, vaulted and sombre, and it was choked to overflowing with the prisoners, who could not get half enough air through the narrow windows. The surgeons, for lack of bandages and medicines, could not attend the wounded, who lay upon the floor.

Where were the fair Mexican promises, in accordance with which they had yielded? Many of the unwounded became so weak from hunger and thirst that they, too, were forced to lie upon the floor. Ned had reserves of strength that came to his aid. He leaned against the wall and breathed the foul air of the old church, which was breathed over and over again by nearly four hundred men.

The heavy doors were unbarred an hour later, and food and water were brought to them, but how little! There was a single drink and a quarter of a pound of meat for each man. It was but a taste after their long fast, and soon they were as hungry and thirsty as ever. It was a hideous night. There was not room for them all to sleep on the floor, and Ned dozed for a while leaning against the wall.

Food and water were brought to them in the same small quantities in the morning, but there was no word from the Mexicans concerning the promises of good treatment and parole that had been made when they surrendered.

Ned was surprised at nothing. He knew that Santa Anna dominated all Mexico, and he knew Santa Anna. Promises were nothing to him, if it served him better to break them. Fannin demanded writing materials and wrote a note to General Urrea protesting strongly against the violation of faith. But General Urrea was gone after Ward's men, who were surrounded in the marshes of the Guadalupe, leaving Colonel Portilla in command. Portilla, meanwhile, was dominated by the younger Urrea, a man of force and audacity, whom he knew to be high in the favour of Santa Anna.

Captain Urrea did not believe in showing any kindness to the men imprisoned in the church. They were rebels or filibusters. They had killed many good Mexicans, and they should be made to suffer for it. No answer was returned to Fannin's letter, and the men in the sombre old limestone building became depressed and gloomy.

Ned, who was surprised at nothing, also hoped for nothing, but he sought to preserve his strength, believing that he would soon have full need of it. He stretched and tensed his muscles in order to keep the stiffness from coming into them, and he slept whenever he could.

Two or three days passed and the Mexican officer, Holzinger, came for Fannin, who was now recovered largely from his wound. The two went away to Copano on the coast to look for a vessel that would carry the prisoners to New Orleans. They returned soon, and Fannin and all his men were in high hopes.

Meanwhile a new group of prisoners were thrust into the church. They were the survivors of Ward's men, whom General Urrea had taken in the swamps of the Guadalupe. Then came another squad, eighty-two young Tennesseans, who, reaching Texas by water, had been surrounded and captured by an overwhelming force the moment they landed. A piece of white cloth had been tied around the arms of every one of these men to distinguish them from the others.

But they were very cheerful over the news that Fannin had brought. There was much bustle among the Mexicans, and it seemed to be the bustle of preparation. The prisoners expected confidently that within another day they would be on the march to the coast and to freedom.

There was a singular scene in the old church. A boy from Kentucky had brought a flute with him which the Mexicans had permitted him to retain. Now sitting in Turkish fashion in the centre of the floor he was playing: "Home, Sweet Home." Either he played well or their situation deepened to an extraordinary pitch the haunting quality of the air.

Despite every effort tears rose to Ned's eyes. Others made no attempt to hide theirs. Why should they? They were but inexperienced boys in prison, many hundreds of miles from the places where they were born.

They sang to the air of the flute, and all through the evening they sang that and other songs. They were happier than they had been in many days. Ned alone was gloomy and silent. Knowing that Santa Anna was now the fountain head of all things Mexican he could not yet trust.

Chapter 18

The Black Tragedy

While the raw recruits crowded one another for breath in the dark vaulted church of Goliad, a little swarthy man in a gorgeous uniform sat dining luxuriously in the best house in San Antonio, far to the northwest. Some of his favourite generals were around him, Castrillon, Gaona, Almonte, and the Italian Filisola.

The "Napoleon of the West" was happy. His stay in San Antonio, after the fall of the Alamo, had been a continuous triumph, with much feasting and drinking and music. He had received messages from the City of Mexico, his capital, and all things there went well. Everybody obeyed his orders, although they were sent from the distant and barbarous land of Texas.

While they dined, a herald, a Mexican cavalrymen who had ridden far, stopped at the door and handed a letter to the officer on guard:

"For the most illustrious president, General Santa Anna," he said.

The officer went within and, waiting an opportune moment, handed the letter to Santa Anna.

"The messenger came from General Urrea," he said.

Santa Anna, with a word of apology, because he loved the surface forms of politeness, opened and read the letter. Then he uttered a cry of joy.

"We have all the Texans now!" he exclaimed. "General Urrea has taken Fannin and his men. There is nothing left in Texas to oppose us."

The generals uttered joyful shouts and drank again to their illustrious leader. The banquet lasted long, but after it was over Santa Anna withdrew to his own room and dictated a letter to his secretary. It was sealed carefully and given to a chosen messenger, a heavy-browed and powerful Mexican.

"Ride fast to Goliad with that letter," said Santa Anna.

The messenger departed at once. He rode a strong horse, and he would find fresh mounts on the way. He obeyed the orders of the general literally. He soon left San Antonio far behind, and went on hour after hour, straight toward Goliad. Now and then he felt the inside of his tunic where the letter lay, but it was always safe. Three or four times he met parties of Mexicans, and he replied briefly to their questions that he rode on the business of the most illustrious president, General Antonio Lopez de Santa Anna. Once, on the second day, he saw two horsemen, whom his trained eyes told him to be Texan hunters.

The messenger sheered off into a patch of timber, and waited until the hunters passed out of sight. Had they seen him much might have changed, a terrible story might have been different, but, at that period, the stars in their courses were working against the Texans. Every accident, every chance, turned to the advantage of their enemies.

The messenger emerged from the timber, and went on at the same steady gait toward Goliad. He was riding his fourth horse now, having changed every time he met a Mexican detachment, and the animal was fresh and strong. The rider himself, powerful by nature and trained to a life in the saddle, felt no weariness.

The scattered houses of Goliad came into view, by and by, and the messenger, giving the magic name of Santa Anna, rode through the lines. He inquired for General Urrea, the commander, but the general having gone to Victoria he was directed to Colonel Portilla, who commanded in his absence. He found Portilla sitting in a patio with Colonel Garay, the younger Urrea and several other Mexican officers. The messenger saluted, drew the letter from his pocket and presented it to Colonel Portilla.

"From the most illustrious president and commander-in-chief, General Santa Anna," he said.

Portilla broke the seal and read. As his eyes went down the lines, a deep flush crept through the tan of his face, and the paper trembled in his hands.

"I cannot do it! I cannot do it! Read, gentlemen, read!" he cried.

Urrea took the extended letter from his hand and read it aloud. Neither his voice nor his hand quivered as he read, and when he finished he said in a firm voice:

"The orders of the president must be obeyed, and you, Colonel Portilla, must carry them out at once. All of us know that General Santa Anna does not wish to repeat his commands, and that his wrath is terrible."

"It is so! It is so!" said Portilla hopelessly, and Garay also spoke words of grief. But Urrea, although younger and lower in rank, was firm, even exultant. His aggressive will dominated the others, and his assertion that the wrath of Santa Anna was terrible was no vain warning. The others began to look upon him as Santa Anna's messenger, the guardian of his thunderbolts, and they did not dare to meet his eye.

"We will go outside and talk about it," said Portilla, still much agitated.

When they left the patio their steps inevitably took them toward the church. The high note of a flute playing a wailing air came to them through the narrow windows. It was "Home, Sweet Home," played by a boy in prison. The Mexicans did not know the song, but its solemn note was not without an appeal to Portilla and Garay. Portilla wiped the perspiration from his face.

"Come away," he said. "We can talk better elsewhere."

They turned in the opposite direction, but Urrea did not remain with them long. Making some excuse for leaving them he went rapidly to the church. He knew that his rank and authority would secure him prompt admission from the guards, but he stopped, a moment, at the door. The prisoners were now singing. Three or four hundred voices were joined in some hymn of the north that he did not know, some song of the English-speaking people. The great volume of sound floated out, and was heard everywhere in the little town.

Urrea was not moved at all. "Rebels and filibusters!" he said in Spanish, under his breath, but fiercely. Then he ordered the door unbarred, and went in. Two soldiers went with him and held torches aloft.

The singing ceased when Urrea entered. Ned was standing against the wall, and the young Mexican instinctively turned toward him, because he knew Ned best. There was much of the tiger cat in Urrea. He had the same feline grace and power, the same smoothness and quiet before going into action.

"You sing, you are happy," he said to Ned, although he meant them all. "It is well. You of the north bear misfortune well."

"We do the best we can wherever we are," replied young Fulton, dryly.

"The saints themselves could do no more," said the Mexican.

Urrea was speaking in English, and his manner was so friendly and gentle that the recruits crowded around him.

"When are we to be released? When do we get our parole?" they asked.

Urrea smiled and held up his hands. He was all sympathy and generosity.

"All your troubles will be over tomorrow," he said, "and it is fitting that they should end on such a day, because it is Palm Sunday."

The recruits gave a cheer.

"Do we go down to the coast?" one of them asked.

Urrea smiled with his whole face, and with the gesture of his hands, too. But he shook his head.

"I can say no more," he replied. "I am not the general, and perhaps I have said too much already, but be assured, brave foes, that tomorrow will end your troubles. You fought us gallantly. You fought against great odds, and you have my sympathy."

Ned had said no more. He was looking at Urrea intently. He was trying, with all the power of his own mind and soul, to read this man's mind and soul. He was trying to pierce through that Spanish armour of smiles and gestures and silky tones and see what lay beneath. He sought to read the real meaning of all these polite phrases. His long and powerful gaze finally drew Urrea's own.

A little look of fear crept into Urrea's eyes, as the two antagonists stared at each other. But it was only for a few minutes. Then he looked away with a shrug and a laugh.

"Now I leave you," he said to the men, "and may the saints bring you much happiness. Do not forget that tomorrow is Palm Sunday, and that it is a good omen."

He went out, taking the torchbearers with him, and although it was dark again in the vaulted church, the recruits sang a long time. Ned sat down with his back against the wall, and he did not share in the general joy. He remembered the look that had come into Urrea's eyes, when they met the accusing gaze of his own.

After a while the singing ceased, and one by one the recruits fell asleep in the close, stifling air of the place. Ned dozed an hour or two, but awoke before dawn. He was oppressed by a deep and unaccountable gloom, and it was not lifted when, in the dusk, he looked at the rows of sleeping figures, crowded so close together that no part of the floor was visible.

He saw the first light appear in the east, and then spread like the slow opening of a fan. The recruits began to awaken by and by, and their good spirits had carried over from the night before. Soon the old church was filled with talk and laughter.

The day came fully, and then the guards brought food and water, not enough to satisfy hunger and thirst, but enough to keep them alive. They did not complain, as they would soon be free men, able to obtain all that they wanted. Presently the doors of the church were thrown open, and the officers and many soldiers appeared. Young Urrea was foremost among the officers, and, in a loud voice, he ordered all the prisoners to come out, an order that they obeyed with alacrity and pleasure.

Ned marched forth with the rest, although he did not speak to any of those about him. He looked first at Urrea, whose manner was polite and smiling, as it had been the night before, and then his glance shifted to the other officers, older men, and evidently higher in rank.

He saw that two, colonels by their uniforms, were quite pale, and that one of them was biting savagely at his moustache. It all seemed sinister to Ned. Why was Urrea doing everything, and why were his superiors standing by, evidently a prey to some great nervous strain?

The recruits, under Urrea's orders, were formed into three columns. One was to take the road toward San Antonio, the second would march toward San Patricio, and the third to Copano. The three columns shouted goodbye, but the recruits assured one another that they would soon meet again. Urrea told one column that it was going to be sent home immediately, another that it was going outside the town, where it was to help in killing cattle for beef which they would eat, and the third that it was leaving the church in a hurry to make room for Santa Anna's own troops, who would reach the town in an hour.

Ned was in the largest column, near the head of it, and he watched everything with a wary eye. He noticed that the Mexican colonels still left all the arrangements to Urrea, and that they remained extremely nervous. Their hands were never quiet for a moment.

The column filed down through the town, and Ned saw the Mexican women looking at them. He heard two or three of them say "*pobrecitos*" (poor fellows), and their use of the word struck upon his ear with an ominous sound. He glanced back. Close behind the mass of prisoners rode a strong squadron of cavalry with young Urrea at their head. Ned could not see Urrea's face, which was hidden partly by a cocked and plumed hat, but he noticed that the young Mexican sat very upright, as if he felt the pride of authority. One hand held the reins, and the other rested on the silver hilt of a small sword at his side.

A column of Mexican infantry marched on either side of the prisoners, and only a few yards away. It seemed to Ned that they were holding the Texans very close for men whom they were to release in a few hours. Trusting the Mexicans in nothing, he was suspicious of everything, and he watched with a gaze that missed no detail. But he seemed to be alone in such thoughts. The recruits, enjoying the fresh air and the prospect of speedy freedom, were talking much, and exchanging many jests.

They passed out of the little town, and the last Ned saw of it was the Mexican women standing in the doorways and watching. They continued along the road in double file, with the Mexican infantry still on either side, and the Mexican cavalry in the rear. A half mile from the town, and Urrea gave an order. The whole procession stopped, and the column of Mexican infantry on the left passed around, joining their comrades on the right. The recruits paid no attention to the movement, but Ned looked instantly at Urrea. He saw the man rise now in his saddle, his whole face aflame. In a flash he divined everything. His heart leaped and he shouted:

"Boys, they are going to kill us!"

The startled recruits did not have time to think, because the next instant Urrea, rising to his full height in his stirrups, cried:

"Fire!"

The double line of Mexicans, at a range of a few yards, fired in an instant into the column of unarmed prisoners. There was a great blaze, a spurt of smoke and a tremendous crash. It seemed to Ned that he could fairly hear the thudding of bullets upon bodies, and the breaking of bones beneath the sudden fierce impact of the leaden hail. An awful strangled cry broke from the poor recruits, half of whom were already down. The Mexicans, reloading swiftly, poured in another volley, and the prisoners fell in heaps. Then Urrea and the cavalry, with swords and lances, charged directly upon them, the hoofs of their horses treading upon wounded and unwounded alike.

Ned could never remember clearly the next few moments in that red and awful scene. It seemed to him afterward that he went mad for the time. He was conscious of groans and cries, of the fierce shouting of the Mexicans, wild with the taste of blood, of the incessant crackling of the rifles and muskets, and of falling bodies. He saw gathering over himself and his slaughtered comrades a great column of smoke, pierced by innumerable jets of fire, and he caught glimpses of the swart faces of the Mexicans as they pulled triggers. From right and left came the crash of heavy but distant volleys, showing that the other two columns were being massacred in the same way.

He felt the thunder of hoofs and a horse was almost upon him, while the rider, leaning from the saddle, cut at him with a sabre. Ned, driven by instinct rather than reason, sprang to one side the next instant, and then the horseman was lost in the smoke. He dashed against a figure, and was about to strike with his fist, the only weapon that he now had, when he saw that he had collided with a Texan, unwounded like himself. Then he, too, was lost in the smoke.

A consuming rage and horror seized Ned. Why he was not killed he never knew. The cloud over the place where the slaughtered recruits lay thickened, but the Mexicans never ceased to fire into it with their rifles and muskets. The crackling of the weapons beat incessantly upon the drums of his ears. Mingled with it were the cries and groans of the victims, now fast growing fewer. But it was all a blurred and red vision to Ned. While he was in that deadly volcano he moved by instinct and impulse and not by reason.

A few of the unwounded had already dashed from the smoke and had undertaken flight across the plain, away from the Mexican infantry, where they were slain by the lances or muskets of the cavalry under Urrea. Ned followed them. A lancer thrust so savagely at him that when the boy sprang aside the lance was hurled from his hand. Ned's foot struck against the weapon, and instantly he picked it up. A horseman on his right was aiming a musket at him, and, using the lance as a long club, he struck furiously at the Mexican. The heavy butt landed squarely upon the man's head, and shattered it like an eggshell. Youthful and humane, Ned nevertheless felt a savage joy when the man's skull crashed beneath his blow.

It is true that he was quite mad for the moment. His rage and horror caused every nerve and muscle within him to swell. His brain was a mass of fire. His strength was superhuman. Whirling the great lance in club fashion about his head he struck another Mexican across the shoulders, and sent him with a howl of pain from the saddle. He next struck a horse across the forehead, and so great was the impact that the animal went down. A cavalryman at a range of ten yards fired at him and missed. He never fired again, as the heavy butt of the lance caught him the next instant on the side of the head, and he went to join his comrade.

All the while Ned was running for the timber. A certain reason was appearing in his actions, and he was beginning to think clearly. He curved about as he ran, knowing that it would disturb the aim of the Mexicans, who were not good shots, and instinctively he held on to the lance, whirling it about his head, and from time to time uttering fierce shouts like an Indian warrior wild with battle. More than one Mexican horseman sheered away from the formidable figure with the formidable weapon.

Ned saw other figures, unarmed, running for the wood. A few reached it, but most were cut down before they had gone half way. Behind him the firing and shouting of the Mexicans did not seem to decrease, but no more groans or cries reached him from the bank of smoke that hung over the place where the murdered recruits lay. But the crash of the fire, directed on the other columns to right and left, still came to him.

Ned saw the wood not far away now. Twenty or thirty shots had been fired at him, but all missed except two, which merely grazed him. He was not hurt and the superhuman strength, born of events so extraordinary, still bore him up. The trees looked very green. They seemed to hold out sheltering arms, and there was dense underbrush through which the cavalry could not dash.

He came yet nearer, and then a horseman, rifle raised to his shoulder, dashed in between. Sparks danced before Ned's eyes. Throat and mouth, lips and his whole face burned with smoke and fever, but all the heat seemed to drive him into fiercer action. He struck at horse and horseman so savagely that the two went down together, and the lance broke in his hands. Then with a cry of triumph that his parched throat could scarcely utter, he leaped into the timber.

Having reached the shelter of the trees, Ned ran on for a long time, and finally came into the belt of forest along the San Antonio River. Twenty-six others escaped in the same way on that day, which witnessed the most dreadful deed ever done on the soil of North America, but nearly four hundred were murdered in obedience to the letter sent by Antonio Lopez de Santa Anna. Fannin and Ward, themselves, were shot through the head, and their bodies were thrown into the common heap of the slain.

Ned did not see any of the other fugitives among the trees. He may have passed them, but his brain was still on fire, and he beheld nothing but that terrible scene behind him, the falling recruits, the fire and the smoke and the charging horsemen. He could scarcely believe that it was real. The supreme power would not permit such things. Already the Alamo had lighted a fire in his soul, and Goliad now turned it into a roaring flame. He hated Urrea, who had rejoiced in it, and he hated Santa Anna who, he dimly felt, had been responsible for this massacre. Every element in his being was turned for the time into passion and hatred. As he wandered on, he murmured unintelligible but angry words through his burning lips.

He knew nothing about the passage of time, but after many hours he realised that it was night, and that he had come to the banks of a river. It was the San Antonio, and he swam it, wishing to put the stream between himself and the Mexicans. Then he sat down in the thick timber, and the collapse from such intense emotions and such great exertions came quickly. He seemed to go to pieces all in a breath. His head fell forward and he became unconscious.

CHAPTER 19

THE RACE FOR THE BOAT

Five men, or rather four men and a boy, rode down the banks of the San Antonio, always taking care to keep well in the shelter of the timber. All the men were remarkable in figure, and at least three of them were of a fame that had spread to every corner of Texas.

The one who rode slightly in advance was of gigantic build, enormously thick through the shoulders and chest. He was dressed in brightly dyed deerskin, and there were many fanciful touches about his border costume. The others also wore deerskin, but theirs was of soberer hue. The man was Martin Palmer, far better known as the Panther, or, as he loved to call himself, the Ring Tailed Panther. His comrades were "Deaf" Smith, Henry Karnes, Obed White and Will Allen.

They were not a very cheerful five. Riding as free lances, because there was now practically no organized authority among the Texans, they had been scouting the day before toward Goliad. They had learned that Fannin and his men had been taken, and they had sought also to discover what the Mexican generals meant to do with the troops. But the Mexican patrols had been so numerous and strong that they could not get close enough to Goliad. Early in the morning while in the timber by the river they had heard the sound of heavy firing near Goliad, which continued for some time, but they had not been able to fathom its meaning. They concluded finally that a portion of Fannin's men must have been still holding out in some old building of Goliad, and that this was the last stand.

They made another effort to get closer to the town, but they were soon compelled to turn back, and, again they sought the thickest timber along the river. Now they were riding back, in the hope of finding some Texan detachment with which they could cooperate.

"If we keep huntin' we ought to find somebody who can tell us somethin'," said the Panther.

"It's a long lane that has no news at the end," said Obed White, with an attempt at buoyancy.

"That's so," said "Deaf" Smith. "We're bound to hit a trail somehow an' somewhere. We heard that Fannin's men had surrendered an' then we heard that firin'. But I guess that they wouldn't give up, without makin' good terms for themselves, else they would have held out as the boys did in the Alamo."

"Ah, the Alamo!" said Obed White. His face clouded at the words.

He was thinking then of the gallant youth who had escaped with him from the dungeon under the sea in the castle of San Juan de Ulua, and who had been his comrade in the long and perilous flight through Mexico into Texas. The heart of the Maine man, alone in the world, had turned strongly to Ned Fulton, and mourning him as one dead he also mourned him as a son. But as he rarely talked of the things that affected him most, he seldom mentioned Ned. The Panther was less restrained.

"We've got a big score to settle for the Alamo," he said. "Some good friends of mine went down forever in that old mission an' there was that boy, Ned Fulton. I s'pose it ain't so bad to be cut off when you're old, an' you've had most of your life, but it does look bad for a strong, fine boy just turnin' into a man to come straight up ag'inst the dead wall."

Will Allen said nothing, but unbidden water forced itself to his eyes. He and Ned had become the strongest of friends and comrades.

"After all that's been done to our people," said the Panther, "I feel like rippin' an' r'arin' an' chawin' the rest of my life."

"We'll have the chance to do all of it we want, judgin' from the way things are goin'," said "Deaf" Smith.

Then they relapsed into silence, and rode on through the timber, going slowly as they were compelled to pick their way in the under-brush. It was now nearly noon, and a brilliant sun shone overhead, but the foliage of young spring was heavy on trees and bushes, and it gave them at the same time shade and shelter.

As they rode they watched everywhere for a trail. If either Texans or Mexicans had passed they wanted to know why, and when. They came at last to hoofprints in the soft bank of the river, indicating that horses—undoubtedly with men on their backs—had crossed here. The skilled trailers calculated the number at more than fifteen, per-haps more than twenty, and they followed their path across the timber and out upon the prairie.

When the hoof-prints were more clearly discernible in the grass they saw that they had been made by unshod feet, and they were mys-tified, but they followed cautiously on for two or three miles, when "Deaf" Smith saw something gleaming by the track. He alighted and picked up a painted feather.

"It's simple now," he said. "We've been followin' the trail of Indians. They wouldn't be in this part of the country, 'less they were helpin' the Mexicans, an' I guess they were at Goliad, leavin' after the business there was finished."

"You're right, Deaf," said Karnes. "That 'counts for the unshod hoofs. It ain't worth while for us to follow them any longer, so I guess we'd better turn back to the timber."

Safety obviously demanded this course, and soon they were again in the forest, riding near the San Antonio and down its stream. They struck the trail of a bear, then they roused up a deer in the thickets, but big game had no attraction for them now, and they went on, leaving bear and deer in peace. Then the sharp eyes of the Panther saw the print of a human foot on the river bank. He soon saw three or four more such traces leading into the forest, where the trail was lost.

The five gathered around the imprints in the earth, and debated their meaning. It was evident even to Will Allen that some one without a horse had swum the river at that point and had climbed up the bank. They could see the traces lower down, where he had emerged from the water.

"I figger it this way," said the Panther. "People don't go travelin' through this country except on horses, an' this fellow, whoever he is, didn't have any horse, as we all can see as plain as day."

"An' in such times as these," said "Deaf" Smith, "fellers don't go swimmin' rivers just for fun. The one that made these tracks was in a hurry. Ain't that so, Hank?"

"'Course he was," replied Karnes. "He was gettin' away from somewhere an' from somebody. That's why he swam the river; he wanted the San Antonio to separate him from them somebodies."

"And putting two and two and then two more together," said Obed White, "we draw the conclusion that it is a fugitive, probably one of our own Texans, who has escaped in some manner from his prison at Goliad."

"It's what we all think," said the Panther, "an' now we'll beat up these thickets till we find him. He's sure to keep movin' away from Goliad, an' he's got sense to stay in the cover of the timber."

The forest here ran back from the river three or four hundred yards, and the five, separating and moving up the stream, searched thoroughly. The hunt presently brought the Panther and Obed White together again, and they expressed their disappointment at finding nothing. Then they heard a cry from Will Allen, who came galloping through the thickets, his face white and his eyes starting.

"I've found Ned Fulton!" he cried. "He's lying here dead in the bushes!"

The Panther and Obed stared in amazement.

"Will," exclaimed the Panther, "have you gone plum' crazy? Ned was killed at the Alamo!"

"I tell you he is here!" cried the boy, who was shaking with excitement. "I have just seen him! He was lying on his back in the bushes, and he did not move!"

"Lead on! Let's see what you have seen!" said Obed, who began to share in the boy's excitement.

The Panther whistled, and Smith and Karnes joined them. Then, led by Will Allen, they rode swiftly through the bushes, coming, forty or fifty yards away, into a tiny grassy glade. It was either Ned Fulton or his ghost, and the Panther, remembering the Alamo, took it for the latter. He uttered a cry of astonishment and reined in his horse. But Obed White leaped to the ground, and ran to the prostrate figure.

"A miracle!" he exclaimed. "It's Ned Fulton! And he's alive!"

The others also sprang from their horses, and crowded around their youthful comrade, whom they had considered among the fallen of the Alamo. Ned was unconscious, his face was hot with fever, and his breathing was hard and irregular.

"How he escaped from the Alamo and how he came here we don't know," said Obed White solemnly, "but there are lots of strange things in heaven and earth, as old Shakespeare said, and this is one of the strangest of them all."

"However, it's happened we're glad to get him back," said the Panther. "And now we must go to work. You can tell by lookin' at him that he's been through all kinds of trouble, an' a powerful lot of it."

These skilled borderers knew that Ned was suffering from exhaustion. They forced open his mouth, poured a drink down his throat from a flask that Karnes carried, and rubbed his hands vigorously. Ned, after a while, opened his eyes and looked at them dimly. He knew in a vague way that these were familiar faces, but he remembered nothing, and he felt no surprise.

"Ned! Ned! Don't; you know us?" said Will Allen. "We're your friends, and we found you lying here in the bush!"

The clouds slowly cleared away from Ned's mind and it all came back, the terrible and treacherous slaughter of his unarmed comrades, his own flight through the timber his swimming of the river, and then the blank. But these were his best friends. It was no fantasy. How and when they had come he did not know, but here they were in the flesh, the Panther, Obed White, Will Allen, "Deaf" Smith and Henry Karnes.

"Boys," he asked weakly, "how did you find me?"

"Now don't you try to talk yet a while, Ned," said Obed White, veiling his feeling under a whimsical tone. "When people come back from the dead they don't always stay, and we want to keep you, as you're an enrolled member of this party. The news of your trip into the beyond and back again will keep, until we fix up something for you that will make you feel a lot stronger."

These frontiersmen never rode without an outfit, and Smith produced a small skillet from his kit. The Panther lighted a fire, Karnes chipped off some dried beef, and in a few minutes they had a fine soup, which Ned ate with relish. He sat with his back against a tree and his strength returned rapidly.

"I guess you can talk now, Ned," said Obed White. "You can tell us how you got away from the Alamo, and where you've been all the time."

Young Fulton's face clouded and Obed White saw his hands tremble.

"It isn't the Alamo," he said. "They died fighting there. It was Goliad."

"Goliad?" exclaimed "Deaf" Smith. "What do you mean?"

"I mean the slaughter, the massacre. All our men were led out. They were told that they were to go on parole. Then the whole Mexican army opened fire upon us at a range of only a few yards and the cavalry trod us down. We had no arms. We could not fight back. It was awful. I did not dream that such things could be. None of you will ever see what I've seen, and none of you will ever go through what I've gone through."

"Ned, you've had fever. It's a dream," said Obed White, incredulous.

"It is no dream. I broke through somehow, and got to the timber. Maybe a few others escaped in the same way, but all the rest were murdered in cold blood. I know that Santa Anna ordered it."

They knew perfectly well that Ned was telling the full truth, and the faces of all of them darkened. The same thought was in the heart of every one, vengeance for the deed, but however intense was the thought it did not approach the feeling of Ned, who had seen it all, and who had been through it all.

"I guess that was the firing we heard," said Smith, "when we thought it was the boys making a last stand at Goliad. I tell you, comrades, this means the freedom of Texas. No matter how the quarrel came about no people can stand such things."

490

"It's so," said the others together.

They did not declaim. They were of a tribe that was not given much to words, but they felt sure that their own resolve to fight until no Mexicans were left in Texas would now be shared by every Texan.

After Ned rested a while longer and ate more of the good soup, he told the full story of the great and tragic scenes through which he had passed since he became separated from them. Seasoned as they were, these men hung with breathless interest on every detail. He told them everything that had passed in the Alamo during the long days of the siege. He told of Crockett and Bowie and Travis and of the final assault.

The Panther drew a deep breath, when he finished that part of the story.

"They were certainly great men in the Alamo, them fellers," he said, "and when my time comes to die I believe I'd rather die that way than any other."

Ned did not linger long over the tale of Goliad. He could not yet bear the detailed repetition.

"I think we'd better make for the coast," said "Deaf" Smith, when he had finished. "Our forces in the field are about wiped out, an' we've got to raise a new army of some kind. We can look for our government, too. It's wanderin' aroun', tryin' to keep out of the hands of Santa Anna. We haven't any horse for you now, Ned, but you can ride behind Will Allen. Maybe we can get you a mount before long."

They remained in the timber the rest of the day, in order that Ned might recover sufficiently for the journey. About the middle of the afternoon they saw a dozen Mexican cavalrymen on the plain, and they hoped that they would invade the timber. They were keyed to such a pitch of anger and hate that they would have welcomed a fight, and they were more than confident of victory, but the Mexicans disappeared beyond the swells, and every one of the men was disappointed.

At night they began their march toward the north, and continued almost until morning. Ned, riding behind Will Allen, scarcely spoke. Obed White, then and afterward, observed a great change in him. He seemed to have matured suddenly far beyond his years, and Obed always felt that he had some unchanging purpose that had little to do with gentleness or mercy.

They slept in the timber until about 10 o'clock, and then resumed their ride northward, still holding to the opinion that the peripatetic

Texan government would be found at Harrisburg, or somewhere in its vicinity. In the afternoon they encountered a Mexican force of eight mounted men, and attacked with such vigor that Ned and Will, riding double, were never able to get into the fight. Two of the Mexicans fell, and the rest got away. The Texans were unharmed.

The Panther, after a chase, captured one of the horses, and brought him back for Ned. They also secured the arms of the fallen Mexicans, one of these weapons being an American rifle, which Ned was quite sure had belonged to a slaughtered recruit at Goliad. They also found a letter in one of the Mexican haversacks. It was from General Urrea to General Santa Anna, and the Panther and his comrades inferred from the direction in which its bearer had been riding that the dictator himself had left San Antonio, and was marching eastward with the main Mexican army.

"I have to inform you," ran a part of the letter, "that your orders in regard to the rebels at Goliad were carried out, in my absence, by the brave and most excellent Colonel Portilla. They were all executed, except a few who escaped under cover of the smoke to the timber, but our cavalrymen are sure to find in time every one of these, and inflict upon them the justice that you have ordered.

"I shall march north, expecting to meet your excellency, and I trust that I shall have further good news to report to you. There are now no rebel forces worthy of the name. We shall sweep the country clean. I shall send detachments to take any Americans who may land at the ports, and, cooperating with you, I feel assured, also, that we shall capture every member of the rebel government. In another month there will not be a single Texan in arms against us."

Ned read the letter aloud, translating into English as he went, and when he finished the Panther burst into a scornful laugh.

"So, the rebels are all killed, or about to be killed!" he said. "An' there won't be one Texan in arms a month from now! I'm willin' to give my word that here are six of us who will be in arms then, roarin' an' rippin' an' t'arin'! They'll sweep the country clean, will they? They'll need a bigger broom for that job than any that was ever made in Mexico!"

The others made comment in like fashion, but young Fulton was silent. His resolution was immutable, and it required no words to assert it.

"I guess we'd better take this letter with us an' give it to Sam Houston," said "Deaf" Smith. "Houston has been criticized a lot for not gatherin' his forces together an' attackin' the Mexicans, but he ain't had any forces to gather, an' talk has never been much good against cannon balls an' bullets. Still, he's the only man we've got to fall back on."

"You keep the letter, 'Deaf'," said the Panther, "an' now that we've got a horse for Ned I guess we can go a little faster. How you feelin' now, Ned?"

"Fine," replied Ned. "Don't you bother about me any more. I started on the upgrade the moment you fellows found me."

"A good horse and a good rifle ought to be enough to bring back the strength to any Texan," said Obed White.

They resumed their journey at a faster pace, but before nightfall they met another Texan who informed them that large forces of Mexicans were now between them and Harrisburg. Hence they concluded that it was wiser to turn toward the coast, and make a great circuit around the forces of Santa Anna.

But they told the Texan scout of what had been done at Goliad, and bade him wave the torch of fire wherever he went. He rode away with a face aghast at the news, and they knew that he would soon spread it through the north. As for themselves they rode rapidly toward the east.

They spent the night in a cluster of timber, and the Panther was fortunate enough to shoot a wild turkey. They made Ned eat the tenderest parts, and then seek sleep between blankets. His fever was now gone, but he was relaxed and weak. It was a pleasant weakness, however, and, secure in the comradeship of his friends, he soon fell into a deep slumber which lasted all the night. The others had planned an early start, but, as Ned was sleeping with such calm and peace, they decided not to disturb him, knowing how much he needed the rest. It was three hours after sunrise when he awoke, and he made many apologies, but the rest only laughed.

"What's the use of our hurryin'?" said "Deaf" Smith. "It'll take some time for Sam Houston to get any army together, an' we might keep in good shape until he gets it. Here's more beef soup for you, Ned. You'll find it mighty fine for buildin' up."

Two or three hours after they started that day they came to a large trail, and, when they followed it a little while, they found that it was made by Mexicans marching south, but whether they belonged to the main force under Santa Anna or that under Urrea they could not tell.

It was evident that the northern road was full of dangers and they

493

rode for the coast. Several small Texan vessels were flitting around the gulf, now and then entering obscure bays and landing arms, ammunition and recruits for he cause. Both Smith and Karnes were of the opinion that they might find a schooner or sloop, and they resolved to try for it.

They reached, the next day, country that had not been ravaged by the troops of Santa Anna, and passed one or two tiny settlements, where they told the news of Goliad. The Panther, Smith and Karnes were well known to all the Texans, and they learned in the last of these villages that a schooner was expected in a cove about forty miles up the coast. It would undoubtedly put in at night, and it would certainly arrive in two or three days. They thought it was coming from New Orleans.

The little party decided to ride for the cove, and meet the schooner if possible. They could reach it in another day and night, and they would await the landing.

"We've got good friends in New Orleans," said Smith, as they rode over the prairie. "You'll remember the merchant, John Roylston. He's for us heart and soul, an' I've no doubt that he's sendin' us help."

"All the Texans owe him a debt," said Ned, "and I owe him most of all. His name saved my life, when I was taken at San Antonio. It had weight with Santa Anna, and it might have had weight with him, too, at Goliad, had he been there."

They rode steadily all the next day. Their horses were tough mustangs of the best quality, and showed no signs of weariness. They passed through a beautiful country of light rolling prairie, interspersed with fine forest. The soil was deep and rich, and the foliage was already in its tenderest spring green. Soft, warm airs swept up from the gulf. Five of the riders felt elation, and talked cheerfully. But Ned maintained a sombre silence. The scenes of Goliad were still too vivid for him to rejoice over anything. The others understood, and respected his silence.

They camped that night as usual in the thickest forest they could find, and, feeling that they were now too far east to be in any serious danger from the Mexicans, they lighted a fire, warmed their food, and made coffee, having replenished their supplies at the last settlement. Obed White was the coffee maker, heating it in a tin pot with a metal bottom. They had only one cup, which they used in turn, but the warm food and drink were very grateful to them after their hard riding.

"Keeping in good condition is about three-fourths of war," said Obed in an oracular tone. "He who eats and runs away will live to eat another day. Besides, Napoleon said that an army marched better on a full stomach, or something like it."

"That applied to infantry," said Will Allen. "We march on our horses."

"Some day," said Ned, "when we've beaten Santa Anna and driven all the Mexicans out of Texas, I'm going back and hunt for Old Jack. He and I are too good friends to part forever. I found him, after abandoning him the first time, and I believe I can do it again, after leaving him the second time."

"Of course you can," said the Panther cheerily. "Old Jack is a horse that will never stay lost. Now, I think we'd better put out our fire and go to sleep. The horses will let us know if any enemy comes."

All were soon slumbering peacefully in their blankets, but Ned, who had slept so much the night before, awakened in two or three hours. He believed, at first, that a distant sound had broken his sleep, but when he sat up he heard nothing. Five dusky figures lay in a row near him. They were those of his comrades, and he heard their steady breathing. Certainly they slept well. He lay down again, but he remained wide awake, and, when his ear touched the ground, he seemed to hear the faint and distant sound again.

He rose and looked at the horses. They had not moved, and it was quite evident that they had detected no hostile presence. But Ned was not satisfied. Putting his rifle on his shoulder he slipped through the forest to the edge of the prairie. Long before he was there he knew that he had not been deceived by fancy.

He saw, two or three hundred yards in front of him, a long file of cavalry marching over the prairie, going swiftly and straight ahead, as if bent upon some purpose well defined. A good moon and abundant stars furnished plenty of light, and Ned saw that the force was Mexican. There were no lancers, all the men carrying rifles or muskets, and Ned believed that he recognised the younger Urrea in the figure at their head. He had seen the young Mexican so often and in such vivid moments that there was no phase of pose or gesture that he could forget.

Ned watched the column until it was hidden by the swells. It had never veered to either right or left, and its course was the same as that of his comrades and himself. He wondered a little while, and then he felt a suspicion which quickly grew into a certainty. Urrea, a daring partisan leader, who rode over great distances, had heard of the schooner and its arms, and was on his way to the cove to seize them.

It was for Ned and his friends to prevent it.

He returned, and, awakening the others, stated what he had seen. Then he added his surmise.

"It's likely that you're guessin' right," said "Deaf" Smith. "The Mexicans have spies, of course, an' they get word, too, from Europeans in these parts, who are not friendly to us. What do you say, boys, all of you?"

"That Urrea is bound for the same place we are," said Obed White.

"That we've got to ride hard, an' fast," said the Panther.

"It's our business to get there first," said Karnes.

"Let's take to the saddle now," said Will Allen.

Ned said nothing. He had given his opinion already. They saddled their horses, and were on the plain in five minutes, riding directly in the trail of the Mexican cavalry. They meant to follow until nearly dawn, and then, passing around, hurry to the cove, where the schooner, without their warning, might be unloading supplies before nightfall into the very arms of the Mexicans.

Before dawn they faintly saw the troop ahead, and then, turning to the left, they put their mustangs into the long easy lope of the frontier, not slowing down, until they were sure that they were at least three or four miles beyond the Mexicans. But they continued at a fast walk, and ate their breakfasts in the saddle. They rode through the same beautiful country, but without people, and they knew that if nothing unusual occurred they would see the sea by noon.

Ned went over their directions once more. The cove ran back from the sea about a mile, and its entrance was a strait not more than thirty yards wide, but deep. In fact, the entire cove was deep, being surrounded by high forested banks except at the west, into which a narrow but deep creek emptied. The only convenient landing was the creek's mouth, and they believed that they would find the schooner there.

Ned, in common with the others, felt the great importance of the mission on which they rode. Most of the Texan cannon and a great part of their rifles had been taken at the Alamo and Goliad. But greater even than the need of arms was that of ammunition. If Urrea were able to seize the schooner, or to take the supplies, the moment after they landed, he would strike the Texans a heavy blow. Hence the six now pushed their horses.

At ten o'clock, they caught a glimpse of the sea upon their right. Five minutes later they saw a cloud of dust on their left, less than a

496

mile away. It was moving rapidly, and it was evident at once that it was made by a large body of horse. When the dust lifted a little, they saw that it was Urrea and his men.

"It's likely that they have more information than we have," said the Panther, "an' they are ridin' hard to make a surprise. Boys, we've got to beat 'em, an', to do it, we've got to keep ahead of our dust all the time!"

"The greater the haste, the greater the speed just now," said Obed White.

They urged their horses into a gallop. They kept close to the sea, while Urrea was more than half a mile inland. Luckily, a thin skirt of timber soon intervened between Mexicans and Texans, and the six believed that Urrea and his men were unaware of their presence. Their own cloud of dust was much smaller than that of the Mexicans, and also it might readily be mistaken for sea sand whipped up by the wind.

Ned and the Panther rode in front, side by side, Smith and Karnes followed, side by side, too, and behind came Obed White and Will Allen, riding knee to knee. They ascended a rise and Ned, whose eyes were the keenest of them all, uttered a little cry.

"The schooner is there!" he exclaimed. "See, isn't that the top of a mast sticking up above those scrub trees?"

"It's nothing else," said Obed White, who was familiar with the sea and ships. "And it's bound, too, to be the schooner for which we are looking. Forward, boys! The swift will win the race, and the battle will go to the strong!"

They pressed their horses now to their greatest speed. The cove and the ship were not more than a half mile away. A quarter of a mile, and the skirt of timber failed. The Mexicans on their left saw them, and increased their speed.

"The schooner's anchored!" exclaimed Obed, "and they are unloading! Look, part of the cargo is on the bank already!"

With foot and rein they took the last ounce of speed from their horses, and galloped up to a group of astonished men, who were transferring arms and ammunition by small boats from a schooner to the land Already more than a hundred rifles, and a dozen barrels of powder lay upon the shore.

"Back to the ship! Back to the ship!" cried Ned, who involuntarily took the lead. "We are Texans, and a powerful force of Mexicans will be here inside of fifteen minutes!"

The men looked at him astonished and unbelieving. Ned saw

among them a figure, clad in sober brown, a man with a large head and a broad, intellectual face, with deep lines of thought. He knew him at once, and cried:

"Mr. Roylston, it is I! Edward Fulton! You know me! And here are Captain Palmer, 'Deaf' Smith, Henry Karnes, Obed White and Will Allen! I tell you that you have no time to lose! Put the supplies back on the schooner, and be as quick as you can! Captain Urrea and two hundred men are galloping fast to capture them!"

Roylston started in astonishment at the appearance of Ned, whom he, too, had believed to be dead, but he wasted no time in questions. He gave quick orders to have the arms and ammunition reloaded, and directed the task himself. The Panther sprang from his horse and walked back to the edge of the wood.

"Here they come at a gallop," he said, "and we need time. Boys, hand me your rifles, as I call for them, an' I'll show you how to shoot."

The Panther did not mean to boast, nor did the others take it as such. He merely knew his own skill, and he meant to use it.

"Do as he says," said "Deaf" Smith to the others. "I reckon that, as Davy Crockett is dead, the Panther is the best shot in all Texas."

The Mexican cavalry were coming at a gallop, several hundred yards away. The Panther raised his long, slender-barrelled rifle, pulled the trigger, and the first horseman fell from the saddle. Without turning, he held out his hands and Smith thrust the second rifle into them. Up went the weapon, and a second Mexican saddle was empty. A third rifle and a third Mexican went down, a fourth, and the result was the same. The whole Mexican troop, appalled at such deadly shooting, stopped suddenly.

"Keep it up, Panther! Keep it up!" cried Smith. "We need every minute of time that we can get."

While the Mexicans hesitated the Panther sent another fatal bullet among them. Then they spread out swiftly in a thin half circle, and advanced again. All the six Texans now opened fire, and they were also helped by some of the men from the boat. But a part of the attacking force had gained cover and the fire was not now so effective.

Nevertheless the rush of the Mexicans was checked, and under the directions of Roylston the reloading of the schooner was proceeding rapidly. They hoisted the last of the powder and rifles over the side, and two of the boats were putting back for the defenders. The schooner, meanwhile, had taken in her anchor and was unfurling her sails. Roylston was in one of the boats and, springing upon the bank, he shouted to the defenders:

"Come, lads! The supplies are all back on board! It's for your lives now!"

All the men instantly abandoned the defence and rushed for the bank, the Panther uttering a groan of anger.

"I hate to leave six good horses to Urrea, an' that gang," he said, "but I s'pose it has to be done."

"Don't grieve, Panther," cried Smith. "We'll take three for one later on!"

"Hurry up! Hurry up!" said Roylston. "There is no time to waste. Into the boats, all of you!"

They scrambled into the boats, reached the schooner, and pulled the boats to the deck after them. There was not a minute to lose. The schooner, her sails full of wind, was beginning to move, and the Mexicans were already firing at her, although their bullets missed.

Ned and Will Allen threw themselves flat on the deck, and heard the Mexican bullets humming over their heads. Ned knew that they were still in great danger, as it was a mile to the open sea, and the Mexicans galloping along by the side of the cove had begun a heavy fire upon the schooner. But the Panther uttered a tremendous and joyous shout of defiance.

"They can't hurt the ship as long as they ain't got cannon," he said, "an' since it's rifles, only, we'll give it back to 'em!"

He and the other sharpshooters, sheltering themselves, began to rake the woods with rifle fire. The Mexicans replied, and the bullets peppered the wooden sides of the schooner or cut holes through her sails. But the Texans now had the superiority. They could shelter themselves on the ship, and they were also so much better marksmen that they did much damage, while suffering but little themselves.

The schooner presently passed between the headlands, and then into the open sea. She did not change her course until she was eight or ten miles from land, when she turned northward.

Chapter 20

The Cry for Vengeance

As soon as the schooner was out of range Ned and his comrades stood up on the deck, and looked back at the long low coastline, which had offered to them so much danger. At first they saw Mexican horsemen on the beach, but as they went further and further out to sea they disappeared.

A strong wind hummed through the sails and the schooner, heeling over a little, went swiftly northward, leaving a long white wake. Ned and his comrades sat on the benches that ran around the sides of the deck. Some of the rich brown colour faded from the Panther's face, and his eyes looked a little bit uneasy.

"I'm glad to be here," he said, "glad to be out of reach of the Mexicans, but I wish I was on somethin' a lot steadier than this."

Obed White, familiar with the waters of the Maine coast, laughed.

"This is just a spanking good breeze," he said. "Look how the waves dance!"

"Let 'em dance," said the Panther, "an' they can do my share of dancin', too. I never felt less like roarin' an' t'arin' an' rippin' in my life."

"Any way, we're getting a fine rest," said Will Allen. "It's pleasant to be out here, where nobody can drop suddenly on you from ambush."

The schooner made another curve to the eastward, the water became smoother and the Panther's qualms disappeared. Food and water were brought to them on deck, and they ate and drank with good appetites. Then John Roylston, who had gone below, as soon as they were out of range, reappeared. He went directly to Ned, shook hands with him with great energy, and said in a tone of deep gratitude:

"I had given you up for lost. But you reappeared with your friends, just in time to save the most valuable of all cargoes for the Texans. I should like to hear now how you rose from the dead, because I had direct information that you were in the Alamo, and I know that everybody there perished."

"I come, nevertheless, as the bearer of bad news," said Ned, with Goliad fresh in his mind.

"How is that?"

Then Ned told for the second time the dreadful deed done by order of Santa Anna, and it seemed to him as he told it that all the details were as vivid and terrible as ever. His desire for revenge upon the dictator and the Mexicans had not diminished a particle. Roylston's face, usually a mask, showed horror.

"It was an awful thing to do," he said, "but it means now that Santa Anna will never conquer Texas. No man can do such a deed and yet triumph. Now, tell me how it is that you are not among the slain in the Alamo." Ned related the story anew, and he dwelt upon the fact that Santa Anna had spared him at the mention of Roylston's name.

500

But when the story was finished, the merchant was silent for quite a while. Ned knew by the contraction of the lines upon the great brow that he was thinking. At last, he broke the silence.

"No doubt you have wondered that my name had so much influence with Santa Anna," he said. "I have hinted at it before, but I will explain more fully now. I am, as you know, a merchant. I trade throughout the whole southwest, and I have ships in the Gulf and the Caribbean. One of them, the *Star of the South*, on which we now are, can show her heels to anything in these seas.

"Earlier in my life I came in contact with Antonio Lopez de Santa Anna. Like many others I fell for a while under his spell. I believed that he was a great and liberal man, that he would even be able to pull Mexico out of her slough of misrule and ignorance. I helped him in some of his young efforts. The splendid *hacienda* that he has near Vera Cruz was bought partly with money that I furnished.

"But our friendship could not last. Vain, ruthless, cruel, but with genius, Santa Anna can have no friends except those whom he may use. Unless you submit, unless you do everything that he wishes, you are, in his opinion, a traitor to him, a malefactor and an enemy, to be crushed by trickery or force, by fair means or foul. How could I have continued dealings with such a man?

"I soon saw that instead of being Mexico's best friend he was her worst enemy. I drew away in time, but barely. I was in Mexico when the break came, and he would have seized and imprisoned me or had me shot, but I escaped in disguise.

"I retained, too, a hold upon Santa Anna that he has sought in vain to break. Such a man as he always needs money, not a few thousands, but great sums. He has been thrifty. The treasury of Mexico has been practically at his mercy, but he does not trust the banks of his own land. He has money not only in the foreign banks of Mexico, but also large amounts of it in two of the great banks of London. The English deposits stand as security for the heavy sums that he owes me. His arm is long, but it does not reach to London.

"He cannot pay at present without putting himself in great difficulties, and, for the time being, I wish the debt to stand. It gives me a certain power over him, although we are on opposite sides in a fierce war. When you gave him my name in San Antonio, he did not put you to death because he feared that I would seize his English money when I heard of it.

"The younger Urrea has heard something of these debts. He is devoted to Santa Anna, and he knew that he would have rendered his chief an immense service if he could have secured his release from them. That was what he tried to force from me when I was in his hands, but you and your friends saved me. You little thought, Edward Fulton, that you were then saving your own life also. Otherwise, Santa Anna would have had you slain instantly when you were brought before him at San Antonio. Ah, how thoroughly I know that man! That he can be a terrible and cruel enemy he has already proved to Texas!"

The others listened with deep interest to every word spoken by Roylston. When he was through, the Panther rose, stretched his arms, and expanded his mighty chest. All the natural brown had returned to his cheeks, and his eyes sparkled with the fire of confidence.

"Mr. Roylston," he said, "the hosts of our foe have come an' they have devoured our people as the locusts ate up Egypt in the Bible, but I think our worst days have passed. We'll come back, an' we'll win."

"Yes," said Ned. "I know as truly as if a prophet had told me that we'll square accounts with Santa Anna."

He spoke with such sudden emphasis that the others were startled. His face seemed cut in stone. At that moment he saw only the Alamo and Goliad.

The *Star of the South* sped northward, and Edward Fulton sat long on her deck, dreaming of the day when the Texans, himself in the first rank, should come once more face to face with Antonio Lopez de Santa Anna.

The Texan Triumph

Chapter 1

Two on the Trail

Two boys were riding across a rolling prairie. They were armed, after the necessity of time and place, with rifle and pistol, and they were dressed in frontier fashion, in tanned deerskin with felt hats, broad of brim to shade their faces from the Texan sun, which could be fiery at times. They advanced slowly, and they watched every point of the horizon with the care that one must exercise when a single step may take him into danger.

One rider, a little the larger of the two, had a face unusually grave and stern for his years. He smiled rarely, and he seemed always to be animated by some great resolve. The acute observer would have said at once that here was a youth who had been through trial and storm. His comrade was of lighter humour, talked more and laughed often.

They crossed the prairie and entered a belt of oaks and pecans. Here they stopped, and sat a little while on their mounts, strong, seasoned ponies. The stretch of forest was clear of bushes, and they looked with pleased eyes at the deep tint of spring on trees and grass. Already the Texan spring was in full bloom, and, the south wind, blowing gently, brought the odour of blossoming flowers. They breathed deeply and the fresh, crisp air brought with it a mental as well as physical expansion. The larger boy raised his head a little, and a glow replaced the sombre look on his face.

"Feels fine, Ned, doesn't it?" said his comrade.

"So it does," replied Ned Fulton. "This coming of spring in full tide seems to make a fellow grow stronger."

But he relapsed in a moment or two into his stern and rather sad mood. Will Allen regarded him with a look of friendship, tinged with respect. Ned's story was strange and romantic to him. He could never forget that this comrade of his had slipped by a singular device from a prison in the Mexican capital, had then escaped from a cell under the sea in the castle of San Juan de Ulua, and had been at the very heart of the Alamo and Goliad, names fated never to be forgotten in Texas.

He even regarded him with a little awe at times.

Ned himself had not returned to the normal lightness of youth. He could not yet forget the terrors through which he had passed. Many a night he saw again the ring of fire at the Alamo, and the Texans in the centre of it, and nothing could ever erase from his mind the treacherous slaughter of Goliad. He not only wished to fight for the Texans, but he wished also to see the punishment of those who had done such great wrongs. Such a passion, allied with natural courage and skill, had made him one of the most daring and valuable scouts in the Texan service.

They remained motionless about ten minutes, and then, seeing nothing, rode down to a little brook by the side of which they dismounted. They drank first, and after watering their ponies, allowed them to graze on the grass which grew thick and high beside the stream.

"Here is another prairie," said Ned, "and as nearly as I can judge it is six or eight miles across. It is backed up by a ridge of high hills which seem to answer to the description, and, I dare say, we shall find there those whom we seek."

"Looks like the place to me," said Will, "but we've had a long ride and I'm willing to rest a while."

"So am I and this is as good a spot as any."

While their horses grazed, they ate venison and bread which they carried in their knapsacks. Then they lay down in the long grass and permitted their nerves and muscles to relax. Ned now and then looked through the trees at the line of blue hills, far across the prairie, but he remained silent.

"Ned," said Will at last, "do you believe that we can really do anything? Don't you think it would be better for the Texans to abandon this country, and to move into new regions further north? We are so few, and the Mexicans are so many."

"Never!" replied Ned with such energy that his comrade fairly jumped. "Give up Texas where so much blood has been shed! We couldn't think of such a thing! Let the Alamo and Goliad pass unavenged! You don't know us yet, Will! It doesn't matter how few we are, or how many the Mexicans are, this war is to the death! Never forget that, Will!"

"The thought merely occurred to me. I didn't take it seriously myself," replied Will in an apologetic tone.

They remounted in an hour and rode across the prairie to the hills which they found densely clothed in timber of good height, with a great amount of undergrowth.

"This brush confirms the description," said Ned. "We'll find a way through here and go to the top."

It was not difficult for their ponies to make a path, and they rode through the dense foliage to the summit of the highest ridge, which rose about three hundred feet above the prairie. They had from this point a splendid view around the whole circle of the horizon. Besides the group of hills about them, there was nothing but rolling prairies everywhere, all clad in the fresh green of spring, sprinkled with many flowers.

They saw neither man nor animal upon the plain, but it was a fact that did not trouble them. It was yet early and there was plenty of time for those for whom they waited.

"We'll camp here and take our ease until it's time to send up the signal," said Ned, the leader.

"So we will," said Will, "and if we had hunted the plains over we couldn't have found a better place. Here's a spring flowing from under this rock. Perhaps it makes the little brook that we stopped by some time ago."

"Whether it does or doesn't, it furnishes all the water supply we need."

They drank of the water, which was pure and quite cold. Unsaddling their horses, they let them, too, drink all they wished, and then allowed them to graze at the end of long lariats. The forest was very heavy about them and in full foliage. No one could see them unless within forty or fifty yards, and, feeling so secure in the covert, they built a little fire and had warm food for early supper, sunset yet being far off. Spreading out their blankets they lay at ease, watching the plain through the foliage, although themselves hidden.

It was necessary for the two to take every precaution. Since the fall of the Alamo, the massacre of Goliad and the flight of the Texan government the whole country was overrun by the Mexicans. A scout, unless extremely careful, might ride, at any moment, into a body of lancers. Santa Anna had divided his triumphant army into three bodies. One under Gaona marched northward on Nacogdoches, another, led by Sesma, was to take San Felipe and Harrisburg, and sweep the coast with a base at Anahuac. Urrea was to rake the whole country between Goliad and the mouth of the Brazos River. Orders were issued to the three generals to shoot all prisoners.

The great and illustrious Santa Anna himself, deeming his conquest complete and his crown of fame safe upon his head, was preparing to return with a brigade of cavalry and a part of the artillery by sea to Mexico. Already he was dismissing the miserable Texans from his mind and his thoughts turned to the capital and a further increase of the power that rightfully belonged to the Napoleon of the West.

There was much warrant for the belief of Santa Anna. Apparently he held the Texans in the hollow of his hand. Their most famous leaders had been slain. They had nowhere an armed force of which he need take any account. They must return to the States, from which they had come, or flee westward and meet the savage mercies of Comanches, Apaches and Lipans.

The two boys were aware of the movements of Santa Anna's three generals, and they fully understood the desperate case of the Texans. They talked of these subjects now as they lay under the shadow of the boughs.

"Santa Anna thinks there's nothing to do but sweep up the remnants or he wouldn't be going back," said Will.

"He's sure of it," said Ned. "You'll remember, Will, that I've seen him and talked with him often. He's cruel and vain to his finger tips. How he must exult over us. Think of that order of his to Gaona, Sesma and Urrea to shoot every prisoner."

"And they'll carry it out," said Will, despondency showing in his tone.

"So they will," said Ned, fiercely, "but he forgets that a day of reckoning may come. Even with the Alamo still fresh in his mind Santa Anna does not yet know the spirit of the Texans!"

He spoke with such bitter emphasis that his comrade stared at him. A little of the awe that he sometimes felt crept over him. He remembered what Ned had seen and endured, and he said nothing.

"The sun is setting," said Ned a little later, "and I suppose it's time to send up our smoke."

A sheet of red and gold hung over the western plains and the sun, a ball of fire, burned not far above the horizon. Will agreed with Ned that the time was at hand, and they collected dry wood, to which they set fire with flint and steel. Then they gathered green leaves and threw them in great quantities upon the fire. On top of these they cast many small boughs that they broke from trees and bushes.

The flames were hidden but a great smoke went up in a spire that grew taller and taller, rising above the trees, and then reaching to the heavens, where it was outlined clearly against the golden glow that preceded the twilight. The two maintained the smoke until the sun set and the swift southern twilight descending blotted out the light.

"They ought to have seen that," said Will.

"They certainly saw it," said Ned. "The eyes that are in the heads of the Panther and Deaf Smith would never miss such a signal, even if they were ten miles away. And as it's likely that they'll want to ride tonight instead of staying here, we'd better saddle up, and be ready when they come."

They put the saddles on the ponies, but allowed them to go on grazing at the ends of their lariats. The twilight, with the speed of the south, turned into black night, and the two boys could not see far among the bushes and trees. With wilderness caution they rolled up the blankets, fastened them across their backs, and sat, rifle on knee, while they waited. When an hour passed, and they heard nothing Will spoke a little impatiently.

"They're a long time in coming," he said, "they could have made fast time over the plain, when they saw that signal."

"Take it easy, Will," said Ned. "They've got to be careful, riding through a country that's sown so thickly with foes. It may be an hour yet before they're here, but you can depend upon it; they'll come."

Half of the promised hour passed, and there was yet no sign. The night seemed to settle down close and dark, as if a huge blanket had been thrown over the earth. Ned himself had grown uneasy, although he did not say so to Will. He wondered at the delay, and he listened eagerly for the sound of approaching hoof-beats.

The second half of the hour passed, and they yet heard nothing. Ned put his ear to the ground, but there was no trace of anything resembling a hoof-beat or a footstep. He felt disappointed.

"It can hardly be possible," he said to his comrade, "that the Panther and the others did not see the signal, when they arranged to meet us here at this time."

"They may have been compelled to turn about in order to avoid a body of lancers," hazarded Will.

"Maybe so," said Ned, and then he added joyfully: "But they didn't! I hear a hoof-beat now, or at least something that sounds mighty like one. There, I've heard it twice, and now I don't hear it any more. Listen your best, Will, and see if the sound comes to you."

Will Allen could hear nothing, and Ned began to believe that he was tricked by fancy. But his strong sense of reality told him that it had not been imagination. In very truth he had heard the sound of a hoof-beat twice—and then there was nothing. The Panther and the others would not come in such a secret manner.

One of the horses suddenly raised his head and neighed. An answering neigh came from the forest on the slope, but the two neighs were followed by silence, just as the sound of the footsteps had been. Ned felt instant alarm. Men were approaching, but they were not those whom they had expected. Will understood, too.

"Shall we jump on our horses and run for it?" he whispered.

"We won't have the chance. We must creep away. There, I hear the hoof-beats again, and they come from two sides now."

"Lancers?"

"Most likely. Our signal happened to be for our foes as well as our friends, and our foes came first. We'll just get out of this as best we can. We'll abandon our horses and creep through the forest toward the western slope of the hill."

It cost them a pang to leave the two good ponies, but there was no other choice and they slipped silently through the brush. They now heard hoof-beats at a half dozen points, and occasionally a low voice. Then they saw a bit of open ahead of them and in the centre sat two Mexican lancers on their horses, motionless, and made gigantic by the darkness. The boys knew well enough that they were on guard there for fugitives, and they crept very quietly away in another direction. But their brief view of the lancers showed that the trap for them had been set well.

When the boys were well beyond sight of the lancers they sank quietly down among thick bushes. Each could hear the other's hard breathing.

"What shall we do now, Ned?" whispered Will Allen.

"We've got to creep through the woods and get off this hill, if we can," replied Ned. "But the lancers probably have surrounded it. I should not be surprised if they were led by the younger Urrea. He is the most daring and energetic of their cavalry leaders, and he hates us all the time. It was like him to read our own signal, and come for our capture."

"They may be in great force," said Will, "but in the darkness it is easier for us who are only two to hide."

"That's so, but we can't rely on hiding, only. We must reach the plain somehow or other. Then we can slip away, though it will be both a loss and a disgrace to us to leave our ponies in the hands of the

Mexicans. Quiet, Will! Sink lower!"

Although Will was making no noise the last words were involuntary as they heard close by a heavy tread, a sound that could be made by not less than ten or twelve men. They fairly crouched against the ground under the bushes and their breathing was suppressed to the lowest pitch. Fifteen Mexicans, led by an officer, walked near them. They were lancers who had evidently dismounted at the edge of the forest, but several still carried the long weapon of the sharp point, with which they prodded the bushes as they passed.

Cold shivers chased up and down the spines of the two boys, when they saw the use to which these lances were put. They would have wormed further away, but they did not dare to risk the slightest noise. Ned was sure that the Mexicans, having found the ponies, were now looking in the bush for their riders. A diligent search would be sure to uncover them, unless they escaped to the plain.

The group passed on and the two heard them pushing among the bushes. Then they rose and crept in the other direction.

"I think a lance is a hideous weapon," whispered Will. "I'd hate to have one of those long things stuck through me by a Mexican, and for a while, when they were so close, I felt as if it had been really done."

"There is no lance sticking through you," Ned whispered back with a certain grim irony. "It's just imagination, but it's not proof that one won't be sticking in you within an hour."

"Here's a gully," whispered Will, "and it seems to lead down the side of the hill. Suppose we crawl along its bottom. It may take us out of this fix."

"Just the thing. We'll try it."

The gully was about four feet deep, but was filled partially with dead leaves, the drift of seasons. These leaves made a soft bed, upon which the boys could tread, making no noise, and they advanced a hundred yards without interruption. Then at a word from Ned who had the keener ear, they lay flat upon the leaves, their bodies blending perfectly with the darkness. Mexican soldiers came into view, and they talked as they searched. Ned understood them perfectly.

"They are much disappointed," he whispered. "They knew because they found only two horses that the fugitives are but two in number, and they do not see why they have not yet overhauled them. But they expect to do it, nevertheless."

"Then we'd better hurry," said Will, resuming the creeping journey over the leaves and down the gully.

"It's not more than sixty or eighty yards to the plain," said Ned. "If we reach it we've got to run for it as fast as we can, in the hope that we may get away in the darkness. Hark! What was that?"

"The howl of a coyote," responded Will. "Isn't it an awfully weird, lonesome sound at such a time as this?"

"Not to me," responded Ned, a joyous note showing in his voice. "That was a most delightful howl. Hark to it again! It grows finer than ever. The wolf that emitted it is a magnificent animal, one of the biggest and grandest specimens of his kind, as brave as a lion, one that would run from nothing."

"Ned, have you gone clean crazy?" whispered Will. "What under the moon are you talking about? You know that the coyote is a mean, sneaking creature. There is never anything noble about him."

"Yes, as a rule, but this one is an exception. He is a grand and noble animal indeed. Listen to him for the third time! On the whole I would say that he is not a wolf, but a panther, a magnificent panther, our own ring-tailed friend."

Then Will understood and he took a quick, short breath of delight.

"You mean it's the Panther himself?" he said.

"The Panther himself and the others are with him, of course. They saw our signal, too, and everything would have come off as arranged, if these Mexican lancers had not happened to cut in. Our friends are riding out of the west, and we must manage to meet them, before they run into an ambush here on the hill. I'm going to take the risk, Will, and answer the coyote. The Panther taught me the trick, and he may understand what I mean."

Will fairly shivered when the yelping, warning cry rose by his side. It seemed to him for a moment that he could feel the teeth of a wild beast in his shoulder, and then he laughed in silent scorn at himself, because he knew that it was only Ned.

After the answering howl the two went down the ravine as fast as they dared. Coyotes were not generally found in forests on the slopes of hills and the Mexicans might suspect. But they stopped further down and Ned gave forth the cry again. Then they hurried on, emerged from the wood into the edge of the plain and saw a half dozen Mexican horsemen before them.

A good moon had come out, and not having the protection of the trees they were now plainly visible. The horsemen uttered a shout and rode at them, long lances extended for the thrust. It was well for the two that Ned, despite his youth, had learned presence of mind in the hardest of schools. He fired instantly at the foremost lancer and emptied his saddle. The others drew rein, and Will raised his own weapon. But Ned pushed down the barrel.

"Save your fire, Will!" he cried. "As long as they know that your rifle is loaded they'll hesitate to crowd us. Now run as fast as you can toward the point where you heard the wolf howl!"

He spoke with such fiery energy that Will obeyed, almost without thought. Ned fired his pistol, causing a horse to fall, and spreading further confusion among the Mexicans. Then he thrust the weapon back in his belt, and ran as fast as he could after Will, reloading his rifle as he sped over the ground, which fortunately was rough and gullied for a little space.

They were a good hundred yards away when the Mexicans, regaining order, began to shout and pursue. But Ned in a moment or two reloaded his rifle and sent back another shot at them. At the same time he shouted at the top of his powerful voice:

"This way, Panther! This way! Shoot over our heads!"

Will, who was still reserving his fire, heard the thunder of rapid hoofs before them and no more pleasant sound ever came to his ears. Figures of men and horses rose out of the darkness, rifles cracked, bullets whistled over his head, and the shout of Texan answered the shout of Mexican.

Ned and Will paused panting, and the horsemen gathered around them. They recognised at once the gigantic figure of the Panther, Obed White, long, lean and red-headed, "Deaf" Smith and Henry Karnes, thick and powerful, and four others.

"The Mexicans saw our signal and came first!" exclaimed Ned. "I think they are led by Urrea, and we have been dodging them in the brush for some time! They seem to be in strong force!"

"They are! We knew it!" replied the Panther. "We've been tryin' to reach you without their seein' us, an' I gave the signal which you answered. Then, when we heard the shots we came at the gallop. They've got your horses, I reckon!"

"Yes," said Ned.

"Then jump up behind Williamson and Hendricks there, who are the lightest, an' we'll leave this place as fast as we can. No use wastin' ourselves fightin' fifty or a hundred Mexicans!"

The boys sprang up behind the designated men, and the little group, wheeling about, galloped back toward the west. But the Mexicans had seen the smallness of their forces, and, uttering loud cries, galloped in pursuit. All their men came from the wood, and, when Ned looked back, he saw that they were fully fifty in number. The Texans, including Will and himself, numbered only ten on eight horses, but three of them—the Panther, Deaf Smith and Henry Karnes—probably could not be matched by any other three riflemen in the world. Ned did not now feel much alarm. His chief regret was for the two lost ponies.

The Panther dropped back beside the pony that bore Williamson and Ned.

"Can you and Will jump from hoss to hoss as we gallop along?" he asked the boy.

"I think we can manage it if the other horse comes close enough."

"Then we'll just pass you two about, that is, we'll distribute your extra weight among eight horses 'stead of givin' it to two. At the same time if them Mexican chasers come too close we'll do a lot of roarin' an' rippin' an' t'arin'. It grinds me plum' to the marrer to have to run away from Mexicans, an' if we had wooded country right ahead of us I'd rather stop an' fight."

"We'd rather fight than run away, but still we may have the same chance some other day," said Obed White. "Ned, we were mighty glad to see you and Will come running from that hill. I thought it likely that the Mexicans would get you before we could come up. Texans are company, Mexicans are none."

"You weren't any gladder to see us than we were to see you," rejoined Ned. "Now, don't you think it's time for me to transfer myself? The oftener we change the better distributed we will be."

"That's the talk. Here, you Langford! You're the third smallest man in the lot, an' you're ridin' the biggest hoss. Move up an' let Ned jump on behind you."

"Good enough," said Langford, and as they checked speed a little Ned sprang lightly from one horse to the other. Will accomplished a similar feat, though not with as much ease. A shout of anger came from the Mexicans who saw this most useful performance.

"Does that trouble your pestiferous souls?" said the Panther grimly as he looked. "Oh, I see you've gained a little. Well, me an' my comrades ain't in favour of your gainin', although it does bring you within range of our rifles. So, I guess I'll have to do a little rippin' an' t'arin'."

He raised his rifle for that most difficult shot, to fire backward from a galloping horse at a galloping enemy in pursuit. But the Panther had not trained his natural gift in marksmanship more than thirty years for nothing. When his rifle cracked the foremost Mexican fell from his horse.

"My time now," said Deaf Smith, and he fired with the same result.

"I follow," said Karnes, and a Mexican fell before the third shot also. The others, in the face of such tremendous shooting, allowed the distance between themselves and the fugitives to widen. Obed White glanced at them with approval.

"A shot to the wise is sufficient," he said, "and I must say, Panther, that you and Deaf and Hank handle rifles as if you had seen 'em and touched 'em before. I reckon you Texans can outshoot anything since the days of Daniel Boone."

"We have to," said the Panther, with a satisfied grin, at the compliment.

"That's so. Down here those who shoot and run away will live to shoot another day, particularly if they shoot straight. Don't you think, Panther, it's about time for those two boys to do that lightning circus act of theirs again?"

"Yes," replied the Panther, "it's the moment for them to jump."

He designated the next lightest pair, and the boys made the second transfer. But it was easier. The Mexicans were now at a respectable distance, and the Texans slowed almost to a walk, until Ned and Will were secure in their new seats.

"I hope that we can keep this up all night," said Deaf Smith solemnly. "It's the finest exercise I ever saw for two sprightly young fellows like Ned and Will. Wonderful training! Makes the eye quick and the muscles spry and strong. I vote, if the Mexicans follow all night and then tomorrow, that we make 'em jump hoops after daylight as they pass from horse to horse."

"Good idee," said the Panther in the same solemn tone. "I always knowed, Deaf, there was a pow'ful lot of hoss sense in that head of yours, though some of it has a lot of trouble gittin' out. But them hoops ought to have paper pasted over 'em same as they do in the circus. Ned an' Will would look pow'ful fine, when their heads an' bodies come through the paper, leapin' from hoss to hoss. It would be finer still, if we kep' the hosses about twenty feet apart."

"I guess they'd rather leap and get away than not do it and never see another day," said Obed White sagely.

"We'll leap as long as there's a leap in us, if it's needed," said Ned.

"Sky is darkening," said Karnes. "Moon's faded quite a lot, an' a heap of stars have left. If we can only strike a patch of woods we can shake off them fellows."

"There's a dark line a little to our right," said Ned of the keen eye. "I can tell in another minute or two whether it's forest. Yes, so it is! I can see boughs and trunks."

They veered, slightly though, in order to give their pursuers no chance to gain, and drew slowly toward the forest. A shout rose behind them and they knew that the Mexicans had surmised their purpose. The increasing hoof-beats showed that the pursuers were seeking to close up the gap. But the Texans knew every wile and trick of border battle.

"We'll show to 'em ag'in that we could hit the side of a house at twenty yards," said the Panther to Smith and Karnes, "an' then, while they're thinkin' it over, we'll dash for the timber."

Now the three rifles flashed together but with the same deadly aim as before. Shouts of anger and pain came from the ranks of the Mexicans. They, too, fired, but in the confusion their bullets flew wild, and, while they slowed down and chattered to one another, the Texans, turning at a sharp angle, galloped rapidly for the timber.

"We'll make it before they get back in shape to pursue in a body," said the Panther, measuring the situation with a critical eye.

They had gained at least two hundred yards before the Mexicans had resumed the pursuit, and then it was too late. The friendly timber received the Texans and they disappeared in its dusk.

Chapter 2

Camp Independence

Ned and Will felt supreme gratitude as they rode into the dark woods. They had had enough of dodging, fighting and running for one night, and many more, too, for that matter. The forest seemed to be extensive, spreading many miles to right and left, and perhaps it had a depth of many miles also. They would be secure there against further pursuit for a while at least. No Mexican force, unless in great numbers, would dare to face the ambush of such deadly riflemen as they had proved themselves to be.

"Havin' rid so far an' havin' rid without harm, I think we ought to get down and lead our horses," said the Panther. "It wouldn't look good if, after havin' escaped Mexican bullets, we was to break our

516

necks over logs in the dark."

Ned and Will, after so many transfers, were glad enough to get down and walk. The others dismounted also, and led their horses, a wise precaution, as they were compelled to choose a way through dense undergrowth and boughs that hung loose. They advanced about an hour without talking, and then the Panther, who was in advance called out to them to halt.

"We've come to a little creek," he said, "an' I reckernize in it an old friend. I know this forest, too, now. It's one of the biggest and thickest in eastern Texas. Twenty years ago I killed one of the most tremenjous panthers I ever saw about a mile up this creek. There are panthers here yet, plenty of 'em, but they won't bother us. What I'm thinkin' about now is a natural camp, one of the finest places of the kind that you ever saw, but it will take us till daylight to reach it."

"Lead on," said Obed White. "I want to find that beautiful natural camp of yours. I grow both sleepy and tired and 'tis sleep that knits up the worn muscles and the weary back. I'd wager, too, that these young friends of ours are tired of the game,—'now the Mexicans see you, now they don't; now you needn't run, now you must.'"

"You are certainly right, Obed," said Will Allen. "I think that just at this minute I'm at least a hundred and ten years old. I could drop right down here in the woods, go to sleep in a second, and sleep a month."

"You don't do any droppin' an' you don't do any sleepin' till I take you to the right place," said the Panther. "I said I had the best of camps waitin' for us, an' I have."

They went on until nearly dawn, and as they advanced the country grew rougher, broken here and there with outcrops of stone. It was nearly dawn, when the Panther led them through forest so dense that they could scarcely force their way into a depression, shaped like a bowl, about twenty feet deep and about two hundred in diameter. The basin contained only high grass and a small clear pool of water on one side. But it was walled in by lofty trees and dense undergrowth. The Panther rode cautiously down a narrow path, followed in the same manner by the others, and then looked around with satisfaction at his comrades.

"It's a reg'lar nest," he said. "I hit on it by accident years ago, an' the Mexicans, who don't know much about this part of the country, haven't one chance in five hundred to run across it. I don't know how such a queer place happened to be here, but I guess it's enough that it is here."

"It must be a crater," said Ned. "There was a volcano here, but it became extinct five or six million years ago. I think that a bowl like this could be accounted for only in that manner."

"I saw two or three such in the forests of northern New York when I was a boy," said Deaf Smith, "an' heard learned men say that they were craters."

"It won't bust out with fire and brimstone while we're here?" said Karnes with some alarm.

"Scarcely," said Obed White, "when the fires have been out five or six million years. Maybe the world then was just full of roaring chimneys, but this place is the nest the Panther said it was, and it won't be long before you'll find me on the grass there, knitting up my sleeves of care as fast as I can sleep."

Great bars of red and gold were now appearing in the east and the dawn was coming swiftly. The crater with its grass and its sheltering woods about it made a powerful appeal to Ned and Will. Both were on the verge of collapse, but this was a better haven than they had hoped. Obed White's shrewd eye was on them.

"Now, boys," he said, "you two begin knitting your ravelled sleeves right away. I don't think you can last a minute longer. Take these blankets, drop down in the grass and off with you."

It was scarcely three minutes before the two were asleep at the side of the bowl just under the overhanging boughs. The men watered the horses at the pool, tethered them with long lariats, in order that they might graze on the grass and also sought sleep. They felt so secure that they set no watch, and soon all were slumbering soundly.

They slept all through the morning. The horses ceased to graze and rested also. There was complete quiet and peace in the crater. A great sun rose high in the blue sky and poured floods of gold over the forest, but the beams did not touch the faces of the sleepers who lay under the thick overhanging boughs.

It was true that the young Urrea led the Mexican band. The most daring of all the Mexican raiders, he had seen the signal and had ridden to capture Ned and Will. He was filled with rage and mortification at their escape and the escape of the men who had joined them. He hunted a while through the forest with his troop, but it was a difficult task, particularly for the lancers. They did not come within miles of the crater, and before midnight he gave up the search, returning eastward.

Obed White was the first of those in the crater to awake, and he slowly drew up his long length. Then he walked out into the centre of the bowl, where the brilliant sun turned his red hair into flame. He drew a long and deep breath of satisfaction. Then he looked at the sleepers and murmured:

"He laughs best who sleeps last. Doubtless Urrea and his men gave up the chase long before we got here and made this camp. But they couldn't have any such cosy nest as ours."

Obed White, despite the light talk that he liked, was a thoughtful man. His mind passed from their present situation to that of all the Texans, and then his face clouded. They had been scouting upon the flank of Santa Anna's forces and it seemed that everything was lost. In that whole region the ten who lay there in the crater were the sole force in arms against the Mexicans. Ninety-nine out of a hundred men would consider longer resistance hopeless and would take flight northward. But his cheerfulness returned as his comrades awoke, one by one. The boys were the last to arise, but they felt as if they had been reborn.

"The sleeves seem to have been knitted up well," said Obed White.

"Never better," replied Ned, joyously, "and our muscles and sinews are knitted together again, too. But I'm hungry, Obed, I'm so hungry that I feel like going up the hillside there, and biting the bark off a tree."

"No need for that," called out Karnes. "I'll have a beautiful fire burnin' here inside of five minutes an' we've got plenty of dried venison to cook. Now, you an' Will just go down to the pool, an' wash your faces like good little boys, an' maybe we'll let you sit at the first table an' eat breakfast with us."

The two boys went to the pool gladly enough, drank of the cool water at the shallow end, bathed their faces at the deep end, and then returned to find the fire burning and three of the men cooking strips of venison over the flames. All ate hungrily.

It seemed to Ned and Will that the whole world had changed. Last night they had been fighting and running for their lives. Now they were suddenly dropped down into a little garden of Eden. Birds sang in the forest all about them. The sound of the light wind among the leaves was like the ripple of flowing water. It did not seem possible that an enemy could be within a hundred miles.

"You have certainly done your duty, Panther," said Obed White, "you have led us to a home."

"I'm thinkin' that we might make it a home shore enough," said the Panther. "Keepin' this as our fort, so to speak, we might do a lot of scoutin' an' if need be, fightin' for Texas. Our people have got to draw their breath before they meet Santa Anna ag'in, an' while they're drawin' it we might do a lot of useful things."

"They're tellin' that Sam Houston won't gather a force, and go after Santa Anna," said one of the men.

"Don't you believe it," said the Panther. "Sam Houston is as brave as a hundred lions, an' he won't strike till he can hit hard. The Texans are all in confusion over the Alamo an' Goliad, but the men that are scattered now will come back ag'in to the lone star flag. Meanwhile we'll decide whether we'll make this our rallyin' point, for the roarin' an' rippin' an' t'arin' that we're lookin' forward to on our own account. What do you say, Deaf?"

"Couldn't find a better, if we looked a hundred years."

"An' you, Obed?"

"A home in the crater is worth two in the bush. Right here I stay."

"An' you, Hank?"

"They made it six million years ago. But they made it just for us."

The other men answered in the same way, but the boys spoke up for the crater as a home before they could be asked.

"That bein' all settled," said the Panther, "I think we'd better look 'roun' a little an' then make our house. We ain't likely to have much bad weather an' this nest is pretty well sheltered, but we don't want to be rained on. It ain't cheerin', an' it wouldn't be no fun, neither, to be hit by a Norther."

Ned was already examining the crater. He had noticed that the water of the pool was unusually cool and fresh, and he found that it was fed by a tiny stream trickling from the base of the hollow. At the deeper end there was a small outlet that carried the overflow into underground regions. Thus the pool was in reality running water, always fresh. It was an important discovery as good water was of the highest value, and a stationary pond might become stagnant or dry up in the sun.

"Good for you," said the Panther, when Ned announced his discovery. "I never stayed here long enough before to look about much. Now I think we'd better see if there's any way of gettin' out 'stead of the one by which we come in. It would be of use if the impossible was to happen, an' we was treed here, so to speak, by Mexicans."

The path by which they had come was not more than a foot broad and very steep, and at the opposite side of the crater they made with the help of their hatchets another, up which the horses might be dragged in an emergency.

The hatchets which all the men carried in accordance with western custom were strong, heavy weapons, and they began at once the building of lean-to shelters, a work which they did with amazing dexterity. Some gathered in the woods above great slabs of bark from oak and other trees. Some cut poles, and they made cabins which would keep out rain, and which with the natural shelter of the crater might even defy a norther. They also made floors of bark, and on the second day they put in wooden pegs and hooks upon which to hang superfluous garments or other articles.

The crater would furnish pasturage for the horses for some days to come, and in the hills beyond they saw two or three fine meadows which would serve later. On the whole they found much that was pleasant in their situation, and, on the third night, their cabins received the necessary test. Ned had noticed a falling temperature in the afternoon, and, by twilight, heavy black clouds covered the whole sky. A cold wind blew, and rain pattered on the leaves and grass.

They had built five cabins, two men to a cabin, and Ned and Will retreated to the one which they shared. There was no door, only an opening large enough to admit them, and two smaller openings for windows. They spread their blankets on either side on the bark floor, and sitting down now, Turkish fashion, listened to the rain and wind.

"We didn't build our mansions any too soon," said Ned. "Hark how the storm drives!"

"I hear it," said Will, "and it's all right if these same mansions will stand on their feet through it all. Do you think our house is rocking, Ned?"

"Not a rock. It does not even shiver. As we are sunk in the crater here I think that most of the wind passes far over the top of the cabin. The storm must be at its height. Hear it whistle!"

"If the cabin stands this, and it's standing it, it can stand anything," said Will. "Now, I'm about to show my confidence by going to sleep. I've worked hard all day, and I'm tired."

He lay down between the blankets and soon slumbered. Ned watched a while longer through the passage that served as a doorway. He saw the rain driving past, and now and then the wind roared as well as whistled. But the little cabin, though only of bark and poles, was staunch and firm. The roof shed the rain, too, and not a drop fell inside. It was pitchy dark without and no sound came from the other cabins. Ned judged that all were asleep except himself, and taking to his blankets he quickly followed them.

When he awoke the next morning the storm had passed, and the day was shining. Beads of rain twinkled on the grass, and the pool was a little higher than usual. All the cabins had stood firm and the horses had found shelter in a cove under thick overhanging boughs. The camp had survived every test, and the little force of Texans felt highly pleased with itself.

"We'll stay," said the Panther in sanguine tones, "an' from this place we'll hang on the Mexican flank an' sting it good an' hard. What do you fellows think we ought to call our home fort?"

"Camp Independence," replied Ned, and all the others promptly endorsed the name, though Deaf Smith added:

"We'll say the crater now and then for short!"

Then they consulted about food. Their travelling rations would end that day, and if they carried on extended operations they must have a considerable supply of provisions ready at any time.

"The woods must be full of game," said Smith. "It would be here, anyhow, and since all the people have been run out of the country it must have increased. At any rate, we'll go out and see."

The Panther, Smith, Karnes and Ned formed the first hunting party, and with a caution to beware of Mexicans they left the crater intending to go toward the south. A score of steps from the edge of Camp Independence and Ned looked back. He could not see a trace of the crater. The dense foliage and undergrowth hid everything.

"It would surely be hard to find if you didn't know it was there," he said.

"You couldn't find it at all if somebody or some-thin' didn't lead you to it," said the Panther. "We'll have to take close notice ourselves to make our way back. But now for the game. It's not early enough in the morning, I reckon, to find the turkeys roosting in the trees, but we may run across a deer."

They walked several miles southward, but started no deer. The forest, save for a little meadow now and then, remained dense, affording a fine covert for the larger animals, but it seemed that luck did not intend to favour them. They came about noon to a big rock standing in a small open place, and the Panther suggested that the four separate, going in different directions, but returning in about three hours to the big rock, where they could make further plans if they were still unsuccessful.

Ned's course lay straight south, and he went forward carefully, eager to be the first who should find the needed prize. Unless they secured a good supply of food they could not, of course, keep the camp in the crater, and Ned, in common with the others, was most anxious that it should remain their base.

He went forward for a long time, carefully examining the ground everywhere for the trail of some big animal. It was a splendid forest, perhaps the finest in all that part of the country, and the density of trees and undergrowth did not decrease as he advanced. Now and then he heard squirrels chattering in the boughs overhead, but they were too small game, and he still looked hopefully for deer.

He came to a fine creek, deep enough for fish, and he knew that in time he and his friends could rig tackle and draw upon its waters for supplies, but it was not available at the moment. He waded it, and midstream the water came almost to his waist. Then he went on, and brought his mind back to the larger game that he sought.

There was a whirr among the tall trees and a magnificent flock of wild turkeys flew away, bearing westward. Ned raised his rifle, but it was too late, he could not get a shot. Then he rushed after them, knowing that the turkey was not a bird of long flight. Once he came almost within range as they alighted on the boughs of a cypress, but they fled once more and although he followed for a time he could not find them.

He was compelled to stop, hot and disappointed and panting from exertion. It was very bitter to him to come so near to such fine game and then to lose it. The Panther, Smith and Karnes would not upbraid him, but they might think him a poor hunter, nevertheless, to lose such a chance. But Ned had the courage, energy and perseverance of which success is made. As soon as he rested a little he resumed the search, bringing into play every detail of woodcraft that he had learned. Once when he came to a place where the forest was thinned he saw tracks that he believed to have been made by a deer and he followed them a while, but they were evidently cold as he roused nothing.

He returned to his main course, and the forest grew thicker again. As he entered a dense clump of bushes he heard a growl and the sound of a startled leap, and a clumsy dark figure whisked itself away. Ned caught only one glimpse but he saw that it was a black bear, already fat in that southern latitude. His rifle leaped to his shoulder and he was about to pull the trigger, but there was nothing to sight at. The bear was gone, swallowed up among the bushes.

Ned lowered his weapon with a cry of vexation, and ran forward on the trail of the fleeing animal. He could follow it for three or four hundred yards, but then he lost it. That bear had vanished as completely as if it had gone from this earth. He hunted angrily for the trail, spending a full ten minutes on the search, and then returned to his main course once more.

He sat down on a fallen log and raged at himself. He ought to have got a shot at the bear. He should have been quick enough. The Panther and Deaf Smith and Karnes would have done it. It was a fine bear, a young bear, a fat bear, and the meat of bear was good. What a savory odour it would have given out, frying in strips over the coals! He was stung by a powerful feeling of hunger.

He recalled his courage and energy once more. He would not be beaten. Two brilliant opportunities had been presented to him and he had missed them, both, but he would not give up. A third chance might come. He rested a little while and then pressed forward, still eagerly examining the earth for traces of what he sought. His muscles felt a little stiff and sore from so much running and walking, but the soreness of his spirit was greater. Yet he compelled himself to hope anew for success.

It was now warm within the forest, or at least it felt so to Ned, who had been suffering such severe tests of body and soul. He wiped the perspiration from his face, and devoutly hoped that the blessed third chance would come very soon. He resolutely crushed the persistent thoughts of bear and turkey, and presently he saw a faint glimmer of silver through the trees. He knew that it was made by the water of another stream, but smaller than the creek, probably a mere brook. He hurried a little, as he had become thirsty and the sight of water drew him.

As he approached he caught a glimpse of a grayish shoulder, and an animal drinking at the stream, uttering a startled snort, made a mighty leap for the woods. Ned saw that it was a deer, and to his excited eyes it was the finest and fattest of its kind that ever roamed the wilderness. The animal, pausing a moment after its first wild leap, presented a good target, and Ned was about to seize the opportunity. But he was standing among thick bushes, and when he started to raise his rifle the barrel caught in one of them. Before he could discharge it the deer was gone, flitting away like a shadow.

Ned did not even pursue. But he was so angry with himself that his heart pounded as if beating a song of ire. His third chance had come and it had been a fair one The deer had stood still for a moment, long enough for a good marksman to send the mortal bullet. He had not done it, but any of the other three would have succeeded. How awkward of him to have let his rifle become entangled at the moment of all moments! The gods had given him three chances and he had not profited by any of them. They would not give him any more. Three was an allowance full and overflowing.

When he sat down this time to rest he remained fully a quarter of an hour. It was his first intention to go back to the point of separation, report his failure when the others should come up, and stand it as best he could.

But fifteen minutes made a change. There was another reservoir of courage and tenacity which he had not yet tapped, and when he rose from the log he turned his face anew to the hunt. It was growing cooler now. The middle of the afternoon had passed, and in the east the blaze was not so brilliant. Ned felt a fresh access of strength, and he thrust his rifle forward with finger on hammer and trigger in order, that he might be ready in a second should the gods grant him yet a fourth chance.

He found nothing, the sun went further and further down the western arch, and the coolness increased in the forest. A light wind arose and the new green leaves sang together. Squirrels leaped about among the high boughs, and Ned fancied they were laughing at him. Once he raised his rifle for a shot at a little tormentor, but he became ashamed of himself and took the weapon down.

Then he saw before him a little prairie, in the centre of which two large dark figures grazed. Ned's heart almost stopped beating, so great was his joy and astonishment. The two big black forms were those of a bull and cow buffalo, wandered far east of their usual range, due no doubt to the abandonment of the country by the settlers.

The gods had indeed given him a fourth chance and one more magnificent than any of which he dreamed. Patience and courage had brought him within range of reward. No carelessness of his should lose it, because it was too much for a fifth to be granted. He crept with exceeding care to the edge of the forest, first noting that the wind was blowing from the animals toward him and could carry no human odour to their keen nostrils.

Both bull and cow grazed peacefully on, and Ned, raising his rifle, picked out a mortal spot on the cow. Despite every effort of the will his hand at first trembled a little. So much depended upon this last chance that the dreadful fear of failure lingered in his mind. But he steadied himself and pulled the trigger.

The crack of the rifle roared in his excited ears like the thunder of a cannon, and a film of white smoke floated before his eyes. He was in deadly fear lest he had missed the mortal spot and perspiration broke out all over him, but when his eyes cleared and the smoke was gone he saw the cow staggering. The bull, un-gallant animal, had already galloped away in fright. Now the cow began to run around in circles and Ned knew that she was done. In a minute or two she fell to the ground and lay quite still.

Ned strode forward, full of pride, and yet with a chastened sense also. He knew that he had won his triumph through sheer courage and persistence, and yet he had come perilously near to surrender. After every failure he had felt the temptation to give up, and after the third it had been almost overpowering.

The prize was indeed a splendid one, a young cow, fat and tender. Here were hundreds of pounds of juicy steaks, enough to last the whole group a long time, but it was too much for him to handle alone. He sent forth again and again the long cry of the wolf that the Panther had taught him, and then waited. After a while the whining cry which seemed to carry unmeasured distances returned to him. Then he knew that his friends had heard and would come. In a half hour they appeared at the edge of the prairie. Deaf Smith carried a wild turkey, but the others had nothing. Ned felt an uncontrollable sense of pride, because he, a boy, had done so much better than these three renowned and daring hunters combined.

The boy was sitting placidly on the body of the cow. Long shadows were already gathering from the western sun, and, the two at the edge of the forest could not see distinctly Ned's splendid prize.

"What is it?" called out the Panther.

"Just you come here and see," replied Ned, purposely making his tone indifferent. "I've shot a rabbit and it's a fine one, too."

"A rabbit," came in disgusted tones from Smith, who was not yet clear of the bushes, "an' you've been howlin' for us to come just for a rabbit!"

"But it's such a fine big one," said Ned, "I thought you really ought to come and see it. I don't believe you can find its like anywhere in Texas."

The Panther, who could see Ned's rabbit now, drew a long breath and called out to Smith.

"He's right, Deaf. It's the finest an' biggest an' fattest Jack rabbit that ever hopped over Texas. It made the mistake of wanderin' over these plains an' up to the muzzle of Ned's rifle."

Then Smith saw and he exclaimed in admiration:

"A buffalo, an' a fat cow, too, by the Jumpin' Jupiter! Who'd have thought it, this far from the range! Why, Ned, there's enough here to feed us for two or three months! You've certainly been the handy boy this day!"

Ned received their congratulations proudly, but beneath the pride he had a little feeling of shame also. He did not tell them how near he had come to complete defeat. But he and the others now quickly turned to the need of securing their royal prize. Night was coming fast. Already the shadows had travelled from east to west and the sun was gone. They decided to make a camp where the cow had fallen and they quickly kindled a fire. Then the hunters, with the skill that comes only from long practice, deftly removed the skin, and with their hatchets quartered the body.

"Although it's early spring, she is one of the finest and fattest I ever saw," said the Panther. "We'll hare to bring three of four horses to carry away our first capture of food, or rather, Ned's."

"I guess we'd better hang it up for the night in the edge of the woods," said Smith. "It will make the wolves howl a lot, but we won't mind that."

They cut strong withes from the saplings and hung up the portions of the buffalo so high that no leaping animal could reach them. They took no rest and ate nothing until this laborious task was finished. Then they broiled the tenderest strips over the coals and ate long and heartily. By this time it was ten o'clock and very dark. Out of the forest from several points came the long mournful howl of wolves, turning from sadness to fierceness on its dying note.

Deaf Smith laughed low but heartily.

"Didn't I tell you," he said, "that the wolves would do a mighty howlin' as soon as they smelt our buffalo. Sometimes I'm sorry for the wolf. It's a terrible thing to be hungry all your life. I don't suppose any wolf ever got enough to eat, an' they have to go rangin' 'roun' over woods an' prairies, snappin' an' snarlin' an' tryin' to trail somethin'. Sometimes they have to turn cannibal, too, an' I'd call that right unpleasant. Tryin' the same thing on ourselves, I'd hate to have to eat the Panther."

"You'd break all your teeth if you tried to eat me," said the Panther complacently. "I've been knocked about so much by wind an' weather, hard ridin' an' hard walkin', hard huntin' an' hard fightin' that sometimes I think even a wolf's teeth would crack on me, though I don't mean to give one the chance. Now, Ned, you tumble over there an' go to sleep. Deaf an' me an' Hank will keep watch by turns."

Ned was willing enough. He was very tired and his day had been full. He stretched himself in a soft place before the fire and slept soundly all through the night. Karnes soon followed him to slumberland, but Smith, who was to have the second watch, sat and talked a while with the Panther.

"I don't ever believe in anything supernatural," said Smith, "but it looks to me as if the killin' of that buffalo was a good sign. Things are goin' to turn for us Texans, an' it seems as if Ned was a kind of flag bearer leadin' us to the right places like one of them water witches, the fellers that walks along the ground, with little forked sticks in their hands until they come to a place where the stick just turns over of itself. Then the farmer digs there an' finds water. Back in the States lots of wells have been located that way."

The Panther glanced at Ned.

"I'm not what you'd call superstitious myself," he said, "but you're bound to believe in signs. If you see a band of Comanches in war paint on the plains, right close to you, ain't it a sign for you to get away, now ain't it, Deaf?"

"It shorely is," replied Smith.

"An' if I've been in a hundred Injun fights an' lots of Mexican fights an' have come out of all of 'em without a real hurt ain't it a sign that I was intended to come out of them that way? Now I ask you, ain't it such a sign, Deaf?"

"It shorely looks that way, Panther."

"Now, just glance at that boy, Ned, lyin' by the fire there! You an' me an' Hank, Deaf, are the best three hunters in all Texas. I ain't sayin' it as any boast, 'cause everybody knows it's true, but just to lay the facts before you. We hunted hard ever since noon over good country, an' we got nothin' but one little old wild turkey. We was just about to give it up an' go into camp, when this boy's wolf howl called us. What do we find when we get here! He has killed the finest an' tenderest buffalo cow I ever saw in my life—an' I've seen a heap —here in this region, where there ain't been any other buffalo for ten year. Ain't that a sign of same kind, now I ask you, ain't it, Deaf?"

"It's p'intin' that way, Panther."

528

"An' go back of that. Wasn't he down there in the City of Mexico with Mr. Austin? Did the bars of a prison hold him? They didn't. He starves hisself thin, cuts his long hair and slips right through. When there ain't no other place to hide, the biggest Mexican church opens itself an' takes him right into its bosom, an' I say that with a mighty lot of reverence, too, Deaf. Then, when he gets hard up ag'in, good Mexicans help him. At last he is took by that black villain, Cos, and he is put in a dungeon under the sea at the castle of San Juan de Ulua. What happens? He is stuck in a cell right next to Obed White, who was a watchmaker, who can pick the biggest lock that was ever made. Obed finds the way out of the dungeons for them, and they discover a boat just waitin' to take them to the mainland. Do you call that just chance? Ain't it a sign, I ask you, Deaf, ain't it a sign?"

"It keeps on p'intin' straight that way."

The fire crackled a little, the two big men stirred and gazed intently at the sleeping boy. From the forest the wolves sent their long howl, always with that fierce undernote. Around them the circling blackness crept up closer and closer to the dying fire.

"An' that ain't the half, Deaf," resumed the Panther.

"A black jaguar, the biggest that ever growed in Mexico, is just reachin' over to bite the boy's head off with his long teeth, when Obed White shoots the heart out of that black jaguar just in time. Other people has escapes, one an' maybe two, but Ned there has 'em all the time. Ned and Obed was treed by Mexicans an' the most terrible storm that was ever heard of comes up ag'in just in the nick of time an' scatters the Mexicans. Again they are driv into a corner by Lipans an' the Texans comes just when they was about to go under. I tell you, Deaf, it wasn't because Obed was there, it was because the boy was there. Ain't them a powerful lot of signs? I ask you, Deaf, ain't they?"

"It shorely looks like it to a man up a tree."

"An' biggest of all, Deaf, think of the Alamo! He was there in that pen o' death. He was there with Crockett an' Bowie an' Travis, an' all the rest of them that's gone to the inside heaven reserved for the bravest of men, where they may be settin' now with Hannibal an' Julius Caesar an' Alfred the Great an' George Washington. Did anybody else outlive the Alamo? No, it was just that boy, layin' there at our feet. They say Davy Crockett sent him out on a false erran' to save him. But who put that thought in Davy Crockett's mind? An' how was it that Santa Anna didn't kill him, when he had him ag'in? The influence of Mr. Roylston's name some might think, but I say you've got to look higher. It looks to me like signs on top o' signs. I ask you, Deaf, ain't it signs on top o' signs?"

"'Pears to me them signs is pilin' up mountain high, Panther."

"An' then he's one of the prisoners at Goliad, when the Mexicans ag'in all good faith an' human natur', surround 'em with cannon an' rifles an' mow 'em down. But the cannon balls an' shells turn aside from him. The rifle an' musket bullets curve over his head an' he comes through without a scratch. Now, Deaf, how can you account for all them escapes, one right after another, so many that you lose count of 'em? I know why they've happened. He's chose, that boy there is chose. He's our luck piece. The signs have piled up till they show it plain. He don't know it hisself, any more than them water witches know where their power comes from, but he's our herald, our flag bearer, an' if we stick to him we'll pull through. Don't you go to savin' it ain't so, Deaf Smith."

"Me! Me say that it ain't so? I ain't dreamin' of sayin' such a thing. I'm thinkin' just like you, Panther. You can't get away from it. It's shorely a sign, an' I'm goin' to stick to that boy. People I reckon are sometimes set apart for particular things without themselves knowin' it. They're magic leaders, always pullin' along the road to victory, an' not knowin' how they do it. We've jest got to keep Ned with us as a luck piece, Panther."

"A luck piece an' a magic leader, Deaf. I like that magic leader name best. It sounds strong an' compellin'."

"An' there's everything to it," said Smith with deep conviction.

"It can't be anything else," said the Panther with conviction equally deep.

Absolute certainty shone from the eyes of both.

"Now you better go to sleep, Deaf," said the Panther. "I'll wake you when my time's up, an' Karnes' turn will come last."

Smith lay down and slept. The Panther sat alone by the dying fire, his rifle across his knees, a huge figure, dark and formidable. The wolves howled again in grief and anger, but they howled in vain. Then the last coal went out, the darkness swept over everything, and the Panther watched in silence.

CHAPTER 3

CAPTURED TREASURE

Far in the night the Panther awoke Smith to take his turn at the watch. But the Panther himself did not go to sleep at once. The great strong borderer, hardened and roughened by many years of wilderness ways and wilderness fighting, had formed a strong affection for Ned. He, too, like Obed White, looked upon him as almost a son, and now came this new and powerful feeling that for some reason the Infinite had made him, unknown to himself, a magic leader. The big man ran over in his mind again the long list of the boy's escapes from deadly peril, and his belief became cumulative. It was a conviction. He regarded the sleeping figure with a trace of awe, then lay down and slept.

When Smith awoke Karnes to take the third and last watch he told him what the Panther had said about Ned and added:

"I believe it just as much as Panther does. Away up there in New York where I came from I knew lots of Iroquois when I was a boy. They believed that certain warriors was born lucky, and that you couldn't kill 'em in battle. An' I tell you, Hank, Indians know a lot. Why shouldn't they? They've had to be smart and quick with ear and eye and hand to live."

"You never said truer words, Deaf, and the same things happen among white men. Look at old Andy Jackson! Don't it stand to reason that he was chose? Think of him a little boy born in a poor little old log cabin up there in the hills of Carolina, away back in the Revolution! Before he is ten years old, a British officer slashes him over the head because he won't black his boots. But the blade turns aside an' just wounds, it don't kill.

"Would you pick out that little feller in a cabin in the hills to be such a terrible great man? You wouldn't an' I wouldn't an' everybody else wouldn't. But somethin' greater than any of us has. He lives through things that would kill most boys. As a man he has to fight an' fight hard, but he always wins an' he ain't any bigger an' stronger than the others. Then he fights the Indians an' he wins. He fights the British an' he wins. You wouldn't think he'd get to New Orleans before the British, but he did an' whipped 'em, too, an' they two to one, an' brave enough, too. It was because he was chose.

"An' they try to keep him from bein' President, sayin' he is a common man from the backwoods. All the fine people, the kind who attack us Texans, 'cause we ain't willin' to let the Mexicans kill us, are ag'in him, an' they do keep him out once, but he goes in the next time an' he goes in twice. He was certainly chose, an' I'm with you an' Panther when you say that Ned is chose, too. No boy could live through what he has unless he was."

Smith went to sleep beside the coals of what had been the fire, and Karnes watched until dawn which came swift and shot with fire, after the southern fashion. The last mournful howl of the disappointed wolves rose in the forest and with the daylight they fled away.

Ned awoke and sat up. He was not conscious that his character had changed in the course of the night, nor that his comrades regarded him with a new respect. They took pains not to show it, thinking it best that he should not know. He yawned, stretched himself vigorously and leaped lightly to his feet. He was too much inured to border life to take harm through sleeping on the ground, and he felt strength pouring through every vein.

"It was a fine sleep, the best I ever had," he said. "Is our buffalo all safe?"

"As safe as can be," replied Karnes. "You can see it hangin' up there in the tree, just as we put it last night, but some mighty hungry an' disappointed wolves have been roarin' 'roun' these woods all night. They raised a real plaintive song now an' then, and I guess they went away powerful sad."

"Which won't keep us from enjoying a juicy breakfast," said Smith. Nor did it.

After breakfast, Smith and Karnes went back to the crater for the horses, returning about noon with four and bringing Obed White with them also.

"It was a hard push for the animals through the thickets," said Obed, "but they made it. And when I heard, Ned, that you'd killed a whole buffalo herd they couldn't keep me from coming along. Unto him that shoots well the game shall be given."

They loaded three of the horses with the dressed and dissevered body of the buffalo, and Smith and Karnes departed with them for the camp, leaving behind the Panther, Obed, Ned and one horse. The Panther had an idea that they might find more wild turkeys, as the forest seemed so favourable for them, and, in case they should, the fourth horse could carry the burden.

Ned did not know that Smith and Karnes, before their departure, had held a secret conference with the Panther.

"You keep Ned with you," Smith had said, "an' if you find them turkeys which you didn't find yesterday, when you was separated, then it's another shore proof of what we already know to be true."

Smith and Karnes had not been gone a half hour before the others

532

heard a faint gobble. The Panther, Obed and Ned followed the sound cautiously, and they saw the finest collection of fat turkeys that they had ever beheld clustered upon the boughs of a great oak. The three stalked them with such ease that it seemed to the Panther that the turkeys awaited them on purpose. By swift and accurate shooting they brought down six before the rest could fly away.

Ned lifted an immense gobbler, with shining bronze feathers, and he guessed his weight at a full forty pounds. He was the biggest and fattest turkey that he had ever looked upon. But their large and easy triumph confirmed the Panther in a belief which was rather conviction already. Ned was their luck piece, their magic leader.

They carried the turkeys back to camp on the horse, which they had left tethered in the forest, and they received a warm welcome. Williamson, a good shot, had killed a deer within three hundred yards of the crater, and that, too, was added to their supply. Experienced hunters, they knew how to jerk and dry, and the crater was filled with proofs of their skill. They found more deer and turkeys and smaller game could be had almost for the asking. They made crude but effective tackle and caught fine fish in the creek that Ned had seen.

Thus several busy days passed. Ned and Will were happy. They were trusted members of a great band, on terms of full equality with such famous men as the Panther, Smith and Karnes, and the wild life and rude plenty there in the forest made a powerful appeal to both. They knew that rougher and more dangerous times were coming soon, but the present sufficed unto itself, and they took their pleasure.

They strengthened their cabins and spread skins over the bark floors, and they added many other comforts, expecting that the crater would long be their base. But while it was a pleasant time for them it was a most sorrowful one for the wolves which, filled with anger at the savor of the plenty that they could not reach, came nightly to the edge of the crater and howled their sorrows. Mingled with their lamentations rose now and then the cry of a panther, so much like the shriek of a woman.

"Some of you fellers could go out there and take a shot at those singers," said the Panther one night when the hungry chorus was unusually lively, "but we ain't got any ammunition to spare. Do you know that we're comin' mighty close to our last bullets? If the Mexicans was to stumble on us here, which ain't likely, we wouldn't have lead enough to put up a good fight?"

"I've been noticin' it," said Deaf Smith, "an' between you an' me,

Panther, we've got to get more lead, an' that mighty soon."

"'Tain't fur away," said the Panther, drooping an eyelid.

"I don't know of any lead mine in eyeshot of us," said Smith, also drooping an eyelid.

"Not just at this minute, I reckon, but we can bring one within eyeshot."

They understood each other perfectly.

"Then we'll do it." said Smith. "And while we're doin' it I reckon we might as well overhaul a powder factory, too. We need one about as bad as the other."

"We'll do that, too, Deaf. Good head, that, on your shoulders."

"Such as it is it's the only one I have, Panther."

They organised an expedition at once. It contained all but Will and two of the men. Will begged to go, but the Panther enlarged upon his responsibilities as a keeper of the camp, and defender of the army's base, and he became reconciled.

The six who departed went on horseback, as their business would lead them upon the plain, and there men on foot would have little chance. They looked very carefully to their arms and scanty supplies of ammunition, and started at daylight for the plains to the westward. It was rough riding through the dense hilly forest, and noon came before they emerged from it. But the knowledge that the belt was so wide made them feel all the more secure about the camp.

Before riding upon the plain they held a short conference. They knew that all the open country was now held by the troops of Santa Anna, and it was important to learn where the nearest detachment lay.

"This is a foragin' not a fightin' expedition," said Deaf Smith, "an' we must slip up on the Mexicans, seize what we want an' get away. This calls for woodcraft and prairie craft and all kinds of craft."

"You never spoke truer words, Deaf," said the Panther. "There can't be no roarin' an' rippin' an' t'arin', but just slidin' an' slippin'. Now I've got to say that about fifteen miles south of here there is, or was, a little settlement called Clay, after the great Henry. It's located on a hill by the side of two big springs, an' last year it had about twenty cabins. I don't know what it's got now, but if it ain't been burned likely a lot of Santa Anna's troops are hangin' out there."

"Then we make for it," said Deaf Smith, "an' if the Mexicans are there we stay about until dark."

"The night hides many a deed that would not be done in the day,"

534

said Obed White, sententiously, "but we intend that ours shall be a good one."

They rode into the open plain, but they kept as far as possible between the swells. Whenever they came to a motte or clump of timber they drew into its shelter, and, for a little while, examined every point of the horizon. They had no glasses, but they had keen and trained eyes. Ned's wonderful vision here came into valuable play again. He could see even farther than Smith or the Panther. After every successive motte he announced that the prairie was clear and they continued their indirect but steady progress toward the former village of Clay.

Shortly after noon Ned announced that he saw figures on the western horizon.

"They are not much more than a dim blur," he said, "but I think they are horses."

"In which case the blurs must be Mexican horsemen," said Obed White. "Nobody else would be riding here."

They waited a little longer and then Ned said:

"I was right. They are horses, but there are no horsemen."

"Horses without riders," said the Panther, musingly. "They can't be wild horses. They were all driven far west of here long ago."

"The meanin' is plain," said Deaf Smith. "Them's the abandoned horses of Texans that had to escape toward the north. It means that the country has been ripped wide open by Santa Anna's men, when you find work horses wanderin' about like wild buffalo."

"True your words are," said the Panther, "but we'll just mark where we've seen them animals. So far, we are ten men and eight horses, an' we need more mounts. We may pick up somethin' else besides powder an' lead on this foragin' trip."

"They've got good pasturage over there an' they won't go far," said Karnes. "We'll look in on that herd on our way back."

They soon left the horses out of sight and gradually approached Clay. Luckily for them the village had been located on a creek, well lined on both sides with timber which they reached unseen. Keeping well under cover they advanced and were rewarded presently by the sight of a spire of smoke. A mile further on and they saw two or three smaller spires beside the first.

"That settles it," said the Panther. "Clay is still standin' an' of course it's the Mexicans who are there. I guess they're havin' an easy time of it, thinkin' that no fightin' Texans are left on the face of the earth."

When within a half mile of Clay they stopped among the trees along the bank and waited patiently for the dark. Then they moved up within four or five hundred yards of the place, and stopped in the densest clump of trees and bushes they could find. There, they dismounted, and, leaving one man to hold the horses, the others crept toward Clay.

The night favoured them, hiding any figure fifty or sixty yards away, and, when they reached the edge of the clearing, they saw that all the houses of the village were still standing. But it was evident that none of the original inhabitants were left. Mexican ponies grazed before the little cabins where the lawns had been. In the square around which the cabins were built a large camp fire was burning. Mexican soldiers were cooking their suppers over the coals and others were lounging near. The watchers reckoned the force at about fifty.

The Mexicans evidently were enjoying themselves. The great and glorious Santa Anna had put his heel upon the Texans and trod them out. They had no more enemies to fight, but they had an abundance of the good things of the earth about them. So, according to their fashion, they dismissed labour and care and rejoiced. The food was cooked and eaten. After that a half dozen took out mandolins and guitars and began to play, while the others lay upon the grass and listened. There was scarcely any order or discipline. They were dreaming of their warm valleys in the south, while the *mandolins* and guitars tinkled on.

"Things are turnin' out fine," whispered the Panther to Deaf Smith. "Didn't I tell you they'd do so if we had him with us?"

He nodded toward Ned, and Smith nodded back in affirmation.

"Where do you think their guns are?" whispered Ned as he approached the two.

"I can see some in the square," replied the Panther, "but it's likely that a lot of them are stacked between the cabins. They are the ones we've got to find, an' the happier them Mexicans get, the finer they think this earth is, the better it is for us. While they're playin' their music I hope a lot of 'em get uneasy feet and take to the *fandango*."

The hunters had now crept very near to the cabins, but they were still in the darkness. Smoke, the spires of which they had seen from afar, rose from four of these cabins, and Ned surmised that most of the officers were inside, doubtless playing some of the games of cards that Mexicans love. All things were relaxed and easy in the Mexican camp.

Their enemies, victorious through overwhelming numbers, were taking the fruits of life. The music had a lilt and swing that told of far-off pleasant places, deep green grass, the trickle of water, the sound of pleasant human voices, and the lilt of the dance. It proved irresistible to the Mexicans too. Men sprang to their feet, clasped one another by the shoulder, and whirled about with all the fire and grace of the south.

"It's right fine to look at," murmured the Panther, grimly, "an' as I said, it suits our plans. If we can't do what we want to do now we can't do it at all."

"But I think we can do it now," said Smith, "that is if they keep on with their music an' dancin'. See that shed there on our left?"

"We see it," said Ned, speaking for all, "and we see the gleam of metal there, too."

"An', as you can see also, that gleam comes from the metal of rifle and musket barrels. They've stacked their guns there, an' where guns are powder an' bullets are likely to be."

"You do reason powerful good, Deaf," said the Panther. "The powder an' lead are sure to be there an' they're our game, the best game that we've ever hunted. We'll just lay quiet here till our time comes."

They crouched close to the earth and waited. Ned thrilled with the tense situation and the excitement of the moment. The music and dancing grew wilder. The Mexicans began to grow excited. They threw more logs on the fire and the flames leaped and crackled as they ate into the wood. The dancers increased to twenty and then to thirty. They sang also a fiery song of the south that had in it the fierce spirit of old Spain. Some of the officers, leaving their cards, came out of the cabins and watched. It was brighter inside the square, but it was darker beyond it.

"I think now's our time," said the Panther. "After all this hullabaloo is over they'll go to sleep, but they'll set a guard first. Now they ain't payin' attention to anything 'cept the music an' the dance."

"Lead on," said Smith, "we'll foller."

"Weak as we are, we do not fear to rush in where the Panther dares to tread," said Obed.

They slid along, keeping well within the shadow of the cabins, and came to the shed. Then their hearts leaped as they saw the trophies to be won by skill and daring. Fully a hundred rifles and muskets were stacked there, enough for twice the Mexican force in Clay. Ned inferred that they were held for fresh troops who were expected.

Lying between the stacks of arms were several kegs of powder and heaps of lead in bars. Some of the rifles were fine weapons of American make. The Panther looked upon the store with pleasure and then he growled.

"There's so much of it," he whispered, "that it makes me mad to think we can't take it all away with us. We'll need them rifles for the recruits we expect to get, an' we need the powder an' lead still more. I guess we'll have to leave the rifles this time. Them kegs of powder will weigh 'bout fifty pounds apiece. We've got to take three of 'em an' the other two of us will load up with as much lead as they can carry. Now be awful careful an' don't drop anything about that will make a noise."

The Panther, Ned and Smith took a keg of powder apiece, while the others helped themselves to as much lead as they could carry conveniently. But the Panther and Smith could not resist temptation and each added a fine rifle to his burden. They also took a considerable weight of lead in order to help out the proportion.

Now everything depended upon their reaching the horses unseen, and bearing their burdens lightly, they stole back to the timber along the creek. Ned's heart was throbbing with excitement, and the pulses in his temples were beating hard. He had hoisted the keg of gunpowder upon his shoulder, where he steadied it with one hand, while he carried his rifle in the other. He was just behind the Panther, whose gigantic frame bore easily the burden of a fifty-pound keg, forty or fifty pounds of lead and an extra rifle.

Ned noted that the music did not decrease. It had the same wild rhythmic swing and the fiery song of the south still swelled. The pulses in his temples did not beat so hard now. They were away from the line of cabins and in another minute they were in the brush. Then the music ceased suddenly and they heard a wild shout.

"They've discovered the loss," exclaimed Smith, "an' they're jumpin' to see what caused it. Now, boys, we've got to make the runnin' good an' get this stuff on our horses quick. They'll naturally look in the timber."

They dashed forward now, careless of noise, and reached the horses. Fastening their spoils on as best they could they leaped into the saddle.

"Up the creek!" cried the Panther. "If we get away we must do it in that direction!"

Ned understood at once. If there was to be a chase they would not lead the Mexicans toward Camp Independence, and reveal its presence. They were galloping now in exactly the opposite direction, and for a little while they made as great speed as the brush would allow. Presently they heard another shout and now it was the combined volume of many voices.

"They've hit our trail!" exclaimed Karnes. "Some of them Mexicans are mighty fine scouts an' trailers, an' we can't do much lingerin', 'specially since Santa Anna has ordered every Texan took to be shot or hanged."

"But we ain't goin' to give up our captured ammunition," exclaimed the Panther. "We've come too far an' we've risked too much for that. I'm ready to do a lot of roarin' an' rippin' an' t'arin' before I let go of these things."

Ned settled his keg of powder in front of him and managed with his belt to tie it securely to his body. He shared the Panther's spirit. He meant to fight to the last for that powder.

"Easy, boys," called the Panther. "Better let the horses have their heads. We can't afford to gallop into a tree or break our necks in a gully, an' remember, that while we have to slow up for them causes, the Mexicans have to do it, too."

There could be no doubt now that a large Mexican troop was in pursuit. They could hear the shouts of officers and the beating of hoofs. A moment or two later they saw the flash of torches among the trees, but the enemy was a full four hundred yards behind. The Texans, had they been willing to give up their ammunition, could have escaped easily, but there was not one in the little band who would do so and they kept on at a good pace, staying well within the cover of the trees along the creek bank.

"Of course," said the Panther, "you fellers understan' that we can't let 'em get within range. We've got here three kags of powder, an' powder can go off with a terrible an' rippin' bang. The Mexican ain't any prize winners on the shoot, but if a bullet was to hit in one of these kags where would we be?"

"Go ask of the winds," said Obed White, "and they'd ask you back again. It's not a fate that I covet, to be spread over the map of Texas by an explosion of Mexican gunpowder, and I think you can rely upon us all, Panther, to keep well ahead."

"I guess you'll try hard enough," said the Panther, grimly.

They rode good horses, bred to the prairie and forest and as they gave them their heads they avoided all the dangers of collision and pitfall. But they still heard the sounds of pursuit and they knew that the Mexicans would hang on. They also saw the torches yet flaring behind them.

"Deaf," said the Panther, "do you think you could carry my kag along with your own for a few minutes?"

"Shorely," replied Smith as he rode alongside and took the keg. The Panther handed the lead to another man, but he kept the extra rifle himself. Then he turned his horse's head.

"You fellows quicken up your pace a little," he said, "an' I'll shoot out some of their lights."

Ned understood that he was about to try a daring experiment, and he could not keep from looking back. The Panther drew his horse behind a bush. The Mexicans came on with a thud of hoofs and four torches flaring. Only the men with torches could be visible to an enemy a hundred yards away. The Mexican scouts, keen of ear, could hear the tread of fugitive hoofs, but they did not see the grim figure that had drawn aside and that sat on his horse beside the bush, for all the world like one of those paladins of old who dared to face single-handed a torrent of men. It was the same spirit. The Texan in the wilderness was as brave and generous of soul as the best armour-clad knight of them all.

There was a spiteful crack from the bush. The foremost torch-bearer threw up his arms and rolled backward off his horse. A second crack and the next torch-bearer did the same. The whole Mexican troop reined in with a jerk. Such terrible shooting at night was uncanny. Nor could they tell just where it came from as the scouts yet heard the fugitive hoofs.

While they were still in confusion the Panther galloped swiftly away and overtook his comrades.

"Good work," said Smith, "we're a full third of a mile ahead now."

"And you've shown 'em," said Obed White, "that there's a flaming sword in the path. He who rides too fast is likely to ride no more."

"If the timber only holds out," said the Panther, as he took back his freight, "I'm certain we can shake 'em off."

"But as I said, the Mexicans have mighty good scouts an' trailers," said Deaf Smith, "an' maybe they have with 'em some of them Campeachy Indians that Ned saw at Goliad. I guess we better keep movin' right lively."

They continued in silence for an hour, the horses going at a trot, and at the end of that time, as they heard no further signs of pursuit, they slowed down to a walk. They were all hopeful that the Mexicans had given up the chase, but no one in his heart was sure. But the easier gait, for the time at least, was very welcome. Ned found that his body was chafed considerably by the heavy keg, and the horses, carrying extra burdens, showed signs of weariness. Finally, at the suggestion of Karnes, they dismounted, let the horses drink at the creek, and rested a while.

It was now midnight or past. The darkness had thinned away considerably and a good moon rode among a host of white stars. If an enemy should appear it would not be possible for them to hide, now, as the belt of timber had become much thinner. They had been going up the stream and the creek itself had shrunk to a brook only a few inches deep and three or four feet wide. Ned walked to the crest of a little hill, and, looking far ahead, saw that the timber continued to diminish in such a rapid manner that it must soon cease.

"I think we will have only the open prairie soon," he said to the Panther.

"Yes, everything shows it, but we can't yet afford to turn back to our forest. If a single one of that gang was to track us to Camp Independence we'd be ruined. We must keep straight ahead, and then if we are not seen, curve about and come into the woods. I guess we'd better be startin' ag'in."

They resumed their flight, both horses and men much refreshed, and as Ned had predicted, soon came to the end of the timber. The creek was now a mere shallow trickle across the prairie, but as the ground was hard they were hopeful they might not leave any trail that could be followed. Just when they were most cheerful, Ned, who was looking back, uttered a cry.

"They are coming!" he said.

He saw a faint moving line on the dusky horizon, and he knew that it was made by the pursuing Mexican horsemen.

"You've got to give 'em credit for hangin' on," said the Panther. "Some people take the Mexicans too cheap. With all these stars an' no trees things are in their favour now."

In half an hour the Mexicans were no longer a mere wavy line. Their individual figures could be seen clearly. The Texans even heard a triumphant shout, brought to them by a stray puff of wind. It was obvious that the pursuit was gaining.

"Do you think we ought to pick out the best place we can an' turn an' fight?" said Deaf Smith to the Panther.

The Panther did not reply for a full minute. Ned, who had heard the question, watched his face but he could read little there. It was so covered with a thick bush of black hair that nothing was visible but his eyes. But those eyes finally flashed as if in triumph and the huge man exclaimed:

"I've got it! It will need delicate handlin', but you an' me can work it, Deaf."

He and Smith whispered together and Smith nodded his head violently in assent.

"It's the only thing," Ned heard him say.

"It will cost us a kag of powder," said the Panther, "an' I hate like pisen to give it up, but it's better to lose one to save the rest."

He slipped loose his own keg and dropped it gently to the ground, where it lay at the very highest point of a swell.

"Now, you fellers slow up," said the Panther, "an' be shore that you don't change a single p'int from the direction in which we was goin' when I dropped the kag. Might be as well to let some of them Mexicans think our horses have pulled up lame."

They rode forward slowly and Ned heard a shout of triumph from the Mexicans who were now only a quarter of a mile away. Smith passed his keg of powder to Karnes.

"Keep three or four hundred yards ahead," he said, "an' if we do what we're undertakin' to do we'll rejoin you on the gallop. But it's a mighty delicate an' ticklish job, an' we don't know yet what's goin' to happen."

Ned looked back all the time, letting his horse have his head. He was quite sure that the Mexicans with their deadly experience of the Panther's rifle would be wary about coming within range of him and Smith. This was just what happened. When the Mexicans saw the two redoubtable Texan horsemen, considerably in the rear of their own comrades, they also slowed down, approaching warily. Then one of them saw the abandoned powder keg, and, as it was out of the Texan range, they rode toward it in a group, uttering another shout of triumph.

The Panther and Smith instantly turned and rode rapidly back toward the Mexicans, until they were within easy rifle shot. Then they stopped suddenly, raised their rifles and pulled the trigger. So swift and so equal in skill were they that the rifle barrels rose together, and the fingers pressed the triggers at the same time. But they had not drawn bead on the Mexicans. They had sent their bullets with unerring aim at something else.

Ned saw a great flash of fire, like the spouting of a volcano. There was a tremendous roar and the whole prairie seemed to shake. Then a huge cloud of smoke arose. Riderless horses, mad with fear or pain, shot from it, and terrible cries came from its centre.

The Panther and Smith swiftly rejoined their comrades.

"Go forward at an easy trot now," said the Panther. "There ain't goin' to be any more pursuit. I reckon, Deaf, that nobody will ever know whether your bullet or mine hit that kag."

But Ned knew that both bullets had struck the target. They were not men who ever missed in such a crisis. He did not look back again, wishing to avoid a sight that would be revealed when the smoke lifted, but gazed straight ahead. They rode in leisurely fashion for a full two hours, when they turned at a sharp angle and made straight for their forest. Then Ned glanced back for the first time. The prairie was clear and silent.

They made no stop, and, an hour or two after daylight, they reached the big forest. Nor did they stop there, until they were several miles within its deep shade. Then they drew up by the side of a small brook, dismounted, watered their horses, and permitted them to graze on what grass they could find among the bushes. They also drank and ate of cold venison.

"It won't do to kindle no fire here," said the Panther. "We must be a full forty miles from Camp Independence, but we don't want to take no risk whatever. Likely enough we'd better stay here all day 'cause our horses are clean fagged out."

"I'm willing," said Ned, with such earnestness that all laughed, including Ned himself. They had been at such high tension that the laugh was a relief. They began now to relax, to stretch their limbs and to get back the easy and natural control of all their faculties.

They felt an immense pride in their exploit and it was justified. They had now a fine store of powder and lead, and, at such a moment, powder and lead were more precious to them than jewels.

"We can spend a lot of good time makin' bullets when we get back to Camp Independence," said the Panther. "I hate to have lost that other kag, but it had to go. It wasn't wasted, either."

But they had done better than their hopes. They spent nearly the entire day by the brook, alternately sleeping and watching, and late in the afternoon they rode along its muddy bottom for three or four hours. This would surely hide the trail from any possible eye as the hoof-prints could not possibly last in the mud and water. When they came out it was on hard ground and they finished their journey without the least apprehension, arriving about noon of the next day at Camp Independence.

CHAPTER 4

DEFENDING A FORD

Will Allen was at the edge of the crater when he heard a swishing among the bushes, and then the sound of horses' feet. Will was naturally of a joyous, impulsive nature, taking most things lightly, but in these dark days of Texas he had learned caution. Perhaps the Mexicans were about to stumble upon Camp Independence. He darted into the thickest of the bush, where he kneeled down and peered in the direction of the sound.

The footsteps came on swiftly and decisively, as if the people who rode knew their way and feared nothing. Will rose a little higher, and the first horseman came into view. He was a man of gigantic stature, with enormous chest and shoulders, and with a great head and face all so covered with thick, black, curling hair that only the eyes were visible. He carried two rifles, a large keg and a heap of metal bars, bound together rudely with withes. Just behind him rode a tall, strong boy, who carried baggage, similar in kind, but less in quantity, and then came others.

Will stood up. Here were the Panther and Ned and all his friends, back safe and sound, evidently bringing with them some kind of spoil. He shouted joyously and ran forward.

"You have succeeded!" he cried.

"What do you think we went for if not to succeed?" replied the Panther gravely. "We had to do a lot of roarin', an' rippin' an' t'arin' an' chawin', but we come back a lot richer than we was when we went away."

"The riches of the Mexicans took unto themselves the wings of the morning and flew into our hands," said Obed White. "We have here, young sir, powder and lead, which are the very cream of the market in Texas at this time."

They dismounted, led their horses down into the crater, unloaded their spoils, and all rejoiced together. The powder and lead were stored in the strongest and driest of the cabins, and they decided to begin the making of bullets at once. All of them had bullet moulds, without which they never went to war, and they built a small but very hot fire in an angle of the cliff. The lead was melted in one of their camp skillets, and, taking turns in fours, they moulded bullets until it was dark.

They resumed the task the next morning, and never ceased until the last pound of lead was turned into bullets, making many thousands in all. The Panther contemplated the shining heaps with great satisfaction.

"With all these bullets an' with all the powder that we've got, we're four or five times as strong as we was sev'ral days ago," he said. "But we ain't strong enough yet. We've got to make another haul soon, an' then we've got to get men. We want to pick up the stray Texan fighters here an' there, an' bring 'em to Camp Independence."

"In order that we may be the skull at the Mexican feast," said Obed White.

"I don't know much about feastin' with skulls settin' by, lookin' at you," said the Panther, "but if you mean makin' ourselves a thorn in the Mexican side an' twistin' it 'roun' an' 'roun', that's it."

"It comes to the same thing," said Obed White.

The men were never idle. Two more deer were shot in the woods, and the meat was jerked. They continued to find the wild turkeys numerous, but they did not shoot many, as they did not wish to alarm the birds and drive them from their haunts. But they caught many fine fish in the big creek. The time not spent in fishing and hunting they devoted to improving their camp. With their hatchets they hollowed out a deep alcove in the side of the hill, lined it with bark, and put their powder in it, where it would be safe from a wetting by a storm of unusual violence, and where there would be no risk of explosion from a stroke of lightning.

They also strengthened and improved their houses, and added two new ones. As they expected recruits, they intended to be ready for them when they came. The crater assumed the friendly aspect of home, although they built no fire of any size, except at night, lest the smoke rising above the trees might be seen by a prowling enemy. But within the entire circle there was every evidence of rude plenty. The horses taken now and then under guard to the little meadows on the hills were sleek and fat. The flesh of deer, wild turkey and other game hung drying from the saplings. Skins also were being tanned, and there were others besides those of deer.

A big panther, driven by hunger, entered the crater late one night and sprang upon one of the horses. Deaf Smith, drawn by the terrified neigh, arrived in time to shoot the panther before he could do any damage to the horse. His skin, a fine one, was added to their collection. The wolves had been a great annoyance, coming to the edge of the crater every night and howling out their anger and grief. Smith and five others, including Ned and Will, stole out of the opposite side of the camp on a moonlight night, approached against the wind, and killed eight of the wolves before the rest could get away.

"Wolf skins are worth having," said Deaf Smith, as they reloaded their rifles, "so we'll just take these."

They secured eight good skins, and returned to the crater. They found the next morning that the survivors had slunk back and had picked clean the bones of their comrades, but they did not come any more to the edge of the crater and howl in the darkness.

"*O, muse, sing no more the wrath of the master wolf,*" said Obed White, "*for his soul is dead and gone down to Hades, and his flesh has served to feed his own comrades, likewise the flesh of seven of his brethren.*"

Then Ned made a proposition.

"Panther," he said, "don't you remember those horses we saw when we were on the expedition after the powder and lead? They are good horses. They had owners once, but none now. Suppose we go and get them."

"I've been thinkin' of it," said the Panther. "They ain't had time to run wild yet, an' you an' me an' Deaf an' Hank will go for them. We may make a good haul."

They mounted their best four horses, took lariats and rode away, reaching the edge of the forest at night and camping there until day. They entered the open prairie the next morning and took the general direction in which they had gone before. Unless alarmed by men or wild animals, it was not likely that the horses would wander from the rich pastures in which they had been seen.

"Buffaloes roam far from north to south and from south to north," said the Panther, "but I don't think wild horses do, an' I know tame ones won't. So we ought to sight 'em within ten miles from where we saw 'em before."

The Panther was a good prophet or reasoner. They found the herd on the banks of a small creek, grazing in a little meadow, and then undertook the delicate task of approach. The four had great experience with horses, and they drew near very slowly, whistling and making all the other equine signs of amity. Perhaps the horses had been scared by panthers, and looked with welcome upon their old friend and employer, man, but at any rate they allowed the four to come among them, and recapture eight of the choicest.

"Waal, who'd 'a' thought it?" said the Panther, fairly exuding triumph. "I guess these horses ain't so much in love with runnin' wild as you'd think they was, or mebbe they think it's better to be captured by Texans than by Mexicans, as one or the other would happen sooner or later."

They kept their new horses in the edge of the timber a day and night, feeding them, watering them, reaccustoming them to the hand of man, and also permitting them to grow friendly with the horses which they already had. Then, cutting their lariats in order that each of them might lead two horses, Ned, the Panther, Smith and Karnes took their way back to Camp Independence, where their arrival created a great stir, and where the new horses soon grew used again to human ownership and became contented members of the herd.

Smith, Karnes and the Panther exchanged notes over their second achievement directly after their return.

"It keeps on workin'," said the Panther, "whenever we take that boy with us we do what we want to do."

"It hasn't failed yet," said Smith.

"'Twould be temptin' Providence to start on anything without him," said Karnes. "Havin' had so much proof, we'd be mighty big fools to go ag'inst all the signs."

"You was never more right in your life," said the Panther.

Several days later, Ned, Will, the Panther, Obed and two others went on a hunting expedition in the deep woods. As the country in the direction they wished to pursue was so broken and so dense with forest and underbrush, they walked, the Panther generally leading the way.

"It's a good thing," said Will Allen, "to have an elephant walking before you when you start through the jungle. He breaks such a nice path that the walking is easy."

"Who's an elephant?" said the Panther. "Is anybody hintin' at me? The next time you call me an elephant, Will, I'll curl my trunk aroun' you, an' throw you up into the top of one of them trees where you'll stick."

As a matter of fact, the Panther was as fine a woodsman as plainsman. His huge form seemed fairly to flit forward, making no sound as it slid among the bushes. The others watched him and studied his craft, wishing to be as nearly as possible his equal in this essential accomplishment.

547

The luck did not prove good. All the big game, warned by the fate of some of their comrades, apparently had fled away. There was no turkey in the tree, nor deer nor bear in the bush. But they persevered.

"All things come to him who hunts long enough for them," said Obed White cheerfully.

"An' havin' hunted so long without findin' anythin'," said the Panther, "we've come to the edge of the woods. Look through them leaves there, an' you can see the green prairie."

"Suppose we try our fortunes on the prairie," said Ned. "The grass is so good that we might find a herd of antelope close by or even run across another buffalo that has wandered too far east."

"The idee ain't bad," said the Panther, "an' we'll take a look anyway."

They emerged from the forest and came out upon the prairie which stretched away, lush, green and wavy as far as the eye could reach. The sky as usual at that period was heavy with clouds, but the gray tint which did not dazzle was more of an aid to Ned's keen eyesight than brilliant sunlight would have been.

They travelled some distance through the grass which often rose almost as high as their waists, and after nearly two hours saw a herd of antelope feeding at a distance of about a mile. Here was tender food, and they resolved to secure it. The Panther had a huge red bandana handkerchief, which Obed, after creeping near enough, was to wave until he attracted the attention of the herd. Then the others approaching from another point were to pick off the fattest with their rifles.

Their campaign began auspiciously. Obed was soon lost to sight in the grass, although they knew that he was advancing toward the herd. Their own progress was sure, and the game showed no signs of alarm. Another hundred yards and they would be within rifle shot, when every antelope, as if by a preconcerted signal, threw up its head, stood still for a moment or two, and all of them fled like the wind toward the western horizon.

"Now, what in the name of all that's cur'us made 'em do that?" exclaimed the Panther. "Obed's too smart to have done any fool thing to alarm 'em, an', besides, here he comes, lookin' as mixed up over it as we are."

"The leader of that herd was a wise old antelope," said Ned; "I see what caused his alarm, and it's about time for us, too, to get away as fast as we can."

He pointed toward the north, and they beheld there eight or ten figures outlined against the gray horizon.

"I see," said the Panther. "The herd got their wind and made off. They are horsemen, an' they're comin' fast in this direction. What do you make 'em out to be, Ned?"

"I don't think they are Texans. They don't ride upright enough. Nor are they Mexicans, because I see neither saddles nor bridles. In my opinion the horsemen are riding bare back."

"Which means they're Indians shorely an' Comanches likely," said the Panther. "It's a raidin' party. Our leaders have been tryin' to keep the Comanches quiet, while we fight the Mexicans, but it's easy enough for the young bucks to gallop over this country, an' hunt plunder an' scalps here an' there. Them warriors have seen us, an' are ridin' straight for us, thinkin' it will be just fun to get our scalps, 'cause they're on ponies an' we're on foot. Make for the motte an' we'll fight it out there, boys. We don't want to run into the woods an' let 'em find out where Camp Independence is, an' bring down on us a big Comanche war band an' maybe a Mexican army, too. I think we can teach these rascals somethin' about fightin'. Are you fellows for the motte?"

"The motte!" they exclaimed all together.

There was a small, but dense clump of trees, about a hundred yards to their left, and they ran for it, at the utmost speed. The Comanches were not more than four hundred yards away, and they uttered a long, ferocious whoop when they saw the flight of the Texans. They were painted horribly, and they threw themselves about in wild attitudes as they urged their horses to a greater pace. Two or three fired, but the bullets fell short.

The next instant the six Texans were in the timber, and the Comanches, halting at a point out of range, began to ride up and down in front of the trees, making hideous gestures and shouting foul taunts at the six.

"I don't know what they're sayin'," said Will Allen, "but it sounds bad. Panther, let me shoot. Please let me shoot!"

"You keep quiet, youngster," said the Panther, laughing. "If you pull trigger, I'll turn you over my knee and spank you. You can't reach 'em, an' so don't waste a good bullet."

"They annoy terribly."

"Our time will come. Just you wait. They're enjoyin' themselves tremenjously, an' when people are doin' that they're apt to be forgetful. Look, now, the nearest fellow that's whoopin' an' cavortin' so is comin' closer than he knows."

The six Texans now lay very low in the little clump of woods, hidden completely from the Comanches, who, nevertheless, knew just where they were. The warriors were doing fancy riding, looking under the bodies or necks of their horses, holding on with heel and toe, and now and then uttering the war whoop. Ned did not know whether their purpose was a taunting display or a desire to get near enough for shots. But he watched closely, and he heard the Panther beside him breathing deeply with satisfaction.

"It ain't a good thing to show off," he said, "when them that you're showin' off to are loaded for you. Mebbe they've miscalculated the power of our rifles and the shoreness of our aim, but in jest about two more minutes of their whoopin' an' cavortin' they'll be in range. They're ridin' in line, an' I'll fire at the first, you take the second, Ned, and Obed the third."

He also assigned other possible targets in order to his other three comrades, and they waited patiently until the howling Comanches came a little nearer. One minute passed, then two minutes, and the Panther cried: "Fire."

Six rifles flashed from the covert and four of the Comanches fell lifeless from their horses. Two others were wounded, and so great and terrific was this surprise that the rest turned and galloped at full speed toward the western horizon, the ponies of the fallen trailing after them. The Panther burst into a great roar of triumph.

"That's about the quickest victory that was ever won," he said, "an' I guess it was Comanche vanity that made it come to us so easy."

"Pride went before the fall of these Comanches from their ponies," said Obed. "We'll gather up their rifles or muskets that fell with them and take 'em to our camp. We'll need 'em for recruits."

"Will the other Comanches return?" asked Will Allen.

"Never," replied the Panther confidently. "They won't even come back to bury them that fell. It was a raidin' band, ridin' pretty far east, an' they'll reckon that they'd better stay on the western border. Mebbe this little victory will save a lot of people besides ourselves."

All the fallen Comanches had Texan rifles, and they carried the four fine weapons back with them to Camp Independence. Deaf Smith agreed with the Panther that the repulse was likely to keep the Comanches out of that part of the country.

Now they organised another expedition in search of recruits and departed upon it almost immediately. Will went with his friend Ned. Two men remained to guard Camp Independence.

"It would be fine to take a big, trained band to Sam Houston when the time comes to strike," said the Panther.

"Houston will strike," said Smith confidently. "I've been throwed with Sam a lot, an' he studies things to the bottom."

"Thrice armed is he who strikes when the iron is hot, and strikes hard and often," said Obed White.

They rode in a great curve to the north and west, intending to pass around Clay, which, beyond a doubt, was still held by a Mexican garrison. They expected to pick up roving Texans, and add them to their band at Camp Independence. All thought it more than likely that they would have a fight before they returned. Now as they advanced northward they saw signs that the Mexicans had passed. Thrice they came upon the ashes of burned cabins, and once they saw where cattle had been slaughtered in sheer wantonness, and left to be devoured by wild animals. About noon they came to another of the burned cabins, and among some bushes near it Ned saw a dark object. It was the body of a man, a Texan, thrust through with a lance.

Ned, when he saw, clinched his teeth, and felt the blood of anger rushing to his brain. Visions of the Alamo, the black flag and the cruel triumph of Santa Anna came back to him. The impression made upon him by the terrible events through which he had passed had not dimmed a particle. The passion for vengeance was as strong as ever, and he felt that the Texans must gather their slender forces and fight anew.

Smith and the Panther carefully examined the ground around the cabin, and then rode forward on a broad trail about a hundred yards. When they returned they announced that the destruction had been done by a large band, at least a hundred men.

"I think it likely that it's Urrea and his cavalry," said the Panther. "We know how active he is, an' he's sweepin' 'roun' through these parts, doin' all the destruction he can."

"Don't you think it likely," asked Ned, "that we can achieve more by following him than by doing anything else? He is seeking prey, of course, and we may arrive in time to save."

"Then the hunter in his turn shall become the hunted," said Obed White. "The thought appeals to me. The ruthless destroyer little suspects that his own time, too, may be at hand. That sounds a little fanciful, but it's what ought to come to pass."

"At any rate, we'll see," said the Panther, as they rode on the broad trail, which they judged to be about twelve hours old. Before night they saw further evidences of devastation. Every house in the Mexican path was destroyed and more animals had been slaughtered. But they did not see a human being. It was evident that the Texans were fleeing northward with their women and children.

"If we keep in the course that we are now takin'," said Smith, "we'll strike the Colorado River tomorrow mornin'."

"And if there are any fugitives ahead of the Mexican cavalry they will strike it at the same time or earlier," said Ned.

"You speak Gospel truth," said Smith, "an' it would be mighty hard for 'em to get away with a big river in front of 'em an' the Mexicans behind 'em."

"I was thinking of that," said Ned. "It seems to me that we're needed."

"Never looked more like it," said the Panther, who was listening. "We'll try to pass around that gang tonight an' see what's ahead. What do you say, boys?"

"Of course," they replied together.

They increased their speed, and they knew by the evidences of the trail that they were gaining fast. Eight can go more rapidly than a hundred.

"It will be night long before we can come within eyeshot of them," said the Panther, "but so much the better. There's lots of buffalo chips about, and they're likely to build a big fire, which will be a guide to us."

The darkness soon showed in the east, and then swept down quickly. Had it not been such a broad trail they could have followed it no longer, but the Texans, strong in experience, kept on steadily in the dusk. Ned, looking straight ahead, suddenly saw a spot of light, which quickly rose and expanded.

"They have stopped for camp," he said, "and there is the fire that you predicted, Panther."

"Correct," said the Panther. "Suppose we shift to the right an' pass by, takin' a good look at 'em as we go."

"It suits us," said Smith, speaking for them all.

They turned their course and rode forward at a more moderate pace, slowing to a walk, when they came within a quarter of a mile of the fire. They did not anticipate very great vigilance on the part of the Mexicans, but they could not afford to be seen by any possible scout or sentinel of theirs.

The Mexican camp seemed to be pitched in one of the mottes or clumps of timber which were frequent on the prairie, and the eight rode toward it at the slowest of walks. Then, sitting on their horses, well beyond the circle of light, they could see clearly within. They beheld many men and horses, and at last Ned saw a figure pass between him and the fire, which he knew to be that of Urrea. Again the blood leaped to his head, and the great pulses throbbed. Here was his enemy and here was another reason why they should defeat the cruel plans of the invaders.

"Their horses look good, better than most Mexican horses," whispered the Panther, "an' the men are all well armed with rifles, muskets and lances. It would take a lot of rippin' an' t'arin' an chawin' to wipe 'em out."

"Those facts indicate that they are riding on a certain errand, and not at random," said Ned.

"'Pears that way. How I wish we had enough men to stay here an' make 'em fight. Only twenty more an' we'd give young Don Francisco Urrea the warmest evening he ever had."

"But we haven't got 'em, so I guess we'd better be ridin' on, an' see what they are chasin'," said Smith.

"Right. You're gen'aly right, Deaf. I've noticed that," said the Panther.

They curved about the camp fire, and they were fully a mile ahead of it when its last gleam disappeared behind the swells. But Ned did not believe that the Mexicans would remain there all through the night. If Urrea was pursuing a definite object he would probably start at two or three in the morning. So it behooved the eight to use speed as they rode.

But they stopped in a half hour and began to search back and forth. There was a fair moon now, and it was not hard to examine the green surface of the prairie. It was Karnes who spoke first.

"This is what Urrea is followin'," he said. "The wheels of ten wagons have passed here, an' there were mebbe a dozen people ridin' horses."

The others agreed with his estimate.

"Texan refugees," said Smith. "I expect them wagons was crowded with women an' children, an' there couldn't have been many men. Urrea would make short work of them all when he came up."

"We're in between," said the Panther, "an' mebbe we can stay in between. Mebbe God started us on purpose to get here at this time."

He spoke in a spirit full of reverence, and the others, too, felt as if a superhuman hand had guided them. The belief strengthened them greatly for the daring task they were about to assume.

"Do you think the Texans know that Urrea is on their track?" asked Will Allen, who was greatly excited.

"No," replied the Panther. "Urrea, most likely, has been keepin' his distance, an' expects to gallop down on 'em when they're penned up ag'inst the Colorado. Then he could slaughter 'em almost as he pleased."

"But we may put a stick between his spokes," said Obed White, in sanguine tones. "Never count your chickens until you've found your nest, and Urrea doesn't know what he's going to find."

The trail of the fleeing Texans was as plain as that of Urrea had been. The wheels of the wagons, evidently loaded heavily, had cut great ruts over the prairie, and the experienced eyes of the scouts and hunters followed it as easily as the ordinary hunter would follow the shining bars of a railway.

All through the night they rode. The moon faded, went out, and then came back again in greater splendour than ever. The clouds drew curtains before the host of stars that danced in the sky, then floated away, and the stars came out more brilliantly than before. Little puffs of wind sped across the prairie, and rustled the leaves in the clumps of timber. But the eight rode steadily on, the ruts made by the wagon wheels always stretching before them.

Ned, near dawn, saw a light far ahead on the prairie. It was faint, but he knew it was no star showing above the crest of a hill. It was the light that came from a camp, and he was sure that the camp belonged to the Texans whom they were following. His comrades agreed with him.

"I guess they're asleep 'cept for a sentinel or two whom they may have out," said the Panther, "but we'll soon bring 'em news that'll make 'em as wide awake as anybody can be."

They drew their horses to a walk, and, as they approached, they saw that their surmise had been right. Ten wagons stood on a little swell, and some horses grazed at the ends of lariats. Two sentinels stood near, rifle on shoulder.

The sentinels took their rifles out of the hollows of their arms, and walked forward a little, when they saw the men approaching. The Panther raised his hand as a sign of amity, and, as they rode closer, cried out in a tremendous voice:

"Friends we are, Texans like yourselves."

They were in the camp the next moment, and men, women and children, some not more than half dressed, were crowding around them, the children gazing with interest and awe at the huge, strange figure of the Panther in his deerskin dress of brilliant dye.

"Who is the leader here?" asked the Panther.

"I am, poor and unworthy though I may be," replied a tall, thin man, emerging from the group. His was a figure even more extraordinary than that of the Panther. He was of great height and very thin, A broad black slouch hat covered his head, but his most remarkable garment was a black frock coat, buttoned closely and falling below his knees. His trousers also were black, but, like the coat, they were well sprinkled with Texas dust. The man's face was long, smooth-shaven and tanned, and, grotesque though the figure appeared, the face was one of uncommon power. The first impulse of Ned and Will to laugh was changed to one of respect.

"I am the Reverend Stephen Larkin," he said. "I have preached at times to the scattered Texas flocks, and I have taught school at times also, though I must confess that the mind of Texan youth runs more to rifle and horse than to history and the higher mathematics. Sam Houston is to them a greater general than Napoleon, and they think more of Crockett and Bowie, just fallen in the Alamo, than of mighty Hannibal and Caesar."

"Can you blame 'em?" asked the Panther.

"No, I cannot," admitted Larkin, "and at such a time as this perhaps it is necessary. And, sir, I do not wish to be too inquisitive, but may I ask who you are?"

"My name is Martin Palmer. Men often call me the Ring Tailed Panther, or the Panther for short."

A grim light flickered for a moment in the eyes of Larkin.

"I have heard of you—often," he said. "I am afraid that you are a sanguinary man, one who has lived a life of violence and strange deeds."

The Panther leaned forward a little on his horse, and stared with his black eyes into the blue eyes of the minister, which stared back, as hard as steel, and never flinching.

"I have killed," said the Panther slowly, "an' I have killed more than once, but never except in self-defence or in defence of those who was too weak to defend themselves. These are not peaceful times, an' this has never been a peaceful country, Stephen Larkin. It's said that Heaven helps them that helps themselves, an' in Texas now when you

555

put up a prayer you want to have a gun alongside it."

A faint smile came into the stern blue eyes of the minister and teacher. He stretched forth a long, big-boned and powerful arm, and his hand and that of the Panther met in a grasp which would have twisted the fingers of ordinary men.

"I meant nothing against you," said Larkin. "The Lord raised up David to fight the battles of His people, and since Satan, whose other name is Santa Anna, is abroad in the land, we must even meet him with his own weapons. My own rifle is in the wagon there. Upon occasion, I can shoot for my people—and I fear me much that the occasion is nigh."

"Here are more men who shoot straight an' true," said the Panther. "This is Deaf Smith, and this is Henry Karnes. There is nobody in all Texas who has not heard of them. And these two boys are Ned Fulton and Will Allen. Ned has been through more dangers than I can tell you about now."

He called the names of the others to the attention of Larkin, and then he added briefly, but very much to the point:

"We've come, Mr. Larkin, to warn you and your people. Francisco Urrea, one of the best of the Mexican cavalry leaders, is following you with a hundred men or more. He is fifteen miles or less behind, but, as we take it, he expects to catch you when you reach the Colorado. You know what to expect from the Mexicans, and most of all from this Urrea."

The face of the Reverend Stephen Larkin whitened a little, but his voice was steady when he replied:

"We are to expect no mercy, but we thank you for bringing us this warning. If we are to be put to the edge of the sword so be it."

The Panther laughed softly through his huge black beard.

"We do more than bring warnin', sir," he said. "We expect to fight by your side. There are eight of us, all good shots, an', although the odds are ag'inst us, your party an' ours may hold the Colorado ag'inst Urrea an' all his band."

"Thrice armed are those whose rifles shoot fast and true," said Obed White.

The steel-blue eyes of Larkin gleamed.

"It is noble of you, gentlemen," he said, "to help the weak, and we may even succeed. There are some stout arms here in our own party."

The announcement of the pursuit by Urrea had caused a hush of consternation among the women and children, but the strong words of the Panther were a tonic, and they began to speak hopefully. The party, including Larkin, had sixteen men and boys old enough to fight, the women and children—children were numerous in Texas—numbering thirty-six. They carried the usual frontier rifles and had plenty of ammunition. Six of the wagons were drawn by oxen and the others by horses and mules. The gait of the oxen would be slow, and Urrea could make three miles to their one. Four of the women, natives of the frontier, big-boned and powerful, could drive, and drive well, leaving more men free for battle if the pinch came.

"How far ahead is the Colorado?" asked the Panther.

"Not more than eight miles," replied Larkin. "We expected to cross it today, and we had begun to feel safe. Not many Mexicans are on the other side, so we hear, and, moreover, we would meet our brethren there."

"The nearer we get to it the better off we will be," said Smith.

"Them's true words," said the Panther. "S'pose we start right now, Mr. Larkin."

Larkin issued his orders quick, but calm and to the point. Ned saw that he was a born leader of men. There had been many such frontier preachers, men who fought as well as preached for what they thought right, and it was obvious that Larkin was a splendid representative of the type.

The wagons began to creak in a few minutes, as they rolled slowly over the prairie. Most of the women and children were under the canvas covers, but several half-grown boys ran beside the wheels. In the rear rode the men, all armed thoroughly with rifles and pistols. The Panther's eyes glistened as he looked over the small but formidable array.

"It will take a lot of rippin' and' t'arin' an' chawin' to wipe us out," he said.

"And the stars in their courses may fight for us," said Obed White.

The Reverend Stephen Larkin nodded approvingly at the semi-biblical quotation, and his own steel-blue eyes glowed with the light of battle.

"Nor will we neglect to fight for ourselves if need be," he said.

The Panther smiled to himself and nodded approvingly. He had recognised a kindred spirit in the tall and stern minister. The wagons moved slowly on. The drivers tried to encourage the oxen to a greater pace, but their increase in speed was only slight. Ned and Will dropped to the rear, and both cast many looks over their shoulders, expecting at any moment to see the sunlight glittering on the Mexican lances.

As yet they saw nothing but the brilliant rays falling on the fresh green of the Texan grass, and far to their right the slender and indistinct figures of animals that Ned took to be antelope. Will, impulsive and always hopeful, thought that Urrea might have lost or given up the chase, but Ned knew better. It was not possible to miss the trail of the wagons, and Urrea would not abandon the prey which he was sure lay under his hand. His scouts might warn him that the fugitives had received a reinforcement, but they could tell him also that it was not large enough to be of importance. They would not know that the redoubtable Panther, Deaf Smith and Karnes were among those who guarded the wagons.

"It's only about five miles now to the river," said Larkin, "and may be they've abandoned the pursuit, after all."

"It's not possible," said Obed White. "Urrea will surely come, but we'll not be discouraged. Faint heart never won hot battle."

"Ah, there he is now!" exclaimed Ned, pointing to a tiny cloud of dust far behind them.

The others could not see it, but in a few minutes it rose on the plain.

"Sister Anna sees it, but it is not made by our brothers," said Obed White.

The cloud of dust broadened and approached fast.

"Tell our people in the wagons not to be alarmed," said Larkin to one of his men. "The enemy draws nigh, but we have trusty friends, and we shall even smite hard."

"Do you know anything about the ford?" asked the Panther.

"It is deep," replied Larkin. "The water will rise to the bodies of our wagons."

"Any timber along the banks?"

"Some, but not much."

"Even if only a little it will help. Will you tell your people, Mr. Larkin, when they get to the river to drive right in. Not to linger a minute, but go straight for the other side. The main attack will be made then, and it will be for us who ride behind the wagons to stop it."

Larkin gave his orders, and, returning to the fighting group, announced that they would be obeyed.

"An old man named Dave Simpkins is driving the first wagon," he said. "He is the bellwether, so to speak, and though far gone in years he has a fiery soul which fainteth not in the presence of danger. He will lead the way."

"Good," said the Panther. "Urrea and his men see us, but they are yet too far away to tell anything of our strength. I take it they won't come so fast now, knowin' that they can pen us with our back ag'inst the river."

"They are slowing down," said Ned. "I see a figure in the front which I think is that of Urrea."

"How I wish I could get a shot at him!" growled Deaf Smith.

About a third of the Mexicans carried lances, and when the brilliant sunlight struck the long blades it seemed to shoot out like a flame. Some of the women and children in the wagons saw this ominous sign, and an alarm spread among them, but it was quickly checked by Stephen Larkin.

"Don't forget," said he, "that the greatest riflemen in Texas stand between you and danger, and perhaps some who are not so good may deal a few body blows in a just cause."

He had a powerful influence. Though different in quality it was in effect something like that of the Panther. He radiated a strength and courage which seemed to flow into the veins of others, and everybody soon became quiet. Every one of the drivers, the women included, carried a rifle on the seat, except old Dave Simpkins, and he had two. There was also a rifle for every long, strong Texan boy of twelve or up, and they would make a formidable reserve force.

Thus the procession moved onward for a full half hour, old Dave Simpkins still in the lead, but wishing that he was back with the mounted riflemen. His fierce old soul blazed for a first chance to get at the enemy. The horsemen in the rear rode in a close group, taking many looks backward.

"Urrea has a glass, and is now watching us through it," said Ned.

"I hope he sees me an' knows me," said the Panther, turning his head full around, and presenting his face squarely to their pursuers. "I want him to know that I'm here, an' that Deaf is here, an' that Hank is here, an' that you're here, an' the rest of us are here."

"It will make him expect a haul that's all the richer," said Ned.

"Let him think it," said the Panther grimly.

A shout came from the first wagon. It was from old Dave Simpkins, and he was announcing that the Colorado was in sight. Urrea must have seen it, too, as the speed of the Mexicans increased rapidly. They also uttered shouts and began to spread out in a much longer and thinner line with lances on either flank. Ned's heart began to throb. Will turned pale, but his hand on bridle rein did not falter. Both quietly awaited the commands of the Panther, who, by common consent, was the leader.

"We'll spread out a little ourselves; we don't want to make too solid a target," he said. "They're goin' to attack in a few minutes."

"And may God defend the right!" said the Reverend Stephen Larkin.

At another time he might have looked a little ridiculous. The broad brim of his black hat, powdered now with dust, stood out straight. The tails of his long black coat fell low on the side of his horse, but there was nothing to laugh at in his face. Two rows of strong teeth were set firmly together, and the steely blue eyes shone with a terrible light. It seemed to Ned that one of Cromwell's Roundheads, reincarnated, was riding anew to battle.

"They're tryin' to flank us," said the Panther. "Deaf, you an' Hank go to the right; Ned, you an' Will come with me on the left, an' I'd like to have Mr. Larkin, too."

They followed his commands, or rather requests, the little party dividing in equal numbers, and wheeling to right and left to face their antagonists. Meanwhile the wagons, fierce old Dave Simpkins still in the lead, were racing toward the river, the oxen having been induced at last by the whip to run. Ned now clearly saw the broad stream shining before them, and he heard the shouts of the Mexicans on either flank charging down upon them.

"Up with your rifles, boys," cried the Panther, "an' don't shoot until you see a Mexican at the end of your sights!"

Ned's heart was still throbbing, but he was growing used to excitement and danger. He held the reins of his horse with one hand and his rifle with the other. Will Allen at his side, knee to knee, did the same. The Mexicans came on fast, the hoofs of their horses beating in rhythmic unison on the prairie. Ned saw that he and his friends had not overestimated their numbers. They were at least ten to one. It would be necessary to shoot straight and fast. Suddenly the red wave that was the Alamo and Goliad rose before his eyes. Then it rolled away, and he saw Urrea, whom he considered the most wicked of all men next to Santa Anna.

Ned raised his rifle, and took aim at the Mexican leader. There was no emotion of pity in his heart, no lack of the wish to kill one whose hands were dipped so deep in treachery and cruelty. The Panther shouted: "Fire!" and he pulled the trigger. His protecting angel, or rather demon, was watching over Urrea. Through some chance he swerved aside, and the bullet struck the man behind him. But the Texans both on the right and left flank had aimed well. A half dozen saddles were emptied, and the two Mexican columns reeled back. While they were still hesitating, the Texans reloaded and fired again.

The second volley was not so deadly as the first, but it was deadly enough. Four or five of the Mexicans fell, and both columns galloped out of range. They, in turn, had been firing, but their weapons were inferior to those of the Texans, and their bullets fell short.

A shout of triumph came from the wagons. The women had lifted the canvas and were looking back at the battle. Now they rejoiced at the triumph of the men who were defending them, but old Dave Simpkins continued to drive his team fiercely for the Colorado, and those behind followed it at the same pace.

Will Allen shouted in his excitement and triumph, but Ned knew that the battle was far from over. Urrea would gather his forces anew, and come on for a fresh attack. The moment when they entered the water was the one most to be dreaded.

"Reload as fast as you can!" cried the Panther, drawing back together the two halves of his force. "We've burned their faces, but they will come ag'in!"

"But we've smitten them hip and thigh at least once," said the Reverend Stephen Larkin, the light of battle shining more brightly than ever in his eyes. "I aimed long, and I trust that I shot well."

"I'm shore of it, Mr. Larkin," said the Panther. "I saw that your arm was as steady as a mountain."

Ned noticed that a strong friendship had been formed already between these two men, so unlike in some respects, and yet so alike in others. He and Will kept close together just behind the Panther and Larkin. He ceased to watch the Mexicans, and turned his eyes toward the wagons. The first was just on the brink of the stream. Then, under the urging of old Dave Simpkins, it gave a lurch and went into the water. One by one the others followed.

But the Colorado was flowing in a wide channel, and more swiftly than usual. The wagons made slow progress, and the obstructed water foamed and boiled around them in a dangerous manner. The Mexicans, seeing the difficulty, gave a yell of triumph and came on again in a solid body.

"Now, boys!" exclaimed the Panther, "we've got to shoot not only for our own lives, but for the lives of them women an' children in the wagons!"

There was a little timber along the bank of the river. Some of the Texans leaped from their horses and took shelter behind the trees, others remained in the saddle, but all of them fired as fast as they could pull the trigger and reload. The Mexicans came on now in the wavering style adopted by Indians when they make a charge. They made the horses shift from side to side, and they sheltered themselves as well as they could behind the necks of the animals and the tall peaks of their saddles. They also opened fire with muskets and rifles.

One of the Texans was wounded dangerously, another slightly and two horses were killed. Mexican numbers were telling, but the devoted band that held the ford fought with coolness and desperation. Ned's own horse was killed, but he sprang clear as it fell. Will's, also, went down presently, but he, too, was alert, and alighted safely on his feet. They secured their ammunition and then fought from the shelter of the trees.

A band of the Mexican cavalry galloped almost upon them. Ned saw a long lance poised and ready for a thrust at Will, who was taking aim at a horseman in another direction. He snatched a pistol from his belt and fired. The lancer reeled from the saddle, breaking his own weapon in two as he fell, and his horse galloped away. Ned reloaded both rifle and pistol. All around him was the crackle of gun fire, the tread of horses' hoofs, and the sudden cries of wounded men. Puffs of smoke arose, now and then hiding the combatants from one another. The Texans with the advantage of the trees and their own indomitable courage held the ground against many to one, striving to keep back the Mexican advance, until all the wagons were on the other side of the Colorado. Ned caught a glimpse of the line of canvas covers toiling through the stream, old Dave Simpkins still in the lead. Then he was compelled to look away, because two mounted Mexicans were charging down upon him.

The boy's rifle and pistol had both been fired again, but a lance dropped by some fallen Mexican lay at his feet. He snatched it up, and, unused to it, swung with it as one would strike with a club. The first Mexican fell with a broken head, and then Ned, remembering himself, thrust with the point of the lance at the second. He shut his eyes, but he felt it strike something, and he heard a terrible cry. Then he was glad that a cloud of smoke drifted between, hiding that which had happened from his eyes when he opened them. He threw down the lance in disgust—he felt that it was no weapon for a Christian human being—and, picking up his rifle again, began to reload.

"Smite the Philistines! Smite them hip and thigh! We will hew them down even as David levelled Goliath in the dust!" shouted the minister, his stern Cromwellian soul burning with a cold white flame of battle. He had been wounded slightly in the shoulder, and the flowing blood made a long red stripe, like a decoration, down his coat.

"Give it to 'em, Philistines or Mexicans; it makes no difference!" shouted the Panther. "Rip an' t'ar an' chaw, boys! That for the Alamo! That for Goliad! That for your cruelty! That for your treachery! That for good count! At 'em, boys! Drive 'em back!"

But Deaf Smith and Henry Karnes fought in silence, leaping from tree to tree, reloading and firing with deadly aim.

Helped by the trees, the bushes and the sloping bank, they still held Urrea back, although two of the men belonging to the wagon train had been slain and several others had been wounded. Now Dave Simpkins reached the far bank of the Colorado, drove fifteen or twenty yards farther, dropped the lines of his team and leaped out, rifle in hand. The other wagons, one by one, followed.

"Drive on out of range!" cried old Dave. "I'm goin' back to help them that have helped us so much."

"An' me! An' me!" cried four or five others.

But the Panther had seen that all the wagons were now across, and, above the crash of the conflict, he shouted to old Dave and those with him:

"Stay on the bank there, an' cover our comin'!"

Old Dave heard, understood and paused. The Panther shouted to his comrades to fire one last volley, and take to the river. Ned looked around for Will. He was just at his elbow.

"The most dangerous part has come," he said. "Jump as far out in the water as you can, run through it as fast as you can, but keep your rifle dry so you can fire back!"

All the Texans, save the two who had fallen, poured in a volley that drove the Mexicans back twenty paces. Then they turned, ran into the stream and rode or waded swiftly toward the farther shore. There was so much smoke and turmoil that the Mexicans did not see the rush until the Texans were halfway across. Then they came on with many shouts of rage, intending to shoot the fugitives down in the middle of the stream.

But they had not reckoned with old Dave and his allies, three or four men, a dozen half-grown boys, and, four or five stalwart women, women and boys, too, armed with the deadly Texan rifles. Firing over the heads of their champions in the river, they drove back the Mexican force which now appeared at the edge of the stream. Not a horseman of Urrea's dared to enter the water. Instead, they fired their rifles and muskets from a distance.

Ned and Will heard bullets pattering near them, and little jets of water spurted up. Once the foam was dashed into Ned's eyes, but he brushed it away, and saw their friends on the northern bank firing over their heads. He was tempted to stop, reload his rifle and take a shot, but the Panther and Larkin were urging everybody on, and he kept his face toward the northern bank. He felt a slight sting in his shoulder, and he knew that he was hit, but he knew also that it did not amount to much. The next moment he forgot it, and then he felt the water shallowing beneath his feet.

At the edge of the stream, and where the water was not more than ankle deep, the Panther and several others turned and fired. Then they rushed in a body up the bank, and, joined by Simpkins, and the others ran for the wagons. The Mexicans sent a scattering fire across the stream, but it did not reach anybody, while the Texans, from the shelter of the wagons, sent back a return that did reach and sting. They could see Urrea and others spurring their horses furiously toward the water, but the Panther merely smiled.

"They won't try to cross," he said. "They ain't thinkin' of such a thing. Urrea is a brave man, I'll admit that, but he knows better than to ride into the Colorado in face of our fire. They'll make a fuss there for a while, an' then go away."

"We left two of our comrades behind," said Larkin sorrowfully.

"They're dead, Mr. Larkin," said the Panther, "an' the Mexicans can't do them no harm. We are lucky to get off with that few down. Many another man is goin' to give up his life before this business is over."

"I suppose you are right; in fact, I know you are," said Larkin sorrowfully. "Now, I think we'd better turn our attention to the wounded, who must number half of our total fighting force. Do you consider it likely, Mr. Palmer, that the Mexicans will cross the river elsewhere and charge upon us?"

"There ain't one chance in a thousand that they will do so," replied the Panther. "They've had enough for one day. They must have suffered a big loss. Besides, there are other Texans this side of the Colorado, and they know that we may be reinforced. S'pose we drive 'till we strike a strong position, halt there an' do whatever we want to do."

Old Dave Simpkins resumed his position as the driver of the leading wagon, putting his rifle by his side on the seat. But there was a satisfied smile on his face when he cracked his whip over his horses.

The mounted men had lost nearly all of their horses, which had suffered more than the riders from the Mexican fire. Both Ned and Will were on foot now. Places in the wagons were offered them, but they declined in favour of those more severely injured, as Ned found that his wound was a mere scratch.

The Reverend Stephen Larkin was a physician, as well as minister and teacher, too—on the border a man had to be many things to live—and he skilfully bound up all the wounds, announcing that none was mortal. He, like the Panther, Smith and Karnes, had escaped without injury.

"About two miles further on," said Smith, who knew the country well, "we'll strike a hill covered with timber. A spring runs out of the side of this hill, and we can make there a camp that we can hold ag'inst any number of Mexicans."

All that Smith said came true. It was a splendid place for a camp, easily defensible, and at the crest they drew the wagons up in a small ring. Several of the men scouted back toward the river, and, seeing no signs of Mexican pursuit, they went into camp and dismissed anxiety for the present.

As the night came on cool they built fires and posted guards. The prairie for at least a mile in every direction was flat and bare, and no enemy could approach without being seen by the sharp-eyed Texans. Ned and Will relaxed completely. They ate heartily of the good food that was given to them, and then sat for a while watching the dancing fires, and listening to the Panther as he told the Reverend Stephen Larkin why they had come and also of Camp Independence.

Larkin stroked his smooth chin and deliberated.

"I have neither wife nor children," he said, "and I feel that as soon as we have led these people into safety I ought to go out with you to that crater and help you in your great service to Texas."

"We'd welcome you an' be proud of you," the Panther said; "wouldn't we, Deaf?"

"If we didn't we'd be mighty big fools," replied Smith.

"Then I'll go," said the fighting minister. "As soon as these people are safe in the north I will return with you to that rallying point which you call Camp Independence."

Nothing more was said, but the hands of the two strong men met in a significant clasp. The Panther and his friends meant to stay with the retreating party two or three days longer, until they were absolutely beyond the reach of the Mexicans.

Ned and Will volunteered for the watch that night, but they were told to find a good place in the wagons and go to sleep. Ned had forgotten that stinging sensation he felt in the course of the battle, but, when he undressed, a bullet fell from his clothing, and there was a big bruise on his left shoulder. He had evidently been struck by a spent ball, and he was thankful for his luck.

There was an abundance of room in the wagons, and plenty of bedding, too, and he and Will slept soundly all through the night. It was announced the next morning that no Mexicans had crossed the Colorado, and the little party of Texans, grieving for the two men lost, but triumphant in its victory, moved on. They were joined the next day by two more fugitive groups which also had extra horses and the Panther and Smith decided that it was not necessary for their own party to remain. Eight of the Texan men, including Larkin, decided to go back with the Panther and Smith to Camp Independence. They were all armed and mounted well, and would make a formidable addition to the party.

But the Panther, Smith and Larkin agreed that Houston ought to know of this band that was forming in the south to help him. The fate of Texas hung so evenly in the scale that a few men might decide it. A messenger should be sent to the Texan commander-in-chief, and Ned, who knew the country well, begged that he be chosen. He seemed the fitting one for the task, because of his acquaintance with Houston and the other Texan leaders, and he was selected for the coveted errand.

Ned had secured a strong and fresh mount, and he was provided with rifle, pistol and plenty of ammunition. He bade his comrades farewell, and eager and full of hope he rode away.

CHAPTER 5

THE TIMELY STABLE

Ned stopped on a swell of the prairie, and waved farewell to the distant group of men who stood on the edge of a grove and watched him. They were too far away for him to make out faces, but he saw a half dozen take off their *sombreros* and wave back to him. His heart filled with emotion. They were brave and trusty comrades, and he was leaving them behind. The thought that he might never see them again occurred to him suddenly. These were terrible times, and, at best, the Texans had but a forlorn hope.

Ned, at that moment, had less confidence in himself than the leaders of the others were having in him. When the men put on their *sombreros*, after waving them to the messenger, Deaf Smith said in a tone of confidence to the Panther, Karnes and the rest:

"If anybody can carry through such a message it's Ned. He's chose, I tell you, he's chose. We've talked that over before, an' we're agreed on it."

"Besides," said Obed White, "he's become one of the best plainsmen there is, which is another way of saying that Heaven helps those who have the strong artillery; but I'm sure with you that he will get through to Houston with the news that the Texans are gathering in the south. They say that Sam Houston, big leader that he is, doesn't value us high enough."

Ned, meanwhile, was riding steadily on toward the Brazos. He had made up his mind not to look back again for fear that his resolution would be weakened. He did not know just where Houston was, and no one had been able to tell him, but he felt sure that he would find him somewhere along the Brazos. It was a big river, swollen by rains, and it would be natural for the Texans to rally there against Santa Anna.

As Ned rode on all his courage returned. In truth, he felt a high elation. He had received a great trust, and he would carry it out in the face of innumerable dangers. He would bring news to Houston that the Texans were coming, that the fighting spirit was abroad everywhere, and then they would gather in the face of Santa Anna.

But Ned's elation came wholly from within. There was nothing around him to encourage cheerfulness. Nature was sullen and gloomy during that famous spring in Texas. He should have been riding at this moment over a carpet of green sprinkled with flowers, varied in colour and innumerable in quantity. Instead there was little sunshine. Heavy, dark clouds hung continually. The rain came down almost every day and night, and sometimes with great violence. The prairie, usually solid, was a morass, in which the feet of Ned's horse sank sometimes over the hoof. There was mud, mud everywhere. The vegetation was scanty and dwarfed by cold winds.

Ned had not been riding more than an hour before the entire sky turned to the colour of lead, and a cold drizzle set in. He had not neglected to provide himself well at the start, and there were two blankets tied to his saddle, a light one of wool, and another heavier, somewhat like a South American *poncho*. He wrapped the poncho about himself from the neck to the knees, while below the knees thick deerskin leggings and *moccasins* kept off the water. He also carried his rifle beneath the *poncho*, and, thus fended from the rain, he urged his horse on over the reeking prairie.

Ned was hopeful that the clouds would break away, but the dismal nature of the day increased. Puffs of cold wind dashed the rain like hail in his face, and, even beneath the folds of the *poncho*, he shivered. He could also feel the horse shivering under him. Now and then, between the swells of the prairie, he rode through water six inches deep.

He plodded on toward the north for a full six hours, and he did not believe that he had covered more than fifteen miles. Although yet dry, he was worn to the bone by the driving wind and rain, and his horse began to stagger from weakness. He felt that he must seek shelter somewhere, no matter how important his errand.

The prospect of refuge was not good. Before him the prairie extended, a vast and desolate morass, without a single tree in sight. He had been hopeful that he would find a cabin abandoned by some fleeing Texan family, but there was none, nor was it likely that he could find any until he reached timber. The pioneers seldom built on the open prairie.

He could only plod on, and Ned's spirits grew very heavy. In reality, danger was less wearing than this eternal mud, rain and cold wind. About the middle of the afternoon he decided to turn toward the east. He knew that numbers of large creeks ran northward into the Brazos. He might find shelter in the timber that always grew along their banks, and shelter and rest he must have if he remained fit to achieve the great task that he had undertaken.

Ned's belief that he might find a deserted cabin in the timber was altogether probable. The Texans had settled rather numerously in this section, in the timber along the creeks, but he knew that after the Alamo and Goliad the flight northward had been universal. Nearly all these settlers were now beyond the Brazos, leaving their empty homes behind them.

Ned urged his weary horse to greater speed, knowing that if he travelled long enough he must come to a creek and timber. But it was a painful task for the worn animal. The morass grew deeper and the rain and cold increased in volume. Finally he got down and walked, pulling himself through the mud beside his horse. An hour of this and he saw a dark line ahead. He could have shouted with joy, because his unfailing vision told him that this was timber.

He remounted, and, as the soil was now somewhat firmer, he advanced much more rapidly. Before him stretched the timber in a long dark line from north to south, and it seemed thick and heavy. Ned was sure that he would find shelter there. The horse's instinct seemed to be similar, as he raised his head, uttered a neigh of satisfaction, and broke of his own accord into a trot.

The trees were merely a darker blur on a dark and desolate day. To the ordinary observer they would have brought no cheer. Nothing could have tempered this savage wilderness to the eye of one who knew civilization alone, but Ned, who had been so long on the frontier, read comfort in that sombre wall against the eastern sky.

He rode into the timber, and, as he expected, he came to a creek, running a deep and yellow flood between low banks. It flowed northward to the Brazos, and the stretch of timber on either side was wide and comparatively free from undergrowth. The trees were fine and tall. They were thick with leaves, which partly protected Ned from the rain, and he rode slowly northward, always watching for a cabin. Some of these buildings were so small and so much hidden that one could pass without ever seeing them.

He came twice to heaps of ashes and fragments of burned wood. He did not believe that their former occupants had set the torch to them when they left, and this destruction must prove that Mexican raiders had crossed the Colorado. Yet they could be only in small parties that travelled fast.

As he left the second heap of ashes and charred timbers he noticed a clump of trees between it and the river, and beyond it a glimpse of rough boards. He rode around the clump and saw a small and rude stable. Evidently those who had destroyed the cabin had not noticed it, but, petty and mean as it was, it was as welcome to Ned as any splendid hotel that ever cheered the sight of a traveller.

The stable, in a way, was more useful to him than the cabin would have been. There was a place for his horse also. It was a good animal that he rode, and he had come long and far through mud and storm. He was not the equal of the great horse, Old Jack, who was wandering somewhere over the Texas prairie, but he had done his duty, and he deserved his reward.

The stable had a rude door made of heavy boards fastened together with cross pieces at the top and bottom. Ned opened it, and gazed into the dusky interior a moment or two, before his eyes could dispel the darkness. The floor was of the native earth, but it was packed hard, and it was dry. Under the sloping roof some planks had been placed across from wall to wall, and upon these was piled considerable hay. Evidently this Texas farmer had been a forethoughtful man, one who, contrary to custom, made a refuge for his stock in winter.

He led the horse inside and closed the door. The horse uttered a gentle neigh of satisfaction. Ned rubbed his nose and stroked his mane.

"We're lucky, you and I," he said, "to stumble upon such a place as this. Our good star, if we have one, is certainly watching over us. We find shelter for both of us and food also for you."

He slipped off the saddle and bridle, and climbed with them up to the planks, on which the hay rested. It was good hay, and he threw an abundance of it down for the horse.

Ned heard the sound of big teeth munching the hay, and he knew that the horse was now in an animal heaven of his own. He realised with acute force that he, too, was very tired and hungry. He carried a pair of stout saddlebags filled with food, and he took out as much as he wished. He disposed his arms and entire equipment about him, and, making a particularly good place for himself in the hay, he lay there and ate until he was satisfied.

He could not recall a time when he had felt more comfortable. Shelter and warmth appeal most to those who have lacked them, and it still seemed wonderful that he should have come upon such a place at such a time. He recalled his singularly good fortune in escaping so often from such great dangers. He did not know that the Panther, Smith and Karnes looked upon him as "one chose," But he did appear even to himself to have a lucky star.

The night was turning colder and the rain grew harder. It beat with a steady musical rhythm on the board roof which was not three feet above him. Often when a little boy he had gone to sleep to that same beating of rain or hail upon the roof, and it was not less soothing now.

The horse, having eaten his fill, half lay on the dry earth, and it seemed to Ned that he was asleep. Then he himself felt sleepier than ever. It was so warm and cosy up there with that cold rain beating on the roof, but unable to get at him. He pulled the hay a little closer about his body and closed his eyes. He had intended to open them again, but when he started to do so the lids felt so heavy that he gave up the attempt. The deep lulling sound of wind and rain quieted every nerve, and soon he was asleep.

Ned did not know how near to collapse he had been. The beating that he had received for a whole day by wind and rain had tried his body sorely, and now he slept the deep sleep of utter exhaustion. But it is an easy task for nature to take care of the young and healthy, and all the hours that he slept it was building him anew. The blood flowed once more in a steady stream through his veins, and his pulse became strong and regular. While he slept, his full strength came back, and his lucky star was watching over him better than he knew.

Ned had gone to sleep shortly after dark, and about two hours later a numerous body of horsemen came riding in the timber up the creek, but on the other side of the stream. They were mostly short and dark, but thick of chest. The man who led them was young and commanding in manner. He wore the uniform of a Mexican officer, and he was none other than Francisco Urrea, who, after his unfortunate encounter at the ford with the Panther, Smith and the others, had daringly crossed the river at another point, and was now seeking to cut off any Texan force that he might find.

Urrea knew well enough that the Texans were in confusion after the Alamo and Goliad, and that the settlers everywhere were abandoning their homes. Now was the time to strike a blow for Santa Anna, Mexico and, above all, for himself. He was young, ambitious, able and energetic, and he had a powerful ally in his uncle, General Urrea. If he could strike some great blow now, there might be two generals named Urrea instead of one. He could destroy villages, he might even seize the fugitive Texan government and have every member of it shot or hanged.

But just at present Urrea and his men were depressed. The rain and wind had taken its toll of them also, and they wished shelter and food. One of Urrea's scouts had seen the burned cabin on the other side of the creek, but he had failed to notice the little stable in the clump of trees. Surely when the Panther, Smith and Karnes heard of this they would repeat anew that Ned was "chose," that he was a magic leader.

The timber was much thicker on Urrea's side of the creek, and he pitched a camp there about five hundred yards from Ned's stable. He had a number of pack mules in his train, and several tents were set up. Patience also produced a fire, which, fed bountifully, burned well in spite of the rain. Then Urrea and his chief assistant, Lieutenant Pedro Tajon, sat in one of the tents and conferred.

"We may yet get the Texans who drove us back at the ford," said Urrea, "and there are some dangerous men among them, whom I should like to slay or take. But it's better, perhaps, to keep on to the north. A quick dash and we may even seize Houston himself."

Tajon's eyes blazed. He was a man of Urrea's own kind.

"Perhaps we can do it," he said. "Houston must be somewhere near the Brazos."

"Beyond a doubt," said Urrea. "If this cursed rain will only cease, and, if the prairie will only dry out instead of remaining a morass, we may get him. In any event, we will continue northward. Except those with Houston himself, I do not believe there is any body of Texans half as numerous as our own."

Then each retired to his own tent and went to sleep. The Mexican common soldiers sheltered themselves as best they could, but they had the advantage of the warming fire, and, with their big *serapes*, they kept fairly comfortable. By midnight they, too, were all asleep save the guards.

Ned, not a quarter of a mile away from his worst enemy, was still slumbering as if he would never wake, and all the while sleep was bringing him new strength and courage for the great dangers that he must face. The rain and wind did not cease until late. Then the clouds walked away like the battalions of an army, leaving behind a clear silver sky, in which myriads of stars sparkled and danced.

A little later Ned awoke. It might have been some movement of his horse that broke his sleep, but he never knew. The Panther or Deaf Smith would have said that it was his guardian angel. He sat up, brushed the hay from his neck and face and remembered where he was and how he had come there. He could no longer hear that lullaby of the rain and wind on the boards. The horse was standing up, and had begun to nibble again at some fragments of hay that he had left on the floor.

Ned let himself down and patted his horse's head.

"Good old fellow," he said. "It's been a better night here than you or I expected."

The horse rubbed his nose against Ned's sleeve and whinnied softly as if he understood and agreed with him. Ned opened the door and looked all about the circle of his limited horizon. The night was not very dark now. He saw the trunks of many trees, the yellow surface of the swollen creek and then beyond it a beam of fiery light. He thought at first that it must be some delusion but it was too clear and intense. He knew that it came from a fire, a large fire, and he concluded immediately that it must be made by a raiding party of Mexicans. He was quite sure there were no Texans in that immediate region, and, whatever he did now, it behoved him to do it with great caution.

Ned watched the red beam for some time and saw it grow. He judged that it was not more than five hundred yards away, and he inferred from the amount of light it shed at such a distance that it must be a large campfire. There was a bare possibility that Texans were gathered around it, but a great probability that Mexicans instead were sitting around the coals.

He fastened the door so the horse could not wander out, looked well to his arms, and slipped away among the trees. The timber grew to the water's edge, but the creek, flooded by the rains, was a swollen yellow torrent, and he could not ford it. Instead, he stopped at a point opposite the fire, and kneeling among the bushes watched long and intently. He was so much absorbed that he did not notice the coming of the day. All the stars went out before the rising sun, and the splendour of the east was appearing. Then Ned saw men going back and forth, their black forms outlined against the ruddy fire. He saw the short, thick figures, the great *sombreros* and he knew that they were Mexicans. It was time for him to leave.

He slipped back to the stable, saddled and bridled his horse, fastened his blankets, ammunition and supplies to the saddle, and made ready to go forth. But in accordance with frontier prudence he first took another look, slipping as before through the dense foliage to the edge of the creek.

It was full day now. The splendour of the east had also become the splendour of the west. Ned, from his point of vantage, heard the sound of many voices, and saw Mexicans coming toward the creek, bringing their horses down to drink. They were in a cheerful mood, these invaders of his beloved Texas, laughing and talking with one another, as their horses lapped up the yellow water. Evidently they had slept well, and Ned's heart was filled half with rage and half with envy. They represented Mexico, immense, powerful and overwhelming, and he a solitary fugitive, hiding for his life, represented the cause of the few and scattered Texans, a cause that seemed to the world lost beyond redemption.

Some of the Mexicans, superb horsemen, rode their horses bare-backed into the deep water, and, in a spirit of bravado, swam them across the creek. It was good sport for the Mexicans, but it might be death for the young Texan who lay among the bushes. Ned felt a mighty warning that it was time for him to get away and to get away fast.

He slipped back to the stable and led his horse forth. He was about to mount and ride away when he heard the voices of Mexicans on his side of the creek. His heart leaped into his throat and the great pulse there began to beat. The Mexicans were around him, and there was not one chance in a hundred that he could ride away unseen. It was his first thought to lead the horse back in the stable and make a last stand, but then came another idea. It was a desperate chance, but he would take it. He dismounted from the horse, took off his saddle and bridle and turned him loose, striking him smartly upon the flank. The horse looked back with great eyes of reproach, but, feeling his freedom, he wandered off among the bushes.

Ned reckoned that the Mexicans would see the horse, but would take him for a waif and stray from some ruined farm about there. It was wholly in accord with probability.

Then with the saddle and bridle on his arm he returned to the stable, left the door wide open, and, climbing in the little loft with the saddle and bridle and his weapons, buried himself and them in the hay. He had left the door open purposely to divert suspicion. There were hoof marks on the earthen floor, but they, too, were wholly probable. A horse, used to the stable and finding the door open, would naturally wander in to seek shelter from a storm.

He drew a light covering of the hay completely over himself and his equipment. But he kept his rifle by his side with his finger on the trigger. He could throw aside the hay at a moment's notice and take aim. He also lay against the wall and there was a little crack between the boards on the side next to the creek, through which he could see anyone who approached from that direction.

He lay there a full quarter of an hour and all that time the distant sound of voices came from several points. Now they approached and then they shifted away. He wondered if they had found the horse, and if so what they would make of his presence there. It seemed possible at last they might go away without seeing the stable. His pulse beat heavily, and it was hard to lie perfectly still. His vivid imagination presented to him the full danger of the ordeal.

The prowling Mexicans did not leave. Ned, through the crack, saw four, muskets on shoulder, come between him and the creek, and then turn toward him. A few moments later, he heard one of them utter a cry of surprise, and he knew the cause. They had penetrated the foliage and they had seen the stable. Presently they came around to the front of the building, and entered the open door.

Ned was forced now to depend upon hearing alone. He did not dare to move or even to breathe heavily, for fear that they would see the slight rising and falling of the hay. But he could hear well through the thin covering, and his knowledge of Spanish stood him in good stead.

The four Mexicans were evidently looking at the hoof prints as Ned heard their comments upon them.

"A horse has been here and but a little while ago, my Miguel," said one.

"Aye, you speak truly, Antonio," said another. "The hoof-prints are not twelve hours old."

"Can it be possible that some Texan has been stabling his horse here, my Antonio?"

"I think not. None would dare delay at such a place, where the Mexican sword and the Mexican firebrand have passed. This stable was overlooked because the trees stood so thickly about it, and likely the horse wandered into it last night, when the storm was at its height. Did you not notice that the door was open when we came?"

"It is so. Then we will get the horse. He must be somewhere near grazing among the trees."

"A fine idea. A good horse would be well worth taking. Thou hast brains, *amigo*, despite thy looks."

The four went out of the stable and Ned rose up a little in the hay. He caught a glimpse of the bright sunshine through the open door. He was tempted to leave his covert and try to steal away, but second thought brought prudence and he sank back into his old lair. There he lay for a quarter of an hour, and he was deeply thankful that he had crushed his first impulse.

The Mexicans were returning. He heard them talking. But he did not hear any hoof-beats and he knew that they had failed to find the horse. They came back into the stable and stood there talking. Their words expressed disappointment.

"It would have been a good horse, I know, my Antonio," said one.

"These Texans have better animals than we and he would have been a fine prize."

"Doubtless he has wandered far down the creek, too far for us to follow, but since we cannot get him we can destroy his shelter. We can complete the work that comrades of ours began."

Ned shivered in the hay. A terrible chill ran down his backbone.

"You speak truly," said another. "It is but a light structure built of boards. A touch of the torch, a rush of flame and it is gone."

Ned shivered again. He knew too well the truth of their words. If fire were set to the stable it would go with a sweep and he would go with it. His brow became wet and cold with sweat. Another of the Mexicans spoke up in approval of the suggestion, and then another, and he knew that the plan would be carried out. What could he do but spring from the loft, and endeavour to dash through them?

It was a terrible problem. The stable made of light boards and with the inflammable hay in the loft would burn up in ten minutes, and he would perish of the fire and suffocation in less than half that time. Even if he sprang down among the Mexicans and succeeded in breaking his way through, the others, drawn by the sounds of the combat, could overtake him easily on horseback.

He could not see any way out, and, while he was hesitating the Mexicans were acting. He heard the rasp of flint on steel, and their talk to one another.

"Strike harder, my Antonio, and strike faster, too."

"Cut more of the thin splinters, Diego. Heap them here, and they will surely catch in a few minutes."

"Then we shall leave nothing of what the Texan built, nothing but ashes."

Ned heard them laugh in unholy glee among themselves, and he also heard, with painful distinctness, the rasping together of flint and steel. Antonio had obeyed the command and was striking harder and faster. Ned knew that the sparks would presently leap forth in a stream, and he raised himself a little in the hay. The dry straws rustled, but the Mexicans, absorbed in their task, did not hear it.

Ned rose a little higher and was nerving himself for the leap, when he heard the mellow and swelling notes of a bugle coming from the Mexican camp beyond the creek. It sounded wonderfully clear in the crisp morning air, and it was an insistent note, too. It said: "Come! Come, on the instant!" It was the summons of Urrea about to take up the march again. One of the Mexicans uttered an impatient little cry, but the others upbraided him.

"Delay not, my Antonio," said another. "When the captain calls it is well to go. Listen, the trumpet still tells us to come, and even if we hasten we shall yet be late. Not another moment. Hurry!"

The rasping of flint and steel together ceased and Ned heard their retreating footsteps. He sank back upon the hay and lay in a cold sweat, so great and terrible had been the tension. Then, calling back his courage and strength, he peered through the crack in the wall, and saw the four Mexicans swimming their horses across the creek. He could hear, too, even at the distance, the jingling of bridle bits, and the loud commands of officers. Urrea was marching and he was saved.

He lay on the hay, and listened until the last of the sounds had passed. Then, after another wait of fifteen or twenty minutes, he lowered himself with his arms and ammunition to the floor. He left the saddle, bridle and blankets where they were for the present at least. It was possible, even probable, that he might find his horse again. But he devoted his first few moments of release from the hay to stretching himself and tensing his muscles. The blood flowed back in a steady tide through his veins, and all his pulses settled down again to a regular beat.

Then he went outside and took long breaths of the fresh air. He felt an immense relief, and he knew also that he had great cause to be grateful. It seemed that Providence had taken him in its special keeping.

He ate food from his saddle bags and waited at the stable a full hour, in order to give the last Mexican straggler plenty of time to get away. Then he began a search through the woods for his horse. He walked down the stream about a half mile. As the timber was dense, giving little room for grass, he returned to his starting point and went another half mile in the opposite direction. There in a little open space near the bank he saw his horse grazing in great content.

Ned anticipated trouble in catching him again, but he found none. It may be that an animal so much used to the presence of man had grown lonely. Ned had brought the bridle only with him and he slipped it over his head. He too was lonely, and it was like seeing a good comrade to find his horse again.

"I've been through more danger than you, old boy," he said, as he stroked his muzzle, "but I've come out of it, and here we are together again. I hope you've fed well, and rested well, and that you are ready now to bear me northward to Houston."

577

The horse rubbed his nose against the boy's arm in assent. Ned leaped upon his bare back, and rode slowly back to the stable. It was the work of only a few moments to saddle him and put all his equipment in place.

Then Ned remounted and rode forward a short distance. When he looked back he could see only a little of the stable, and he might not have noticed that, had he not known of its presence. Whether placed in such concealment by accident or intent, it had served him well. It was to him at least the finest stable in all the world.

Then he rode slowly up the stream until he could find a good point of approach, where he swam his horse across the deep waters. Curiosity took him back down the shore toward the Mexican camp. He saw that it had been a good one, well sheltered by the timber and the nature of the earth, and he also saw about many fragments of food, indicating that Urrea's men fared well. Ned's face grew dark with wrath. He knew that most of their supplies were plunder taken from the Texan settlers, and he feared that Urrea would do much greater harm before some stronger force drove him back across the Colorado.

He followed a little while on the Mexican trail. About a mile lower down it left the stream and turned northward.

CHAPTER 6

THE CAMPEACHY PURSUIT

Ned decided to water his horse before following further on the Mexican trail, and turned back into the timber to the creek's edge. Here, as the bank was rather steep, he dismounted in order to lead the horse down. But he paused at the brink when he caught sight of other hoof-prints and footprints there. Unshod hoofs had made one set of prints, and feet, that turned in at the toes, had made the other.

The Mexican horses were shod, and the feet of the Mexicans, like those of other white men, did not turn in at the toes. What did it mean? It was certain that other people had brought their horses to this place to drink, but who were they and what were they? All at once he recalled the Campeachy Indians who had been with General Urrea at the taking of Fannin's men. Yet he had not noticed any of them in the band of the younger Urrea. He looked again at the prints. They were very fresh. It seemed as he examined them more closely that they could not be more than an hour old. No, they were not more than a half hour old.

Ned suddenly sprang back in the bushes, drawing the horse with him by the bridle. Then he stood there in the thick green of the foliage, looking and listening with all the might of his faculties. He had become aware of a presence. It might be that a bush had moved suddenly, or it might have been the sound of a footfall. He did not know what, but he did know that he was not alone.

The sound, if sound it was, had ceased, but Ned felt that whatever had made it was creeping nearer. He could not tell from what direction it approached, but he felt with the full certainty of his five senses that it was coming. Had he not held the bridle of the horse he would have dropped down in the bushes, and have endeavoured to creep away. It was, in truth, his first impulse, but if he were not lost now he would be lost later without the horse.

While he hesitated, he saw a naked and yellow shoulder appearing among the bushes not twenty yards away. Then he saw an upraised and bent arm upon which the muscles stood out in surprising fashion. Recognition came in a flash and he dropped like a shot. A great bow twanged, and a steel-headed arrow flashed above his head, burying itself deep in a tree beyond. Had he not dropped it would have gone through him like a bullet.

When he felt the rush of wind above his head Ned sprang up, and another leap carried him to the back of his horse. A second arrow and a bullet also whizzed through the bushes. Ned struck the sides of his horse violently with both feet, and the startled animal rushed toward the prairie. Behind him rose a long and triumphant war whoop, dying away in a wolfish whine.

Ned knew at once the danger. The Campeachy Indians were there, probably a roving detachment now, under no command and seeking scalps and plunder, wherever they could find them. He urged his horse to full speed for eight or ten minutes, before he looked back. They were eight in number, yellowish, powerful savages, naked save for waist cloths, and bearing more resemblance to Asiatics than to the Indians of the States. Only four of them carried rifles or muskets, the rest being armed with bows.

Eight to one, and the wide prairie before! Ned felt a surge of courage. His horse was running steady and true, the powerful muscles rippling away under his shining coat. He remembered another time, when the Lipans had hung for days upon the trail of himself and Obed White. But these Campeachy Indians could not follow so long a time.

This was Texas, and, at any moment, Texans might come. No, Ned was not afraid of this new danger. The Providence that had watched over him was with him yet.

As he sat in the saddle with the racing horse beneath and the racing Indians behind he was quite calm. He looked back again, and saw that their firearms were muskets not able to carry far. It was likely that the bows were more dangerous. Even as he looked one of the savages drew his bow to his ear and let fly. It was a powerful weapon, and the arrow, grazing his horse's flank, sank far beyond the head into the prairie.

The savages uttered a shout at this proof of their marksmanship, and Ned, feeling that the arrow had come uncomfortably close, urged his horse to a little more speed. It showed his wisdom as three or four more arrows that were fired fell short. He fingered the trigger of his rifle, but he concluded to reserve his fire. In a burst of speed the Indians would have no chance with him, but they would hang on with all the tenacity of death itself. He saw that they rode strong and wiry ponies used to great journeys.

Ned was very glad now that Urrea's band had left the creek, turning in another direction. Otherwise the pursuit would have driven him into the very thick of enemies as dangerous as those behind him. At least he had a fair field for flight. He eased his pace again, keeping just out of range, and rode steadily on for a long time, noting with pleasure that his horse showed but little signs of exhaustion.

It was a golden morning. There had been a vast and brilliant sunburst, and the earth was flooded with yellow rays. The green of spring was dyed to deeper and more vivid hues. On his left the prairie rippled away with the young grass already growing high, and shy little flowers in early bloom. On his right the timber along the creek was a mass of dark green. In his face a crisp fresh wind blew. Despite his situation his spirits rose again, rose to a higher point than they had been at any time since the Alamo and Goliad.

Ned, usually a silent youth, never given to boasting, turned now and taunted. He shouted to them in Spanish, which he thought they would understand. He called them poor warriors, sluggards who could not overtake a single enemy. When they began to urge their ponies to a greater speed he saw that they understood, and he laughed aloud. It was an easy matter for him to shake out the reins on his own horse, and preserve the distance between them.

But this look back revealed, in all its deadly intensity, the purpose of the Indians. They meant to run him down, if it took forever, and they were surely a hideous lot of savages. He had seen ugly people, but these were the ugliest of all. Their yellowish faces and their flattened noses seemed to tell him of Asiatic cruelty. He pulled a little more on the reins of his horse. Then he raised his rifle and fired at the leader. He saw the Indian fall backward from his pony, then, urging his horse to renewed speed, he did not look back again for a full quarter of an hour. He heard the Indians shouting in rage and anger, but he was busy reloading his rifle, and watching the country ahead.

A half hour later the pursuing Indians uttered a shout which sounded like a note of triumph. He looked back at them, and, then looking ahead again, he saw the cause. While he had been engaged in some slight readjustment of his equipment the Indians had noticed it first. A few hundred yards further on the creek suddenly took a sharp angle to the left. He was now riding straight for the timber and the swollen stream, and if he turned to the left also to avoid it, the Indians, by taking the diagonal line of the triangle, could cut him off without doubt. They had good cause for their shout of triumph, and he recognised the fact at once.

Ned's mind never acted more quickly. His desperate resolve was made in an instant. He would take a last chance, and try to swim his horse across the flooded creek. He returned a cry of defiance to their own shouts of triumph, and rode straight toward the timber. He struck at once a flooded bottom in which the water was six or eight inches deep. He pressed on through it, but the Indians on their lighter ponies gained fast. He had not foreseen this morass, and it was a terrible impediment. The horse had to struggle not only through water, but through mud, which was worse. Once he stumbled, and only a hard pull on the reins kept him from falling.

Now the Indians began to shout continuously in savage glee. This was a sure victim. It was likely that they could get him even before he reached the timber. They were within range now and they began to fire both with bows and muskets, though somewhat wildly. Ned heard bullets and arrows whizzing near, and of the two he dreaded the arrows more. They made such an unpleasant sound.

But the timber was very near now. Once within its green shade he would not make such a conspicuous target. Suddenly he felt the horse shiver all over and then stagger. He looked back and saw an arrow standing out in the animal's body just behind the saddle. It was buried deep, far beyond the feathered shaft, and Ned shuddered with horror.

The machinery beneath him jarred and shook, and he knew that his good horse was gone. The triumphant cry of the Indians, rising now to greater volume, told him that they knew it, too.

But it was a gallant and faithful horse. He made a last effort and plunged into the timber. There he stopped short in the green shade and began to shake violently. Ned, rifle in hand, leaped to the ground. His powder horn and bullet pouch were over his shoulder, and the pistol, hatchet and knife which completed the equipment of the borderer were in his belt. His saddle bags filled with food and his blankets strapped to the saddle he was compelled regretfully to leave.

The horse shook again, more violently than before, and then fell crashing. The arrow had found his life.

"Goodbye, faithful friend," said Ned, heavy of heart. He plunged into the densest of the timber, near the edge of the creek and ran up the stream. He was hopeful that he might dodge the Indians among the trees and bushes, but, as he ran, he listened. He heard one shout when they came to the fallen horse, then the thud of the hoofs of their own ponies, followed by silence.

He believed it likely that some of the Indians would dismount and hunt through the timber, while others on horseback would ride along its edge, keeping a watch. He ran swiftly, always keeping well hidden among the bushes, and as he advanced the soil became much softer from the overflow. He was always stepping in either mud or water. It annoyed him at first, but he soon recognised its advantage. The soft mud closed over his tracks in a few moments and he was leaving no trail.

Ned continued thus for more than two miles. He was wet to the waist, and the water was mixed with mud. As he ran he had splashed the water and every time his feet were pulled from the mud there was a soughing sound. Had Indians been within a hundred yards of him they could easily have heard these sounds, but he did not believe they were anywhere so near, and he did not take any precaution against noise.

When Ned rested, he sat on the roots of a huge live oak, with his back against the trunk. Bushes and grass, now flooded about the roots, grew all around him. The creek, in ordinary times not more than a foot deep, flowed a swollen yellow flood a hundred feet across and twelve or fifteen deep. Brush, old logs, weeds and other debris floated on its bosom. Wild fowl darted here and there. But it was not a beautiful stream. The flood was dark and ugly and the melancholy foliage of live oaks hung just above the current.

As Ned sat panting, there was a slight movement in the water near him, and he drew himself up swiftly and with a shudder. A short thick water moccasin swam slowly away. In five minutes he rose and plodded on, always keeping to the deep bush, where he was compelled to wade through mud and shallow water. Such travelling was hard, and, although his rest at the live oak had restored him somewhat he found himself growing weary again. But he dared not leave the bush and swamp for the open as he knew that the Indians on their ponies were galloping up and down there and would see him at once.

He looked longingly at the creek. He could swim it, but he had to carry his rifle and other weapons and he could not afford to get his ammunition wet. But there was much greater chance of safety on the other side. He walked perhaps a hundred yards further, and then listened for sounds of pursuit. He heard none, but he knew that the Indians would have no thought of abandoning the chase. In fact, they had every right to consider him an almost sure victim, and he knew it.

He saw one of the large decaying logs, so numerous in any wild forest, lying at the very edge of the deep water, which was pulling hard at it. Only the stumps of its boughs held it, because here the stream was flowing swiftly. The solution of his problem was presented at once to Ned's quick and ready mind. This was his boat.

He secured his rifle, other weapons and ammunition across his back, broke off one of the longer boughs to be used as a sweep, and, then walked astride the log until he was in water nearly up to his waist. He pushed hard against the bottom with the broken bough, and the tree, coming loose, floated with the stream. But it was a very damp and uneasy craft that Ned bestrode. It wobbled wildly under his weight, and only his dextrous use of the bough kept it from turning over with him. Once or twice he was in alarm lest he should go, despite his sweep, but knowing that he would be helpless with wet ammunition he struggled hard and kept his balance.

The current bore the boy and his strange craft slowly down the stream, and, as he had to devote so much of his time and effort to keeping it steady he could divert it only by inches toward the northern shore. But the strong and skilful use of his sweep told, and he saw himself going slowly in the direction that he wished. Yet it was a tremulous time. The Campeachy Indians might appear at any moment, and, sitting astride a dead tree, there in the midst of the current he would be perfectly helpless. But they did not come. Kindly Providence was still watching over him.

Now the current was growing swifter and he noticed a swirl of water around the flooded trunks of the trees on either shore. Three or four minutes more and the increase of speed was decided. He also heard a faint murmurous sound which grew louder as he went along, and he knew that he was approaching a fall, a most unusual thing in that prairie region. It might not be much of a fall, very little indeed in ordinary times, but with the present flood it would be dangerous. It would, in very truth, be impossible for him to ride any kind of a fall on that shaky and rolling dead tree.

He bent all his efforts now toward reaching the northern bank. He risked everything, and the very speed of the current helped him, shooting him in suddenly toward the shore, where his tree struck among the trunks of some living trees, and began to rock in a way that was beyond the control of his sweep. He made a prodigious effort, drew himself up bodily on the rolling log, rested his feet there just an instant, and, then leaping, grasped a bough of one of the trees.

It was a good strong bough, hanging low over the water, and, with another mighty effort, he drew himself upon it. He sat there a few moments trembling from the physical effort, and watched his rude raft, its purpose served, float swiftly down the stream sucked away by the current. He heard the rush of water distinctly now, and he knew that the fall was very near.

The trees were very dense at that point and he was able to pass from one to another until he reached a place where the water was not more than a foot deep. Then he dropped to the ground and waded until he came to fairly solid earth. Still keeping in the timber he went down stream a little further and saw the fall, only a few feet high, but with a great volume of flood water, pouring over it. His tree would certainly have overturned there, and he was doubtful whether he could have escaped with his life.

While he stood among the trees watching the fall he saw several of the Indians on horseback appear on the further shore.

The timber was now much more dense on his side of the stream and it was easy for him crouching among the bushes to escape observation, and yet watch them as they rode up and down the shore, searching for him about the fall. At last, they disappeared among the trees and bushes further down the stream, and, judging that they would continue in that direction some time, he went back the other way.

Ned now felt fairly safe for the present, but his situation was full of hardship. He was wet, muddy and exhausted. He had lost all his supplies of food in the swollen creek and his good horse was dead. Many a lad would have given up, but it was never in his heart to yield. He left the timber and went out far enough on the prairie to get the full benefit of the sunshine, until his clothing was dried completely. Vigorous walking also kept up the circulation of his blood and the warmth of his body.

But that famous spring in Texas was cold, dark and rainy, and this day was no exception. Heavy clouds came, the sky grew sombre and the air chill. A cutting wind began to blow and Ned was afraid of a norther. He turned back into the timber which gave fair shelter from the wind, and, finally coming to a hillock, where the earth was dry he sat down with his back against a tree.

He did not become conscious, until he stopped walking, of his nearness to exhaustion. With his back against the tree he seemed to collapse like a body without a spine. He breathed heavily and jerkily for a long time, but finally the beat of his heart became steady, and then he felt a great peace. The sense of rest and safety pervaded his whole being. Danger was very far away now, and, for the present, he need think little about it. The wind which was cold on the prairie blew soothingly among the woods where he sat. It was a pleasant music, softening everything and lulling him to deeper rest. While never intending it he fell asleep, back to the tree, and slept a long time.

Ned was awakened by something cold dashed in his face, and he sprang to his feet. It was quite dark and the rain was falling again. A pain shot through his joints, but as he walked vigorously around the tree and stretched himself it disappeared. He had no idea what time it might be. No moon and stars shone. The one dominating fact was the unpleasant rain.

Ned for a few moments was at the verge of despair, but he summoned his courage anew. He recalled the stories of the vast border that stretched northward to Canada, how men, and women and children even had triumphed over hardship after hardship, over danger after danger. Weak human bodies had survived impossible sufferings and had achieved impossible tasks. It was not for him in the very flower and bloom of youth and strength, to lie down there and die.

He sought some place where he might find shelter from the rain, but as he found none, plunging about in the darkness, he decided to take to the open prairie. There, at least, he would not break his neck or a leg in the timber. He was glad when he left the last bushes behind, and, pressing on far enough, found himself standing on firm ground. As nearly as he could judge by the faint light he had reached a swell of the prairie, but he saw that he must keep moving. The cold wind was coming with cutting force, and the rain was driven before it in sheets.

He remembered to keep his powder dry under his clothing and he staggered on, not knowing in what direction he was going, nor how long he went. Several times, as he passed between the swells, he waded through water six or eight inches deep. It seemed to him that there was water everywhere. His weary brain reckoned that it must cover all Texas, except the mountain tops.

The rain lightened by and by, and, later on at some unknown hour, he saw a red spark in the darkness and storm. It was such an incredible, such an impossible thing that he winked his eyes fast, and then rubbed them. The red spark was still there, a star of hope amid illimitable gloom. He walked toward it, and knew now that it was a light, the light of a camp fire. Only a number of men could keep a fire going amid so much water.

Star of hope, though it might be, Ned was very wary. The Texans were further northward and it was likely that it was made by Urrea's band or some portion of it. But he would not turn away. It was better to take the risk than to perish in the night and storm. As he drew nearer, he saw that the fire was in a deep dip of the prairie sheltered partially by mesquite. Nearer yet, and he saw dark figures outlined before the red blaze. It was easy to approach unseen. The darkness covered him and his feet made no sound in the soft earth.

Ned paused at a little distance, and looked at the dusky figures, hovering in a close ring about the fire. They were seven in number. All were wrapped closely in blankets, but the faces of those on the far side were outlined distinctly by the red blaze. He saw yellowish complexions and high cheek bones, and he knew that here were the Campeachy Indians, minus the one who had fallen to his rifle.

They too had crossed the creek, perhaps in search of him, or perhaps to join Urrea. As he looked, one of them threw old buffalo chips on the fire and then all hovered more closely, basking in the warm and grateful heat that defied wind and rain. It was not likely that any of them dreamed of the presence of another human being near, in all that vast and desolate wilderness.

Ned's heart was filled with envy. Savage and cruel though they were, he would have been glad to sit with them in that hovering circle about the fire. He would have rejoiced to touch elbows with a savage on either side, if he could only have bent his face over the glowing coals, and have felt the glorious warmth penetrating through every bone.

It was with a genuine sigh that he turned away. Then he stopped. Where were their ponies? They were bound to be somewhere near. There was not room for them in the little dip where the fire shone, and, at last, searching everywhere with his eyes, he saw them tied with lariats to some mesquite, and crouching close together for warmth. Then Ned took counsel of courage and resolved to stake everything on one last attempt.

He was skilful with horses, knowing how to soothe them with touch and voice, and now he began a slow and cautious approach to the huddled group by the mesquite. Doubtless those Indian ponies had gone through many a storm and many another hardship, but it was evident to Ned that they had had enough for one night. Their disconsolate heads were lowered, and they were continually crowding together. If they heard Ned they paid no attention to him.

The wind rose and howled over the prairie in a strange weird chorus, like the hungry chant of wolves. Ned cast another look at the dip, and he saw that the Indians were bent so far over the fire that at the distance their heads seemed to touch. Wrapped in their blankets they sat there silent and immovable around that single core of light in the immense wilderness. How could they dream that anyone, especially the one whom they had hunted so lately, could be near!

Ned approached more boldly. He uttered a low, soft whistle unheard by the Indians because of the shrieking wind, and he saw one pony hold up his head. A little nearer and yet a little nearer and the whistle lower than before, soft, musical and soothing, was repeated. Ned cast a last glance at the Indians in the dip. Not one of them had moved a fraction of an inch. They made the same silent ring around the fire.

Now Ned ceased to whistle, and spoke softly as he came very near to the ponies. He used to them soothing words in Spanish and English, he told them that he was their friend, that he had come to do them good, that he would release them from ignominious servitude under hard and savage taskmasters. He would do more, he would give freedom to all except one, but the exception should be chosen not as the servant, but as the friend of one who knew how to treat a horse well.

The ponies moved about a little, but made no effort to get away from him. He reached out a hand and stroked the nose of the one that had heard him first. He was a fine, strong mustang, made of steel wire, and when his nose was rubbed he rubbed back, uttering a grateful sound like the purring of a cat. Then Ned stroked his mane, and their friendly relations grew. The other ponies crowded near, finding comfort perhaps in the human relationship.

Ned cut the eight lariats one by one. Then he sprang suddenly on the back of the first pony, kicked violently one on each side with either foot, and, uttering a series of tremendous shouts thundered away over the plain, with the seven riderless ponies racing madly ahead of him.

He heard a whoop and then a long whining cry from the dip, but the rest of that wild ride was a series of almost unrelated but vivid impressions. He gave the pony his head—in fact he had nothing but the lariat with which to guide him—knowing that the wary mustang would not trip or fall, and let him run in a direction which he sanguinely reckoned was toward the north. The other ponies streamed out in front, their great eyes distended, their manes flying, their swift feet urged on continually by the wild youth who rode behind them.

The pony had no saddle, but Ned was a sure rider, and he kept his seat with ease and certainty. He took only one flying glance backward, but he saw nothing. The spark of fire had gone long since, and the warriors on foot were too far behind to be heard. Before him was only the dark prairie, but he did not care. Something in his head had given way, and while the wind and rain lashed him he shouted continually, urging on his own horse and the ponies ahead of him to greater speed. Occasionally he turned his head and sent backward in the darkness a long, defiant shout. Whether the Campeachy Indians heard or not he never knew.

Ned's excitement, and it was of a joyous kind, grew fast. The slipping of that little spring in his head had upset all the rest. He was trembling all over, but it was not from fear or weakness. It came from the certainty that he had triumphed over such tremendous difficulties. The ponies ran on for a long time and then slackened to a walk. Ned had collected his mind sufficiently to know that the Indians were many miles behind, and could not possibly overtake him that night. Indeed the chances were great that he would never see them again. His stampede had been a brilliant success.

He pulled himself together slowly. The something that had gone wrong inside his head was going right again. His eyes had been hot with fever, but now they grew cool. The mustang, despite his frame of steel and his endurance, was now trudging along wearily. He was wet, but despite his wild flight, he had kept his weapons and ammunition dry under his deerskin hunting shirt.

It was still raining, and he yet heard the long-drawn shriek of the wind, as it swept through the swells, but he was rejoicing so much over his brilliant feat that he did not think of the wet and cold now. He could make nothing of the country. As far as he could see in the darkness, it seemed to be the usual alternation of dips and ridges.

His horse comrades, now that he had ceased to shout and no panic was driving them, began to drift away. Perhaps they had been wild horses when seized by the Indians and now they took their chance of freedom. Presently Ned was alone with the one that he rode and he did not care. He guided his own horse easily with the lariat, and perhaps the mustang was too tired to seek liberty for himself.

The night was still very dark, but his eyes had grown so used to it that he could see a short distance, and he noticed for the first time a slender dark coil tied around the neck of the mustang. He took it off and found, to his intense delight that it was jerked venison, enclosed in a strip of deerskin, a yard long, amply sufficient to meet around the neck of his horse. The Indian's choice of a way to carry his food had been a godsend to Ned.

The boy ate eagerly, but the nature of the jerked venison kept him from eating too fast. He chewed resolutely on the tough strips, and let his horse wander as he would over the prairie. The food brought back fresh strength, warmed his blood anew, and encouraged him for the great risks that were yet before him. Truly, if the Panther, Smith and Karnes had seen him that night and had known all through which he had gone with so much success they would have acclaimed him anew, and with yet greater emphasis as their bringer of luck, their magic leader, chosen for the purpose, although wholly unconscious of the fact himself.

The rain abated after a while and the wind died. Ned saw something gleaming in front of him, and then the horse turned aside. It was a shallow lake made by the heavy rains, and he could not see across it, or the end to either right or left. But he let the mustang turn to the left and walk on until he passed around it. He was still chewing the tough venison, and the task was so grateful that he did not care where the horse carried him.

Near morning he reached a clump of timber and decided to stop there. He tied his mustang securely with his lariat, and, despite his wet clothes and the wet earth, lay down and slept. He believed that he was so hardened now to weather that he could not take any further harm. When he awoke the day was several hours old, and a bright, warm sun was shining.

Ned felt a little stiffness and his clothing was still wet, but he was refreshed and strong. The captured mustang was eating grass within the circle of his lariat. The boy was about to begin his breakfast on the jerked venison, when he caught a glimpse of bronze among the boughs of a tall tree fifty yards away. He knew that it was a wild turkey, that unintentional friend of the pioneer, and fresh wild turkey was far more juicy and succulent than tough strips of dried venison.

He stalked the tree, which contained a dozen turkeys, and shot a fat hen. Then began the long task of lighting a fire with flint and steel, one achieved with the greatest difficulty under such circumstances, but it was done at last. Then he cooked and ate. Meanwhile the sun had dried his clothing, and, remounting, he resumed his journey, keeping a northward course by the sun.

Chapter 7

Across the Brazos

Ned intended to reach the Brazos, and he believed that it was not far ahead. The increasingly watery nature of the country made him think so. He saw many of the shallow lakes, like the one that he had passed in the night, and he saw also the little prairie streams swollen to creeks and even rivers. He was descending perceptibly, and it was sure proof to him that he was coming into the Brazos bottoms. Unless he had passed Houston further back toward the Colorado he would surely find him somewhere along this river, which the spring floods had made a giant stream.

Ned was surprised that he had not already encountered some Texan outpost. He did not know then how far the Texan retreat had gone, and with what energy the overwhelming Mexican columns were pressing forward. Santa Anna had changed his intention to return to the City of Mexico. Assured by Almonte and Filisola that the Texans were not yet conquered, and, receiving definite news that a new Texan army was gathering, he had recalled the portion of his troops who were to have been sent home, and was now concentrating all his fiery energy on the task of destroying Houston and the remaining Texans. With the Alamo and Goliad so fresh in his mind, he had no doubt of his swift success. It was only a detail and a delay.

But Ned, as he rode along knew nothing of Santa Anna's movements. The day was fortunately clear and bright, one of the few in that brief but epic period, and, with those uncommonly keen eyes of his, he continually scanned every point of the horizon for horsemen. It was far in the afternoon when he saw a single figure to the west, just a dim blur against the blue sky that touched the ground. Eyes, less good and less trained than his, would have passed it unseeing, but he knew that it was a man and a horse.

He stopped and watched the low shadow against the sky a long time. Was it a Mexican or was it a Texan? And if a Mexican, were there other shadows behind the single one that he could see? He became sure that it was not moving and he concluded the man was an outpost. Hence it was likely that he was not alone. Armed with his good rifle and abundant experience he was not afraid of a single man and he rode boldly toward the figure.

He laid his rifle across the mustang's shoulders, from which he could raise it, take aim and fire with a single continuous motion, and kept steadily ahead. Now the figures of horse and man became distinct against the low blue sky. The rider had seen Ned, too, as he was facing him with the muzzle of a rifle thrust forward. Except for turning his horse about he had made no motion whatever, but sat steadfast, gazing intently at the boy on a bare-backed mustang who was coming straight toward him.

Ned was now sure that the man was a Texan. The signs were unmistakable. Those great shoulders and that length of limb did not belong to a Mexican. Nor would a Mexican sit thus silent and motionless, awaiting the coming of a probable foe. It was a Texan! It must be a Texan! And a Texan was a friend. He held his rifle aloft in sign of amity and shouted:

"I'm a friend! I come from the south and I'm looking for Sam Houston!"

"That's a Texan voice, an' I'm a Texan, too," said the man. "Come on an' tell who you are!"

Now Ned's last little doubt disappeared, and he rode forward at increased speed. He saw a man in early middle age, sun-browned and powerful, riding a large American horse and armed thoroughly for battle. The countenance was not wholly unfamiliar to Ned. Suddenly he remembered that broad benignant face, and the kindly blue eyes.

"You're Jim Potter," he cried, "yes, I know you are! We were together for a while in the San Antonio campaign! Don't you remember?"

The man was staring at him in the deepest astonishment, an astonishment that increased as Ned drew nearer.

"I remember the San Antonio campaign," he said, "but I don't remember you. I don't believe anybody would remember you. You have the human shape an' your voice sounds like that of a human bein', but you don't look like one. I don't see nothin' much but a bundle of rags stuck together with mud, an' hung astride an Indian mustang that ain't got on any saddle or bridle."

But Ned was not daunted at all. He was too full of joy and excitement.

"But you will remember me, Jim Potter," he said, "you have to do it. I'm Ned Fulton. I was in prison in the City of Mexico with Mr. Austin. You and I fought together in the San Antonio campaign, and then I was in the Alamo and at Goliad."

"Thunderation!" Potter exclaimed, staring at him open-eyed. "Yes, I knew that Ned Fulton, and a fine boy he was! Your voice sounds like his, an' now that I rec'lect your figger under all that mud looks like his, an' by thunder you are him. Give us your paw, Ned. I'm terrible glad you're alive, though you are the finest scarecrow I ever saw in all my life."

Ned grasped the powerful hand and he laughed in his excitement and joy.

"I know I'm no beauty," he said, "and you wouldn't be either if you'd been through what I have. But tell me first where is Houston?"

"In the bottoms of the Brazos, on this side, when I was sent to keep watch out here, but I guess he ain't there now. He was meanin' to cross and camp in the bottoms on the other side. But it's been rainin' like all tarnation nearly every day since I left. The Brazos must be runnin' like a sea through all the bottoms on both sides, an' I guess Houston an' his men have lit out for higher an' drier ground on the far shore. Now, Ned, boy, what news do you bring?"

"I'm on my way to Houston to tell him that there are Texans in the south, a strong body, who have gathered there to help him. They are cutting in as much as they can on the Mexican flank and rear, thinking they could do more good that way than any other, but the moment

Houston wants them to join him they'll come."

"That's good! That's good!" exclaimed Potter joyfully. "I tell you, Ned, every fightin' man is now wuth his weight in gold. We need them men an' we need 'em now. We've got to send south for 'em right off."

"In what way?" asked Ned. "I can't turn around and go back, until I've seen Houston."

"No, you can't, that's sure, but if you'll tell me where this party has gathered I'll do it myself. There's another sentinel about ten miles on, an' I'll take you to him. Then you'll tell me exactly where this Camp Independence of yours is, an' I'll ride straight to it."

"All right," said Ned, "lead on."

Potter at once turned his horse northward and the two rode side by side at a brisk pace. Presently Potter's face broke into a broad grin.

"Ned," he said, "if we had time you could stop and wash your face with profit to your looks. I can say also that if I had 'em I'd lend you a lot of clothes. And I'd lend you a saddle an' a bridle, too. I've seen some tough looking specimens in my time, but I think you're way ahead of all the others on tough looks."

"I know I'm no beauty," said Ned, "but I'm alive. I've lived, Jim, when it was something just to keep on drawing your breath."

"You've done what not one man in a thousand could do," said Potter in a deep and hearty tone. "It just looked to me, Ned, when you told me all about it, that you was watched over by somethin' more pow'ful than Santa Anna or anything on this earth."

Here it was again. Jim Potter, although he had heard no such suggestion from them, was sharing with the Panther, Smith and Karnes the belief that Ned had been chosen for a task, and that a supreme power was watching over him, while he was doing it. But no such thought entered the mind of the boy.

"I had luck," he said, "lots of it, or I wouldn't be here."

"Seems to me that luck was dead ag'in you," said Jim Potter, shaking his head, "an' that by miracles you crawled through all them dangers. But that ain't neither here nor there. We've got to git you to Houston an' I've got to git down to Deaf Smith an' that crowd. There are two bands of Texans that need joinin' bad, an' if we do git 'em together we may ketch the Mexicans both comin' an' goin'."

"I take it from what you say," said Ned, "that things are moving fast."

"They shorely are. That devil Santa Anna is pushin' 'em on. He thinks he'll clean us out in short order. Anyway, there's goin' to be a big mix-up before long. Now just beyond that clump of timber that you see on the hill in front we ought to find Stump."

"Stump! Who's Stump?"

"Stump is Bill Burke, though lots of people don't know his right name. When you see him you'll understand why we call him Stump."

Potter put two fingers a little apart against his mouth and blew a shrill, piercing whistle between them. A reply in kind came from some point beyond the trees.

"That's him," said Potter. "Ol' Stump is where he belongs. Come on, Ned."

They rode forward rapidly. A horseman, emerging from the shelter, came to meet them, giving Potter a friendly hail as he came, but the hail was uttered in an extraordinary voice. It seemed more like the roar of a lion than the tones of a human being. Ned, too, saw instantly, as Potter had predicted, why he was called Stump. His body was exceedingly short, and his feet rested in shortened stirrups, but the thickness of him was something tremendous. He had a huge head, with the hair cut very close, contrary to the border fashion, and shoulders and chest such as one sees in old statues of Jupiter. The hand that held his bridle rein looked like the paw of a grizzly bear.

"I know why you call him Stump," said Ned.

"Did a name ever fit better?" said Potter, laughing, "an' I want to say to you, Ned, that he's an oak stump, too, just the toughest an' most endurin' oak that you ever heard of or that ever was growed. When he sets his feet in the ground it takes forty oxen an' a log chain to drag him out."

"Hello, Jim!" thundered Stump, "what in thunderation have you got there? Is it the great horned gyascutis of the mountains or is it a mud image that you've made, an' set on a mustang for company?"

"'Tain't neither. An', first you quit your roarin' an' bellowin', Stump. If you've got to talk that way when you talk out between your teeth, just you whisper. This that's ridin' by the side of me on the mustang that you speak of so disrespectful is a boy, a big boy an' a live boy that you've heard of. A boy that's already done more wonderful things than you've ever done, an' you've done a lot. He's Ned Fulton, the one that went through the Alamo an' a thousand other dangers afore an' since. He's come to tell us there's a crowd of Texans in the south, an' I'm goin' back to git 'em, while you take him on to Houston with your news."

"Yes, I've heard of you, Ned, an' I'm glad to see you," thundered Stump.

The unfinished colossus grasped Ned's hand in his tremendous paw, and gave it a shake that made him quiver all over.

"You're a good fighter, I've heard, an' I'm proud to know you," he said. "I like brave people, but I ain't a fightin' man, myself. I won't fight at all unless I'm driv to it. I'd rather be back in the States, ploughin' corn an' talkin' peaceful to the old mule than be here. Jim, what do you reckon ever made a coward like me come to Texas?"

"I guess it was because you thought you'd be safe under the rule of Santa Anna. He's such a good kind man that he wouldn't let any feller speak harsh to a tender little lamb like you, an' you knowed it. You come a-runnin' as soon as you heard that Santa Anna was here to protect you."

"I reckon that was it," said Stump resignedly. "I do the best I can, Ned, though it's pretty hard on a feller who's most skeered to death, night an' day. But I guess we ain't got any time to lose. Come on, an' I'll be your brother, since you're losin' Jim, who has to go back for them other fellers."

They lingered only a few minutes. Ned gave Potter explicit directions about Camp Independence, and, as the man knew the country, he was sure to find it quickly, unless he was taken or slain by Indians or Mexicans. But Potter rode away confidently, and waved them good-bye from a distant swell.

"There goes a brave man," said Stump with a sigh. "I wish I was as brave as he was. Do you think, Ned, that we're goin' to have a big fight?"

"It's bound to come sooner or later."

"An' I suppose I'll have to be in it," again sighing.

"I think it likely," said Ned, a twinkle in his eye. "They need strong men like you."

Stump's face was illumined immediately. Evidently Ned had touched him in his proud spot.

"I am strong," he said. "I reckon I'm the strongest man in all Texas 'cept the Panther, him that you've been runnin' with. I wonder why I was sawed off so short."

"I suppose," said Ned, in his most flattering tone, "it was because they began to build you on such a great scale that the material of the high quality needed gave out before they were through."

Stump's face brightened.

"Do you really think that's so, Ned?"

"I've no doubt of it."

"It makes me feel good to hear you say so, so I reckon it's true. Now, take a look from this hill, Ned. You see that sheet of yellow water stretched out there, with trees and bushes growin' out of it. Somewhere in the middle of all that water the Brazos River is runnin'. The rest of it, I guess, is a lake made by the big spring rains. You an' me have got to cross it to reach Houston, but as it is two or three miles wide here we can't swim it with our horses."

"Then how are we to get across?"

"There's a ferry lower down, where a black fellow would take us in his boat, an' if we think we can't get down to him soon enough I know where there's a canoe hid among the bushes, that'll take over a coward of a man like me an' a brave boy like you. At that place the horses can swim, restin' on the little islands here an' there."

"Is there any reason why we can't go on to the ferry?"

"I've a notion from what you say that Mexicans are somewhere pretty near the Brazos. Maybe Urrea an' that band of his are already on the bank, an' I'm plum' skeered lest we run into 'em. Anyway we can't cross before mornin', cause you an' me, Ned, have to ride mighty careful. Take this blanket of mine an' double it under you. It ain't no fun ridin' a bare-backed horse for a month or two."

Ned took it gladly.

"Now," said Stump, "I think we'd better go down stream an' take it slow for a while. I ain't got any taste for runnin' into a swarm of Mexicans. It don't suit a peace-lovin' man like me, an' besides you an' that pony of yours need rest."

Ned was not at all averse, as his limbs had begun to ache from so much riding, and they let their horses go at a moderate walk, keeping on the firm ground, away from the flooded valley of the Brazos.

"Terrible things have been done this spring in Texas," said Stump, "an' I guess God has made the weather to suit. Rain an' rain an' rain. Wind an' hail an' black days an' Northers. It may cloud up ag'in in an hour or two, an' bust loose like all the imps of Satan unchained. Now, Ned, what would you say that was shinin' 'cross the prairie there?"

"It's the flash of sunlight from the long blades of Mexican lances. I've seen it before often, and I can't mistake it."

"I was sure of it myself, but thinkin' that mebbe your eyes was keener than mine, I asked you. Trouble is shorely comin' for a peaceful man. I wish I was back in North Caroliny where I come from, and I wish it hard."

"No you don't, Stump, and you can't make me believe that you do."

Stump took off his hat and shook his head with a peculiar threatening motion. Immense, round and clipped close it was a formidable head. Ned saw the great nostrils swell as if the man already smelled battle.

"Do you reckon, Ned, that it's Urrea's band, the one that gave you so much trouble?"

Ned looked long before he answered.

"No, I don't think it is," he replied. "This force is too big to be Urrea's, Stump. There must be two hundred lancers alone besides infantry. And I think too, Stump, that I see a cannon."

"So do I, Ned. If it ain't a cannon it's somethin' else on wheels, an' it makes me shake all over with fear. I reckon that one of their generals with a big force is about to reach the Brazos."

"It would appear so, but we must look further into this, Stump."

"Of course. That's what we're here for, at least I am. We'll keep among these cottonwoods, an' we'll go as near as we dare. I reckon we'd better keep on walkin' so our horses will be fresh for a dash, if we have to gallop for our lives."

Luckily the timber was very heavy along the Brazos, and keeping in its shelter they edged gradually toward the advancing Mexican force. They soon saw that their surmises were correct. The new body assumed the dimensions of an army, outnumbering by far any that Houston could possibly have.

As Ned and Stump looked from their covert in the bushes they saw the division go into camp on a broad expanse of high ground. The horsemen dismounted and tethered their horses. Rifles, muskets and lances were stacked, the cannon were drawn up in a row, and men began to build fires.

"I guess it's the division of Gaona or Sesma, an' to think of me standin' here, shakin' in my shoes an' lookin' at a whole Mexican army," whispered Stump.

"No, it is not the division of Gaona, nor is it that of Sesma," said Ned. "It is the army of Santa Anna himself, because I see him now, and I ought to know him."

"Where? Where?" asked Stump eagerly. "I never put eyes on Santa Anna an' I'd like to see him."

"There, under the great cottonwood, the little man in the fine uniform and the big cocked hat. See how all the others bow to him."

Stump raised himself in the bushes and strained his in a devouring gaze upon this man who seemed to the Texans a very arch-demon. Santa Anna, with his back against the great cottonwood, was occupying a seat that the soldiers had made hastily for him. His uniform, though stained with mud, was of the most splendid material, heavy with gold epaulets and gold stripes. His great cocked hat shaded his dark face, but the face itself, despite its darkness, was tinged somewhat with pallor from a long and exhausting march. He had drawn his troops forward with all his energy, seeking to capture the last of the Texans.

The heart of Santa Anna, at that moment, was full of evil passion. He hated the Texans with all the power of a strong and malignant nature. These wretched interlopers had interfered too much with his plans, and it hurt his pride all the more, because they were so few. He had destroyed them at the Alamo and Goliad, but they persisted. His officers told him that this fellow Houston was still on the Brazos, with a ragged band, and he, the great, the illustrious Santa Anna, the lord of a land as large as half Europe, was compelled to hunt him down. He must toil through the mud here and delay his splendid triumph in the streets of the great capital.

Santa Anna leaned his head against the tree and looked around at his army. Surely such a force as this would soon put an end to the miserable Texans. He drew a small gold box from the inside of his coat, took from it a pinch of a dark drug and put it in his mouth. Soon his weariness vanished under the influence of the opium, and splendid visions came. He was the greatest man in the world, since Napoleon Bonaparte, and there was no limit to what he might achieve. The taking of Houston and the last of the Texans became but a trifling incident that he would dispose of within a week.

Meanwhile, Ned and Stump were watching him from the bushes with the fascinated eyes of those who gaze between the bars at a great tiger. Ned remembered that terrible morning at the Alamo, when he had been forced to look on at the slaughter of his comrades. He had seen Santa Anna then as Satan, and he seemed no less evil now. He saw Bowie and Crockett and Travis and the others again and a red mist came before his eyes. The great pulses leaped, and began to beat hard. He hated this man. He hated him with a concentrated power and energy of which he had not believed himself capable.

"An' so that's Santa Anna," whispered Stump. "I never before saw a little man look so big. What was the stuff that he slipped in his mouth, Ned?"

"Opium. I've seen him take it before."

"Opium? Well, we Texans don't need any drugs, but he is cert'nly wicked lookin'. Still, Ned, skeered as I am of fightin' I'd like to have him out here in the bushes for about five minutes. There'd be one devil the less in the universe."

"You can't get at him, at least not now, but our time may come, Stump; it may come. Ah, there is Almonte! See him, the tall young man. He is a Mexican whom you would like. He treated me kindly, when I was a prisoner among them, and he is a brave and humane man."

"I think we've looked long enough," said Stump. "You an' me know what's here now, an' we know what threatens Houston. It's time we was crossin' the Brazos with the news. We've got to take the canoe that I told you of, an' let our horses swim from island to island."

"You're right, Stump," said Ned. "Now that we know what we've got to expect, the sooner we leave the better."

They slipped from the bushes, mounted and rode rapidly up the stream. Already the day was waning. Behind them they saw the fires of Santa Anna's camp, and ahead they saw the coming twilight. It was about two miles, so Stump said, to the place where the canoe lay hidden, and they did not spare their horses.

The twilight had passed, and the night had come, when they reached the hiding place of the canoe. The wind shifted, the clouds came and drizzling rain began to fall again. It seemed to Ned that it was forever raining in that famous spring in Texas, and it was a fact that had a deep influence on the great events to come.

They were compelled to ride their horses through shallow water, the overflow of the Brazos, before they reached the bushes in the edge of the main stream, among which the canoe had been sunk.

"S'pose it ain't here," said Stump, "s'pose the risin' waters have carried it away, or some prowlin' scamp found it an' took it before the waters riz. Me bein' of a despondent nature, it clean fills me with fear to think of it."

"What shall we do if we don't find it?" asked Ned.

"If we don't find that canoe, then you an' me hev got to cross the Brazos some way or other, stay on our horses as long as they can swim an' then if they give out take to the water, an' swim the rest of the way ourselves."

Ned laughed outright.

"What you laughin' at?" asked Stump suspiciously.

"It seems to me that for a coward you've marked out a pretty bold and grand attempt."

"I'm bein' pushed on. I tell you, Ned, I'm bein' an' you're bein' pushed on, if ever men was. When I looked on that devil, Santa Anna, settin' there in all his triumph, I felt like we was the few Greeks that I've heard of in the old histories, an' that he was the king of the Persians comin' with a hundred to one. What was his name, that old king?"

"Xerxes," said Ned, upon whose mind the simile cut deep, "and I tell you, Stump, you've got it. That's just the way it is. Santa Anna is like that old Xerxes. He's come with his overwhelming numbers. The Alamo was our Thermopylæ, and Goliad was the sack and burning of Athens. But we'll beat him yet, as the Greeks beat Xerxes."

"Of course we will, Ned. A man ain't ever beat, 'cept when he gives up, an' you don't have to give up. Glory, here's the canoe all right, an' the paddle in her. The risin' waters haven't taken her away or hurt her either, two things of which I was afear'd. Ned, you must have brought us luck. Things are runnin' smoother with me now since you come. Help me bail out the canoe, an' I'll do the paddlin' while you rest. You need it an' you've won the right to it."

They stood in water to their thighs, until the canoe was bailed out completely. Then they climbed gingerly into the frail and rocking craft, laying their rifles beside them. Stump took the paddle, and Ned took the lariats of the two horses which were to follow, wading at first, then swimming. Paddling a canoe is a delicate task at any time, and it was complicated by the horses which might pull on the lariats, and upset them.

"You keep up close as you can, Ned," said Stump, "with a lot of purchase on the lariats, so they can't give too sudden a jerk. You an' me have just got to get across this river, an' we'll need the horses afterward. I tell you, Ned, we must reach the other side, if it was a thousand miles away, with the news that Santa Anna an' all them hordes of his are at hand."

He spoke with fiery energy. His assumed manner of timidity was wholly gone. The man's vast shoulders and chest seemed to swell through his clothes, as courage and resolution poured into every vein. He settled himself squarely in the centre of the boat and grasped the paddle in powerful hands.

"Now, Ned," he said, "you handle them lariats, as if you was the greatest horse breaker the world has ever seen, an' keep 'em straight behind us. They'll have to wade quite a piece before they strike the main stream of the Brazos."

"I'm ready," said Ned, full of confidence. "I can manage them."

Stump gave the paddle a sweep, and the canoe emerged slowly from the bushes. It was not his intention to go fast at least at first, owing to the difficulty about the horses. But Ned spoke soothingly to the animals. He called to them softly, he encouraged them to come on and he pulled gently on the lariats.

"That's right," said Stump, "talk to 'em, call 'em nice names, tell 'em they're the finest horses in the world, tell 'em that the Brazos may be in flood an' two miles wide, but they can swim it, an' they're the only two horses in the world that can. Horses are like people, flatter 'em an' you've got 'em."

Ned obeyed. He continued his mild and soothing talk to the horses, and they followed without hesitation, wading deeper and deeper into the yellow stream, until the water rose to their bodies. Then they began to swim, easily and powerfully, following the boat steadily, as if the fortunes of their masters were their own. The canoe itself, so great was Stump's dexterity and strength, scarcely rocked in the current. But full need had he of his skill that night. Entire trees, bushes and quantities of other debris came down on the current, but he always avoided them or pushed them aside.

In the tensity of those moments Ned had forgotten that the rain was sweeping against them. Overhead the menacing clouds were trooping across the sky. Far off, the wind was moaning and now that they were in the deep water, and, beyond the line of flooded trees and bushes, Ned felt the full majesty and desolation of the great scene spread before him. They were in the midst of a sea of yellow waters, broken both on the near and far sides by little islands which in reality were knolls covered with clumps of trees.

The scene was indescribably impressive to Ned. The great yellow river flowed slowly on, trees and bushes upon its bosom, its surface broken into waves by the wind which was now blowing steadily from the west. Far off on the horizon there was a dull low muttering of thunder, and, now and then, a stroke of lightning flared across the sky, bringing into vivid relief the yellow river, the black forests on either shore, and the lone canoe, with its two occupants, and the horses swimming behind them. Once or twice, the lightning was so vivid and intense that the surface of the river was turned from yellow to red.

"Here's an islan'," said Stump. "It's what would be a high part of the bank in low water, an' I think we'd better let the horses rest on it a while. I tell you, Ned, I'm mighty glad you're along with me. A timid man like me, alone in all this, would be terribly scared."

"It's certainly a nice, balmy summer night," said Ned.

Stump paddled the canoe to the knoll, merely the crest of which showed above the water, and pushed it among the trees, which held it against the drawing power of the current. The horses stood close to the canoe, not much above their knees in water, panting and evidently anxious to keep human companionship. Stump looked at them pityingly.

"We've got to give 'em a good rest here," he said, "'cause we're about to enter the main stream of the Brazos. It looks like it's flowin' slow, Ned, but all that mighty mass of water will pull at us awful hard. I think we'd better make for that bunch of trees, stickin' out 'bout a quarter of a mile down. You can see it the next time the lightnin' comes. We've got to go partly with the stream."

The lightning flared again across the broad waters, and Ned saw the dark projecting line of the trees that Stump had indicated. This was one of the uncommonly vivid flashes and the whole surface of the water between them and the trees blazed with red, the same tint of red that had surcharged the air at the Alamo and Goliad. He was no less glad than Stump that he was not alone. This shortened Hercules was just such a comrade as he would have wished at such a time.

They remained a full half hour on the knoll, in order to give the horses a good rest. Then Stump paddled the canoe into the main channel, seeking a diagonal course across it, and paddling with all his power toward the point that they had selected, and which they saw frequently by the increasing flashes of lightning. He felt now the immense power of that slow huge current pulling at them through the thin sides of the canoe. Yet he was not afraid. Somehow, his mind, bent upon so great a task, became attuned to the tremendous might of nature around him.

The horses swam steadily and powerfully. There was no danger now that they would pull on the lariats, as they kept close to the canoe, ever seeking that human companionship which seemed to them to hold them secure amid dangers.

The wind rose, and Ned felt the canoe swinging. He swayed, too, to preserve the balance, and all the while the peerless canoeman, the shortened Hercules, kept the balance of the tiny craft, and drove it surely toward the further shore. Soon they were in the middle of the stream, and Ned's pulses throbbed with awe. The low rumble of thunder on the far horizon had become terrific crashes directly overhead. Stroke after stroke of lightning blazed across the river and all the waters were now red.

There came a tremendous crash that stunned Ned's ears and the lightning flamed all about him. Both he and Stump were so startled that they jumped in their seats, and the canoe rocked dangerously. But Stump recovered himself quickly, and, by rapid and skillful use of the paddle, steadied it again.

"Must have struck the Brazos itself," said Stump. "It shorely hit close by 'cause I smell fire an' brimstone. I reckon it smells that way at the gates of them infernal regions."

Ned, too, either in fancy or in fact, smelled fire and brimstone, and his anxiety to reach solid land redoubled. Fortunately the horses had been too much frightened by the bolt to struggle, and swam after the canoe, as if they would keep their very noses against it, and in touch with its human occupants. Ned's nerves steadied again. Stump suddenly turned the canoe down stream and held it almost straight, while three or four trees matted together and torn by the roots from the soft earth floated past. Had they struck the canoe it would have gone down in an instant.

When the trees were well out of the way, Stump turned the canoe once more toward the original point of destination. Now all his skill was drawn into play, as the wind had grown more violent and the waves ran high. Well it was for them that nature had exhausted herself on the mighty shoulders and arms and chest. The muscles on his arms bunched up in huge knots as he swung the great paddle. Despite the rain and cold, beads of sweat stood out on his face. The huge volume of water continually drove against the canoe, trying to send it down the stream, but his strength always served. The canoe never swerved from its course, keeping directly for the dark projection of trees into the water.

Ned could see the trees now. They grew upon a relatively high peninsula of land, and behind this peninsula there was sure to be a cove of comparatively still water, where the current could not pull at them.

"I can make out the trees," he said to Stump. "They're on a neck of land. Paddle in behind it, and we will be safe."

"That's our harbour," replied the indomitable man, "an' I'll be mighty glad to get there. Restin' time is at hand ag'in."

The canoe now crossed the last reach of the main stream, and drew in slowly behind the peninsula, keeping on until its point touched soft mud. Then Ned and Stump stepped out upon a little patch of earth, ten or fifteen feet square, and the horses, wading up afterward, drew close to their human comrades. Stump leaned against the wet trunk of a tree, and wiped his great brow.

"I reckon that's about the best paddlin' I ever done," he said. "How that lightnin' flashes, Ned. I thought I was about gone, when that thunderbolt hit in the river beside us. I never expect to make such another crossin' as long as I live."

Ned looked back and he too was appalled.

"I don't know how we ever did it," he said, "but one thing is sure, we did do it."

"We've got at least a half mile or maybe a mile of overflow to go through yet," said Stump, "but before we start it we'll have another rest, one longer than the first we took."

"I'm willing," said Ned.

While they waited there, he patted the heads of the horses and talked to them and soothed them. He also examined their weapons and ammunition, which they had wrapped in Stump's blankets, and found that everything was dry and secure.

"Ned," said Stump, "you an' me ought to be pretty good comrades by the time we get to Houston. When two fellows share such dangers as we've left behind, an' such as we have comin' it makes 'em feel mighty near to each other."

"It certainly does." said Ned. "You must join our band. There's the Panther, and Obed White and Deaf Smith and Henry Karnes and Will Allen and the Reverend Stephen Larkin and Potter and others that are ready to die at any time for Texas."

"I know all them people that you've named, 'cept Allen an' Larkin," said Stump, "an' they're true blue, every one of them. We're shore to j'in in one band, as soon as Potter brings 'em up. Now, I reckon, Ned, we'd better be startin' ag'in."

They resumed their places in the canoe, and picked a channel through flooded forest. Sometimes the horses swam, but oftener they waded. Stump, who had some knowledge of the ground when it was not flooded, chose their path. They were compelled frequently to turn around masses of bushes and vines, but after midnight they reached solid earth, beyond the reach of the risen river, and hid the canoe in the densest brush they could find.

"It's done us a good turn that little canoe of mine," said Stump, "an' we'll leave it here, where it may do us another some day."

"Have you any idea where we are?" asked Ned.

"Just an idee, but it may be a close one. Houston's camp when I left him was in the Brazos bottoms five or six miles down, but I take it that they have become flooded since, and he must have moved back toward higher ground. Anyway you an' me, Ned, must make toward that place, as soon as we git rested. We're clean fagged out now, an' it's likely, too, that the horses are all done up."

They did not have the heart to mount their worn animals, but led them out on the prairie, until they came to one of the usual islands of timber. Here they forced their way into the close mesquite, tethered the horses, and, despite the rain, despite everything, slept.

CHAPTER 8

ON THE MEXICAN FLANK

Stump awoke first. He was conscious that he had not slept more than three or four hours, but the dawn was coming, and it was time for them to be up and on their way. The horses were grazing at the ends of their lariats, and seemed to have suffered no harm. Ned was asleep, his head on his arm, looking very worn and weary and Stump was sorry for him. But he must awake and go. He shook Ned and the boy sprang up grasping at his rifle.

"It's all right, Ned," said Stump. "There's no enemy. It's just you an' me. I was sorry to drag you out of your nice warm bed, with them nice feather pillows under your head an' them silk covers over you, but it had to be done. You an' me must be on the go ag'in, 'cause there are ferries lower down an' the Mexicans may be crossin' this very minute. I've got a knapsack full of good meat an' bread, an' we'll eat as we ride along. You take my blankets for a saddle ag'in, an' hop on your mustang."

Ned's body was somewhat stiff and sore, but the condition soon wore off. It seemed to him that his frame was so much toughened that he could stand anything. He even forgot that his clothes were still wet, and he felt a fair degree of comfort and much courage, as he rode beside Stump. The morning was warm and the rain had stopped, for a while, at least. Under the grateful heat and dryness their muscles regained their elasticity.

Ned looked at Stump and laughed.

"It's a fine thing to be happy," said Stump, "but I don't see nothin' to be laughin' at."

"Of course you don't, because the joke is in both the literal and material sense."

"I don't understan' them big words, but what do you mean when you say the joke's on me?"

"It's on your face. It's all over you. You remember how Potter told you he laughed at me when he first saw me coming. Said I had the shape of a man, but I looked more like a mud figure. Well, you're one, too. You've had muddy water splashed all over you and it's hardened there. You're a clay image, Stump."

"Then we're a pair of 'em. I don't mind since we're both safe an' sound. That was a terrible crossin' last night, Ned. I don't see how I ever got up the courage to try it with you. I know my hair has turned gray. See if it hasn't."

He took off his *sombrero*, and Ned looked at his head critically.

"It's more than that, Stump," he said in a sorrowful tone. "It's all silver white, what there is of it, an' what's worst of all, a lot of it has fallen out. Right on top of your head there's a perfectly bare spot as large as a saucer."

"You don't mean it! That can't be true!" exclaimed Stump, dashing his hand to his head. "Ned, you skeered me so bad I nearly fell off my hoss."

"I fancy I scared you more than you were scared at any time last night," said Ned laughing. "But don't be unhappy, Stump, you haven't a bald spot and, as well as I can see, not a single gray hair."

"I forgive you this time," said Stump, "but don't you do it ag'in. Now, Ned, we ought to strike some houses pretty soon. I know of three or four along the higher ground, but most likely their owners have run away. Good cause they've had for runnin', too."

His prediction was justified. They came to three cabins, but they were all deserted and silent. Then they turned back toward that point in the Brazos bottoms where Houston had been encamped, when Stump left him. But they did not go very far, soon reaching the area of flooded ground. Stump shook his head.

"If Houston is still camped there," he said, "he an' his men are standin' or settin' in three or four feet of water, an' as nobody could stan' that very long they just ain't there."

"What shall we do now?" asked Ned.

"Reckon we'd better keep on down the Brazos, an' watch for the crossin' of Santa Anna. The news of him is the best thing we can carry to Houston."

A half mile further and Ned, who was a little in advance, noticed a broad trail in the soft prairie. He called Stump's attention to it, and the latter announced at once that it had been made by Houston's force.

"Here go the wheels of the wagons," he said. "An' the whole trail leads straight from the edge of the shallow water. Houston has shorely crossed somewhar or other, an', as I guessed, he's moved to higher ground for a dry camp."

Ned felt relief. The fact that it was Houston's trail meant that no Mexican army was yet across the Brazos.

"Five more miles along the stream an' we come to the ferry at San Felipe de Austin," said Stump. "Maybe Houston has gathered his force there to dispute the crossin'. We ain't got no time to follow his trail, which may wind about every which-a-way, but must make straight for the ferry. I'm thinkin', too, Ned, after what we saw last night, that we'd better gallop."

They touched up their horses, and rode as fast as they could toward the ferry at the tiny place that bore the large name of San Felipe de Austin. Stump knew this part of the country thoroughly and he led the way. He explained as they galloped along that the river could not spread out to such width there, and, if the Mexicans had seized the ferry-boats, they could cross with ease. Ned felt a great fear. He knew the celerity and energy of Santa Anna and his anxiety to crush the last of the Texans with the utmost speed.

The wind was blowing toward them, and as they drew near to the ferry Ned heard a faint sound like the distant tapping of a light hammer. He knew that it was made by the firing of rifles or muskets.

"Do you hear?" he said.

Stump nodded.

"Maybe they're across already and are attacking," Ned said.

"No, it can't be that. If Houston an' his army was there the firin' would be a long ways bigger. If they ain't there an' Santa Anna was across then the Texans would be too few in number to hold their ground an' would retreat quickly. No, Ned, Santa Anna is still on the other side of the Brazos."

Stump's logic seemed sound to Ned, and the truth of it was confirmed by the fact that the fire soon died, merely to be renewed a minute or two later in a feeble and desultory manner. Then they galloped headlong toward a little group of men, and an officer on horseback rode forward to meet them. Stump held up his hand.

"You're Captain Baker," he cried, "an' you know me well. Under this coverin' of mud I'm Bill Burke, known to most people as Stump, 'cause God changed his mind an' made my legs shorter than He intended. This boy is Ned Fulton, him that was in the Alamo with Bowie an' Crockett an' Travis, an' all them gran' men who are gone."

"Yes, I know you well, Stump," said Captain Baker, a gallant man, "and I've heard much of Ned Fulton from Mr. Austin and General Houston. Coming as you do you must come with news. What is it, Stump?"

"Me an' Ned saw Santa Anna, old Satan himself, yesterday on the other side of the Brazos, an' he had with him a big army an' cannon. He's after Houston. We crossed the Brazos last night in the storm, an' we've galloped here to tell you. Ned himself has come from the other side of the Colorado to bring the news that a band of Texans has gathered there to help."

"So he's at hand!" exclaimed Baker. "Some Mexicans have appeared among the burned houses on the other side of the river, and we've been exchanging shots with them, but we did not know whether they were merely a band of scouts. See those scattered ruins across there. That's San Felipe de Austin, but we burned it to keep it from sheltering the enemy."

"And that's Santa Anna himself on the hill just out of rifle shot," exclaimed Ned. "I know him! Ah! how well I know him! See him there on the horse with the big military glasses to his eyes!"

The Texans circled around him, and their eyes followed Ned's pointing finger with intense curiosity. Not many of them had seen Santa Anna, but they had a good view of him now. Evidently he had not suffered greatly from the storm, as his uniform was fresh, and gorgeous. He sat upon a powerful white horse, and scanned the Texan band leisurely with his great glasses.

"He looks mighty sassy," said Stump.

"He regards us as easy prey," said Baker bitterly, "and perhaps he has cause to do so."

"Where's Houston?" asked Ned.

"I don't know," replied Baker. "When I left him he was still on the other side of the Brazos."

"But he must have crossed yesterday or the day before," exclaimed Ned. "We saw a big trail that couldn't have been any but his."

"Maybe he has," said Baker, still showing great feeling. "He has a little cotton steamer, the *Yellowstone*, which could take the men across without much trouble. But we wanted him to quit falling back. We had a chance to attack and destroy Sesma's column, but we didn't do it. Then I took a hundred and twenty men and came here to guard the ford. He didn't want us to do it, but we came anyhow. We were right, for there is Santa Anna now, looking at us. Do you know, Fulton, the young officer who has ridden up beside him?"

"That's Colonel Almonte, a brave man and a kind one. I know, as I was in his hands. He received his military education mostly in the United States and he is probably the best officer that Santa Anna has."

Baker looked around at his troop, one hundred and twenty lean, weather-beaten and resolute men.

"There's not a bad marksman in this command of mine," he said, "and Santa Anna cannot cross here. He may bring up boats, but they cannot face such riflemen as these."

Santa Anna sat long on his horse, and the Texans made ready with their rifles and ammunition. Almonte rode away presently, but Santa Anna remained. Baker provided Ned with a saddle and bridle for his mustang. The boy and Stump remained together on the left flank of the Texan force.

"Now, if it wasn't for that big river between me an' Santa Anna," said Stump, "I'd be skeered to death. At the same time I wish it wasn't just quite so wide, then I could topple him off that horse with a bullet, an' things would look a lot brighter for the Texans."

"He'll take care of himself," said Ned. "He won't expose himself unless he has to do it as a last chance. Look, Stump, what they're bringing up now!"

"A cannon, as shore as thunder!" exclaimed Stump. "I reckon they expect to drive us away with it an' then launch their boats, crossin' under cover of the cannon fire."

"It looks like it," said Ned.

The cannon was now observed by Baker's men, and they all drew back from the river. There was no doubt that a cannonade was about to begin, as the Mexican gunners were making ready.

"Ride back a little further, boys, just over the crest of the ridge," said Baker. "We are not afraid of their cannon."

There was a flash of fire, a gush of smoke, a roar and a solid shot ploughed up the ground near them.

"Try ag'in!" thundered Stump derisively.

The cannon was reloaded and fired a second time. A shell burst to their right but did no damage. The Texans then galloped forward and sent a volley at a dozen Mexicans who had appeared at the edge of the opposite shore. The range was too great, but a spent bullet reached one of the Mexicans, stung him, and they fell back.

The Texans retreated to their shelter behind the ridge, and the cannon reopened its fire, sending both shot and shell.

The Texans contented themselves with an occasional rifle bullet. Thus time wore on. Santa Anna disappeared from the hill, and did not show himself again. Ned wondered at the long delay. The Mexicans were certainly making no strenuous effort to cross. In fact the crossing, in spite of the cannon, was impossible, and it seemed strange that they should linger there, wasting so much time. It occurred to Ned that they might have some other object in view and he mentioned his suspicion to Stump.

"Does look queer," said Stump. "Santa Anna, as we know, is the kind that's always pushin' on, but here he is fiddlin' an' fussin' with us. He must know that he can't get across while we're here. Why, they haven't even tried to start any boats."

"And we don't see Santa Anna now, nor do we see Almonte," said Ned, "and the whole Mexican force looks smaller than it did a while ago. Stump, is there any other ferry near here?"

"There's one at Fort Bend, lower down, but all the boats there have been brought to this side of the river."

"Then, Stump, as sure as you and I are here, Santa Anna and Almonte have gone there to cross. While they have been popping at us with that cannon they have set about the real work elsewhere."

"Ned, I believe you're right! You've hit it! While the side show has been goin' on here, the main circus is down the river at the Fort Bend ferry. Old Santa Anna is all that they say he is. He's tricked us."

They told their suspicions to Captain Baker. He, too, was alarmed, but he was not willing to leave the ferry, which he had undertaken to defend.

"I hope you may be wrong. You must be wrong," he said, "but if I left this place they would come across here, and so I have to stay."

"Then me an' Ned are goin' to ride down there an' see," said Stump. "I'm a timid man, Captain Baker, an' I've got a fear in my heart that they're workin' a trick on us."

"Go and luck be with you," said Baker.

Ned and Stump galloped away. As they were compelled to make so many circuits avoiding morasses and flood water it was a long road. But the further they went the more certain Ned was that they were right. Santa Anna and Almonte would neglect no device. The younger Urrea also might be present with his band and he was full of craft and resource. The two were silent for a long time and when the boy spoke at last he said to his comrade:

"Stump, we're surely going to find that we've been outwitted. But if they are across we can go back in time to warn Baker and his men."

When they drew near the second ford Ned uttered an exclamation and he and Stump instantly galloped into the cover of some trees. He had seen the blades of lances shining on their side of the river, and they knew at once that their worst fears were justified. The Mexicans were across. As they stood there, they counted numerous cavalry and artillery, with cannon already gathered on the bank, and Ned thought he saw the figure of Urrea.

He learned afterward that Santa Anna's easy crossing there had been due to Almonte. The boats had been withdrawn to what was for the moment the Texan shore, and had been left in charge of a negro. The young colonel had appeared and hailed him in excellent English, insisting that he was a Texan officer, who would be captured if he could not cross, and the negro went back for him. Of course other Mexicans appeared, and seized the boat the moment he touched the bank. After that, Santa Anna brought his army across without difficulty,

"What do you think we'd better do, Stump?" asked Ned. "Go back and warn Captain Baker?"

"I don't think so," replied Stump. "Baker will take care of himself. You can't surprise a lot of Texans on horses. Besides, Ned, I don't think Santa Anna will bother about Baker an' his men. It's far more likely that he will push on after Houston or our government. The president, I think, is at Harrisburg. Wouldn't Santa Anna like to seize Mr. Burnet and then swoop down an' destroy Houston?"

"If he did that our last hope would be gone," said Ned, "and I think, Stump, that you and I had better stay here and watch Santa Anna."

"It makes me shiver to think of the danger we'll run," said Stump, "but it was just what I was goin' to propose. Anyway, as the day is growin' late, an' the march through the Brazos bottoms is somethin' terrible, I don't think he'll start till tomorrow."

Ned did not feel that they were in any great danger of being captured. The nature of the country, made a morass by the incessant rains, would keep the Mexicans close to their camp. Even Urrea and his horsemen could do but little scouting in that vast area of swamp.

He and Stump found a fairly firm spot, where they tethered their horses and watched the growing light of the fires that Santa Anna's army was building. Stump spoke with bitterness.

"Everythin' goes ag'inst us," he said. "We took San Antonio an' we crowed too much. Now Santa Anna sweeps everythin' before him, an' it seems that about all you an' me can do, Ned, is to stand 'roun' in mud an' water an' watch his triumphal progress."

"Our time will come," said Ned earnestly. "I feel sure that it will come. You forget Houston and all the brave men who are yet alive."

"I hope you are a good prophet," said Stump somewhat despondently. "All the same, here are you an' me in the mud, an' over there are the Mexicans by their fires, warm and dry."

"I'm going over to join them," said Ned.

"What?"

"Not to stay, either by choice or force. Don't think that. You know, Stump, I speak Spanish and different kinds of Mexican-Spanish. I'm burnt almost as dark as an Indian by months of life wholly in the open, and I can pass for a Mexican. I'm going over there to talk to some of those fellows."

"For the Lord's sake, don't think of such a thing!" exclaimed Stump. "They'll nab you, shore, Ned, an' in just about ten minutes Santa Anna would have you shot."

"I can risk it," said Ned, "because I want to find out just what they are going to do. Besides, it isn't as dangerous as you think it is. Mexican armies are always disorderly, with crowds of men loafing about the fringe of them. You stay here, and I'll be back safe and sound inside of an hour."

"Don't do it, Ned," pleaded Stump. "Think how terrible lonely an' skeered I'll be here by myself. An' then if you'd never come back!"

Ned smiled at Stump's reference to his loneliness. His mind was quite made up.

"I know that you're not the least bit afraid on your own account," he said, "and you need not be on mine. Even if they should suspect me I could dodge away in the morass, and escape them in a minute."

"I'll go, too."

"No, you could never pass for an instant. There's nobody in all Mexico who looks like you."

"That's so," said Stump, with a sigh. "Besides, my Mexican won't bear close inspection."

Ned waited a little, until the night deepened, and then he walked away among the trees. He had decided already upon his manner of approach. The fires would have to be fed continually with fresh wood, and he would appear as one accomplishing that task. He pulled up an armful of fallen wood, walked boldly forward, and cast it upon the largest fire. Then he dropped back in the dusk, and ranged about as if hunting for more.

This process soon brought him into contact with real Mexicans, and he exchanged words with them, at first in an inconsequential fashion, but soon drifted toward the object of their march.

"We start early tomorrow toward the place that these Texan rebels call their capital, for the moment," said a dark Mexican from Oaxaca. "Then we turn and destroy the greatest of the rebels, the one named Houston. And I say to you, *amigo*, I shall be glad when it is all over. The illustrious Santa Anna who leads us, and who is with us, is terrible in the battle, and he is likewise terrible on the march. My poor feet have trodden thousands of miles of hard ground in Mexico and soft ground in Texas. And it is always raining. When I put my head on the ground to sleep the rain falls in my face, and when I awake it is still falling. We cross great rivers and we wade vast marshes and morasses. I shall be glad when the wicked Texans are all dead, and we can return to our own Mexico where the sun is warm and shines so much. From what region dost thou come, *amigo*?"

"Vera Cruz, about ten miles back of the city," replied Ned readily, remembering that he could describe from his own knowledge the surroundings of that place, "and I shall rejoice like you when I can return. Are we close upon the heels of these flying Texans?"

"It is said that we're but a day's march behind," replied the Oaxacan. "I hear that the general is to start very early in the morning, and to take a picked force with only one cannon. He intends to travel fast so that no matter how light the heels of the Texans may be, they cannot escape. It will be a great sight when the rebel leaders are brought in with the halters around their necks."

"A great sight, truly," echoed Ned, although he shuddered as he said it.

The two then walked forward together, and threw more wood upon the fires which cast a ruddy light as they crackled and leaped. Ned, under his apparently careless manner, observed everything about him. He saw a great white tent a little to his left, and he knew that it had been erected for Santa Anna. Officers entered and others passed out as he looked. He saw the brilliant young Almonte, and he turned his head aside, lest those keen eyes should notice something un-Mexican in his appearance. Then he saw Francisco Urrea, Urrea older and more cruel than ever. Urrea passed within ten feet of him but took no notice.

Now Ned went back to the forest in search of more wood, and as he continued his search he gradually drifted away from the Mexican camp, and back toward the place at which he had left Stump. He hailed him in a loud whisper through the bushes.

"Stump! Stump!" he said. "It is I, Ned Fulton! I have gone into the Mexican camp, as I said I would, and I have come back safe!"

"You're more than welcome," said Stump, stepping into the light. "You've been gone over two hours, an' I thought, every minute, I'd hear the Mexicans yellin' triumph over your capture. Did you learn anythin', Ned, that was worth the risk?"

"I learned a lot," replied Ned. "It was fully worth the risk. For the sake of speed they're going to split up in the morning, and Santa Anna, taking the picked men and one cannon, is going to hurry forward on Harrisburg. They think our wandering government is there, and they feel sure of capturing it."

"I'm thinkin' that the president an' all his cabinet are there," said Stump, "an' if you hadn't done this thing they might have been s'prised an' taken. You shorely have sing'lar ideas, Ned, an' they 'pear to work out right, just when they're needed most. Now I guess we've got another night of hard ridin' before us. Seems to me that I've just growed to my horse."

"Lucky we are to have horses to grow to," said Ned, as he sprang upon the back of his faithful mustang.

"You let me lead the way," said Stump; "not that I'm more fit than you are, or that I'm intended to be a leader, but I know this country, an' we've got to be mighty keerful until we reach higher ground."

The way was exceedingly difficult, almost wholly mire for a long distance, but fortunately they were spared another night of rain. There were clouds, it is true, but they saw the moon and some of the stars all the time. Stump therefore was able to lead, with a fair degree of certainty, through the vast marsh, although they were compelled at times to let the horses rest.

Finally they drew out upon the firm prairie, and Ned saw it in the moonlight, the green touched with silver rolling away, until it sank out of sight in the darkness. He and Stump heaved mighty sighs of relief, and dismounted.

"We'll give our animals a long breathing spell here," said Stump, "an' then we won't stop till we get to Harrisburg. I wonder what old Santa Anna would have said if he had noticed you there, helping to feed his fires for him."

"He probably would have said, 'Seize him at once; cut him down!' and then the slash of a sword or the thrust of a lance would have been the end of me. The name of a great merchant, John Roylston, protected me once when I was in the hands of Santa Anna, but I doubt whether it would do so now."

"I doubt it, too. I doubt whether any Texan fallin' in his hands would live. So we jest won't fall into 'em."

Their stop lasted nearly an hour, as they wished their horses to recover their full strength. Then they mounted and rode swiftly toward Harrisburg. Ned's destiny was ever taking him northward. Santa Anna was breaking down every line of defence in turn, but the boy shared the dauntless spirit of the men with whom he rode and fought.

"When can we reach Harrisburg?" he asked.

"Before night anyway," replied Stump.

"You're sure that the members of our government are there?"

"They were three days ago, anyway, an' there was no talk of their leavin'. They hadn't heard of the advance of Santa Anna an' maybe nobody but you an' me, Ned, yet knows he is across the Brazos. We'll give President Burnet an' the others news that is news."

They rode swiftly but mostly in silence, each realising to the full the tremendous importance of that for which he rode. They overtook several fugitive wagons, bearing Texans and their families, fleeing northward before the ruthless Mexican advance. Ned and Stump gave no words of consolation to them, but bade them hasten their flight.

"Santa Anna an' his whole army are across the Brazos," said Stump to one of them, "an' nothin' can stop him. But you bend a little to the west, 'cause Santa Anna is headed for Harrisburg."

The man asked no questions but took Stump's advice at once. His wagon was drawn by powerful mules, and he turned them from a northerly to a north-westerly direction. In a few minutes he was out of sight beyond the swells of the prairie.

"That man has a heap of sense," said Stump approvingly. "How I wish I was with him in that wagon, fleein' off to peaceful scenes, 'stead of goin' to Harrisburg right in the thick of danger."

"You're the king of prevaricators, Stump. You couldn't be kept from going to Harrisburg."

"I don't know what a prevaricator is, but I do know that I'm terrible skeered. I guess it's your company, Ned, that keeps me from runnin' away from our task."

True to their original intention, they made no stop on their way to Harrisburg. Their horses, trained to long distances, and not pushed unduly, went on without a weakening stride. Now and then they crossed swollen brooks, and once or twice they were compelled to ride around lagoons made by the heavy rains. But the sun forced itself at intervals through the clouds, and then the earth looked very beautiful. There was a delicate shade over the green grass, and, wherever they had a chance, the early flowers had thrust into bloom. The timber, which was often heavy, was shrouded in great masses of dark green foliage. It occurred to Ned, in their flight, that it was a country worth fighting for.

They topped a long swell, and Stump pointed straight before them. Ned saw two or three thin columns of smoke rising.

"Follow them lines of smoke down to the places they start from, an' you'll find Harrisburg," said Stump. "In another half hour we'll be there an' between you an' me, Ned, we won't arrive a minute too soon."

Well inside the half hour, and covered with mud, they galloped into the little town. Their horses' hoofs splashed the mire in the unpaved streets, and they made straight for the largest house in the place.

"The president, is he here?" exclaimed Ned to a man who stood before the open door of a log cabin.

The man pointed at the house toward which they were riding.

"What is the"—he was asking, but Ned and Stump were out of hearing, and a moment later drew rein before the large house. They sprang from their horses, ran to the front door which was closed, and Ned beat upon it. An armed Texan threw it open and exclaimed:

"Who are you, and what do you want?"

"My name is Ned Fulton, and the man with me is William Burke, generally called Stump. You must know him! Everybody in Texas knows him!"

"I know him, and I have heard of you, too, Fulton," said a grave voice. "Come in and tell us the news that you have ridden so hard to bring us."

He who spoke was a handsome man, dressed neatly, none other than David G. Burnet, the first president of the new Texan republic. Behind him were Hardiman, Carson, and other members of his cabinet. They had been sitting at a table examining papers and talking, when Ned and Stump made their violent intrusion. Every one of them knew instinctively that the two had ridden far and hard—they bore all the signs of it—and the message they brought, whatever its nature, must be important.

Stump stopped. His inborn respect for education made him wait for Ned to speak.

"Perhaps you have news about Santa Anna?" said Burnet in the same calm, grave tone.

"We have," said Ned. "He is on this side of the Brazos with his army and artillery."

Burnet paled a little, and a murmur arose from the others.

"How do you know this?" asked the president.

"Mr. Burke and I saw the Mexicans apparently trying to cross at San Felipe, but the ferry there was held by Captain Baker and his men. We suspected that it was a feint, and rode to the other ferry at Fort Bend, only to find that Santa Anna and his army were already across at that point. They camped for the night in the bottoms of the Brazos, and, as I can speak Spanish, I passed for a Mexican, and talked with some of their men. I learned their plan. Even now Santa Anna with his picked troops and one cannon is pushing as hard as he can for this place, in order to capture you, Mr. President, and your cabinet."

"And Houston is not here to defend the Texan government," said a man bitterly. "He is continually retreating before the enemy. He does not trust our Texans."

"Patience," said Burnet soothingly. "We may disagree about the actions of General Houston, but he is a soldier and he may be right. Doubtless it is unwise for him to meet Santa Anna until his army is larger. Remember, gentlemen, how much depends upon the battle whenever it is fought. If Houston is beaten, the last hope of Texas is gone."

But some of the men still murmured. Houston in those terrible days was much criticized, because he continually retreated before Santa Anna. The valiant but impatient Texans wished to meet the dictator

617

at once in a final combat.

"What time do you think Santa Anna can reach Harrisburg?" asked Burnet.

"Not before night, in any event," replied Ned. "He has to force his way with his cannon and horses through the Brazos bottoms and the mud is very deep there. The prairie too, is soft."

"Then it will give us time for another flight," said Burnet sadly. "Gentlemen, I suggest that we retreat now to Galveston Island. Santa Anna cannot reach us there easily. The water will defend us, for a time at least. Mr. Fulton and Mr. Burke, on behalf of the people and the government I thank you. It is likely that we should have been surprised here without your warning. Go into the next room and I will see that you have food and fresh clothing."

Ned and Stump obeyed willingly. Good food was brought to them and they discarded their muddy garments for clean ones. They also stretched their limbs and felt the soothing influence of rest. But they heard, too, the bustle of hurried preparation for flight. Many of the people were gone already, but they saw through the window large wagons drawn up to receive women and children and household goods. The president was harnessing a horse to a wagon, with his own hands, and nearly all the members of his cabinet were engaged in a similar task. It was very crude, very homely, and few would have suspected the beginnings of a great state in these small and dangerous surroundings.

Ned had eaten enough, and he stood at the window gazing with a melancholy interest at the work that was going on before him. He was reminded of the hop-skip-and-jump of his childhood. That was the way now the Texans seemed always to be going. They scarcely tarried long enough in one place to draw a good breath. Even as he looked several wagons, loaded to the last pound, rolled away. Then President Burnet opened the door and said to them:

"I am about to depart. If you wish to go with me I shall be glad to have you come along."'

Stump glanced at Ned and the boy replied:

"We thank you, Mr. President, but we want to remain here a while longer. We have good horses. My friend, Mr. Burke knows the country, and we can escape with ease. We will follow tonight, but it is our intention, sir, to join Houston later."

"You could do no better," said Burnet. "I pray that all our Texans will rally around him. Meanwhile we owe you great thanks. If the opportunity comes to me, and we save this Texas of ours you shall be rewarded."

Then he was gone. His wagons and those of his cabinet disappeared down the muddy road, carrying with them records of the new government and heavy hearts. Other wagons soon followed them, and the little town was left lonely and desolate. Ned and Stump left the house, and went down to the edge of the yard that surrounded it, where their horses were tethered to posts.

Twilight was coming now, and the abandoned town was in deep stillness. They thought they were alone, but Ned presently saw a ray of light from a window. He knew that it was made by a candle burning inside, but as all the other people had gone away in the day it was obvious that it had been lighted by someone who was taking no part in the flight.

Ned's curiosity was greatly aroused. He walked toward the low frame building and he saw painted over the doorway the sign: "The Harrisburg Telegraph." Other words added that it was the greatest newspaper in Texas and the southwest. Ned called to Stump and the two, pushing open the door, entered.

They found themselves in a large room, the counterpart of many weekly newspaper offices in the more isolated regions of the United States. In one corner stood a small hand press. The floor was littered with old newspapers, "exchanges," which had come mostly by water and land from New Orleans. On a desk was a pot of paste, a large pair of scissors and some clippings. There was a chair at the desk but it was vacant. Some of the windows had been broken and greased paper had been pasted over the holes. In the corner of the room, opposite the press, stood several printers' cases and over three of the cases bent men, hard at work, setting type. Over each case burned a candle, and the printers did not look up, as Ned and Stump entered.

It was a startling and incongruous scene. It seemed that for all they knew or cared Santa Anna and his men might be a thousand miles away.

Ned walked across the floor and tapped the oldest of the printers on the shoulder. The man looked up.

"What do you want?" he asked.

"Don't you know that Santa Anna and the Mexicans are expected at any moment, and that all except you three are gone?"

"You and your friend have not gone."

"No, but we are scouts and we have good horses at hand. We can escape easily."

"I do not know that Santa Anna is coming," said the man. "We have heard before that he was coming, but he did not come. We have type to set that will take us until midnight. It was given to us by the president himself and it must be done. Who has seen Santa Anna?"

"My friend here and I both saw him," said Ned, with great emphasis. "We saw him and his army this side of the Brazos, marching straight upon this town. You must go at once. Why, the president, himself, who gave you that manuscript to set, has gone. I repeat to you that, saving ourselves, you are alone in this town and Santa Anna is at hand."

"It's in my mind to finish this job," the man said to the others. "Do you want to stay with me?"

The two nodded and went on setting type. The older printer resumed his task also and paid no further attention to his visitors. Ned urged them again to go, but the only answer they got was from the same man, who said:

"You mean well, and we thank you, but we intend to stay and finish the job. You can make yourselves at home here, if you want to do so, as the editor and proprietor have run away. You'll find New Orleans papers not more than two weeks old, and some from St. Louis not over three weeks."

"I'll take some from New Orleans, if you don't mind," said Ned, gathering up a half dozen and sticking them inside his jacket, "but while we thank you for your hospitality we can't stay. Won't you listen to one last word of caution?"

The man shook his head and Ned and Stump went out.

CHAPTER 9

AHEAD OF SANTA ANNA

It was about nine o'clock, and outside the same deep stillness held the town. Ned, looking back, saw again the faint light from the windows of the newspaper office. He could imagine the men inside, bent over the cases and silently setting type. Stump shook his head.

"I don't understand it," he said. "Seems to me that job could wait. Even if I knew how to set type a timid man like me would shake so hard that he'd throw the alphabet all over the floor."

"It would surely be a hard test," said Ned, "but maybe they don't know Santa Anna as well as we do. I vote we go out a little distance, and see if he is coming."

The two rode nearly a quarter of a mile along the road which they knew Santa Anna would follow, but as yet they saw nothing. The wind moaned across the prairie and through the timber, but it did not bring the clank of the cannon or the rattle of bayonets. Nor could they see anything moving in the dimness. Behind them the town itself was lost in the shadows, and they seemed to be wholly alone once more in the black wilderness.

"Not a sound to hear and not a thing to see," said Stump, "but he'll come just the same."

"As surely as the dark follows the day," said Ned, "and he will be in Harrisburg, too, before those printers finish that job. You know the way down to Galveston Island, don't you, Stump? We've got to secure our line of retreat."

"Don't you bother about that. I can lead you all right. I s'pose we'd better walk our horses back to this deserted town an' wait."

They rode slowly into Harrisburg, and still heard no sound on the road by which the invader would come. But the candles yet burned in the office of the Telegraph. Everything else was in darkness. Ned and Stump rode quietly about, but they did not disturb the printers again. They had fresh supplies of ammunition and food, and felt ready to dare any new peril if it were thrust in their way.

It was nearly ten o'clock when they saw a faint light far out on the road from the Brazos. The two beheld it at the same time, and they knew in an instant what it meant.

"It's Santa Anna," said Ned.

"True," said Stump, "an' he an' his force are comin' fast. Now you can hear the beat of their horses' hoofs. In five minutes they'll be here. I think you an' me'd better retire, Ned. I hope he won't hang or shoot them printers the moment he takes 'em."

"Maybe he won't," said Ned. "He may think they will be valuable for exchange. There the Mexicans are now. Don't you see them by the torch that one of them carries?"

"Yes," said Stump, as they rode softly toward the far edge of the town.

In fact it was Santa Anna himself at the head of a chosen detachment. Knowing that the members of the Texan government were in Harrisburg, practically undefended, he strained every nerve to capture them. Deep was his rage when he found that all were gone, save the three printers whom he took at their cases. He would have had them killed, but, in accordance with Ned's hopeful surmise, he considered them useful for exchange, and spared their lives for the present. They were lucky enough to be retaken later.

Feeling that it was useless to continue the pursuit that night Santa Anna waited until his cavalry under Almonte and Urrea came up. Then he found quarters in the house which President Burnet and his cabinet had left not many hours before, and by midnight his whole force, cavalry, infantry and cannon, was gathered in Harrisburg.

Ned and Stump meanwhile were watching from a bit of forest just beyond the edge of the town. They saw the lights coming and going, and now and then the figures of passing Mexicans. The two were on their horses, ready for flight at a moment's notice, but they soon saw that Santa Anna would go no further until the next day.

"I guess he an' his men are wore out by their long day's march," said Stump, "an' as it is now about midnight, they'll rest."

"But we can look for him in the morning," said Ned. "He won't be satisfied with the capture of Harrisburg. The taking of the nest after the bird has flown will mean little to him."

"Then carryin' out the task that we've chose to do, it means that we must keep on watchin'?"

"That's just it. I propose, Stump, that you and I spend the rest of the night somewhere near Harrisburg, but not near enough to be taken by any scouting cavalry of Urrea or Almonte."

"It's likely that we can find an abandoned cabin somewhere near in the woods, as everybody has run away." They found such a cabin about a half mile from the town on a hill rather higher than usual and girdled with trees. They could see from it the Mexican lights in Harrisburg, but they were in total darkness themselves. They tethered the horses as usual, and, as Ned insisted upon keeping the first watch, Stump went inside, lay down on the floor in his blankets, and was soon asleep.

There was a wooden bench beside the front door of the cabin, and Ned sat there, with his back against the wall and his rifle across his knees. He was neither sleepy nor tired, tension and excitement sustaining him both physically and mentally. Hence it was a long time before his mind and body relaxed. But the silence and the darkness were compelling influences at last.

The tension relaxed, but with its relaxation came sobering thought. He and his comrade, in reality, were fugitives keeping just ahead of a leader and an army that swept everything before them. Ned looked back to those brilliant days when the Texans, himself among them, had taken San Antonio, the seat of the Mexican power in the north. It was all victory and glory then, but how brief had been that time! Santa Anna had come and nothing had been able to resist his overwhelming march.

Ned's heart swelled with bitterness. He had been taught that it was Christian not to hate, but Santa Anna appeared to him a very king of Hades. He had seen him in his evil hour of triumph. He had seen how barren he was of mercy or of consideration for a gallant but defeated foe. How could he keep from hating such an enemy?

He saw three or four lights in the town, doubtless the flame of fires built by Santa Anna's troops, but, around the cabin, the silence and desolation remained complete. The sky seemed heavy and low. But a few stars twinkled in it. Fog and mist rose from the damp earth.

Ned's position on the bench, with his back against the wall was comfortable. After the first half hour, as the heavy damp of the night was chilly, he had wrapped his blanket about his body, bringing warmth and making the wall softer to his back. While he let the past year, which seemed many years, so crowded was it with great events, run vaguely through his mind, he did not forget to watch well with eye and ear.

Ned did not move. In the darkness of the night the keenest eye would scarcely have noticed his dark figure against the dark wall. He had learned in Mexico how to rest completely, how to sit absolutely still like the Hindoo, and let the world pass.

Something stirred in the bushes. He merely slid his hand down to the hammer of his rifle, but only arm and hand moved. His body remained blurred against the dark wall. A figure, made gigantic by the dim moonlight, came from the bushes and was followed by another and then others. Ned did not yet stir. It was only a herd of cattle wandering now without masters. They passed on and were lost in the bush. He wondered if their rightful owners would ever come back to claim them.

His despondent mood passed after a while. Surely the tide must turn some day. The Texans were a valiant people. None more so. Great things had been said of Houston, and he had done great things in the past. He must be somewhere, out there in the darkness, gathering an army to meet this terrible Santa Anna.

But Ned, all unconscious, took his own experiences as a good omen. He had escaped everything. He had passed through all kinds of dangers. The sword was always turned aside, just when it was about to fall and he was here, free, armed and strong. If it should happen so to him why should it not happen so to Texas. Still unknowing, he was ascribing to himself the qualities that the great hunters and scouts had already given to him, those of the magic leader.

It was beyond the appointed hour when he called his comrade to take his turn at the watch. Stump looked up at the heavens, and sniffed the air as if he could tell the time by its quality.

"It's not more'n a couple of hours or so till daylight, an' you've let me sleep too long, Ned," he said.

"I wasn't sleepy," replied the boy, "and it has been so quiet here that I've been getting almost as much rest awake as you were asleep."

"Then nothin' has been goin' on?"

"A herd of cattle passed. That was all. The Mexican fires in the town have sunk pretty low, but you can see them yet. I suppose that the soldiers are asleep all about them."

"Like as not, but now you go into the cabin, spread out your blankets an' sleep. You may think you're made out of steel, Ned, but you ain't. Nobody is—unless maybe it's the Ring Tailed Panther."

Ned slept quickly, and when he awoke he saw that it had been day several hours. Stump explained.

"The Mexicans in Harrisburg," he said, "haven't moved, an' so we didn't have to move either. I let you sleep on, as you wasn't needed yet."

"It is now eleven o'clock at least," said Ned. "What do you suppose has kept Santa Anna in the town?"

"Perhaps some of his army didn't come up last night an' he's waitin' for the rest of it."

"Have you seen anything of Almonte's cavalry?"

"The cavalry haven't stirred either. I've been keepin' my eye out for Almonte and Urrea. Our horses, saddled and bridled, are hitched just behind the house, an' the provisions are strapped to the saddles, too. We could leave in thirty seconds."

They decided to stay at the cabin, until they saw some movement in the town. The two sat side by side on the bench, watching and listening. They did not speak for an hour or more, and then Ned, pointing toward the town, said:

"See, Stump, what kind of a war Santa Anna is making upon us. He means nothing but destruction and death for Texans."

A long flame shot up, and then stood out, like a red spear against the golden sky. Another and then many others rose, and by and by

624

they seemed to blend. Stump sighed.

"It's a pity," he said, "to see what cost so much work vanish in the smoke of an hour. But as you say, it's Santa Anna's way."

Burning Harrisburg was now one mass of flame. It was the order of Santa Anna to spare nothing and his men obeyed gladly. The wind picked up sparks and brands, and carried them as far as the cabin before which Ned and Stump sat. Ned fancied that he could hear the roaring of the flames. He knew that the entire town was gone. It was another charge in the Texan bill of vengeance, if the day of accounts should ever come.

"There's Santa Anna an' his army south of the town," said Stump. "See 'em all drawed up, most of 'em mounted an' with the cannon in front of 'em. Ned, I wish I had a cannon bigger than any cannon that was ever made, loaded with ten thousand pounds of broken steel an' iron in all shapes an' sizes, an' trained straight on that Mexican army, so it couldn't miss. Then, Ned, I'd touch it off. I'd touch it off, lingerin'ly an' lovin'ly, in order to make the pleasure last, 'cause it would be a bigger an' keener pleasure than any that I've ever yet had in my life."

"I don't blame you, Stump," said Ned, whose feeling against Santa Anna quickly rose again. "You'd take many lives with that monster cannon of yours, but you'd probably save many more. They're marching now, headed south, and I fancy that Santa Anna still expects to take the president and his cabinet."

"Maybe he will unless they are warned to push on still faster."

"And it is for us to give the warning."

They sprang upon their horses, and, keeping well in the timber, undertook a circuit about the Mexican army. Stump thought it likely that the fleeing Texans would stop first at the village of New Washington, and, if they did so, Santa Anna would almost surely overtake them.

"The president has got a house near that village," said Stump, "an' of course he'll stop to take his family away. Ned, it makes me shiver from the top of my head down to my toes to think of what may happen."

"But your shivering won't keep you from doing the utmost that any man can do."

They rode now at great speed and the spirits of both rose with action. They expected to complete their half circle and be in front of Santa Anna in a short time.

"He must have nigh a thousand men," said Stump, "an' the speed of two, tryin' just the same, is at least twice that of a thousand. Besides, there's the cannon which will sink deep in the soft earth."

But they were compelled to make a wider curve than they had expected. Santa Anna had a numerous and efficient cavalry under Almonte, with Urrea and others as capable lieutenants. The horsemen spread out on either wing of the main army, guarding the flanks and examining the country, not so much for fear of any foe numerous enough to be dangerous, as from a desire to snap up Texan fugitives who may have lingered too long.

Ned and Stump were forced to draw away much further, and they were thankful that their horses were so swift and enduring. The risk was great, but nevertheless they still hung on the flank of the Mexican cavalry. Once they were sighted by Urrea's command, and a trumpet sounded pursuit.

"We'll gallop through the woods straight away from them," said Stump. "Urrea can't tell who you are at this distance, an' he'll think we're just stragglers, waitin' a little late to get out of the way."

Stump's surmise was correct. The cavalry did not follow them far through the timber, presently turning at a sharp angle, and riding toward the main road to rejoin Santa Anna. When they were out of sight, Ned and Stump turned at the same angle and followed. They advanced somewhat slowly, as there was danger that the cunning Urrea would lay an ambush. Fortunately the timber while heavy proved to have little undergrowth, and as the eyes of both were keen they soon increased their pace.

"Here goes Urrea's trail," said Stump. "Look how his horses' hoofs have torn up the soft earth. We ought to strike his junction with Santa Anna in another mile."

Stump was right again. In a few minutes they came to the place where the two trails joined, and led on as one. It lay before them straight and wide, hundreds of footprints and hoof-prints, cut by the deep ruts made by cannon and wagon wheels.

"Now, Stump," said Ned, "I think we'd better try to get ahead again, don't you?"

"Ke-rect. Come on!"

They curved deep into the timber and rode at a rapid pace once more. In a half hour, they caught sight of moving heads and heard the hum of a marching army. They drew a little nearer, and plainly saw the forces of Santa Anna toiling through the mud, but making good time, nevertheless. Santa Anna rode near the head of the line. They could not recognise his figure at the distance, but they knew him by his great white horse.

"Where is this place, New Washington?" asked Ned. "Is it on a river?"

"No, it's on the edge of Galveston Bay. Like as not the President and the cabinet will take ship there for the island."

"It would seem the natural course."

Then Ned suddenly uttered a gasp of alarm.

"Do you see? Do you notice?" he exclaimed.

"Do I see? Do I notice what?"

"The cavalry of Almonte is gone. Only a few lancers are marching there with the army. What does it mean, Stump? What does it mean?"

"The cavalry gone?" said Stump in bewilderment. "Why, we saw their trail come back and join that of Santa Anna. But, by thunder, they're gone, as shore as we're livin'. What does it mean?"

Now the meaning came swiftly to Ned.

"Knowing that there is no force to resist him," he said, "Santa Anna has detached Almonte and the cavalry and has sent them on at speed to capture our government. Now, Stump, we've got to ride."

"You're right, Ned! You're right both ways! It's bound to mean that Almonte's galloped on ahead, an' it means that we've got to ride for Texas."

They spoke sharply to their horses, shook out their reins, and sped ahead, keeping about a quarter of a mile distant on the flank of Santa Anna's army. They took no precautions to hide themselves from any possible skirmishers thrown out by Santa Anna. They knew that they could leave behind anything in that army, and it was time to hasten, paying no attention to trifles. Haste! Haste! And ever more haste! The fate of the republic might turn upon an extra ounce of speed! Truly Santa Anna had been crafty and far-seeing to send forward Almonte and the swift horsemen!

They did not spare their horses now. "Hurry! Hurry! Hurry!" rang incessantly in Ned's ears. He strained his eyes for a sight of Almonte's waving plumes and saw nothing. He looked back, and caught a bare glimpse of a great white horse, bearing the little dark figure of the Napoleon of the West.

That fleeting glimpse incited him to greater endeavour. He not only wished to save his own, but the desire to thwart Santa Anna became a passion, a fever. He and Stump would accomplish it, even if it

627

were thrice impossible. He spoke sharply to his horse again, and the good mustang leaped forward.

"Not so fast! Not so fast!" said Stump, warningly. "We can't afford for our horses to spend themselves so soon. What's got in you, Ned?"

The boy recalled himself. He saw that he was letting his passion run away with him, and he pulled his willing mustang in to a lower rate of speed.

"I was thinking of something," he replied.

Stump glanced curiously at him, but said nothing. It may be that the shortened Hercules guessed what was passing in Ned's mind.

"When there's so much dependin' on a race always nurse your horse for the last spurt," he said. "Look! See, the lance heads shinin' on top of that hill ahead of us! It's the men of Almonte! They're goin' fast, but we'll pass 'em yet! I tell you, Ned. we'll pass 'em!"

Ned saw the shining lances for only a few moments, and then they were gone over the brow of the hill. But it was Almonte's cavalry, beyond a doubt, and now he and Stump knew how they stood.

"It's goin' to be touch an' go," said Stump. "We've got to pass around 'em, but we needn't take a big curve. They're in such a hurry that they won't have time to pay any attention to us. I know just how much speed there is in these two ponies of our'n, Ned, an' if nothin' out of the way happens we ought to beat Almonte into New Washington by about fifteen minutes."

"That's cutting terribly close," said Ned.

"But it may be edge enough."

They swung in a little nearer to the Mexicans, but a line of trees between sheltered them from view. Their horses were running strong and true, and despite Almonte's speed were surely drawing level.

"Another fifteen minutes an' we're up with 'em!" said Stump.

"A second fifteen, and we're ahead!" said Ned.

"Now we can let 'em out a little more," said Stump.

They urged their horses anew, and their speed increased. Galloping on a parallel line with Almonte's troop they saw them on even terms, within the fifteen minutes allowed by Stump. Then they drew ahead, and when a long narrow hill, covered with thick timber, intervened between them and the Mexicans they curved back toward the direct road to New Washington.

"If we come out well ahead of Almonte," said Stump, "we don't care whether they see us or not, because it's goin' to be a race from now on to the town, an' Almonte can't go any faster. The speed of his slowest horses is the speed of them all."

The wood lasted a mile, and when they came out into the main road, they saw the lances of Almonte a quarter of a mile behind them. It seemed that fortune was showing to the Texans at least one little favour. Before them lay a stretch of level country, and now the wisdom of Stump in nursing the strength of their horses became apparent. They heard presently the echo of a cry behind them, and they knew that the Mexicans had seen them. It was obvious also that the Mexicans would take them to be messengers of warning.

"They are trying to increase their speed," said Ned, "I see them beating their horses! Ah, a score or so of horsemen shoot out from the group, and they are led by a man whom I know from his figure to be Urrea!"

"They are sendin' forward their swiftest," said Stump, "an' as you say they're about twenty, but they can't catch us. But if our people at Harrisburg haven't gone they may catch them."

"Shouldn't we go a little faster? The horses can do better than this."

"Not yet. We'll nurse 'em ag'in, an' then we'll let 'em out to the last link. Urrea an' his twenty are not gainin' on us. Our mounts are better than theirs."

They settled down now into a long, easy stride, and rode knee to knee. The day was now more brilliant than any other in weeks. The sunshine filtered like molten gold through the trees, and deepened the tints of the grass. A fresh breeze with the strong tingling flavour of salt, the very breath of life, blew in their faces, and Ned knew that it came from the sea. They must be near the town now.

"Isn't it time to let out that last link?" he asked. "I feel the sea on my face, and when we reach the town we want to be as far ahead of Urrea as possible."

"Right you are. You've chose the moment, Ned. Now for runnin' that is runnin'!"

Stump rode a large and very powerful horse—he needed one for his great weight—and at the crisis had talked to him, soothing, encouraging and flattering. The good horse responded nobly, and Ned's mustang, with the lighter weight upon his back, kept by his side. The two fairly ran away from Urrea. Ned and Stump could no longer hear the shouting of the Mexicans, and when they looked back they saw no lancers. The pursuit had been lost behind the swells.

But the two horsemen did not abate a particle of their speed. They had divined that every second was precious, and the gallant horses always responded to their urging. They were wet with foam, but their spirit was as strong as that of those they bore. The air rushed past, and Ned felt that stinging flavour of the sea grow stronger and stronger. The scattered roofs of houses appeared and between them the glitter of a bay. Then all the little village sprang into view and Stump uttered a cry of disappointment.

"Look! Look!" he cried. "See the sailin' ship in the bay, an' the men loadin' things on her! The Texans haven't gone, an' in ten minutes Almonte's men will be here!"

"It is so," said Ned, "and that is President Burnet himself standing on the wharf! But the town seems abandoned. All have gone but these!"

"Yes, but think what such a capture will mean! How under the sun could they have delayed so long?"

President Burnet had not foreseen the swift march of Almonte. He lived near by, and he had lingered to take off his family and some of their effects in a little sailing vessel, which would carry them down the bay to Galveston. The last of their baggage was going aboard as Ned and Stump on their foaming horses galloped up, shouting:

"Almonte's horsemen are at hand! You have not a minute to spare! Be off! Be off!"

It was no time to be respectful, even to a president, and they repeated their urgings over and over again. The sails of the vessel were up, the wind had filled them, and she was straining at her cable, but President Burnet delayed yet another moment.

"And you!" he cried. "Jump from your horses and come with us!"

"No, we can escape down the side of the bay!" cried Stump. "There's still a good run in our horses! Don't stop another minute! It's for Texas! Look, the Mexicans are here already!"

They heard the rapid beat of hoofs and Urrea's horsemen appeared in the town, setting up a great shout of triumph, when they saw the men on the wharf, and the vessel still tied to it. Behind them quickly appeared other Mexican cavalry, showing that the full force of Almonte was at hand.

"For God's sake go!" cried Ned.

Seeing that the two would not come with him Burnet leaped aboard the vessel, and, snatching up a hatchet, cut the cable with his own hand. The vessel slowly began to move, and the water appeared between her and the wharf. But the foremost of Almonte's horsemen under Urrea were almost at the sea's edge. As the vessel slid away and her speed began to increase they opened fire from their saddles with rifles and muskets.

The president, standing upon the little deck, was within easy range and fully exposed. It was well for him and Texas that day that Ned and Stump had galloped in with their warning, and well for them, too, that the Mexicans were poor marksmen. Bullets struck upon the deck. One hit the mast, others clipped spars or went through sails, but the president stood untouched. Ned and Stump gasped more than once, thinking he would surely fall, but the eagerness and haste of the Mexicans made them wilder than ever in their shooting. Urrea had galloped to the very edge of the water, and was firing his pistols. Almonte was also at hand now, urging on his men.

The sails stretched taut with the wind, and the speed of the little vessel increased fast. The bullets were still striking upon her, but that stretch of water between her and the shore was growing wide. The Mexicans were now firing fast. One more bullet struck upon the deck, and then there were many little jets of foam, when they fell in the water. The little vessel passed out of range. The Mexicans upon the bank, raged and watched the figure which still stood erect upon the deck, but beyond their reach.

"I don't suppose there was ever a closer call than that," said Ned to Stump.

"I reckon somethin' must have been helpin' us to get here just in time," said Stump, gravely, "an' now that we've done what we came to do it's movin' time for you an' me."

They had ridden behind a small warehouse from which they could observe both the flight of the boat and the Mexicans. But they knew that the place would not hide them long, as Almonte's men would now begin to rage through the little port. Hence they rode boldly away from the bay. Their horses were tired, but not more so than those of the Mexicans, and they felt sure that they could make good their flight.

They were not seen until they reached the crest of a little hill. Then the Mexicans set up a shout, and, pursued for a little distance, but soon gave it up. Their worn horses would go no further.

"Our horses are just a little better than theirs," said Stump, "but that little bit saves us. I guess the little bit is all the difference there is between a common man and a great one."

"But we'd better be improving that little bit into a large one," said

Ned. "As soon as his horses have recovered, Almonte is sure to send out troopers looking for us."

"We'll dive into the woods," said Stump. "The forest is the best refuge when you're not strong enough to fight. S'pose we ride into that grove of cottonwoods. We can rest there a while an' at the same time keep a watch for anybody who may be comin'."

It was a splendid grove, and they were well hidden among the trunks, where they dismounted, and rubbed down their horses, as well as they could. They owed much to these gallant animals and they meant to take the best possible care of them. While they were engaged in the task they caught glimpses of the bay through the trees and they saw afar upon it a black speck which seemed to be without motion. But it was moving, nevertheless. It was the little sailing vessel, which, in a sense, carried the fortunes of Texas. Certainly the capture of the republic's president would have been a crushing blow, following so close upon other great disasters.

They were left so thoroughly alone in the cottonwood grove that they remained there a long time. They could hear no sound from the distant town, nor did they see any spire of flame to indicate that the Mexicans were burning it. Ned thought it likely that Santa Anna would not reach it until the next morning and Almonte, who was a humane and enlightened man, would not destroy the port, unless the dictator ordered it.

"I propose," said Ned, "that we hang about here and watch what Santa Anna does. They have no need for us on Galveston Island. The government can take care of itself now. We've got to work for Houston. We're only two, but even two count. And then we can look soon for the Panther and that crowd from down below."

"You talk sense, Ned," said Stump approvingly. "We'll hang on to Santa Anna. There's lots of forest 'roun' here. We'll go further on an' sleep in a thicket."

They left the grove, and passed through country, part of which was cultivated, coming finally to the deeper forest. They selected a hilly point in it, from which they could get a distant view of New Washington, and there made their camp. They reasoned that if they saw a fire at the port it was proof that Almonte was burning it and moving on; if not, it was proof that he was resting there, and awaiting the arrival of Santa Anna.

They saw no flames, and relaxed, lying on their blankets under the trees. As usual there was grass, and the horses grazed in content at the end of their lariats. Food of their own they still had in plenty and they ate it cold. When night, soothing and without rain, came Ned kept the first watch, and Stump the second. Nothing to disturb them occurred during either watch.

Chapter 10

Old Comrades Again

Ned and Stump were awake and about early the next morning. The good sleep had restored strength to their bodies and nerves. The horses having grazed to their full content were lying peaceably at the ends of their lariats. The two ate breakfast, and, then measuring their food, calculated that they had enough left for twenty-four hours. Something ought to happen within that time.

Ned climbed one of the tallest trees, and, while Stump stood guard below, he took a good view of the little port.

"What do you see?" Stump called up.

"I see horse, foot and a cannon arriving in New Washington. At the head of them is a big white horse which carries a little man in a brilliant military uniform. I cannot see his face or tell much about his figure, but I know that he is Santa Anna."

"So he has joined Almonte, has he? I think, Ned, that he will send for the rest of his men under Sesma, wait until they join him, and then march against Houston."

"So do I, and that being the case I'll come down. Then we'll ride for Houston, wherever he may be."

The two, a-horse once more, rode in a wide circle around the little port that now contained the Mexican leader and his army, passed by the ruins of Harrisburg and around the bayou on which it was located and to the other side. But they had been only partially right in their guess. It was true that Santa Anna had sent back to Sesma, but he had directed his brother-in-law, General Cos, who was with Sesma, to come up as fast as possible with the pick of the rear guard. Santa Anna intended then, with the combined forces, to reach Galveston Island, and yet capture the Texan Government. He would bring up ships and boats, and he was sanguine of success.

Thus the Texans and Mexicans were moving for the present in ignorance of the plans of each other, but circumstances more powerful than the will of either Santa Anna, Houston, Burnet or any one else would soon draw them together. Ned and Stump rode hard. They met a scout, sent south, who told them that Houston lay northward near the San Jacinto River, that his force was very small, and that there had been great dissension among the leaders. The more fiery spirits among the Texans had been upbraiding Houston with his unwillingness to fight.

Baker and Martin, after their unsuccessful attempt to hold the ferries, had returned, wild with anger against the Texan leaders. Their companies had refused for a long time to go into line with the rest of the army. They were borderers, free of speech and action, and as they could not be coerced Martin and his command were sent to the region along the Trinity to face the Indians, who were threatening an attack on the flank of the Texan settlements. This had reduced the little army still further, but, nevertheless, it was marching south toward Santa Anna.

"We've had a terrible time," said the scout, whose name was Redding. "The news that Santa Anna had reached the Brazos was brought to Houston eleven days ago, an' it made a big stir, I can tell you. The general issued a proclamation, telling us that the crisis was at hand. He told us to remember the Alamo and Goliad. Then we prepared ourselves for the enemy but we did not know just where he was. A week ago two cannon, sent all the way from Cincinnati, reached us. It was said that a great merchant raised most of the money for them, and he has come with them into camp."

"Was his name Roylston, John Roylston?" exclaimed Ned.

"Yes, that's it. He's with Houston, and he joined the others in urging him to fight. We didn't have ammunition for the cannon, but we made it. We've cut up horseshoes and every kind of old iron that we could find. We've tied these pieces in bags, and we mean to spray the Mexicans with them just as if they were shrapnel or canister. The day after the cannon came we learned, for sure, that Santa Anna and his army had crossed the Brazos. So we crossed ourselves on the steamer *Yellowstone*."

"And then?" said Ned, with the most intense interest.

"Four days ago our army started to the south to meet Santa Anna. But it don't look like an army. It's covered with mud. The marching is awful. The horses' feet sink deep in the mire. The wagons go down to the hub. The cannon do the same. Why, I saw General Houston himself get off his horse and push at one of the cannon wheels."

"When did you leave the army?" asked Ned.

"Three days ago."

"For what point was it making?"

"For Buffalo Bayou, just across the bayou from Harrisburg."

"Harrisburg has been burned by Santa Anna," said Ned. "We saw it done."

Redding set his teeth.

"One more notch on the stick to remember," he said. "I tell you, fellows, there's going to be a bad time, when Santa Anna and the Texans come together. Our men back there are now just mad to get at him. So much blood has been shed, and so many of our people have been massacred by the Mexicans that you can't hold 'em any longer. Maybe Houston was right in keeping back so long, but that time is over."

"Does Houston know that Santa Anna himself is here?" asked Ned.

"No, but when you tell him it will make the men wilder than ever to get at him. I have to stay here to watch, but if you keep straight on you ought to reach our army before dark."

"We'll make it," said Ned. He and Stump shook Redding's hand and resumed their ride over the prairie. Their eagerness to reach Houston was now intense, yet their progress became slow. Here, the country seemed to be in even worse condition for travelling than it was further south. The mud increased in depth, and it had a singularly waxy and tenacious character. Their horses sank in it half way to the knee, and when the hoof was pulled out the mud closed back with a sighing sound. At noon they were compelled to seek comparatively firm ground among some cottonwoods, and give their horses a long rest.

Just as they were remounting they heard the sound of a shot to the north. On the horizon they saw one figure fleeing and two others in pursuit. The figures were so far away that only eyes as keen as Ned's could tell that they were men and horses.

"It may be that it is one Texan chased by two Mexicans," said Ned.

"Not likely," said Stump. "The way our people feel now one Texan would never run from three Mexicans, much less from two."

"Then it's two Texans chasing one Mexican, and in either event we ought to take a hand. Anyway it's likely to be forced upon us as they are galloping straight in this direction. Come on, Stump!"

The two rode from the trees to the plain, and went forward at a great pace. The fugitive did not see them as he was bent over on his horse's mane, and was beating him with hands and feet, desperately urging him to greater speed. The two pursuers were within easy rifle range, and Ned and Stump now saw clearly that they were Texans. It was equally obvious that the fugitive was a Mexican.

"Hold up, Stump," said Ned, "I don't think we're needed. The Texans could shoot the man, if they cared to do it, but I suppose they want to take him alive."

"You're right, Ned," said Stump. "I can see the foremost of the Texans uncurling his long lariat from his saddle bow."

Ned gave a great start of surprise.

"Stump," he said, "I know those Texans."

"Who are they?"

"I'll tell you in a minute. Wait and see what happens."

The two Texans were gaining rapidly. Presently the one with the lariat whirled it swiftly around his head, and then threw. The fleeing Mexican heard it hiss over his head, and bent flat upon his horse's neck to escape it, but the wily Texan, foreseeing such an evasion, had thrown for the animal's head instead. The loop fell true, and, as it tightened around his throat, the horse stopped. His rider sprang to the ground and reached for a weapon, but the other Texan covered him with a rifle and he threw up his hands. The first Texan sprang to the ground, and quickly bound the prisoner's arms behind him.

Ned and Stump, who had looked silently at the capture, rode slowly forward.

"Mr. Burke," said Ned with formal politeness, "I wish to present you to two old friends of mine. Mr. Burke, Mr. Smith; Mr. Burke, Mr. Karnes."

Deaf Smith looked up in astonishment and pleasure.

"If it ain't Ned Fulton his very own self!" he cried. "Alive an' kickin'! An' old Stump, too. You needn't call him Mr. Burke, Ned. His best name and right name is Stump. We know him."

"So you do," said Stump joyously, "but Ned knew who you was first. I didn't reckernize your faces under an inch of mud. Give us your hand, Hank Karnes, you old mud horse."

Karnes shook hands with both, and grinned with pleasure.

"You think it strange to see us here, Ned," said Smith, "but just a little after you left we got uneasy an' hurried north. Hank an' me galloped on ahead an' reached Houston. As you hadn't arrived an' we didn't know what had become of you we was afraid you was dead or captured."

636

"Where are the Panther and Obed White and the rest now?" asked Ned.

"Somewhere near here on their way to Houston. Like as not they're not ten miles from this spot. Now, Ned, before we talk any further an' hear your tale, we'll examine this prisoner. We think he's a courier with messages from one Mexican general to another."

Smith turned to the Mexican who had been standing by with his arms bound. The prisoner when he saw that he was about to be searched broke away and started to run, but a raised rifle and a stern command stopped him.

"We're not goin' to murder you," said Smith in Mexican. "We're not like Santa Anna's cutthroats, but we're goin' to see what you have on you. Make up your mind to that and stand still."

The Mexican stopped, and Smith went through his clothes deftly. He took none of the Mexican's personal belongings, but when he drew from an inside pocket a strong buckskin bag, and felt of it he knew that his search had been rewarded. He cut it open with his hunting knife and exposed papers.

"Ned," he said, "you're the best Spanish an' Mexican scholar among us. Just open these an' read 'em out aloud. Everybody here is to be trusted."

Ned took the papers and read them one by one. There were many dispatches from officers in the City of Mexico and from General Filisola. They told of conditions in the capital, and in that part of Texas overrun by the Mexicans. They spoke confidently of General Santa Anna's speedy crushing of the rebels, and of his return in triumph to his capital.

"An' so," said Smith to the courier, "Santa Anna is here with his army. We did not know for sure, where he was. Some said that he had gone back to Mexico."

The Mexican, knowing now that his life would be spared, looked defiantly at Smith and said: "I will not answer."

"It is not necessary for him to answer," said Ned. "Santa Anna is down the bayou at New Washington with his own troops. Stump and I have seen him more than once in the last few days, and we saw him as late as this morning. We cannot be mistaken."

"Then I guess that's settled," said Smith. "So much the better! I'm glad Santa Anna is with his army. When we strike at the wolves we want to strike hard, too, at the king wolf of them all. Now, Ned, tell us your story."

Ned ran over his tale rapidly, but he could not tell it without tell-ing of the remarkable way in which he had escaped so many dangers. More than once in the story, Smith and Karnes glanced at each other and muttered under their breath: "He is chose, he is certainly chose."

"Hank an' me have got to go straight back to Houston with this prisoner and his dispatches," said Smith. "If you an' Stump want to come along we'll be glad of your company, but maybe you'd rather cut across country an' join the Panther an' the rest of our crowd as they come up. If you ride to the north an' east you're sure to meet 'em or strike their trail."

"I think we'd better join the Panther," said Ned, and Stump also signified his assent. Then Smith and Karnes put the prisoner on his horse and rode away with him and the dispatches.

"This is big news, Stump," said Ned. "It looks to me as if things were beginning to draw to a head. I'm glad the Panther and the oth-ers grew impatient and started north so soon. They came just when they are needed."

"An' there go Smith an' Karnes an' their prisoner," said Stump. "Look how fast they ride. They are shorely eatin' up the trail to Hou-ston's camp. Now they look like nothin' but dwarfs; now they're littler than dwarfs; now they're gone."

"They've cause to ride fast," said Ned. "Houston will be wanting to know what they have to tell, and you and I, too, Stump, ought to be driving the same way, if we expect to catch the Panther."

Turning at a slight angle from their original course they rode north and east through a country partly prairie and partly wooded, searching all the while for the sight of horsemen. Much of the region through which they rode was flooded, and they were continually crossing brooks swollen almost to rivers and wide lagoons, where in summer not a drop of water would be seen.

Both Ned and Stump kept a sharp watch for trails, and they saw several, but in every case it was the track made by a single horseman, until at last they came to one of width where many hoofs had trod. They followed it for a little space and came to a herd of cattle grazing on one of the prairies, ownerless and wandering as they pleased, new evidence that fire and sword had swept through the land.

They turned back to their original course, and, about the middle of the afternoon, Ned saw afar a single figure on a swell of the prairie, outlined distinctly against the western horizon which was a blaze of red from the declining sun. It was so distant that it seemed nothing more than a black dot, but as Ned watched it his heart began to leap. It was moving and the tiny black figure seemed to suggest something familiar.

As he and Stump watched, another figure appeared behind the first on the swell, then a third, a fourth, and more. The horsemen rode in Indian file and the steadiness with which they kept on indicated that they knew where they intended to go.

"Either it's Mexicans, some band sent out by Santa Anna," said Stump, "or it's them that we're lookin' for. It makes me shiver to run the risk of a mistake, but I guess we've got to ride forward an' see who they are."

"Your shivering won't hurt you, Stump. I notice that it never does. We'll go straight toward that line of men, and unless I make a big mistake we'll find friends and not foes."

Ned rode forward boldly, and Stump rode by his side with equal boldness, scanning the black line with the greatest curiosity and interest. The horsemen were now standing out more clearly on the prairie and Ned counted fifty-two.

"'Pears to me," said Stump, "that the fellow leadin' is a big man."

"He is a big man, Stump, a very big one. You can see now that he rides a very big horse, also. Only a horse of the greatest size could carry such a man. Notice his breadth of shoulder and chest. I should say, Stump, that he is the only man in Texas who is stronger than you are."

"It's only 'cause he's taller, which makes him heavier an' gives him a wider sweep," said Stump quickly. "I ain't so sure that he could lift more than I can, 'cause I stand mighty close to the ground, an' I don't have to pull from so great a height."

"Then we are agreed as to the identity of this striking figure?"

"We are. It's the Ring Tailed Panther an' nobody else."

"It is surely he, and the man behind him, whom you do not know but whom I do, the one with the long body and the long legs, is Obed White, once of Maine, as brave and true a man as I ever knew. Just behind him is Will Allen, my comrade, and as you and I now see, Stump, these are the men for whom we are looking."

"An' mighty glad we are to find 'em," said Stump as they galloped from a clump of chaparral, giving a joyous shout and waving their hats in welcome.

The line of men stopped at once and faced about. When the Panther saw who was coming he opened his mouth, and emitted a mighty roar.

"If it ain't Ned Fulton!" he cried. "An' unless I'm blind the fellow with him is that sawed-off Bill Burke, whose right name is Stump and who pretends to be a strong man."

It was a joyous reunion for Ned. He rode down the line, shaking hands, and then came back by the side of the one who was of his own age, his comrade, Will Allen. All had given him the warmest of welcomes, and none was warmer than that of the Reverend Stephen Larkin. Like the rest he was in full panoply of war. The tails of his long black coat fell down on either side of his horse, but he carried a rifle across the pommel of his saddle and a pistol and other weapons were in his belt.

"Deaf Smith and Hank Karnes went on ahead," said the Panther. "Have you seen or heard anything of them?"

"We saw them both this morning," replied Ned, "and we saw them take a Mexican herald who had a buckskin bag crammed full of dispatches from General Filisola to General Santa Anna. They learned from them that Santa Anna is here in the field and they've gone with the news to Houston, but Stump and I knew it already."

He recounted once more what they had seen and the Panther roared.

"Now the time for rippin' an' t'arin' an' chawin' has come an' no mistake," he said. "By the great horn spoon we'll settle accounts some day with the Mexicans or stretch ourselves on the Texan sod."

"It was permitted to the hosts of Israel to smite the unbeliever," said the Reverend Stephen Larkin, "and since nothing else availeth we'll smite our treacherous and cruel enemy with all the strength that is in our arms."

The Panther shook his great figure in fierce joy. They were only fifty-two—fifty-four with Ned and Stump—he said, but they were all hardy, experienced, and good marksmen. They had arrived in time for the great fight that was surely coming.

"A fight in time may save nine," said Obed White soberly. "I'm thinking that we'd better hurry on to join Houston. United we stand, divided we're broken to pieces, stick by stick."

"Do you know just where Houston is?" asked the Panther.

"We can't tell exactly," replied Ned, "but we learned from Smith and Karnes that he did not cross the Brazos until Santa Anna had crossed it first and had advanced toward Harrisburg. Stump here thinks that he will be found somewhere toward the San Jacinto River."

"Looks likely," said the Panther thoughtfully. "Anyway, there's so much country here an' so few people in it that we won't hardly run across him in two or three days. The best thing for us to do is to look for a camp. We've been marchin' so long through mud an' water that mighty few of us have felt like rippin' an' roarin' an' t'arin'."

"Though my fancy often deceives me my eyes seldom do," said Obed White, "and I think I see a cottonwood grove far ahead. We're likely to find dry ground and shelter there."

"I see it, too," said the Panther, "an' we'll make for it."

But distances are deceptive in the thin clear air of Texas, and it was nearly night before they reached the wood, which proved to be of some extent, covering a broad and long hill, and composed of large, well-grown trees. Its eastern base was washed by a creek, small in dry weather but now swollen by the rains into the measure of a river. It evidently emptied into some bayou not far away.

Every man in the company felt relief when they rode among the trees. The horses even seemed to show fresh life and vigour when their hoofs pressed the firm soil. The men dismounted and quickly began to build fires. The Mexicans might be near or they might not. The Texans knew little of fear, and sometimes not much of caution. But the twilight had come and they were cold, wet, mud-bespattered and hungry. They intended to eat and be dry.

Ned and Will worked together dragging up brushwood for the fires. They were glad to be together again, but they were not demonstrative.

"Since we last met much water had flowed under the places where the bridges ought to be," said Obed White, as he joined them.

"But it has not been many days," said Ned.

"If you count them as ordinary days you're right," said Obed, "but every one of these days amounts to a week at least, and I'm thinking that we'll remember 'em as such. Meanwhile we'll seize the fleeting hour, dry ourselves and get supper. Man wants but little here below, but food and sleep are always on the list."

The fires were now burning well, and cast forth a grateful light and warmth. Many of the men had taken off their boots and sat with their upturned feet to the coals. Others as they stood within the area of drying warmth were carefully scraping the mud from their clothes. The cooks already were at work and the savour of deer, buffalo, wild turkey and smaller game came to Ned's nostrils. Evidently the men had provided themselves well before leaving Camp Independence.

Ned felt one of those great bursts of elation to which his usually calm nature was sometimes subject. He could not help it, now that he had rejoined his friends, and light and warmth were all about him. Physical and mental exaltation were at work upon him at the same time.

"Set down here, Ned, an' tell me that tale over again" said the Panther. "I want to hear for the second time about all them marvellous risks you run through without turnin' a hair, after you left us with the messages for Houston."

He moved along the fallen log, on which he was sitting and Ned took a comfortable seat there, with his back against an upthrust bough. He held in his hand a sharpened stick and on that sharpened end was a savoury piece of broiled venison. He might have stood, or rather sat, as an emblem of supreme content. But at the request of the Panther he went over the story again, suppressing himself as much as possible and dilating rather upon circumstances. Obed White sat on the other side of the log and listened carefully.

Both the Panther and Obed were silent, as Ned talked, and they were also silent for a little while, after he had left them and joined Will Allen.

"We was right, back there in the woods at Camp Independence," the Panther at length said solemnly. "You'll notice, Obed, that whenever he gets into trouble he gets out ag'in. Now, it seems more than nateral that he should have got out of prison in the City of Mexico the way he did an' should have come so far an' through so much without turnin' a hair. Don't he always turn up, too, jest in time to tell us where we ought to go an' what we ought to do? An' it ain't always 'cause he's aimin' to do it. It's 'cause he's driv to it. He shorely is chose. He's our leader without knowin' it."

"It certainly looks like it," said Obed White, in the same grave tone. "Maybe it's the dawn instead of the sunset of life that gives us mystical lore, although the one who has the mystical lore may not know that the gift is his. At any rate, he's tremendously lucky."

The news soon spread among them all that Ned carried luck with him. Borderers, like Indians, are prone to superstitions and a certain sort of fatalism. All people who are much alone in the wilderness acquire such beliefs. His manner, rather more grave than his years warranted did not invite familiarity from those who did not know him, and from this time, also, the men began to throw a guard about him. It seemed to them that in guarding him they were also guarding

642

themselves. Ned himself was interested in a lively conversation that was going on between the Panther and Stump.

Stump had taken the seat beside the Panther that Ned had left vacant, and he was measuring himself against him. Sitting, Stump was but little inferior to his mighty comrade. The huge head was only slightly smaller, the great spread of shoulders was only a little less, and the arms and hands bore the same resemblance to the paws of a grizzly bear. Yet Stump was sad.

"Panther," said he plaintively, "you an' me are about the same age, an' a great mistake was made when we was born. You got my legs. I tell you, Panther, I was cheated. I was cheated big. Them's my legs that you're wearin' now, walkin' 'roun' on every day of your life an' standin' up six feet an' a half, while cheated of my true rights I've got to walk about sawed off."

"They're my legs, Stump," said the Panther. "I've used 'em all my life an' I don't think I could do without 'em now. I'm sorry, Stump, but I've got a genooine title, made fast by possession, an' I can't give 'em up at this late day."

"I know you can't, an' that's the worst of it, but they was intended for me all the same. Look how they'd fit me an' become me. Anybody can see as we set here with shoulders almost touchin' that I'm as good a man as you are an' maybe just a leetle bit better."

"Don't you worry, Mr. Burke," said Stephen Larkin. "When it comes to riding a horse you are better built than our great friend here, Mr. Palmer. You're about as big above the saddle as he is, and you are much easier on a horse. And we have to use horses much in Texas."

"I 'low that the parson speaks the truth," said the Panther, looking at his rival contemplatively. "You're a powerful strong man, Stump, an' you wouldn't break a horse down as quick as I would."

"All the same," said Stump, "you take mighty good care of them legs when you go into battle. Remember that they belong by rights to me."

"I'll shorely do it for both our sakes," said the Panther perfectly willing to be agreeable. "Do you think, Stump, we're likely to have a brush with the Mexicans before we reach Houston?"

"Like as not. The cavalry under Almonte and Urrea is mighty active, prowlin' everywhere. Santa Anna expects to snap up Houston in a few days, an' I guess his horsemen are out in front."

"Then let 'em come," said the Panther defiantly. "We'll shoot as they shot at the Alamo. We've had a long march an' our men need a big rest which they're goin' to get right now an' here. Here, you Will Allen, you're so young and spry, rush 'roun' an' gather more brush for our fires."

The same defiant spirit animated all the men. They felt that they had been running and hiding from Mexicans long enough. They were going to rest that night, and show their colours, which for the time were furnished by great beds of coals and leaping flames. Will Allen willingly pulled up more brush and fallen boughs. Ned helped him and so did others, Stump among them. It was wonderful to see the way in which the short Hercules worked. He picked up boughs which Ned and Will together could scarcely have lifted. He was like some huge, squat wild animal crushing and tearing away in the brush. He would carry a whole log upon his shoulder and cast it among the flames. The Panther, who was not working, regarded him with admiration.

"Stump," he said, "you're shorely a mighty man. Even walkin' as I do on what you claim to be your legs, I'd hate to have to fight it out with you, shoulders and arms and fists."

Stump smiled a gratified smile.

"Them are cert'inly pleasant words comin' from a man like you, Panther," he said. "Maybe if I had been finished I wouldn't be the timid sort of fellow I am, shiverin' at every sound in the woods."

The Panther laughed deeply and heartily. He had a great regard and also a great respect for Stump. Meanwhile the fires grew fast and the flames leaped and roared. Sparks shot up and died in the air above the trees. A glorious drying warmth beat back the chill wet air of the night.

Ned felt very happy. His part of the work was finished and he was now lying on one of the blankets between two fires. Will sat Turkish fashion not far away, and they were talking of what each had seen and done in the last week. The men, all except the sentinels posted at the edge of the forest, were busy mending their clothes or cleaning their weapons. Like Will and Ned they were light-hearted and happy. It was characteristic of the borderer, a condition of his life, in fact, that he should seize the passing hour, and make as much of it as he could. It did not take much to make him happy. Often it was the mere gratification of physical needs, so easy in civilization, but many times an affair of life or death in the wilderness. For that reason they frequently took what seemed to the dwellers in sheltered regions great and rash risks.

Now the Texans beside the fires in the wood paid little heed to Santa Anna and his men. He might be near or he might be far. It was all one to them. He was, for the time, not in their thoughts. They were spending the hours in luxury and they refused to be troubled.

The Panther, who by tacit agreement was the leader, nevertheless kept a vigilant guard. Ten sentinels were posted at equal intervals along the edge of the wood, and the night was to be divided into three watches, ten men to the watch. Will Allen fell into the second watch, but Ned's time did not come until the third. It was then one o'clock in the morning and the night was dark. Ned felt the usual wet chill in the air, which the fires dispelled only within a short radius, and he saw the banks of clouds which seldom ceased to hover throughout that famous spring.

His beat was at the northern corner of the wood next to the flooded creek, and here he paced back and forth, not in quite such high spirits as he had been at the beginning of the night, when the fires were leaping and talk and laugh were passing.

It was dark, raw and a bit lonesome. He was glad when he met the sentinel next to him. But they could exchange only a word or two, each then returning on his own beat. Ned usually stopped longest at the bank of the creek. It was yellow with earth, swept away by the flood, and seemed to be at least seven or eight feet deep. There was no forest on the other side, only a ragged patch of bushes, with the bare prairie beyond.

Ned kept a close watch on the region beyond the creek, or at least as far as his eye could range. Down there, somewhere, but still in Harrisburg, no doubt, the forces of Santa Anna and Almonte lay.

The faint cry of a night bird came from some far point. The water splashed lightly against the bank, as a tree torn up by its roots, floated slowly by. He often heard little noises in the stream. So much debris was floating down that now and then it struck against the bank and the high water itself rippled and gurgled.

He heard by and by a splash a little louder than the rest, but when he looked he saw only the uneasy yellow flood, and he went back down the beat until he met the man next to him. Then he returned, walking slowly toward the creek, which here was lined thickly with bushes. He paused a moment at the brink, and then he felt a sudden chill in the blood as he heard a light step behind him.

Ned wheeled about and he was confronted by a face that he never forgot. It was yellowish, painted, and hideous with evil passions. Long black hair fell back from the low forehead, and the muscular hand, already upraised, held a long-bladed Spanish knife.

Ned knew in an instant that it was one of the Campeachy Indians whom the Mexicans had brought from the far south, as scouts and skirmishers and the splash that he had heard, had been made by the savage swimming the creek. He acted now wholly by impulse and instinct. There was no time for reason. He dropped his rifle, seized the uplifted wrist of the Indian in one hand, and grasped at his throat with the other. The Indian endeavoured to spring backward. Neither uttered a cry. They writhed in each other's grip for a moment or two, and then as the soft bank crumbled away beneath their weight they plunged head foremost into its deep and muddy water. They came up still locked fast, and instinct caused Ned to utter one piercing shout of warning. Then they sank again.

They rose for the second time, still hanging together, but the force of the current had already carried them to a point some distance beyond the camp. Ned shook the water from his eyes and saw the savage still confronting him, but more horrible than ever. Long coarse black locks hung down on either cheek and the yellow water was running from them. How it happened he never knew, but he yet clutched the wrist of the Indian's hand that held the knife. The savage was paddling with his other hand to keep himself above water.

Ned, still guided by instinct, suddenly remembered the knife at his own belt. He snatched it and then shutting his eyes struck with all his might and struck home. He heard a gurgling sigh. The wrist grew limp in his grasp and then was gone. Weak and nerveless he was barely able to keep himself afloat, and he did not remember to shout again. He was much beyond the camp now and everything was dark about him.

The creek seemed to be flowing more rapidly. He guided himself as best he could to the nearer bank which happened to be the one farther from the camp and, drawing himself up with difficulty on the farther shore, fell unconscious.

Chapter 11

The Miraculous Escape

Ned came back to consciousness, when somebody prodded him in the side with the butt of a lance. Two men in soiled Mexican uniforms were holding him up by the shoulders. Muddy water was running

SEIZED THE UPLIFTED WRIST OF THE INDIAN IN ONE
HAND, AND GRASPED AT HIS THROAT WITH THE OTHER.

from his hair and his clothing in streams, large enough to make a little pool at his feet. It was dark about him, and he knew that he could not have been unconscious more than a few minutes. Behind him he heard the sharp crack of a rifle shot and then the sound of three or four more. A moment's silence, and then came the deep thrilling note of the Texan yell. His cry had warned his comrades in time, and straightening himself he looked at those who held him.

The men who had him by either shoulder were undoubtedly Mexican regular troops. In front of him stood three more and it was one of these who had prodded him with the lance butt. Five horses held by another man were standing somewhat back of them in the bushes. Ned surmised at once that they belonged to Almonte's cavalry.

"Who are you?" asked a Mexican who looked like a petty officer.

"A Texan," replied Ned briefly.

"So I can see," said the man, glancing at his height and fair hair. "It was your cry, I think, that warned the Texans in the woods of our coming."

"I hope so and I have every reason to believe so."

"A red knife was clutched tightly in your hand when we found you."

Ned shuddered.

"I am afraid that it meant the end of one of your scouts, a Campeachy Indian," he said. "He was the ugliest fellow I ever saw, and I had to strike."

The Mexican smiled faintly.

"They are not beautiful, those Indians," he said, "and I do not grieve much because he is gone, although he and his comrades have been useful as scouts and skirmishers."

"Well," said. Ned, noticing now that all his arms had been removed from his belt, "I am your prisoner; what do you intend to do with me?"

"Take you to our captain. Bind his arms behind him, Xavier."

Ned knew that it was not worth while to resist and Xavier quickly made his arms fast, although in a manner that was not painful.

"Now, march ahead as we point," said the officer, "and I warn you that at the slightest attempt to escape we will shoot instantly."

Ned shrugged his shoulders and answered with a coolness that was not wholly assumed:

"Don't worry. I may get shot some time or other. I don't know, but I don't want to get the bullet in the back."

He walked firmly in the direction indicated by the point of the lance, and the Mexicans rode close behind him. A minute or two took them out of the bushes into the open prairie, and here Ned's heart leaped again he heard the deep Texan yell behind them, followed by a crackling rifle fire. He looked over his shoulder.

"It appears," he said, "that my people are holding the wood in which they encamped. My friends appear to be making trouble for your friends."

"You are not wanting in intelligence, Texan," said the Mexican, who seemed to have a sense of appreciation. "As I judge, your camp was aroused in time and is making a good defense. The Campeachy Indian whom we sent across the creek to scout was too fond of shedding blood. He lingered to take your scalp, and, in so doing, destroyed himself and injured us. Those who want too much hurt not only themselves but others."

Ned looked back again. This seemed to be a good-natured man, and he might be a friend at a time when he needed him most. The orders of Santa Anna were to shoot or hang all prisoners. He suddenly remembered it with a shudder.

"Keep straight ahead parallel with the stream," said the officer. "Presently we shall turn back to the creek, and cross it. We are alone on this side, and we came here primarily to scout."

They rode about a mile, and all the while Ned listened attentively for the sound of shots. He heard only two or three, but they were enough to tell him that his friends had not been rushed successfully. Hope returned.

They turned back to the creek at a point where it was wider and shallower than above.

"Can you swim?" said the officer to Ned.

"When it is necessary."

"Unbind his arms, Xavier, and let him follow behind our horses as we cross. It will not make you any wetter than you are, *señor*, and when the water grows deep you can hold to the tail of one of the horses. It is a great help in swimming, as I know from personal tests that I have made."

"Go on," said Ned. "Your statement about the help that a horse's tail gives to a swimmer is true. I appreciate the kindness of your offer."

The officer regarded him curiously.

"You are a young man of spirit," he said.

Ned returned the gaze with equal curiosity. He had noticed that the officer spoke almost pure Castilian Spanish and now that they were out of the bushes he saw that he was quite young. He was fairer than usual among Mexicans, the brow was high and the eyes were set wide apart.

"If I had a spare horse you should ride him," said the officer, "or you should ride double if it were not too much for any of our horses."

"Go ahead," said Ned, smiling a little. "The tail will suffice. I've been living in mud and water the most of the time in the last two or three weeks."

The officer without another word rode into the stream. Ned waded after him and the other horsemen came behind. The water rose to his knees, then to his waist, then to his shoulders. The horse in front of him began to swim and Ned, laying hold of his tail with one hand, kept himself afloat with the other.

"Is it all right with you, Texan?" asked the young Mexican, looking back.

"It is as easy as a ferry boat," replied Ned with calculated carelessness. "If it were not for getting wet I should always choose this method of crossing deep water. It requires so little preparation."

The officer laughed.

"*Señor* Texan," he said, "I saw from the first that you were a young man of good spirit. It appears also that you have a high humour. I could wish that you were Mexican instead of Texan, and I can wish it now especially."

He sighed, and Ned understood. He was referring to Santa Anna's order to shoot or hang all Texans who presumed to resist the power of Mexico. The thought came to him a second time that the young officer might prove to be a friend whom he would need very badly indeed.

They passed the deeper part of the stream, and now the water was not above Ned's, waist. He released the horse's tail and waded to the shore, following the officer. The other Mexicans came behind. When they stood upon firm ground the young officer locked contemplatively at Ned.

"I would offer you dry clothing if I had it," he said; "but since I do not have it, *señor*, you must go to our camp as you are. My name is Montez, Philip Montez, and what I can do for you I will."

"Mine is Edward Fulton," said Ned, not to be surpassed in polite-

650

ness, "and since I have fallen into Mexican hands I am glad that those hands are yours."

Montez gazed with renewed interest.

"Fulton! Fulton!" he said. "I have heard the name from both Colonel Almonte and Captain Urrea."

"And it is Urrea who is in command of the vanguard which is now attacking our men?"

"It is he. Almonte has not come up yet, nor do I think he will arrive for two or three days. You are the prisoner of Captain Urrea."

Ned noticed a trace of sadness in the officer's tone, and he understood perfectly. It was one thing to be the captive of Almonte, and another to be the captive of Urrea.

"I will not bind your hands again," said Montez. "I will spare you that indignity. My men will be on all sides of you, and we will proceed as quickly as possible to camp. Hark to the attack! Hear those shots! Your Texans are still holding out, but I do not think that Urrea will press home the attack tonight. It will be done tomorrow, and you will surely be overpowered."

Montez did not speak in any spirit of boastfulness or to taunt his prisoner, but rather as if he were announcing a fact to himself and Ned, recognising it as such, attempted no reply. The way led for some distance across the prairie, and Ned, at length, saw a light burning ahead. He knew that it was Urrea's camp fire. When they came closer a figure walked forward and stood revealed against the blaze.

It was Urrea himself, in a fine uniform splashed with mud. It seemed to Ned that he had grown much older in the last month or two, and that the face was much more sinister. There was no trace of that open and seemingly frank smile which had marked him, when Ned first knew him. A dozen other Mexicans, some of the officers, were standing about the fires. More were in the background, but the main Mexican force was a quarter mile in front, keeping up a desultory fire on the Texans who lay in the wood.

Urrea did not recognise Ned at first. Ned himself did not know how near he came to being in disguise. His face was covered with muddy sediment and his hair hung in strings. But he held himself very erect and met Urrea's look without fear.

"What have you here, Lieutenant Montez?" asked the leader.

"A prisoner, one of the Texans. Our Indian scout attempted to kill him from behind. There was a struggle and they fell in the creek. Only one reappeared and we have brought him to you. His name is

Edward Fulton and he is a member of the Texan force in the cotton-wood grove."

Urrea's eyes lighted up with malicious joy. He took a step forward and laughed.

"Santiago, but it is so!" he said. "I recognise him now, although he comes to us in singular plight. Well, young Señor Fulton, we welcome you. You could have brought no more acceptable gift, Lieutenant Montez."

Montez moved nervously. It was evident to Ned that he did not like Urrea's tone.

"Suppose we let him dry himself," he said. "As you see, the water is running from his clothes."

"Take him to one of the fires," said Urrea, "but bear in mind, Lieutenant Montez, that the orders of our illustrious president and commander-in-chief, General Santa Anna, are severe and must be obeyed."

"I do not forget them," said Montez, flushing a little, Then he walked with Ned to the nearest fire, and told him to stand there until he was warm and dry. Ned, paying no attention to the curious glances of the Mexicans, stood close to the blaze. He was growing chill from his wetting and the fire was very grateful. Montez with a friendly word left him there, but other Mexicans, arms in hand, stood about, and there would be no chance to make a break for liberty.

He assumed a careless manner. He devoted himself entirely to the drying of his clothing. When the steam arose from one side he turned the other, like a roasting apple, revolving before the blaze. Presently Urrea came. But Ned was completely dry now, and the dryness and warmth at such a time seemed to add an especial stiffness to his backbone. He took no notice of Urrea until the Mexican spoke.

"I deem it an omen of good luck that you have fallen again into our hands," said Urrea. "You slipped away smoothly before, but the fact that fate has brought you back indicates that you were not to escape our hands permanently."

"It's hard to read the future," said Ned placidly.

"But sometimes one may determine events twenty-four hours ahead. For instance, there are the orders of President Santa Anna that all Texan prisoners be hanged or shot. I believe that you saved yourself at the Alamo by some sort of claim made upon him in the name of the merchant, John Roylston. But that claim would be too tenuous now. Moreover, General Santa Anna will not overtake us for several days and orders are orders."

"I understand," said Ned, "that you are threatening me with a quick death."

"Your life is absolutely in my hands," said Urrea, "but I mean to use you. For that reason you can sleep here, and we will give you food in the morning."

Ned's feelings were far from pleasant, as Urrea turned away. He knew the cruel nature of the Mexican, and how intensely he hated the Texans. Yet it did not seem possible to him that the end had come at last after he had been saved miraculously more than once. Resolved to appear as indifferent as possible, he sat down before the fire and stared into the coals.

He was not molested for some time, and gradually his pulses returned to their normal beat. The fitful sounds of combat ceased. Evidently the last shot for the night had been fired and more Mexicans gathered about the fires. Ned could hear them talking and he judged that the force under Urrea numbered at least two hundred, or four to one against the Texans.

Montez came a half hour later and offered him a blanket. Ned accepted it and was grateful for the courtesy.

"The time may come when I shall be able to repay you, Señor Montez," he said.

"It may," said the lieutenant in a philosophical tone. "It would seem impossible now that such a time should come, but the wheel of fortune turns fast. I may have to hold you to your promise, Señor Fulton. Now sleep well. *Adios*."

Ned did sleep. Exhaustion and a splendid constitution brought him slumber in spite of everything. He was awakened early in the morning by Montez, and the Mexicans gave him a good breakfast of corn cakes, bacon and coffee. From the point where he sat he could see the grove in which the Texans lay, but it was impossible to discern figures at the distance. About half way between, a patrol of fifty Mexican cavalry rode about the wood, taking care, however, to keep well out of rifle shot.

Ned's eyes glistened as he looked. He saw that Urrea would not dare even with four to one to rush the formidable body of Texans who lay under cover among the trees. The Mexicans knew too well the deadly nature of the Texan rifles.

Urrea on horseback stood on a little knoll, watching the grove through a strong pair of glasses. As Ned and his guards came near he put down the glasses and said to the boy:

"I told you last night that I would have a use for you. I will tell you what it is. We have about fifty of the Texans surrounded in this grove, and we wish them to surrender. I say to you frankly that if we were to attack the grove we should probably suffer heavy loss. But it is not necessary for us to do so. We can surround the men, pick them off, or starve them out. It is also true that our illustrious general will be here presently with cannon, and we can rake every corner of the wood, while ourselves remaining out of rifle shot."

"This being so, what need have you of me?" asked Ned.

"Tell the men, your comrades, to surrender, and I will secure terms for them from General Santa Anna. I will see also that your life is spared. I have great influence with our commander-in-chief. I can say it without boasting."

Ned looked up at Urrea and gazed straight into his eyes. His soul was stirred with a fiery and honest indignation.

"I was at Goliad," he said, "and our men surrendered on the promise of life and speedy liberty. What was the promise worth? It was worth as much there as it is here. You know it."

Urrea flushed deeply and his hand flew to the hilt of his sword. But he quickly regained control of himself.

"They were rebels," he said.

"If they were rebels, so are we," said Ned.

"Then you refuse to bear this message and to tell the Texans the terms I offer."

"I refuse to help in any way to set a trap for them."

Urrea considered.

"You refuse to bear this message," he said at length, "but nevertheless you shall be present at a conference that I intend to hold with them. If you do not go forward willingly you shall be dragged. Your presence, silent though it may be, will add weight to what I have to say."

"I do not object to being an innocent spectator," said Ned. "You will not have to drag me."

"Hoist the signal, Montez," said Urrea.

The young lieutenant raised a handkerchief on the end of a lance, but no attention was paid to it. They waited some time, but nothing moved in the wood.

"I would advise you to ride forward out of the range of your own troops," said Ned dryly. "The Texans in the wood also remember Goliad."

Urrea flashed him an angry glance, but he adopted the suggestion. He had Ned's hands bound behind him again and then he, Montez and two others rode slowly toward the wood, with the boy marching between the horses of the two officers.

As they advanced Ned saw three figures issue from the wood, and come forward to meet them. The Panther led, looking, on his horse, like a gigantic black knight, and just behind him came Stump and Obed White.

As they drew near the Panther called to him cheerily.

"Is that you, Ned, or is it your ghost? We heard your cry an' it made us jump to our arms, but we was afeard you was dead."

"It is I in the solid material flesh," Ned called back, "but I am, as you see, a prisoner, and I am merely here as a witness."

The two little groups met and the Panther frowned darkly at Urrea. It hurt him to see a friend of his walking a prisoner between triumphant Mexicans on horseback. He also hated Urrea, whom he regarded as a spy and a traitor.

"You are Urrea," he said. "You would have betrayed us to death while pretending to be our friend. Well, what do you want?"

Urrea smiled superciliously. He seemed to be greatly satisfied with himself.

"I overlook your bluster," he said, "because I know that it is idle. I have had this white flag raised in order that we may talk with the rebels and save needless bloodshed."

"We don't mind your callin' us rebels," said the Panther. "Words don't hurt. But we are here, waitin' for you to tell us what you've got to say."

"We have come to demand your surrender. We have here a force outnumbering yours at least eight to one," said Urrea, doubling his numbers. "General Santa Anna himself will be up soon with plenty of artillery. It will be easy for us to take you."

"Then if it so easy to take us," said the Panther, "why do you demand our surrender?"

"If you surrender without bloodshed I shall intercede with General Santa Anna for your lives which are forfeit as rebels."

"We know Mexican mercy," said the Panther. "Besides, even if we trusted you we wouldn't dream of surrenderin'. Just you come an' take us, Captain Urrea. Santa Anna may come up as you say, but we ain't so shore that he won't have his own hands full before long."

"You can surrender or not, as you choose," said Urrea, "but in the end all of you who are left alive will be taken and you will be executed duly as rebels. I wish to remind you also that I have here a prisoner, a youth of importance among you, and unless you yield it will be my duty to hang him between our lines where you can see it done."

"You wouldn't do that!" exclaimed the Panther, horrified.

"It would be the deed of one worse than a savage!" said Obed White.

"I shall certainly do it," said Urrea. "This is war, as you Texans are finding to your cost. Fulton's life is forfeit."

Then Ned spoke up. Like the other Texans he had the glow and fire of a great resolution, the resolution to fight to the last.

"Pay no attention to him, Panther," he said. "You cannot surrender a strong Texan force on my account. I've got to take my chances."

"No, Ned, I won't surrender," said the Panther, "I can't do it. I've got no right to do it, but it just t'ars me to pieces 'cause I can't."

Then he turned fiercely to Urrea.

"Urrea," he said, "what you are proposin' is the lowest down thing I ever heard of."

"Your opinion is of no importance to me," said Urrea.

"Panther," said Ned earnestly. "Don't you think of doing as he asks. They can never take your force. He has already lied about his numbers. He has only four to one. Not eight to one, and Texans do not mind four to one."

Urrea swore furiously, and raised a little riding whip that he carried. The Panther lifted a huge finger warningly.

"Urrea," he said, "you can't strike a prisoner, one of our own people, here before us. We are under the white flag, but if you let that whip fall upon Ned I'll blow your head off as shore as the sun is shinin'!"

Urrea paled, then looked savagely at the Panther. He saw immutable resolution in the eyes of the gigantic plainsman, and he lowered the whip.

"I do not strike prisoners," he said lamely.

"An' I've got this to say, too," said the Panther. "You think that everything's your way, an' that the last of the Texans will be wiped out in a few days. Well, mebbe you're wrong. I'm thinkin' that you're mighty wrong, an' your time may come. You may fall into our hands an' then what you've done to this boy we may do to you. He's got strong friends, men that have been made hard by many dangers, an' when they get their hands on you they won't spare you."

The Panther spoke with a fiery energy that was convincing. A deep pallor overspread the face of Urrea and, for a moment or two terror bit like an arrow at his heart. But he recovered himself and replied:

"I do not fear threats, particularly from those who are in no position to carry them out."

"You won't forget what I've told you," said the Panther. "Ned is in your hands, but we're watchin' over him, even from a distance. Now, if you've said all you've got to say we'll return, an' you can begin your attack on the wood as soon as you like. Ned, we'll get you back. Don't forget that we'll be thinkin' of you most of the time."

"I'll be all right," said Ned, with an assumption of cheerfulness. "I'm lucky. Goodbye."

"Goodbye," said the Panther, Obed and Stump together. Then they rode slowly back to their own lines. But Ned's phrase, "I'm lucky," stuck in the minds of all three. It merely strengthened anew their conviction that he was indeed born under a lucky star, and that he would come safe out of this new danger.

Ned himself walked back with the Mexicans, Urrea and Montez on either side of him and the others in the rear. Urrea was in a savage humour, and he nervously flicked his horse with his whip. Montez gave Ned a look of sympathy but said nothing. Urrea himself did not speak until he was nearly back to his own force.

"Montez," he said, "we must take those Texans in the wood. It would be a great achievement for us and would immensely help our credit with the general. He is anxious to return to the capital as soon as possible, and this capture and a few more like it would end the Texans."

"It is so, my captain," said Montez. "Now what shall we do with this prisoner?"

"Let his arms remain bound and put him in the middle of the troop. He cannot get away."

Ned sat down on a little hill, where some of the Mexican horsemen were grouped about him. As the air was somewhat chill they had dismounted and built a fire, before which they stood holding their horses by the bridle and waiting orders. Ned turned his back to the fire and stood waiting also, but not knowing what he awaited. His intense excitement kept him from noticing the raw chill of the day.

Ned had divined the savage and implacable nature of Urrea. He knew that the Mexican, while he might be daunted for a moment by the Panther's threats would be inflamed by them later on. He felt that he was in great danger, and he could only hope and pray that some-how he would come through safely.

Urrea's cavalry, except the reserve, spread out and opened a distant fire upon the grove. It was not returned for a long time. Then two rifles flashed from the forest and two cavalrymen fell from their sad-dles. Ned laughed. It was not a laugh of amusement, but a laugh of the nerves and of triumph. He was keyed to an intense pitch, and, at every touch, his nerves responded like the strings of a violin. Yet he did not notice that it had grown much colder, and that heavy clouds were massing in the west. The sun of which the Panther had spoken but a half hour before was almost gone.

The Mexican attack drew off, and Ned saw Urrea sitting on his horse a short distance away, apparently deep in thought. Presently he called Montez and the two rode toward Ned.

"The Texans are stubborn," said Urrea, more to Montez than to Ned, "and we must teach them a lesson. We must put the fear of Santa Anna's wrath into their souls. We must show that there can be no mercy for rebels."

"I would not do it, my captain," said Montez. "It will only make these Texans more fierce and resolute in resistance, and it will go hard with us should any of us be so unfortunate as to fall into their hands."

"Enough, Montez," said Urrea brusquely. "We do not fear the Tex-ans. I am in command here and what I see fit to order shall be done."

Montez was silent, but his manner was still disapproving. The two halted before Ned, and Urrea beckoned to several soldiers.

"Get a lariat," he said to one.

Ned heard him, and a shudder ran through his whole body. But he said nothing.

"Bring the prisoner," said Urrea to the men, "and follow me to the oak that stands in full view before the Texan grove."

"Captain, I entreat you," began Montez.

"Silence!" shouted Urrea.

Ned himself marked the oak, a stout tree with stout branches, stand-ing between the two lines, but out of Texan rifle shot. He understood Urrea's meaning well enough, and again that shiver passed through his body from head to foot. But he summoned all the resources of his will and walked with unfaltering step.

Now in very truth it appeared that his time had come. He could see no possible way of salvation. If the Texans issued from the wood to save him they would be cut down by overwhelming numbers. The elements themselves were in accordance with the event, and were drawing a funeral pall over his final moments. It had turned very cold. The last segment of the sun was gone, and the clouds, massing in heavy battalions, suffused all the air with a deep, sombre tint. A vast wind was moaning far away on the rolling plains.

They reached the tree, the Mexican with the lariat climbed it quickly and fastened one end of the rope to a bough. A shout came from the grove, and many rifles cracked, but all the bullets fell short. Ned saw horsemen at the edge of the wood, apparently about to gallop forth on a desperate forlorn hope. But he took no hope from such an attempt. It could not possibly succeed.

"Make the rope fast around his neck," said Urrea to another of the Mexicans who was more than willing.

The man carefully made a loop and approached. Ned shrank away, and, as he did so, glanced at Urrea to see if he were really going to carry out such a horrible plan. But he was unable to read anything in the face of the Mexican, because the air suddenly had grown so dark that he could not discern his features. The vast wind that had been moaning afar was coming nearer, and leaves and twigs, picked up on its edge, began to whirl past.

The man with the noose took another step forward, and Ned shrank back again. Then the norther struck in all its blackness and fury. There was a rush of dust picked up on far western plains. A vast cloud black as Egypt swept over them, while the wind moaned in their ears. The air itself was like the touch of ice.

Ned was dazed for a moment by the suddenness of the transformation. Then he felt an edge of steel cold against his wrist and his thongs, cut in two, fell to the ground.

"Run! run for your life!" exclaimed the voice of Montez in his ear. "This will pass in a few minutes, and I cannot see you die such a death!"

The words were like the charge of an electric battery. Uttering a fervent "Thank you!" Ned sprang away. He had been conscious for a moment of trampling hoofs about him, and of the shouts of the Mexicans, but he could see nothing, so great was the darkness, and so dense was the cloud of dust that had filled the eyes of them all. But he was conscious of an immense and devout joy. Nature herself had interfered at the last moment to save him.

He ran blindly at first and then chose a course which he thought would lead to the wood. The darkness was as deep as ever, and hail had begun to fall, pelting him on the back and head, and driving him to a greater speed. The roaring of the wind was so great that he could hear nothing else, and he did not know what had become of the Mexicans. Twice he stumbled over roots and bushes and fell, but each time he sprang up again and ran on as fast as ever.

He had been running at least twenty minutes before he recollected himself and stopped. If he had been going straight toward it he could have reached the cottonwood grove in half that time. It was obvious that in the darkness and confusion he had taken the wrong course. But he was out of the hands of the Mexicans. That at least was achieved. He decided to keep on, though at a somewhat slower pace, until he found the cover of forest, and bushes, in which he would lie, until there was light enough for him to return to his comrades.

But he went much further than he had thought would be necessary. He tripped again and fell, and once he went for thirty or forty yards through water that sometimes reached to his knees. He judged that it was a lagoon formed by the overflow from the creek, and that consequently he must be very near the timber. He veered in a little in the hope of reaching it at once, but he encountered neither bushes nor trees until a full half hour later.

Then he ran into a clump of bushes, and, as he pushed his way through them, he felt trees. Presently both forest and underbrush grew very dense, and he crouched down in the thickest portion that he could find. He was partly protected there from the wind and hail which were still driving hard. As he sat between the great roots of an oak, with a thick clump of bushes guarding him like a palisade, he felt a deep and intense thankfulness. Truly a miracle had intervened in his behalf, when there were only thirty seconds between him and death. He could never despair again.

He remained a long time between the roots of the tree. The darkness did not pass as quickly as he had expected, and the wind, charged at intervals with hail, blew with great strength for three or four hours. But he was still insensible to cold and wet. His nervous system, taxed to the utmost by mental tension, was unconscious of physical hardships.

When he felt the darkness thinning away, and the wind dying he rose and peered over the bushes. He could see but dimly, but he knew that no great light would come, as another dusk, that of twilight, was creeping up. He was glad the night was at hand, as it would afford a good cloak of concealment, and he felt confident now that he could rejoin the Texan band.

He waited a while longer, and the hail ceased entirely. The wind sank to a murmur and the artificial darkness was succeeded by that of night. Then he stepped forth from his covert, and tried to locate himself. He saw nothing familiar, merely the wet forest and bushes, and beyond them a sodden morass.

He was sure that he was somewhere near the Texan grove, but whether above or below it he could not tell. When the norther struck there was so much confusion of the elements and of his senses that he could not remember in which direction he had run.

The clouds were now passing rapidly away, leaving a fine blue sky sown with stars. The air grew warm again, and had the remarkable purity and clearness that always follows a norther.

He went deeper into the woods and found the creek, but there was nothing familiar about its banks. Yet he could not be more than two or three miles from the Texans. But up or down! Up or down! That was the question. It would not have been so serious a problem had he been armed. But he was without rifle, knife, hatchet or pistol. He had nothing with which to defend himself except his bare hands.

It was likely that Urrea had sent out men to find him, as soon as it was light enough. Doubtless he had with him more of the Campeachy Indians and he would have their skill as trailers and their savage lust of blood to fear. He resolved therefore to cross the creek and hunt from the other side for his friends. So broad a body of water would serve to hide his trail from the keenest eyes, for a while at least.

Ned dropped softly into the water. The stream at this point had spread out to much width, but yet was deep enough to require swimming. He waded as far as he could, and then swam a distance of twenty or thirty feet, when he struck the shallow water, approaching the further shore. He let down his feet and stood on the bottom, the water reaching to his chin. Then he looked back toward the bank from which he had come, and a chill ran through him.

Ned had feared the trailing of the Campeachy Indians, and with justice. One of the savages stood now on the bank looking eagerly for the fugitive. He was much like the other whom Ned had encountered in the water, a short heavily built man, yellowish in colour, his hair black and long and his clothing limited now to a waist cloth. He carried only a long knife, and, in a darting ray of the moonlight, its edge looked so keen that Ned shuddered. The Indian doubtless knew that he was unarmed, and considered the knife sufficient.

Ned, without a single weapon, felt helpless. He sank a little lower in the water, immersing himself to the nose, through which he breathed. The spreading bough of a large oak cast a darker shadow upon the stream where he stood, and he hoped that the Indian would not see the blur upon the yellow water which was the boy's head.

The savage looked a long time up and down the stream, and then hunted a little along the bank. But he came back to the point from which he had been observing the creek. Evidently he had found some trace of Ned's trail, and was now convinced that he had gone into the water. The boy sank a fraction of an inch lower, and the water almost bubbled into his nose. He hoped that he might yet escape discovery, but the Indian suddenly uttered a low cry, and sprang into the stream.

Ned instantly rushed for the land. But it was slow progress running through deep water. He looked back and saw the Indian swimming swiftly and almost silently, his knife held between his teeth. He was a brave youth, but an unarmed fugitive cannot delay when the pursuer is a bloodthirsty savage. Ned felt his whole body quivering as if the Indian were already upon him. He fairly leaped through the water, and with a mighty effort gained the bank. There his feet sank deep in the mud, but he pulled them out again, and dashed into the bushes.

He cast one fleeting glance and saw the Indian also reach the shore and stand there for a moment, outlined in the moonlight, the water running from his yellow body. Then Ned used his utmost speed because he knew the Indian would hang upon his trail like death itself. He doubled and turned in the brush, always running lightly, and, pausing now and then, to crouch in the shelter and listen. He did not hear anything, but he knew as certainly as he knew he was alive that the Indian was following him.

He came finally to a point where the bush was very dense, and crawling into the centre of it he lay there, panting. He looked at his empty hand and he was overcome by a sort of horror. He would have given a year of his life for a weapon of any kind. Then he could have turned and faced this terrible, trailing savage. It was a beautiful moonlight now, with all the crispness and freshness that follows the norther, but he hated the silky blue sky and the myriad of dancing stars. Before, there had been little but rain and mud and storm, and he had prayed more than once to be delivered from them. Now he could pray with equal fervour to have them back again.

Suddenly he sank down lower in the brushwood. His acute ear, attuned for any foreign sound, heard a soft step, as light almost as that of a fox. The Indian stepped gently into the undergrowth and stood looking about, and Ned, his imagination alive, had never seen a more utter savage. The Indian's gaze was roving around and suddenly he caught a glimpse of Ned. The boy, who was watching him intently, saw the cruel light spring up in the eyes of the savage, and, making a mighty leap from the undergrowth, he ran as he had seldom run before in his life.

His impetus was so great that he left the savage staring for a few moments at the place where he had been. Then he doubled and turned again, and once more he lost his pursuer in the shadows. But Ned knew that he would hang on. The single glimpse would encourage the savage to hunt him all night, if need be. He stopped again panting and wished with the very essence of his soul that he had a weapon.

Looking among the trees and bushes, he saw the savage again following his crooked trail in the moonlight. But the Indian had not seen him this time, and he slid softly away in the other direction. Now he was among large trees, and the ground was littered with old and fallen boughs. His foot struck against a stick and he picked it up. It was two or three inches in diameter and four or five feet long, a natural club.

When Ned felt the club in his hand, his whole figure stiffened, and courage poured back into his veins. He was not defenceless now. He was one with a weapon, and the hunted would become the hunter. He stepped behind a large tree and crouched there, lately a fugitive for his life, but now a formidable figure.

The Indian came on, carefully trailing the footsteps in the soft earth, and, when he was opposite the tree, Ned sprang forth. The savage uttered no cry, but as quick as the spring of a tiger thrust with the long knife. It was well for Ned that he too was quick and that he was keyed for the crisis. He brought the club down with a snapping stroke on the Indian's right arm and the knife fell to the ground. Then he struck again straight at the savage head, and the Indian went down without a cry. Ned did not know whether he was dead or not. He never knew, but snatching up the knife he dashed away again through the brush, free now from the fear of that relentless and deadly pursuit.

He must have gone a half mile, when he felt a sudden attack of faintness. The earth rocked and everything grew black before his eyes. He lay flat upon the ground, until his nervous system relaxed, and the earth grew steady again. Then he resumed his feet and found that the swimming in his head was gone.

Ned returned to the edge of the creek, and, noticing that it was wider here than at the Texan camp, he concluded that he was much farther down the stream, and nearer to the bayou into which it emptied, where it would naturally spread out. Hence the camp would be back up the creek, and, acting upon his logic, he went in that direction.

Now the moonlight helped him. Keeping in the timber he always scanned the opposite shore with the greatest care, and, after nearly two hours' walking, he saw trees that he believed he knew. They must be the cottonwood grove, but he watched some time before he saw a light, a faint one apparently in the very depths of the wood.

Ned sat down on the bank and gave forth a long, melodious whistle. He waited a while and there was no reply. Then he repeated it, and, after another wait, a similar whistle came from the grove. Then he stood up boldly and called aloud:

"It is I, Ned Fulton!"

He saw a gigantic figure upraised in the dusk, and back came the cry:

"Where are you? Who did you say you are?"

"I am Ned Fulton, and I'll be with you in a minute, Panther."

Then Ned sprang far out into the stream and swam to the bank.

CHAPTER 12

THE BATTLE WITH URREA

When Ned climbed up the bank and stood there like a dripping young river god it was not alone the Panther who met him. Obed White, the Reverend Stephen Larkin, Will Allen and others also faced him.

"Is it you, really you, Ned?" exclaimed the Panther.

"Just my own self," replied Ned, rejoicing at the sight of these friendly faces. "I've been on a trip."

"And a lively trip it must have been," said the Panther. "When we last saw you Urrea was just gettin' ready to hang you up to a nice oak tree."

"So he was," said Ned, "but at that moment, as you saw, about the blackest norther that was ever known in these parts swooped down upon us, and under its cover I managed, with a little help, to escape."

"I knew it; I knew it!" exclaimed the Panther fervently.

"Knew what?" asked Ned.

"Never mind," replied the Panther. "Just you come into camp now an' we'll give you some dry clothes. I guess you've had enough of this muddy creek to last you a long time."

Ned did not take the time then to tell how he had fallen into the creek with the first Indian, and how he had been pursued by the last one, but he changed quickly into dry clothing, lay down on dry boughs and fell fast asleep. The Panther and Obed stood by, talking, while the boy slept soundly.

"If I had any doubt left," said the Panther, "this would settle it. All of the Mexicans an' Indians in Texas can't kill that boy. Think of his standin' there with the rope tied 'roun' his neck, an' that norther, black as pitch, comes rushin', an' b'arin' him away from the Mexicans right in the middle of it! Then he comes swimmin' back into our camp, just as good as he was when he went away."

"It does look curious," said Obed, "and I don't fathom it. There are more things in the woods and creek tonight, Panther, than are dreamed of in our philosophy, and we'll let it go at that."

Will Allen, after shaking Ned's hands violently many minutes, had gone back to sleep. The Reverend Stephen Larkin had spread his blanket anew, but the Panther and Obed watched until day.

Since the storm the Texans had improvised some rude fortifications, having drawn up tree trunks and brush wood to such an extent that the grove would be impervious to a cavalry charge. The two men now and then saw moving lights on the plain in front of them, but they did not anticipate any night attack even by skirmishers. The Texans at the ends of the wood, behind their log barricades, were far too formidable riflemen to be faced by any Mexican band unless in great force.

But the Panther and Obed were far from being pleased by the siege. They wished to be up and away. They wished to join their force as quickly as possible to Houston's. Little it was, that is few in numbers, but half a hundred skilful, daring and resolute men such as those who constituted the "Panther's Claws," were a force with which one would have to reckon, and which might turn the scale of a desperate battle. The two debated several times the wisdom of swimming the creek in their rear, and of then galloping northward to Houston. But as vigilant a commander as Urrea would be sure to have out scouts who would detect the movement and then the Texans would be taken at a fatal disadvantage when in the water. Their chief consolation lay in the fact that while they were held in waiting there, a strong portion of the Mexican force was held in a similar waiting.

Ned was permitted to sleep longer than the rest, and when he awakened a specially good breakfast was ready for him. He was treated with a deference which at first he ascribed to their fear that he had been overcome by an overwhelming succession of hardships and dangers. When it was continued, after they were sure that he was well and right, he wondered a little, but in the press of events he soon forgot all about it.

The Texans had extra arms, some of which had been captured, and Ned was equipped anew. His rifle was of Kentucky make, a fine weapon with a long, slender barrel, and he was confident that he could do good work with it.

The morning was somewhat overcast and grayish, but it was not cold. Ned, from the cover of the wood, clearly saw the Mexican position about a quarter of a mile away. Most of Urrea's men were dismounted there at the edge of some bushes, but on either flank about twenty horsemen rode up and down, prepared for any sudden movement by the Texans.

"The emissary of Satan has laid his plans well," said Stephen Larkin to Ned. "He does not intend that we shall escape and if he should capture us or we should surrender, no matter what the Mexican promises might be, our fate would be the fate of those who died at Goliad, prisoners of war, butchered ruthlessly. It was the hand of God that saved you yesterday from a cruel and ignominious death, and I believe that the same hand will be stretched forth now to save us all."

Although the Reverend Stephen Larkin carried a rifle on his shoulder and a pistol, hatchet and knife at his belt, he spoke with deep religious fervour. A minister, one who looked upon himself as the humble mouthpiece of a message, he was nevertheless one of the best fighters in all that little band. The Mexicans seemed to him to be heathen, savage heathen at that, and where the Bible failed it was necessary to lay on with the sword.

But it was in very truth a strange time throughout Texas. After the terrible massacres of their people the air appeared to the Texans to be surcharged with red. It affected their vision and heated their brains. They could not think of normal things. Always before them was that image of Satan, Santa Anna, and around him were his demons.

"What do you think they will do, Mr. Larkin?" asked Ned.

"They will not charge straight at us. Of that we may be sure. Urrea, as I hear, is very crafty, and he will not waste his men. Doubtless he is waiting for reinforcements."

An hour passed and they saw no movement whatever within the Mexican lines. The horsemen on the flanks still rode back and forth as a guard upon the Texans, but there was no further evidence of life in the camp of the foe. Will Allen joined Ned, and now he was all of his cheerful, optimistic young self.

"It's a case of checkmate," he said. "If Urrea holds us here we hold him out there."

His reply came quickly. There was a flash in the bushes near Urrea, a deep roar, a column of smoke shooting upward and a cannon ball sang so near the boys that they felt the rush of air, and instinctively sprang aside. But the ball had already passed them, tearing the side of a tree trunk, ricocheting to the ground, and then bounding in a series of great leaps through the wood, whence it landed in the middle of the creek and sank hissing.

"Reinforcements for the Mexicans arrived in the night and they've brought up a cannon!" exclaimed Will.

"Evidently," said Ned.

The Mexicans uttered so great a shout after the shot that the Texans in the wood heard it. They recognised at once that this was a new and formidable danger and they acted promptly. The horses, which they could not afford to lose, were taken to the farthest edge of the wood, the one nearest the creek, and were tied there, where the danger of the fire from the cannon would be reduced as much as possible. The men themselves were ordered to take refuge behind the logs and trees and to throw up little earthworks with their knives and hatchets.

Ned and Will were together, and they worked busily, scooping out the ground. They reckoned that the Mexicans would not fire again for at least five minutes, and two active youths with such a spur upon them could make quite a hole in that time. Then when they saw the flash in the Mexican lines they threw themselves flat upon their faces in their excavation, heard the mass of metal whistle near them, go entirely through the grove, pass over the creek and bury itself in the earth far beyond.

The Mexicans again raised their great shout of expected triumph and the Panther, Obed and Stephen Larkin debated the problem very seriously. The Mexicans might not be good artillerymen, they had not yet hit any of the Texans, but if they kept on firing they must do so in the end.

"It's an eighteen pounder at least," said Obed, "and they'll get the range in time. It's a long shot that doesn't hit anything."

"We've got to reach them gunners somehow or other," said the Panther. "If we can get within range with our rifles, an' they carry a long way, we can soon leave that cannon without a friend around it."

"What about the high grass running off from the left of the grove?" asked Ned, who stood by.

There was a narrow dip leading from the grove toward the Mexican camp, and, in it, the grass had grown much taller than elsewhere, standing at least a foot above the ground. The Panther surveyed it critically.

"If we can get to the end of it," he said, "we can reach the cannon with our rifles, but to get there we've got to do some mighty good creepin' an' crawlin'. It's worth thinkin' over."

But they did not think about it long. A third shot from the cannon slightly wounded two of the Texans, and showed that the Mexicans were getting the range.

"We've got to do it!" exclaimed the Panther, "'cause there ain't nothin' else to do."

He chose the best ten marksmen in the group, including himself, Obed White and Ned, for the creeping and crawling up the grassy gully. Stephen Larkin was left in command of the main force, with instructions to begin a scattering fire in the direction of the Mexicans, and to shout a great deal.

"The more smoke of all kinds you start the better," said the Panther, "'cause it will help to cover up our own movements."

A fourth shot from the cannon made it timely for them to reply, and the rifle shots of the Texans were reinforced by such a tremendous yelling from these marksmen that the Mexicans themselves, despite the great range, began to fire their rifles and muskets.

"Now is the time for us!" exclaimed the Panther, and, hurrying to the edge of the grove, he dropped almost flat on his face, and began to creep up the gully. Ned, imitating him, kept by his side, and just behind them came Obed and the others. As they crept forward they heard a fifth shot from the cannon, but the ball flew high above their heads. The Panther had spoken only in a casual and hopeful way of the smoke, but it really came to their aid. Nearly all that caused by the cannon and rifles drifted in their direction, and, as there was no wind, hung there for some time.

"Now boys," he said, "the chances are certainly with us. We've not only got the grass to hide us but the smoke is doin' it, too. That bein' the case we can afford to go faster."

It was hard and tiresome work, dragging oneself along with hands and knees, taking care of weapons at the same time, but their need was urgent, and they advanced rather rapidly through the grass. The Panther grinned more than once as he listened to the firing and to the shouting of the Texans. Above it could be distinguished the tremendous voice of the Reverend Stephen Larkin, calling down maledictions upon the heads of a cruel foe. Mr. Larkin also had a great vocabulary and marvellous facility of speech. The way in which he disposed of the Mexicans was wonderful, and it appealed with great force to the Panther in the grass.

"He beats any dictionary I ever saw," he said to Ned. "If words was bullets Mr. Larkin could send such a storm of lead on the Mexican camp that it would be wiped out."

"If the pinch comes he'll be as ready as anybody with the lead," said Ned.

"Not a doubt of it," said the Panther. "Funny how the smoke keeps on hangin' right over our heads an' hidin' us."

He cast a superstitious glance at Ned, and muttered thanks to himself that he had brought the boy along.

"We must be comin' within range," said Obed White. "It's a long gully that goes on forever, and I noticed from the wood that at the end of it we could reach the Mexicans."

"Another minute an' we're there," said the Panther.

The Panther gave the word within the appointed time, and all stopped. The grass was still more than a foot high, and as they lay upon their stomachs with their heads raised to see, they were yet well concealed. The Mexicans had fired two shots from the cannon, while they were creeping through the grass, and they were preparing for another. The whole crew of the gun were standing about it.

"Now, boys," said the Panther, "we must do our work. We must teach them Mexicans that the most dangerous thing in the world they can do is to touch that cannon. I'll take the rammer; Ned, you take the sponger; Obed, you take the one at the lanyard."

He continued assigning members of the crew one by one to his sharpshooters, and then he counted, "One! two! three! Fire!"

The ten rifles crashed as one, and the entire gun crew went down smitten by a deadly hail. Some were killed, some wounded and with a shout of fear and horror the whole Mexican force rushed away from the cannon.

"Now boys, reload as fast as you can!" cried the Panther. "They'll come back in a few minutes, an' we must be ready for 'em again."

A second gun crew, driven by the Mexican officers, ran forward, but like the first it was shot down. Nothing could live in face of the deadly rifles that were concealed in the grass, but, before the Texans could reload anew, a number of the Mexicans seized the gun and ran it rapidly far back in the bushes.

"We've done our work," said the Panther. "They can't do good shootin' with that cannon from the bushes an' from a place so far. It'll be out of real action for some time at least."

"And that being the case, I suppose it is now our duty to go back to our little home in the wood!" said Ned.

"It's our duty an' our pleasure, since you put it so beautiful," said the Panther. "Face about boys, and crawl on the back track."

Ned did not think that they would return unmolested. He knew the inquiring and suspicious mind of Urrea who would seek to know from what point the deadly rifle shots had come, and who would naturally pick the grassy dip as the only available ambush. But they were at least half way back, although still within range, when Urrea with his glasses noted the moving grass.

The Mexican leader gave an impetuous order and many bullets began to cut down the grass. But it was hard to hit a target indicated only by waving stems, and, while Ned and his comrades heard the frequent hiss of bullets, none struck within ten feet of them.

"Hurry along now, boys!" cried the Panther. "We've done our work, an' we don't want to be struck down after it is over."

Just as he spoke one of the Texans ceased to crawl, and lay quiet and motionless on his side.

"Elwell's gone," said Obed White. "A bullet entered his temple."

"Catch hold of his body on one side, Obed," said the Panther, "an' I'll take the other. We've got to bury him decent. Ah, that's good."

The Mexicans in their eagerness were rushing forward, and the Texans suddenly issuing from the wood opened a heavy fire upon them, at the same time protecting their retreating comrades. The Panther and his men then escaped to the trees, carrying with them the body of Elwell. The Mexicans, standing in healthy awe of the Texan rifles, retreated to their own lines, and the cannon, drawn to the rear, remained silent.

The exultation of the Texans over their achievement was saddened by the death of Elwell to whom they gave decent, Christian burial. They dug out a grave with hatchets and knives, covered him over and the Reverend Stephen Larkin spoke a solemn burial service. The scene was deeply impressive to both Ned and Will, as they stood by with bared heads.

"This man," said Stephen Larkin, "has fallen in the doing of his duty. He fell with weapons in his hands but human wickedness gave him no choice but to carry arms. He bore them to defend the innocent, to defend women and little children, and he died that they might live. Because of these, his great virtues, we ask Thee to forgive his little sins, and we ask for him Thy mercy, Oh, God!"

Then they covered him up and left him there in his nameless but heroic grave.

"He is not the only one who will go," said Obed White. "We've got to make up our minds to that. We can't fight such odds as are now against Texas and not have a lot of our men that we have left fall."

Ned and Will, who were listening to him, felt the full gravity and truth of his words. They realised, despite the temporary repulse of the Mexicans, that their situations was indeed desperate. Moreover, it would be desperate even if they escaped from the grove. Santa Anna with a formidable force was steadily advancing. Nothing had been able to stop him. Even if they were able to join Houston their chances would still be desperate. He had only a few hundred Texan frontiersmen and hunters against the powerful army of the Mexican dictator.

"What are you two lookin' so gloomy about?" asked Stump. "We ain't thrashed yet. Not by a long shot. An' haven't we just made 'em pull their cannon so far back they can't get no aim at us at all?"

"It's so, Stump," said Ned, "but we're thinking of poor Elwell."

"Sooner or later the turn of every one of us will come," said Stump philosophically. "His just happened to come sooner. Set down here and rest yourselves. When you're on the defence you can afford to be quiet, if the enemy is, too."

The boys lay down willingly enough on last year's autumn leaves which were thick in the grove and listened while Stump talked, telling of old adventures with buffaloes, bears and Indians. The shrewd frontiersman saw that both of them were keyed rather high, and he was soothing them with his talk.

"This Texas of ours will be a great country as soon as we drive out the Mexicans," he said. "Nobody knows how big it is, but I guess you could ride either north or south or east or west for a month an' not cross it. That would give galoots like me an' the Panther lots of room for rangin' about. It's a big country an' a fine country, with mountains an' plains an' rivers an' creeks, an' Indians an' buffaloes an' panther an' deer an' antelope, just the kind of country I mean to spend the next fifty or sixty years in, but I want our flag to wave over it."

"There should be great chances in Texas if we ever drive out the Mexicans," said Ned, thoughtfully.

Stump opened his arms their widest and waved them about.

"Chances!" he exclaimed. "They're so many nobody can count 'em! Here in the east there's room to build up all the cities and towns one can ever need, while the west and the great plains go on almost forever. We're not many, Ned, but we're shorely fightin' for a great, big empire."

"Your vision is none too large, Stump," said Obed White, who had joined them, "but at the same time there is a great contrast. You are talking of empires and at the present moment we have only an acre or two of cottonwood that we can call our own. Truly, Mr. Burke, you have a flourishing fancy."

"I'm glad of it," replied Stump. "I like to imagine things. Some times when I'm settin' by the camp fire all fed up on good game an' with my back comfortable ag'in a tree I can imagine fine things happenin' to me, an' they're almost as real as the real ones. I can see myself lickin' the Panther, who is the only man in Texas stronger than me; not lickin' him so that he would be crippled up long, but just to have him stretched flat on his back on the ground, with me settin' a-straddle on his chest pushin' his face back whenever he tries to raise it up, an' givin' him a friendly dig now an' then in the side with my heels, not to hurt him, but just to show him that I'm the better man. I know it will never happen, but I imagine it a lot of times, which gives me a heap of pleasure without troublin' Panther any, which is mighty satisfactory all 'roun', 'cause me an' Panther are the best of friends."

"Is that the limit of your fancy, Stump?" asked Ned.

"Not by a long shot. When I look into them coals I see myself ridin' a big black horse, bigger an' stronger an' faster than any that was ever bred in Texas. I'm the greatest hunter of buffalo an' deer that the world has ever seed. I can whip six Indians or six Mexicans any time all by myself, an' if they should happen to be fifteen or twenty in a gang my big horse with me a-straddle of him would leave them behind, same as if they were tied to a stake. I see myself the best rifle-shot in the world, the best that ever was or ever will be. I see myself the best scout, trapper, hunter an' trailer in the world, the best that ever was or ever will be. I know more about woodcraft and prairie craft than all the Indians an' all the other white men put together.

"When I get tired of people, as everybody does sometimes, I mount my big horse, lay my rifle across the pommel of my saddle, an' ride away into the west, right spang into the eye of the settin' sun. I don't ride for just one day or two days or three, but for weeks an' weeks an' months an' months, until I come squar' ag'in the mount'ins. Then I ride up among them an' I shoot the grizzly bear an' the big elk, an' I breathe the air ten thousan' feet up, an' when my notion changes I ride back ag'in. I tell you, Ned, that's life! I wouldn't swap places with no king that lives or that ever has lived or that ever will live, 'cause I'd be a king of the whole world, without havin' to take care of any of it."

Stump's eyes glowed as he spoke. Underneath the frontiersman's speech and rude garb lay a highly imaginative nature, and Ned sympathized with him.

"If ever we drive the Mexicans out I think that most of your dream is likely to come true," he said.

The Panther joined them a moment or two later, and Mr. Larkin came, too. Then they discussed the possibility of a retreat across the creek. They were safe from the cannon for the present, but they believed that Santa Anna and his whole army would arrive on the next day. Then the wood would become untenable. If only the rain and storm that had persecuted them so long had continued they could escape under their cover, but now when they needed black skies most they were blue and clear.

The danger was urgent. It was not sufficient to beat off Urrea and his band. They must get away and they must join Houston. The Panther and his council discussed the question long and anxiously.

"If the night is dark at all we must try swimmin' the creek. We wouldn't do it before, but there ain't nothin' else to do now. Urrea, of course, will be on watch, an' if we lose some men we have to lose 'em. We'll hope that the rest can break through an' get to Houston."

The plan was announced speedily to the men and they agreed. They were tired of the grove and they wished to be on the march. The rest of the day passed with occasional shots between skirmishers and no damage. The night came on fairly light but with some little clouds drifting here and there. The Texans from the trees saw the Mexican sentinels riding up and down, and they had no doubt that the watchful Urrea had also posted a sufficient number on the other side of the creek.

The Texans lighted no fire, but ate their cold food in the dark, looked to their arms and ammunition, saddled and bridled their horses and waited. The time passed very slowly for Ned and Will who as usual were together. They watched the clouds hoping that they would increase in size and number, but they remained the same, light drifting masses of gray. It became evident that the night was not going to make any change to help. Nor would it be against them. It was just neutral.

A moon came out and faded in its proper time. It was dark within the grove, but the Mexican sentinels outside could have seen anybody coming from it. Then the Panther gathered his men together in the deepest shadow of the trees near the creek. Only Elwell was left behind and he would never know. Every man was on his horse with his weapons ready.

"Boys," said the Panther, "we have agreed to swim the creek an' tackle whatever is on the other side. We want to get into the water as gentle as we can, an' at the place where the swimmin' is best not more than six can go abreast. I'll go with the first six an' in the last bunch I name Obed, Stump and Mr. Larkin. If that three ain't as good then I miss my guess by a long shot."

The three men whom he called smiled to themselves, pleased secretly at the flattering but truthful words. Ned and Will went with the Panther and they rode their horses as gently as possible into the stream. Nevertheless, as the bank was steep and the animals were soon swimming, there was much splashing and noise.

"If they're keeping good watch at all," whispered Ned to Will, "they're bound to hear us. But if part of us gain the bank we can drive them off and help the others to reach it, too."

While they were yet swimming they heard rapid hoof-beats near the shore that they were seeking, a loud shout, and then a shot which Ned knew by its hollow roar to be that of a smooth-bore musket. Here was full evidence that the Mexicans were neglecting the watch in no particular.

The Panther urged his horse on with great energy, and every one in the line of six did the same.

"Make the bank! Make the bank!" he cried. "If they pen us up in the stream we're lost!"

More shots were fired and two or three bullets whistled over their heads. Others splashed in the water. Another, better aimed than the rest, struck a Texan full in the heart. He fell quietly from his horse and drifted away with the stream. Now they heard faintly the shouts of Mexicans behind them and they knew that Urrea, warned by his sentinels, was charging upon the grove with the full force of his cavalry.

"Will we ever make it?" exclaimed Will.

"We surely will," said Ned. "Now our horses' feet touch bottom. We are wading and we go faster."

Another second or two and the horses of the first six climbing the steep bank stood among the grass and bushes. The second six were hard upon their heels and then came the others. The Panther, raising his rifle, fired at a shadowy figure on a pony and Ned sent a bullet at another.

Then the Panther loosed his mighty voice. He called upon his comrades to charge, to ride down the skulking cowards, he said that one Texan was worth ten Mexicans. His thunder encouraged his comrades and they galloped swiftly forward through the bushes, the Mexicans who were not in large force on that side of the stream, melting away before them.

But a crash arose behind them. Urrea and his cavalry galloping through the wood had opened fire across the creek. The great rear guard of six that included Obed, Stump and Mr. Larkin, had turned and were sending bullets into the dark mass. More of the Texans quickly turned also and they sent back such a hail of bullets that Urrea and his men did not dare the crossing. Ned's hasty glance over his shoulder showed them hovering on the brink, fearful of the plunge. Then the Panther, swelling with triumph, sung his war song.

"Come on, you Mexicans!" he roared. "If there's any rippin' an' t'arin' an' chawin' to be done we're the people for you! Ho, you Urrea! If you are there, you slaughterer of unarmed prisoners, spur your horse into the creek an' come to meet us! You won't come, will you? Well, we're the Texans, an' we're goin' to join Houston! Then we'll come to meet you! Don't forget it, Urrea, if you're there! A lot of us have accounts to squar' with you an' we're goin' to squar' 'em!"

But the Mexicans, notwithstanding their large force, still did not dare the stream, and the detachment before the Panther and his men was too weak to stop them. After hurling back their defiance they scattered the Mexican horsemen on the shore and though three men were slain, falling amid the bushes, the rest made good their flight to the open prairie, where they rode steadily northward, despite the fact that they lost two more men killed and several wounded. It was a time in which men could not mourn long over the fallen, they must think of the living.

They rode for a full hour before stopping, and then struck forest again. When they were well within its shadow they stopped and could neither hear nor see any sign of the Mexicans. Undoubtedly their bold dash had shaken off Urrea for the time, and they cared little about his pursuit now. They were flushed with victory, their horses were good, and they could leave the Mexicans behind while they sought Houston.

They took an hour's rest in the edge of the timber, every man dismounting, rubbing down his horse and also stretching his own muscles. The wounded received the rude but efficient surgery of the plains, and spoke scornfully of their hurts, considering themselves as good as anybody else. Meanwhile Ned and several others, keen of eye, kept watch upon the plain, but saw nothing.

When the men remounted they rode through the woods at a walk, but the strip of forest was narrow and in two miles, soon after dawn, they came out upon another prairie, extremely marshy now, and cut by many flood-time springs. Its passage would be very hard for the horses and they were drawing together to debate it when Ned's eyes caught a flash, like a tiny imitation of the modern searchlight. The flash moved quickly across his face, appeared against the woods, and then disappeared. He called instant attention to it and then it reappeared several times, a beam of brilliant light playing through the air.

"I think it comes from that hill on the far side of the prairie," said Ned to the Panther.

"I'm shore it does," replied the Panther, "an' it's a signal throwed by a burnin' glass held in the rays of the sun. I feel shore no Mexicans are ahead of us, an' it must come from Texans. Mebbe they can see us from the hill. I'm sorry we ain't got any glass to talk back with, but we'll ride straight for the hill."

They put their horses into the muddy prairie and as they advanced slowly the burning glass still played upon them at intervals.

"Suppose it should be a Mexican trap," said Will.

"If it is," said Ned, "we'll just break out of it as we did out of the one in the cottonwood grove. But I don't think it's any trap. I begin to make out figures now. Panther, two men on horseback are standing on that hill and waiting for us."

"Can you tell who they are?" asked the Panther, who had immense confidence in Ned's eyesight.

"Not yet, but the figures look familiar. I must have seen those men somewhere before."

Ned shaded his eyes with his hand and was silent for a minute or two as they rode forward.

"Yes, I know them," he said. "The one on the right is a hunter and scout. Some of you Texans may have heard of him. He was born away up north in New York State, but there isn't a better Texan anywhere in the world. He is a little bit deaf, but it doesn't seem to interfere with him."

"Deaf Smith!" exclaimed the Panther joyfully.

"And the other was born in Tennessee, a thick and very strong—"

"Nobody but old Hank Karnes!" interrupted the Panther, "the finest pair in the world, an' they've been waitin' there on the hill signallin' to us. Forward, boys! Gallop if the mud will let you!"

They put their horses to the run, and the Panther, curving his hand in a trumpet about his mouth shot forth words that carried like rifle shots.

"Ho, you Smith and Karnes, are you there 'cause you're the only ones left, or are you there to watch for us?"

Every heart in the little troop beat hard and fast, as they waited for the reply. They saw Karnes put his own hand trumpet-shaped to his mouth, and back came his reply in words, also like rifle shots:

"We're just waitin' for you. Houston an' his men are on ahead, an' you're needed badly!"

In a few minutes more they were at the hill and were shaking hands with the two scouts. The Panther told them rapidly of their encounter with Urrea and of their escape.

"Thank God we've found you so quick!" exclaimed Smith, who almost for the first time since Ned had known him showed excitement, "We came out to look for you. Every Texan is needed now. Things are closin' in, boys! I tell you they're closin' in!"

"You got back safe to Houston with them dispatches and the news that Santa Anna is here?"

"We did, an' we didn't lose no time in reachin' him either. We found Houston an' our men on the side of Buffalo Bayou opposite Harrisburg. Our Secretary of War, Colonel Rusk, was with the general, and so was that big merchant, Mr. Roylston. When I gave that bag full of dispatches to the general an' they had read 'em an' I had told, too, what I heard from you, there was a stir that would do your heart good.

"Houston an' Rusk had a conference, an' it wasn't so mighty long, nor was it so mighty private. 'I think we've talked long enough,' says Houston, 'you want to go out an' fight the Mexicans an' so do I.' 'We're agreed,' says Rusk, an' that ended it. The boys were terrible pleased. Houston had been doin' so much retreatin' that they were afraid he'd keep on at it. I believe that to the very last he's been underratin' us."

"Then what happened?" asked Ned.

"When the boys were thinkin' that Houston would lead 'em off toward the Trinity he called 'em together, an' standin' there among 'em, said: 'This army is goin' to cross the bayou an' it will meet the enemy. Some of us will fall, and some must fall. But, my Texans, re-member the Alamo, the Alamo, the Alamo!' It was a short speech, but he couldn't have made a better. You ought to have seen him standin' there with the fire jumpin' in sparks from his eyes. Every one of the boys was touched with fire, too, as he heard them words. Then Colo-nel Rusk stood up to make a speech, and he was talkin' fine, when he suddenly broke off right in the middle an' says: 'Boys, there's no need to say more. I'm done.' He saw that the fire in the veins of the boys was mighty hot now an' didn't need any more fannin'."

"What did they do next?" asked the Panther eagerly. He was be-ginning to share Smith's excitement.

"I think our boys then were mostly mad with the wish to get at Santa Anna, when they heard that he was comin' within reach. They began at once to cross the bayou so there wouldn't be deep water between him an' them. Buffalo Bayou is flooded an' it's runnin' like a deep river. Everybody fell to work. We made rafts of the timber an' we pulled 'em across the stream with ropes. We made the horses swim. Houston stood on this side of the bayou, callin' to the men to come on, an' Rusk stood on the other, tellin' 'em to hurry. But they'd have hurried anyhow. It was twilight when the last horse an' man were across."

"Did they stop there?"

"Not a bit. They pushed right on through the dark in the direction they thought Santa Anna was. Just think of that, boys! Men anxious to march all night to get it the enemy, after spendin' a whole day buildin' rafts an' crossin' a big flood. They went on until a lot of 'em got so weak they just tumbled ag'inst one another an' fell down in the mud. Then we rested two hours, but even before the time was up the Tex-ans were callin' out loud to be led on ag'in. They kept up the marchin' until mornin', when they camped on the wet prairie. Then Houston sent Hank an' me on, thinkin' that mebbe we'd find you fellers an' bring you in. We've found you an' God knows you're needed. In two more hours you can be in Houston's camp."

"Somethin' led us the right way," said the Panther solemnly, "an' I guess that God, after puttin' us through so many trials, is goin' to give us a chance."

"The hour is at hand," said Stephen Larkin, in deep and solemn tones.

Ned felt a thrill so keen that it made him shiver. Houston! Houston! How often they had heard that name. Some had attacked it and to some it had appeared a tower of strength. Now it was the tower of strength. Houston, with all his force, was coming forward and Santa Anna was advancing to meet him. Texas was to be won or lost on a single cast.

"Will," said Ned, "we'll soon be members of Houston's army. Let's stick together whatever happens."

"Of course," said Will.

"We'll all stick together," said Stump, who overheard them. "You two an' me an' the Panther, an' Obed an' Smith an' Karnes, an' we'll make a team, too."

"United we stand, divided we're grain for the scythe of the reaper," said Obed.

"We'll rip an' t'ar an' chaw together to the end," said the Panther.

But they did not waste much time in talking. Smith and Karnes, rejoicing greatly over this hardy reinforcement, led the way. Urrea was far behind, and there could be no further danger from him. Apprised by his scouts that Houston was not far ahead, he would turn back or would await Almonte and Santa Anna.

It seemed to Ned as he rode forward that it had all come about as if both Texans and Mexicans had been moved by a master hand in a great and terrible game that meant destruction for the loser. The Mexican orders from Santa Anna were to spare no prisoners and the Texan blood was up.

Both sides had been moving almost blindly about the vast spaces of Texas, but that master hand was now bringing them together. Ned had a supreme conviction that the end was approaching, whatever it might be.

In an hour they saw dim lights over the prairie and Smith and Karnes said that they were made by the camp fires of Houston's army. Then they rode forward at a rapid pace.

Chapter 13

In Houston's Camp

Ned and Will could not restrain their impetuosity. They rode forward rapidly and the whole troop swung ahead with them. They saw many fires burning on a prairie and about them men cooking food. Other men were eating or were rubbing down horses or were lying on blankets resting after their tremendous labours of the night and day. Some slept soundly amid all the noise of a camp.

A tall man of middle age stood near one of the fires. His hands were folded behind his back and he was looking thoughtfully into the blaze. He wore an old black coat, through which his shoulders were almost bursting, a waistcoat of faded black velvet and tight pantaloons, snuff in colour. His high boots were worn and covered with dried mud. He held in his hand a hat of broad brim, much dilapidated like the rest of his attire. A sword in a silver-plated scabbard hung from his belt, but the scabbard itself was fastened to the belt with strips of buckskin. It was a plain and simple figure but no one interrupted him as he looked into the fire, and, even had he not seen him before, Ned would have known that this was Houston.

Houston looked up when he heard the shoutings and the hoof-beats, disclosing a worn and weary face. The lines running from either side of his nose to the corners of his mouth were sharp and deep and there were networks of fine wrinkles about his eyes. There had been enough in the last few months to age Sam Houston and give him sleepless nights. He carried upon his shoulders the fate of a whole vast region. The Texans were to win or to go to a cruel death, according to his judgment. Hence he had hung back. He had retreated and he had seemed to waver. Used in his early youth to the iron rule of Andrew Jackson he had, perhaps, underrated the desperate valour of the Texans, and had feared their lack of discipline.

His lieutenants had taunted him to his face. They said that their wives and children were left at the mercy of a cruel foe, while he retreated continually before Santa Anna. He had borne it all patiently. But he would bear it no longer, and he had agreed with Rusk that the time for battle was at hand. But his numbers were small, very small. His soul was tortured with fear for the result, and the terrible consequences sure to follow, if they failed.

But when Houston looked up and saw half a hundred new men riding into his camp the whole weary face was illuminated with a smile. He knew these riders of the plains. He knew Ned, the brave and brilliant youth, who had done so much. He knew the Panther, that gigantic figure, strongest of strong men, the hero of a hundred battles. He knew Stump, looking almost as large in the saddle as the Panther himself. He knew Obed White, the long, lean, clever, red-headed man with his cheerful philosophy, and he knew that those who rode behind them were fearless and able, too, a powerful help to his army that was all too small.

Houston stepped forward. All the men sprang from their horses and saluted respectfully. The Panther, holding his horse by the bridle, was the spokesman, as became him.

"We've come, gen'ral," he said, "to do whatever you tell us to do. We started as fifty-four an' we come in as forty-eight. But as we've had a brush with the Mexican cavalry I reckon we've done well to lose only six. I'm not boastin', sir, but the other forty-eight, if it's needed, are ready to die in the same way for Texas."

Houston smiled again. It was a rare, ingratiating smile that warmed the hearts of men. He liked this candid giant, and he liked the help he brought. He and the Panther shook hands warmly, and then Stump and the others were made welcome in the same way. To Ned he said:

"Your very arrival here, my boy, after so many dangers, is a sure omen of victory."

The Panther and Obed glanced at each other significantly. But Ned did not notice them. He had seen another figure, that of an elderly man, with a clean-shaven face, and a great brow, intellectual and magnificent. Ned ran forward to meet him.

"Mr. Roylston!" he cried.

"Yes, it is I," said the merchant, taking the eager hand, "I did not think that we should meet again so soon, nor did I dream that we should ever meet under such conditions, but here we are."

"What made you come?" asked Ned.

"Doubtless the same reason that made you do so. I am a merchant, and it seems strange that I should be here on what promises to be a battlefield, but my feelings and a large part of my business are wrapped up in Texas. Briefly, I could not stay away."

Ned surmised that the merchant had furnished a large part of the sinews of war to the Texans. He had heard much from Smith and Karnes of the "Twin Sisters" that had come all the way from Cincinnati, the gift of the people, to help the desperate colonists, and he knew that Roylston's hand had been largely behind the gift. Presently he saw these famous "Sisters." They were only little six-pounders, but the Texans had polished them until they were bright and terrible.

Near one of the Sisters Ned found that same Alfonso de Zavala, the sympathetic young Mexican who for a brief space had been one of his jailers in the City of Mexico. Now his father, Lorenzo de Zavala, a Liberal Mexican, with great estates north of the Rio Grande, was vice-president of the new Republic of Texas, and he had come some days before into the Texan camp with eighty men to fight for Texan freedom.

Ned and young Zavala greeted each other warmly, and after the words of welcome the gallant young Mexican began to laugh heartily.

"I notice that your hair is rather long," he said. "Isn't it about time to have it cut again. I remember you best by your lack of appetite at the capital and your long hair. Ah, it was a clever trick, and, as you may now surmise, I am glad that you escaped. My father could not stand the tyranny of Santa Anna and fled for his life. I, too, have come joyfully, and we and some other Mexicans fight side by side with the Texans for liberty. May I present you to my father?"

"I should be glad to see him if he is willing," replied Ned.

Lorenzo de Zavala, vice-president of Texas, was sitting on some brushwood, but he rose and received Ned most kindly. He was a grave and dignified man, the highest type of Mexican, universally liked and respected by the Texans. He was of absolute integrity and great ability, and they had put him in their second highest office. His calmness, penetration and resolution had already been of great help to them. He had a northern residence and estates near the San Jacinto, and no man of all those present was likely to suffer more than he in case the Texans were defeated. He smiled as he laid a friendly hand upon Ned's shoulder.

"I have heard of you from my son, Alfonso," he said. "You are a brave and ingenious lad and I trust that you and he and the youth whom you have with you will be the best of friends here, where we are united so closely by one common bond, that of victory or death."

He spoke gravely, and with so much fervour that Ned was deeply moved.

"I know, sir, the position in which we stand," he said, "and I also shall be glad indeed if your son will honour us with his friendship."

Unconsciously he adopted the courtly style and somewhat precise words characteristic of the high-bred Mexican gentleman. But his feeling was deep, nevertheless. Making a salute to the vice-president, he went away and wandered through the camp with young Zavala and Will Allen.

It was a rude camp on the wet prairie. There was not much to it except the men who made it, and they were one of the most extraordinary little groups ever gathered in the world's history. In them all was the spirit of the Alamo, the same spirit that animated the Grecian three hundred when they stood in the pass and faced the millions. They did not speak of odds or the need of caution. They thought of their slaughtered brethren, of broken faith and massacres, and of the desolation that Santa Anna had made where he had passed. He was to them the arch-demon, Satan himself, and now, having made up their minds to measure their last and utmost strength with him, all fear passed. They felt the singular calm that comes when we know things are unalterable.

Yet they were a rude lot to look upon. They were clad mostly in the buckskin of the border, and whether buckskin or not their clothes were old and frayed. They were spattered with the mud through which they had marched so long, but their arms were clean and bright.

Ned found the Texans quiet in manner. They had shot some wandering cattle that morning and they were cooking a late breakfast. He and Will and Zavala were welcomed at the fires, and they ate tender steaks with men whom they had never met before, but who were already comrades for the battle. Ned was asked many questions and the answers were awaited eagerly. He had seen Santa Anna more than once, then how did he look, what was his manner? Was it true that he killed prisoners with his own hand?

While Ned answered as well as he could they heard the faint sound of shots on the horizon. The whole army sprang to its feet and looked off there in the sunlight. The Texans saw light puffs of smoke and many of them ran to their horses. But Houston gave orders at once. He quickly detailed fifty men to ride toward the firing, see what it meant, and do what was needed. Mirabeau Lamar, later on president of the Texan Republic, led the detachment and Ned, Will, Zavala, the Panther, Obed and Stump could not be kept out of it.

It was a scattered firing, but it continued. There were numerous puffs there on the horizon, where the sun shone so brightly, and the fifty Texans rode fast. It was a rifle fire, increasing in volume, and it might mean that the whole army of Santa Anna was at hand. He was a man of boundless energy—they gave the arch-demon his due—and he was full of surprises.

"Some of our sentinels are scouting in that direction," said Lamar, "and undoubtedly they have been attacked."

"An' there's nothin' but Mexicans to attack 'em," said the Panther. "It's a Mexican vanguard. It's bound to be."

They increased their speed, and the puffs of smoke grew more distinct. They also saw flashes of fire, and then men on horseback withdrawing slowly, but wheeling every minute or two, and firing from long rifles.

"Those are our sentinels," said Lamar.

"An' they are givin' a mighty good account of themselves," said the Panther. "They can't be more'n a dozen, but you'd think from the way they was firin' that they was fifty. An' you can see off there the puffs of smoke from them that are attackin'. Ned, you've got the best eyes, can you make out who they are?"

"I see horsemen, at least a hundred," replied Ned, "and I catch the sun glinting now and then on an epaulet. They are the Mexican cavalry."

"Almonte or Urrea, or both," said the Panther.

"Which means," said Lamar, "that it is only their vanguard. If Santa Anna is within striking distance he would push forward in full force, instead of having a cavalry skirmish."

"But that doesn't keep us from takin' a hand in the business before us," said the Panther.

"Not at all," said Lamar, as they quickened the pace of their horses again, and drew up on a level with their own scouts.

"We were attacked a few moments ago by Mexican cavalry riding out of the forest," said one of the scouts hastily, "an' they're pressin' us hard. They seem to be a hundred in number, but I don't know what's behind 'em."

"Neither do we," said Lamar, "but we'll show 'em what's behind you. Now, men, turn and we'll do a little attacking ourselves."

The Texans formed in a line across the prairie and awaited the Mexican advance. Their long rifles were held parallel with their horses' heads, and they were ready, on the instant for the command to fire. The Mexicans were not far away, but they halted when they saw the increase in the Texan force, and gathered more closely together.

"I see Urrea!" exclaimed Ned. "Look! He is near the centre, the man with the gold epaulets!"

"I see him, too," growled the Panther. "I wish my rifle would carry a hundred yards further."

"We've no orders to charge them," said Lamar, "but General Houston told us to do whatever seemed needful, and as a charge looks to me like the right thing now we'll make it. Forward, boys, and drive 'em away!"

He shouted the command, and the Texans, already eager to get at the foe, uttered a roar. Then they galloped forward in a curving concave line. Before the astonished Mexicans could collect themselves the Texans were within range and firing. But Urrea again showed himself a capable cavalry leader. Although men and horses were falling already he issued quick orders, made his force spread out and return the Texan fire, at the same time retreating slowly.

The combat proceeded wholly on horseback, but the Mexicans, although two to one, were no match for the Texans. Their muskets did not have the range of the Texan rifles, nor were they by any means such accurate marksmen. But they were superb horsemen, and they protected themselves, as far as possible from the bullets with the necks and bodies of their mounts. Sometimes the Texans were forced to shoot the horses themselves, but the Mexicans always leaped lightly away, as agile as bull fighters, and sprang up behind some comrade.

"We'll drive 'em back on the wood soon," said Lamar, "and we'd best not follow them there."

"No," said the Panther. "We must not run into any ambush. I guess Sam Houston doesn't want to lose any men now."

Urrea and his force reached the forest, and, from its shelter, shouted defiance and maintained a heavy fire.

"We'll let 'em keep that up if it suits 'em," said Lamar, "and we'll ride back to camp with the news that we've met the Mexican vanguard."

"They won't follow us," said the Panther, looking at the wood. "They've seen how we can rip an' t'ar an' bite."

The Panther was right, as the Mexican cavalry remained in the wood, after the Texans began to withdraw, continuing to shout defiance and to fire an occasional shot.

"Let 'em keep it up," said the Panther with satisfaction. "It don't hurt us an' the more powder an' lead they shoot away the less they'll have for the big battle that is comin'."

Now they rode at a fair pace back to their own camp. As only two of their number had been wounded, and they not badly, they felt much encouraged by their success in the skirmish. Houston, Zavala and Rusk were waiting for them.

"It must surely mean that Santa Anna intends to attack us," said Houston. "Perhaps he is now at the ferry. And if we were mistaken and he should be going to Anahuac for a movement on Galveston he would have to take the same ferry."

"Then suppose we march at once to the ferry," said Rusk.

"A wise suggestion," said Houston. In fifteen minutes the army which had already done so much marching was on the march again for Lynch's Ferry at the point where Buffalo Bayou and the San Jacinto River united. The men, although not half rested, made no complaint. Those on foot plodded sturdily on, and those on horseback rode by their side in the mud. At intervals infantry and cavalry exchanged places. Houston was near the head of the column, Rusk was in the middle and Zavala at the rear. Now and then these three men so high in office dismounted like the rest and gave their saddles for the while to footmen.

The Twin Sisters, drawn by strong horses, were near the front, side by side. Their wheels cut deep in the mud, and sometimes sank to the hub. Houston once more put his own shoulder to the wheel and pushed with the others, until the gun came from the deep mud with a sticky sigh. Then he plodded on, his snuff-coloured trousers thrust into his high boots, the mud flying over him as it flew over everybody.

Ned thought the Mexican horsemen would be watching on the horizon, but he saw none. He concluded that Urrea had merely been making a scout in force, and that he had now withdrawn to join the main body under Santa Anna. But he made no comment, because now the little army had ceased to talk, yet there was plenty of sound, and it was mostly a vast sigh as hundreds of feet were dragged out of the famous, sticky Texas mud.

But the men thought most of the cannon. They loved the Twin Sisters. They handled them carefully, they helped them through the bad places, and they watched, that nothing might interfere with their mechanism of working order. They could not bear to see them muddy all over, even on the march, and when the flying mud struck upon their shining metal barrels somebody always wiped it off.

Ned, Will and young Zavala called it the Muddy March, a name that stuck, but the men were far from unhappy. Action, a sense of an impending great event, keyed them up. After a while, tiring of the human silence, they whistled and sang. The songs were mostly sentimental, like others of the time, and told of their true loves at home, sighing at the windows, until they should come. It is a singular or perhaps a reasonable fact that men going into battle knowing that death may be near grow sentimental.

But the songs dampened their spirits no more than the mud. The steady march went on. Never for a moment did the pace diminish. When the whistling chorus began it increased perceptibly.

"How far away is this ferry?" asked Ned of young Zavala. "I hope it's not more than a thousand miles."

"It's something under a thousand miles," replied Zavala, "but on such a deep and sticky soil as this I think we should measure by time and not by distance. We ought to get there in two hours."

But after the next hour Houston ordered a short pause for rest. He did not mean for his troops, when overwhelmed with exhaustion, to meet Santa Anna and his vastly superior numbers. He must take every precaution now, because the last weapon of the Texans was in his hand.

They resumed their rapid march, both horses and men greatly refreshed, and Stump announced to the boys that the ferry was not far away.

"What will we do if we find Santa Anna and his army there?" asked Will.

"Pitch right into it," said Stump. "I'm a timid man myself, but sometimes things drive me right on in spite of myself. Besides, I've got to keep with the Texans and do whatever they do."

"I see water," cried the Panther, who was a little ahead, "an' as shore as I'm a livin' sinner there's a boat in the stream, too. Mebbe Santa Anna an' his army are crossin'. No, they ain't! It's just one boat, a big flatboat, an' I see no troops on the shore!"

"Gallop forward and seize the boat!" cried Houston.

A hundred Texans, Ned and Will with them, put their tired horses to the run and in a few moments they were in full view of the deep stream. A dozen Mexicans were trying to row rapidly away a great flatboat, which swayed in the middle of it.

"Spoils! spoils!" cried the Panther. Then he shouted to the Mexicans: "Bring it to the shore if you know what's good for you!"

When the frightened Mexican oarsmen saw the muzzles of many rifles turned upon them they obeyed as quickly as anyone could wish. The flatboat grounded against the bank, and then the Texans saw that they had in truth taken a prize. Ned, the Panther and others leaped on board, and found that it was loaded with supplies of all kinds.

"Here's beef!" cried Ned.

"An' here's bread, an' lots of it!" said the Panther.

"An' here's a big pile of blankets!" said Stump. "I'm willin' to sleep under 'em, even if they are made in Mexico."

"And here are ten barrels of powder!" said Will. "We'll use it against its owners."

"And here are medicines," said Obed White, "and we're likely to need 'em. Mexicans heal the Texans!"

They also found considerable quantities of lead which they would melt into bullets, further supplies of provisions, including venison, flour, meal and dried fruits, the whole constituting a most valuable capture for the Texan Army. The Mexicans meanwhile stood on the bank, under guard, and shivering with fear. They expected to be shot in a few minutes, feeling sure that the Texans would treat them as Santa Anna had ordered all Texan prisoners to be treated. The Panther noticed that their faces were yellower than ever, and that their teeth were knocking together.

"We're only poor boatmen, *señor*," one of them said as the terrific figure loomed over them.

"Yes, I can see that you are boatmen, an' a pretty poor lot, too," said the Panther, "but all the same, if I was Santa Anna an' you was Texan boatmen, no matter how poor, your lives wouldn't have more than five minutes to run. Now, don't begin to beg an' pray. There ain't no Santa Anna here and we ain't goin' to kill you. 'Stead of that we're goin' to make you work. Jump right in, help take the stuff out of that boat, an' then help load it on our horses."

The prisoners, assured of their lives, obeyed gladly enough. Everything of value was taken from the boat, and put on the horses. While they were engaged in the task Houston and the main army came up, and this little triumph spread a feeling of elation among all the soldiers. Houston learned from the boatmen that the supplies were being held at the ferry for Santa Anna who was now on the same side of the river that Houston was, and who was expected there that day.

The news that Santa Anna was coming, that he might arrive at any moment, spread fast through the little army and it was welcome. All their wrongs, all the massacres, the memory of all their kin and friends, and of all the treacheries crowded upon them. Now they would do or die. There was not a coward among them.

Ned, Will and young Zavala were on foot now, their horses being loaded with the spoils from the boat. As they stood together they saw Houston, the elder Zavala, Rusk and John Roylston draw together for a brief conference. Every one in his turn spoke quickly and earnestly, and Ned noticed that the merchant received equal deference with the others.

Houston presently gave orders and they marched about a half mile to a grove that grew thickly on the banks of the bayou. It was a fine grove, one that drew Ned's admiring eye, one that he was destined never to forget. It was composed wholly of huge live oaks, from which the weeping Spanish moss hung in great quantities. There was no undergrowth, but instead a carpet of fine clean turf.

The men entered the grove of live oaks joyously, and the horsemen, dismounting, took their horses to the rear, where they secured them. But Ned returned with all speed to the edge of the grove, and examined the country. Before them lay a prairie that undulated away gently for about two miles. Beyond it were the marshes of the San Jacinto River, which he could mark by the line of tall timber curving away to the south. The prairie was unbroken save by two clumps of trees four or five hundred yards in front of their position, but the grass upon it was exceedingly tall, owing to the heavy and continuous rains. Everywhere the vegetation was full and luxurious, and, now that the sun was shining, it glowed in many brilliant hues.

Ned scanned the horizon long and carefully, but he saw no human being. The vanguard of Santa Anna had not yet appeared. Then he went back into the grove, where the men were quietly placing themselves in order with the deep and broad bayou in their rear. Ned marked the significance of the battleground that Houston had chosen. There could be no retreat. They must win or die. Fugitives would find the unfordable bayou before them. But there would be no fugitives. He saw the spirit of the Alamo shining forth once more in its full glory.

The Twin Sisters under their chief, Neill, were advanced to the edge of the grove, where they were planted with their muzzles pointing across the prairie. Solicitous hands wiped their wheels clear of mud. They must be clean, bright and fresh for the battle. The gunners gathered around them, each detailed to his place, and ready at a moment's notice.

But there was yet no sign of Santa Anna, and Houston ordered the noonday food to be served to the men. They ate, sitting about the grove in groups, and were calm enough also to lie down on the soft turf, and wait until they should be called. They knew that the scouts at the edge of the wood would see the first advance of Santa Anna.

Ned sat near Stephen Larkin and he saw the man's lips moving, although he uttered no word. The minister was praying. The harrying of the Texans, the ruthless slaughter had stirred him to the very core of his soul. He was praying God now to make mighty the arms of the Texans that a land might be free.

But Stump was cheerful for such a timid man. He saw both sides of the shield.

"Ned," he said, "it's a lot of pleasure to know that all our marchin' through mud is about done. I was never so tired of anything in my life. Skeered as I am, I'd ruther stop an' fight Santa Anna an' have it all over, one way or the other."

"I feel that way, too," said Ned.

"The time for runnin' has passed an' the time for rippin' an' t'arin' an' chawin' has come," said the Panther sententiously.

"It's a long lane that has no Mexican at the end," said Obed White.

Ned left them after a while and went to the edge of the live oaks, where he found John Roylston who was attentively watching the prairie, which still showed nothing but the tall and waving grass. The merchant put his hand upon Ned's shoulder, and his manner was that of a father to a son.

"Ned," he said, "the battle is at hand. We cannot doubt it. We must triumph, but in case we should not I am willing to fall with the others. Now I am glad you have joined me here, because I have something to say to you which I shall keep from everybody else. You will guard the secret until after the battle, will you not?"

"Of course," said Ned, much impressed by the manner of the merchant, who never spoke without cause.

"You are ingenious and brave and you are to be trusted," said Roylston. "I have, as I have intimated to you before, furnished much of the money for this war. Literally, I have financed the Texans. I have done it for many reasons. Sam Houston and I were friends in boyhood, although I am the older of the two. We were together at the Horse Shoe Bend, when Andrew Jackson fought the great battle with the Creek nation. I helped to nurse Houston back to life. We are knit together by ties that nothing can break. I am bound to help him, now that he is the leader in a war for home and life.

690

"Moreover, I am deeply interested in the fortunes of Texas. I have risked most of my life's earnings in its growth and development. If it were subjected again to Mexican rule I should be ruined. And above all, the Texan people have my deepest sympathies. They have been harried and decimated by a cruel and relentless foe. It is the dearest wish of my heart to see them victorious, the few against so many. I have smuggled arms and ammunition for them from New Orleans, and I glory in it. I have come myself, and now after this rather long and perhaps boastful peroration I reach the meat of what I have to say."

The man who rarely smiled smiled now. It was a noble smile, illuminating his broad, stern countenance, and giving to it, for the moment, a wonderful softness. Ned waited in silence.

"As I have told you before," he continued, "I have great sums of money on deposit in foreign financial institutions in Mexico, which Santa Anna cannot touch, though he would dearly like to do it. But I cannot touch them myself unless I send the proper authority. These authorities are letters of credit and bills of exchange, signed duly. I have them upon my person and if they fall into Mexican hands they could be used, even if those who used them had to resort to clever forgery in order to transfer them. And if I were dead nobody would be interested in disproving or disputing the forgery."

Ned did not yet understand, but he continued to wait in silence.

"What I want you to do, in case I fall," continued Roylston, "if you do not fall too, is to secure these papers from my body, and if necessary to destroy them. I brought them with me, because I cannot go back now to New Orleans. I foresaw that I might have to go to one of the British ports in the West Indies to raise money for the Texans, places where I am personally unknown. I suspect that Santa Anna and one or two of his lieutenants know that I am here and what I have. Therefore since you are ingenious and clever I wish your help to save this money from the dictator. If you were to fall into his hands he might spare you, for a while at least. Be the first to search my body and destroy the letters of credit and bills of exchange."

"Mr. Roylston," exclaimed Ned vehemently, "don't talk of our defeat and your death!"

"I am not expecting them," he replied calmly. "I am merely taking a precaution. I have your promise?"

"Certainly," replied Ned.

"Then," said Roylston, with quiet satisfaction, "I have something more to add. Take this and put it in your pocket where you are sure not to lose it."

He took from his own pocket a small sealed envelope and handed it to Ned, who put it without a word in the inside pocket of his coat.

"I am glad you have not asked me what it contains," said Roylston, "but I will tell you. It is my will, a holographic will, but perfectly good. I make you my sole heir, on condition that you carry on my business as soon as you arrive at suitable age. Meanwhile it will be in the hands of capable lieutenants."

Ned gazed at him too much astonished to say a word.

"Your heir!" he exclaimed at last. "Why do you do this?"

"I have already examined myself on that point," replied the merchant, "and I have arrived at my conclusion. We come from the same State, and I have discovered that there is a distant kinship between us like the thread that runs through great groups of people in Virginia or Kentucky or Tennessee. Certainly I have no kin closer, but that does not count for so much. You will remember that you saved my life, when no chance seemed to be left. But while I am greatly grateful, that in itself is not the cause, or the chief cause."

He paused and examined the youth with his slow and thoughtful gaze.

"I have never married," he said, "but I crave someone to stand in the place of a son to me and to take up my work when I am old. I do not care to heap up money for strangers. I should like to know while I am alive that the enterprises I have founded will go on when I am dead. Although the tie of blood between us is but slender it has seemed to me that nature has chosen you for this position. You have decision, courage and mental grasp, you have also truth and honesty which are powerful weapons in the battle of the world. I have not made any rash choice. I have weighed it, and thought over it long. Nor can you remain a wilderness rover and hunter. When this war is over you must choose a career, and I offer it to you."

Ned could hardly think what to say. Certainly it was a brilliant position that the merchant painted for him.

"If we survive," he said at last, "I will go with you. And if I say nothing more now it is because I do not know what to say. But I feel the magnitude of your offer and I hope that my gratitude will be equal to it."

The merchant smiled.

"Then it is agreed," he said. "Now I won't keep you here any longer. Go with your friends. I have something to say to General

Houston."

Ned walked back to his friends, thinking intensely. Amazing things were continually happening to him, but this perhaps was the most amazing of them all. He was very quiet, but as the others were very quiet, too, no one took any notice of his manner. He and his friends were sitting in a group under one of the great live oaks, when a shout from a sentinel at the edge of the grove drew their attention.

As the Texans crowded forward the other sentinels also gave the alarm, and the whole army gathered at the border of the wood, forming a solid mass to right and left of the Twin Sisters, which were in the centre. Ned saw horsemen on the plain, short, thick men under wide *sombreros*, and he caught the glint of lances. He also saw behind these a solid dark line, extending far across the prairie. His heart began to leap and black specks danced before his eyes. Santa Anna had come and the two armies were face to face at last on the narrow land between the waters. It was then about two o'clock in the afternoon of a bright day, full of sunshine.

All the Texans were now on foot, the horses tethered securely in the rear, and doubtless there was not one heart in all their force that did not throb as Ned's did. They felt the same thrill, the same eagerness to have it out with the ruthless dictator whose hands were red with so much blood that they held dear.

"It's the cavalry of Urrea an' Almonte," said the Panther. "Ain't that what you make 'em out to be, Ned?"

"Beyond a doubt, and don't you see, Panther, the big dark mass behind them? The whole Mexican Army is here."

The Panther's face glowed and his great form seemed to expand.

"At last! At last!" he said under his breath.

The Texans formed for battle, but the Mexican cavalry stopped and the long line of their infantry advanced very slowly. The Texans said grimly to one another that the Mexicans were in no haste to rush them. They heard the hostile trumpets calling, and they saw their cavalry spread out on the wings, but they saw no sign of a charge. Ned exulted. He told himself that Santa Anna remembered the Alamo and feared the Texan rifles. He began to wonder now in just what way the attack would come. He began to watch Houston, Rusk and Roylston, who were gathered on the highest point at the edge of the grove. They had glasses and were closely watching the Mexican movements. But this was a democratic army, and many of the soldiers crowded around the leaders, anxious to know what they saw, and asking eagerly.

693

"They're bringing up cannon and putting them in position, lads," said Houston. "They'll open fire on us presently, but don't you be worried. I doubt whether they could hit the side of a mountain at that distance."

The soldiers laughed and cheered, and the Panther nodded approvingly.

"Old Sam is right where he belongs now," he said. "He's been retreatin' an' retreatin', 'cause he thought it wise to do so, but now he smells the fight, an' he's as keen for it as anybody."

He used the adjective "old" as a compound of affection and admiration, not as implying age—Houston was only forty-three that day. The next moment he uttered in imperious cry:

"Duck, boys, duck!"

He had seen a distant spurt of white smoke, and then a cannon ball crashed into the wood, but hurt nobody. Nevertheless the Mexicans were shooting better than they had expected. The Twin Sisters were silent. They were smaller guns and their range was not so great. Their crews stood around them, silent and attentive.

The Mexicans, aiming with great deliberation, fired more shots which made a great crashing in the wood, but the Texans laughed until one of the balls wounded Neill, the commander of the artillery. That gave them a shock. Some wanted to fire the Twin Sisters, but Houston decided to send forth a hundred mounted riflemen.

Ned rode by the side of the Panther, with Deaf Smith on the other side and they galloped forth with a mighty shout. Two cannon shots were fired at them, but the balls went far astray. Then the riflemen drove back the Mexican cavalry, and, as in the case of Urrea's siege, began to pick off the gunners around the cannon. The guns were quickly unlimbered, and withdrawn, and then the riflemen rode back. Santa Anna remained out of range, and seemed content with the situation.

"It's really the middle of the afternoon now," said the Panther, as he glanced up at the sun, "an' I guess he don't mean to attack today. I wonder why."

"Maybe he is waiting for reinforcements," said Ned. "I think he was expecting a force under Cos or Sesma."

"Which would make it much worse for us," said the Panther. "But at the same time, it wouldn't do for us to leave the wood now an' attack him. I guess we've just got to stand quiet an' see."

They were welcomed by Houston who gave them warm words of approval, and then the Texan Army sat down to wait.

CHAPTER 14

NED'S NIGHT JOURNEY

Ned, Will and young Zavala were sitting on the grass, under one of the great live oaks at the edge of the grove. The mournful Spanish moss hung above them, and swayed in the wind that blew lightly from the west. The Texan Army settled into silence again. The polished muzzles of the Twin Sisters projected from the wood, but all seemed peaceful there, despite the arms. The men, lying down mostly, were talking in low tones and here and there two or three were writing on faded sheets of paper with stubs of old lead pencils. They were making wills, taking the chance that if they fell their last words would some day reach the hands of friends.

Now that the great event was at hand it was almost like a dream to Ned. The people around him, the forest, the prairie and the dark line of the Mexican Army were scarcely real. It was difficult to feel that after all the marchings, strivings and risks the mightiest of moments —for them—had come. He stared long at that dark line. Urrea was there. Almonte was there, and Santa Anna was there. Little mercy would the dictator show the Texans if they were beaten. It would be Goliad over again, but without hesitation. Santa Anna was raging, because these miserable Texans kept him from his capital, the great city in the south, where he could enjoy the luxuries and splendours that he loved, and parade himself before his own admiring people.

Ned looked around with a certain curiosity at the Texans. it seemed to him that he had never realised before how very few they were. Only seven or eight hundred to stand as a barrier against the Mexican millions, and to fight a battle which, should they win it, would prove one of the great, decisive combats of history. Now the sense of it pressed upon him. He was one of the few there in the grove, under the drooping Spanish moss, who thrilled not only with the certainty of coming battle, but with the magnitude of its issues.

The Panther, who had been walking along the line, sat down with them. His gaze followed theirs.

"They're in no hurry to attack," he said, "an' it means one of two things. Either he thinks he's got us secure here, lookin' on us as a rat in a trap, or he's a little afraid an' is waitin' for reinforcements. You said, Ned, that Sesma or Cos was comin' with more men."

"That's what I learned."

"Then I think the last guess is the right one. Santa Anna is waitin' for his army to grow. He knows that we can't get out of here without a fight, but he don't know that a fight is the very thing we're lookin' for. So he bides his time, an' won't attack until his numbers are overwhelmin'."

"It seems to me that his policy is a good one for his side," said Ned.

"So it is," said the Panther, "but we may stir him up. See, Houston an' the other officers are talkin' it over."

Houston, Rusk, Sherman, Millard, Bennett, Burleson and others had gathered under one of the trees, and were talking earnestly. Ned watched them, hoping intensely that they would agree upon immediate action. He felt sure that Santa Anna's full force was not in front of them, but that other troops would soon come. If the Texans attacked now their chance of success would be greater. Nor were the men yet wearied by waiting. Their spirit was at the highest, and, as he thought, would achieve the most at this very moment. Were the fiery Texans right when they had asserted so often that Houston delayed too much?

The council broke up, and an order was sent to the cavalry to mount at once and ride toward the enemy with the purpose of bringing on a general battle. Colonel Sherman commanded, and Ned and all his friends were in this force. The Panther was on one side of him and Will on the other. Just behind him rode Obed, Stump and young Zavala.

The reins in their left hands, their rifles in their right hands, the brave horsemen rode from the wood and out upon the prairie, where the grass in places rose to the knees of their horses. The afternoon was near the middle, and the sun was at the brightest. Brilliant rays poured down upon this little band of men who rode knee to knee. It was like a spectacle, a dramatic effect, the result of chance and not of arrangement. Behind them Houston and the larger part of the army were watching intently, and before them Santa Anna and his army were not missing a single movement.

On went the horsemen with measured tread, the hoofs making a soft rhythm as they sank in the high grass. The eye at such times often takes almost unconscious note of details. Ned saw that the prairie was very beautiful. The grass was uncommonly fresh and tall. Wild flowers were blooming everywhere, and the forest afar was a great mass of living green.

His eyes, after following the curve of the prairie and the woods, came back to the Mexican lines, and he saw a movement there. Horsemen were riding out, presenting a front double that of the Texans. Ned heard a low cry of satisfaction from the Panther. It was evident that the Mexican cavalry would meet the Texan, and the general battle so much desired by the Texans might follow.

He noted that the Mexican cavalry was in great force, far outnumbering the Texans, but Sherman led on steadily. The boy was able to recognise a figure riding at the head of the Mexicans. It was the gallant and enterprising Almonte, and he believed that another not far away was that of Urrea. The Mexicans came forward in a diagonal course, and it seemed to Ned that they were trying to cut off the Texans from their own army in the wood. He was about to whisper his suspicions to the Panther, but Sherman also noted the plan, and turned the course of his own men. This brought the two columns much closer together and they began to fire at each other.

Ned heard the bullets singing and hissing through the air. A Texan near him was wounded mortally, but a comrade held him on his horse. Another nearby was hit badly, but maintained his own seat, and sent bullets in return. The conflict grew warmer. The horsemen steadily came to closer range, and the great numbers of the Mexicans gave them an advantage, enabling them to overlap the Texans. Moreover they were picked men, and Almonte and Urrea led them well.

Now they came so close together that the lines were involved. Several Texans were cut off from their friends and were about to be surrounded. A youth named Lane was wholly separated from his comrades, and his death or capture would have been a matter of seconds when the gallant Lamar rode his horse straight at the Mexicans, knocking down with his own horse one Mexican horse and rider, cutting down a second man and compelling a third to surrender, galloping back to the Texan group with his prisoner and the rescued Lane. It was an extraordinary exploit comparable to those done by the knights of chivalry when, clad in steel they fought in front of their armies. But Lamar's coat was of buckskin not of steel.

Ned had been a breathless witness of this deed which was done in a minute, and he joined in the mighty cheer that greeted Lamar and Lane as they rode up. Houston, watching anxiously from the edge of the wood through his glasses, had seen it also, and he had noticed, too, the superior numbers of the Mexicans. He instantly ordered a body of infantry to support his cavalry.

Ned, Will and Zavala kept together. They were not in close enough contact with the Mexicans to watch for the sword and lance, but they were firing their rifles and pistols as fast as they could reload into the mass of Mexican cavalry. A dense cloud of smoke was gathering over their heads and about them, interfering with the order and method of the battle.

Ned at last caught a glimpse through the smoke of the Texan infantry advancing to their support. Almonte and Urrea saw also. Fearing a deadly Texan fire on their flanks they drew back slowly, and the Texans began to shout in triumph.

"Now, we're goin' to have the big battle!" shouted the sanguine Panther.

But he was wrong. Houston, either deeming the hour too late or for some other cause, would not make the venture. When the Mexican cavalry retired he sent orders for his own cavalry and supporting infantry to withdraw also. Disappointed and chagrined, they retired slowly to the grove of live oaks. When they were well among the trees, the Panther threw himself from his horse.

"It was our chance, an' we let it go!" he exclaimed.

"But the general has to think of everything," said Obed White. "Too much haste sometimes spoils the broth, and we've got only one kettle of broth to be spoiled."

Ned, although he felt disappointment too, thought Obed was right. But he did not say anything, merely unsaddling and tethering his horse at the rear of the grove. He went back to the edge of the live oaks and looked across the prairie toward Santa Anna's army. It was obvious that no battle could be fought that day because the first haze of twilight was already appearing in the east. A few minutes later, lights sprang up in the forest on the other side of the prairie, and he knew that they were the camp fires of the Mexican army.

Fires were rising behind him, too. The Texans, despite their disappointment, were showing great patience. They were cooking their suppers now, and discussing the morrow. Then the great battle would surely be fought. It could not be delayed any longer. But Ned's attention returned to the prairie. He stood there a long time, watching the twilight thicken into the dusk, and the night come trailing after. Imaginative, always intensely alive to everything that surrounded him, he was in an excited and exalted state. It did not show itself in words or nervous movements. Externally none was more calm, but inside the soul was working at white heat.

Ned was taking a great resolution, one that involved his life, but he felt that this was the greatest chance to serve his people that had ever come to him. With his knowledge of Spanish and its Mexican variants he was the very one for the work. Yes, he would do it, he must do it, and he put away the last doubt. But he did not move until the whole curve of the world was in darkness,

Houston and his chief officers were sitting about a fire, when Ned approached and saluted respectfully:

"What is it, my boy?" asked Houston kindly.

"I have been much in Mexico, as you know, general," replied Ned, "and I not only understand the Mexican tongue but I also understand the Mexican ways. You want to know what force Santa Anna has with him and what he expects. This information is vital. I hope you won't think I'm presumptuous, sir, but all the men say it is."

"You are neither wrong nor presumptuous," said Houston. "Go on."

"I would suggest, sir, that with your leave I go to the Mexican camp and find out."

Houston stared at him a moment and then shook his head.

"Your life would not be worth a moment's purchase in the Mexican camp," he said. "It shall not be told of me that I sent a boy to his death."

"But, general, I do not take any very great risk," Ned persisted. "I have been so much among the Mexicans that I can easily pass for one. There is always a great deal of disorder about a Mexican camp. A single man can wander almost as he pleases. Let me go. I know, as all the men know, that the crisis of Texas is at hand. What happens tomorrow will mean the life or death of thousands of people. It will mean whether Texas shall become great and powerful, or cease to exist, and the knowledge that I can bring tonight may swing the balance in our favour."

Ned spoke with much earnestness, and with such complete forgetfulness of self that his words sank deeply into the mind of Houston. The frontier general was a keen judge of men. He read Ned's mind by his flushed face, and his voice, so sincere that it trembled. He hesitated, and then looked at Rusk who looked back his assent.

"Go, my boy, and God bless you," he said. "You make us a great offer, and I devoutly hope that you will come back safe."

He and his officers rose, and, one by one, shook Ned's hand. It was at once a farewell and a hope to see him again. Ned left them and quickly made his preparations, the Panther being his chief aid.

He was so much browned by sun and wind that the matter of complexion presented no difficulty. A Mexican hat and an entire Mexican costume were secured for him, piece by piece, from the other men, many of whom were dressed much like the Mexicans. While the brief transformation was being made, the Panther showed no apprehension for the youth whom he liked so much.

"Come back safe? Of course he will," he said to Obed White. "Don't he always come back safe? Hasn't he passed through things that would have been the end of you an' me, an' him only a boy, too. He's chose, Obed, you know that. He's our magic leader. Some bigger power than any that we see has put in his head the idea of goin' into Santa Anna's camp tonight, an' he's shore to bring back the very things we want to know."

"I hope you're right, you must be right, Panther," said Obed, "but it's an awful risk, and I hate to see him go."

But the Panther seemed to have never a doubt. He was the last to grasp Ned's hand in goodbye, and he said confidently:

"I'll be waitin' here at the edge of the trees when you come back before mornin'. I've only one piece of advice and it's to watch out for that fellow Urrea."

"I'll bear it in mind," said Ned as he left the grove and slipped away in the long grass. There, as he bent low, he became quickly invisible to his friends, who were watching at the edge of the grove, although he did not look back toward them. His course at present was toward the first clump of woods which stood in the prairie between the two armies.

The night was normal. If the Mexicans had out spies they might or might not see him. But he could not yet discern any figure against the dusky horizon. He advanced very swiftly now, and passed within the shadow of the first group of trees. They were not many in number, just a dense little cluster shooting up from the prairie, but it was very dark in them, and, straightening himself, he stood erect and listened.

He heard night birds calling softly to one another in the boughs high above, but he heard nothing else. Satisfied that he was alone there he left them, and crossed the grass to the second and larger clump where he sank down instantly behind a big oak. But he rose the next instant. He had seen a human figure among the trees, a short dark man in Mexican dress with a musket on his shoulder. He knew that he was a spy from Santa Anna's army and he thought it a good time to test his own skill.

Ned whistled softly. The startled Mexican whirled about and thrust forward the muzzle of his musket.

"What do you find, friend?" asked Ned. "I am of Almonte's cavalry and I have been sent here on foot to look at the Texan army. I have crept in the long grass almost to the wood in which they lie. Most of them are asleep, but a double guard watches."

"I am Miguel Marrin of the corps of Castrillon," said the man, sinking his gun muzzle and looking much relieved. "I knew that other scouts were out, but I was not told where I should meet them."

"We're likely to meet anywhere," replied Ned. "Do you go on toward the Texan camp?"

"Even so. It is my duty, a perilous one, but I fear to disobey."

"Trouble yourself but little, friend," said Ned. "It is easy enough to approach the Texan camp through the long grass. *Adios.*"

"*Adios!*" said Miguel Marrin, going on toward the task that he did not like. Ned took the other direction, and, curving a little toward the right, made for the left flank of Santa Anna's army.

The test had been a complete success. His Mexican had been perfect both in language and manner. Miguel Marrin had never suspected for an instant. Much emboldened he kept on toward the camp fires which were now growing brighter. He saw dusky figures passing before them and presently he heard the trampling of horses.

Knowing that it was unwise to go straight into the Mexican camp he veered further to one side, and struck the swamps, which now spread far out from the San Jacinto. They gave him a good line of approach and he decided that he would be a common soldier who had been sent out to look for strayed cavalry horses.

He walked in the deep mud, getting himself well spattered, which was entirely suitable to his design and came into the outskirts of the camp. He saw at once that it was in much disorder. Many of the men had thrown themselves down here and there, and hundreds were already sound asleep on the grass.

Others, however, were at work and Ned observed with grim satisfaction the task upon which they were engaged. They were building breastworks in front of the army. Many boughs of trees had been cut and they had been formed into a sort of abatis, reinforced with boxes, saddles, and all kinds of baggage. But a wide opening had been left in the centre and through it pointed the muzzles of Santa Anna's cannon.

"And so he is afraid! The great, the powerful Santa Anna is afraid!"

said Ned to himself. "He fears that the miserable Texans whom he has denounced so much will rush him in his own camp. The Mexicans would shun the battle, while the Texans seek it."

This was a great and important fact to be carried back to Houston. Santa Anna, the magnificent and invincible, was afraid, afraid of a tiny Texan army! He kept repeating it to himself, because men who are afraid do not win battles. But he must know more. He must also go back with definite details. He made his way to one of the fires where some men were eating, and, sitting down boldly, asked one of them for meat. The soldier with a casual glance passed him a piece of beef.

"Whence do you come, comrade?" he asked. "You have much mud upon your person."

"From the swamps," Ned replied in a tone of deep complaint. "I belong to the corps of Castrillon, and I was sent to look for strayed horses down in the marshes. And what marshes! The continual rains and the floods have given them a depth of which you can't conceive, comrade. I verily believe that some of them go all the way through the earth and open out on the other side in China, Japan or some other heathen country. And they are yellow, black and brown. You can see the mud on me."

All the Mexicans around the fire laughed at his vehemence. They liked him and passed him another piece of beef.

"Did you find any horses?" one of them asked.

"No, they wandered far, and after falling into one marsh after another I came back lest I should tumble into one that would swallow me up. What are the Texan cattle doing?"

"Keeping to their grove, where we will make the slaughter tomorrow. It was thought that a battle would be brought on before sunset, and the rebels seemed to wish it, but the general preferred to wait. He seems to be without his usual great courage and energy."

"That cannot be," said Ned, waiting eagerly for the answer.

"But it is so," said the man with some emphasis, proud of his information and not wishing it to be questioned. "Did I not see it myself at the place the rebels call New Washington, when our Captain Barragan brought him the news that the Texans under Houston were near? He sprang upon his horse and galloped at full speed among our troops, knocking down his own men, sending them flying right and left, and shouting aloud: 'The enemy are coming! The enemy are coming! Houston is at hand!' Ah, comrade, this singular conduct of our general who is the greatest man in the world, frightened us terribly. We were in confusion. Many of us were about to run, whither we knew not, nor from what. But he grew calmer after a while. The brave officers, Castrillon and Almonte, worked hard. Order was restored and the men were put in line. We saw no enemy, but we marched across the prairie until we did see one. See, you can behold their lights in the grove, if you stand up and look!"

Ned stood up boldly. His *sombrero* was drawn low down over his eyes and the *serape* with which he had provided himself was around his chin.

"I can see the lights," he said. "There will be merry doings tomorrow, and I shall be there and have a part. I have missed much today, through exploring those wretched swamps for horses."

"Good lad," said the man of much information. "You show a right valiant spirit, and you will have a better chance to show it tomorrow. These Texans die hard. Our officers tell us that they are cowards, but I know better. Who should know it better than I? I was at the Alamo, and perhaps my eyes shall never again look upon such another sight. All the Texans died with their faces to us, and many, very many of us died first."

"At the Alamo?" said Ned, almost in a whisper.

"Aye, at the Alamo," said the man proudly. "I was in the division of Cos then. Never can I forget that Sunday morning when we made the last charge. The band played the *Deguelo*, and we rushed forward to the sound of the music. The Texans fought like the devils they are. We left a stream of dead and dying behind us, and they fought us from room to room, until the last of them was gone."

Ned was silent for a little while. His memories were too strong.

"When will Cos be here?" he asked at length, but not wholly at random. He knew that Santa Anna would strive to reunite his divided army.

"He is expected at dawn with the pick of Sesma's army," replied the man.

Ned now remained a long time in silence. He knew all that was needed, the condition of Santa Anna and the fact that Cos would be at hand before a battle could be fought. But he was too shrewd to leave the fire now. His rifle was across his knees, he stared into the blaze, and after a while his eyelids began to droop.

"The swamps have winded you, comrade," said one of the men.

"They have, truly," said Ned. "I wish never to see or hear of a swamp again. I have to make report to my officer, but there is no

703

hurry since I bring nothing. Let me stay here a little while longer, comrades, since the fire and rest are good."

They were willing for him to stay as long as he liked, and he sank into an easier position, from which he did not stir for a full hour. Then he rose and with a word of thanks slipped away. But few of the men heard him. They were asleep.

Ned saw that he could not pass the breastworks where the guard was strong and wary, and he turned aside again for the marshes, but a great white tent drew his notice, and he stopped. He knew that it was the tent of Santa Anna, and he hoped to see the dictator himself.

In the general lack of order in the Mexican camp it was not difficult to approach the big tent. Two guards stood on either side of the entrance, but the flaps were swung wide and within twenty feet of it soldiers lay on the ground, sleeping soundly. Ned lay down with them and counterfeited sleep. Then when no one was noticing he gradually edged forward until he was within ten feet of the tent.

Ned knew that he was taking a great risk, but the desire to see Santa Anna and to learn perhaps a more intimate knowledge of his plans was overwhelming. His head lay upon his arms and from his lowered lids he could look into the tent. Then he saw Santa Anna.

The dictator, the man who in his own florid announcements marched only from one triumph to another, had changed. His manner did not now show the immense satisfaction that had always marked him hitherto. The yellowish tint of his face had deepened. There were black pouches under his eyes, which showed a greenish tint when the light from the candle on the table in front of him fell on his face. His gorgeous uniform of white and gold was splashed plentifully with mud. He seemed nervous and restless, moving his head from side to side. He reminded Ned of the black jaguar that he had faced once. Presently he put his hand inside his coat and drew out a little gold box. He opened the box, took from it a pinch of something that Ned could not see, and put it in his mouth. He closed the box, returned it to the inside pocket, and soon grew calmer.

Santa Anna had been alone in the tent, but when Ned had been watching him about ten minutes the sinewy figure of a handsome young man entered. It was Juan Nepomuceno Almonte, as Ned easily saw, and the young colonel saluted respectfully. He was followed soon by General Castrillon and other officers, including Urrea, and they all talked earnestly with Santa Anna.

Ned lay in such a position that Santa Anna faced him across the blaze of the candle. The change in the face of the man was extraordinary. Evidently he had taken a powerful dose of the drug and its effect had been rapid. His eyes were brilliant and sparkling. His whole face was flushed and Ned saw that he was talking with rapidity and confidence, although he could not hear the words he said.

They talked for a long time. Ned strained his ears, but he caught only an occasional word. But the others seemed to be inspired by the confidence of Santa Anna, and, when they left the tent, their steps were more springy than they were when they had entered.

The officers departed in different directions, and Ned hugged the earth very closely now. Urrea was coming in his direction. He walked so close to him that his feet almost touched Ned, but he never suspected that a Texan lay there among these soldiers, who, strewed upon the ground, slept through very weariness. He walked on and Ned felt relief when he was gone.

Ned looked into the tent again and he saw that Santa Anna's head was drooping over the table. The drug had spent its force already, and he was collapsing. He rose presently, as if with an effort, and Ned saw that his face was haggard. Then he gave an order to the soldiers at the entrance and the flaps were closed.

Ned, convinced that he had seen all that he could see, rose, and walked staggering, like a man yet half asleep who seeks a better couch. No attention was paid to him. Other men were wandering, engaged in a similar pursuit, or doing some task. He turned gradually away towards the marshes of the San Jacinto. The Mexicans had no guards there, knowing that an army could not come that way, and Ned was interrupted only once. A petty officer asked him his errand and he repeated the fiction about the horses. He had not been able to find them, he said, and his captain had sent him back to hunt for them again, even if it took all night. The man sympathized with him.

"A hard task," he said. "One should have some sleep before a battle."

"Aye, sleep and rest," said Ned bitterly, and with an "*Adios*" he passed on. Five minutes later he was in the marshes among bushes, tall grass and weeds, where a hundred soldiers might have hunted long without finding him. But he was able to see the Mexican camp fires' from his concealment. They were burning low now, and Ned knew that the army gathered about them had been in a disorganised state. If Houston had only pushed the attack that afternoon, when the skirmish was on, they could surely have won the victory. If he had

705

only known! But Santa Anna and his troops would be refreshed in the morning, and Cos would be there with enough new men almost to double the Mexican force. Now that he knew everything with such absolute certainty, his disappointment became intense.

But he was not one to brood over anything, and, as nearly as he could, he retraced the same circuitous route through the swamp by which he had come. His knowledge did not save him from mire and one or two falls, but in another hour he emerged from the swamps, well plastered with black, yellow, red and brown mud, and stood once more upon the comparatively solid ground of the prairie.

He lingered a while before venturing the passage of the open ground. The Mexican spies might still be abroad, and he did not wish to have trouble with any of them. He saw the low lights of Houston's camp burning on the far side of the prairie and his heart throbbed. Overhead sounded the low note of a night bird, calling.

He did not see any human figure in the tall grass of the prairie and now he ventured boldly, cocking his rifle and holding it ready for instant use. He reached the clump of timber nearest to Santa Anna's camp and paused there a while. Convinced after a period of looking and listening that nothing was moving on the prairie, he advanced to the second clump and thence to his own camp. But he took proper precautions. Before entering the wood he crouched low in the long grass, and uttered a soft whistle. The note was answered instantly from the live oaks, and, rising, he walked forward without further effort at concealment. A gigantic figure stood in the shadow of the first live oak, and an eager voice said in a loud whisper:

"Is, it you, Ned? Is it really you?"

"Yes, it's really I, Panther."

"An' have you been in the Mexican camp or did you have to turn back?"

"I've been in the Mexican camp, Panther, and I saw Santa Anna himself. He did not see me, or if he did, he did not know who I was. I've been lucky, Panther, lucky beyond our hopes."

"I knowed you'd have the luck," said the Panther with deep sincerity. But Ned did not know the basis of the Panther's confident belief.

"I've got information," he continued rapidly, "big information, information of the first importance, and I must see General Houston at once."

"He left orders that you was to be brought to him the moment you came, if you did come. This is the way, Ned."

The Panther led to a small tent, with one end open. They saw Houston lying upon some blankets. The tent contained nothing else besides his clothes and arms. The Panther called without hesitation:

"General Houston! General Houston!"

Houston sat up instantly. He had not been asleep and was at once keen and alert. He was a striking contrast to that other general in the camp on the far side of the prairie.

"Is it you, Palmer?" said Houston, peering into the dark.

"Yes, general," replied the Panther, "and the boy, Ned Fulton, is here. He has been in the camp of Santa Anna, he has seen Santa Anna himself, an' he comes back with important news."

There was a thrill of pride in the Panther's voice. Ned's exploit was an exploit by one of his own. Houston saw the shadow behind the Panther's great form, and he called quickly:

"Come in, Fulton! Come in, Ned, boy! And you have succeeded! I feared that you would never come back."

He wrung Ned's hand and then sent for Rusk and one or two others high in command. He had the Panther stay also, and then they listened to Ned's story. He told it clearly and in detail. Houston frowned a little as he listened.

"We have missed an opportunity," he said, "I concede that, gentlemen. Tomorrow we shall have Cos also to fight, but we can whip them both. We will go out and smash them on their own ground."

But Rusk demurred.

"When the division of Cos comes they will outnumber us perhaps three to one," he said, "and we should await them in our position here, which is very strong."

The other officers were silent. Ned inferred that they wished to reserve their opinions until the morning.

But Houston was sanguine. The change in him was marvellous. The man who had delayed so much, even in the face of fierce criticism, was now the most eager of them all to fight. Yet the conference was not long, and they agreed to make no decision until day came. Everyone in turn thanked Ned and praised him until he blushed, and was glad to withdraw with the Panther from the tent. Houston gave them both a caution as they went out to say nothing about the arrival of another Mexican force under Cos.

"All our boys are sleepin' over here under the limbs of one of the big live oaks," said the Panther, "an' I think we'd better j'in 'em. You an' me, Ned, want to be fresh for the battle tomorrow. There's goin' to be one. I know it now. It wasn't worth while for them in the tent back there to be discussin' it. It's settled. Them are times, Ned, when things keep gatherin' an' gatherin' on a certain point. They may hang back an' there may be delays but at last they all crash together, an' you can't hold 'em back any more. You gen'ally feel the time when it comes an' I feel it now."

"So do I," said Ned.

"Do you think you could get the Texans away from here now without a battle?" continued the Panther. "Houston and all the other officers might order an' order, but they wouldn't go. They are just ragin' an' b'ilin' with all that Santa Anna has done to our people, an' they're goin' to have it out with him."

"I know, but I mean to sleep if I can. I am very tired, Panther."

"Well, here's the place, an' look at the boys stretched on their blankets, an' snoozin' so beautiful!"

Ned lay down. He was suffering now from mental as well as physical exhaustion, and the blanket on the grass was wonderfully soft and soothing. He saw the dim figures of the sentinels walking back and forth at the edge of the wood, and once again came the call of the night bird, but he was soon asleep.

CHAPTER 15

SAN JACINTO

Ned did not sleep long. His emotions had been keyed to too great a pitch. He wished to rise at dawn, and strangely enough it was the song of birds that awoke him then. Many of them, some coloured brightly, were flying among the boughs of the live oaks above him, careless of soldiers and battle.

He threw off the blanket and stood erect, fully clothed and eager. The sun was rising a brilliant globe in a cloudless sky. The early beams sparkled on the waters, and touched the tall grass of the prairie which waved gently under the soft wind. There were no human beings yet upon that expanse, but beyond he saw lights still burning in the camp of Santa Anna.

Ned glanced around. Already he heard the hum and murmur, the sign of preparation. He saw General Houston asleep on the grass, his head resting on a coil of rope used for dragging the Twin Sisters. He had taken only two hours of sleep, just before morning. Now he arose, and, with all his faculties alert, began to look to his army.

"We're goin' to have a fine day for a fight," said the Panther, looking up at the sun, and not meaning to be either humorous or ironic.

"No, there'll be no rain today," said Stump. "We can't put off the battle."

"The long lane has come to its turning," said Obed White.

The whole army now awoke and stood up. Every pair of eyes was turned toward the far edge of the prairie, but neither horse nor foot came from the forest there, and nothing indicated that they would come. Santa Anna was still afraid, the Texans said, but surely he would gather his courage and advance.

Houston and his officers walked among their men, telling them to cook breakfast, make coffee and eat and drink. Rarely has such another band been gathered together and they went about everything with coolness and deliberation. They dragged up more fallen wood, lighted the fires, and began the day as if they were in their own homes.

The sun went up, very slowly it seemed to the two boys, but it was fulfilling its early promise. Not a cloud yet appeared in the sky. The waving grass was a shimmer of gold. Nothing stirred in the Mexican camp. For all the Texans could see, their foes were yet asleep. The men began to grow impatient at last. If the Mexicans would not come to them they would go to the Mexicans. The murmurs grew loud. Why would not Houston lead them forth? But he was walking up and down the edge of the grove, looking through his glasses and he paid no attention. Ned shared the impatience of the men, but he said nothing, guessing much that lay in Houston's mind and knowing the tremendous weight of his responsibility.

On went the sun, and the tall grass on the prairie still waved in peace. The Texans, while growing more and more impatient, were now moving about but little, and the birds were singing wonderful songs among the live oaks over their heads. The singing of the birds was one of the details that impressed themselves so deeply upon Ned's memory. It seemed so strange at such a time, and yet it seemed natural, too.

A man suddenly uttered an exclamation, and pointed to the north. A long file of men had come from under the horizon, and were marching toward the Mexican camp. Ned knew very well that it was the army of Cos, coming to the help of Santa Anna and so did the Panther, who stood beside him. But Houston, who knew too, put down his glasses and said in a casual tone:

"Clever trick that of Santa Anna to march part of his men around a rise of the prairie and then march them back again, in order to make us think he is receiving reinforcements. But he won't fool us that way, will he, boys?"

He spoke loudly and most of them heard. One, a grizzled hunter, replied for them all in dry tones:

"No, general, he won't fool us."

Houston looked sharply at him, but the man's face expressed nothing.

"They know," whispered Ned to the Panther. "Their eyes have told them that those are new troops coming for Santa Anna. It's Houston who has failed to fool them."

"They know, but they don't care," the Panther whispered back. "Not a man has batted an eyelash. They are ready to meet Santa Anna whether he has one army, two armies or three. I reckon nobody was ever more willin' to fight than this little band of ours."

Ned looked along the lines again, and he could not doubt the full truth of the Panther's words. Every face showed the desire to rush forward.

The long line of Cos' army filed across the plain and into the camp of Santa Anna, where it disappeared from the view of the Texans. And still there was no movement on the part of the armies. The plain was once more clear of human beings, and the high sun showed that the morning was far on the wane. Even the Panther growled.

"Waitin's good enough," he said. "It ain't wise to be in such a hurry that you fall over your own feet, but you can't wait forever."

"I'd like to get it over an' be done with it," said Stump. "I can't tremble all day long."

But Santa Anna was still immovable. Ned expected that with the army of Cos joined to his own he would now march out and engage the Texans, but he seemed to be as peaceable with Cos as he was without him. Houston, apparently showed the same temper. They were unlike Mahomet and the mountain. If Santa Anna would not come to him he would not go to Santa Anna. The murmurs among the men rose again, and now they were louder than before. They demanded battle.

Ned, who had been watching the prairie, stepped back among the live oaks. He saw Houston there, walking back and forth under the shade of a great tree. He had taken off his old white hat and was fanning his face with it, but he showed no sign of nervousness or impatience. Houston beckoned to Ned.

"Call Major Forbes for me," he said.

Ned quickly brought the officer.

"Major," said Houston, "you have in your command axes for cutting firewood and for other uses; now I want you to bring me two of the heaviest and sharpest of them, and, if, on the way, anybody asks you what you are going to do with them tell him you don't know, which will be the truth."

The major departed instantly on his errand, and Houston beckoned again to Ned.

"Find Deaf Smith," he said, "and bring him here."

Smith was lying down under one of the live oaks, apparently asleep, but he sprang to his feet before Ned had spoken three words.

"I think this means something," he said.

Forbes arrived with the axes just a few moments after Ned came with Smith.

"Smith," said the general, "I want you to choose a good comrade for an errand of importance, somebody who is quick, skilful and brave like yourself."

"Will the task take long, general?"

"Two or three hours."

"I know a lot of good men. There's the Panther, Obed White, an' Hank Karnes, but they wouldn't want to go away from here for fear of missin' the fight."

He stopped a moment and glanced at Houston, as if the word "fight" might bring an expression of his intentions, but the face of the general was impenetrable.

"I think," continued Smith, "that I'll choose Denmore Reeves. Him an' me have scouted together often, an' he's the true metal."

"Very well, then," said Houston. "You and he are to take these axes an' keep yourselves and your horses near, in order that you may obey any command I may give you, without a moment's delay."

Smith stared at him, mystified, but Houston walked to the edge of the grove, and began to look again through his glasses at the enemy. Ned rejoined the Panther and his friends, but he did not say anything about the axes. Yet he felt that some important thought was stirring in Houston's mind. He must have reached at least a tentative decision.

But there was yet no movement. The sun, poised almost directly overhead, was pouring down showers of golden beams. It was now noon and the democratic little army which had its own opinions, and which was not afraid to speak them even to its commander, could conceal its impatience no longer. The rebellion against waiting communicated itself to the officers, and they began to gather and talk about it. Ned stood with them, and listened with their full consent. They decided to go to Houston at once, and try to come to some decision.

One of the officers went to the general with the request for the conference and he consented. It was composed of Houston and Rusk, the secretary of war; Burleson and Sherman, colonels; Bennett and Millard, lieutenant colonels; and Major Wells. Houston told Ned to stand by as a sort of secretary. At a little distance, many of the men stood watching, although they were too far away to hear. Others at farther points in the grove did not know that the conference had been called.

"Well, gentlemen," said Houston with the formality of a presiding officer, "will you put the question which you wish to discuss?"

"It is quite simple," replied Rusk. "We take it for granted that sooner or later there is to be a battle here. Shall we attack the enemy in his position or shall we await his attack in ours?"

His comrades nodded.

"Yes, that is the question, that and no other," said Houston, gravely, "and I wish to hear the opinion of every one of you. Mr. Rusk, will you speak first?"

Ned glanced at Rusk. He was one of the older men, and naturally he turned to conservatism.

"We must wait here for Santa Anna," he said. "We have a strong position, and, since we are the last hope of Texas it would be foolish to go out of it. Santa Anna has veteran troops. Ours are not men used to discipline, but are farmers, hunters and trappers gathered together hastily. They know nothing about military rules. It is an unheard of thing for militia to charge seasoned veterans. It is also an unheard of thing to charge over an open prairie without bayonets against a fortified enemy. Our position is strong. Let us remain in it. Here, we can whip all Mexico."

He spoke with great earnestness, and Ned was deeply impressed. All the older officers supported him, asserting that they could not afford to yield anything to impatience, and, since they carried the fortunes of Texas in their hands, they must secure every advantage for this last chance. These were solemn words and there was much reason for saying them. Ned was bound to admit it, although he longed for the attack.

But the younger officers favoured an immediate assault upon Santa Anna in his own position. They pointed out the eagerness and impatience of the men. They said that neither the numbers nor fortifications of their foe mattered. So great were the ardour and courage of the Texans that they would triumph over everything. The speakers showed all the fire and zeal of youth, and Ned swung back to their side, which was his own side.

While the men were talking, giving their reasons why a charge should or should not be made, Ned attentively watched the face of Houston. Whatever the officers might say the decision rested with him. But his expression never changed. He neither nodded nor shook his head at anything. They talked until every one in his turn had told what he thought and then Houston said:

"I have heard you, gentlemen, and now we will dissolve the council."

The officers looked at him inquiringly, but, as he said nothing more, they walked reluctantly away. When they were beyond earshot, Houston beckoned to Ned.

"Bring Deaf Smith," said the general.

Ned ran for the scout and brought him within a minute, Smith still holding in his hand the axe that had been given to him. Houston said to him in sharp, rapid tones:

"Smith, you and Reeves ride at full speed and cut down the bridge over Vince's Bayou!"

A deep smile overspread the weather-beaten face of the scout.

"This looks a good deal like a fight, general," he said.

The stern face of Houston also was illuminated by a smile.

"Ride, Smith, ride!" he said.

Ned's heart gave a great leap. He too knew what this meant. What he and all the men wished with all their hearts was surely coming to pass. Vince's bridge was the only bridge over a bayou eight miles to the north, and running into Buffalo Bayou which was at their backs. Texans and Mexicans in turn had crossed it as they came into the peninsula between the San Jacinto and Buffalo Bayou. When the bridge went down the two armies would be held in by deep unfordable waters and like angry lions in a cage must fight.

Smith and Reeves leaped upon their horses, and held the great shining axes at their saddle bows.

"You must hurry, boys, if you would get back in time for what is about to happen," said Houston.

Smith and Reeves struck their horses sharply, and galloped away to the north. Ned saw them urging their mounts to greater speed, and, in a few minutes, they were lost beyond the swells of the prairie. He turned away, and met the Panther, in whose eyes shone an eager light.

"What does it mean, Ned?" asked the giant.

"They are to cut down the bridge over Vince's Bayou and there is no getting out for either Texans or Mexicans."

The light of curiosity in the Panther's eyes turned to the light of battle. Clenching his mighty fist he shook it at the far woods.

"We're comin', Santa Anna, we're comin', an' we'll remember the Alamo and Goliad!" he said between his teeth.

A sharp eager cry resounded through the wood. It was the single note of welcome from the men. They had heard. Now they began to make the last preparations, to take the final look at rifle and pistol, to see that the ammunition was there. They loosened the big bowie knives in their belts, the terrific weapon, that every Texan carried for close quarters. The Twin Sisters were dragged from the edge of the wood, and their crews stood beside them.

Ned felt an extraordinary thrill. His head and his feet alike seemed light, and tiny red motes in myriads danced before his eyes. The voice of his comrades sounded far away, and yet, despite the strangeness of everything, it seemed to him that the most vivid, the most real moment of his life had come.

"To the saddle, boys!" cried the Panther, leaping upon his powerful horse.

Ned, the Panther, Obed White, Stump, Will Allen and Stephen Larkin were in the little body of cavalry, the command of which was given to Colonel Lamar, because of his gallant exploit the day before. Less than a hundred in number, they formed on the extreme right of the line. Next to them were the Twin Sisters under the command of Hockley. Then came the infantry of Millard. The regiment of Burleson occupied the centre, and that of Sherman formed the left wing. Houston was in the centre with Burleson's men, and Rusk was on the left with Sherman's.

All faced the prairie. The preparations had been deliberate, and it was now a long time since Smith and Reeves had gone with their axes. It was more than mid-afternoon, and the sun, declining from the zenith, was shining with uncommon splendour. In the east, great terraces of rose and pink were heaped, one upon another. The red motes had gone from Ned's eyes and he saw a glowing golden world. His heart was beating very hard, but he felt a mighty impulse to go on, the same impulse that was driving up the whole army, ready to launch it like a thunderbolt.

Ned felt Will's knee touching his. Will's face was glowing a deep red with tension and excitement, but his hands were steady on the reins.

"There's no turning back, Ned," he said.

"No, Will, there's no turning back now."

Ned shaded his eyes with his hand, but he could see no movement on the other side of the prairie. What were the Mexicans doing? Would the Texan army rush into an ambush? It seemed strange that no Mexicans should appear when their foe was about to attack. There was a deep breathless silence in the Texan lines, which was at last broken by Houston, who said:

"Begin the music, boys!"

Two odd figures stepped forward. One was that of a tall thin man and the other that of a boy. The man carried a fife, and the boy an ordinary drum. Both were dressed in ragged homespun, but they were the band.

"Play, boys, play!" shouted Houston.

Then the drum and fife began a quaint old tune: "Will you come to the bower?" None who heard the song played that day by a single drum and fife could ever again hear it without emotion. Now, for a few moments, the steady roll of the drum and the wild wailing notes of the fife above it were the only sounds heard on the prairie. Then Houston shouted:

"Forward!"

The little army lifted itself up and marched out upon the prairie into the tall grass. On it went, the horsemen holding down their horses to the pace of the infantry, while over and above everything the shrill voice of the fife wailed and wailed. That piercing note cut into the drums of Ned's ears. He felt it putting a new and sharper tang into his blood, quickening the leap of his pulse, and making him eager to rush on. The myriads of red motes began to dance again before his eyes. The hoofs of the horses beat regularly, and the weapons of the infantry often rattled together, but Ned heard nothing save the insistent tune: "Will you come to the bower?"

It was hard for the horsemen to keep back in line with the infantry. The song of drum and fife and the supreme tension of the moment seemed to have communicated themselves to the horses, which quivered under their riders and tugged at the bits. But the front of the Texan force remained an even line, and they could not yet see any movement in the camp of their enemy.

"It's not possible that Santa Anna has gone away?" said Will.

"No, there is no way for him to go," replied Ned,

Further and still further and yet no sign in the Mexican camp. No horsemen charged on either flank to meet them. Where was Almonte? Where was Urrea? Ned was amazed, but he had little time to think about it. The piercing note of the fife incessantly urged him on.

Now they were coming close to the hostile camp, and the men quickened their pace. They were almost in a run, and the stocks of rifles were leaping to shoulders. Houston ran up and down the lines. His old white hat was clutched in his right hand and as he waved it about he shouted continually to his men:

"Hold your fire! Hold your fire! Wait till we are closer! Wait till we are closer!"

Ned heard the thunder of swift hoofs behind, and he saw Smith and Reeves galloping toward them, their horses covered with foam.

"Fight for your lives!" shouted Smith. "Vince's bridge has been cut down, and there is no retreat!"

"An' now, boys, up an' at 'em!" roared the Panther, unable to contain himself any longer. "There's livin' fire behind us, an' deep water before us. Come on, you sons of battle!"

A tremendous shout burst from the Texan army. Up went the rifles, and then a sheet of fire blazed along the whole front. Before the smoke of that deadly volley could lift the Texans rushed forward shouting their terrible battle cry:

"Remember the Alamo! Remember the Alamo! Remember the Alamo!"

It is likely that no other body of men ever charged with more zeal and fire. Every human emotion and passion which can rouse the desire for victory drove them on. It is but truth to say that the ghosts of the Alamo and Goliad rode with them at their saddle bows.

And the god of battles was with them. The vigilant, the energetic Santa Anna had expected no combat that day. Perhaps he had not dreamed that the Texans would march across the prairie, and attack him in his own camp, when his army outnumbered theirs more than two to one and was led by the greatest captain in the world, His enormous egotism overcame his strong intelligence. At three o'clock he had entered his tent and gone to sleep. He was still sound asleep when

716

the Texans began their charge across the prairie. The whole Mexican army was relaxed. Some of his best officers were sleeping like himself. Many men were lazily cooking supper for the army, others were cutting wood to feed the fires.

Cavalrymen were watering their horses, muskets and rifles stood in stacks and three or four strummed upon *mandolin* and guitar, singing at the same time sentimental love songs of the south. Upon such a camp burst the flaming front of the Texans, and, in a moment there was a scene of wild and terrible confusion.

The Twin Sisters were wheeled at short range and fired point blank into the Mexican mass, smashing down the weak barricades. Then the Texans, reloading and firing another volley, closed in and were upon their foe. The Mexicans were not yet in line of battle. General Castrillon on the right flank was striving to get them into order, Colonel Almonte on the left was seeking to do the same. Santa Anna had rushed from his tent, and, standing near the centre, was shouting to his men to lie down and avoid the Texan fire. Other Mexican officers gave contradictory orders. Castrillon succeeded in getting up the gunners for a cannon, but half of them were shot down at once by the Texan riflemen, and the rest fled.

The Texan army was like a tornado. Hurled forth by the fiercest of human passions its very speed made it the more deadly to the Mexicans, and caused it to suffer less harm itself. Ned, when the charge broke into a run, leaned far forward on his horse and fired beside his head. The rifles and pistols were crashing fast, and lines of light ran continually along the front of the Texan force. He heard the heavy breathing of the men about him, and he saw the manes of the horses tossed backward as they galloped toward the Mexican camp.

The steady roll of the single drum and the shrill wailing of the fife went on all the time, still heating the blood and adding fresh fire to the passions of the men. "*Will you come to the bower?*" "*Will you come to the bower?*" rang in Ned's ears through all the roar of the battle, the shouts of men, the beat of horses' hoofs, and the fire of cannon and rifles.

They were almost in the Mexican camp, when Ned felt his horse stagger, then stop suddenly and shiver all over. He had been hit in a mortal spot by a Mexican bullet and Ned, holding his rifle, sprang clear, as the good mustang fell dead upon his side. The cavalry passed on in an instant, but he was in the thick of the infantry.

Behind the remnants of the earthwork was the dark and confused mass of the Mexicans, and in an instant the Texans, clubbing their rifles and drawing their huge bowie knives, were among them like a thunderbolt. Castrillon, still struggling to get his men in line, was killed by a rifle bullet. Some of Santa Anna's veteran regulars tried to use the bayonet, but the clubbed rifles dashed them down, and the Texans rushed over them.

Ned could never recall more than a few details of that dark and awful fifteen minutes. The red motes before his eyes fused into a solid red blaze, dimmed now and then by the clouds of smoke and vapour which were rising fast. He still heard the wailing of the fife, driving him on to action, but whether real or fancied he never knew. He saw the dark avenging faces of the Texans, the great knives uplifted by bare and brawny right arms, and the huddled mass of the Mexicans, yellow with fear, while over everything swelled the shout in a sort of terrible measured beat: *"Remember the Alamo! Remember the Alamo!"*

Ned's own brain was heated. He struck fiercely with his clubbed rifle at heads showing through the smoke. The Alamo and Goliad came back to him once more in a red vision, and he struck again and again. The Texans were now pressing body to body against the great mass of the Mexicans. The huge knives were flashing fast, and still the Texans pushed harder and harder. There was no longer any firing. The clubbed rifles and the bowie knives were doing the work. The Texan officers ceased to give orders, and rushed in with the rest.

The smaller but far more terrible force was swiftly destroying the larger. The Mexican army, merely a confused mass, now was doubled up and hurled back upon itself. All the time those terrible knives were flashing along the whole front, and the Mexicans were falling so fast that the survivors hearing that terrible and incessant battle cry began to shout in terror: *"Me no Alamo! Me no Alamo!"*

Ned collided in the smoke with a huge figure. It was Stump, also on foot now and fighting shoulder to shoulder with the Panther, dismounted, too, the only man whom he considered his equal in strength. Nothing could resist them. They drove like a wedge into the solid Mexican mass and split it apart.

What was left of the Mexican army—half had been slain in that awful quarter of an hour—broke up and dissolved. Officers and men fled. Some rushed upon the prairie, but the bullets overtook them in the long grass. A portion fled northward for Vince's bridge, which they did not know had been cut down, and were destroyed by the cavalry.

The bravest of the Mexicans were appalled by the Texan fury which, burning within so long, now burst forth with the most awful force. It seemed to them that they were attacked by demons rather than men. The chosen veterans of Santa Anna, who had been with him in all his victories, threw away their weapons, and ran as they had never run before. Even then they did not escape. The Texans reloaded their rifles, and shot them as they ran.

In this crisis Almonte, ever the bravest and most gallant of the Mexican officers, strove to get some of the men together, not to make effective resistance, but in order that they might make a formal surrender before all were killed. He succeeded in gathering at last a frightened crowd of about three hundred, and they hoisted not one but a dozen white flags.

Ned was still driving with his comrades at the main mass of the Mexicans, which was now melting fast away. Soon, only scattered clumps of Mexicans were left standing in what had been their camp. Now, Ned saw General Houston who had ridden on horseback in the charge with the front line of the army, galloping about the field, and calling upon his men to show mercy when quarter was asked.

He noticed that one of the general's ankles was stained with blood, and that his horse also was bleeding in several places. The horse suddenly staggered and fell to the prairie. Ned rushed forward and dragged the general clear. Houston was white with pain.

"So it's you, young Fulton," he said. "Always at the right place! Was there ever such another victory?"

"Are you badly hurt, general?" exclaimed Ned, tense with anxiety.

"A ball in the ankle. I received it when we were charging the breastwork, but what difference does that make on a day like this! Tell them to give the Mexicans quarter. The victory is complete, and we are not mere slaughterers."

Other Texans ran up. They assisted Houston to a place, where he might recline and yet see the battlefield, which was now covered with the bodies of the fallen and with running men. But the Texan fury which in fifteen minutes had destroyed an army more than double their own force was abating. The surrender of Almonte and his men was received. Prisoners were brought in from the prairie, the woods and the morasses of the San Jacinto. Most of them were stupefied with terror, and made not the slightest resistance. Among many of them the legend persisted years afterward that they had been attacked at San Jacinto not by men, but by devils in human form.

Ned saw a young Mexican officer standing alone with drawn

sword, and a Texan rushing at him with clubbed rifle. He caught one glimpse of the Mexican's face and he sprang between.

"Stop!" he cried to the Texan. "This man is my prisoner!"

The man swerved without a word and rushed off in pursuit of others.

"Montez," exclaimed Ned, "don't you know me? At last I'm able to repay you!"

"Fulton!" cried the young Mexican. He handed Ned his sword and then suddenly burst into tears.

"Oh, my God, what a rout!" he exclaimed.

The firing now died to scattered rifle shots, and soon ceased altogether. The clouds of smoke and vapour rose, disclosing the whole battlefield. Ned was appalled at the sight. The Mexican dead lay upon the prairie in hundreds and hundreds. Most of them had been slain at close quarters, and with the bowie knives. The Texan loss was almost nothing, and, so sudden and terrible had been their rush, that the Mexicans had not been able to fire a single cannon shot.

The prisoners were gathered at one edge of the field under heavy guard, and Ned sent Montez in with the others, sure now that he was safe. The Texans, just beginning to realise the immensity of this triumph and its meaning, spared the prisoners. Their fierceness did not continue after victory, yet many could not keep from flinging taunts at the dark and huddled mass of Mexicans.

"Do you remember the Alamo? Do you remember Goliad?" they shouted at the terrified men. "Where is Santa Anna? Where are your generals? Where is your army?"

Ned looked for his friends. Not one of them was hurt, but Deaf Smith had escaped narrowly. His horse had stumbled so violently at the breastwork that he had been hurled over his head. A Mexican soldier rushed forward to thrust him through with the bayonet. Smith, while still lying on the ground drew a pistol and pulled the trigger. The cap snapped but Smith, quick as lightning, threw the pistol into his face. As the Mexican staggered back the Texan leaped up, wrenched musket and bayonet from his hands and charged with the rushing infantry into the Mexican camp.

Now the Texan officers began to institute order for the coming night and to gather up the spoil. The Texans collected a thousand good rifles and muskets which the Mexicans had thrown away in their flight, besides hundreds of sabres. They also took five or six hundred horses and mules, besides great quantities of ammunition, clothing, provisions, all sorts of camp equipage, and a treasure of $12,000 in silver, a great sum in a region in which money was so scarce.

Ned and Will Allen had been helping to heap the spoil together. Now they rested and were joined by the Panther.

"I saw your horse fall when he was shot, Ned," said the Panther, "but I knowed that nothin' would happen to you."

"How did you know that?" asked Ned, astonished.

"I just knowed it," replied the Panther in a tone of deep conviction.

The twilight was now at hand. The Texans lighted many fires and rejoiced hugely. They did things that may seem wild to those who sit safely in their homes. But they were in the darkness of a wilderness prairie, and they had just released themselves with their own valour from the apparently immutable threat of desolation and death that had hung over them so long. The rebound was tremendous.

They joined hands and danced in circles around the fires. They brought out the fifer and the drummer again and they sang: "Will you come to the bower?" and the other songs they knew. The twilight passed into the night. Thick darkness crept over forest and prairie, but the whirling forms were outlined clearly against the fires. Someone discovered a great store of candles in the Mexican camp. They were brought out quickly, distributed among the men, and the wild dance was resumed, every one holding aloft in his hands a blazing candle, as he whirled and whirled about his fire. Occasionally they uttered all together a tremendous war whoop, and now and then they shouted for Santa Anna, who was not there, and who could not be found, dead or alive.

"He is running away on his hands and feet like a dog and dressed like a common soldier," said Houston as he lay on a blanket, his leg bandaged tightly.

The dancing ceased by and by and the Texans returned to their sober selves. They ate and spread their blankets. The heavy guards were kept about the prisoners, but the rest of the victors lay down and slept. Quiet and deep night settled over the epochal field of San Jacinto.

About the middle of that terrible fifteen minutes, a little man in a gorgeous uniform who had been rushing about among the Mexicans, shouting orders, and then other orders that contradicted them, stopped suddenly and looked once more at the bristling front of the Texans. Dazed at first, he was now recovering his judgment. But no one noticed amid the crashing of rifles and shouts and all the vast turmoil of smoke and noise that he was the great, the unconquerable Santa Anna, dictator of Mexico and Texas, the Napoleon of the West.

He saw that the battle was lost, and terror, invincible terror, was the king of his soul. These men rushing down upon him with terrible shouts and far more terrible knives in their hands were the Texans, all of whom he had sentenced to one common death, when taken. He, too, remembered the Alamo and Goliad, and he had no wish now but to be gone.

He fled through the press and turmoil to the rear. He was not noticed, because others were fleeing also and the smoke was everywhere. He paused an instant, snatched out the little gold box, took from it the last of the drug, and thrust it into his mouth. Then he flung the gold box from him, sprang upon a powerful horse and galloped northward, incessantly urging the horse on with shouts and blow of fist and heel. Terror was still his ruler. Brave at times, he was in a complete panic now, and judging the Texans by his own standards he had great cause for fear.

He regretted now his brilliant uniform. He wrenched off his gold epaulets and threw them upon the ground, and he tore at the lace on coat and trousers. But merciful darkness was coming down. He heard more than once the sound of pursuit to find it only fancy. The shadows of his foes that made him tremble so violently were only those of trees and bushes.

He stopped at last. His horse was panting and covered with foam. The rider still quivered. He felt in his pocket for the gold box, but it was gone and he remembered. A part of his terror disappeared. He could hear no sound about him, but the light rustle of the wind among grass and leaves, and the mournful call of a night bird. He had left them all behind him. His men had perished, but he, Santa Anna, the illustrious and invincible, had escaped.

He urged his horse anew, more confident now and made straight for Vince's bridge. He had noticed the country well in coming down and he knew the way. Confidence grew.

He rode from the bushes and approached the bridge. Then he stopped aghast. There was no bridge. It was fallen in and only the piers remained, between which flowed the deep waters of the bayou. He divined instantly that the Texans had done this, and even now they might be lying there in wait for him. He began to tremble again. He was shut up on that narrow triangle and the Texans would surely find him on the morrow.

Terror grew and this very terror itself made him act. He drove his horse at the bayou, through the deep mud of its bank. The animal's weight sank him in the thick mire, and he struggled in vain to go on. Santa Anna shouted at him and cursed him, but the poor horse only sank deeper.

The dictator sprang from his back, and although he sank in mud to his knees, reached the water, swam it, and climbed to the prairie above, never looking back at the lost animal.

Santa Anna stood a while on the bank of the bayou, sunk in the depths of the blackest despair. His army was destroyed, and he was alone, and on foot in the depths of a vast wilderness, where any man whom he might meet was sure to prove a foe. It was incredible, impossible, but it was true. He, Santa Anna, a few hours before a dictator, a triumphant commander, a ruler over a territory half the size of Europe, was a solitary fugitive from a foe to whom he had set the example of no mercy.

The false strength that had come from the drug was going, but he walked slowly over the prairie, until he discerned in the darkness the outline of a forest, which he entered, feeling more secure among the trees. He went a few hundred yards further, and saw a little clearing in which stood a house. The march of his army had passed near, and he surmised, with good cause, that the house was abandoned.

But he approached very cautiously, and it was sometime before he dared to enter. The house was dark and silent, and by the moonlight at the windows he saw that it was in disorder. Evidently its owner had left in haste. He found scraps of food in the kitchen, and he devoured them eagerly, but in another room he discovered what he wanted most. Some old clothing hung on hooks in the wall, and quickly he took off his muddy but gorgeous uniform, rolling it in a bundle and tossing it into a corner. He even got rid of his cavalry boots.

He put on a rough cloth cap, a blue cotton jacket, yellow linen trousers and a pair of red worsted slippers, made by some thrifty Texan housewife. Now he felt a gleam of satisfaction. Surely his star was favouring him again. No one would detect in this poorly-clad Mexican *peon* the great Santa Anna.

He would have been glad to stay in the house for the rest of the night, but he was afraid. The owners or the Texan soldiers might come and he went out into the thickets. There he wandered around for a while, and then, lying down near the edge of a ravine, tried to sleep.

CHAPTER 16

THE GREAT CAPTURE

Ned awoke early the next morning. It seemed as if he had emerged from some terrific dream, but there was the field yet covered with bodies, and off to his left was the group of Mexican prisoners, some sitting up and others still sleeping. He felt much pity for them. All his passion against them was gone. It had burned out in that dreadful fifteen minutes of yesterday. If the Texans wanted vengeance they had certainly taken it to the full. He saw Almonte, and, moved by a certain pity, he went to him and addressed him.

There was nothing gay or gallant about Almonte now. He had been sitting with his face in his hands, and he looked up sadly when Ned spoke.

"Ah, Señor Fulton!" he said. "The Texans have triumphed! Most of our men are dead, and the rest are prisoners!"

Ned did not reply.

"If you have any influence at all with the Texan generals," Almonte exclaimed, "I beg that you intercede with them for these poor men. It was not they who ordered Goliad. You know that."

"Where is the man who did order it?" asked Ned.

"I do not know," replied Almonte. "I saw him in the battle, but not when we surrendered. He must have galloped away, since you have not found him."

Ned was sure that he was speaking the truth.

"Colonel Almonte," he said, "I was your prisoner once, and you treated me kindly. As far as I can, I shall return your kindness. I don't think your men have anything to fear from the Texans; they don't murder prisoners."

Ned brought food for both Almonte and Montez with his own hands, and he also brought them assurances from Houston that the prisoners were safe. The general himself was lying on a pallet, suffering great pain from his wound. He had slept but little in the course of the night, but despite his shattered ankle, he was giving orders and gathering up all the loose ends of the victory.

Scores of the Texans were already at work burying the dead. Parties were sent out to hunt down the last Mexican fugitive. Most of his friends were already gone on such expeditions and Ned, a man named Sylvester and three others started on a similar journey to the northward.

Ned was glad to get away from Santa Anna's camp. The sight of so much death repelled him. He felt an immense relief, when the woods and the swells of the prairie hid it from view. He rode a captured Mexican horse of excellent quality, and as he and the others galloped northward it was good to feel the rush of wind past his face and to breathe untainted air.

"For what point are we making?" he asked Sylvester.

"For Vince's bridge, or rather the place where it stood. It would be natural for the Mexicans, not knowing that it was cut down, to run toward it."

"That is true. We may pick up some fugitives there," said Ned.

They saw nobody on the way, but, when they came to the stream and the fallen bridge, they decided to swim their horses to the farther shore, and continue the search there. Sylvester led them to a place, free from deep mud or quick-sands, and they crossed safely to the other side.

They saw before them an alternation of forest and open grassy country. Ned suggested that they look in the woods, as fugitives would naturally hide there, and, Sylvester agreeing with him, they rode among the trees. They came to a ravine and continued down its side. Sylvester, who was in advance, suddenly stopped his horse.

"What's the matter?" called Ned, riding up by his side.

"I saw something in the brush at the edge of the ravine that looked mightily like a man. I don't see him now, though."

"But I do. It's a man, sure enough, and he's dropped down on his hands and knees in the bushes to keep us from seeing him, which, I suppose, means that he's a Mexican trying to get away."

"We'll soon rout him out and see," said Sylvester, and they rode quickly toward the point where the man was crouched on all fours in the grass in a vain attempt to escape observation. Sylvester caught sight of a blue cotton jacket and yellow linen trousers.

"A *peon*," he said; "which means that he was only a common soldier, if he was any soldier at all, but we'll take him, anyhow."

The man, who had remained crouched on hands and knees as the Texans approached, now straightened up, and prepared to run. But Sylvester raised his rifle and cried sharply:

"One step, and I shoot!"

The man stood still except for a violent trembling.

"He's a *peon*, sure enough," said Sylvester, "and a badly scared one, too, at that. Come out of those Mr. Mexican, and give an account of yourself."

The man walked forward slowly and reluctantly, and, when Ned saw his face, he fairly jumped in the saddle. San Jacinto was complete! Here was the last detail to make it so. Never had victory been rounded out more thoroughly. But, from motives of curiosity, a desire to hear what this prisoner would say, he remained silent, for the present, and turned his own face away.

"Throw up your hands and come out of those bushes," repeated Sylvester sharply. "We're not going to kill you, but we're going to see who you are and what you're doing here. Where are your weapons?"

"I have none," replied the man. "I'm just a common soldier. I threw them away in the defeat and flight. I hope, good Texans, that you will spare me. Like most of my comrades, I have nothing against you. I was compelled to come here and fight you."

"That's just as it may be," said Sylvester. "You seem to have made good time from the battlefield, and you look as if you hadn't got over your scare yet."

The man was silent, and again Sylvester examined him closely.

"How does it happen," he asked, "that a common soldier, such as you say you are, has on a fine linen shirt, with big diamond studs in it?"

The man began to tremble violently again, and tried to hide all of his shirt front with his blue cotton jacket.

"I am not altogether correct when I call myself a private soldier," he said. "I was an *aide* on the staff of General Santa Anna."

Sylvester studied him with inquiring eyes. Ned turned his head, and gazed squarely at the prisoner.

"Mr. Sylvester," he said, "this is General Santa Anna himself. I have seen him often; I have been his prisoner more than once, and I know him well."

A deep pallor overspread Santa Anna's face, and he trembled from head to foot.

"It is false!" he cried. "I am not General Santa Anna! I do not know where he is!"

Sylvester glanced at Ned, and then looked back at Santa Anna.

"Ned is right," he said decisively. "You are Santa Anna, himself, and nobody else. Ned could make no mistake about you, and you answer all the descriptions of you that I've ever heard. Thunder, but what a haul we've made! You're the man of the Alamo and Goliad, but things have changed a lot since then!"

726

Santa Anna stood silent. A deadly and sickening fear assailed him at the names Alamo and Goliad. These Texans, in revenge, might shoot him down at once. What an extraordinary turn the wheel of fortune had taken! He, the mighty Santa Anna, the greatest man in the world, to be the prisoner of five wandering Texans in buckskin! Then he recovered himself a little, and thought of gold. He began to offer them bribes, vast sums of money, to let him go. He would see that it reached them when he returned to the City of Mexico.

"Stop that!" said Sylvester sharply. "Not another word of such stuff. You're afraid that we're going to kill you. Well, we won't do it, but we're going to take you to General Houston and Secretary Rusk, and let them decide it. Now, you march! Keep just ahead of us, and, if you try to dodge or run, all five of us shoot, and we don't miss! Go toward the bayou!"

Santa Anna started, walking in his red worsted slippers, with the five horsemen close behind him, their rifles cocked. What an indignity! To be forced to walk ahead, while five of the miserable Texans, whom he had despised, rode behind him, his captors! He began to limp badly.

"What is the matter?" asked Sylvester.

"My foot is very sore," replied Santa Anna.

Sylvester considered a moment.

"Ned," he said, "you ride the biggest and strongest horse. Take him up behind you."

Ned felt an instinctive repulsion, but he could not refuse.

"Help him up," he said.

He did not wish to touch Santa Anna himself. But Sylvester put an arm under the Mexican General's shoulder and he scrambled up behind Ned, coiling an arm about his waist to steady himself. Ned shivered with loathing, when he felt this man's arm pressing against him. Santa Anna was to him a black and treacherous murderer.

"And now for the camp," said Sylvester. "The boys will open their eyes when they see what we bring."

Ned felt Santa Anna trembling, but he was silent now. They started, Sylvester leading, Ned and Santa Anna following, and the others close behind. Ned forgot the loathing that had stirred him so deeply. A feeling of immense exhilaration took its place. After the slaughters, the suffering, the desolation, and seemingly the utter ruin of Texas it was reserved for him to ride into camp with Santa Anna, the author of all this destruction, his prisoner.

They swam the bayou on their return and rode forward at a good pace over the prairie. It was now afternoon, the sun, shining in full glory, as if to light up the Texan triumph. Santa Anna did not speak again, and the Texans were silent, too. After a while they saw the two clumps of timber on the prairie and then the figures of men and horses. Santa Anna began to tremble once more, but presently, by an effort of the will, he stopped.

Several Texan searching parties returning to camp, some with prisoners and some without, saw Ned carrying the prisoner behind him, but they took no particular notice. They had been bringing in prisoners since sunrise. Sylvester and his men rode on, and they passed close to the great group of the captured. The Mexicans saw the man riding behind Ned, and, recognising him at once, they set up a great shout.

"*El Presidente! El General Santa Anna!*" they cried.

An uproar arose at once in the Texan camp. At the cry of "The President!" and "General Santa Anna!" scores of the men rushed forward, the Panther, Stump and Obed White among the foremost.

"Yes, it is Santa Anna himself," said Ned. "We found him disguised and in hiding beside a ravine beyond Vince's Bayou."

"An' Ned comes ridin' into camp bringin' Santa Anna hisself behind him," said the Panther to Obed. "This caps it all."

The uproar, the disjointed sounds among the Texans, ceased suddenly, and, in its place, came a deep, sinister growl, like the threat of an enraged wild beast. Santa Anna shook more violently and now clutched Ned with both hands.

"It's well you tremble an' shake!" boomed the deep voice of the Panther. "You're thinkin' of Goliad!"

The mutter grew more menacing and the crowd pressed closer. But Rusk, Lamar and others ran up.

"Keep back!" they cried. "He must be taken to Houston!"

Ned and his comrades leaped from their horses and Santa Anna, half dead with fear, was taken down and put upon his feet. Ned on one side of him and Sylvester, on the other, carried him to Houston, with the menacing crowd following close behind.

Houston had been lying in a doze on his pallet of blankets. Now he was awakened and sat up, his wounded leg, held stiffly in front of him. Santa Anna, the fear of immediate death gone, made one of those sudden recoveries that were possible in him. An abject coward at times, he had at other times the greatest assurance. When he saw Houston, he stepped forward, made a low and dramatic bow, and said in Spanish in full rounded tones:

"I am General Antonio Lopez de Santa Anna, and I claim to be a prisoner of war at your disposal."

Houston did not understand Spanish, and with a gesture of his hand told Santa Anna to sit down on an ammunition box that lay a few feet away. Then he sent for Colonel Almonte to interpret. Ned and Sylvester could have interpreted, but, wishing to keep in the background, they did not volunteer.

Santa Anna sat down on the box. All around him was the ring of threatening faces, and his false courage deserted him again. He moved nervously on the box. His black eyes wandered furtively and fearfully over everything. The yellowish tint of his face deepened, and he pressed both hands against his sides as if he were in sharp pain there. Ned saw clearly that Santa Anna was in great fear.

Almonte arrived at this moment, an erect and handsome figure, but his face fell, when he saw the man sitting on the ammunition box, and he uttered a low exclamation. Santa Anna seemed to be somewhat relieved when he saw him, and spoke to him rapidly. Almonte turned to Houston.

"General Santa Anna wishes some opium," he said. "His condition is bad. Can you not get it for him?"

Five grains of opium were brought from the stores, and were given to him. He took it eagerly. Presently he began to grow steady and some colour returned to his face. All the time the black and threatening ring of the Texans stood around him. Ned now saw a man in mortal fear, dreading the thunderbolt of a just vengeance, but the sight was not good. Houston sat silently by, until Santa Anna recovered himself. When some of his courage had returned the Mexican lifted his head and said in pompous and theatrical tones:

"That man who has conquered the Napoleon of the West may consider himself born to no common destiny. It now remains for the victor to be generous to the vanquished."

A faint smile passed over the face of Houston, which immediately became stern again.

"You should have remembered that at the Alamo," he said.

Santa Anna paled, and then burst into a torrent of words. He made excuses so fast that Almonte, translating, could scarcely keep up with him. He said that he had been acting under the orders of the government of Mexico, that is its Congress, which had decreed that all Texans taken in arms must be treated as pirates. He claimed that he did not know that Fannin had surrendered at Goliad under assurance of good treatment. He said that as soon as he was released he would have General Urrea shot for the massacre. He proclaimed himself a white angel, and he charged all the treacheries and massacres to his subordinates.

Houston, through Almonte, reminded him that he was the government of Mexico, its autocrat, and dictator. Everything had been done according to his wish and order. But the stream of Santa Anna's eloquence was not to be broken. He suggested to Houston that they treat at once for his release and terms of peace. Houston replied that he was merely the general in command in the field, and that he must talk to the government of Texas about such matters. Then Santa Anna proposed a truce, to which Houston agreed, provided the Mexican sent letters to his generals still in the field to cease operations at once.

Santa Anna called eagerly for pen, ink and paper and he wrote orders to General Filisola, General Gaona and General Urrea to release all Texan prisoners and retire at once. Deaf Smith departed immediately with the letters. Houston ordered a tent for Santa Anna to be pitched beside his own. He also put in it his personal baggage which had been found in the camp, and knowing well the feeling of the Texans, he surrounded the tent with a triple guard.

When Ned saw Santa Anna disappear within the canvas he felt intense relief. The strain of the last half hour had been hard upon the nerves. And the murmur still ran through the Texan camp. Many of the men did not like Houston's polite treatment of Santa Anna. They had the arch-demon under their heel now. Then why not crush him? Already a group was gathered near the heaps of captured baggage.

"Let's hear how they talk," said the Panther to Ned. They walked over to the men and were joined there by Will, Obed White, Stump and young Zavala. A fiery Texan was making a speech. He demanded the death of Santa Anna. Had not the dictator brought mourning to nearly every home in Texas? Was there any principle of honour or faith that he had not violated? Was he not the blackest murderer above ground?

A tall figure suddenly pushed through the group. It was that of the Reverend Stephen Larkin. He still wore the long black coat, but a portion of one tail had been slashed off by a Mexican sabre. Minister though he was, he had been one of the first to charge into the Mexican camp, and now the Texans gave way to him with respect. He spoke to them rapidly and earnestly. He said it was not for them to pass sen-

730

tence on Santa Anna. It was true that he had violated all the laws of God and man, but they had no right to take vengeance in their own hands. They must behave like enlightened and merciful human beings, and leave Santa Anna to the government. And he shrewdly added that Santa Anna alive and a prisoner might be worth more to them than Santa Anna dead. He had already sent orders to all his generals bidding them to cease the war, and Deaf Smith was bearing the messages.

The men listened and the fury of hate and vengeance died in them as the fury of battle had died with victory the day before. The group dispersed slowly, and Ned and his friends also walked away, although the Panther was growling under his breath.

"It was hard for the boys not to string him up," he said, "but I reckon Steve Larkin was right."

"He truly was," said a voice beside them, and they saw John Roylston for the first time since the battle. He had joined like any common soldier in the charge, sustaining a slight wound which had compelled him to lie quiet that night and most of the day. But he was now up and strong, and they greeted him gladly.

"All of you have escaped without harm," he said, "and it was a most glorious victory, more glorious and complete than anything of which we dreamed, capped as it was by the taking of Santa Anna. That minister was right when he said that Santa Anna, alive and a prisoner, was worth more to us than Santa Anna dead. Ned, have you seen anything of young Urrea?"

"I have not," replied Ned. "I was unable to find him among the prisoners, and I did not see him among the dead."

"But the dead were buried in great haste," said the merchant, "and we are not really sure whether he was or was not among the list. I wish I knew."

"I suppose the war is over, is it not?" said Ned.

"Without a doubt. Most of the Mexican veterans have been destroyed. Filisola, Gaona, and the elder Urrea have, combined, a force several times larger than ours, but the blow that we have struck here at San Jacinto has been hard, very hard, so hard that its echo will be heard throughout the world. The Mexicans, no matter what their numbers, will not dare to face us and Texas, I think, will soon be free of the invader."

They remained where they were some time, and, three days after the battle, Ned saw a little party of Texans riding into camp, bringing with them a prisoner, a thick, very dark man, whose appearance was familiar. He looked again and saw that it was Martin Perfecto de Cos, the brother-in-law of Santa Anna, he who had broken faith after his surrender to the Texans at San Antonio, he who had joined his chief the morning of San Jacinto, merely bringing more victims to the slaughter.

"There's Cos," he exclaimed to the Panther.

"Aye, so it is," said the giant. "One by one we sweep 'em up."

The Texan scouts had found him alone in the bottoms of the Brazos trying to rejoin the remainder of the Mexican army. He, too, had fled from the field of San Jacinto in time, but he was not to escape. The two brothers-in-law were put together to obtain what consolation they could from the society of each other, and the Texans rejoiced over another important prisoner.

Ned was one of the messengers who carried the news of the victory to the government on Galveston Island, where the president and his cabinet had made ready for another flight, in case Houston was defeated. He came back with them to Houston's camp, where the Panther greeted him with a long face.

"Mr. Roylston is missing," he said. "Some think that he has gone to one of the towns without takin' the trouble to leave word, but that don't seem natural. Houston is worried about him, but he's got so much to do now with Santa Anna, the government and the treaty of peace that he can't do anything for him. Ned, we must find Mr. Roylston."

"Of course we must," said Ned, as he suddenly remembered what Roylston had said to him before the battle. Great events had crowded it completely out of his mind, but now it came back, vivid and clear in every word. He did not doubt that Roylston had been taken by some wandering band of Mexicans. It might be that Urrea was alive and had done it; then with all the prophetic power of instinct he felt sure that it was so. It was obvious that his friends and he must act at once. He secured a brief interview with Houston, who said briefly but with intense earnestness:

"Go, in God's name. Take what men you and the Panther wish, and bring John Roylston back. Texas owes him too much."

Ned and the Panther quickly made up their party, which included Stump, Obed White, Will Allen and fifteen others, twenty all told, but every one a daring horseman and sharpshooter. Roylston had been last seen on the mainland side of Vince's bridge which the workmen were repairing. He was on horseback and so far as the workmen knew he seemed to be merely taking a look at the country.

The Panther, who naturally assumed the command of the little troop, searched the vicinity long and carefully for the sign of a trail. He had skilled scouts with him, and they spread over a wide space, looking for traces that might have been left in the soft earth by shod hoofs. Stump finally picked up the evidences of a trail that led to the south, and they followed it two or three miles until they came to forest. Here it was joined by the hoof-prints of other horses, twenty perhaps in number, and the tale was plain to the Panther.

"You all believe that trail was Mr. Roylston's don't you?" he asked.

"We do!" they replied together.

"So do I, an' these trails that join his were made by Mexicans. They came upon him here an' took him. Look everywhere, boys, an' see if Mr. Roylston hasn't left a sign of some kind. He's a smart man an' he'd help a rescue all he could."

A half hour's search and one of the men found a small handkerchief lying in some bushes, which, so the Panther believed, was the sign.

"Mr. Roylston is one of the few men in these parts who carry handkerchiefs," he said, "an' this is his. Now, boys, we ride straight on the trail."

The little company moved forward at a swift pace.

CHAPTER 17

ROYLSTON'S RESCUE

The trail led steadily south and west, and, even Will Allen, who had less wilderness experience than any other in the company, could follow it easily. The ground was soft, as it had been throughout that memorable spring, and the hoofs of the horses cut deep, leaving a ploughed track behind. They came to numerous creeks and brooks, still swollen by the floods, but they always picked up easily the path of the retreating band on the other side.

Thus they rode for many hours, but late in the afternoon, Stump, who was in the lead, stopped suddenly and pointed to the trail.

"What have you seen, Stump?" asked the Panther.

"Unshod ponies have rid into the main trail here," replied the timid one. "Six or seven of 'em came down from the north."

The Panther rode up by his side and examined the rivulet of hoofs that had flowed into the chief stream.

"You're right, Stump," he said. "You're always right about these things. Them tracks was shorely made by ponies that wore no shoes."

"Isn't it likely," said Ned, "that the Campeachy Indian scouts have joined Urrea here? They would certainly have cleared out, as soon as the Texans smashed into the Mexican army, and they would naturally make for Mexico."

The Panther slapped his huge thigh.

"That's it," he said. "I haven't a doubt of it. The Campeachy Indians are snaky fellows an' we'll have to look out lest we run into an ambush. If it's Urrea that's leadin' these Mexicans—an' it's shorely him—he'll keep the Indians in the rear watchin' for pursuit."

"But we're something on the scout ourselves," said Obed White. "Having put our hand to the plough we'll continue to cut a wide furrow until we overtake this Urrea, and have a final settlement with him."

"Since Santa Anna has agreed on peace how will Urrea dare to keep Mr. Roylston prisoner?" asked Will Allen.

Obed White laughed.

"Urrea will claim that he never heard of the peace," he replied, "and if he can gain any advantage from his exploit Santa Anna will wink at it. If Santa Anna should be released he would break the treaty himself on a moment's notice, if he thought that he could make a new and successful attempt to conquer Texas. Urrea is safe from any punishment by Mexican authorities."

They followed the trail the rest of the day, and as far into the night as the moonlight sufficed, taking it up again the next morning. They were sure that no harm had yet been done to the merchant, or they would have found some trace of it by the trailside. But it was unlikely, however, that Roylston would be subjected to foul play. As a hostage he was almost as valuable as his letters of credit and bills of exchange.

They resumed the pursuit in the morning across a beautiful country, an alternation of forest, heavy in leafy green, and of prairies, on which the grass grew tall and thick. As if to celebrate the Texan victory, spring was now doing its best, showing every colour it knew in tints alike the richest and most delicate. The heavy rains also ceased to trouble, and they had now and then only a slight shower which did not trouble them at all. They rode nearly all the time through brilliant sunshine.

Ned's sensitive temperament also responded to another note in the atmosphere. It was that of liberty and freedom. The sombre cloud that had hung so long over Texas was lifted and he felt sure that it could never come again. The victory had been too complete, the Texans had shown that they were invincible in battle, and the Mexicans would not dare another trial.

There were visible signs that the same feeling was spreading over Texas. The news of the great victory had been carried fast. The fugitives into the north were returning. Men were bringing back their women and children and household possessions. Smoke was rising again from the chimneys of the cabins deserted so long. The Panther's party met three such groups, returning on the very heels of victory, and while the Mexican lances were yet on the eastern side of the Brazos.

The Brazos itself had subsided somewhat, but they crossed at a ferry which had been restored only a few hours before they came. They obtained valuable information from the ferryman who, hidden in the bushes two days before, had seen a Mexican force of about thirty men, including six or seven Indians, build a rude raft and cross on it, letting their horses swim behind. They had with them one man, who looked like an American, obviously a prisoner, and their leader was young, sharp and imperious in manner.

"This settles it," said the Panther. "There ain't a single doubt left. The prisoner was Mr. Roylston and the description answers to Urrea to a dot."

They found the wide trail again, leading on from the Brazos to the Colorado, and followed it at increased speed. Shortly before noon they met no less a person than Deaf Smith, on his way back to Houston, after delivering Santa Anna's letters commanding peace to his generals. They exchanged news, and Smith was sorry that he could not turn about and join them in the pursuit.

"It's young Urrea, of course," he said, "and he will avoid the Mexican army below in order not to be involved in any armistice. He will make straight for the Rio Grande with his prisoner, an' since there is peace for a while at least, that makes him a brigand. Don't you trust any of the Mexican leaders. Even now they are up to all sorts of tricks."

"What do you know?" asked the Panther.

"I had Santa Anna's letters to Filisola and Gaona. They had heard of Santa Anna's defeat before I got there, but at first they wouldn't believe it. I don't blame 'em. The full truth looks almost past believin'. But when a fugitive officer of Santa Anna's own army, who swam his horse across Vince's Bayou, reached them they had to believe it. So I found 'em a bit humble when I got there.

"Gaona and Filisola had already joined their forces, an' Gaona also had recalled a portion of his troops which had crossed the Brazos. Then they fell back to Victoria, where they were joined by General Urrea with his men. Although they have a big force yet, they had decided to retire beyond the Colorado before I got there with Santa Anna's letters which made them hasten their movements. But they are tricky to the last. They've sent General Woll to negotiate with Houston for cattle for food, while they are retreatin', but I got sure proof while I was in their camp that Woll's main object is mighty different. He's goin' there to gather all the information he can about our intentions, strength an' condition. Mr. Woll is goin' to be badly fooled, 'cause I'm goin' to see that Houston holds him for treachery."

"You do it," said the Panther earnestly. "They brought in Cos just before we left, an' if we keep on we'll have one of the finest little collections of Mexican generals ever made."

"If the war was to go on we'd add to it right along," said Deaf Smith. "There are Gaona and Sesma and Filisola and Urrea loose yet, but we'd gather 'em in. Panther, if we've got the right kind of leaders we can lick the Mexicans anytime, no matter what the odds. That was the only trouble with Houston. He wouldn't believe it of us, but we've proved it now. May the best luck go with you, boys. Mr. Roylston is a mighty fine man."

Smith went reluctantly on his way but paused on the summit of the last swell to wave them farewell. The Panther led his men toward the Colorado along the plain trail that the Mexicans had left. But it soon veered to the east and kept in that direction a long time. Ned surmised that Urrea wished to keep well away from Victoria, where the Mexican generals and their forces had gathered, and, thus not hearing directly of the peace, he could keep on with his prize to the Rio Grande and beyond.

They entered a country that was wholly desolate, the Texan settlers not having returned, and they saw by the appearance of the trail that they were gaining. Perhaps Urrea now considered himself safe from pursuit, and in that lay their greatest advantage. The following night they came to a large camp which he had made.

Big fires of mesquite had been built, and a deer, shot by one of their hunters, had been cooked. The hoofs and horns and bones, licked clean by the wolves, were found on the ground.

As the camp was located in a good place in the woods the Texans decided to occupy it themselves. For the sake of cooking and cheerfulness they built up a new fire of mesquite, and gathered about the blaze. Soon the horses began to whinny and show uneasiness. Long ferocious howls came from the forest.

"Wolves, not coyotes," said the Panther, "but big wolves, timber wolves. It's strange how quick they learn. Six months ago you wouldn't have found a timber wolf in this region, but somehow or other they've found out that all the people have gone away, and here they are ag'in. How they howl! They must he hopin' for somethin' here."

The wolves showed so much boldness that Ned, Stump and the Panther crept through the bushes and shot two of them. They left the bodies where they lay, but, before they were back at the fire, they heard a terrible growling and snarling.

"Cannibals," said Ned with a shudder.

The next morning they found that only clean bones were left. But they forgot the wolves in their pursuit of the trail which ever grew fresher. The Panther believed they would overtake Urrea not far beyond the Colorado, and, when they reached the forest, lining the banks of that stream, they advanced with great caution. The condition of the timber showed that the Mexicans had made another raft and had crossed, but the raft itself had floated away.

The Texans could make a raft also for passage, but they hesitated. The appearance of the trail showed that the Mexicans had not been across many hours. They might be lying ambushed in the trees on the other side, and if they caught the Texans in midstream they could shoot them down at their leisure.

As they reached the river late at night, they decided to make a camp in the thickest of the timber, and remain there until day. Then they would decide upon their procedure. The whole troop halted in an opening in a dense growth of bushes and tethered their horses. They did not light any fires, fearing that the blaze might be seen by a possible enemy on the further shore, but made themselves comfortable on the grass and ate cold food. Four sentinels were posted, and these in due time were to be relieved by others.

Most of the men soon went to sleep in their blankets. Since San Jacinto they had no fear of Mexican attack, and, even should it come, they felt supreme confidence in their ability to defeat any odds. But Ned, although it was not his watch, could not sleep. Mr. Roylston was all the time in his thoughts. He felt that he owed much to the great merchant who intended to take him into his house and business as a son, and that they must rescue him quickly, both for his own sake and the sake of Texas. He was confident that Urrea was now in the deep woods on the other side of the river, perhaps not more than a mile away, and there should be some method of taking Roylston from him that very night.

Restless and trying to think of a way, Ned walked from the bushes to the water's edge. The swollen flood of the river, like all the others at that time, was yellow with the soft earth, washed from the channel, and the current flowed deep and strong. The further shore was high and thick with forest. Ned watched it attentively, as if he might see something moving against that solid black wall. He was joined there by the Panther, who also gazed at the forest on the far shore.

"You think Urrea is over there, don't you, Ned?" he said.

"I feel sure of it."

"So do I. The Mexican trail was not very old, when it reached the river, an' the woods, an' high ground on that side would make a splendid place for a camp. A leader, if he had any sense, would stop right there, an' Urrea is no fool."

"No, he is not. Look, Panther! Is that a light on the hill or a low star?"

A faint silvery light, barely showing through the foliage, had just appeared. The Panther watched it at least a minute before replying.

"It's a fire, Ned," he said, "but I don't think it's been built for either warmin' or cookin'. Now it's gone! An' now it comes back! It's for signalling Ned. Somebody holds a blanket before it an' then takes it away. Between you an' me it has somethin' to do with us. Mebbe Urrea has learned that we're on his track an' has sent back spies. Let's go up the river a piece."

Leaving word with Stump they moved through the bushes a quarter of a mile up the stream, examining the bank minutely, and then turning back to their own camp. Half way there and Ned's attention was drawn by a splash in the water.

He sank down instantly and dragged the Panther's huge bulk after him.

"Look at the river," he whispered. "Don't you see the two heads?"

"Yes, I see 'em," the Panther whispered back. "It's them Campeachy Indians."

The two Indians side by side were swimming strongly to the bank. They carried knives in their teeth, and packages tied on their heads.

"They are the spies I was thinkin' about," said the Panther. "They're comin' over here to look at our camp, an' mebbe to answer, too, the signal that we saw on the hill."

"I haven't seen the signal since we left our camp."

"Mebbe they was just practicin'. Ned, it's a pow'ful temptation to fire at them swimmin' heads, but we mustn't do it. We've got to see what the Campeachy fellers do."

"Of course."

They lay almost flat on the ground among the bushes where the eyes of the Indians, no matter how keen, could not see them, and watched. The two Indians reached the bank and stood up, the water falling in black beads from their naked yellow bodies. They unfolded the packages from their heads and laid them down under the bushes. Ned saw that each consisted of a blanket, a little bundle of sticks and flint and steel. These could not be intended for anything but signals, and the Panther was right. One of the Indians sat down under the tree, beside the blankets and other apparatus and the second slipped away among the bushes.

"Don't try to follow him," said the Panther as he put a restraining hand on Ned's arm. "These men haven't come armed for fightin', they're ready for spyin' only. I guess they want to find out how many we are, an', when Urrea learns that his force outnumbers ours, I reckon he'll try to lay an ambush for us or hold the ford ag'in us."

The Panther's logic seemed very sound to Ned, and he sank back again; resuming his watch upon the warrior under the tree. These Campeachy Indians were snaky creatures, and this fellow made a most sinister figure. He was crouched against the body of the tree with his hands clasped around his knees, which rose almost as high as his head. His arms were unusually long and powerful. His yellow face was immobile, absolutely without expression, and he did not move. A full half hour passed and Ned was never able to see that the Indian stirred an inch.

The second Indian returned and whispered a few words to the other. Then they rapidly built a small fire. When it blazed up they passed a blanket back and forth before it several times.

"Look at the far shore, Ned," whispered the Panther.

Ned looked, and saw the light there appearing and disappearing. The two fires were talking together, but he could only guess what they said. He guessed that the Indians on this shore told the Mexicans on the other shore that the Texans were in small force, and could not cross the river in the face of a much more numerous foe.

The signals continued five minutes. Then the Indians put out the fire, refolded the blankets, put the packages back on their heads and slipped back into the river. Ned saw their black hair just above the water, until they reached the middle of the stream when darkness took them.

"Ned," said the Panther; "I think Urrea, after he hears the report of the Indians will stay on the bank where he has such a great advantage an' fight us."

"I've formed the same opinion."

"But you an' me an' Stump an' Obed have got to go over tonight an' bring Mr. Roylston back. The Indians have showed the way. Then Urrea, if he feels like it can cross an' fight us."

"What's your plan, Panther?"

"We'll swim the stream, but, as we've got to go armed we'll roll one of the fallen trees into the river, an' use it as a support."

They were soon back with the others, and quickly made their preparations. Stump and Obed were eager for the trial, and nobody made any objections. Wayland, an experienced man, was left in charge of the camp. All the men were to be awake and ready to help their comrades. Every wilderness forest is full of brushwood, and fifty feet from the bank they found a suitable fallen tree with many of the boughs still on. They rolled it as gently as possible into the water, and the bold adventurers made ready.

The four took off all their clothing except their trousers and belts. Knives and hatchets which the water would not harm were left in the belts, but they placed their rifles and ammunition on the tree. Will Allen watched them as they made ready. He gave Ned's hand a strong clasp, but he said nothing.

They slipped into the water, giving the tree a slant with the stream, and swam gently, not intending to reach the farther shore until they were at least a half mile below Urrea's camp. Their faces were hidden behind the trunk and boughs and even the wary Indians would have taken the tree to be harmless, floating like many others down the flooded Colorado.

"I wish all crossin's was like this," whispered Stump. "Cur'us how little it takes to hold you up in the water."

"It's more than a tree," Ned whispered back. "It's a ship and it's carrying us in safety and dignity. I don't believe anybody could suspect that this is not the harmless tree it looks."

"It's an omen," said Obed White. "It's Birnam wood going to Dunsinane, and it means that we'll beat Urrea. You never read Shakespeare, Stump, but he said some good things, one of which fits our case."

"Whisper as much as you like, boys," said the Panther, who believed in keeping cheerful, "but don't raise your voices. Do any of you see a light in Urrea's woods?"

"Nothing is there except darkness," replied Ned.

"Then he's hopin' that we'll try to cross in the mornin', an' he'll wait until we get into the middle of the river, when his men will open fire. He's a smart man, but we're smarter. This is a lovely boat, Ned, an' no mistake. She moves nice an' gentle."

The tree under its artful direction moved smoothly on, floating down the stream, but always bearing slightly toward the farther shore. The stream curved a little, passing around a hill, and they increased the slant. Now, no one of them spoke. Darkness and the wilderness seemed to prevail absolutely. Ned heard the wind among the trees, and the water lapping against the shore. He felt to its fullest extent, the hazardous nature of the task they were attempting.

"Turn it a little more now," said the Panther, "an' in a minute or two we'll be at the bank."

The shore at the point they reached was low, and they pulled the tree wholly out of the stream, in order that it might be ready for them should they need it again. Then the four, dripping water but carrying their rifles and ammunition, stepped into the woods. The Panther led the way, Ned followed, behind him came Stump, and Obed was at the rear.

They found the forest even more dense than on their own side of the river, but it suited their purpose, hiding their bodies and not keeping them, accomplished woods men as they were, from advancing without noise. Their path led up the hill, and when they reached its crest the Panther stopped. The others moved softly to his side and looked into a fairly large open space, where men lay about sleeping. Horses were tethered on the far side, and half a dozen sentinels, walking around in a circle, kept watch.

They were looking into the camp of Urrea, but they made no movement until they located Roylston. Ned finally saw him sitting in a leaning posture against a small sapling, his arms bound. To their great joy he seemed to be awake. And yet it was not so singular. He must have seen the Mexicans signalling, and he must have inferred from it that the Texans were near.

"How far would you say it is from the trees to him?" whispered the Panther to Obed White.

"Not over twenty feet," replied Obed, "and I want to say, Panther, I'm so long and slim that I make less shadow on the ground than the rest of us. S'pose I creep up to Mr. Roylston, cut him loose and run with him. Mexican sentinels are always bad. Those fellows are probably walking in their sleep, and we can at least get a good start."

"I reckon it's the only way," said the Panther. "We'll wait here an' cover you with our rifles, but be careful, Obed. Be mighty careful!"

Obed, his knife in his hand, dropped down upon the ground, and seemed to disappear in the shadows. Merely a slight line marked where his long thin body writhed forward like a snake. Ned on his knees in the bushes watched breathlessly. The sentinels walked back and forth, but it was apparent that they had neither seen nor heard anything. The time seemed very long, but the line that was Obed still moved forward, reached Roylston, and then stopped. Ned saw the merchant move a little. He also saw the flash of a strong blade and then the merchant and Obed, half rising, walked swiftly toward the wood. Obed had not asked Roylston to creep back as he had come knowing that he could not do it, and he deemed it better to make a bold rush, trusting to the protecting rifles of his three comrades.

They were half way to the trees, when one of the sentinels saw them, and uttered a shout of alarm. The others echoed the cry, adding that the prisoner was escaping, and, in an instant, the Mexican camp was in an uproar.

"Run, Mr. Roylston, run!" shouted Ned.

The merchant, with such an inducement, showed great speed for a man of his years, and in another instant was in the forest. Several bullets, fired in haste at him and Obed cut the twigs above the heads of fugitives and rescuers, but the rifles of Ned, the Panther and Stump flashed in return, and the Mexicans began to shout in alarm that a great Texan force was upon them.

"Now's our time!" cried the Panther. "Make for our tree, Obed, an' start across the river; The rest of us will hold the Mexicans back!"

Ned caught a glimpse of the merchant's face. It was white but composed. His great intelligence had comprehended everything in an instant. He said nothing but in one flashing moment he looked his gratitude and was gone with Obed. The Panther, with Ned and Stump, drew off slowly, and in a slightly different direction. They heard the Mexicans crashing after them for a few minutes, and then sink into silence, not knowing by what numbers they were assailed and evidently fearful of an ambush.

The Panther led, and suddenly he came out on the edge of the hill overlooking the river, where his gigantic figure was disclosed in the moonlight. Stump and Ned were yet in the bushes, when they heard a shout of triumph, a pistol shot, and saw two Mexicans rushing upon the Panther, upon whose sleeve a red spot leaped, where the blood had been drawn by the wound below. But the Panther's own pistol flashed, one of the Mexicans fell, and springing forward he grasped the other in his powerful arms.

Ned had but one glimpse of the Mexican, who had been seized in that terrible clutch and he saw that it was Urrea. The next moment the Panther whirled him aloft and hurled him outward. Ned heard a crash on rocks below and then came a moment of sickening silence. He knew that Urrea had been killed instantly.

"Come on!" cried the Panther. "Their leader's gone, an' they won't be eager in the pursuit!"

They ran along the river's edge and found Obed and Roylston already launching the tree. All pushed it off and swam and drifted to the other shore. The Mexicans, cowed by their leader's death, fled with speed the next day, and the Texans prepared to return northward in triumph.

But before they began their return journey Ned asked the Panther to ride westward with him in the direction of San Antonio. That part of the country seemed to be free now from Mexicans and Indian raiding bands, and there was little possibility of danger.

"I want to find a horse," said Ned, "the best, most intelligent and greatest horse that anybody ever rode."

The Panther went with him gladly and they travelled a night and day, until they came to a wide plain, heavy with grass and watered well.

"It was somewhere near here that I abandoned Old Jack," said Ned, "and it seems to me that if we hunt around a while we ought to find him."

"Like as not we'll run across him," said the Panther. "Besides the buffalo, which migrate, not many of the animals in this country go very far from their reg'lar runs."

They hunted nearly all the next day, and, toward its conclusion, they approached a deep dip in the prairie with a small stream running down it, and, ending toward the north in a fine grove of oaks. It was an ideal place for an animal home, with grass, water and shelter all close together, and the Panther considered it highly probable that they would discover Old Jack in the dip.

When they rode down the swale to the brook they saw nothing, but the Panther pinned his faith to the fine oak grove at the end.

"It's comin' on toward night," he said, "an' like enough Old Jack, havin' eat an' drunk his fill, is now thinkin' about goin' to bed."

They rode toward the grove and Ned caught sight of a great, dark figure at its edge, standing under the boughs of a large oak. His pulse leaped. Despite the distance, he recognised the figure. It was his faithful friend, Old Jack. The Panther had also seen him and he turned to Ned and said:

"Ain't that your hoss?"

"Beyond a doubt it's Old Jack his very self."

"Shall we try to ketch him with lariats or can you talk him up?"

"I think I can toll him to me, Panther. At least, I'd like to try. It would be an insult to him to pursue him with ropes."

The Panther understood. In some matters the great brusque plainsman had extremely fine and delicate sensibilities.

"I'll wait here," he said, "'cause I guess you'd like to go on alone. He don't know me as well as he does you and I might skeer him."

"Thanks, Panther, I think it would be best."

The Panther wheeled in behind a clump of bushes, where he was hidden, and yet could watch, and Ned rode on alone.

The great dark figure under the tree did not move. The sun was now setting in a sea of red and gold, and poured a vast stream of light directly upon the grove, where the horse stood in the very centre of it. Old Jack was magnified. He seemed to grow to twice his height. His body and legs were colossal.

Ned rode slowly forward, uttering the long deep whistle which had been his call to his best and favourite horse. He saw the gigantic figure move and then stretch forward a great neck. At the same time he saw behind other horses, a group gathered closely together, and evidently much afraid. Ned divined at once that they were wild horses, and that Old Jack, by virtue of size, strength and power, had already become their leader and king.

He continued to ride slowly forward, all the time uttering that melodious, persuasive whistle which Old Jack had learned to know as the signal from the best of masters. Ned knew that the great horse was trembling, that training was pulling him one way, and nature and

744

instinct the other. But that wonderful, melodious whistle never ceased to come from his lips, and at last Old Jack, issuing from the wood, walked slowly forward.

As the great horse, hesitating but still advancing, came nearer, Ned began to talk to him, and to call him all the old familiar names. He told him that he was the finest and greatest horse that lived, that ever had lived or that ever would live. Old Jack turned his head and glanced two or three times at the wood where his herd yet lingered, and came, more slowly still, yet he came.

He was so near at last that Ned reached out his hand, and stroked his glossy mane and his nose. Old Jack whinnied softly, and nuzzled his master's hand. Then Ned, full of gratitude for great services done and of sympathy for horse nature, said:

"I merely wanted to see you once more, Old Jack, and thank you for saving my life. May bridle or saddle never rest upon you again!"

He struck Old Jack smartly upon the flank. The horse uttered a deep, thrilling neigh, and galloped back toward the wood and the herd, of which he was leader. Ned saw their forms disappearing in the shadows and at that moment the sun set behind the high swell of the prairie.

"Why did you do it?" asked the Panther, when Ned rode back.

"Because he is a king and I want him to keep his kingdom."

"I'd have done it, too," said the Panther.

They heard often in the years afterward of a great black stallion, leading a splendid herd of wild horses, which many an expert with lariat sought in vain to capture. It was said that the stallion had a wisdom almost uncanny, that he seemed to add human and reasoning qualities to the acute senses and instinct of the wild animal. He gradually led his herd further and further westward until they disappeared in the canyons of the mountains and were seen no more by men.

John Roylston was deeply grateful for his rescue and he insisted that Ned should join him, as his adopted son and coming partner, as soon as the war was over. But Ned served until the close, when the last Mexican soldier had disappeared from the soil of Texas. He took part in the controversy over Santa Anna, when a large number of the Texans insisted on his execution, but, from motives of policy, he opposed it. He was glad when the government decided to give him to the United States, which sent him back to Mexico, and, singularly enough, he and most of his close comrades faced him ten years later at Buena Vista, when the Americans, who now included the Texans, beat him again, although the odds were five to one in his favour.

Ned, with Will Allen his chief assistant, became a great merchant with John Roylston. Their trade filled the southwest and they had many ships upon the Gulf and Caribbean. His most daring captain in the field, whether of fleet or wagon train, was a long, red-headed man from New England named Obed White. But trade and riches had no temptations for the Panther and Stump. They took to the great west, and their fame as hunters and scouts rose to an unparalleled degree.

Ned, now and then, for the sake of relaxation, joined them on a big buffalo hunt on the plains, or a search for the grizzly bear in the mountains. When he was with them they never failed to find the game they wished, which merely confirmed the belief of the Panther and Stump that he was "chose," that he was in very fact and deed a magic leader.

CPSIA information can be obtained
at www.ICGtesting.com
Printed in the USA
LVOW12s0504051117
555065LV00001B/10/P